THE MAGIC OF EYRI

by Daniel J. Hogan

The Magic of Eyri – Daniel J. Hogan

For Mom, Dad, Uncle Jim & Uncle Karl

This book is intended for entertainment purposes only. Anyone who thinks otherwise should please have their head examined.

This is a work of fiction. Characters, names, places and events are the product of the author's overactive imagination, and should not be considered real (that is usually what 'fiction' means). Any unintended resemblance to places or persons (living, dead or undead) is purely coincidental.

Honestly.

To buy a copy of this book (or a few dozen extra), contact the author, to see some neato artwork or to learn more about the book please visit:

www.magicofeyri.com

Special Thanks

My artists: Michael (**www.drakered.com**)
Romel (**www.danieljhogan.com/romel**)
& Kevin (**www.prettyokayproductions.com**).
Please visit their websites.

Sarah for editing this thing. I can't thank you enuff.

And Brooke, for telling me about NaNoWriMo. This is all your fault.

<u>**More exciting than the Michigan tax code!**</u>

<u>**More action than the phone book!**</u>

<u>**Funnier than a root canal!**</u>

What happens when Steve, a smart-mouth suburban teen from Michigan and his Uncle Shameless get whisked away to the bizarre fantasy world of Eyri? (pronounced AIR-EE) An adventure beyond logic and reasoning, *that's* what. Follow young Steve as he reluctantly partakes on one of the wackiest quests ever written.

Will he fulfill The Prophecy? Can he defeat the Hawk-King and free all of Eyri from the yoke of tyranny? Why *IS* his uncle called Shameless?

Find all this out and more in,

The Magic of Eyri
"Your Next Favorite Fantasy-Comedy-Adventure Book"
by
Daniel J. Hogan

www.magicofeyri.com

www.danieljhogan.com

–Pronunciation Key–

Eyri (AIR-EEE)
O'Jec (OH-JECK)
Istrio (IST-REE-OH)
Zaa (ZAA)
Zuu (ZOO)
Hawken (HAWK-IN)
Swanta, Swantan (SWAN-TA, SWAN-TAN)
Fiach-Ra (FEE OCK-RAH)
Fel-Ra (FELL-RAH)
Da'Rahga (DA'RAH-GAA)
Arx Vena'Tor (ARKS VEN-AH'TOR)
Uth (OOTH)
U'Nala (OOO'NALL-AH)
Delu, Uled (DI-LOO, OO-LID)
Pyrix (PIE-RICKS)
Eira (EAR-AH)
Zeroth (ZIR-OATH)
Gladius (GLAD-EEE-US)
Tal (TAL)
Mininat (MINI-NAT)
Arx A'Quila (ARKS AH'QUIL-AH)
Daniel J. Hogan (HACK)

1

Once upon a lunchtime a few afternoons ago, a young boy watched a grown man pick a fight with a duck.

The fight was not without reason. The duck had flown above the man while he was eating a sandwich and skillfully knocked it out of his hands. A chase ensued as the man ran after the duck, the sandwich clasped tightly in its bill. The irritated (and hungry) man chased the duck down the bank of the Grand River, where he had been enjoying his lunch prior to its being stolen. The chase eventually led the pair out into the waters of the slow moving river.

The man had forgotten ducks could fly until it hovered safely over his head while he thrashed around in the water. After finishing the man's sandwich, the duck foolishly let its guard down long enough for the man to grab it out of the air. He grasped the duck's neck in one hand and started to drunkenly express the wrongness of stealing someone else's lunch.

"Listen here pal, you can't just go 'round stealin' what ain't yours!"

The duck, still caught in the man's vise-like grip, ignored all of this alcohol-soaked lecturing.

"I don't steal all the bread people throw in the river for you guys, do I?" the man asked the beady eyed mallard,"...Well, there was that one time...but *that* was an emergency! I was trying to make this really big sandwich...and big it was! Y'see, I had made a bet with this wicked banker that I could make the biggest sandwich ever."

The silent duck gave the man a confused look. "Well, how else was I going to save the orphanage?!" finished the man.

By now, a crowd had formed on the banks of the river. The young boy shook his head and continued to watch the watery spectacle. Whispers worked their way through the crowd as the man in the river continued spinning his tall tale for his feathery prisoner.

"Oh, it's Shameless Harrier, I might have known," said a rotund man with a beard "Who else in River City would pick a fight with a duck?"

"What kind of name is Shameless?" asked another rotund man, this one without a beard.

"He's real name is Shamus, but everyone in River City calls him 'Shameless' because he is a shameless drunk," explained a skinny man with a moustache.

"Yes, but he does tell a good story," added a fat woman with a bad haircut.

As good as Shameless was at telling stories, the duck had lost interest long before Shameless had even finished listing the Ark-like ingredients of the mythical sandwich.

"An' so I also put in deers, antelopeses, mooses, an' various things. But I also made sure to put on plenty of OUCH!" screamed Shameless as the duck bit his nose. He awkwardly thrashed around in the river with the small duck clamped firmly to his sniffer, as the crowd collectively shook their heads and walked away.

The young boy also shook his head, as he watched Shameless finally let go of the duck as he fell backwards into the water. The duck triumphantly flew away, its quacking echoing off the stone ledges along the Grand River.

The young boy sighed, picked up the blanket he had been laying on, and walked over to Shameless as he stumbled out of the river. The soggy man reached out with a drenched arm and wrapped the blanket around himself.

"Ah, thank you boy. Yer a good caddy," whispered Shameless before he collapsed down onto the ground drunk, wet, and exhausted.

The boy shook his head as he watched over the soaked man.

"You're welcome, Uncle."

Steve hated River City.

In fact, he hated it so much that he spent a whole afternoon looking up synonyms for 'hate' just so he did not run out ways of expressing it in his phone calls to his parents (his favorite was 'abhor').

Steve Harrier was from the suburbs of a big city on the east side of Michigan, and was not accustomed to small town life in the mid-Michigan town of River City. Instead of skyscrapers and luxury malls, there were farm silos and sidewalk sales.

Being from the suburbs, Steve was not accustomed to being surrounded by nature all the time. His yard back home had one tree, and it was the same tree everyone on his block had. Everyone also had the same house in his hometown of Beacon Pines. He liked it that way; he could go over to a friend's house and already know where the bathroom was.

That was, if he had any friends. There weren't many children on his block; most of his neighbors were elderly couples who had lived there since Beacon Pines was built decades ago. This was part of the reason his parents had sent him to live with his Uncle Shameless for the summer (yes, even his family called him Shameless).

His parents hoped that spending a few months in a small town with other children around would help him act more like a regular kid.

For his age, Steve took life very seriously. He almost never smiled. He also had no use for make believe or imagination. His parents blamed the schools, for they had stopped all arts and music programs because they were tired of the children acting 'childish.'

The schools also banned all storybooks – namely those dealing with far away magic lands, space adventures, and wizards (especially wizards). As a result, all of the children had the creativity and personality of a room full of soap salesmen.

Not too long after arriving in River City, Uncle Shameless witnessed Steve's ailment first hand as he tried to entertain his nephew with a popular Michigan myth.

"...An' so, this huge mother bear waited an' waited for her cubs," Uncle Shameless held out his arms as far as he could to suggest the size of the bear, "An' she's still waitin' till this day, only now she's covered in sand. That's why the dunes are called Sleepin' Bear."

"Let me get this straight," countered Steve, "This mountain sized bear lived in Michigan?"

"Yup! It was so big you could walk across it for a fortnight and still not see the other side. Huge it was! Mammoth even!"

"That's impossible. The eco-system in Michigan could never support such a huge creature. A bear's primary food is fish, there would have to be whale sized fish in the Great Lakes. Simply impossible," said Steve.

"Ah!" winked Uncle Shameless "But how do you know there weren't fish that size, eh? They are called the *Great* Lakes after all."

"Easy. There is no evidence of such creatures in the fossil record," answered Steve proudly.

Uncle Shameless placed a hand on Steve's shoulder, "Steve my boy, never let the facts get in the way of a good story."

The serious young boy had similar problems when trying to socialize with the children of River City, especially when it came to playing make believe.

"Want to play with us?" asked a redheaded boy with mismatched sneakers. He gestured to his rag-tag group of friends nearby.

"Not rea-" began Steve before he was cut off.

"Great!" exclaimed the boy with the sneakers "Me, Alex and Kevo will be pirates. You, Tony, and Benny will be cowboys!"

Steve gave the boy with in the sneakers a confused expression as he continued setting up his scene "An' we're attackin' your Moon Fortress! Here's your Moon Sword."

Steve held up his Moon Sword and examined it skeptically, "This is just a stick…" he began.

The boy ignored him "Ready? Go!" he yelled as the teams broke up, one side yelling "Arrr!" and "Avast!" the other screaming "Giddy-up!" and "Draw!"

Steve stood in the middle of the group, not moving, "This is ridiculous," he said "Pirates and cowboys were separated by hundreds of years –not to mention hundreds of miles - and last I checked you couldn't sail a boat or ride a horse to the moon," Steve explained expertly "And like I said, this is just a stick."

Steve broke the stick over his knee and stormed off to go read a lengthy essay about holes in space, leaving the group of boys to wonder if insanity ran in his family.

River City earned its name from the fact that the Grand River ran through the middle of downtown. The cozy little town used this to its advantage, building parks around the river and in some cases on many of the little islands on the Grand River itself.

"Steve, you see all of these islands up and down the Grand River?" asked Uncle Shameless one day while at Islands Park.

"Yes."

"Want to know where they came from?"

"I *know* where they came from," answered Steve "Geological formations built up over time, probably caused by glacier moveme-"

"No, no, no," interrupted Uncle Shameless, "Y'see, many years ago there was a woman travelin' down the river in a boat with all her children."

Steve sighed and listened.

"Anyway, the boat caught fire-"

"Caught fire? In a river, how?" interrupted Steve.

"Don't interrupt me boy...now where was I?"

"Boat on fire."

"Oh yes. *Anyways*," continued Uncle Shameless "In order to save them, the woman threw each of her children into the river...and wouldn't you know it? Each of the children turned into an island!"

Steve stared at his uncle with his mouth open in shock, "T-that's-"

"Impossible?" finished Uncle Shameless.

"Yes! People can't turn into islands!" screamed Steve.

"Well," mused Uncle Shameless "Folks were different back then. They musta had a high fiber diet."

Uncle Shameless lived on a farm along the bank of the Grand River. He hadn't always been the town drunk, he used to run a successful farm and apple orchard. Sadly, he could not compete with huge farms owned by faceless companies. It was a good year if his farm would break even and that had rarely happened towards the end.

The local markets in and near River City that would buy his crops went out of business under the heel of the nation wide super store chains that began to sprout up everywhere. These *super*-super markets opened up near River City and ran the local mom and pop shops into the ground, mostly by selling crops grown overseas.

Uncle Shameless, then known only as Shamus, shut his farm down and survived by renting space on his land to roadside billboards, most of which advertised the companies that had put him out of business.

One bright and sunny summer day, Uncle Shameless walked up to Steve while he was under a tree reading an essay about bio-diesel.

"Boy, I just had a fantastic idea."

"That must have hurt," mumbled Steve.

"We're gonna go on a canoe trip down the Grand River!" slurred Uncle Shameless.

Steve looked up from the essay "A what trip?"

"Canoe," answered Uncle Shameless.

"Can I what?"

"Huh?"

"You said 'can you,' and I asked can I what," relied Steve.

"I said canoe."

"I know, can I what?" asked Steve again, growing impatient.

"No, I said canoe," continued Uncle Shameless, his faced crimped in confusion.

"I know! And I keep asking you, can I what?"

"...It's a boat," explained his uncle.

Uncle Shameless walked Steve down to the small wooden dock by the Grand River and pointed to a beat-up aluminum canoe.

"That's a canoe."

"Oh," said Steve.

"They were created by the first peoples of America, an' were used to tame the angry lakes and rivers," Uncle Shameless told his young nephew. "In fact," he continued, pausing to take a long drink from a bottle "They were used by Lewis and Clark when they fought the Aztecs during the War of 1812!"

"Wow...wait, what?"

Ignoring Steve, his uncle continued, "Yes, that canoe in front of you," he drunkenly pointed to worn out craft in front of them "is the pride of the Harrier Fleet."

Steve looked around, searching for other boats, finding none he said, "It *is* the Harrier Fleet."

"Exactly!" exclaimed his uncle, not getting the boy's sarcasm.

That night, while sitting outside under the starry sky, Uncle Shameless told Steve his plan.

"What we'll do, is get in that canoe and go down the river seein' the sights, hearin' the sounds, and smellin' the smells," he finished as he winked at Steve. He leaned too far while he did and fell out of his chair.

"Smells?" asked Steve.

"Yes! Smells!" proclaimed his uncle. He stood up and dusted off his torn flannel shirt and equally torn and tattered blue jeans.

"Haven't you ever smelled nature?"

"Can't say I have."

"Well, then you're in for a treat!" bellowed Uncle Shameless excitedly. He stretched as far as his forty-five year old body would let him and rested his large, calloused hands on his tangled mess of hair.

"I'm cold. How 'bout a little fire, Steve?"

"...Isn't it a little too warm out for a fire?"

"Nonsense!" Uncle Shameless yelled "Plus it'll give' me an excuse to show you how to build a fire. Now, first things first. Have you seen my gas can?"

Uncle Shameless wandered around, gathering up random pieces of wood and other burnable objects.

"This isn't necessary," pleaded Steve.

"No-no, no problem at all!" he heard his uncle yell from the darkness, followed by a loud symphony of heavy objects crashing to the ground.

Eventually Uncle Shameless returned, and began pilling up the wood and paper he had found in front of Steve. Uncle shameless then grabbed his old, dented gasoline can and poured the entire contents over the pile. He fumbled through the pockets of his torn jeans until he found a book of matches, lit one and threw it into the pile of gasoline soaked wood and paper.

A pillar of flame shot up with a loud WOOSH! before it descended quickly and burnt itself out. Steve looked at his uncle, still in the same position, however now Shameless' entire front side was blackened and smoking.

"Y'know boy, yer right, it is too hot out for a fire. Let's go inside."

Steve was awoken early the next morning by his uncle's poorly improvised, off-key singing.

"All-a-wet-yeah, gonna get all-a-wet-yeah!
All-a-wet-yeah, down the river we go!
Don't be cold river, cuz I don't wanna shiver!
Gonna eat some fishes, cuz they is de-lish-es!
All-a-wet-yeah, gonna get all-a-wet-yeah!
All-a-wet-yeah, down the river we go!"

Steve groaned and pulled on his jeans, striped t-shirt and black high top canvas sneakers. He picked up his black plastic frame glasses from the nightstand next to his bed and slipped them on. Eye problems ran in the family. Uncle Shameless even had his own aliment, a lazy eye.

Steve ran a brush through his wavy brown hair and went to go meet his uncle.

Calling the canoe a *canoe* was being nice. Most of the original silver aluminum had been punctured or busted. There were more white semi-transparent patch jobs on the canoe than aluminum.

This fact did not escape the critical eyes of Steve, "…Is it bad that we can see through the side of the canoe like that?"

"Oh pa-shaw, it's fine boy. Did I ever tell how that happened?"

"No, and I don't need-"

"I was out on the Grand River, and the river was angry that day, let me tell you!" began Uncle Shameless, ignoring Steve's protest "The currents were like nothin' I had ever seen, an' rapids were all 'round me!"

"What were you doing on the river when it was like that?"

"Ah! But there's the rub! It was a nice day like this, but I was out fishing you see, and I snagged a whopper of a catch!" he picked up a nearby paddle and pretended it was a fishing rod.

"I tell you she was seven feet long if she was a foot! And it fought like a devil on a bad day, she did!" He sat on the ground and pretended he had the fish on the end of his make-believe rod, "A huge spiny fin, and a mighty mouth with teeth like daggers! A fish like that I have never seen before or since!"

"…What does this have to do with bad currents?"

"Well, you see this fish was so large that her thrashing 'round on my line caused the river to churn an' swirl all crazy like!"

Steve rolled his eyes, but his uncle continued.

"It pulled me up stream! Then down stream, and then side ways! Catching this fish was a feat worthy of Hercules it was!"

"I bet," snickered Steve.

"Don't interrupt…where was I?"

"Side-ways."

"Oh yes, well hours – no – days passed and I was finally able to reel it in close enough. I was about to knock it cold with my paddle, but in one last panic attack it swung its mighty tail at my little canoe," he pointed to the large patch spot on the side of the canoe, "And it busted the side! Water came screaming in! Down I went, and it got away," finished Uncle Shameless with a nostalgic grin.

They loaded everything they needed on to the canoe, causing the little craft to rest low in the water. Uncle Shameless took a drink from a flask and entered into the canoe. It rocked and swayed in the water against his movements as Steve tried to keep the canoe steady.

"Easy there!" yelled Uncle Shameless to no one in particular.

After he was settled, Uncle Shameless picked up his paddle and pushed off from the dock. He started rowing, gradually rowing harder and harder.

"The current sure is strong today! We're barely gainin' any speed!"

"Uh, Uncle-"

"Mercy this current is strong! I don't think we've moved at all!"

Steve turned around and yelled at his uncle "That's because we're still tied to the dock!"

After untying the canoe, which resulted in Uncle Shameless falling into the river a few times, the pair was on their way down the Grand River. The shallow, slow moving river cut a snake-like path through the wild Michigan countryside, taking the boy and his uncle through heavily wooded areas far from civilization. Lush green forests surround them on either side and seemed to go on forever into the horizon.

"Steve-o, did you know that the Grand River is the longest river in Michigan?" asked Uncle Shameless, who was causally steering from the back of the canoe.

"Yessir, when Lewis and Clark discovered it after the Indiana Purchase they thought they had found the North-West Passage!" continued Uncle Shameless "Hundreds of miles long! It is called the Grand River for a reason after all."

"...Was that before or after they fought the Incas?" asked Steve, who mumbled something about the Indiana Purchase under his breath.

"Fought the Incas? Don't be silly boy!" bellowed Uncle Shameless from the back of the canoe "They fought the *Aztecs*!"

Steve stared out at the river, taking in the scenery. He had never seen anything like this before. They floated past a group of rocks sticking out of the water. A large turtle sunned itself, while dragonflies buzzed around it. Steve did a double take when he thought the turtle smiled at him. He rubbed his eyes, convinced they were playing tricks on him.

All of a sudden, Steve heard a crash in the forest not too far from the canoe. "What's that?"

Uncle Shameless looked over the top of Steve's head. A group of deer cautiously pushed their way out of the forest and entered the water. "Are those deer?" asked Steve, amazed.

"They ain't rabbits," smiled his uncle.

"What are they doing?" Steve asked as the deer walked into the river and started making their way across it to the next bank.

"Why, swimmin' of course," answered Uncle Shameless.

"That's impossible, deer can't swim," said the city boy.

"'Course they can! In fact, George Washington and his men rode a herd of 'em across the Mississippi to fight off the Huns!"

Steve and Uncle Shameless floated by in time to watch the last of the deer exit the water and run into the woods. "Haven't you ever seen any animals in the wild before?" asked Uncle Shameless.

"No, the big city zoo doesn't have animals anymore. They couldn't afford to keep any real animals after the Mayor used all of the budget money for a party on Mackinaw Island for his dog," lamented Steve.

Uncle shameless scratched his head "Well, what *do* they have at the zoo?"

"Cardboard cut outs of animals, and in some cases people in suits. But the people in suits have a really good union so they are in hibernation most of the year," explained Steve.

Uncle Shameless was about to ask for details about the people in suits' union, when a large shape flew overhead. A shadow covered Steve's face as he looked up and saw a funny looking bird with a long neck and long legs. It swooped down in front of the canoe and landed on a nearby branch sticking out the water.

"A blue heron!" yelled Uncle Shameless.

Steve studied the interesting looking bird. It had a body like a blue football with a pair of skinny legs shooting out from the bottom. He wondered why the bird's eyes were totally white and without irises. He did not know much about birds, but he was pretty sure that was not normal.

"Weird," whispered Steve.

"That's a sign of a healthy river, seeing a heron y'know," said Uncle Shameless.

Steve looked at the majestic bird, it stood on its perch watching the river flow by. Then it looked at Steve. The boy took his glasses off and cleaned them on his shirt. He was positive the blue heron had just winked at him, but he knew that was not possible.

"Yessir! I bet that heron will follow us all the way down the river!" Uncle Shameless bellowed, his words echoing around him.

Sure enough, whenever the canoe got within a few feet of the blue heron, it would fly a few yards down the river only to perch itself again until the canoe caught up with it.

Unfortunately, this only prompted Uncle Shameless to continue bellowing his blue heron theory. Every time the blue heron would land at a new spot along their path, Uncle Shameless would yell, "Yessir! I bet that heron will follow us all the way down the river!"

This continued until Steve could not take anymore and begged his uncle to talk about something else, which Steve knew was a dangerous thing to say.

"Hey Steve-o, have you ever seen a pelican?"

"No," answered Steve, watching the blue heron fly ahead of them. Once again, his serene moment was spoiled by Uncle Shameless' bellowing.

"Strange bird the pelican! Its beak holds more than its belly can!"

Steve ignored Uncle Shameless and kept looking at the spell-binding blue heron, until once again, "Strange bird the pelican! Its beak holds more than its belly can!"

Steve groaned, knowing well enough the situation was only going to get worse. *Please don't start singing,* Steve thought to himself.

"Y'know Steve-o, I feel like singing. How 'bout you?"

"No!"

"Oh *yes!*" his uncle exclaimed as he drew in a long breath,

"Well, the Deacon went down!" sang Uncle Shameless "C'mon boy you're suppose to sing what I sing," instructed Uncle Shameless as he prodded Steve in the back with the tip of his paddle.

Steve sighed, knowing there was no way of avoiding this, he slowly spoke "Well, the Deacon went down." "There you go!" smiled Uncle Shameless and then he continued:

"To the cellar to pray!"

"To the cellar to pray," sighed Steve out of tune and time

"He had a jug!"

"He had a jug," repeated Steve.

"C'mon boy, once more with feeling!"

Steve sat up and in his best fake-enthusiastic voice re-repeated the line "He had a j-"

Unfortunately (but fortunately for Steve), he was interrupted by a loud cry.

An explosion of brown and white blasted down from the sky, letting loose another shrill shriek. The shape flew like a spear towards the river, aiming its decent at a mother duck and her ducklings not too far from the front of the canoe.

"A hawk!" exclaimed Uncle Shameless from behind Steve.

Sure enough, the brown and white blur slowed enough for Steve to make out the sharp hooked beak and the lethal talons as they lashed out to grab a hold of an unsuspecting duckling.

The boy turned away as the swift-striking hawk carried away its prize.

"That poor duck…" Steve said.

"That's the way of nature boy. Nothing you can do about it," explained Uncle Shameless as he tried to make Steve feel better, realizing the event had upset his young nephew. "But, that little duck's loss will help its brothers and sisters."

"How?"

"Well, now when they hear a hawk cry, they'll know there is danger," replied Uncle Shameless.

"So, you're saying that everything happens for a reason?"

"Well, maybe. But it's more like what that philosophizer guy said, 'What don't git us kilt, makes us stronger.' I think his name was Necktie, or Nacho or somethin.'"

Steve quietly nodded, even though he was positive he had never heard of a philosopher named Necktie or Nacho, and paddled a few strokes as he watched the blue heron in the distance. Steve was convinced the sun was getting to him; the blue heron had just winked at him again.

"What about losing your farm? Since that didn't kill you, did it make you stronger?"

Uncle Shameless took an extra long drink from his flask, and answered in a hollow voice "Who said it didn't kill me?"

Looking to change the subject, Uncle Shameless spoke again in a happier tone, "Did you know that hawks have some of the best eye-sight of all the birds? Yessir, I betcha that hawk had been following those duckies for a long time, just watching 'em from up high. Those poor duckies never knew it either. That's where the sayin' about watching someone like a hawk comes from."

Steve scanned the sky, looking for any other birds of prey, hoping he wouldn't be on their menu. Uncle Shameless noticed the concerned look on Steve's face and patted him reassuringly on the back, "Don't worry boy, I'll protect you if some hawk tries to carry you off," he said with a warm chuckle.

"Yessir," continued Uncle Shameless as he leaned back in the canoe "Ya can't hide from a hawk, they can see everythin.'"

2

Hours passed and the pair continued with their trek down the Grand River. It was getting close to dusk, and the muscles in Steve's arms began to ache. "Are we going to stop sometime soon?" he whined.

"Soon enough."

"Where are we going anyway?"

"To this convenience store down the river," explained Uncle Shameless "It use to be a speakeasy back in the ol' days!"

"How far is that?" Steve asked.

"Hey, look! Swans!" bellowed Uncle Shameless, ignoring Steve's question.

Steve looked at a group of large white birds floating contently near the river's edge.

Steve was getting tired of being told the life story of every single animal they came across on this trip. He wanted to go home. In fact, he didn't even want to go back to his uncle's farm; he wanted to return to the suburbs of Beacon Pines. At least in Beacon Pines there weren't any dangerous creatures dropping out the sky. The only dangerous creatures there had four wheels and broken turn signals.

Uncle Shameless carefully steered the battered canoe towards the group of swans. Up above, the blue heron watched with interest through its ghostly white eyes.

A large swan floated closer to the canoe. Steve reached out to touch it. The swan quickly hissed at him and bit his hand with its black ringed orange bill.

"Wha!" Steve cried, falling backwards and rocking the canoe, rubbing his sore hand.

"Git outta here!" called Uncle Shameless as he splashed water at the swan, protecting the boy from further attacks. The irritable swan hissed again before floating away.

Uncle Shameless inspected Steve's bit hand, and finding no damage done, gave the boy a warm smile and patted him on the head.

"You'll live," he said to the shocked city boy. "Yessir, swans are mean suckers," explained Uncle Shameless as he started rowing again "They may look pretty, but they are nasty and they like to bite. In fact, that's how your dad got bald."

"Huh?" asked Steve, still watching the swan. The white bird continued hissing at the canoe as it floated away.

"It's true, a swan flew at him and ripped all his hair out."

"But-"

"Hey look at that!" said Uncle Shameless, pointing up to the blue heron "Didn't I tell you it would follow us all the way?"

As it grew later Steve was getting very tired. His legs were cramped and felt like they were made of stone. Uncle Shameless however, was busy entertaining himself with more poorly improvised, off-key singing:

"Riv-er! Nutthen but riv-er!

No, I ain't no quit-er, cuz I'm canoin' this riv-er!"

Steve sighed as he listened to his uncle take sips from his flash in-between verses. He would stop at random moments to bellow nonsensical things:

"Strange bird the pelican! Its beak holds more than its belly can!"

Or

"Hey Steve!"

"...What?"

"Are you hot?!" bellowed Uncle Shameless. Steve tried to ignore him.

"I said – ARE YOU HOT?!"

Steve's face crimped in an expression of annoyance "...Yes," knowing the punch-line to this oft-used routine.

"Well then take yer shirt off!" bellowed Uncle Shameless as he laughed at his own joke.

Or just random words and sounds Steve was convinced his uncle made up: "Moo-ha!...Woor-ba!...Bru-ha!"

Thankfully, this last volley of nonsense ended as they rounded a bend in the river. In the middle of the river was very small island with a single tall, bare tree. All of the other trees along the river and on the other islands were in full bloom, this was the only tree that Steve had seen without leaves. However, this was not as remarkable as what was *in* the tree.

Resting at the top of the tree, on a skeleton-like branch was a large bird, around the size of a big dog sitting on its hind legs. Its massive talons clenched the limb of the tree aggressively as it scanned the river with its large eyes. Steve wondered why the bird's eyes had a faint blue tint to them.

"What is the deal with the birds' eyes on this riv-" started Steve.

Uncle Shameless gasped loudly "An eagle!" cutting off Steve's question "An' look at the size of it! I bet it's a female!"

"How can you tell that from here?" asked Steve as he squinted at the massive bird.

"Female eagles are bigger and stronger than males," explained Uncle Shameless "And that one is bigger than any eagle I've ever seen."

"Have you ever seen one with blue eyes?" asked Steve. He studied the eagle's eyes again – they were almost entirely blue now, where they had been only tinted moments ago.

"Uh..." Uncle Shameless searched his memory for anything about eagles with blue eyes "Can't say I have."

The river fell silent and even Uncle Shameless ceased his bellowing for several moments. The eagle turned quickly away from the canoe before screeching loudly and flapping its mighty wings. It loosened its grip on the tree and took flight.

"Let's follow it!" cried Uncle Shameless as he started paddling faster. Steve did the same, somehow forgetting how tired he was.

Meanwhile, behind them the blue heron followed the battered canoe.

Uncle Shameless and Steve paddled the old canoe faster and faster, ignoring the pain in their arms. Ahead of them, the eagle effortlessly soared over the river.

"Man is it *fast*!" cried Uncle Shameless. They quickly dodged fallen trees and pointed rocks in their path. Steve wondered if the bird would ever stop. They rounded another bend, and a few yards in front of them they saw a fork in the river.

"Huh, I don't remember seein' that fork b'fore," said Uncle Shameless.

"Oh c'mon, it's not like a fork in a river could just pop up over night," said Steve.

On the right side of the fork, Steve could see the back of the convenience store in the distance. On the left all he could see was a dark shaded area running under a large group of over-hanging trees.

"Follow the eagle!" Uncle Shameless cried to Steve.

"What? I can see the store up ahead, let's call it a day."

"Adventure Steve! The unknown! C'mon, paddle!"

Steve sighed and started paddling harder and harder. The eagle coasted towards the left fork and sped ahead until it disappeared under the cover of the trees. As the eagle entered the darkness, Steve thought he saw its body give off a faint blue glow.

"Okay...a glowing eagle," said Steve flatly "That's it. I'm going home."

"Hurry!" screamed Uncle Shameless as he paddled furiously and ignored Steve's observation. Water flew everywhere, and splashed into the canoe. Steve was getting soaked by both water and sweat as they approached the shaded fork in the river.

From the depth of the shadows within the tree-covered river, they heard the eagle cry again. Steve felt Uncle Shameless start to paddle even faster, and soon they penetrated the darkness of the shadows. Specks of light here and there poked through the thick tree canopy, igniting the dust in the air.

"Where are we going?!" called Steve, trying to navigate in the near darkness.

"Don't worry, we'll come out the other side and loop 'round back to the convenience store," answered Uncle Shameless.

The pair heard the eagle cry again, and they also heard a faint roaring sound growing closer and closer. They carefully avoided a trio of large rocks before the roar grew louder.

"I can see the eagle!" yelled Steve, noticing again the faint blue glow surrounding its body.

They were finally gaining on the eagle when it swooped up and perched on another dead tree in front of them. They both watched the eagle look back at them. This time its eyes were totally blue and glowed brightly in the shadows.

"Can you please explain why that eagle's eyes are glowing like two blue headlights?" asked Steve "I'm pretty sure that isn't normal."

"I don't know, maybe it grew up under power lines," suggested Uncle Shameless. Steve thought about that for a moment as the constant roar grew louder and louder until-

"A waterfall!" yelled Steve, fear overtaking him.

"That's impossibl-ahhhh!" screamed Uncle Shameless as the small canoe went over the waterfall, tossing its passengers into the swirling waters below.

They fought against the current, which was too strong for their exhausted bodies. The strong water pulled them to a whirlpool in the center. Steve did his best to stay afloat. But when he could not fight the current anymore, his body gave in and he was carried away. Uncle Shameless hurriedly swam after his nephew to save him from the whirlpool.

"Grab my hand!" yelled Uncle Shameless to the boy as he stretched as far as he could. Their fingers were only inches apart when the force of the whirlpool grew stronger and pulled them to the churning funnel.

No one heard their cries, except for the eagle that only watched with its eerie glowing eyes. It watched until both the man and boy were sucked under the waves and disappeared. It then cried loudly, and disappeared further into the shadows, the glowing of its eyes and its body fading away with it.

Shortly after, the blue heron flew from the shadows. It coasted down to the whirlpool and landed on the broken wreckage of the canoe to croon an eerie song.

Water splashed against the shore, breaking the silence. Wind rustled through the trees, carrying smells and sounds of nature.

However all of this was lost on young Steve, who was crawling through sand and mud to the shore. His head broke the surface of the water, air rushing to his burning lungs. He dug his fingers into the mud and kept pulling himself closer to the shore. Once he was close enough, and mostly out of the water, he collapsed onto the rocky surface of the beach.

Steve was exhausted, drenched, and very angry with his uncle. It dawned on him suddenly that he had better look for Uncle Shameless, otherwise he wouldn't have anyone to complain to. Steve wearily lifted up his head and looked around.

Thankfully Uncle Shameless had been washed ashore by the waves on to the small beach. This made Steve feel a little better; he didn't think his thirteen-year-old body could handle dragging his uncle out of the water.

When Steve could not stand lying on the rocky beach any longer, he summoned up his remaining strength and slowly walked towards his uncle.

"Follow the eagle, bah!" cursed Steve as he wrung out his striped shirt. Water gushed out of his black canvas high tops with each step he took. In a moment of panic, he reached up to his face and felt for his glasses.

They were gone.

"No!" he cried, trying to focus his weak eyes on the blurred images around him. No matter where he looked, all he could see was fuzzy blurs. His glasses could be right next to him and he wouldn't even know it.

While blindly searching, he remembered Uncle Shameless telling him about the excellent eyesight of the hawk and silently wished he were blessed with such a gift.

"This can't be happening," he cried again, tears began to well up in his eyes. He fought to hold back the tears, but failed.

"What's a-matter sonny?"

"Oh good, you're awake," Steve said towards Uncle Shameless as he fought back tears.

"Well of course I am! I'm not one for sleepwalkin'. Now, what's wrong?"

Steve wondered how long Uncle Shameless had actually been awake, and turned to the blurry outline of his uncle, who was still lying on the beach. "I lost my glasses," sniffed Steve.

"Oh, well that's no good. I'll help you look."

Steve kept looking for the next few minutes and eventually turned back to the blurry shape of Uncle Shameless, which had not moved at all.

"I thought you said you were going to help?"

"I am, sonny, I am."

He must be crawling on the ground, Steve thought to himself, he could have sworn it sounded like his uncle's voice had come from near the ground.

Steve ignored the thought and kept blindly feeling the ground in front on of him. The grass was soft and smelled fresh. It smelled different than the grass lawns back home in Beacon Pines, which all had a distinct chemical smell to them. This grass was long, uneven, and grew wildly and would have made his lawn maintenance obsessed father go crazy.

"Found 'em sonny!"

Steve was knocked out of his daydream. Eager to get his glasses back on he carefully maneuvered over to the sound of his uncle's voice. He wondered if Uncle Shameless was injured at all, because his voice sounded slightly different. So different in fact, that it sounded almost nothing like him.

"Where are they?" asked Steve, trying to see through the blurs in front of him.

"I'm holdin' 'em out for ya here. No a little to your left," directed the voice "There ya go!" Steve quickly grabbed the glasses and put them on, at the same time wondering how his uncle had gone to the beach without moving.

"Thanks," said Steve as he slid the glasses over his ears. He glanced around behind him and noticed Uncle Shameless was still where he had been before. Confused, Steve turned around.

"Gah!" the boy yelped, falling backwards.

In front of him stood a brown squirrel, but unlike any he had seen before. This squirrel was standing on its hind legs like a person, and was as a big as a medium sized dog. Adding even more to his confusion was the bowler hat it wore, cocked to the side to allow one long pointed ear to poke out from underneath.

"What's the matter sonny?" asked the squirrel politely.

"You aren't my uncle!"

The squirrel cocked its head in confusion, "I should hope not. I don't know how I'd explain that one to the wife."

Steve rubbed his eyes, making sure he wasn't seeing things. Sure enough the squirrel remained, and it kept looking at him.

"You can talk!" exclaimed Steve, who pinched himself to make sure he wasn't dreaming.

"Thanks, but I didn't know I needed your permission," joked the squirrel.

"You have a wife?"

The squirrel walked closer to Steve, "Oh yes. We've had five years of happiness together...but we've been married for ten! Ha-*ha*!" laughed the squirrel who playfully punched Steve in the arm. "Good one, eh?" It turned to walk away.

"Wait!" called Steve, "What's your name?"

"O'jec. O'jec of the Squirrels. No relation to O'jec of the Bears tho! Ha!" O'jec winked at Steve and quickly ran off into the woods.

"Take care sonny! Be careful next time you decide to swim in the sea!"

Steve's eyes widened, *Sea?* he thought, *what was that squirrel talking about?*

"Squirrels can't talk, I just swallowed too much water, that's all," the boy said aloud.

"Wha's that 'bout a talkin' squirrel?" a familiar voice uttered painfully.

Steve spun around to see his uncle attempting to sit up and moved over to help him. "Nothing, I was just hearing things that's all," explained Steve.

"Oh, I hope it was nothin'," started Uncle Shameless "I'd hate to think you'd gone – nuts! Ha! Get it?" Uncle Shameless' laughter was quickly drowned out by Steve's loud groaning.

"I don't know where that waterfall came from. Last I checked, there really weren't any on that stretch of the Grand River," explained Uncle Shameless as he began wringing out his torn flannel shirt.

"Well it couldn't have just appeared. It has obviously been there for years, you probably never noticed it or that crazy fork."

"Listen Steve-o, I've canoed that river for years an' I ain't never seen that fork before, let alone a big ol' water-fall."

Steve sat down on a rock and looked out onto the water. "Well, it was dumb to have followed that weird…eagle…" his words trailed off into to stunned silence.

"But it isn't too often you get to see such a majestic critter nowadays, or a even one that glows…what are you lookin' at?" Uncle Shameless turned around and followed Steve's gaze out onto the water.

He almost fainted.

Uncle Shameless had expected to see the other side of the river, as the Grand River was not that wide where they had been canoeing. Instead, all he saw was an endless sea of crystal blue water. Uncle Shameless stepped back and looked around. Only now did he realize that the trees around them were enormously tall, wide and rather spooky looking.

"Wh-wh-where are we?" he stammered.

"I was hoping you knew that," said Steve.

Uncle Shameless looked desperately for his flask, only to find it was empty. He cursed under his breath, and with a shaky hand brushed back his damp mess of hair.

"We ain't near River City, that's for certain. Heck, I don't even think we're in Michigan," Uncle Shameless said with a hint of concern. Steve stood up quickly, "Impossible! There is no way we can't still be in Michigan. We just got washed far down river, that's all."

The boy looked up at one of the large spooky trees. "I dunno, maybe we found that Northwest Passage you were talking about," joked Steve. Uncle Shameless walked up to one of the large trees and ran a hand along the coarse bark. He looked up until his neck wouldn't go back any further, and still couldn't see the top of the tree.

Uncle Shameless turned around and leaned against the tree.

"What are we going to do?" demanded Steve.

"Only thing we can - just start movin' an' see what happens."

"What?!" yelled Steve, his voice echoing through the tall trees. "Can't you think of something? You are the adult here, you are s'pose to have all the answers."

Uncle Shameless stuck his hands in the pockets of his torn jeans, "Steve, a lot about growing up is learning to think on your feet. You know what your grandfather told me once?"

"'Strange bird the pelican, it's beak holds more than its belly can'?"

"No!..Well...yes that too, but he told me that I had to be able to adapt, improvise, and to overcome."

Steve pouted and kicked at a loose rock. Uncle Shameless walked over and wrapped a caring arm around the boy,

"But don't worry, you got yer ol' uncle here to protect you," Uncle Shameless said with a wink as he gave the boy's shoulder a hearty squeeze.

A weak smile crept across the boy's face. Even though Uncle Shameless was fond of drinking, he was even fonder of looking after Steve, and the boy knew it. Uncle Shameless, having no children of his own, had always treated Steve as more of a son than a nephew.

The pair tried their best to maneuver through the thick trunks of the tall trees. They were so tall that neither of them could see the sky above. Steve kept wondering if he should tell Uncle Shameless about O'Jec of the Squirrels or not. He was still convinced he had only been hallucinating, he knew very well that squirrels did not get that big, nor could they talk. Plus, why would it be wearing a hat?

The blue heron with the blank eyes and eagle that glowed in the dark had been bad enough, running into squirrels with hats that cracked bad jokes about being married was much worse.

Eventually they came to a small clearing in a grove surrounded by the tall trees.

"What's this?" said Steve, after entering the clearing.

"Don't know...but it don't look natural," said Uncle Shameless as he pointed to some of the trees along the edge of the clearing. Steve noticed that the sides of the trees facing the clearing were stripped of leaves and branches, creating a perfect circle. Not one leaf or branch hung into the circular clearing.

Steve stopped dead in his tracks, "Look!" he shouted and pointed to the middle of the clearing.

In the exact center of the clearing stood three stone columns. They were arranged in a triangle shape. Steve inspected them closely. All three were badly damaged, chucks of rock were missing here and there. Each column had a large rune towards the top. Under the runes were etchings of what looked like humans, birds, and other creatures Steve did not recognize.

Uncle Shameless and Steve cautiously entered the center of the triangle and both looked down to see an ancient looking stone floor covered with more runes and etchings.

"What is all this junk anyway? It all looks like left over set pieces from a heavy metal stage show," Uncle Shameless said, kicking away dirt from the stone floor "Speaking of heavy metal shows, did I ever tell you about the time I met the lead singer of Mëtryk Systëm?"

"Not now please. I'm tired," yawned Steve as he began to lie down on the stone floor. He had not felt tired a few minutes ago but all of a sudden he really wanted to go to sleep.

Uncle Shameless yawned as well, "Yeah, it's been a long day, I'll save that story for later," Uncle Shameless fell down on the floor and was asleep in a matter of moments. Steve quickly fell asleep as well. He began to dream about humans, birds, and other creatures he did not recognize.

Steve opened his eyes. He quickly wanted to shut them, but he could not. He was floating in mid-air over a large castle. It stood atop a mountain and overlooked the surrounding land. It was early morning and everything was quiet.

He blinked and the castle was engulfed in flame. He heard people screaming from all directions. He blinked again and he was closer to the castle walls. He could feel the flames as they towered higher and higher.

The flapping of hundreds of wings filled the air. As he turned, he saw hundreds of flying creatures descending upon the castle walls. The images flashed by him too quickly for him to make out any exact details. Everything was blurry and Steve felt like he was watching flames dancing in a fire, or an out of focus movie projector. The creatures carried spears and swords. He saw other blurry shapes too, but these looked like humans. These human shapes had started fighting the flying creatures, but were losing.

Steve blinked again and he was floating through the air in what looked like a throne room. He heard the sounds of weapons clashing. Steve saw another ghostly, blurry person. This was an old man, even older than Uncle Shameless. He wore a crown on his head and was fighting someone or something.

Steve blinked again and saw the man with the crown being stabbed by a flaming spear held by one of the flying creatures. Only this flying creature was different, it was much larger and it frightened Steve. Unexpectedly, the ghostly creature turned slowly and looked right at Steve with horrible fire-filled eyes.

Flames poured out of the creature's burning red eyes and reached almost to the top of its head. As fire filled the background of the throne room, it let loose a horrific soul-shattering shriek. Steve covered his ears and screamed.

Steve woke up.

He was still lying on the stone floor, and looked skyward, it was night. Steve screamed, shocking Uncle Shameless awake.

"It wasn't me!" Uncle Shameless blurted randomly. Gaining his composure moments later, he looked over at Steve.

"What's wrong?"

Steve speechlessly jabbed a finger rapidly to the night sky. Uncle Shameless looked up. "Crackers!" he yelled.

In the night sky above them shined two moons.

"Okay. I can honestly say we ain't in Michigan," said a confused Uncle Shameless as he looked up at the two astral bodies.

Seconds later Steve regained use of his voice and his sense of logic "Yes we are! That's just the reflection off one of the Great Lakes! That's why we're seeing two moons!" Steve said as he tried to come up with a reason to explain the lunar anomalies.

"Ok Mr. Know-It-All," replied Uncle Shameless, "Then how do you explain that each of the 'reflections' is a different phase of the moon?"

"Well-"

"And that one is larger than the other?"

"It's-"

"*And* that one is square shaped?"

Steve paused and tried to recall the essay he had read about holes in space, but nothing he could remember would explain this.

"...Uh, swamp gas."

Uncle Shameless crossed his arms and stared at Steve with his lazy eye. "Well, if we aren't in Michigan, then just where the heck are we?" asked Steve.

"*Eyri*," said a voice inside both of their heads. Both Steve and Uncle Shameless jumped and looked around, but they could not see anyone.

Without warning there was a loud CRACK, and a pillar of blue light began to grow in the center of the three columns.

"Oh, I am *definitely* gonna need a drink," whispered Uncle Shameless.

3

The pillar of blue light grew larger and larger until a shape appeared in the glowing light. Steve could make out the hazy outline of a figure wearing a cloak.

"What the...?" Steve gasped.

A voice with a refined, scholarly male tone began to speak. Steve thought he heard what sounded like a large group of people going 'aaaaaah' together in the distance.

"And on high it was written long ago 'And lo, The Boy shall come. He who will extinguish the Flame of Evil-"

Frightened, and not knowing what was going on, Steve reached for a rock and threw it directly at the figure in the pillar of light.

"'The Flame that has burned in Eyri for'-" the rock hit the figure in the forehead with a loud WHACK! " – OW! Son-of-a-Motherless-hawk *that hurt!"*

Immediately the blue light disappeared, and the 'aaaaah'ing stopped. However the figure remained in the center of the columns, holding a hand to his forehead, and looking very irate.

"Zaa's Talons!" he cursed. "What's your problem kid?!" yelled the figure in a less refined voice. He left the center of the columns and entered the pale moonlight.

Steve and Uncle Shameless gasped in unison.

In front of them stood a blue heron, but not just any blue heron. This one stood and walked like a human and was dressed in blue robes that reached the ground. He was as tall as Uncle Shameless, but lanky, with long thin arms that ended with hands of clawed fingers. Steve noticed that unlike the birds back in Michigan, this one had no wings.

The blue heron's face was old and wrinkled, with a beak that was long and straight. On top of his head was a cap of black feathers that formed a sort of natural headdress. The bird-man reminded Steve of drawings of Egyptian gods, human-like but with animal features. As he walked closer, Steve noticed its eyes were blank pools of white.

Steve spied a slight hunch on the blue heron's back underneath his long robes. He grumbled like an old grandfather as he shambled towards the pair.

"Kids today," he grumbled "No respect for their elders!"

Once he got to Steve, he poked the boy in the chest with a long thin finger.

"Listen, I don't know where you get off throwing rocks at me, but if you weren't part of The Prophecy," thunder sounded in the distance, despite the sky being clear of clouds "I'd teach you a proper lesson! Here I am, making my first appearance in over 300 years, risking great personal danger just to give you a little back story, and you throw rocks at me!"

Steve looked at Uncle Shameless and they both shrugged.

"And another thing-" continued the blue heron as Steve reached out to pinch the angry bird-man. He yelped in pain, swatting away the boy's hand.

"What's the big idea?! By the Wings of Zaa, do I even have the right person?" the blue heron said sarcastically. "Some hero you'll make!"

"I just wanted to see if you were real," explained Steve.

"Of course I'm real!" screamed the blue heron.

"He looks real to me," added Uncle Shameless.

"Thank you!" replied the blue heron, as he pointed to Uncle Shameless, "You could learn a lot from your uncle there."

Steve was about to ask how he knew Shameless was his uncle but the blue heron walked away. His head bobbed with each step, before he finally took a seat on a tree stump.

"Bah, I need a drink," said the blue heron bitterly.

Uncle Shameless' ears perked up, "That sounds like a good idea to me!"

"It would," joked Steve.

"No need for that, young Harrier," scolded the blue heron in a slightly (but not much) less irritated tone. Steve's eyes widened. "H-how do you know my name?" he asked.

The blue heron looked at him with an expression that made Steve feel a little silly, "Oh, just The Prophecy," thunder boomed in the distance again "You know, the one I came all this way to tell you about."

The blue heron reached inside his robe, searching for something as he shook his head.

"What Prophecy?" asked Steve as thunder cracked in the sky again.

"Gee, I don't know," said the blue heron in a sarcastic tone "I think that hit on the head might have made me forget about it."

"That happened to me once," said Uncle Shameless. "I was kicked in the head by a cow and I forgot how to chew."

The blue heron tilted his head towards Uncle Shameless and blinked his blank eyes, "Really?"

"Oh yes. I was on a liquid diet until I could remember how to chew again."

"That explains a few things," Steve said with a snicker. The blue heron ignored Steve, "How did you remember how to chew again?"

Uncle Shameless walked over the blue heron eagerly, "Well, I had to remind my mouth what it was s'pose to do. So, I tied a bunch of rubber bands together to make one HUGE rubber band and ran it from the bottom of my jaw to the top of my head."

The blue heron leaned closer, gripped by the story. "Then what?" he asked with great interest.

Uncle Shameless smiled, "Then, I would put food in my mouth and then I would pull down on my jaw," he demonstrated with his hands "An' the rubber band would pull my jaw back up, making my mouth chew. I had to do that over and over. Finally, after days – no…weeks of doing this, I was able to chew normally."

"Amazing," replied the blue heron with an amused smile.

"Aw shucks, it was nothin.'"

"You bet it was nothing – because that's not what happened at all," Steve explained truthfully. Both Uncle Shameless and the blue heron looked at Steve. "When you got kicked by cow it broke your jaw. It was wired shut until it healed. That's all that happened, not some nonsense with a giant rubber band," Steve explained smartly.

Uncle Shameless rolled his eyes at his logic minded nephew. The blue heron shook his head, "But that isn't as good a story. You don't always want to hear all the boring details. "

"But that's the truth," explained Steve.

"Some times fiction is better than the truth," said the blue heron.

"That's what I keep tellin' him!" added Uncle Shameless. "Lighten up boy!"

The blue heron reached into his robes again. Finally finding what he was looking for, he pulled out what looked a sewn leather bag.

"What's that?" asked Steve.

"Haven't you ever seen a water skin b'fore?" asked Uncle Shameless. "Sorry, I'm from the suburbs. All of my water comes in plastic bottles, not stitched up animal skins," countered Steve.

"Right you are Shamus," said the blue heron as he tossed the water skin to Uncle Shameless, who was surprised that the blue heron had called him by his real name.

"Eldercherry wine," explained the blue heron with a nod towards the wine-skin.

"I dunno, I'm not much of a wine cona...cona...uh...carnasaur," stuttered Uncle Shameless.

"*Connoisseur*," corrected Steve.

"What he said," added Uncle Shameless.

"I think you'll like it, it has a nice kick."

Uncle Shameless removed the stopper from the wine-skin and took a drink, "WOOO!" Uncle Shameless bellowed. He took another sip. "I'll do my best to make it last."

"No worries," explained the blue heron "That wineskin will last longer than you think."

The blue heron stood up, "Well, since you told a story, I guess I should tell one...seeing as that's the *reason* why I came here – until I was interrupted," he said with a nasty stare towards Steve.

"Wait, what's your name?" asked Steve.

"Oh, contributing to the conversation now are we?" snapped the blue heron. "My name is Istrio, I am an Elder Mystic of Zaa."

"Yousawhatnow?" Uncle Shameless slurred.

"An Elder Mystic of Zaa."

"A Mystic of Fa?" questioned Uncle Shameless "What is that, some kind of musician?"

"Not Fa, Zaa," explained Istrio.

"What's a Zaa?" asked Steve.

"Look - if you two will pipe down, I'll tell you!"

"Sheesh, *excuse me*," said Steve.

Istrio made a quick gesture with his hands, and both began glowing with a pale blue light. As he moved his hands in small circles while chanting, Steve noticed a light blue mist filling the air around them. Suddenly an orb of blue light appeared in between the three stone columns in the middle of the clearing.

Istrio started speaking, his blank white eyes began to glow a faint blue. "Long ago, eons before Eyri existed-"

"Before what existed?" interrupted Steve.

"Eyri," Istrio the blue heron sighed "It is where you are."

"What, this forest?"

"No, not the *forest*."

"Oh, you mean the *clearing*," added Uncle Shameless.

"Not the *clearing* either!" snapped Istrio.

"I thought this was a more of glen than a clearing," added Steve.

"Naw, a glen is more like a valley," said Uncle Shameless. "You're thinking of a meadow."

Istrio's blanks eyes narrowed in frustration.

"Oh that's *right*," said Steve, slapping himself on the forehead.

"Ahem," said Istrio, clearing his throat loudly to get their attention "I'm trying to give a little exposition here. May I continue?"

"Sorry," said Steve and Uncle Shameless in unison, sounding like a pair of disciplined grade-schoolers.

"Since I *have* to be specific – You are in the northern part of the world of Eyri, which is littered with kingdoms, cities, villages and shanties. Happy?

Steve shrugged. Uncle Shameless helped himself to some more Eldercherry wine.

"As I was saying," continued Istrio, his voice shifting to its refined tone once more, "Eons before Eyri existed, there was only...*The Nothingness*."

"'The Nothingness'? Oh, *c'mon*," said Steve.

"Shh!" said Uncle Shameless, showering the boy with spittle.

Istrio continued. He waved a hand and two eagle-like shapes made of light appeared within the blue orb.

"Out of The Nothingness came the two Great Eagles...Zaa the Great Eagle of Water, Zaa the Waterbringer, Zaa the Protector..."

Steve crossed his arms and rolled his eyes.

"And Zuu the Great Eagle of Fire, Zuu the Firebringer, Zuu the Destroyer."

"Just how many names do these things have?" interrupted Steve.

"Don't interrupt!" yelled Istrio. He gestured to the shapes in the orb. One was a bright blue, the other a bright red. Flames jumped all around Zuu's fiery body, reminding Steve of his nightmare.

"The two Great Eagles created Eyri along with everything and everyone in it." The orb showed a vast land forming from the blackness, followed shortly after by plants and animals.

"But not long after that came *The Rift*," said Istrio with an added spooky tone.

"Oh, were they going sailing?" asked Uncle Shameless, who was beginning to have a hard time standing up thanks to the wine.

"*Rift*, not raft," corrected Steve.

"My mistake," apologized Uncle Shameless with a sloppy curtsy. Istrio shook his head and continued. "As I was saying, then came *The Rift*."

"Which was?" asked Steve.

"The disagreements that would lead to the divide between the worshipers of Zaa and Zuu, and change the course of Eyri's history."

"Yes, I get it, and?" asked Steve, growing impatient.

"Zaa decreed that the week should start on Ookday, while Zuu decreed that the week should begin on Ushday," explained Istrio in a very serious tone. "Additionally, Zuu also declared that no one was to receive presents on their birthday, but Zaa disagreed. Thus The Rift between the two Great Eagles was formed."

Steve's jaw dropped, "What?"

"Yes, I know. Silly isn't it?" answered Istrio.

"Very."

"You're telling me. Starting the week on Ushday. Pure madness," finished Istrio, not getting Steve's sarcasm.

"No presents on your birthday?" added Uncle Shameless. "That's no fun."

"...Does any of this have a *point*?" sighed Steve, wishing he had a watch to look at to stress his boredom.

Istrio rolled his blank eyes, "I'm getting there...then came The War of Fire!" yelled Istrio. The orb showed Eyri breaking out in war, "Zuu took the form of Atrox the Warrior and Zaa took-"

"Can't you summarize all of this?" interrupted Steve.

Istrio sighed loudly, "Fine. Then came the War of Fire. Events happened-"

"Events happened'?" laughed Steve.

"Well you weren't happy with the short version, so now I have to do the *short*-short version."

"*That* was the short version?" questioned the boy.

Istrio ignored Steve and continued his hastened history of the world of Eyri, "Then came The Great Union. Events happened. Then The Peace, in which slightly fewer events happened, because after all we were at peace. But, although Zuu and his followers had been fought back during The War of Fire, he still pined for the day that all of Eyri would worship him."

"By having the week start on Ushday and not giving out birthday presents?" replied Steve condescendingly.

"Exactly!" exclaimed Istrio, again missing Steve's sarcasm.

"Then, 313 years ago, Zuu got his chance. There was a young Hawken warrior who was tired of having the week begin on Ookday and also tired of living under the gift-giving ruler Fel-Ra, the Owl-Queen."

Before Steve could ask who or what a Hawken was, the orb showed a creature that had the body like a man, but the head and clawed feet of a hawk. Feathers covered its body, even though it had a human like chest and limbs. Unlike the blue heron, huge feathery wings extended from its back.

"...I s'pose they couldn't just recall this Fel-Ra, huh?" joked Steve. The blue heron glared at him.

"The young warrior sought out others who shared his ideals and found the last remaining Mystics of Zuu, not seen since the War of Fire. While with the Mystics, Zuu appeared to the young warrior, Fiach, in a vision. In this vision, Zuu told Fiach that he alone had been chosen to make Zuu's wish a reality. The Firebringer told him to travel far away to his abandoned temple of Zooris Gol, which was built at the base of Mount-"

"Is this going anywhere?" asked Steve "I'm already losing track of all these names, I mean c'mon, Zaa, Zuu, Fiach, Fel? I can't remember which is which. They're all running together, don't you have more than two letters when it comes to names around here?"

Istrio pouted and glared at Steve. Uncle Shameless glared with his lazy eye. Steve glanced at the floating orb, the faces of those represented in it were glaring at him too.

"Sheesh, sorry...go ahead," said Steve.

Istrio continued, his hands glowed once more as the he went on with the story. Again.

"And SO...it was at Zooris Gol that Fiach recovered the Spear of Zuu, lost since The Wa-

"War of Fire, yes," sighed Steve.

"-A horrible weapon that granted him great power," continued Istrio without missing a beat "It increased his strength a hundred fold and he flew away to build his army."

The orb showed the hawk warrior flying through the sky engulfed in flame, wielding a large spear with an obelisk shaped blade.

"Ooooo!" crooned Uncle Shameless as he watched the orb.

"He did not build his army overnight, but Fiach preached the frailty of Zaa and her followers to those among his kind who would listen." The orb flashed to scenes of an energetic Fiach working a crowd of Hawken into a frenzy as he spoke, waving the Spear and what looked like a crude calendar around in front of a pile of burning birthday presents. Steve noted the fire pouring out of Fiach's eyes.

"After winning over his fellow Hawken with promises of power, a proper week, and no obligations to buy presents, Fiach traveled to Swanta, home of the ancient enemies of the owls – the Swantans," the orb showed a mass of brawny, swan-like bird-people in full armor. Steve had a feeling they did more than just hiss and bite.

"With his army finally in hand, Fiach struck the owls without warning during the day-"

"Why during the day?" asked the boy, his eyes fixed on the orb. "That's when owls sleep silly," explained the boy's uncle "Seems kinda unsporting if ya ask me."

"Right you are Shamus," said Istrio "Fiach usurped Fel-Ra's throne and crowned himself Fiach-Ra, Hawk-King."

"With the owls conquered and the animal kingdom under his control, Fiach-Ra turned his army against Donal the Mighty, the human king."

Guessing this wasn't going to end anytime soon, Steve made himself comfortable on the ground. Uncle Shameless was already beginning to nod off.

"Just as before, Fiach-Ra combined the foot solider Swantan army with his flying Hawken and launched a ghastly surprise attack against Donal's castle-"

"How was he able to keep getting away with all these sneak attacks?" interjected Steve, finding it hard to believe that a large army of loutish bird-people dressed in full battle armor could sneak up on anything.

Istrio hesitated for a moment. "Magic."

"Magic? You *can't* be serious."

"Well that, plus Donal and Fel-Ra had both grown old and a bit...*comfortable*," explained Istrio carefully "They kind of let their guard down. But it was mostly magic. Mostly. Really, it was."

"Sure it was," said Steve, rolling his eyes as Istrio motioned to the orb. The boy watched as flying Hawken warriors descended upon the castle walls, and opened the gates from the inside to allow the ferocious Swantan army to enter on foot.

The orb flashed after a few seconds and showed a castle burning while humans fought both Hawken and Swantan warriors. Steve looked at the orb and a shiver ran down his spine.

They were the same images from his dream.

"Wait," said Steve, confused. "I thought Zuu was the water-eagle-great-aunt-thing, why would this Frittata guy have a flaming spear?"

The blue heron sighed, "Are you even paying attention? Zaa is the Waterbringer...and Zuu is the...," Istrio looked at the lost expression on Steve's face and decided to sum it up "Ok – Zaa is good, water is good. Zuu is bad, fire is bad and it's Fiach-Ra...not Frittata. Got it?"

Steve shrugged, "I guess. It's just hard because they both have 'Z' names."

"This reminds me of the time I met two men named Smith," said Uncle Shameless, who was losing both his grip on language and balance thanks to the Eldercherry wine.

"Y'see, both of 'em would stand by this fork in the road and gave people directions to town..."

Steve groaned, but Uncle Shameless continued "But da kicker was that one always told the truth and one always lied," Uncle Shameless slurred something unintelligible "...and *anyways*, that's how I met my *last* wife."

Steve glanced at Istrio, he was repeatedly rubbing his temples and muttering 'why me?'.

"Will you please let me finish? We are on a bit of timetable here people." The blue heron Mystic stressed this point by producing an hour glass and pointed to the sand falling.

"Timetable? For what?" asked Steve.

"The Prophecy!" yelled Istrio as thunder roared in the distance.

"Why does thunder roar whenever you say 'prophecy'?" asked Steve, who waited for it to happen again and was surprised when it didn't.

"Oh," said Istrio "That's a standard thing."

"Wait, how come it didn't thunder just now when I said 'prophecy'?" asked Steve.

"Because, you just said the indefinite version of 'prophecy,' you must refer to The Prophecy for the thunder to roar."

And sure enough, thunder boomed once more in the distance.

Steve shook his head, "This is ridiculous, there's no way a word can create thunder. It's all a coincidence."

Realizing that they were way off topic, the blue heron tried to continue his lengthy exposition, "Stop getting me off the subject kid…Blast, I've lost my place…where was I?"

"Birds fighting people," mumbled Uncle Shameless.

"Oh yes. Thank you Shamus."

Istrio continued his storytelling and began gesturing again, causing different places and people to appear in the floating orb nearby.

"And so, Fiach-Ra fought Donal in his throne room. Fiach-Ra was after the Sword of Zaa, which was wielded by Donal." Steve watched as a ghostly visage of Fiach-Ra and Donal appeared in the orb and began to fight each other.

Istrio continued, "They fought endlessly, because Donal knew that if Fiach-Ra took the Sword of Zaa he would be unstoppable."

"Oh, of course," said Steve, shaking his head as he yawned.

"Knowing he was no longer strong enough to defeat Fiach-Ra, Donal decided he had to hide the Sword of Zaa."

Istrio gestured, and the orb showed the pair fighting even harder. Donal was wounded, but made a desperate attack and swung the sword towards Fiach-Ra's unprotected face, slashing at his left eye. The Hawken warrior howled with rage and pain.

"Ouch," said Steve, watching with interest.

"Yes, well this gave Donal enough time to run away and to give the Sword to one of his Mystics." The orb showed Donal running through the castle to what looked like a small stone chapel. Steve watched in surprise as he saw Donal give the sword to Istrio.

Steve turned and faced the blue heron, "You?!" Istrio nodded and gestured back towards the orb.

Fiach-Ra stormed through the castle, setting anything and everything aflame with streams of burning fire that shot from the tip of the Spear of Zuu. He left eye was healed, yet a long scar through the eye remained.

"Fiach-Ra's evil magic saved his eye, elevating him to demigod status among his Hawken warriors."

"Why?" asked Steve.

"Because the Hawken value their hawk-sight above everything else. The greatest disgrace in their society is to be blinded. That is why Donal made the attack he did, hoping at least Fiach-Ra would be disgraced. His magic saved his eye but he was scarred."

The orb then showed Fiach-Ra reaching the chapel where Donal and Istrio were. The blue heron grasped the sword and disappeared in a flash of blue light just as Fiach-Ra kicked in the door. Donal spun around to face his attacker, weaponless.

Fiach-Ra's large frame was too tall to fit through the door, so he stooped down and entered the room. His massive wings blocked the exit. He stared down at Donal with his evil burning eyes and raised his flaming spear to throw it –the orb went black.

"Wait, what happened?" asked Steve as Uncle Shameless began snoring next to him. Istrio lowered his head, "Donal sacrificed himself to protect the Sword of Zaa, which he knew was the only thing that could ever stop Fiach-Ra."

Istrio continued, "After the fall of the human kingdom, the surviving humans were banished to the swamps in the east and the owls were…well, an even worse fate befell them. Fiach-Ra built his evil castle, Arx Vena'Tor, and his new city Da'Rahga in the west. Now the only realm free from Fiach-Ra's rule is the sea, which is still controlled by the Wurms. Fiach-Ra has since ruled over Eyri for 313 years as tyrant-king."

"So…what does this have to do with me?" asked Steve, skeptical, but glad the lengthy exposition was over. He elbowed Uncle Shameless, forcing him awake.

"It was seen by the Three Sisters in a vision that a boy and a man would come to Eyri, brought here by Zaa, to free us from the yoke of tyranny."

"Huh?" said Steve and Uncle Shameless in unison. The blue heron sighed, "You two must find the Sword of Zaa and defeat the Hawk-King."

"Oh, come on!" yelled Steve "I'm from the suburbs, I don't know anything about looking for lost magical swords!"

"You can do this, it says so in The Prophecy," explained Istrio over the thunder in the distance.

"I don't think so," said Steve, "I don't even like nature, and the last thing I want to do is go prancing around in the forest looking for some rusty oversized letter opener. Besides, that Donal guy gave it to you. Don't you have it?"

The blue heron shook his head, "For the record, no one said anything about prancing…but I gave the Sword to the Three Sisters. You must find them to find the sword."

Steve crossed his arms, "And where are they?"

The blue heron shook his head again, "You must find that out for yourself. But first you must go east to Uth, The Last Human Village, located deep within the swamps of the Forbidden Forest.

"...If the forest and the swamp are both forbidden, why do people live there?" asked Steve.

"Look, it's just a name," explained Istrio. "You must complete this quest. You are the one destined to free Eyri-"

"Yeah-yeah. From the yoke of tyranny, I heard you the first time," sighed Steve.

"So, you will fulfill The Prophecy?" asked Istrio with a slight cheer in his voice. Steve waited for the thunder in the distance to stop roaring. "I guess," he sighed.

"Count me in!" said Uncle Shameless, who was sprawled out on the ground..

"Splendid!" exclaimed Istrio as he walked over to Steve. The Mystic produced an amulet from a pocket and put it around Steve's neck.

The amulet had a silver chain, while the amulet itself was made of blueish-silver. It had oddly shaped projections on the outside edge that reminded Steve of a broken clock gear or a circular saw blade. The amulet was composed of three rings. In the center of the amulet was a blue heron's head, and the eye was a small sparkling jewel.

Surrounding the blue heron's head in the center of the amulet were three triangular shaped holes, one near the top of the head and one on either side of the bottom.

"This will protect you on your journey," explained Istrio as he patted Steve on the head, messing up his hair, much to the boy's frustration.

"Wha-what 'bout me?" asked Uncle Shameless, who was on the ground waiting for the sky to stop spinning.

"Ah, but you have the wine I gave you," said Istrio with a long smile as he reached down and helped Uncle Shameless stand up. "That will help you on your journey."

The blue heron looked at his hourglass, "Well, I suppose that's about it then, I should be going. Good luck boys, and don't worry. I'll be keeping an eye on you."

"Swell," mumbled Steve.

The blue heron's body started to glow in a pale blue light, "There are crossroads beyond the clearing in that direction," he said in a ghostly, reverb filled voice as he pointed south. "Head east towards

Uth for the Last Human Village..." his voice trailed off as he disappeared in a flash of blue light.

"Phew," sighed Steve, "I though he'd never leave."

4

"I dunno Steve-o, I think we should do what the nice bird-man asked us to," slurred Uncle Shameless as they headed south to the crossroads through the odd looking forest.

"Forget all of this nonsense about magic eagles and bird-men with pointy sticks. I wanna go home," stated the boy.

"But, you told him you would help."

"If I hadn't, he would have kept going on and on. Seriously I thought that little back-story of his would *never* end," said Steve. "I don't believe any of this, its all just someone messing with us."

"I dunno, he looked pretty real to me," said Uncle Shameless as he stumbled around next to Steve.

"This can't be real. There's no such thing as walking, talking birds," added the boy.

"But you just spent the last hour with one."

"Was that all?" joked Steve "It felt more like six hours with that crazy story with all those weird names."

They finally reached the edge of the forest and passed through the last of the giant trees. The land outside of the giant tree forest was brown and dry with blight. The grass and plants were all brown, and the regular sized trees were twisted into odd shapes. An eerie silence surrounded them; a silence that suggested something bad was about to happen.

"Never seen that happen to a tree b'fore," said Uncle Shameless, looking at a barren tree twisted into a figure eight.

"Ah, who cares? It's just a side effect of pollution run off or something. Let's just get out of this crazy place," said Steve.

As they walked on the brown grass, it cracked under their footsteps, leaving visible footprints behind them. Steve's footprints were in a straight line, whereas Uncle Shameless' were in circles and curls as he stumbled through the grass after his nephew.

The pair eventually reached the crossroads. A simple dirt road ran from East to West in front of them. In the center of the road rested a tall metal pole.

"Ew!" cried Steve.

Attached to the pole was a skeleton – of what, Steve could not tell - with its arms crossed at its chest. Its right hand pointed to the west, and its left hand pointed to the east.

The skeleton still had tattered clothing hanging from it, and burning candles were resting in its eye sockets. Small hand-painted signs hung from each of its hands and rocked gently in the night air.

Steve motioned to the sign that pointed west to Da'Rahga.

"Let's go there. Birdo said it was a big city. I'm sure we can find someone to help us, or at least get to a phone."

Uncle Shameless motioned to the other sign that read Uth, The Last Human Village, "I dunno Steve, that heron guy said to head east."

"To that *forbidden* swamp in the *forbidden* forest?" Steve said, showing his contempt for the idea of a 'forbidden' place that people actually lived in. "I don't think so, I'm not going into a swamp to look for people. No thank you." Images of stereotypical backwoods river people with three teeth, overalls, banjos and a preference for watery, mass-produced beer popped into the boy's head. Steve grabbed Uncle Shameless by his tattered flannel shirt and headed west towards Da'Rahga.

Da'Rahga, or The City of Flame as it was also known, was where Fiach-Ra had built his wicked castle Arx Vena'Tor on the ruins of the seat of the former human kingdom. Fiach-Ra's throne room was at the top of the high towering castle.

The Hawk-King's city was called The City of Flame because of the magical Wall of Fire that encircled its perimeter, protecting the city from would-be rebels, attackers, solicitors and children selling cookies.

The Wall of Fire glowed brightly in the dark night as Steve and Uncle Shameless approached. The brightness of the magical wall was part of the reason everyone who lived in the city was always in such a bad mood, and its residents had a reputation for being rather curt with each other.

It was impossible to get a good night's sleep in Da'Rahga. The Wall of Fire glowed so brightly at night, that it was like trying to go to sleep in the middle of a summer day. Then there was the noise. The Wall of Fire made as much noise as a small camp fire, except multiplied by a million times and piped through one of those super-fancy sound systems that movie fans only dream about.

The quickest way for one to find themselves on the business end of a sword in Da'Rahga was to ask a citizen how they slept last night.

Steve and Uncle Shameless shielded their eyes when they came closer to the wall. Steve looked as closely at the Wall of Fire as he could; it was around fifty feet high. He watched the flames dance around, snapping and crackling loudly.

"Crackers!" Uncle Shameless yelled over the noise of the burning wall "The city is burning!"

Steve looked around again, and noticed buildings through the flames. They reminded him of adobe buildings. They were all a light brown color and square shaped. "I don't think the city is burning, I don't see smoke," Steve observed.

"Phew, sure is hot though," added Uncle Shameless. "Steve, are you hot?"

The boy ignored his uncle. "Are ya hot?!" his Uncle yelled over the roar of the Wall of Fire.

Knowing that Uncle Shameless would keep this up for hours, Steve gave in and told his uncle what he wanted to hear "Yes," he sighed as he spoke the words slowly, "I am hot."

"Well, then take your shirt off!" laughed his uncle. Steve groaned.

The boy scanned the wall. He spotted an entrance not too far from where they were standing and started walking over to it.

"Strange bird the pelican!" bellowed Uncle Shameless randomly, in a wine fueled stupor. "Its beak holds more than its...uh," Uncle Shameless stumbled over the last line.

"Belly can," finished Steve.

"Oh yes, that's the one. Sorry this wine sure packs a punch, it's makin' me feel a wee bit odd."

"You've *always* been a wee bit odd," joked Steve, while keeping his eyes on the Wall of Fire.

"We're all a wee bit odd boy, some are just a wee bit more than others."

As they approached the gate, Steve noticed a pair of guards. One was short, just under Uncle Shameless' height of six feet. The other was almost seven feet tall. Both were bird-men. The short one had the face and wings of a hawk.

Its body was built like a man's, except the head, which was like a bird's. The other guard was the same, except instead of being covered in brown feathers, it was covered in white feathers. This taller bird-man did not have wings, and instead of a sharp hooked hawk beak, it had a rounded orange swan bill with a ring of black around it.

Steve guessed that the tall bird-man was a Swantan and the short one was a Hawken. Both were clad in armor; the Swantan had heavy plate armor, and the Hawken wore light chain mail. The Hawken warrior proudly held a menacing looking spear, while the Swantan stood alert with a large sword strapped to its back.

The guards had not yet noticed Steve and Uncle Shameless. The boy pulled his uncle aside.

"Look, I'm sure these guys will let us in if we say we need help. Let me do the talking, I'll use the old 'helpless kid' act." Uncle Shameless looked at Steve with concerned eyes and put a comforting hand on his shoulder.

"Steve..." he spoke slowly. Steve tried not to stare at his uncle's lazy eye.

"Yes?"

"Are you hot?"

Steve rolled his eyes and peeled his uncle's hand off as Uncle Shameless started roaring with laughter.

The two guards stood vigilantly at their post, which was mostly for show since the Wall of Fire protected the city from nearly any peril - except for one instance involving a overly dedicated cookie sales-kid and a catapult. To say the position of gate guard was ceremonial would be a great overstatement. It was the lowest of lowly jobs in Fiach-Ra's army.

If one were to look at a hierarchy flow chart of positions in Fiach-Ra's army, the gate guards would not even be there – but ditch diggers would. The job was so low, that those stuck with it had to look up to look down.

The short Hawken warrior stretched his wings and clicked his hooked beak.

"I tell ya Kaz, this is only temporary. I have an idea to get out of this boring military job," the Hawken said to his Swantan partner. Kaz rolled his beady, swan-like eyes, growing tired of the conversation that he knew was going to follow.

"Remmit, you say that everyday, but your plan won't work."

"You say that now, but I'll show you. My idea will make this city better, you'll see."

"Blindfolds and earplugs? No one will buy 'em. I don't think they'll help people get a good night's sleep like you say."

Remmit sighed, a few of the feathers on his head ruffled up. He pushed them back down with a clawed hand before continuing.

"Look big guy, to get ahead you have to be an idea person. Big ideas make the world go 'round. The blindfolds and earplugs will block out all the light and racket from the Wall of Fire. Everyone 'round here will be able to get a good night sleep for first time since that thing was put up. I'll corner the market on sleep aides in Da'Rahga, retire young, and build a cozy nest on the northern coast."

Kaz thought hard for a few moments, which was difficult since Swantans were not known as great thinkers, mainly due to the small brain that rattled around in their cavernous skulls. Their enemies would use this to their advantage by lobbing simple word problems at the large bird-men. By the time a Swantan would figure it out, their enemy could be long gone.

"...The world goes 'round?" Kaz finally said. Remmit buried his face into his free hand and decided to change the subject.

"Are you doing any planning for the future?"

"Well, I was thinking that after my shift I might go down to Wheezy's House of Pies-"

"Not that," sighed Remmit.

"What do you mean?"

"Y'know putting money away. Investing. You're no spring swan y'know, you're gonna have to retire eventually," explained Remmit.

"Swantans don't retire. They die in battle," stated Kaz proudly. Remmit sighed again, "What happens if you can't find a battle to die in? There haven't been too many battles around here lately."

"That isn't true, we had a battle last week, remember?"

"I don't think chasing away kids that were throwing rocks at the Wall of Fire counts as a battle."

"But they were *big* rocks..."

"Face it my flightless friend," said the hawk, flapping his wings slightly, "Gate Guard duty is a slow death."

Kaz sighed, knowing this was true. The real action was within the raiding parties that the Hawk-King sent out to keep the population of Eyri in line. The job was to randomly show up at a city, town, village, or shanty and cause wanton destruction.

The idea was that this destruction would keep the population of Eyri afraid of Fiach-Ra and his armies, thus keeping everyone on their best behavior.

Kaz cracked the knuckles of his large hands and looked at his partner, "The answer is yes," he said eventually.

"Oh, you're going to start bathing more? That's great because-"

"No!" yelled the angry swan-man, his heavy plate mail rattling, "I mean, yes I've been planning for the future."

"Excellent!" exclaimed Remmit, clapping a free hand to the Swantan warrior's armor covered shoulder, like a drummer hitting a cymbal.

"I've been keeping part of my pay under my bunk in the barracks," Kaz said proudly. Remmit shook his head, "No, no. You have to invest. Make the money work for you."

"Huh?"

Remmit turned to look at Kaz, "You should make a budget for all your expenses each week, and whatever you don't spend, you should invest into-"

Remmit quickly turned to face the down the path, in the distance he saw two shapes approaching and they appeared to be arguing. Even though he had the gift of hawk-sight, it did not fare too well at night. *That* ability was granted to the owls. He would have to wait until they moved more into the light cast by the Wall of Fire to get a better view.

"What is it?" asked Kaz.

"Trespassers!"

A sinister smile crept across Kaz's bill as he slowly drew his sword from the scabbard on his back.

"No, let *me* do the talking," pleaded Steve over and over.

"Now now, don't worry m'boy. I'm quite apt at talking my way into places," Uncle Shameless patted the boy on the head and walked in front of him.

As they walked closer to the gate, the heat from the Wall of Fire gradually increased. Sweat began rolling down Steve's back. It was not caused by the heat, but rather by his concern about getting into the city. He wanted to go home. Even if these creatures were real – which he still refused to believe – the whole idea of saving this land from a winged tyrant did not really appeal to him.

Remmit watched as the dark shapes approached. He wondered if they were solicitors, in fact he hoped they were. The guards had free reign to dispose of solicitors as they saw fit according to their supervisor, a lazy Hawken officer by the name of Lexa.

Finally, the shapes entered the brilliant light put off by the Wall of Fire.

"Hu-mans!" exclaimed Remmit as he studied the pair with his expert vision. The tall one with shaggy hair started tucking in his tattered shirt, which Remmit guessed was a poor attempt to impress them. Kaz held his sword out in front of him; Remmit gripped his spear with both clawed hands.

Uncle Shameless grabbed Steve's hand and shushed to him to keep quiet, showering the boy in cherry-scented spittle.

Remmit narrowed his eyes; he wondered what a pair of humans were doing this far from the swamps.

Kaz studied the pair and wondered what 'invest' meant.

"Keep quiet and follow my lead," winked Uncle Shameless as he took a quick drink from his wineskin. He gripped Steve's hand tighter and started walking faster. The guards tried their best to look extra menacing, which was not too hard. Learning how to look as mean as possible was a standard part of basic training in Fiach-Ra's army.

Uncle Shameless and Steve walked right up to the guards…and then walked right past them, heading towards the large twin doors several yards down the wide hallway.

Remmit and Kaz looked at each other confused and wondered why the humans had not stopped. Remmit, thanks to his small agile frame, quickly maneuvered in front of Uncle Shameless and blocked his way with his spear.

"Where do you think you are going hu-man?" asked Remmit in a deep menacing voice.

Uncle Shameless stood up straight, looked the Hawken warrior straight in the eye, and said with great confidence, "Don't you know who I am?"

This caught Remmit off guard. A human had never spoken in this manner to him before. When humans did speak to him, it was mostly something like 'Not in the face!' or 'I'm a bleeder!' He wondered if he was supposed to know who these humans were, he didn't remember hearing about any important people arriving when he'd had his daily briefing with Lexa prior to the start of his shift.

Not that his daily briefing was anything noteworthy anyway. It was more a technicality than anything, like telling a wall to hold up a house. Remmit clicked his beak and looked past the strangers to Kaz for a sign that perhaps he knew the humans.

Kaz only shrugged, which did not surprise Remmit. "No, I don't," admitted the Hawken slowly.

Uncle Shameless sighed and shook his head, "Well, I s'pose I can let it go *this* time." He effortlessly pushed the heavy spear aside, much to Remmit's surprise, and continued walking down the hall.

Now Remmit and Kaz were even more confused. *Just who was this man?* Thought Remmit. He was not intimidated by the Hawken or the Swantan at all, which was odd for a human. Remmit motioned to Kaz to bring up the rear behind the strangers and took to the air in the high ceiling of the entryway and flew down in front of the strangers with a WOOSH of air.

"I said halt, hu-man!" yelled Remmit.

Uncle Shameless did not even blink, and continued his act.

"Look here Mister...?" he said bitterly, like someone who had visited a store's complaint department one too many times.

"Remmit."

"Look here Mister *Remmit*, I don't even want to be here," he jabbed Remmit's chain-mail covered chest with his index finger to stress the point, although it felt to Remmit like he was being punched "But I *have* to go inside."

"What is your business inside, hu-man?"

"*That* is classified. Look, just let me in so I can do my business and get out of here. I don't wanna say this is a bad city, but I've been thrown out of better places then this dump."

Again Remmit foolishly looked to Kaz for an idea about what to do. All Kaz did was pantomime cutting their heads off. Even though that would have pleased Remmit, something about this situation told him it might not be a good idea.

"Are you going to let me in or not? I have *things* to do," stated Uncle Shameless, never once breaking eye contact with the guard.

Remmit clicked his hooked beak repeatedly, trying to figure out what to do. Uncle Shameless grew impatient and decided to up the ante.

"Let me speak to your supervisor," he said quickly. Behind him Steve let out a hushed yelp, Remmit's eyes widened in surprise, and Kaz dropped his sword.

The only thing the Hawken officer Lexa liked more than not doing his job was a good night's sleep. But such a thing was a rare commodity in Da'Rahga since The Wall of Fire, necessary for protection of the city and those within (or so they were told), was a major public nuisance. The noise and light emitted by the wall were such an annoyance that lately it had become common practice for warriors and officers to disobey orders in hopes of getting reassigned to some remote region of Eyri and finally get some decent sleep.

Several other soldiers went another route; and did their best to get thrown into the dungeons of the castle Arx Vena'Tor. Sadly, these soldiers had forgotten that being thrown into the dungeons was the first stop before being thrown into The Pit of Big Nasty Things.

Lexa however, was closing in on his goal of getting reassigned. He had been acting poorly for the past few weeks, and only recently had been demoted to supervising the guards of the main gate. The gate guard position was a joke since the Wall of Fire kept the city far safer than two lowly guards ever could, especially the pair guarding it at that very moment.

Supervising this position was even more of a joke, because there was next to nothing to supervise. Still, to keep up with his plan to be reassigned out of the city, Lexa did his best to do less.

He had gone from being a high-ranking advisor in Fiach-Ra's favor, to the supervisor of the lowliest position in the city in just over a fortnight, which was a new record.

All Lexa needed was one more major failure and he was free from the noise and light of the Wall of Fire.

Kaz stayed behind to watch the strangers while Remmit flew quickly to Lexa's quarters to fetch the officer. Lexa lived in a small square shaped adobe house that rested on the top of a pole close to the castle, Arx Vena'Tor.

Lexa had lived in the castle itself until recently, but with his demotion came a change in living arrangements. The noise and light from the Wall of Fire had been bad enough when he was living high above the city in Arx Vena'Tor, but it was considerably worse in his new dwellings.

Luck, however, seemed to be on Lexa's side that night as Remmit landed outside Lexa's door and knocked sharply.

"Sir? We need you at the gate. We have a…situation."

"Go away," barked the Hawken officer from inside.

"But sir-"

Remmit heard Lexa get up and walk towards the door. His talons clicked against the floor as he walked. Lexa flung open the door and stared at Remmit.

"I don't care what's going on. I don't want to deal with it."

Lexa figured if he ignored the problem, it might just add to his getting reassigned.

"But sir."

"Good night," said Lexa as he started to close the door

"Sir! Two hu-mans are at the gate and demand entrance to the city!" pleaded Remmit, the feathers on his neck sticking up.

Lexa's eyes opened to the size of saucers and he smiled broadly with inspiration. Lexa clicked his beak and thought to himself that surely Zuu was smiling upon him.

The two Hawken warriors took flight and headed toward the gate, their mighty wings flapping loudly in the night air. Lexa was older than Remmit and had white feathers around parts of his head intermixed with the regular brown.

Lexa had taken the time to put on his full officer trappings; the traditional Hawken loincloth decorated with Fiach-Ra's emblem and colors, silver shoulder armor, chain mail vest similar to Remmit's, and lastly long silver wrist guards that identified him as an officer.

The winged pair quickly reached the gate and descended upon the strangers and Kaz. Uncle Shameless was busy telling Kaz a story to past the time, "And then what happened?" asked the swan-man, who listened intently while leaning on his sword.

"Well, the boy's dad an' me finally show up at the party...and my nose is broken. So I says, I says 'Oh, we were moving a dresser downstairs and-"

Lexa screeched as he landed, getting the group's attention. Steve had been sitting on the ground, ignoring his uncle's story. The giant hawk's screech made him jump, reminding him of the hawk attack on the Grand River.

Lexa approached Uncle Shameless and extended his wings to their full span with a loud FLAP! Lexa walked slowly towards Uncle Shameless, his light chain mail rattled but was barely heard over the crackling from the Wall of Fire.

Lexa towered over Uncle Shameless and looked him over. He was unimpressed to say the least. He had hoped the humans were burly looking adventurers, or at least disgustingly cute cookie sales-kids.

Still, he thought, these humans might help him get relocated that very night.

"These are the hu-mans who demanded entry the city sir. They claim to have business here but won't tell us what it is," explained Remmit from behind Lexa.

Lexa clicked his mighty hooked beak at Uncle Shameless, "Is this true hu-man?" asked the Hawken officer.

"Yes, and if you don't mind I'd like to get on with things," said Uncle Shameless.

"So," mused Lexa while walking around Uncle Shameless and Steve, examining the rag-tag pair, "I'm to believe that a hu-man dressed in shabby tattered clothes, reeking of wine, and dragging along a child has classified business within the city?"

"That's correct," lied Uncle Shameless without blinking.

Lexa leaned down until the tip of his beak was mere inches from Uncle Shameless' face. His large hawk eyes stared deeply into Uncle Shameless'. Steve wondered if the bird-man was going to bite his uncle's nose much like the duck at Islands Park had. Uncle Shameless returned the bird-man's iron stare without so much as a flinch.

"Very well," said Lexa eventually, rising to his full height "Let them in." Both Remmit and Kaz were shocked "But Sir!" they cried in unison.

"I take full responsibility," said the officer "They are being let in on my authority and my authority alone" he bellowed, secretly savoring a chance to finally bellow a command of any kind "If anyone – especially higher ranking officers – asks who let them in, let it be know it was I."

Lexa turned and poked Uncle Shameless in the chest with a long clawed finger. "Also," he continued, "If anyone asks *you two* who let you in, or if you get into trouble," Steve thought he saw the Hawken wink at his uncle, "Inform them that it was Lexa who granted you entrance to Da'Rahga. I have spoken hu-man."

Lexa flapped his wings open "Enjoy your visit," he said before flapping his expansive wings again for take off. Remmit and Kaz called after him, but their cries were drowned out by the Wall of Fire. The two guards looked at each other and then looked at Uncle Shameless and Steve. Uncle Shameless had a very smug grin on his face.

Remmit sighed, "Right this way please...*sirs*," and lead the pair through the long entryway.

High in the air Lexa laughed. He had found a sure-fire way to get out of Da'Rahga. Once his superiors found out he had allowed two humans into the city, he would be reassigned for sure.

It would only be a matter of moments until they were discovered by someone else and arrested. Once they followed the paper trail back to him, he would be kicked out.

Lexa decided to go back home and start packing.

Uncle Shameless and Steve walked down the stone path leading into the center of the city. All of the buildings were made of drab colored adobe bricks, and each building was a boxy square shape.

Steve could not believe what he was seeing, mainly because he did not want to believe any of it. Next to him Uncle Shameless walked proudly, gloating over his success on getting them into the city.

"Yessir, didn't I tell you I'd get us inside? Eh?" Uncle Shameless elbowed Steve in the ribs lightly over and over until the boy caved and agreed.

"I've used that routine more times then you know. Y'see, the trick is you, just walk in like you own the place and you are s'pose to be there."

Steve listened while looking at the stacked buildings along the path leading to the center of the city.

"Most of the time they just have some Johnny Punchclock workin' the door who doesn't wanna get into any trouble if you really are some VIP."

Uncle Shameless brushed back his mangled hair with a free hand. "Yessir, it's about actin' smooth and it's all about plannin'."

The pair rounded a corner (in Uncle Shameless' case, stumbled) and found themselves in the center square of the city. It was deserted; the only thing within the square was a large statue in the middle. It showed a Hawken warrior standing proudly on statues of a smaller, prone human and owl-person. In its right hand was a large, menacing spear.

"That must be that Fi..Feefifofum guy," said Uncle Shameless.

"Fiach-Ra," corrected Steve who studied the statue. He had never seen any statuary in person before, the art museum in the big city near Beacon Pines had closed down after the mayor lost all the artwork in an euchre game with a mayor from Ohio.

"I'd guess that the statues underneath his feet represent those he stole power from, Donal and Fel-Ra," noted Steve.

"You certainly remembered that pretty well for not believing it," said Uncle Shameless.

Steve shrugged. He had always been good at remembering useless trivia and he definitely considered *this* useless trivia. Steve glanced around and noticed other pieces of artwork – murals, mosaics, and posters all showing Fiach-Ra with his standard sinister scowl.

"This guy must really like looking at himself," said Steve as he inspected a mural that depicted Fiach-Ra teaching Hawken hatchlings to read, which Steve thought looked rather odd and unnatural.

Uncle Shameless looked up past the statue into the sky above the city "Now," he said to Steve as he lightly grabbed the boy's head and tilted it slowly upward, "would you mind tell me what *that* represents?"

Steve's eyes widened as he gazed upon the sight of Fiach-Ra's castle and home inside Da'Rahga, Arx Vena'Tor. The castle had a huge wall separating it from the city. Steve could barely make out movements on the top of the wall, guessing they were guards. The castle was in three sections, the center main section extended the highest into the sky and on either side of the center section were two shorter arms of the building.

Extending high into the air from the center of the castle was a giant egg shaped dome. It was what was on top of this dome that Uncle Shameless wanted him to notice.

Perched on top of the dome was an enormous stone eagle. It was so large it blocked out the view of both moons in the sky. The stone eagle clenched the top of the dome with its giant talons and stood overlooking the city with its wings fully extended.

The stone eagle's jagged beak was open in a hideous snarl, and Steve noticed flashes of fire and flame deep within the dreadful mouth. Running from the top of the head down to the talons was a huge mane of fire that extended many yards away from the body, burning in the night air.

"I think it's that Zuu fire-eagle thing," he guessed.

"Well it ain't the blue bird of happiness," responded Uncle Shameless.

"Let's go and see if we can find someone to take us home," said Steve, reminding his uncle of their goal.

"I still think we should go to that place in the swamp..." Uncle Shameless did a complete about-face from the castle after noticing a sign out of the corner of his eye.

"Is that a pub?"

Less than twenty minutes later, as they were being led to the dungeon of Arx Vena'Tor by a group of Swantan guards, Steve shook his head at his uncle.

"So…what happened to 'just walk in like you own the place' or 'it's all about being smooth'?"

"Silence hu-man!" yelled a Swantan guard behind Steve.

Uncle Shameless was in front of Steve and was being held up by two guards. In fact, he was such bad shape that he was practically being carried. Uncle Shameless tried his best to look behind him so he could talk to Steve.

"Steve – are you hot?" he rambled.

His nephew just shook his head and tried to walk fast enough not to be run over by the giant swan-men escorting him.

Uncle Shameless and Steve had entered the bar easily enough, as there was not a bouncer or guard. Uncle Shameless walked right up to the bar and sat down. Everyone in the bar stopped what they were doing and watched the pair of humans.

Muttering filed the room and Steve could feel the tension growing by the second.

Uncle Shameless looked around at the crowd with his back to the bar and loudly pounded on the wooden countertop. Steve thought he saw splinters fly from the force of the impact and wondered if the bar was made of shoddy wood. Uncle Shameless had drank a lot of Eldercherry wine before coming into the bar, and he was having a hard time staying balanced on his seat. His lazy eye rolled like a ship lost at sea.

The room was nothing more than a swirling group of colors and sounds to Uncle Shameless. Steve had a sinking feeling that nothing good would come of this.

The pounding on the bar continued, and the bar started to make cracking sounds, adding to Steve's confusion.

"Easy friend!" cried the bartender from behind Uncle Shameless "You're breaking my bar!"

"Oh you're cray-zee," slurred Uncle Shameless, watching the crowd with his back to the bartender.

"I'll give you a drink if you just stop beating on my bar," pleaded the bartender to the back of Uncle Shameless' head, "I'll even make it on the house."

This caught Uncle Shameless' attention, as he was never one to turn down a free drink. He slowly turned to face the bartender, but it took a few moments for his lazy eye to catch up.

"I like the way you do business mister..." Uncle Shameless stopped in mid sentence after seeing the bartender. A duck the size of a small child stood on top of the bar counter on little squatty legs. His feathers were a dull green, he wore a stained apron and was smoking a pipe.

"Good! Glad we could come to an agr-aaagh!" choked the duck as Uncle Shameless clutched his neck in a vise-like grip. Uncle Shameless pulled the small duck to his face and yelled "Gimme back my sandwich!"

Steve gasped, realizing what had happened - the feathered bar keep had reminded Uncle Shameless of duck who stole his sandwich at Islands Park.

Uncle Shameless started shaking the duck forcefully. His pipe went flying through the air and landed in the pint of a very hefty Swantan foot soldier, splashing his scarred white face with ale. The Swantan and his drinking buddies quickly jumped from their seats and tackled Uncle Shameless. A pile of feathers, flesh, and armor promptly built up in front of Steve.

Surprisingly, Uncle Shameless was able to push his way out of the pile up, which was impressive since there were several hundred pounds of guard and armor on top of him.

"I'll tear ya apart! I'll smash ya ta pieces!" yelled Uncle Shameless, but he quickly dove after the duck bartender who was quickly waddling away "But first, gimme back my sandwich!"

One of the Swantan troops knocked Uncle Shameless out with a hit to the back of his head with the hilt of his sword. Steve thought about running, but did not have time as he was immediately grabbed by the big Swantan with the scarred face, ripping open his shirt and revealing his blue heron amulet. A large group of Swantan guards escorted the two humans out of the bar.

The bartender eyed Steve's amulet with great interest, as did a Hawken solider seated in the back of the bar.

"Toss 'em in cell six!" barked the head jailer, an older Swantan who had grown squishy around the mid-section after years of greasy dungeon food.

The cell door slammed shut in front of Steve. His uncle lay sprawled out on the floor of the dirty cell in Arx Vena'Tor's dungeon.

Steve helped his uncle sit up against the cell bars. Steve slapped his uncle's face lightly to wake him up.

"Steve..." mumbled his uncle.

"Yes?" answered Steve, very concerned.

"Are you hot?!" Uncle Shameless bellowed before passing out, his head hit against the bars with a loud CLANG!

"Why *do* they call you Shameless?" asked Steve sarcastically.

The Hawken warrior who had spied Steve's blue heron amulet flew to Arx Vena'Tor without haste. He knew he had to inform the Hawk-King about the appearance of a human child with a blue heron amulet. However, instead of heading straight to the Hawk King, he decided to stop at the dungeon in order to bring the boy with him. The slow thinking Swantan warriors who had brought the boy in would have never noticed the amulet, or even known what it signified.

The duck bartender who had noticed the amulet as well was also moving quickly to the dungeon to get his hands on The Boy before anyone else did.

Steve dropped to the dirt floor with a loud sigh. Uncle Shameless was still out cold. The boy glanced around the dank, dark cell. It smelled like Uncle Shameless' old barn and was lit by a single candle hanging on the wall outside the cell. He tried to think of a way out. He stood up and walked to the cell door and yelled to the dozing Swantan warrior keeping watch.

"Hey!" the boy yelled, the guard stirred in his seat and looked at Steve with tired beady eyes.

"Silence hu-man!"

"I want my phone call!"

The guard shot Steve a confused look.

"F...fone call?" he said, doing his best (which for a Swantan was commendable) to pronounce the strange words.

"Yeah! I want a telephone!" yelled Steve.

"What is a fone, and why do you want to tell it something?" asked the guard, now even more confused.

"UGH," grumbled Steve. "I want a tell-a-phone!"

"You want to tell a fone what?" the guard asked again, trying to think if there was some rule that let him kill prisoners that spoke in riddles.

"That won't help," said a voice from within the cell.

The boy spun towards the direction of the voice. He hadn't noticed before that there was someone else in the cell. The prisoner was sitting in one of the dark corners, clothed in a black robe with white piping, his face hidden within a hood. The hood hung low over his face, a beak just barely stuck out of its folds.

"Who are you?" asked Steve, struggling to make out any features of the prisoner in the darkness.

"No one of importance. I've been here so long even I don't remember why I was stuck here in the first place," answered the prisoner.

Steve thought the voice sounded oddly familiar.

The Hawken warrior landed near the entrance of the dungeons of Arx Vena'Tor and quickly walked inside. On the way down, he thought he heard slow footsteps behind him. He ignored them, since he was concerned with getting the prisoners and being able to present them to Fiach-Ra, especially The Boy. He wondered how two humans were even able to get inside the city.

While walking down the dark circular steps that led to the subterranean dungeons, he thought he felt something brush by his leg. Even his keen hawk-sight could not aid him in the dark cramped stairwell. It was hard to maneuver quickly with his large wings, and cursed whoever had built the stairs.

As Uncle Shameless started to wake up, Steve turned his attention from the stranger to his uncle.

"Ugh, what happened?" asked Uncle Shameless.

"You were on the business end of a beating, courtesy of some of our new swan friends."

Uncle Shameless stood up slowly, sobered by the fight and hits to the head,

"I feel like I lost a fight with a jackhammer."

From the shadowy corner, the other prisoner spoke again, "Why not take another drink from your wineskin? I'm sure that would help." Without giving it a second thought, Uncle Shameless took out his wineskin and drank many gulps

"Haven't you run out yet?" asked Steve. "You've been drinking that stuff nonstop since you got it."

"It's the craziest thing. I know I've seen it get almost to the bottom a few times. But when I go to drink more, it's filled back up again!"

"Impossible, it's just an optical illusion," explained Steve, who was eyeing the prisoner again.

"Perhaps it's a magical wineskin?" pondered the other prisoner aloud.

"I doubt it," said Steve "There's no such thing as magic."

"You don't believe in magic?" asked the prisoner.

"No," said Steve. "It's all nonsense. Everything can be explained by science."

"Who gave you that wineskin?" the prisoner asked Uncle Shameless.

"Uh, some blue bird fellow?"

"A blue bird? I doubt that, they aren't fans of wine," corrected the other prisoner, who almost sounded offended.

"It was a blue heron," explained Steve.

"Ah, then it *must* be a magic wineskin. Those blue herons are crafty folk."

"*Were* crafty folk," said a deep voice from the shadows outside the cell. Everyone turned and watched as the Hawken warrior from the bar stepped into the light near the cell door. He looked to the now alert Swantan guard.

"Leave us," he said, and the Swantan quickly walked away from the cell door leaving the Hawken warrior alone with the trio.

"Every hatchling knows the blue herons disappeared over three hundred years ago. No one has seen a feather of those foolish wizards since," said the Hawken warrior proudly.

He scanned the group in the cell carefully, "Yes, it seems that after the fall of the owls and the humans, the herons disappeared. Long gone are the Mystics of Zaa, hiding in their cowardice, dreaming of starting the week on the wrong day and unnecessary gifts."

Steve noticed the other prisoner move for the first time as he shifted uncomfortably where he sat on the floor.

"Speaking of blue herons," continued the Hawken warrior "That is an interesting amulet you are wearing, young hu-man."

Steve reached down in surprise to realize for the first time his shirt had been ripped and his blue heron amulet was hanging out.

"Oh this? It's nothing important," he said, stuffing it back into his shirt.

"Ah, well the Hawk-King enjoys jewelry very much. Perhaps if you let him have it, he would let you liv..leave Da'Rahga with your," he glanced at Uncle Shameless, who still drinking his wine greedily *"Charming,* companion" the warrior finished sarcastically.

"Really? We could go home?"

"I'm certain of it, the Hawk-King is a powerful magic user, and a favorite of the Great Eagle Zuu. He is not some mere trickster like the weak blue herons. He could easily use his magic and power to send you home."

Steve looked at Uncle Shameless with hopeful eyes. His uncle however was less impressed by the deal.

"Steve-o, I don't know...didn't that heron guy say the king here was not too nice?"

"It all depends on who is telling the story," replied the Hawken warrior "When told by the *losers,*" he stressed the word and shot it in the direction of the prisoner in the black robe, "He would be described that way. But I assure you he is a just and fair ruler, unlike the unscrupulous former Queen Fel-Ra and her human counterpart, the weakling Donal."

"Don't do it young Harrier," said the prisoner.

"Will the both of you stop with the political posturing for a moment so I can think?" Steve said to both the Hawken and the prisoner.

The warrior came right up to the bars and extended a clawed hand between the gap and spoke to Steve "I'm offering you my aid, and by extension the aid of the Hawk-King. You have my word, you'll be allowed to go home after you give him your amulet," he said in a soft voice, sounding like a crocodile luring a zebra into its mouth.

Steve slowly walked to the bars, right next to the Hawken's arm. It was lean, muscular and covered in tan dotted feathers.

"Don't do it!" pleaded the prisoner from the shadows.

"Yeah, get away from my nephew bird brain!" yelled Uncle Shameless, who realized later that insult did not carry the same weight in Eyri.

In a quick motion the Hawken grabbed Steve with his clawed hand by the neck and flung him against the bars. He skillfully drew a knife with his free hand, and held it to Steve's neck.

"I *was* going to take you alive to meet Fiach-Ra, but I suppose it does not matter," laughed the Hawken warrior.

"Guard! Return! I wish to remove this prisoner!" bellowed the Hawken towards one of the dark corridors. His words echoed off the stone walls.

"Look, you can have the dumb amulet," pleaded Steve. "I don't see what the big deal is!"

The Hawken laughed, "How amusing. You do not realize the threat you pose."

"Is this that Prophecy thing again?" asked Steve, hearing thunder in the distance. "Look, I don't believe in any of that, you have nothing to worry about from me. I'm from the suburbs, I don't know anything about toppling evil rulers."

"You may not now, but part of the Prophecy says you'll-"

"Duck!" screamed Uncle Shameless in anger towards the darkness outside the cell as thunder roared in the distance.

Steve ducked his head, not realizing this was not what Uncle Shameless meant.

"What?" said the Hawken, who turned his face in time to have it be on the receiving end of the flat side of a spear. The warrior's body went limp as he was gripped by unconsciousness and fell to the ground. As Steve moved away, rubbing his sore neck, he heard the spear fall to the ground with a clatter.

"Looks like I got here jus' in time, I hate these dungeons, they are nothing but a maze," said a gruff little voice.

Into the light walked the duck bartender, still garbed in his stained apron. He stood to only Steve's waist on his squat little legs. He moved his small pear-shaped body to the cell door.

"No hard feelings about earlier friend," said the duck to Uncle Shameless. "It's a good thing you came into my bar, I should have realized sooner who you were," he finished, casting a glance to Steve.

"Who are you?" asked Steve.

"My name is Mudd," said the duck proudly.

"That's a...uh, nice name."

"Why, thank you. It was my mother's."

5

"We had best hurry," said Mudd as he cast a concerned glance to the fallen Hawken. "Where are the keys?"

"I think that Swanky guy has them," said Uncle Shameless, who took a drink from his wine-skin.

"The Swantan guard has them, he means," said the other prisoner "Who will be returning shortly. I suggest you break out."

"How will we do that?" asked Steve as he touched the metal bars "There is no way to get through these bars."

"You better think of something, I hear the guard comin'," whispered Mudd while looking for something to use to open the door.

"Shamus," said the prisoner from the blackness of his hood, "Why not try bending the bars?"

Uncle Shameless blushed, "I know I look like I work out, but I really don't."

"Yes, there is no way he could bend those metal bars with his bare hands," added Steve.

"You do not really have a choice young Harrier, and you never know unless you try. Take another drink of your wine first," suggested the prisoner.

Already feeling the euphoria of the wine, Uncle Shameless took the advice and drank some more. He felt it run through his body.

He hiccupped. "Yeah, yeah why not then?" he said, "I shshsh-sure can do that!" He hiked up his tattered pants, which promptly fell back down to their original position, and strutted to the bars. He spit on both his hands, rubbed them together, and grabbed two of the bars.

"This reminds me of the time I was birthin' a calf. Y'see the darn thing was coming out side-ways and upside down! So I –"

"Just do it!" yelled Steve, hearing the Swantan guard rapidly approaching. "Okay, okay." Uncle Shameless took a deep breath, closed his eyes and tried to move the bars.

"Wor-bah!" he yelled, this was followed by the sound of metal bending, as he successfully moved the bars.

"I'll be a monkey's uncle!" he looked to Steve, "Sorry boy. I did it!"

Steve, in shock, admitted, "Yes you did – but you pushed them together! You were suppose to pull them apart!" he yelled angrily.

Uncle Shameless looked down and sure enough he had in fact pushed the two bars closer together instead of moving them apart.

"Oops."

"Do it again, hurry!" pleaded Mudd who was keeping a look out for the guard.

Uncle Shameless gripped the bars again and pulled them apart with ease. "Wor-bah!" he bellowed in exertion.

Steve crawled through the gap in the bars, and Uncle Shameless followed.

"Aren't you coming?" Steve turned to ask the prisoner, but he was gone. A faint blue light rapidly faded away where the mysterious prisoner had been sitting.

"Hurry!" cried Mudd as the trio ran down the halls. Mudd, who could not run that fast, was almost left behind several times. Uncle Shameless reached down for Mudd.

"Please, I don't have your sandwich!" pleaded Mudd, afraid that Uncle Shameless was going for his neck again.

"Easy there," slurred Uncle Shameless as he gently picked up Mudd and put him on his shoulders.

"Now, where do we go?" asked Uncle Shameless, who was having a harder time keeping his balance with the duck on his shoulders. From his new vantage point, Mudd directed them where to go. They rounded a corner, and the Swantan guard was right in front of them.

"Halt hu-mans!" he bellowed, drawing his sword.

Instinctively and without hesitation, Uncle Shameless punched the Swantan in the face. The guard was sent flying through the air like he had been hit by a battering ram. Uncle Shameless paused and looked at his fist.

"I never knew I had it in me," he whispered.

Mudd patted the top of Uncle Shameless' head, "C'mon let's keep moving! This way!" He pointed down a dark corridor.

"Where are we going?" asked Steve as he panted heavily.

"To the aqueducts!"

"Not more ducks," whined Uncle Shameless, still secretly bitter about his lost sandwich.

"No, aqueducts," corrected Steve.

"What, are these ducks better swimmers?"

"They aren't ducks at all!" yelled Steve, his voice echoing through the dark stone corridors.

"Oh," thought Uncle Shameless aloud. "Are they geese?"

Steve and Mudd looked at each other and shook their heads.

The intrepid trio finally came to a heavy wooden door. Steve tried the handle, but it was locked. Uncle Shameless took Mudd off his shoulders, he looked at Steve, "Did you bring the key?" he joked

Steve rolled his eyes.

"Not to worry!" bellowed Uncle Shameless as he hiked up his pants, he backed up several feet and ran straight at the door.

Just as he was approaching the door at top speed, it opened suddenly to reveal a room full of Swantan guards. Uncle Shameless had his eyes closed and kept running, and charged right into the group of guards, knocking them and himself to the floor.

"Oh great," said Steve after seeing the room full of guards dressed in plate armor and holding nasty looking swords.

"Son of a Motherless Hawk!" cursed Mudd, "We're in trouble!"

Uncle Shameless picked himself up and noticed he was surrounded by guards. "Don't worry lads, I'll make short work of these baddies!" he cracked the knuckles of his right hand and threw a punch at the nearest guard's face.

However, it was like punching a pile of bricks. The guard was not sent flying like the last time had punched one. His fist was stopped dead by the guard's granite-like face.

"Owwww!" whined Uncle Shameless, who quickly started rubbing his hurt hand. He did not understand why it had not worked like before. The guards closed in and tackled him to ground. They took turns punching his unprotected body. After a moment they threw him aside and began walking towards Steve and Mudd.

Suddenly, Steve realized why his uncle's punch had no effect. He quickly ran to his uncle and fished out his wineskin and uncorked it. "You need to drink more wine!"

"Ugh, bluga...No mom, I didn't eat dad's headcheese," rambled the beaten Uncle Shameless. Steve tilted his uncle's head back and poured wine into his mouth until he started swallowing it.

"Help!" cried Mudd, Steve looked over to see one of the Swantan guards holding him upside down from one of his short little legs.

Uncle Shameless shot up like a bolt of lightning and made his way to the guards. He tapped one on the shoulder, "Excuse me, you dropped something," he said, pointing down to the ground. The slow thinking guard looked down and Uncle Shameless hit him with a swift uppercut.

The guard was sent flying through the air, and before he even landed, Uncle Shameless punched out the guard holding Mudd, and grabbed another and threw him into the last standing guard.

All of the guards let out moans of pain. Uncle Shameless dusted off his hands and his tattered clothes. He reached down and picked up Mudd, placing him back on his shoulders.

"Sh-shall we move on?" he slurred. Steve surveyed the room in awe; his uncle had taken out all of the guards in a manner of seconds. He handed him back his wineskin.

"I think this wine gives you super-strength," said Steve. He had always been rather observant.

"What kind of wine is it?" asked Mudd from Uncle Shameless' shoulders.

"Red," blurted Uncle Shameless.

"Elder something," said Steve.

"Eldercherry!" exclaimed Mudd.

"Yes, is that important?" asked Steve as they continued trekking to the aqueducts.

"Very!" stated Mudd, "Eldercherry wine is the drink made by the blue herons, the Mystics of Zaa. I have heard it grants humans special abilities, but I had always thought that was only a legend."

"So, let me get this right…the drunker he gets, the stronger he is?" asked Steve, thinking this brought a whole new meaning to the phrase 'drunk with power.'

"Exactly!" exclaimed Mudd.

"Now that's my kind of magic!" said Uncle Shameless as he stumbled down the corridor.

"It's not magic," said Steve "It's probably just some kind of reaction to the wine. Perfectly logical."

"But boy, what's logical about it being made by talking bird-wizards?" asked Uncle Shameless.

Steve ignored his uncle and kept walking towards the aqueducts, thinking to himself that nothing here was exactly logical.

Meanwhile, back at cell six, the Hawken warrior woke up. He rubbed his sore head and slowly stood up. In an instant he realized the prisoners were gone. He ran to look for a sign of them, and found the Swantan guard Uncle Shameless had punched out.

Not knowing where they could have run off to, he decided he should inform the Hawk-King of the situation. If he was lucky he might be rewarded.

Or at least not thrown into The Pit of Big Nasty Things.

Finally, the trio made it to the door leading to the aqueducts. Uncle Shameless pulled the locked exit door off its hinges and threw it to the ground with a loud CRASH.

"We're trying to be stealthy here friend," said Mudd. "Ripping heavy doors out of walls isn't going to help with that."

"Oh, sa-sorry" Uncle Shameless slurred. Dawn crept through the doorway.

"It's good to see the sun again," admitted Steve as they left the underground caverns of Arx Vena'Tor. They were at the rear of the castle foundation, set on a mountain. A long stone aqueduct ran from the foundation down to the valley below the back of the mountain. Steve noticed that the aqueduct was very old; most of the rock face was chipped and faded, yet it looked incredibly sturdy.

"This was built by the humans hundreds of years ago," explained Mudd. "It is one of the few remains of the human kingdom. Fiach-Ra and his armies destroyed most of everything else."

Steve watched the rushing water flow down the ancient aqueduct and suddenly had a thought.

"Um...now what?" he asked.

Mudd pointed to a section of the castle that extended out right next to the aqueduct.

"You'll have to climb out there and jump into the water, don't worry it'll dump you into a lake in the valley," said Mudd.

"Ain't you comin'?" asked Uncle Shameless to the duck on his shoulders.

Mudd shook his head, "No, I must stay here. I may learn information that could come in handy. Besides it's good to have someone on the inside of the city."

"...Are you planning for something?" asked Steve.

"Well of course. You will save all of Eyri from the – "

"Halt hu-mans!" bellowed a voice from the door leading out to the aqueducts. Mudd ran and hid in a nearby bush, "Hurry, jump into the water!" He pointed to the flowing aqueducts.

Out of the doorway burst a Swantan guard, flanked by a trio of Hawken warriors.

"Crackers!" yelled Uncle Shameless, he grabbed Steve and headed towards the ledge.

"Oh, no! I've had enough of water!" protested Steve, thinking back to the waterfall.

Uncle Shameless paid no attention to his nephew's objection and, thanks to his Eldercherry wine induced strength, picked up the boy with ease and jumped down into the flowing water. They landed in the water with a large SPLASH, and were quickly carried away by the current.

The three Hawken warriors spread their large wings and took flight after the escaping pair. They easily kept pace in the air as Uncle Shameless and Steve were carried down the series of canals.

The group of Hawken warriors split up, one of the Hawken flew under the curved arch of the aqueduct and waited further down the canal, waiting for Uncle Shameless and Steve. The other two opened fire with their bows, launching volleys of arrows. Thankfully, the roaring water caused Uncle Shameless and Steve to roll around, making them difficult to hit. Several arrows ricocheted off the stone close to Steve.

They were rapidly approaching the Hawken who was waiting for them further down the aqueduct. As they were swept by, the hawk-man lashed out with his talons to grab them. He snagged part of Steve's shirt and scratched Uncle Shameless' chest with curved wicked talons, but was unable to grab onto them.

The warrior, out of anger threw his heavy spear, and severely missed. It landed several yards ahead of Uncle Shameless, stuck into the rock of the aqueduct. The warriors regrouped and flew further down the incline to wait for Uncle Shameless and Steve.

Uncle Shameless had an idea, as he approached the spear stuck into the aqueduct he timed his reach just right so he could grab it.

"A-ha!" he yelled.

"What are you going to do with that?" asked a soaked Steve, desperately holding onto his uncle's waist.

"Did I ever tell you I tried out for the Olympic Javelin Team?"

"No. What happened?" asked Steve.

"I didn't make it."

Steve rolled his eyes; Uncle Shameless took a quick swig of his wine and spun the spear around so that the blunt bottom was facing out. He pulled back his arm and waited until all three of the Hawken warriors ahead of them were close together.

With a bellowing "Bru-ha!" he hurled the spear, bottom end first, towards the group. It split the air like a lightning bolt and hit the front Hawken right in the chest like a truck. The force knocked him back into the other two Hawken and all three were knocked out of the air into the trees below.

Steve noticed the aqueduct ran through a series of low hanging trees, so he lowered his body as best he could.

"Duck!" yelled Steve to his uncle who was still sitting up in the flowing water.

"I thought he stayed behind-," asked Uncle Shameless, before being knocked down by a thick low hanging branch.

Steve sighed as the other trees passed quickly overhead, and he wondered what else he was going to have to put up while he was here.

"Sir?" asked a young Hawken to his larger, older superior who was sitting in a nearly empty room meditating. The observant young Hawken quickly realized that meditating, however, does not usually involve loud snoring.

"ZZZ...hrmm?"

"Sir, I'm sorry to bother you but – "

The older Hawken stood up quickly, his old bones cracked and popped as he moved. However, this did not stop him from swiftly moving to the younger warrior and picking him up by the neck.

"You dare to interrupt U'nala, Wing-Master of Fiach-Ra's army during his daily na...meditation?"

"I'm sorry sir, but I have important information!" gasped the young Hawken.

U'nala threw the warrior to the ground in a crash of armor and feathers.

"Speak, tell U'nala of this news that could not wait."

The young warrior stood and rubbed his neck, wondering how such an old warrior could still be so fast and strong.

"Yessir, the –"

"What is your name, warrior?"

"Irek, sir."

"Irek, do you know what U'nala's duties are as Wing-Master?"

"Sir?" asked the jittery warrior, who was starting to get annoyed with U'nala referring to himself in the third person.

"Answer U'nala."

"You command all the Armies of Fiach-Ra, and are second in command only to the Hawk-King," answered Irek like a school child reciting the ABCs.

"Exactly, and do you have any idea how much paper work U'nala has to do because of his position?"

Irek hesitated. "Uh. Sir?"

U'nala ignored him, "Let me tell you, it's quite a bit! U'nala grows tired of it quickly. He works hard, but it keeps piling up," he sighed. "In fact U'nala is probably going to have to fill out even more because of this meeting. Thank you for the extra work, Mr. Irek!"

Irek knew that U'nala was a tad eccentric, but had no idea he was this bad.

U'nala walked into the lone pool of light in the room, and Irek finally got a full look at the Wing-Master. He was taller than the average Hawken, and his feathers had started to go white and gray with age. Irek then noticed U'nala's trademark feature, his left wing had been sliced off, leaving him with only one working wing.

The legend was that the injury had happened during the attack on the human kingdom, and none other than the human king, Donal, had cleaved U'nala's wing off with the Sword of Zaa.

Irek knew that even though U'nala was technically Wing-Master, he very rarely went into battle because of his 'situation.' Rumors circulated that the only reason he held the second in command position was because he and the Hawk-King had been friends since they were hatchlings.

U'nala continued his work-related lament,

"Even though U'nala works hard all day every day filling out forms, completing paper work and sending out memos, he is only allowed one hour a day of personal time. Now, you are taking away his free time, so you better have a good reason."

Irek motioned behind him and the Hawken warrior that had tried to steal Steve's blue heron amulet walked into the light.

"Sir," he bowed, "The Boy has appeared."

U'nala's mouth dropped, not because of this The Boy person, he had no idea what that even meant, but because he had a feeling he was going to have to do a lot of extra paper work because of it.

Steve covered his face as they continued sliding down the aqueduct through the trees. The low hanging branches scratched his arms, and his shirt was getting covered in leaves. He did his best to keep Uncle Shameless' head propped up since he had been knocked out by a low hanging branch. Thankfully, his uncle was starting to come around.

"Uhhh...What hit me?"

"A very fierce tree," said Steve.

"We have to fight trees now? Well, at least we know their bark isn't worse than their bite!" joked his uncle.

Steve groaned.

Finally the branches cleared away and the boy could sit up in the flowing water again. He was getting sick and tired of this crude water slide and wanted to get out.

Steve gasped as he looked ahead and realized he was going to get his wish. The aqueduct emptied into a small lake...and the lake was a good twenty feet below the end of the aqueduct.

"Oh no! Not again!" Steve yelled remembering their disaster with the Mystical waterfall on the Grand River.

Uncle Shameless grabbed a hold of Steve,

"Hang on ta me boy! An' take a deep breath!"

Neither of the duo was able to hang onto the other, or even manage to take a deep breath. Instead, they screamed as the bottom fell out from under them and they plunged to the water below.

Darkness surrounded Steve on all sides after he entered the cold water. He tried to swim, but did not have any more strength and gave up. His vision blurred and everything thing went black.

"What's your name warrior?"

"Nevik," said the Hawken who had just told U'nala about The Boy appearing.

"Nevik, do you realize the gravity of this situation?" said U'nala as he paced around the room.

"Yes Wing Master, it has been said that The Boy appearing is harbinger of change to-"

"Never mind any of that," interrupted his one-winged superior "Do you realize how much paper work U'nala is going to have to do now?"

U'nala studied the young Hawken's fully intact wings with great envy. He longed to be able to soar on his own again and to rain down destruction no those below – like in the good old days. Memories flooded his mind of terrorizing those on the ground as he showered them with flaming arrows, deadly spears and dirty looks.

A nostalgic tear welled up in one of the old Hawken's eyes. Today, the only way he rained down destruction was with his 'rejected' stamp on helpless vacation request forms.

He was thankful Fiach-Ra had not disposed of him after he had lost his wing, as was the usual custom in Hawken society. Still, some days he wished the Hawk-King had put him out of his misery. Especially during budget season.

"If you go around telling everyone about this, U'nala will have to spend sleepless nights putting together paperwork to ready the use of reserve troops, to allow the use of war time provisions, and all kinds of nasty things! U'nala does not even want to think about it!" he moaned as visions of reams of parchment needing signatures in triplicate filled his head.

U'nala still had no idea who this The Boy was, but he had learned over the years that bad news always equaled more work for him.

Fiach-Ra's way of dealing with problems in his kingdom was comparable to using a war hammer to crack a nut. The Hawk-King's temper would usually get the better of him and he was prone to being somewhat excessive when it came quelling rebellions, insurrections, and charity bake sales.

Nevik and Irek shared a confused look.

"Sir...? Do you mean you do not *want* me to inform the Hawk-King about this?" asked Nevik, wondering if personality problems were a prerequisite for working in administration.

"Now now, U'nala is *not* making you *not* say anything. There are all kinds of reports that have to be filed when a superior officer forces a warrior to lie," he held a clawed thumb and finger several inches apart, "A stack this big!"

"But sir-"

"This big!" yelled U'nala as held up his thumb and finger again. Nevik continued, "I think the Hawk-King should know. Since it does sort of signal the start of the Prophecy."

U'nala looked confused at the mention of the Prophecy, and was even more confused when he heard thunder roaring outside.

"Which prophecy is that?"

"*The* Prophecy," said Nevik as thunder cracked yet again.

"U'nala knows not of what you speak," replied the Wing-Master. He walked to door towards the back of the meditation room, opened it and bellowed "Send in a Mystic!" as he tried to not think about the Mystic Request form he was going to have to fill out.

Steve was dreaming again.

He was in a village. He looked up to the sky and saw the vile burning eyes of Fiach-Ra as he descended from the air. The ground quaked as the Hawk-King landed. Two fiery creatures were on either side of Fiach-Ra; Steve could not make out what they were, like before the images were blurry and sketchy.

The Hawk-King pointed at the boy with the Spear of Zuu, and the creatures opened their mouths. Streams of white-hot fire shot out towards Steve.

He felt it burn.

"Bah!" Steve gasped loudly, waking himself up.

"Back with us are you?" said a calm female voice.

Steve rubbed his eyes; thankfully this time he still had his glasses. He was almost afraid to stop rubbing his eyes, he wondered what odd creature had helped him this time. Perhaps, it was some manner of woodchuck or marmot.

"Take it easy," said the voice as a soothing hand wiped his forehead "You're lucky I was around to see you two fall in, otherwise…Well, I'd rather think about what might have happened."

Steve looked up to see his rescuer. She looked like a pelican, but like the other bird-people of Eyri, she stood up like a human and did not have wings. Her head was a mix of white and brown feathers. The rest of her body was light brown except for her thin, yellow legs and webbed feet. She was dressed in a light gray poncho and wore a large backpack.

"Who are you?" asked Steve

"My name is Eira," the pelican-lady replied in a soft voice.

Steve noticed that her poncho was soaked. "Did you have to dive in to save us?"

"Think nothing of it," she said patting Steve on the head with a soft-feathered hand "We pelicans are excellent divers. In fact I stopped by this lake for a quick swim anyway."

"Huh…that is…*convenient*," mused Steve.

"Well the funny thing is, I was not planning on it at all and then suddenly I had the urge to go for a swim," explained Eira.

Steve furrowed his brow and was about to go on about coincidences when he was distracted by a loud groan from Uncle Shameless.

"They oughta charge for a ride like that," Uncle Shameless said, rubbing the sore spot where he had been hit by the tree. He looked over at Steve and Eira, "Oh, hello."

"This is Eira the pelican, she saved us," explained Steve.

Uncle Shameless' eyes lit up, "A pelican huh?"

Steve quickly saw where this was going. "No! Please don't!" he pleaded

Uncle Shameless ignored his nephew as his voice shifted into a boisterous tone, "Can your beak hold more than your belly can?" he asked.

Eira looked at Uncle Shameless plainly and eventually laughed, "My, what a charming man your father is."

"That's my uncle, we call him Uncle Shameless."

Eira walked over to Uncle Shameless to help him up, Steve notice she used a walking stick.

Eira helped up Uncle Shameless, "Hello," said Eira as she gently shook his hand.

She looked back at Steve, "And what is your name?"

"Steve."

Eira smiled, then she looked at Uncle Shameless' chest and noticed the wounds caused by the Hawken warrior's talons. "Zaa's Beak! You're wounded!"

Uncle Shameless looked down at his cut up chest, only just now realizing it. "Hm, I hadn't noticed," he said as he began to take a drink of wine.

Eira stopped him, "No need for that. I have something that will heal the wound." She dropped her walking stick and took off her large backpack. She rummaged around inside for a moment until she pulled out a small glass bottle.

The glass was the color of blue crystal and a thick silver liquid swirled around inside.

"This will fix you right up, my own special recipe," Eira said as she poured some of the silvery liquid into her hand and rubbed it into Uncle Shameless' wounds.

Steve watched in amazement as the wounds quickly began healing over.

"Wow, thanks!" said Uncle Shameless.

"No problem. That is what I do, I'm a healer. I was actually on my way to Uth, the Last Human Village when I had that urge to go for a dive in this lake."

Uncle Shameless shot Steve a look that seemed to say 'well how 'bout that?' The boy rolled his eyes.

"Mind if we tag along?" asked Uncle Shameless.

Back at Arx Vena'Tor, U'nala and the other Hawken warriors waited for a Mystic of Zuu to show up and explain The Prophecy.

All U'nala could think about was how this was cutting into his free time for the day. He already had a mountain of paper work to fill out from yesterday's raids on a western farming village.

He longed for the clash of battle again. There had not been any epic full-scale battles in decades and he was growing tired of sitting in the castle doing all of the government paperwork for the Kingdom.

Eventually the door leading into the meditation room opened and in walked a Mystic of Zuu. He was a short squat vulture. His head was bald of feathers, and he was dressed in the red robes of Zuu. His eyes were solid spheres of white with tiny black dots in the center.

"You requested me, Wing-Master?" asked the fat little vulture.

"Yes, U'nala wishes you to explain this prophecy nonsense to him," said U'nala as he finished filling out a Mystic Request Form.

The vulture waddled up to the Wing-Master and dropped a large, heavy book onto the table in front of him. He opened it up to the middle and started reading,

"Which one?" asked the Mystic in a snippy tone.

"U'nala does not understand what is meant by 'which one.' Explain."

The Mystic slammed the large book shut with a loud BANG, causing both Irek and Nevik to jump. He then took off his ridiculously large monocle and starred right at U'nala.

"This whole book," said the Mystic, pointing to the large red book on the table "Is filled with prophecies. You'll have to be a *tad* more specific."

U'nala sighed, "U'nala is not amused Mystic."

The Mystic scoffed, "I'm quite serious. I'm afraid they were rather prophecy mad back in the old days. In fact, this copy is just the abridged version!" he said, picking up the book and letting it drop to the table again with another loud BANG to prove how thick it was.

The Mystic started turning to random pages and reading aloud the various prophecies written down.

"Here listen to this one, 'And so it shall take place that after the sunsets, there will be nothing but darkness until morning.' Oh yes, they really worked hard on that one."

He turned a few more pages, "Or how about this? 'So it was written that there will be many rains in the rainy season,' dear me I don't even know why we keep these secret."

U'nala started rubbing his eyes, and then looked at Nevik, "Tell him what you told U'nala."

Nevik stood up, "We wish to know about *The* Prophecy! I have seen The Boy!" yelled the warrior. Thunder cracked violently outside as the Mystic cast them a knowing look. He reached inside his robe and pulled out a locked small red book. He took a key from a chain around his neck and unlocked it.

He read the contents aloud to the three Hawken.

6

The Mystic closed his little book containing The Prophecy with a quick SNAP.

"Hmm. This concerns U'nala," said the large Hawken as he stood up. "Perhaps we *should* inform the Hawk-King."

He pointed to Nevik, "You come with U'nala, the rest of you…leave."

Nevik bowed and followed U'nala to the stairs leading up to the throne room of the Hawk-King.

"You did well, young warrior, by coming to U'nala. I'm sure the Hawk-King will also be very thankful."

They reached a door at a landing, "You must wait here until U'nala returns."

"Is something wrong sir?" asked Nevik.

"U'nala still has fifteen minutes of personal time left, and he wishes to spend it alone before having to visit the Hawk-King to talk about this The Boy business."

Nevik nodded and stepped aside as U'nala maneuvered his large frame through the door and closed it behind him. Nevik heard the clunk of a lock, followed by silence.

Nevik had never been to the throne room before, nor had he ever been within close distance of the Hawk-King. He thought about the different rewards he might be granted, perhaps even a different post outside of the city, away from the annoying Wall of Fire.

Nevik's daydreams were interrupted by a loud banging sound coming from U'nala's room. It sounded like metal being hit by a hammer; he wondered what U'nala was doing.

Like clockwork, fourteen and a half minutes later U'nala exited his room.

"U'nala's personal time has expired for the day. Let us go."

As he walked up the stairs, Nevik wondered to himself how such an peculiar, deranged Hawken could be the Hawk-King's second in command.

As U'nala walked up the stairs, he wondered if his meeting with the Hawk-King would count as overtime.

Nevik nervously waited outside the main doors of Fiach-Ra's throne room as U'nala talked with the Hawk-King inside. On the wall across from him there was a large mural showing Fiach-Ra leading his Hawken troops into a grand sky battle against the owls and their allies.

Fiach-Ra and his troops were on the right, with their targets on the left. The caption underneath read 'Fiach-Ra, Favorite of Zuu, Smites the Enemies of Zuu.' Nevik then turned his gaze down the hall to see a massive stained glass window of the Hawk-King looking vigilant and holding an ornate calendar as a pile of birthday presents burned behind him.

Nevik inspected another piece of artwork, this time an elaborate tapestry showing Fiach-Ra with a fishing net and various bird peoples (but no owls or blue herons) surrounding him in awe. The title read, 'Fiach-Ra, Favorite of Zuu, Invents Fishing.'

This caught Nevik by surprise. He was not aware that the Hawk-King had invented fishing, but he figured that if it was in the tapestry it *must* be true. Although he was fairly certain that the Hawk-King never went anywhere near the sea because of the Wurms and their watery magic.

But the young Hawken merely shrugged and figured that any thing was possible during a reign of over 300 years.

The next tapestry astounded him even more. It showed Fiach-Ra sitting at a desk with books and parchment around him. The title read 'Fiach-Ra, Favorite of Zuu, Invents Words.' Nevik had no idea that the Hawk-King had invented words!

The young Hawken started walking down the rest of the Hall of Accomplishments (as the hall outside of the throne room was so named) and inspecting the remaining several dozen tapestries that lined the walls, each showing one of Fiach-Ra's Accomplishments.

Suddenly, the large wooden doors of the throne room opened.

"U'nala commands you to enter," said U'nala "And to bow before your King."

Nevik swallowed nervously. He left the tapestry he was looking at (entitled 'Fiach-Ra, Favorite of Zuu, Invents Gravity') and walked into the main throne room. The massive room was dome shaped because it was on top of the castle right underneath the stone effigy of Zuu. Fiach-Ra's Royal Guard lined sides of the domed room. Ceremonial winged helmets covered their battle scarred faces, their piercing eyes hidden in the depths of the metal.

Equally beautiful light armor covered their bodies. The entire Royal Guard held their spears upright and perfectly still, like they were statues. Nevik knew from rumors that if anyone tried to attack Fiach-Ra in this room, they would never even reach the throne.

Nevik walked to the center of the throne room and kneeled. Above him was a large circular opening in the roof. Nevik could just barely make out the bottom of the statue of Zuu sitting not too far from the edge of the opening.

Light poured into the throne room from the hole in the ceiling, illuminating the tile floor Nevik was kneeling on. He glanced down at the floor to see a large tile mosaic showing the Hawk-King wielding the fiery Spear of Zuu.

"Raise," commanded an ominous voice that sent chills down Nevik's spine.

The warrior slowly stood up and looked towards the Hawk-King. His throne was actually several feet above the floor, accessed by a narrow staircase ascending towards it. Even though light filled most of the chamber, Fiach-Ra was blanketed in shadows. All Nevik could see from his lower position on the floor were Fiach-Ra's two fire filled eyes and the Spear of Zuu.

Nevik was surprised to see that the Spear was not aflame, as it was often depicted in artwork of the Hawk-King. Instead, it looked like an ordinary spear with a long obelisk shaped blade made of stone.

U'nala stood near the bottom of the staircase leading up to Fiach-Ra's elevated throne.

"Tell Fiach-Ra, Favorite of Zuu, Hawk-King of Eyri, what you told U'nala," but before Nevik could speak U'nala added, "By the way, this was during U'nala's personal time, he is wondering if he'll be compensated since the interruption was business-"

"Silence!" bellowed the Hawk-King as he pounded the stone floor with the butt of his spear, it sounded like crack of thunder and echoed deeply in the expansive rotunda.

"Speak," said Fiach-Ra from his throne in a powerful, yet calm voice.

"Highness, I have seen The Boy from The Prophecy!" Nevik ignored the thunder roaring above and continued, "He was here in Da'Rahga, and he wore a blue heron amulet!"

Nevik watched in amazement as Fiach-Ra's fire filled eyes burned brighter and brighter. The flames poured out of his eyes and reached up past his shadow covered head. Then Nevik noticed the stone tip of the Spear of Zuu began glowing, as if it were in a hot forge. A sizzling sound filled the domed room, and abruptly the tip of the spear became engulfed in flame.

From this flash of fire, Nevik caught a glimpse of Fiach-Ra's face, and his scarred eye that burned with endless rage.

"Where is The Boy now?" demanded Fiach-Ra from high atop his elevated throne.

"He has escaped, I was knocked out in the dungeon and when I awoke he was gone," explained Nevik.

Fiach-Ra slammed the butt of his spear into the ground once more. "*Who* let this boy into my city?" bellowed the angry king from his shadowy throne.

U'nala produced a leather bound book and began flipping through pages. "What was yesterday?" U'nala asked the nearest Royal Guard, forgetting that the Royal Guards were not allowed to speak unless commanded by Fiach-Ra.

U'nala kept waiting for the answer, he jabbed the guardsman in the arm with clawed finger.

"Hello? U'nala, Wing-Master of Fiach-Ra's army is addressing you!" There was no response. "Listen here guardsman," said an angry U'nala to the unmoving guard "Just where do you get off thinking you can give U'nala the cold shoulder! And in front of the Hawk-King no less! The nerve you have! Why I have half a mind to-"

"Yesterday was Dasday sir," interrupted Nevik.

"You see?" said U'nala pointing to Nevik "He follows U'nala's orders! You could learn a lesson from him. That young Hawken is going places!"

U'nala cleared his throat and found the information he was looking for.

"Ah yes, the gate guards and the supervising officer last night were..."

Remmit and Kaz sat in the city square near the statue of Fiach-Ra enjoying some personal time until their next shift at the gate began. Kaz was sharpening his sword, while Remmit worked tirelessly sewing together sets of blindfolds.

"You're wasting your time," sang Kaz "No one will buy your silly blindfolds."

"That's what they said about the fellow who invented the writing quill, and look what happened to him."

"Wasn't he branded as a heretic and forced into exile?" asked Kaz.

"Yes, but before that he had a nice house. Besides, it was eventually accepted…of course, that was after the execution."

Kaz shook his head and went back to sharpening his sword. Remmit looked over at the Swantan "Given any thought to my offer?"

"I don't know."

"C'mon you can invest that money you're just sitting on into my company; I'll make you an even partner."

Kaz shook his head, he was unsure of giving his hard earned money to the enterprising Hawken. He did not think there would be much of a market for sleep aides in Da'Rahga even with the noisy and bright Wall of Fire.

"Haven't you noticed that I've been more alert and relaxed lately?" said Remmit.

"No, but I have noticed you have been more *annoying*," admitted Kaz.

Remmit ignored the muscled headed Swantan, "It's because I've been using my very own blind-folds and ear-plugs!" exclaimed Remmit proudly, "I've been getting a good night's sleep for the past couple nights."

Kaz sighed, and was about to say he would consider trying the sleep aides when their conversation was broken up by a series of loud hawk cries.

The pair of warriors immediately stood at attention as four members of the Royal Guard and a Hawken officer landed in front of them. Kaz and Remmit looked at each other nervously. Remmit discreetly hid the blindfold he was sewing.

The officer, clothed in a chain mail vest and a long black cape, opened a small scroll and began reading, "Guardsmen Remmit and Kaz you are hereby called to the Court of Fiach-Ra to answer to charges of –"

"It wasn't my idea!" pleaded Remmit as he pointed to Kaz. "He was the one that said we should sneak into the kitchen and steal the gruel!"

Kaz turned and stuck his face next to Remmit's, "But you were the one who came up with the plan to do it!"

The Hawken officer stood with a confused look on his face, "This is not about stealing gru-" he started to say before he was interrupted.

"Wingless savage!" Remmit shouted at Kaz.

"Mama's boy!" countered Kaz.

Remmit's eyes widened and his hands closed into fists, "You leave my mother out of this!" yelled Remmit.

"Y'know, I never thanked your mother for the meal she gave me last time I stopped by - *while you weren't home!*" parried Kaz.

Remmit jumped at Kaz and tackled him. Implying a Hawken's mother fed you while they were not around was one of the greatest insults in Hawken society. Historians had been unable to pinpoint the origin of this put-down, because every time the question is raised, someone thought they were being insulted.

The pair began fighting on the ground, throwing punches in between insults. The Hawken officer crumbled up his scroll, tossed it to the ground and sighed loudly.

Lexa put the last of his belongings into a large sack and tied it shut. He had spent the evening packing up all of his things in hopes that he would finally get transferred out of Da'Rahga.

He had even put out word that he wanted to sell his home. He was hoping to make a little extra traveling money. His house was nothing special, it was the basic adobe cube on a tall pole that all the other officers of his rank were given.

Still, he thought to himself, it was worth a shot. There was a loud knock at the door, "Ah, a prospective buyer," said Lexa with a smile as he walked to the front door, but thinking to himself 'that was fast.'

Lexa opened the large circle shaped front door, "Hello-ooooh dear," he said as he saw a pair of Royal Guardsmen silently standing outside his door. He loathed the Royal Guard, their silence always made him uneasy.

Lexa stared at them for a second, "I'm guessing you are not here about the house."

Lexa looked over the pair of identically dressed elite soldiers, "Which is shame, because the two of you make a cute couple."

At the throne room of Arx Vena'Tor, Remmit and Kaz were led inside by the group of Royal Guardsmen who had brought them to the castle. After escorting the captives, the guardsmen returned to their places along the perimeter of the rotunda. Lexa was to remain outside with his escort until after judgment had been passed on Remmit and Kaz.

Remmit and Kaz were terrified. They did not know why they had been brought to the castle. Laws changed almost daily in Da'Rahga, mostly depending on Fiach-Ra's mood. Lexa on the other hand knew why he had been brought in and waited impatiently outside of the throne room. He could not wait until he was reassigned out of the city and away from the Wall of Fire.

Remmit and Kaz stood nervously in the pool of light pouring through the hole in rotunda at the base of Fiach-Ra's throne. Remmit's keen hawk eyes darted around the throne in panic, he tried not to look at the Hawk-King but his eyes kept landing on the pair of burning eyes sitting in the shadows.

U'nala stomped in front of the pair and began to speak,

"Gate Guards Crammit and-"

"Th-that is Remmit sir."

U'nala's eyes widened at the insult, and he stomped over and stuck his face near Remmit's, "How *dare* you imply that U'nala is wrong, U'nala is never wrong, U'nala is infallible!"

"So...you never fall down?" asked Kaz, confused at the word.

"Wh-what?" stuttered U'nala as he moved over to Kaz and shoved his large hawk face next to Kaz's swan-like head.

"No it doesn't mean U'nala never falls down! But just for the record," U'nala looked over at the court scribe, a determined raven with a writing quill sitting at a stone writing desk "Scribe! Put this in the record!" he looked back at Kaz and Remmit "U'nala *never* falls down," he bellowed, his voice echoing around the rotunda.

"It means U'nala is never wrong! That is what infallible means! Now, where were we?" continued U'nala as he walked back to his place, reading his parchment with the guards names written on it.

Since he was not paying attention to his steps, U'nala took a bad step on a loose stone on the floor, tripped, and fell over with a loud CRASH.

"I guess he is fallible," Kaz whispered to Remmit.

The silence was broken by the court scribe ripping out the last page of paper from the court record.

Remmit thought he heard Fiach-Ra let out a disappointed sigh from high atop his throne as U'nala stood up and brushed himself off.

"Gate Guard Crammit," U'nala continued as if nothing had happened. "Remmit," the Hawken guard said again.

U'nala stormed over to the court scribe and shoved the parchment into the raven's face, "Is that a 'C' or an 'R'?" he asked the scribe who was also in charge of writing down the guard schedules.

"It's an 'R,' Wing-Master," said the raven as he wrote quickly to add their conversation to the court record.

U'nala examined the parchment again carefully, "You call that an 'R'? U'nala is not impressed by your so-called quill-skills. This is nothing but chicken scratch."

"It's not chicken scratch," answered the scribe.

"Why not?"

"Because, I'm a raven."

The Court had a twenty-minute recess while members of the Royal Guard went to fetch a new court scribe as Fiach-Ra chastised U'nala for wasting a perfectly good one.

Twenty minutes later, they tried again from the beginning. U'nala stood in front of Remmit and Kaz at the base of the stairs leading to Fiach-Ra's throne.

"Now, Gate Guards –" he pointed to Remmit.

"Remmit," answered the Hawken.

"And-" continued U'nala, pointing to Kaz.

"Kaz," said the Swantan.

"Good…you are hereby charged with – "

"Whatever it was we did, it was *his* idea!" yelled Remmit, pointing to Kaz.

"Whatever we did, it was *his* plan!" yelled Kaz pointing at Remmit.

"Grounder!" Remmit screamed at Kaz, once more attacking the Swantan lack of flying.

"Mama's boy!" countered Kaz, causing Remmit to tackle him. They began fighting and insulting each other on the floor in the throne room.

U'nala ripped up his parchment with the charges written down, crossed his arms and sighed.

Fiach-Ra brought everything back to order by ferociously slamming the butt of his spear into ground, causing the rotunda to shake. U'nala once again fell down.

After everything was brought back to order, U'nala quickly questioned Remmit and Kaz about letting Steve and Uncle Shameless into the city.

"Did you let two hu-mans into the city?"

Remmit and Kaz looked at each other, "Oh…is that what this is about?"

"Yes!" bellowed U'nala

"Yes, we did," answered Kaz, nodding his long-necked swan head.

"Why? Do you not know of The Prophecy?" demanded U'nala as thunder boomed overhead.

"Sort of," lied Remmit.

"Then why did you let them in? U'nala demands to know!"

Kaz looked at Remmit, "They said we had to."

U'nala's jaw dropped,"...You let a pair of hu-mans into the city because *they* said you had to?!" screamed U'nala "Why?!"

Remmit shook his feathery head, "They couldn't tell us."

Kaz nodded, "That's right. They said it was *classified.*"

Over the next few moments the new court scribe, this time a loon with a writing quill, quickly grew tired of writing 'curse deleted' over and over into the court record as U'nala expressed his great disappointment with the two guards.

U'nala then asked the pair to explain themselves before he had them thrown into The Pit of Big Nasty Things. Remmit and Kaz took turns retelling their encounter with the charismatic Uncle Shameless and the quiet young Steve.

"And then he said 'I've been thrown out of better places than this dump', and he demanded to see our supervisor," finished Remmit.

"A dump! He dared to call Da'Rahga, City of Flame, jewel of Fiach-Ra's Kingdom, a dump! Of all the nerve! If U'nala ever finds this hu-man, U'nala will..." U'nala glanced over to the court scribe.

"What is a dump anyway?" he asked the scribe. The loon shrugged. U'nala looked to Remmit and Kaz to see if they knew. They also shrugged.

Remmit continued, "So I went to fetch Lexa, our supervisor. He returned with me and he made the choice to let them into the city."

Kaz added "Yes, and he said he took full responsibility."

In a blur of motion, the throne room doors were thrown open, Remmit and Kaz were tossed into the hallway, Lexa was pulled into the throne room and the huge doors slammed shut.

"Well, we got out of that one," sighed Remmit.

"No thanks to you," Kaz said with a glare.

"Grounder!" insulted Remmit.

"Mama's boy!" Kaz yelled back.

The sound of the fight in the hallway was drowned out by U'nala's reading off the recent misdeeds by Lexa. The whole time, Lexa tried to hide his smile.

"U'nala is not pleased with your recent habits Wing-Commander Lexa," said the angered Wing-Master after reading ten minutes worth of screw-ups, mistakes and blunders.

Lexa decided he better play up the part of a lazy commander in front of U'nala in order to guarantee his reassignment out of the city.

"Well, y'know I just haven't been the mood to be a good commander lately," confessed Lexa.

U'nala was dumbstruck; he had never witnessed such apathy in a Hawken officer. At least not since the last one they transferred to a Zuu-forsaken post in the southern sunny regions of Eyri two days ago.

The recent trend of Hawken officers getting transferred out of Da'Rahga had not caught on with U'nala. He chalked all of it up to the current crop of young commanders being part of the same lazy, shiftless generation.

U'nala secretly loathed this entire generation (secretly in the sense that he only complained about them in a normal tone voice, instead of yelling), and figured they were all lazy and took the Kingdom for granted because none of them had actually fought for it over 300 years ago.

It never occurred to him that all of these officers and warriors were doing this only to get away from the distracting Wall of Fire.

"So, you are telling U'nala that it was *you* who let in the hu-mans?"

Lexa nodded calmly, "Yep."

"Even after one of the hu-mans referred to our lovely city as a...as a," U'nala glanced over at the loon scribe.

"Dump," answered the loon.

"Yes. A dump!" U'nala hollered as he turned back to Lexa.

Lexa did not know what U'nala meant by that, but nodded anyway. He figured that if it got the old Hawken so worked up that it must be something bad.

U'nala bellowed, "And you let them in knowing of this The Boy person mentioned in The Prophecy?"

Lexa slowly nodded again as thunder cracked in the sky above, "Yep." He knew his wait was going to be over, he'd be out of this city within the hour because of this!

U'nala clicked his beak and flapped his single wing on his back out of frustration.

"Treason!" yelled U'nala "You knowingly let in this The Boy, the one destined to free all of Eyri from the yoke of tyranny!"

From atop his throne, Fiach-Ra cleared his throat loudly.

U'nala realized is poor choice of words and quickly tried to remedy his mistake. "…According to the blasphemous, Ookday loving, present buying followers of Zaa, of course!" the Wing-Master quickly added, bowing in front of Fiach-Ra's throne several times.

Lexa liked where this was going. He might even be kicked out of the army for this. Treason! Why hadn't he thought of that sooner? If he was kicked out, he could go wherever he wanted and do whatever he wanted.

He had thoughts of opening a nest and breakfast on the coast – a nice adobe cube in big tree with a good view of the Ralk Sea. This was going better than he had hoped.

U'nala walked up the stairs to Fiach-Ra's throne and kneeled at the Hawk-King's feet.

"Fiach-Ra, Favorite of Zuu, Hawk-King of Eyri. U'nala, Wing-Master of your armies, hereby charges Wing-Commander Lexa with treason for allowing this The Boy person into Da'Rahga, City of Flame," U'nala took a deep breath before continuing "Fiach-Ra, Bringer of Fire, Wielder of The Spear of Zuu, what punishment do you pass onto Lexa?"

U'nala was getting tired of having to list all of Fiach-Ra's titles whenever they held court or during other formal and informal occasions. The Hawk-King was fond of them and U'nala felt that almost every week he had to memorize another batch of extravagant titles.

The worst of it came on the twenty-second day of summer when U'nala had to read all the Hawk-Kings titles at a lengthy, long-winded tribute for Fiach-Ra's Hatch Day. This always resulted in U'nala losing his voice for at least a fortnight afterwards, much to the pleasure of his staff of underlings.

Fiach-Ra stood up and walked slowly down the stairs until he was halfway down. The large wings on his back cast an equally large shadow upon Lexa. Each heavy step echoed throughout the rotunda as he walked.

Lexa thought he heard choral chanting as Fiach-Ra descended from his throne, but thought that was impossible and made a mental note to see a healer before he left the city.

Fiach-Ra pointed the Spear of Zuu at Lexa, "Kneel," he commanded.

Lexa obeyed, he figured it would be the last command he was ever given. He looked up at Fiach-Ra's cruel face. His pupilless, fire-filled eyes glared back at him. The Hawk-King's hefty muscular body was outsized only by his large wings. Unlike other Hawken, Fiach-Ra wore no armor and was bare-chested, garbed only in an elaborate loincloth that reached his knees.

Then there was his scar, the terrible scar through his left eye. That scar was the only thing about Fiach-Ra that even hinted at mortality.

"Wing-Commander Lexa, because of your *repeated* incompetence," exhaled Fiach-Ra, his deep voice reverberated around the rotunda at the top of Arx Vena'Tor, "You are stripped of your rank."

Yes! Thought Lexa, *I am out of here!*

"You are no longer part of my glorious army."

Lexa kept thinking of his freedom and night after night of energizing sleep away from the Wall of Fire.

Lexa looked up proudly, "I accept this punishment, O Favorite of Zuu. I shall leave Da'Rahga at once."

Lexa stood up, wondering if he had time to sell his house before he had to leave.

Fiach-Ra snapped his clawed fingers. Several Royal Guards moved to block the exit; two more came over to Lexa and grabbed a hold of his arms, restraining him.

"I was not finished," Fiach-Ra spoke softly, yet with a sinister tone.

Lexa was confused. He wondered what else the Hawk-King had in store for him. He tried to move but the Royal Guards tightened their grip upon him.

Fiach-Ra raised the Spear of Zuu and gripped it with both hands; the obelisk shaped stone head of the spear began to slowly glow. Its color quickly changed from its normal stone gray to a glowing red-orange. A hissing sound filled the rotunda.

Lexa did not like this at all. He had only seen the Spear do that once before and that was when...

His eyes widened and Lexa dropped to his knees as he watched the head of the Spear of Zuu burst into flame.

"For your treason, you shall suffer the greatest punishment," spoke Fiach-Ra as he swung the spear around so that the tip pointed in the direction of Lexa.

"I should have just bought one of Remmit's lousy blindfolds," Lexa whispered as a stream of blazing fire shot from the Spear of Zuu.

As servants swept away the ashy remains of Lexa, a strong gust of wind blew into the throne room through the hole in the roof (making the task of sweeping all that more difficult). With the wind came a pair of misty clouds.

The ghost-white mists swirled throughout the throne room, over and around everyone until they reached Fiach-Ra. The mist-clouds came to a stop on either side of the Hawk-King and floated in mid-air, each taking a long vertical shape.

"Well?" asked the Hawk-King in the direction of the twin mists.

A pair of white disks formed in each of the clouds and flashed brightly. In an instant, the clouds split down the middle like pea-pods and the mist was ripped away like capes. The mists *were* in fact capes, worn by Fiach-Ra's loyal spies, a pair of identical raven twins – Delu and Uled. As the twins' capes were pulled away from their bodies, they turned from mist into green leather-like patchwork.

Across the room, U'nala scoffed silently (silently for him. Which was about a normal volume for anyone else). He did not enjoy the company of the sickly raven twins. He narrowed his eyes as the twins' thin, lithe frames turned from magical mist back into feathers and bone.

Deep down, he was jealous of the Caper Capes that gave them their ability to turn into mist, which also allowed the wingless twins to fly literally like the wind. However, he did not envy the price the twins paid for using the capes. It was said that the using the Caper Capes drained the life force of the user; hence the ever-present sickly state of the twins.

"Humph! They deserve whatever they get!" blurted U'nala, who did not realize he was thinking aloud. He quickly tried to act as if he was talking to one of the silent Royal Guards when the Hawk-King and his spies turned in his direction.

Fiach-Ra turned his gaze from his boisterous second-in-command to the glowing white eyes of the twins.

"Well?" he asked a second time.

"Highness," began Delu in a voice like a nail on a chalkboard "It is true-"

"-The Boy *was* in Da'Rahga," finished Uled with an equally eerie tone "And has-"

"-Since escaped," finished Delu.

This was another thing about the raven twins that U'nala despised – the way they talked.

"Who do they think they are, talking like that?" U'nala said somewhat quietly (which was an accomplishment). "U'nala can not believe the manner in which they speak, finishing each others sentences. U'nala does not like it. No, U'nala does not like it one bit."

The Royal Guard next to U'nala broke one of the rules and rolled his eyes under his winged helmet.

Fiach-Ra slammed the butt of his spear into the ground to accent his rage after hearing his spies' confirmation of The Boy being in his city. He had dispatched the twins after hearing Nevik's story.

"Where did he escape to?" asked Fiach-Ra.

"We had but little-"

"-Time to search Highness, but we heard-"

"-That he escaped by way of-"

"-The rear of the castle," finished Delu (or Uled. They were *identical* twins after all).

Fiach-Ra climbed back up to his throne. The twins joined him on either side; their thin black-feathered bodies seemed to almost float up the staircase.

"Find him."

"Of course Highness, but-," whispered Uled into Fiach-Ra's left ear.

"-Even as mists, we can only-," continued Delu into the Hawk-King's right ear.

"-Travel in two directions at once. We'll need Hunters," said both of the twins in unison. Fiach-Ra sighed and reluctantly nodded.

"Very well. Hire Hunters if you must – U'nala!" barked the Hawk-King.

His one-winged second in command halted his complaining of the raven twins to the nearest Royal Guard and ran hastily towards the throne, tripping in the process. After slowly getting up and dusting himself off, he kneeled at the base of the steps.

"Yes?"

"Give the twins money to hire Hunters to aid with their search," said the Hawk-King.

"Highness…is this really necessary?" questioned U'nala, thinking of the paperwork for such a request "I would have to take it out of the Petty Treasure-"

"Are you questioning my command?" countered the Hawk-King, as he narrowed his fire-filled eyes at his old friend.

U'nala's eyes widened. He was one of a few-if any-that could actually debate with the Hawk-King. But he was still very careful about doing so. Fiach-Ra demanded absolute obedience, and took any thing else as disloyalty. The Hawk-King had no tolerance for disloyal subjects, as Lexa had just learned.

"No, no," U'nala finally answered after his heart began beating again, "I just thought, why out source this task when we have legions of Hawken and Swantans around the castle?"

"Using troops-"

"-Would attract too much attention," the twins said. Fiach-Ra nodded, agreeing with the twins.

This was yet another trait of the raven twins that U'nala detested. Whatever they said or suggested, Fiach-Ra usually agreed with – which usually resulted in U'nala handing over money.

U'nala also hated using Hunters. They were expensive enough to begin with, but when they were hired by the Kingdom they would always add several zeros to the end of their going rate. Plus Hunters were usually shady characters. They were anything from outcasts to criminals to assassins or any thing in-between, even former diplomats.

U'nala shuddered at the thought of hiring Hunters, but decided not to voice his disapproval anymore today since he did not like the idea of being swept up off the floor.

Some time later, the raven twins stood by the door leading out of the castle that Uncle Shameless had easily ripped out of the wall. They were joined by three other figures, dressed in hooded cloaks. One of Hunters was garbed in a black cloak and wore a long yellow scarf tied around his neck.

Only the tip of an oddly shaped hooked beak peaked out from under the blackness of his hood. The bird-man ran a clawed hand covered in black feathers over the severely damaged door frame.

"A *human* did this?" he asked calmly, his yellow scarf flapping gently in the breeze.

"Yes, a hu-man," said Delu. Or maybe Uled. None of the three Hunters could tell the difference, or cared.

Whichever twin it was turned to the other and cast a sly smile. The twins had managed to find not just three Hunters, but a band of

Hunters. They called themselves The Five (even though there were only three of them).

Delu and Uled had learned from experience that hiring Hunters was all about luck. Skill levels ranged greatly when it came to Hunters, as did price. The selection of Hunters available depended greatly on which of them were in the city at that moments, or even still alive.

Another reason the twins had demanded the aid of Hunters was that neither of the pair was physically strong enough to handle the likes of Uncle Shameless and his super strength. Before reporting back to Fiach-Ra, they had interrogated several of the beat-up Swantan guards and learned what Uncle Shameless was capable of.

The twins were good at sneaking around and knifing people in the back and all that sort of nasty business, and could handle average humans but that was about it. The twins could not be touched in their mist form, but neither could they touch anyone or anything. The Five looked like they could more than handle Uncle Shameless.

The yellow-scarfed Hunter walked back over to the leader of the band, a large shape covered in a forest green cloak. A pair of battered, old antlers jutted out from under his hood and an equally battered and old looking longbow was slung across his body.

The two talked quietly while the third, who had remained silent the entire time, watched the twins with unblinking black eyes from under his brown-gray hood.

A snort from the leader of The Five broke the tense silence and he threw back his hood, reveling an aged deer face.

"Awright," said the leader, an old deer by the name of Cam, in an oddly enthusiastic tone of voice, "My second here tells me that we ain't dealin' wit no regular human. And yous guys said there was two of 'em?"

The twins sighed in unison.

"That is correct, we-" started Uled.

"-Believe that the older hu-man-" continued Delu.

"-Has extra ordinary strength." finished Uled.

Delu crossed his long thin arms under his Caper Cape, "The other is only a boy, he should-"

"-Not pose a threat," finished Uled.

Cam crassly cleared his throat and spat something large and wet to the ground before walking over to the twins. His aged hooves clicked on the stonework. He gave Delu (or maybe Uled) a wild-eyed look.

"But how do we know that fa sure?" asked Cam as he cracked the knuckles of his elderly fingers.

The twins sighed again, already guessing where this was going.

"…We do not," the twins said together.

"Aw, so my boys an' me could be goin' up a'gain *two* extra ordinary humans! Is that what you are sayin'?"

The twins looked at each other and then turned their piercing gaze back to Cam and his band.

"How-" started Uled.

"-Much?" finished his brother.

Cam turned his back to the twins, "Well, it's hard ta say, I ain't never dealt with no *extra* ordinary humans b'fore…" he quickly glanced at his second in command in the yellow scarf, who stealthy flashed him three clawed fingers "But maybe for five-"

He was cut off by the sound of a sizeable sack of coins hitting the ground and making a loud THUD. Cam spun around on his hooves and looked down at the bulging sack.

"Well. I reckon that'll work too."

"So, ya got all of that?" Cam said later to the Hunter in the yellow scarf.

The other Hunter nodded, "The twins check to the north and south. You an' Arbal," he cast a quick glance to the silent mourning dove Hunter in the brown-gray cloak, "will head to the west. I'll go east."

"You gonna be okay by yerself?" asked Cam, giving his second in command a knowing wink.

"I'll be fine, I've Hunted humans before."

"So have I Zeroth, but none that could rip a door clean outta stone wall," replied Cam "G'luck and mind yer temper, ya hear? They want 'em in one piece."

A sly smile crossed Zeroth's beak as he nodded.

The raven twins pretended to clear their throats in a sickly chorus. "Awright ya bums!" cursed Cam as he trotted over to the twins "Arbal! Stop screwin' around wit yer toy!" Cam yelled at the dove-man, who was busy winding up the steel bow of his gigantic crossbow.

The crossbow stood upright as Arbal's feet held it in place while using the large crank at the rear of the weapon. After it was properly wound, he slung the beastly weapon onto his back and quietly chased after Cam. Zeroth had questioned the use of such a weapon when Arbal had joined the band, since it did not seem worth the hassle. Since then Zeroth had witnessed the damage the heavy weapon could easily inflict. Cam hated the weapon and the smaller hand-held repeating crossbows that Arbal kept under his cloak. The old deer-man was happy with his longbow and savored the expertise and skill required to use it, unlike Arbal's point and shoot weapons.

Cam was fond of accusing Arbal's weapons of taking all the fun out of Hunting, but he could not really argue about the results. Business had been much better since Arbal joined the band, even if the dove hardly spoke and seemed to enjoy the job a little *too* much.

"They couldn't have gotten too far," Cam yelled to Zeroth and the twins, "Use the Signal Stones if ya find 'em!"

Signal Stones had been decided on in case the twins ran into the humans while alone. All one had to do was break a Signal Stone against the ground and a column of smoke would be released. The smoke would climb high into the air and could be seen for miles.

Unfortunately, the smoke could also be *smelled* for miles.

For whatever reason, the inventor of the Signal Stones was in such a hurry to get them on the market that he did not bother to perform any tests first. He realized too late that the ingredients he used created an extremely foul odor when combined together and exposed to air. The smell was so bad, that some cities had outlawed their use, even outside of the city (especially those downwind).

Zeroth had been wary of using Signal Stones ever since he had tripped and fallen hard on his supply while sneaking after a target some years ago. It was many weeks before he could enter a town again, let alone sneak up on anyone.

A chill ran down Zeroth's feathered spine as he watched the twins wrap their Caper Capes around themselves. When not using them, the capes hung loosely off their backs and looked only like stitched leather. Zeroth knew better though, he had heard the stories of the creatures the skins had come from – Capers. They were fearsome creatures that could turn into mist at will and were fond of ambushing travelers.

Like the twins, Capers could only be hurt while flesh and blood, making them very hard to hunt. Zeroth did not know how the twins had come across the mythical capes, let alone two.

As the twins wrapped the capes around their bodies, they instantly turned into clouds of hazy-white mist. Their blank white eyes glowed for a moment, then blended into the rest of their misty bodies. The twin clouds took to the air and flew into the distance, one headed North and the other South.

Zeroth waved a final good-bye to Cam as the old deer and his mourning dove companion headed off into the distance.

Zeroth wandered around the exterior of Arx Vena'Tor until he came to the old aqueduct. His sharp eyes caught the faint remains of a pair of footprints near the edge of the old stone waterway.

The bird-man had never seen prints such as these before as he was not familiar with sneaker and boot treads. What confused him even more than the wavy lines in the dirt was the seemingly random number printed inside of the smaller of the two sets of prints.

Zeroth did not know who this 'Six' was, or why he and the owner of the larger tracks had such strange footprints. But Zeroth did not care. A pair of black wings swung out from under his cloak.

The Hunt had begun.

7

Eira, Steve and Uncle Shameless walked slowly toward the Forbidden Forest on their way to Uth, The Last Human Village.

The companions took frequent breaks as Eira looked for trail markers. Steve did not know how anyone could tell one forest from another; they all looked the same to him.

"Why are you going to Uth?" asked Eira eventually.

"We're not from around here," answered Steve as he tried unsuccessfully to ignore his tired feet. "We were told to go there."

"Who told you?"

"A friend," said Uncle Shameless.

"I wouldn't go that far," added Steve, thinking bitter thoughts about Istrio and the mess the blue heron had gotten him into.

"I see," said Eira, walking slowly but steadily with the aid of her walking stick, "Tell me, does it have anything to do with that amulet around your neck?"

Steve and Uncle Shameless stopped in mid-step. They turned and looked at each other.

Eira leaned on her walking stick, "I am not a fool. I know what that amulet means."

"I'm glad someone knows," said Steve as he held up his hands in protest, "I didn't really agree to anything at all. This was all kind of dumped on me."

He shook his head; "I think the whole idea of me bringing change to your world is a bit silly."

Eira walked over to Steve and placed a feathery hand on his shoulder, "You may think that now, but you will learn to believe in 'silly' things."

"Yeah, maybe you'll even start believing my silly stories," added Uncle Shameless with a goofy smile.

"Such as?" asked Eira "I like a good story, as do most around here. Silly or not."

Uncle Shameless' eyes lit up. "Well, there was this one time I had to punch out a cow-"

Steve shook his head, "Please don't encourage him. *Please*."

"Well, you see there was this cow and-" started Uncle Shameless.

"Did you hear that?" asked Eira as she glanced around.

"'Course I did, I said it!" answered Uncle Shameless.

"No, no," replied Eira "I thought I heard something in the woods."

Steve looked through the trees, and all he saw was more trees. He shrugged, unimpressed. The trees in this part of the forest were sickly and almost barren, like the rest of Eyri that he had already seen.

He was fairly certain he had not seen any green or healthy looking plants during their trip so far. The trees around them looked like wooden skeletons with a few leaves pasted on here and there.

Zeroth landed near the small lake at the end of the aqueduct moments later. From the blackness of his hood, his eyes spotted Eira's tracks and the two drag marks coming out of the lake. He quickly figured out what had happened, and considered charging the twins extra for having to take care of a third target.

That was the beauty of having a government contract, he could easily charge for extras such as disappearing an additional party.

'Six' and the larger human had been here. He could see more of their bizarre footprints. He was positive he was on the right trail and considered signaling the others, but he was tempted to see if he could handle this extra ordinary human the raven twins spoke of by himself.

As he climbed a nearby tree he realized that he had not been in a good scrap in a long while, and that Arbal would probably make short work of this extra ordinary human before he could have any fun.

Zeroth smiled as he drew his sword and took to the air once more, his yellow scarf flapping madly after him.

Later on, the trio decided to stop for a rest. Eira and Steve sat on a fallen tree (they actually had quite the selection to chose from) while Uncle Shameless decided to collapse on the ground.

"Why is it called the Forbidden Forest anyway?" asked Steve.

"Oh, it's just a name. That's all," answered Eira, yawning and stretching out her long bill. "The first map of Eyri was drawn by an owl named Datts Forbidden. She took a few liberties with some of the names and named the forest after herself."

"That sounds like something *you* would say," Steve said to Uncle Shameless, who was taking a few sips from his wineskin. Uncle Shameless nodded at Steve's comment.

Steve smiled, "But see it's like I told you, there was a logical reason for the name, not because people go in and never come out. There's no such thing."

"Oh, there's a forest like that," remarked Eira.

"What's it called?" asked Uncle Shameless.

"Treasure Forest."

Steve groaned. *This place is getting weirder by the second*, he thought.

As they all stood up to leave, motion in the trees caught Steve's eyes – he thought he saw a blur of yellow among the drab-brown branches.

Zeroth watched the trio with great interest from above. He assumed the taller human was the one with the extra-ordinary strength. Although, for someone who was so strong he seemed to have great difficulty walking. In fact, to call what he was doing walking was a great overstatement. It was more like a stumble with a dash of stagger.

The boy, who Zeroth determined was 'Six' by spying the footprints he left behind in the dirt, did not look like a threat and neither did the pelican from the lake.

Zeroth tightened his grip on his sword and prepared to attack.

"Look, I just wanna go home," Steve explained to Eira. She had been trying unsuccessfully to get Steve to accept his role in The Prophecy.

"But you were visited by a blue heron, a Mystic of Zaa! They haven't been seen in –"

A branch snapped loudly in the woods. Eira stopped in mid sentence and looked in all directions.

"What's-"

"Shhh!" said Eira as she hushed Steve. "We aren't alone," she held up her walking stick like a weapon. Following her lead, Uncle Shameless took a few extra swigs of wine and felt the extra-ordinary strength fill his body.

A large thrashing sound came from a closely packed group of trees nearby. "Get ready!" said Eira.

Steve looked around, "For what?" he said nervously.

A giant blur of brown fur exploded from the trees in front of them and hit the ground with a reverberating stomp.

Eira shouted "Run quickly!"

Steve looked at her, "What is it?"

His words trailed off as he looked at the bear sized creature in front of him. Its large tooth filled mouth was salivating all over the forest floor, creating several gross looking pools.

Its powerful muscular legs clawed at the dirt, readying a charge. Eira grabbed Steve, "We must go! They eat anything, and I mean *anything!*"

The revolting creature roared loudly. The stench of its foul breath filled the air around them. It looked right at Eira and Steve, and suddenly began to charge towards them with snapping, menacing jaws. Salvia flew from its gaping mouth as it aimed its long snout in their direction.

Steve did not know what to do; he could not believe such an odd creature was attacking him. It looked to Steve like a giant shrew. An animal like this could not exist, he told himself. Shrews were normally very small animals, about the size of mice.

"Don't worry," slurred Uncle Shameless as he stumbled into the creature's path "I'll handle this." He hiked up his pants and pulled back his fist. Unfortunately, blinded by drunkenness, Uncle Shameless threw the punch while creature was still a few yards away and swung carelessly into the air. The force of his swing caused him to spin around and to collapse to the ground in a cloud of dust.

"Thanks for nothing," said Steve.

The giant shrew continued its charge, ignoring Uncle Shameless who was sprawled out on the forest floor. Steve and Eira were backed up against a tightly packed group of trees, and there was no way out for the trapped pair.

The giant shrew closed in, its hungry jaws snapping. Steve felt the creature's hot breath upon him. Suddenly, there was a loud hawk cry from the sky above. The giant shrew slowed its charge as a shadowy shape fell from the sky in front of him and rested on a pair of clawed bird feet. It flapped a pair of black wings and cried its shriek again, only louder this time.

The giant shrew turned and fled, frightened by this new creature. Zeroth pulled back his hood and spun to face Steve, Eira and Uncle Shameless.

Steve gasped as he found himself staring into a pair of menacing Hawken eyes.

Eira spotted the triple ringed Hunter's pendent around Zeroth's black feathered neck and tightened her grip on her walking stick.

"A Hunter!" she snapped.

"Guilty," said Zeroth coldly as he bowed mockingly.

"Excuse me-" started Steve, who was afraid that this was going to lead to a bunch of boring information.

"He's a what-now?" asked Uncle Shameless as he slowly stood up.

"A Hunter!" said Eira again "They are bounty hunters, assassins, mercenaries-"

"Oh, here we go..." sighed Steve, who was already looking for a comfortable seat.

"-Thieves, kidnappers, and all around nasty people," continued Eira.

"If you are about finished," barked Zeroth as he approached with attitude "I would like to wrap this up quickly. And for the record, I have never assassinated anyone."

"Why?" asked Uncle Shameless, earning him a confused look from his now seated nephew.

"I could never pass the licensing test. It is a tad difficult."

Eira maneuvered herself in front of Steve, "For some reason, I don't believe that."

"Look here," said Zeroth as he placed his hands on his hips "My contract did not specify I bring you in alive, and if you are going to get snippy I might have to exercise that option."

"But I thought you said you failed the licensing test," responded Uncle Shameless as he sipped some more wine.

"Assassinating someone is a whole other thing, trust me I know, I had to read three thick volumes explaining it." The Hunter held his five fingered clawed hands apart to suggest the size of the volumes.

Uncle Shameless scratched his head, "I'm confused now."

"The short answer is, assassinating is signing a contract just to kill. But, if I were to kill you while having contract that *preferred* to capture you alive but did not specifically request it, that is something completely different."

"That doesn't make any sense," said Uncle Shameless.

"I agree," snapped Steve from his somewhat comfortable seat on the ground.

"Yes, I know it is a bit of a gray area, but I didn't write the Hunter Code," replied Zeroth as he stabbed his sword into the ground and leaned on the hilt, "However, we are getting away from the task at hand."

"Which is?" asked Uncle Shameless as he tried to focus his lazy eye on the bounty hunter.

"To bring you two humans in, especially Six over there," he pointed a clawed finger at Steve.

Steve looked around, half expecting to see someone else, "Me? My name isn't Six."

"Then why is it written on the bottom of your funny looking shoes?" asked Zeroth, referring to Steve's black canvas high-tops.

The boy looked at the bottom of his sneakers and sure enough saw a '6' printed on the heel. He rolled his eyes.

"That's my shoe size, not my name!"

"Shoe...size?" said Zeroth, tripping over the words.

The whole concept of footwear was alien to most of the bird-people of Eyri, as they never had any need for it. Plus the variety of feet among the bird population made it impossible for even the most enthusiastic cobbler to attempt making designer footwear for them.

This is not to say that no one had tried, because it was a vastly untapped market. But those that did all failed, became bankrupt, and went insane (but not always in that order).

"That's right, my name is Steve!" snapped the boy.

"Very well, Steve then," replied Zeroth coldly as he pulled his sword free from the ground and thought to himself what an odd name 'Steve' was.

"Wait!" pleaded Steve.

Zeroth sighed and narrowed his hawk-eyes at the boy, "Yes?"

"What was that thing that attacked us?" asked Steve, referring to the giant shrew-like creature that Zeroth had scared off.

"Oh, just a solicitor," answered the Hunter.

"But we have solicitors back home and they aren't like that," explained Steve as he thought of annoying salespeople.

"Well around here 'solicitor' is an old word for 'savage ravenous beast," said Zeroth.

"Hmm...actually, that kinda makes sense," said Uncle Shameless.

Zeroth, deciding the lesson was over, continued his approach towards the trio. "Wait!" Steve pleaded again.

Zeroth sighed louder this time, "Yes?"

The boy looked over the bounty hunter, "What *are* you anyway?"

The Hunter was certainly unusual looking, the boy thought to himself.

He was taller than a Hawken and more muscular, but shorter and leaner than a Swantan. His beak was longer than a hawk's but hooked like one and had a ring of black around it, looking like a swan's. He had the piercing eyes of a hawk, but also had orange webbed feet equipped with razor sharp talons.

His wings were not the sizeable, majestic-looking tools of flight that the Hawken had, they were considerably smaller and looked rather weak. The parts of his body that were not covered by his cloak were covered with black feathers. Steve decided that the Hunter looked like some sort of a hawk-swan hybrid.

Zeroth tightened his yellow scarf and seemed disturbed by the question. "I'm..." he stumbled as he looked for the right words "Look, I don't know."

"Oh," breathed Steve in a disappointed tone.

"Oh my," added Eira.

"Whaddyamean ya don't know?!" bellowed Uncle Shameless loudly; earning cross looks from Eira and Steve.

Zeroth narrowed his eyes at Uncle Shameless, "All I know is that because of the way I look, I am an outcast. Happy?" snapped the Hunter, anger rising in his voice. Steve was certain he saw faint tint of red flash in the Hunter's eyes.

"Now," said Zeroth, his voice switching to a deeper and more sinister tone "You two humans will be coming with me – and like I said before – dead or alive."

Steve jumped to his feet with a loud yelp and started running away. At least he tried to. Before he was a few feet away, a pair of bolas wrapped around his legs and arms.

Zeroth seemed to produce the webs of rope with attached weights from nowhere, and as Steve fell to the ground he was already spinning another over his head.

Eira rushed over as fast as she could with her walking stick to help the disabled boy but quickly fell victim to a third bola as it pinned her arms to her body. Unable to balance herself, the pelican fell to the ground.

Zeroth turned his aim to Uncle Shameless and readied another bola. The events of the past few moments took several seconds to reach Uncle Shameless' wine soaked brain. When they eventually did, he figured out that he was in trouble.

Sadly, by this time Zeroth had already wrapped a bola around him. Uncle Shameless looked down at his bindings, "Dang-nab-it!" he cursed.

"Indeed," said Zeroth, a little disappointed that no one had even tried to put up a fight.

Uncle Shameless closed his eyes in concentration and seconds later let out a loud "Wor-bah!" as he broke through the ropes holding him.

The weights and ropes fell to the ground with several loud thuds, causing Zeroth's beak to drop open in surprise (and thankfulness).

Uncle Shameless tucked his wineskin into his old leather belt after a quick drink and began cracking his knuckles.

"A'ight birdie-boy – let's go," he challenged "No one messes with *my* nephew."

A sly smile crossed Zeroth's beak and he sportingly put away his sword (for now). The Hunter struck a fighting pose (which reminded Uncle Shameless of a repulsive dance he had seen at a recent wedding), and beckoned Uncle Shameless to make the first move.

The man in the tattered jeans and faded flannel shirt charged the odd-looking bird-man. Uncle Shameless threw a wild punch at the Hunter, which was dodged. Zeroth kneed Uncle Shameless in the ribs, causing the man to stumble backwards.

Zeroth jumped at his target and was surprised when Uncle Shameless performed a super strong jump and tackled the bird-man in mid-air.

"Oof!" gasped Zeroth as they crashed to the forest floor. Uncle Shameless threw a punch at Zeroth's head, but he rolled away, letting the human's fist shatter a rock next to him. Zeroth rolled away from his prey and picked himself up. It had been a long while since he had such a challenge – let alone from a human. Uncle Shameless lunged towards Zeroth again, but the bird-man spun and grabbed him, effortlessly throwing him to the ground.

This amazing spectacle of mortal combat was lost on Steve, as he had landed facing away from the fight. He tried to roll over to see what was going on but the weights on the bolas made it difficult. Eira did her best to describe the action to him.

"Well your uncle was just thrown to the ground, and now the Hunter is kicking him in the ribs, and now he is kicking him in the – oh my..." she said, her words trailing off.

"Where?" asked Steve, but after hearing the epic length of curses coming from his uncle seconds later he made an educated guess as to the region of Zeroth's last kick.

Steve quickly decided that being tied up wasn't all that bad compared to the alternative.

Uncle Shameless threw dirt in Zeroth's face, giving him enough time to stand up as the bird-man brushed out his large eyes. Uncle Shameless lined up Zeroth in his mental sights and charged full-speed at the Hunter. Recalling the five years he played high school football, Uncle Shameless tackled Zeroth with all of his might.

Uncle Shameless plowed into Zeroth like a truck, knocking both of them back several yards. The tackle knocked the wind out Zeroth's lungs, leaving him prone for several moments. This was enough time for Uncle Shameless to pick the bird-man up and to hurl him high into the trees.

It was at this moment Uncle Shameless remembered that Zeroth had wings.

"Oh, crackers!" blurted Uncle Shameless as he watched Zeroth flap open his wings and fly away from the trees. Unlike the Hawken that had flown after him and Steve in the aqueducts, Zeroth appeared to only be gliding. The Hunter was several yards above them in the air and looked to be rummaging around in a small leather pack at his side.

Zeroth almost pulled out a Signal Stone, but changed his mind. He wanted a few more minutes to see if he could wrap this up himself. Instead, he pulled out a flash bomb and lobbed it near Uncle Shameless. It went off, momentarily blinding the human.

Zeroth tucked in his small wings, dove at the dazed human, and kicked him squarely under the jaw. The blow knocked Uncle Shameless back a few feet to the ground, but he got up in time to avoid a taloned webbed foot aimed for his head.

Zeroth was back on the ground again and this evened things up for Uncle Shameless, or so he thought. The Hunter stood in place several yards away from Uncle Shameless with one arm tucked under his cloak. Uncle Shameless paid no attention to this and ran towards the Hunter while winding up a mighty punch.

Seconds before the punch would have connected with Zeroth's chest, the Hunter pulled out his arm from under his cloak – along with a large shield. Uncle Shameless' fist crashed head on into the thick shield, leaving a slight dent. Uncle Shameless stumbled backwards, rubbing his sore hand.

"No fair!" cried the human.

Zeroth chuckled as he held up the shield with one hand and adjusted his yellow scarf with the other.

"And having extra-ordinary strength is fair?" countered Zeroth.

"That's diff'rent!"

"Now what's happening?" asked Steve, still unable to see the fight. "Well, the Hunter just pulled out a shield from under his cloak and-" started Eira.

"He what?" gasped Steve, who did not believe the pelican.

"He pulled out a shield, a rather large one too...I don't know where he was hiding it."

Steve shook his head in disbelief as best he could since he was still lying on his side and tied up. He was positive he would have noticed a large shield hidden on Zeroth's body, as he was not that bulky. Steve pushed aside that paradox for a moment.

"Now what is happening?" asked Steve as he heard a series of loud clangs.

"Your uncle keeps punching at the Hunter, and the Hunter keeps blocking the punches with his shield."

Steve let out a loud, audible sigh.

"Your uncle isn't a quick learner is he?" asked Eira as she watched Uncle Shameless repeatedly connect punches with Zeroth's mysterious shield.

"His heart is in the right place," sighed Steve, "I just wish his brain was."

Zeroth could not explain it, but it seemed that the human's punches were grower weaker and weaker. The first batch had left noticeable dents in the shield, but now the shield was barely flexing under the blows. He decided to exploit this opportunity.

A very exhausted Uncle Shameless wound up one more punch and threw it towards Zeroth. The Hunter side-stepped at the last moment and bonked Uncle Shameless hard on the head with his heavy shield. Uncle Shameless turned to face Zeroth and appeared very cross. For a moment Zeroth thought his plan had backfired.

But after a quick stagger, Uncle Shameless' eyes rolled towards the back of his head and he folded like a card table.

"Uh-oh," gasped Eira.

"What do you mean, 'Uh-oh'?" asked Steve, although he had a pretty good idea what she meant.

"You Uncle is-"

"Down for the count," finished Zeroth smugly as he approached the pair. He less than gently sat Eira and Steve up. The boy could see that Zeroth had tied Uncle Shameless up with several lengths of chains. Like the shield, their origin was a mystery.

Zeroth walked back to Uncle Shameless and dragged him over to the others. He then retrieved his shield and pulled back part of his cloak to reveal a small leather pack at his side. What happened next broke every law of science Steve had ever learned (and he had learned quite a few, even the unpopular ones).

Zeroth opened the top of the pack, which was about the size of a small loaf of bread, and proceeded to shove the much larger shield into it. Steve's eyes bugged out as he watched the large shield quickly disappear into the blackness of the pack's compartment. Afterwards Zeroth snapped it closed like nothing out of the ordinary had happened.

"Impossible!" yelled the boy.

"Look, it isn't my fault your Uncle is a lousy fighter-" began Zeroth.

"No!" corrected Steve "The shield! The pack! How?!"

"Hrm?...*Oh*," realized Zeroth.

The Hunter tapped the top of the pack with a clawed finger, "Magic."

"But-but-but," stuttered Steve "H-h-how?" The boy felt all of his knowledge of science quickly becoming worthless.

Zeroth shrugged, "I'm no wizard. All I know is that it holds as much as a room. Pretty handy actually, 'specially for smuggling."

"H-h-hhh-h-" started Steve again, sounding like a parrot in an earthquake "h-how?"

Zeroth shrugged again, "Stuff just goes in and when I want something out of it, I just stick my hand in and think of it. Easy."

"Where did you get something like that?" asked Eira.

"From some adventurer," reminisced Zeroth with a sly smile "As I recall he was rather... *reluctant* to give it up."

Zeroth finished tying up the trio with a series of ropes and chains he produced from his science-defying pack. For a moment he considered letting Eira go, but decided to see if he could get more money from the twins instead. He did not feel like dragging all three of his prisoners back to the castle, so he fished around in his pack for a Signal Stone.

He hurled it a few yards away, cracking it open against the trunk of a brittle looking tree. A dark yellow column of smoke began slowly crawling up through the canopy of sickly trees.

The smell however, moved considerably faster.

"Yuck!" choked Steve, his eyes beginning to water.

"Ugh!" added Eira as the tendrils of stench wove around her.

"…Jimmy?" mumbled Uncle Shameless as he began to come around.

"Quiet down," ordered Zeroth as he did his best not to inhale the rancid fumes.

"What was that?" asked Steve as he tried not to breathe.

Zeroth held his scarf over his beak as he walked over to the boy, "A Signal Stone, so the rest of my band knows where I am."

"Band? You're musicians?" asked Steve, confused.

"No, we're a band of Hunters not musicians," explained Zeroth, sounding a little annoyed.

"There are more of you?" asked Eira.

"There are three of us. We're called The Five."

"Wait a minute," interrupted Steve "Why are you called The Five if there are only three of you?"

"Cam was never that good at counting."

Zeroth leaned against a gnarled tree as he waited for his bandmates and the raven twins.

"Why'd you come after us anyway?" asked Steve.

"We went over this already. I'm a Hunter. I was paid to find you. Nothing personal."

"Do you know *why* you were paid to find this boy?" asked Eira as she fought against the ropes restraining her.

Zeroth stretched and scratched his neck, "No, and I don't really care. I don't ask questions about Prey."

"Look at this boy, doesn't he look odd to you?" asked Eira.

"Hey!" objected Steve.

Zeroth decided to humor the chatty pelican and walked over to Steve. He certainly did look odd, the bird-man thought. His clothes were not typical human clothes and then there were his odd shoes with numbers printed on the bottom.

"He dresses funny. So what?"

"What?!" protested Steve.

Eira ignored Steve and continued, "Haven't you ever heard of The Prophecy?" she asked as thunder cracked overhead. Zeroth thought for a moment, "Aren't they the band of Hunters out of Eaner? No, wait. I'm thinking of Prophet's Profits-"

"No!" scolded Eira "*The* Prophecy!" exclaimed the pelican-lady over the distant thunder. Zeroth narrowed his eyes in deep thought. This 'The Prophecy' business sounded oddly familiar, but he could not remember why.

He seemed to remember Cam going on and on about that one night over a fire. The deer-man was full of knowledge regarding folklore and myths, although Zeroth often thought he was just full of something else.

"Too bad Cam isn't here," Zeroth said with a shrug.

"Aw, ya miss me already?" called a gruff voice from deep within the forest.

Zeroth snapped to attention as Cam and Arbal emerged from a group of trees several yards away. The old Hunter walked steadily towards Zeroth, bow in hand. Behind him Arbal walked silently, his gigantic crossbow at the ready.

"That was fast," said Zeroth, surprised at the elderly deer's quick appearance.

"Fah," mumbled Cam as he came to a stop next to his odd-looking second in command "I knew which way these guys went right from the git go."

Steve thought he saw Arbal give Cam a nasty look. At least as nasty a look an overgrown mourning dove *could* give someone.

Before Zeroth could ask how he knew where to go, Cam pointed to his graying deer snout. "Yap, I smelled 'em from the start," he explained. "Humans tend to stick out when it comes ta smells. 'Specially that one." He pointed to Uncle Shameless.

"He's got that right," joked Steve.

"Why didn't you say so?" asked Zeroth.

"Don't me give that," said Cam "You know you wanted to tangle with that super-human yerself. I just gave ya the chance."

"Excuse me," interrupted Steve "Who is this 'super-human' you are talking about?"

Cam pointed a furry finger at Uncle Shameless, "Him."

"Him?!" questioned Steve.

"Believe it, kid."

Uncle Shameless slowly opened his eyes and focused on the gruff features of Cam.

"Yer a deer!" yelled Uncle Shameless.

"Aw, yer pretty terrific yerself," joked Cam. Steve and Zeroth both groaned at the bad joke.

Zeroth pointed his sword at Steve, "The pelican says there is something odd about this boy."

"'Sides the way he dresses?" asked Cam, earning a loud 'Hey!' from Steve.

"Something about a prophecy."

"Oh, fergit that. I'm more worried about profits, see?" Cam joked with a wink. Uncle Shameless laughed.

"Somebody shoot me, now. Please," sighed Steve, growing tired of the all the bad jokes he was hearing.

Arbal, not recognizing the figure of speech, stared at Steve with cold dark eyes and aimed his crossbow.

"Gwaaah!" blurted Steve. Cam swung his bow and knocked Arbal's massive weapon away before he could shoot.

"Arbal, remind me to give ya raise so ya can buy a sense of humor."

Eira scooted around on the ground until she faced Cam. "Not just a prophecy, *The* Prophecy!" yelled Eira as thunder cracked in the sky.

"What is with the weather today?" started Zeroth "Cam do you know what...Cam?"

Cam's eyes widened and his furry hands shook as he looked over Steve once more. "Is this...The Boy?" he said, almost gasping for air.

"I have a name," started Steve.

"He is. Look," said Eira as she glanced to Steve's neck.

Cam kneeled down and reached for the blue heron amulet around the boy's neck. His fur covered fingers stopped just before it as the amulet began to glow light blue. Cam pulled back his shaking hand and stood up as quickly as he could.

The amulet stopped glowing.

"Let 'em go..." gasped Cam.

Arbal and Zeroth both looked at their leader, confused by Cam's command.

"Bad for business," snapped Arbal coldly with a shake of his head. Zeroth's beak almost dropped open. He couldn't remember the last time he had heard Arbal talk.

"I said let 'em go!" ordered Cam in a rare display of authority.

"But..." started Zeroth.

Cam snorted and pushed Zeroth aside as he pulled out a long knife from his belt and began cutting the ropes holding Steve and Eira.

"C'mon Cam!" pleaded Zeroth "What's going on?"

"The Prophecy!" yelled Cam as he helped Eira stand before moving on to Steve.

Zeroth waited for the thunder to stop before asking, "What's the big deal about it?"

"This boy will free Eyri from the yoke of-"

"Yes, tyranny," sighed Steve. He then realized he did not even know what a yoke was.

"It says that he will yargh!" yelled Cam.

"Yargh? What are you talking..." Zeroth's words trailed off as he watched Cam slowly fall to the forest floor.

Arbal swung his spent weapon onto his back and pulled out a small handheld crossbow and aimed it at Steve.

"You are not going anywhere," ordered Arbal, the cold words oozing out of his beak.

"What did you do?!" screamed Zeroth as he kneeled next to the mortally wounded Cam.

Arbal did not answer. He pulled back on the lever of his repeating crossbow, firing a small arrow at Zeroth's sword arm and readying another shot with the same motion.

"Arbal..." hissed Zeroth as he covered the wound with his hand, which was only a graze, but still painful. Arbal walked over and kicked Zeroth in the face, knocking him to the forest floor alongside Cam.

Arbal loaded another harmful bolt into his colossal crossbow. Steve was frozen by fear, not knowing what to do. Cam had freed him and Eira, but Uncle Shameless was still wrapped in chains. Steve figured that the three of them could at least run away, but was worried about Arbal shooting them in the back, as he had Cam.

The wind started to pick up, blowing leaves and the smell of the Signal Stones around everyone.

"The twins!" gasped Zeroth.

Steve didn't know who the twins were, but he had a feeling he wasn't going to like them. The boy looked down at Cam. The old Hunter met the boy's gaze and softly spoke, "Run."

"What?" whispered Steve.

"I said," whispered Cam "Run!" he yelled as he rolled with all his remaining strength and stabbed Arbal in the foot with an arrow.

As the injured dove-man screamed in pain, Steve and Eira ran off. Uncle Shameless, still chained up around his arms, did the best he could to follow after them. Zeroth picked himself up and tackled Arbal as the traitor tried to free his staked foot from the ground.

"Arrgh!" yelled Zeroth, his eyes flashing red with rage as he did his best to pummel Arbal with his good arm.

Suddenly, wind gusted around them and a ghostly-white cloud shot through the air towards Zeroth. Saucer-like eyes flashed for a moment in the cloud as Delu (or maybe Uled) solidified long enough to kick Zeroth in the beak before returning to mist once more.

The blow knocked Zeroth off of Arbal, giving the dove enough time to painfully remove the arrow from his foot. The cloud, now joined by its twin, circled around the Hunters before finally solidifying into the raven twins.

The sickly twins stood to their full height and surveyed the scene before them. Uled (or maybe Delu) looked at Zeroth and shook his head.

"We should have known-"

"-You'd turn against us," finished the raven's twin.

"This wasn't planned or anything," interrupted Zeroth as he kept his eyes on Arbal.

"So it would seem," said Delu as he looked over the wound in Cam's back "But it is still-"

"-Treacherous," finished his brother.

Zeroth got up slowly and reached inside his cloak for his sword. He stopped after Arbal pulled out a small crossbow and pointed it at him. The dove gestured for Zeroth to put his hands up. The bird-man sighed and complied.

"How could you?" Zeroth shot back at Arbal even though his eyes were on Cam. The old deer had not moved since stabbing Arbal in the foot, but Zeroth thought he could just barely see him breathing.

Arbal stared into Zeroth's eyes without blinking and did not answer. Zeroth narrowed his eyes at Arbal, "You miserable-" he was cut off by Arbal firing an arrow just inches away from his head.

"Enough," snapped the twins in unison.

"You, dove," ordered Delu "Bring back the hu-mans. We'll-"

"-Handle this one," finished Uled with a sly look at Zeroth.

8

"You can't be serious," pleaded Steve as he tried in vain to loosen Uncle Shameless' chains.

"As serious as a heart attack," countered the boy's uncle "Those two helped us, we should return the favor. It's only common courtesy."

"If I recall correctly, only *one* of them helped us, and he was shot in the back," said Steve.

"But the odd looking one would have helped us after he knew what was going on," explained Eira, "I'm sure of it."

"So let me get this straight," said Steve as he messed with the heavy lock that secured Uncle Shameless' metal bindings, "You want to go back and help two bounty hunters that only moments ago were ready to turn us over to the Hawk-King?"

"Pretty much," answered Uncle Shameless.

"That's the idea," added Eira.

Frustrated with the unyielding lock, Steve let it drop from his hands "Am I the only one that finds that a just a little bit silly?"

"C'mon boy," jabbed Uncle Shameless as he stood with his arms still chained against his torso, "You know what they say – one good turn deserves another."

"They also say, get while the getting's good."

"Pa-shaw," scoffed Uncle Shameless. "Honor, boy. It's all about honor."

"I don't see what getting good grades has to do with-"

"No!" blurted Uncle Shameless. "Not honor roll - honor! Pride! Chivalry! Respect!"

Steve crossed his arms, "Go back there and be target practice for that trigger happy mourning dove? And what about those twins the weird looking one was talking about?"

"Who knows, they could be cute," answered Uncle Shameless with an exaggerated wink.

"Something tells me otherwise," sighed Steve as he stared at the ground. He looked up and saw Uncle Shameless giving him a sad puppy dog look.

"Oh no, don't-"

Uncle Shameless increased the magnitude of the look.

Steve moaned in aggravation, "Fine!"

"Bully!" exclaimed Uncle Shameless. "But first things first – get me outta these chains."

"I don't think so," snapped Zeroth as Arbal started to hobble away.

"You are in no position-" started Uled.

"-To give orders," finished his brother.

Without hesitating, Zeroth quickly reached into his cloak as he jumped towards the nearest twin. Arbal spun around and rapidly fired off a volley of several arrows. His hand was a blur as he moved the lever on his repeating crossbow back and forth.

The arrows safely deflected off the shield Zeroth pulled from his magical pack. Before Zeroth reached the closest twin (he was pretty sure it was Uled) the raven turned into mist, causing the Hunter to pass harmlessly through him.

"Oh yeah…" sighed Zeroth as he rolled to avoid another volley of arrows, having momentarily forgotten about the twins' ability. He reached in his pack for a bola and ignored the pain in his arm as he wound it up.

He let it fly at the second twin, hoping to catch him by surprise. Like the first twin, the raven turned into mist. The bola flew through the eerie cloud, wrapping itself around a very confused tree.

"This might be harder than I thought," confessed Zeroth as more arrows flew in his direction.

"Ow. Ow. Ow. Ow," sang Uncle Shameless as Steve banged the lock with a rock. The boy rested and inspected the hunk of metal, barely finding a scratch.

"I give up," sighed Steve as he tossed the rock to the ground.

"Maybe if we had something to pick it with," suggested Eira as she took off her large pack and began looking through it.

Uncle Shameless collapsed to the ground, landing on his knees.

"I'm thirsty," he said.

"Then drink something," answered Steve as he racked his brain.

"Kinda hard with my arms tied up-"

"That's it!" yelled Steve as inspiration struck him. He reached through the chains and grabbed his uncle's wineskin.

"Hey, you ain't old enough for that!"

"I'm not going to drink it," explained Steve "Open your mouth."

Steve's eyes watered as he got close to his uncle's open mouth, "Your breath could peel paint. When's the last time you brushed your teeth?"

"Give me a break boy, my toothbrush is back in Michigan!"

Steve shook his head as he lifted up the wineskin and aimed it at Uncle Shameless' mouth.

"I don't think that's a good idea," interrupted Eira.

"It'll be fine," said Steve as he gave the wineskin a hard squeeze. Crimson colored wine shot out and struck Uncle Shameless between the eyes.

"Pbbbt!" sputtered Uncle Shameless as Eldercherry wine ran down his face "Watch where you're aiming that!"

Steve ignored him and fired again, this time hitting him in his lazy eye.

"Stop! Stop!" pleaded his Uncle.

"Here, let me," said Eira softly as she took the wineskin away from Steve. Before Uncle Shameless could ask what she was going to do, Eira pushed his head back and shoved the spout into his mouth. "Drink," she said as she began to slowly raise the wineskin. After a few moments she pulled the wineskin away. "How do you feel?"

Uncle Shameless shook his head like a dog coming in from the rain. Excess wine flew everywhere. He looked at Steve and Eira as his head began rolling around.

"I feel like a million deer!"

Steve rolled his eyes, "He's fine."

Eira gave him a confused look, "I don't understand-"

"He means bucks. He feels like a million bucks."

"Oh," replied Eira. She thought for a moment. "I still don't understand."

"It's a human saying. A buck is another word for a dollar," explained Steve.

"Ah, I see," smiled Eira. She thought for another moment. "What is a dollar?"

Zeroth was in a tight spot. Not literally of course, but he might as well have been since it could not make things any worse. Not only did he have a crazed partner-turned traitor shooting arrows at him, he had to try and fight a pair of foes he could not even touch. This would certainly go on his list of Most Challenging Battles, right behind his brawl with Lake Artus.

The speed with which the twins could travel in their mist form caught Zeroth off guard. They easily zipped around him, sporadically materializing to kick him in the back or something equally dirty.

He had to keep moving; otherwise he'd be an easy target for Arbal's devastating large crossbow. The other problem was that he did not want to abandon Cam.

Zeroth's thought process was interrupted by a sharp punch to the back of his head, followed by a ghostly snicker.

"Alright, that's it!" bellowed Zeroth "Stop fighting dirty and face me fair and square!"

The bird-man's challenge was answered by a large rock being dropped on the top of his head.

"Ugah..." slurred Zeroth as he stumbled around in a daze. In the distance, Arbal lined up the stunned Hunter in the sights of his crossbow.

Overhead, Delu and Uled watched Zeroth with their misty eyes. As they swirled around they decided to swoop down to attack Zeroth from both sides at once. Uled aimed for his spot on Zeroth's body and dove quickly. His saucer like eyes flashed for an instant and his body began to fade back into blood and bone.

Uled suddenly felt very odd and missed Zeroth completely as he crashed to the forest floor. Over the years he had grown used to the odd sensation of switching forms but this was a different feeling altogether. It was a feeling he had not felt in a very long time and as he tried to catch his breath he thought of what this feeling was.

Then he remembered. Pain. Uled slowly looked down to see an arrow poking through his unprotected chest. He quickly returned to his mist form, expecting the arrow to simply fall out. As he awkwardly floated skyward, he remembered that his powers did not work that way. Anything on, or *in*, his body changed right along with him.

Uled's loud curse was drowned out only by the very loud splat his solid lifeless body made after it struck the forest floor.

"Cam!" cried Zeroth as he made his way to his mentor, now sitting up and wheezing heavily. His spent long bow lay on the ground next to him. Behind Zeroth, Delu flew to his fallen brother. Arbal fired off more arrows at Zeroth with his small crossbow, only to have them deflected by the bird-man's shield.

Zeroth kneeled behind his shield next to Cam. "How did you hit that raven?"

Cam groaned loudly as he tried to remain sitting up, he spoke in-between heavy breaths.

"Timing…is…everything," explained the wounded deer.

Zeroth risked a glance over at the fallen raven twin and understood what Cam meant. He had timed his shot just right so that it was passing through Uled as he was changing back to his normal form.

"You never fail to amaze me," praised Zeroth.

Cam forced a gruff laugh before breaking in to a loud hacking fit. Zeroth gripped his mentor tightly, "Hang on, I'll get you out of here."

"Oh, don't make me laugh," joked Cam weakly. "Yer wounded an' outnumbered."

Zeroth started to protest but Cam held up a weak hand, "Listen…"

"But-"

"Listen will ya?!" snapped Cam in-between coughs "Just because I was shot don't mean I can't still rough ya up."

Zeroth smiled and held Cam closer to him as more of Arbal's arrows bounced off his shield.

"You aren't going to get all sentimental and charge me with some oddball task because you think you are dying, are you?" sighed Zeroth, "Or tell me some big secret about my past that really isn't all that shock-" Cam slapped Zeroth upside his head, surprising the bird-man.

"Shuddup and listen!"

"Yessir."

"Protect The Boy," wheezed Cam.

"What?"

"Protect…The…Boy," pleaded the bird-man's mentor.

"But why?" asked Zeroth. Cam fell silent, and his body relaxed "Cam? Cam! Why?"

Zeroth closed his eyes and fought back tears until his moment of silent grief was interrupted by Cam slapping him upside the head one more time, "Just do it, ya bum!" yelled the old Hunter with his final breath.

Uncle Shameless charged through the woods. After Steve finally caught up with him and told him he was going the wrong way, Uncle

Shameless quickly turned around and started charging in the other direction.

Zeroth rested Cam's body gently on the ground. Then, blocking all pain from his mind he quickly pulled out his sword and ran at Arbal and Delu. The mourning dove Hunter glanced up from Uled's body in time to see Zeroth swinging his sword for his head. Arbal brought up his heavy crossbow, the sword dug into the thick wood of the weapon.

Arbal twisted his crossbow, forcing the sword from Zeroth's wounded and weakened arm. Undeterred, Zeroth charged Arbal with his shield and knocked the lanky dove over. Too enraged to reach into his magical pack for different weapon, Zeroth resorted to trying to hit Arbal with his old shield.

Delu looked up from his twin's body and pulled out a long, nasty looking dagger from within his Caper Cape. After a sickly cough, his eyes flashed and his body began fading away into mist as he made his way toward Zeroth's unprotected back.

Zeroth swung his shield at Arbal. The dove-man ducked under the wild swing and brought his heavy crossbow up under Zeroth's chin, knocking him off his feet. Arbal stared at Zeroth coldly and without any sign of hesitation aimed his gargantuan crossbow at Zeroth's heart.

Suddenly, a loud bellowing echoed through the trees, followed by an equally loud "Wor-bah!" Arbal looked up from Zeroth to see a spider-web of heavy chains flying right toward him. Unable to move quickly enough, the chains struck Arbal and knocked him over.

A very boastful Uncle Shameless jumped into the clearing and ran to Zeroth. But when he was only a few feet from the Hunter, Uncle Shameless saw two saucer like eyes light up in front of him.

"Who the...?" said a confused Uncle Shameless.

He was even more confused when Delu quickly materialized in front of him, brandishing a dagger.

"Crackers!" yelled Uncle Shameless as he skidded to a stop. Delu slashed at Uncle Shameless with his dagger wildly, though he did not really want to fight the human with extra-ordinary strength.

"Go..." started Delu, forgetting he did not have a twin to finish his sentences anymore.

"Go where?" asked Uncle Shameless.

"Go..." barked the raven once more.

"I don't think so," countered Uncle Shameless as he quickly grabbed a loose chain off the forest floor and began swinging it.

Moments later, Steve approached the edge of the clearing with Eira right behind him.

"Oh, you have to be kidding," sighed Steve as he watched his uncle having what looked like an old time gang fight with a sickly raven in an ugly cape.

Eira limped up next to Steve. She spied Cam's lifeless body and saw Zeroth trying to get to his feet as he shook the cobwebs from his brain. She gasped as she watched Delu slash once more at Uncle Shameless.

"Oh no!" she yelped.

"Now what?" asked Steve as he watched Arbal pull the heavy chains off himself.

"That's one of the raven twins!"

"And they are…?"

"The Hawk-King's spies!"

"Ah," Steve said dryly "Yes. I could see why that would be bad."

"C'mon birdo," taunted Uncle Shameless as he swung his chain at the raven like a veteran street fighter. Delu's milky eyes flashed as he turned to mist. The chain passed harmless through him.

"Hey!" objected Uncle Shameless, almost neglecting to dodge a dagger aimed at his back as Delu materialized behind him.

"What!" exclaimed Steve from his hiding spot, having just witnessed Delu turn into mist and then back into his normal solid state.

"Magic," explained Eira quickly. "Their capes allow them to do that. They are made of the skin a magical creature-"

"So you're telling me that ugly cape lets him turn invisible?"

"No, of course not," answered Eira.

"I knew it-"

"Don't be silly. It just lets him turn into *mist*."

Steve narrowed his eyes at the helpful pelican and started shaking his head.

Delu slashed at Uncle Shameless again, nicking his arm.

"Ow!" yelled the human, *"That's it!"*

Uncle Shameless whipped his chain quickly at Delu, wrapping it securely around the raven's thin arm. He tugged hard on the chain and brought the raven close towards him and fired off a quick punch. His fist never reached the raven's face, however. Delu turned to mist in an instant.

Unfortunately for Delu, Uncle Shameless turned into mist along with him.

Zeroth's senses returned just in time to see Uncle Shameless disappear along with Delu. He snapped back to attention after hearing the telltale sound of Arbal loading a box of dart-like arrows into his small repeating crossbow. Zeroth rolled out of the way in time to avoid being turned into a living bull's-eye.

Zeroth instinctively reached for his sword, only to forget he had lost it earlier. He picked up his shield once more and charged at Arbal. Zeroth reached into his magical pack and tried to think of any other weapons he had stored inside.

That was the trick of the magical pack; he had to think of what he wanted to take out of it. A thought flashed through his mind and he felt his hand grab onto something. Without waiting to see what it was, he attacked Arbal with his new weapon.

From the bushes Steve watched Zeroth and scratched his head in confusion.

"Why is he fighting with a coat rack?" he asked Eira.

"I have no idea," answered the equally confused pelican.

Zeroth cursed his luck. Of all the items in his magical pack, he had to think of the coat rack first. He had been given the ornate, brown wooden coat rack as payment some time ago. If he had known ahead of time that the village of Nary used coat racks as a form of currency, he would have never taken the job.

The odd-looking bird-man swung the coat rack at Arbal, nearly striking the dove's head with the quartet of hand decorated metal hooks that crowned the rack's top. Arbal was aware of the abilities that Zeroth's pack had, but he was still surprised at being attacked with such a random weapon.

Zeroth would have had an easier time attacking with the makeshift weapon if had not been for the four long 'feet' that spread from the bottom of the rack. He finally decided to risk putting away his shield to use both hands with his new weapon. With a quick maneuver, the large dented shield disappeared into his magic pack, and Zeroth gripped the coat rack with both of his clawed hands.

"You're sure that isn't some weird Hunter custom?" Steve asked Eira as they watched Zeroth continue to thrust with the handcrafted decorative coat rack.

"I am fairly certain it is not," answered Eira.

To aide in his fight, Zeroth quickly broke off the four 'feet' of the rack, making it look more like a staff, albeit a staff with four ornamental coat hooks on the top. As Zeroth snapped off the last of the 'feet,' he could almost hear a banker crying in Nary.

Zeroth swung the rack expertly, gaining speed and keeping Arbal guessing as to where he would strike. Zeroth caught Arbal off guard and struck the dove hard on the wrist, forcing him to drop his small crossbow. Arbal countered with a high kick to the enraged Zeroth's head, but the blow was blocked by Zeroth's improvised staff.

The dove surprised his attacker by quickly doing a high back flip through the air. Before reaching the ground again several yards back, the dove pulled out his second small crossbow and fired a pair of shots before landing on the ground in a cloud of dust.

Zeroth spun the coat rack, letting one of the small arrows bury itself in the wood instead of his face. He missed the second, causing the tiny missile to painfully graze his leg.

The injured Hunter winced as he leaned on the coat rack for support, "This just isn't my day."

Uncle Shameless felt very strange. He had experienced many odd feelings and sensations over the course of his life, but never anything like this. The only thing he had experienced before that came close to this feeling was the time he had tired to make salad dressing.

Not being much of a cook, or even a person that reads directions carefully, he had mistakenly used five entire heads of garlic to make one small bottle of dressing.

Despite what the doctors told him, the hallucinations weren't all that bad. He had really enjoyed playing charades with Socrates and Richard Nixon.

But this feeling was in a league of its own.

It had all started after he wrapped his chain about Delu and tried to punch the raven. Before his fist even hit the raven, the bird-man started disappearing. Then Uncle Shameless also started disappearing.

Now Uncle Shameless knew what it felt like to change from a solid to a gas, and he was pretty sure he did not want to ever feel this way again. But now he was flying through the air, and through the trees and anything else.

Delu climbed high into the air and dove into a fierce spin, trying to think of a way to shake Uncle Shameless loose. He chastised himself for not realizing that the human was connected to him when he began to change forms. Their misty bodies flowed around each other, causing great disgust to the bird-man.

The giant cloud of mist shot high into the air, dozens of feet over the tree tops. Delu's eyes flashed as he and Uncle Shameless turned back to their normal forms. The pair floated in the air for several seconds before gravity found its hold on them and dragged them towards the ground once more.

Uncle Shameless began screaming and held tightly onto the chain. Delu looked over at his stowaway, "Let..." started Delu, forgetting again that his twin was not around to supply the rest of his sentences.

"Let? Let what?" yelled Uncle Shameless as air screamed all around him. Delu bellowed and slashed at Uncle Shameless with his knife, but missed. Uncle Shameless tugged on the chain with extraordinary strength, causing Delu to slam into his body. The force of the blow knocked the knife from the raven spy's hand.

The pair began plummeting to the ground below. Uncle Shameless wondered why the raven-man didn't turn them back into mist. He looked down to see Delu's ghostly eyes shut, and his body limp. Slamming into Uncle Shameless had knocked out the weak bird-man.

As the ground began catching up with them, and not knowing how Delu turned them into mist, Uncle Shameless decided he had better do something fast. He carefully slapped the raven across the face a few times and shook him.

"Wake up! C'mon! I don't wanna be buried in a pizza box!"

Delu started to come around, his milky eyes focused on Uncle Shameless. Then his clawed hands focused on Uncle Shameless' neck.

"Ack!" choked Uncle Shameless "St-Stop it! Look!"

Delu paused his strangling long enough to realize they were moments from being considerably flatter. With a disgruntled huff, Delu turned them back into to mist and flew towards an unsuspecting Zeroth.

The raven turned himself and Uncle Shameless back into their solid forms with a thought and the entangled pair slammed into Zeroth, creating a huge pile up of bird and man.

"Get off!" scolded Zeroth as he tried to move his pinned down arms.

"Ughh..." was his only response from both Uncle Shameless and Delu. Forgetting about Arbal and his crossbow, Steve ran out of his hiding place to help his Uncle. Eira called after him as she limped after the boy.

Arbal stared at the boy with his cold black eyes and skillfully dropped his small repeating crossbow and readied his large crossbow in one quick motion. The dove Hunter aimed at Steve as a clawed finger lashed around the trigger of the foul weapon.

Zeroth struggled under the weight of Uncle Shameless and Delu. Normally he would not have a problem lifting the pair off him, but they were lying on top of his coat rack, which pinned down his arms and made it almost impossible to move.

His sharp eyes caught Steve running over to him and Zeroth quickly looked over to see his former partner readying his devastating crossbow.

Remembering Cam's final wish, Zeroth summoned all the strength he had left and tried to free himself. He managed to painfully free one arm, but realized he had only seconds to act. Without haste, he reached into his magical pack, thought of an item and skillfully hurled it at Arbal.

Steve heard Eira calling after him, but he ignored the pelican. He wondered what she wanted. He was halfway to Uncle Shameless when he realized he had a pretty good idea what Eira had been yelling about.

The mourning dove Hunter looked up at him with eyes like two black marbles and gave him a chilly stare. Time slowed to a crawl. Heart beats seemed to last minutes. Steve watched as the dove dropped his small crossbow from his hand.

An eternity passed before the weapon hit the forest floor, and by then the dove had unshouldered his massive crossbow and was aiming it at Steve.

Everything around Steve froze as the dove flicked a switch and a simple crosshair target popped up from the body of the large instrument of destruction.

Steve's breath stopped in his lungs and his eyes locked as the dove squeezed the trigger of the crossbow.

As slow as the past few moments had passed, the next few moments passed with swift vengeance, as if making up for lost time.

Just as the giant spring in the crossbow shook before releasing, the bag of Signal Stones exploded against the dove's hard beak, blasting the Hunter with a cyclone of noxious smoke, causing Arbal to wretch and twist. His crossbow twisted with him right as the large bolt was let loose by the massive weapon.

The bolt screamed through the air and missed Steve, finally burying itself deep within a nearby tree. Once Steve's breath returned he ran over to Uncle Shameless, Zeroth and Delu. The boy pushed Uncle Shameless and his raven adversary off of Zeroth, finally freeing the bird-man.

"Uh, thank-," exhaled Steve, trying not to breath in the putrid fumes of the Signal Stones.

"You can thank me later, *run*," barked Zeroth as he picked up Uncle Shameless and slung him over a shoulder.

As Steve and Zeroth turned to get away, Arbal stumbled blindly within his own personal tornado of ugly smoke and ugly smells.

The pair ran from the clearing and zipped past Eira, who had finally caught up with them.

"We're leaving," snapped Zeroth as he headed for the deep woods, still carrying Uncle Shameless.

"What he said," added Steve as he chased after the helpful Hunter.

Eira stopped to protest, but after getting a whiff of the giant cloud of Signal Stone smoke, she quickly changed her mind and trotted after the them.

9

Zeroth had taken many strange jobs over the years, but this one would certainly land near the top of the list. It might even beat out the time he had to be a bodyguard for the Prince of the Potato People of Tubor, and that was saying a lot.

The Hunter sighed and scanned the horizon from his lookout spot at the top of a tree. The forest had been silent for a long while now, and the cloud of Signal smoke back in the clearing had all but disappeared. After running away from Arbal and Delu, Eira had healed everyone's wounds before Zeroth decided that they should hide until it was safe to travel again.

Zeroth stretched and looked for any signs of danger. Not seeing any, he decided it was safe to return to the forest floor.

"Alright, we've hid long enough," said Zeroth as he flapped open his wings and jumped from the tree top. He caught the wind with his wings and glided back to the clearing where he had fought Arbal and the raven twins.

Normally he would not risk going back to where he had run away from, but he wanted to bury Cam's body and to find his sword. After landing, Zeroth cracked his knuckles and reached into his magical pack.

Effortlessly, he pulled Steve out of the small leather pack and dropped the boy on the ground.

"Okay. That was really weird," confessed the boy, thinking that he never wanted to be hidden away in a magical pack again. He now knew what a toy in one of those mechanical crane games felt like.

Without answering, Zeroth reach into the pack again, this time pulling out Eira.

"I had no idea you were so organized," complimented the pelican, referring to the neat interior of the pack.

"When you have a pack that holds as much as a room, you have to be," explained Zeroth. He reached into his cloak and pulled out a small book and showed it to Eira. The book was divided into several sections, each with a different category followed by a listing of items.

"I have to keep an inventory of everything I have. Otherwise I forget what's in there." He snapped the book shut and put it away before reaching into the pack for Uncle Shameless. Zeroth pulled the man out of the pack by his hair, Uncle Shameless seemed rather upset.

But he was not upset because he was being pulled out by his hair. As he was being pulled out of the pack, Zeroth noticed he was holding several playing cards and yelling.

"That's total bunk! There's no such thing as a Full Flush!"

Confused, Zeroth dropped Uncle Shameless to the ground.

"What are you yelling about?"

"He cheats!" yelled Uncle Shameless, throwing his playing cards to the ground in disgust.

"Who cheats?"

"Stu!"

"Who is Stu?" asked Zeroth.

"The woodchuck!"

Zeroth's eyes narrowed.

"…Woodchuck?" he finally said before reaching into his pack, his arm up to his elbow disappearing into the opening. This time he pulled out a raggedy looking squatty woodchuck, dressed in worn out clothing and an equally worn out top hat. He too was holding several playing cards, and was smoking a pipe.

Stu was small, about half the size of Steve, but looked very old and well traveled. He looked like the woodchuck version of a hobo. Zeroth held the little furry hobo by the back of his shirt as he dangled in front of the angered Hunter.

"Hullo," said Stu, taking a second to tip his tattered hat to the bird-man.

"What were you doing in my pack?" demanded Zeroth.

"Well, it's a funny story-" began Stu, but he did not get to finish it. Enraged by the stowaway, Zeroth wound up his arm and hurled Stu far into the forest. As Stu soared through the branches and trees he took the time to call Zeroth several unpleasant names.

"That explains why all of my things have smelled like pipe smoke lately," sighed Zeroth.

"What a mean thing to do," scolded Eira.

"I'll say," started Zeroth "I hate free loaders."

"I was referring to *you*."

"He should have known better after reading the label," replied Zeroth as he lifted up the lid of his pack and pointed to a label. His three companions all took a turn reading it.

"'Irregular'?" asked Steve "I don't get-"

"The other one," interrupted Zeroth. The Hunter pointed to a hand stitched label that said 'No Trespassin'.'

"So, what is your name anyway?" Steve asked finally.

"Zeroth," answered the Hunter as he searched the clearing for signs of Arbal and Delu. He realized at that moment however that Delu could be in his mist form and he would not know it.

"That's a funny name," replied the boy.

"And Steve isn't?" countered Zeroth, "Six I could have understood, but what is a Steve?"

The boy tried to answer the question but decided to just keep his mouth shut as Uncle Shameless and Eira introduced themselves to the Hunter. Steve joined Eira and Uncle Shameless as they watched their new protector search the clearing.

"Uh-oh," said Zeroth moments later.

Steve figured this was the last thing he wanted to hear from an elite mercenary that had been charged with keeping him alive.

"What do you mean, 'uh-oh'?"

"It is a casual expression, usually meaning something is wrong-"

"I know the definition!" yelled Steve "I meant, what's wrong?"

Zeroth spun around and motioned to the floor of the clearing, "Do you notice anything missing?" he asked urgently.

Steve sighed and was about to say 'wasn't that the reason we came back here?', when he glanced at Uled's body and noticed that his ugly magic cape was gone.

"Uh-oh."

"Glad we agree," replied Zeroth as he searched the area for his lost sword.

"So what?" said Uncle Shameless as he stumbled around the clearing "Someone swiped his cape, big deal."

"That cape is what let him and his brother turn into mist," explained Eira.

"And Arbal is gone too," finished Zeroth as he pointed to the dove's foot prints leading up to Uled's body.

Uncle Shameless looked over at the dove footprints leading to the raven and then looked at Uled. He thought for a moment, took a sip of wine and looked at Uled once more and then glanced at the Arbal's footprints, realizing that there were not any footprints leading *away* from the raven's body.

"So that means he-"

"Yes," finished Zeroth.

"And now he can-"

"Yes."

"Uh-oh."

Uncle Shameless helped Zeroth bury Cam, thankfully Zeroth had a pair of shovels in his pack. Luckily for the Hunter (but unluckily at the time of the job) the mining town of Quid used shovels as currency. Zeroth carved Cam's name into the shaft of his coat rack, which he had found nearby, and used it as an improvised headstone.

Zeroth then took his mentor's trademark long bow and hung it on the ornate hooks at the top of the coat rack. Steve thought he saw the battle hardened warrior's eyes full of tears but Zeroth quickly pulled up the hood of his cloak, shrouding his face in darkness. The boy was sure he saw the Hunter's eyes flash red briefly from the depths of his hood.

The bird-man searched the clearing for his trusty sword, but could not find it. Steve and the others helped, but they could not locate the weapon either. Zeroth sighed and took out his pack's inventory book and flipped to the section labeled "Weapons – S thru T."

He quickly snapped the little book shut in a loud huff.

"What's wrong?" asked Eira.

"I'm out of swords," sighed Zeroth, embarrassed.

"You don't have any more in that crazy pack of yours?" asked Uncle Shameless.

Zeroth explained that he had recently traded the last of his spare swords at an outpost for some rare herbs and spices.

"Why'd you do that?" asked Uncle Shameless.

"Well you can't really make ve'anti without ayke leaves now can you?" countered Zeroth.

"Uh..." thought Uncle Shameless, having no idea what either ve'anti or ayke leaves were "Uh...well, no...I s'pose not."

"You like to cook?" asked Eira.

Zeroth nodded, "When you wander for a living, you don't really have a choice."

"I know the feeling," added Uncle Shameless.

"Oh please," sighed Steve, "Your idea of cooking is canned soup and pancakes."

"Hey, I made fish the night before our canoe trip," countered Uncle Shameless.

"Fish? I thought that was meat loaf."

"Where are you headed?" asked Zeroth after saying goodbye to Cam one last time.

"Uth," answered Eira.

"Ah, yes. The swamp. We'll need to get moving soon. But first, you two need some armor," said the Hunter, as he motioned to Uncle Shameless and Steve to come closer.

"That wine may give you super-strength, but it doesn't really protect you at all," said Zeroth. The bird-man looked through his pack inventory and studied the section labeled "Armor." Finding what he was looking for this time, Zeroth replaced the book and reached into his pack.

He effortlessly pulled out a large metal breast plate and handed it to Uncle Shameless. Eira helped him put it on over his ripped flannel shirt and tattered blue jeans as Zeroth pulled out armored elbow pads, fore arm guards and boots.

"Don't worry, I didn't forget about you," Zeroth said to Steve as he handed the boy a chain mail vest. Eira helped Steve lift the heavy vest over his head.

"It's too big!" complained Steve. The large vest reached past his knees and looked more like a dress than a piece of armor.

"It's magical," explained Zeroth "So is your uncle's. All you have to do is imagine it fitting you correctly, and it will shrink."

"But-but," whined Steve.

Zeroth shook his head, "Just try. Haven't you used your imagination before?"

Steve tried to think of a time he had to imagine anything like this, but he could not.

"No problems over here!" yelled Uncle Shameless. Everyone looked over at Uncle Shameless, and saw his armor fitting him perfectly.

"Very good," applauded Zeroth.

"Thank you," Uncle Shameless said as he treated himself to a sip of wine. Zeroth turned back to Steve, "Now, you try."

Steve closed his eyes and tried to picture himself in his mind's eye. He could not; all he saw were the inside of his eyelids. He tried again and again, but had no luck.

Zeroth patted him on the head, perhaps a little too hard, but said "Don't worry kid, you'll figure it out." Steve wasn't so sure.

There was a loud THUNK, causing everyone to turn around. Uncle Shameless was lying on the ground. One of his elbow protectors had grown to the size of large rock, which made it very difficult to keep his balance.

"Uh, a little help?" he cried.

"But anyway, what are you going to use for a weapon? A shoe tree?" asked Steve.

"That's not funny," snapped Zeroth.

"I wasn't joking," said Steve, pointing to Zeroth's coat rack.

"Oh. Right," replied Zeroth "Don't worry, the swamp will provide us with weapons."

Steve did not know what Zeroth was talking about, but he had a feeling it would be something gross. He figured anything that lived in a swamp *had* to be.

The companions headed out of the clearing and made their way to the swamp in the center of the Forbidden Forest. Steve tried not to trip on the long chain mail vest that nearly reached his feet.

The boy would try to imagine the armor fitting him as Zeroth had instructed, but he could not conjure up the mental image. He was not accustomed to using make-believe.

Steve was getting tired, he was not used to so much walking.

"Can't we rent horses somewhere? I'm tired of all this walking," he said. Eira and Zeroth looked at each other, then at Steve.

"What is a horse?" they asked.

"A horse is well...a *horse*," explained the boy as he tried to think about the best way to describe a horse.

"It's a large animal that you can ride, it has four legs," described Steve. Eira and Zeroth shook their heads, Steve continued, "They have big swishy tales, and long faces? You ride on their backs?"

The bird-people shook their heads once more.

"You don't have horses here?" asked Steve, amazed by the lack of equines in Eyri.

"That reminds me of a joke!" bellowed Uncle Shameless proudly.

"No, please," begged Steve.

Uncle Shameless ignored his nephew, "So, this horse got elected to Congress right? But he wasn't very popular with the people..." Uncle Shameless waited for someone to ask him 'why'.

After several moments of silence, he looked at Eira. "Ask me why."

"Oh," replied Eira with a long smile "Why?"

"Because he always voted 'neigh'! Ha!" Uncle Shameless rolled on the ground with laughter. Steve covered his face in embarrassment.

"I do not understand," confessed Eira.

"What is a Congress? A place for horses?" asked Zeroth, also confused by the horribly bad joke.

"Well, parts of horses anyway," answered Uncle Shameless with a wink.

As they came closer to the outskirts of the swamp, the ground began getting squishy and wet. Steve's black canvas high-tops quickly became soaked in the muddy ground.

"Gross!" the boy yelled.

Steve decided to try and take his mind off his less than pleasant surroundings, "So, how does that pack of yours work anyway?" he asked Zeroth.

The bird-man shrugged as he led the way towards Uth, the Last Human Village.

"It works because I *believe* it works, not unlike your armor," answered Zeroth, his yellow scarf flapping in the air as he moved. Steve wondered what exactly Zeroth meant by that remark.

They marched on through the thick underbrush until they came to a stagnant marshland that was littered with small pools of murky water and tall grasses.

"Ick!" cried Steve as he skipped along the soggy ground, trying to avoid the dark pools of water.

"What kind of weapon are we going to find in a swamp? Some sort of blood sucking, slimy creature?" asked Steve as he noticed creatures swimming in the small dark pools near him.

Zeroth looked over his shoulder to the boy again, "Swordfish."

Steve stopped in his tracks, "Swordfish? You have to be joking," said Steve as he tried to think about using a live fish for a weapon. He didn't like the idea of having to hit someone with a big, smelly fish, and couldn't see how it would be that helpful.

Zeroth kneeled next to one of the larger pools of murky water.

"Come 'ere," he said to Steve. Zeroth pointed a clawed finger at one of the dark shapes darting around in the water.

"That's a swordfish, they are pretty common around all parts of Eyri."

"...So what do you do with it? Throw it at bad guys and hope they are allergic to fish?"

"You'll see. But first we have to catch some," explained the Hunter.

"If they are so common, how come none o' those hawks an' swans warriors were usin' 'em?" asked Uncle Shameless.

"They're hard to catch," explained Zeroth as he walked towards Eira. "You, pelican, catch us some."

"My name is Eira, and you *could* ask nicely," she said, a little irritated.

Zeroth sighed, "Fine...Eira, catch us some fish."

"That wasn't what I meant," she said firmly.

Zeroth sighed again, only louder, "Eira, would you *please* catch us some fish?"

Without saying anything, Eira slid off her bulging backpack, headed towards the pool and jumped in. Steve watched as she chased a school of the squatty, cylindrical swordfish around in the shadowy water.

Suddenly, Eira exploded out of the pool in a shower of murky water. She landed next to her companions and shook the excess water off herself. She then hunched over slightly and opened her beak, now filled to the brim with water. Steve peered into Eira's open beak and watched the odd looking fish dart around as best they could in their organic prison.

The swordfishes' black-blue bodies were around six inches long and came to an end with a fan-like triangular tail. Their eyes were large disks on either side of the head and were parallel with their mouths. They looked nothing like the cardboard cutout swordfish Steve had seen at the zoo back home.

Zeroth nodded to Eira's mouth, "G'head, grab one," he said with a slight chuckle.

Steve wondered what the Hunter thought was so funny and started to reach inside Eira's engorged beak. He stopped suddenly,

"How does it live outside of water?" he asked, not wanting to hurt the odd creature.

"Don't worry 'bout it," explained Zeroth "Once they are out of water they go into a sleep-like state. They stay that way until they get into water again and then off they go."

"So they don't get hurt out of water?" asked the boy. Zeroth shook his head.

Steve decided that sounded all right to him and he reached into Eira's beak and tried to grab one of the swordfish. He felt one of their scaly bodies brush against his hand and quickly zip away.

"This is gross," whined Steve. If Eira could have spoken, she would have said 'At least no one is reaching inside *your* mouth.'

Steve almost caught one of the crafty fish, but once again it slipped through his fingers.

"They're too fast!" he complained. He now had a pretty good idea about what Zeroth had been laughing at.

"Try wigglin' your fingers," suggested Uncle Shameless with a wink to Zeroth.

"Why can't she just dump them onto the ground?" asked the boy logically.

"Just keep wigglin' your fingers," ordered Zeroth.

Steve grumbled under his breath and did as he was told.

"I don't see how 'wigglin'' my fingers is going to –OUCH!" he screamed as a pair of swordfish clamped onto his hand. Steve jerked his hand out of Eira's mouth, bringing the two swordfish with it. Just as Zeroth said, once out of the water, the swordfish froze and stopped moving. Steve easily pulled the frozen creatures off his fingers.

Uncle Shameless and Zeroth started laughing, much to the annoyance of the young boy. Eira walked over to the pool and released the rest of the swordfish from her beak.

"You knew they would bite my fingers if I started wigglin' them, didn't you?" asked Steve.

"'Course. Fish think wigglin' fingers are worms," explained Uncle Shameless.

"Especially around here, since the worms *look* like fingers," added Zeroth with a final laugh.

"So, now what?" asked the boy after Zeroth grabbed one of the swordfish, half-expecting the creature to shoot lighting from its mouth.

"This," snapped Zeroth, squeezing the swordfish's midsection. The creature's square shaped mouth split open with a loud BLEAH! releasing a five-foot long, pointed blade.

"That's its tongue?!" exclaimed the boy.

"Man, talk about being sharp tongued," joked Uncle Shameless.

As the Hunter held the swordfish, Steve realized now that with its mouth open the fish's body resembled the hilt of a sword, forming the familiar T shape. Its stiff, deadly tongue looked exactly like the blade of a sword, and shined like steel.

"So let me get this straight," began Steve as his sense of logic started up once more "These tiny fish all have a really long sword-like tongues inside them?"

Zeroth nodded, swinging the swordfish around to get accustomed to its weight.

"But...*how?*" asked Steve as he studied the swordfish's improbable tongue.

"Maybe it's like one of them party favors," suggested Uncle Shameless "Y'know the kind that are all rolled up until you blow into 'em?"

Steve flicked a finger against the shining blade and sure enough it felt like real steel. He did not see how that would be possible, considering that the tongue was more than three times the size of the swordfish's body.

"What happens when you are done with it?" asked Steve.

Without saying anything, Zeroth quickly squeezed the swordfish's cylindrical body once more. There was a loud SLURP! as the swordfish's tongue was sucked back into its small body. Its mouth slammed shut, and its body no longer formed a T.

"...Okay," said Steve finally "But how sharp is it?"

Zeroth ran towards a low hanging tree branch and squeezed his swordfish. The creature's tongue shot out with its signature BLEAH! and the Hunter slashed at the snarled tree branch.

"Big deal, nothing happened," said Steve "The branch wasn't cut."

Zeroth reached over and lightly tapped the branch. There was a low groan that quickly grow to a very loud groan as the branch fell to the ground, cleanly cut in two.

"I'd say that's pretty sharp," said Uncle Shameless, impressed.

10

Steve held one of the unmoving swordfish in his hand.
It was lighter than he expected, and its body had a metal like feel to it. He could not believe he was standing in a swamp, wearing an oversized chain mail vest and holding this bizarre fish.

The boy tried again to imagine his chain mail vest shrinking to fit him as Zeroth had instructed.

He had never had to use his imagination in school, and was unaccustomed to imagining things. He closed his eyes and thought hard, trying to visualize himself in the vest but all he could think about was a physics lesson from last fall.

Steve remembered the lesson plain as day, it was on thermal expansion. The class learned that when an object is exposed to heat, it expands and likewise when it is exposed to cold the object will contract.

The teacher, Mr. Antater, demonstrated this by showing the class an ice cube. The ice cube was frozen and was contracted into its current shape. He then exposed the ice cube to heat and it started melting and expanding.

Steve wondered if he exposed the chain mail to extreme cold if it would contract and fit him better. He started thinking about ice fishing with his dad on Lake St. Clair near Beacon Pines, and how extremely cold it had been.

He thought of himself wearing the chain mail in that situation, and how the cold might have made it shrink.

"Over here," called Zeroth, who was standing several yards away, his swordfish at the ready.

Steve's thoughts disappeared as he walked over to his new companion. Zeroth was going to teach Steve how to use his new weapon, but the boy was not really looking forward to it. He never had much success with any kind of physical activity.

Steve thought that he must be finally getting used to walking in the baggy chain mail, since he was having an easier time walking with the oversized armor.

What he failed to realize was that his armor had shrunk slightly.

"What do you mean don't know how to hold a sword?" asked a surprised Zeroth moments later.

Steve shook his head, "I'm from the suburbs. The only thing I know how to hold is a remote control."

Behind the boy Uncle Shameless nodded, he remembered the dreadful afternoon he had asked Steve to help him chop wood. Uncle Shameless went to go check on his nephew later in the day and found that he had not chopped a single piece, but had managed to break one in half.

Steve had been hitting the wood with the wrong side of the axe blade.

Zeroth stood next to Steve and showed the boy what to do.

"Hold it in your hand like this. No, point the mouth away from you, otherwise you'll make it really easy for your opponent to defeat you. Now squeeze the middle."

Steve squeezed the midsection of the hilt-shaped fish tenderly. It was an odd feeling, like squeezing a canvas bag filled with loose change. His swordfish opened its jaws just slightly and only stuck out its tongue a couple of inches.

Zeroth shook his head and reached over and squeezed Steve's hand hard, the swordfish's deadly tongue shot out with a loud BLEAH!

"You won't hurt it, so squeeze it like you mean it," instructed Zeroth. Steve squeezed the swordfish again and retracted its steel tongue with a loud SLURP.

"Excellent," applauded Zeroth dryly. "Now its time learn to fight. Ready?"

"Wait!" begged Steve, fumbling with his swordfish.

"Begin!" yelled Zeroth as he and Steve squeezed their swordfish at the same time in a chorus of BLEAHs.

Steve frantically swung his swordfish at Zeroth, who dodged the wild blows easily since they came nowhere near him or anything else for that matter. Zeroth countered with a quick strike to Steve's swordfish, knocking it to the ground. The impact caused the swordfish to suck its tongue back in.

Zeroth walked up to Steve and placed a clawed hand on the discouraged boy's shoulder.

"Part of being a good swordsman is believing in yourself, remember that," he whispered to Steve.

Zeroth looked over at Eira and Uncle Shameless,

"You two had better build a fire. We're going to be here for awhile."

"Good idea!" bellowed Uncle Shameless, "Now, where's your gas can?"

Much later, Uncle Shameless and Eira sat near the fire, still watching Zeroth try to teach Steve to sword fight. Over the sound of Steve either having his swordfish knocked out of his hand or being knocked down himself, Uncle Shameless chatted with the kindly pelican healer.

"Alright Eira, I have to know. Why do some of you bird people have wings on your backs, like the Hawken do, and some don't?"

Eira shrugged, "I do not know. Why are some humans left-handed?"

Uncle Shameless thought hard over the sound of the swordfish striking each other and could not answer Eira's counter question.

He shrugged, "Because they just are, I s'pose."

Eira nodded "The same goes for us. But in some cases the lack of wings is intentional. Like the Swantan."

Uncle Shameless stopped in mid-sip,

"What do you mean? Do they cut theirs off?"

Eira laughed, "No no, they have bred their wings out of themselves over the centuries. The Swantans always preferred ground combat, and lived for fighting. They found that their wings got in the way."

"That's crazy."

Eira shrugged, "They come from the city of Swanta, and their main goal is generating perfect soldiers and having the best warriors."

"Yeah, well they certainly don't have the best thinkers," added Uncle Shameless.

Eira laughed again and nodded.

Zeroth's yelling at Steve quickly caught their attention. The Hunter kept yelling "again!" over and over to his reluctant student each time ending with Steve or his swordfish being knocked to the soggy ground.

Uncle Shameless got up to go watch Steve practice but changed his mind after his nephew's weapon was knocked from his grip and nearly hit him.

Eventually Zeroth yelled at Steve to stop and retracted his swordfish's blade-tongue as he approached Uncle Shameless and Eira.

"How is he doing?" asked the pelican with a hint of motherly concern.

"Well," Zeroth searched for the polite thing to say. Not being able to think of one, he went with his first reaction, "He isn't...he isn't *good*," sighed Zeroth as he shook his head and tried not to think of the countless lessons he was going to have to give the boy.

Zeroth turned back and yelled at Steve, "C'mon then! You best get some rest, you'll need to have your wits about you come tomorrow!"

Steve slowly and sorely made his way towards the others. He was pretty sure he had used several dozen muscles he hadn't been aware he had until learning to swordfight, and all of them were rebelling against him.

Steve sat next to Eira and started dozing off. He fell towards her and she set his head on her lap.

"Do you have any children...er...hatchlings?" asked Uncle Shameless.

"I did, a long time ago," she whispered in a somber tone.

"Oh, an empty nester eh!" joked Uncle Shameless. The humor was lost on Eira who continued to watch over Steve as he slept.

The group woke early the next morning to Uncle Shameless bellowing at the top of his lungs and stumbling around while having philosophical debates with shrubs or rocks. Occasionally he would imagine his armor being a different size and cause a big ruckus until he changed it back to its normal size again.

Five minutes later he would repeat the entire process.

Eventually they were on their way to Uth, the Last Human Village. As they moved closer to the village, the terrain became progressively more soggy. No longer was the ground merely a little mushy, now it was turning to one giant mud pit.

Scraggily shrubs and bushes replaced the dense trees of the Forbidden Forest. The buzzing of insects and the croaking of frogs filled the air with their deafening symphony.

This part of the quest reminded Steve of a time his dad had taken him fishing to a small lake that was nothing more than a swamp. They stood on soggy, insect covered ground for hours attempting to fish. They only thing they caught was a nasty rash.

The swamp in the Forbidden Forest was not at all different from the swamp he had visited in Michigan, though in the swamp back home he knew that the animals weren't going to talk to him. Steve was reluctant to swat at the insects buzzing around his face out of fear he might get yelled at by a swarm of vengeful relatives.

A thick fog covered the swamp, which limited their vision and made their traveling slow and difficult.

"Ick!" complained Steve after stepping in something that looked like green oatmeal "Zeroth can't you find us a better path?"

"Not in this fog."

"I thought you had hawk-sight?" asked the boy, referring to the Hunter's hawk vision.

"Yeah, and I can see a lot more fog than you can," snapped Zeroth. "Just keep quiet and stay close."

Steve grumbled under his breath and grabbed onto Uncle Shameless' belt so he wouldn't get lost. He soon realized this was a bad choice, given Uncle Shameless' frequent stumbling, as he found himself being led over and through every disgusting thing in the swamp.

"Ugh!" yelled Steve as something wet and spiny crawled over his canvas sneakers.

"Shh!" shushed Zeroth "We're coming up to the village."

"Oh, how can you tell?" asked Steve skeptically.

Zeroth pointed to a sign up ahead that read, "Uth, the Last Human Village."

"Well…that's convenient," mumbled Steve as the fog began to clear, revealing the outskirts of the village.

"I don't even know what I'm s'pose to do here," said Steve. Istrio had not given him instructions on what to do once he arrived in Uth, the Last Human Village.

"We'll figure it out," replied Uncle Shameless as he patted the boy on the head.

"Yes, just keep quiet," ordered Zeroth as he raised his hood.

"Why are you covering your face?" asked Steve.

"The humans here don't exactly put out a warm welcome for Hawken."

"But you are not a Hawken," said Eira "You're…you're…well, you're *you*."

"I look close enough to one to cause a problem. Not to mention there are probably a few humans in this village that aren't too friendly towards Hunters either," finished Zeroth as he tucked away his Hunter's medallion.

Zeroth turned to Eira, "You said you were coming to the village before meeting these two, can you think of any reason why Steve was told to come here?"

Eira thought hard for a moment until a revelation came to her.

"I think I know why," she said finally. "There is supposed to be a well known oracle in this village."

"That has to be it," finished Zeroth, already thinking of a plan for getting into the village.

"An oracle? Let me guess, some old crazy hermit with a bizarre personality trait?" Steve said sarcastically.

Eira, not understanding sarcasm, had a surprised look come over her face,

"Oh, you've met?" she asked seriously.

Steve shook his head, "Never mind," he sighed. He had a feeling he was going to be in for another long, boring story involving people and places with multiple bizarre names.

The intrepid companions continued onward as Zeroth described their cover story.

"Eira you were coming here anyway, so just act normally," he explained "And say that we are your body guards."

The pelican nodded.

"I don't think they'll believe I'm a body guard," said Steve.

"No foolin'," replied Uncle Shameless.

"Yes, the humans here aren't *that* foolish," answered Zeroth knowingly. "You just say you are my apprentice, and Shameless..." he turned to the boy's uncle, who was swaying back and forth as he tried to keep his balance, "Can you control yourself for few minutes?"

"What do I look like, a moron? I can blend, don't worry," Uncle Shameless answered nonchalantly as he hiked up his pants and ran a hand through his messy hair.

Zeroth turned back to face Steve, "Good I'm glad I can count on you Shameless, now it's important that –"

"Uh!" cried Uncle Shameless.

Everyone turned around to see one of Uncle Shameless' armored boots, now five times larger than its normal size, sinking into the mud.

"A little help?" he pleaded as he sunk further.

The companions made their way through the parted fog and Steve could see water ahead. Beyond that, he could just make out an island in the middle of the swamp. He saw the tops of shacks and other buildings on the island.

When the group came to the water's edge, they saw a rickety wooden bridge leading out to the island. A lone guard stood by the bridge. He held a large pitchfork and leaned against a sign that said 'Troll Bridge.'

"'Troll Bridge'?" asked Steve aloud. Zeroth hushed him as they approached the guard, who looked up at the group.

"Greetings travelers. If you want to get to Uth you have to pay to cross the Troll Bridge," explained the robust man with limbs like tree trunks.

Steve thought for a moment, "Don't you mean toll bridge?"

The guard looked at the boy, "Oh no, Troll. This swamp water is filled with Swamp Trolls. Only way to get to Uth without getting hurt by the Swamp Trolls is by using this bridge," he explained proudly "And that'll cost you."

"What is a Swamp Troll anyway?" Steve asked the guard.

"You don't' know?"

Steve shook his head, "I don't get out much."

"Y'see young man, they are these wicked little creatures that live in the water and – "

"Don't listen ta him!" called a voice not too far from the bridge. The group turned and looked to see another man and, surprisingly, another bridge – several yards away.

"You don't want to use his bridge! It's not reliable!" bellowed the voice.

"Who are you?" called Zeroth.

"My name is Enry, come over and use my bridge. I'll give ya a discount!" bellowed Enry from his own bridge.

The guard in front of Steve and his friends grew angry and bellowed back at Enry, "Back off Enry, these are my customers!"

Enry yelled back, "You're not fooling anyone Yerlist! Everyone knows your bridge is made of lousy lumber!"

The group looked at Yerlist's wooden bridge and sure enough his looked very rickety and hastily put together.

"Come down and use my stone bridge, it costs a little extra but its safe and roomy!" bellowed Enry.

"At least he didn't hire folks from outside the village to build his bridge!" cried a third man on the other side of Yerlist's bridge. This man also had his own bridge.

"I hire all my workers from the village and only use the best supplies!"

"Oh, hush up Lime!" Yerlist bellowed to the third man.

"Three bridges and three different men selling passage over them? How ridiculous," said Steve.

"Yeah, especially since they all get you to the same place," added Uncle Shameless.

Steve nodded; sure enough all three of the bridges went to the exact same spot on the island.

After listening to the three men advertise back and forth about which bridge they should take and why, the group grew tired of all the nonsense.

Also, they did not have any money, which made their choice a little easier. Steve walked to the edge of the murky lake and looked into the water. He did not see any Swamp Trolls, but then he realized he did not really know what one looked like.

"This is stupid," he said aloud "Swamp Trolls. There's no such thing."

Uncle Shameless nodded, "I think yer right boy! This is all just a scam! A con! *A FIDDLE!*" and with that, Uncle Shameless charged towards the water.

Zeroth looked away from Yerlist, who was trying to set the bird-man up with a line of credit and yelled "What is he doing?!" as Uncle Shameless jumped into the lake and began swimming rapidly.

"...Am I the only one who is wondering how he can swim with all that armor on?" Steve asked aloud.

"Hush," scolded Eira.

Uncle Shameless continued to swim far out into the lake, when suddenly he saw a large shape heading towards him from the east side of the island. It's craggy, putrid face was adorned by what looked like a gnarled mess of dead lake weeds.

"S-s-ss-swamp troll!" he blurted out, swallowing lake water in the process.

Terrified by the Swamp Troll's hideous features, Uncle Shameless quickly turned around for the shore. He cut through the water, gaining speed thanks to the wine and his fear. Uncle Shameless gained enough speed that he actually began to run across the water.

Steve's eyes bulged in disbelief. He wished he had a science book so that he could throw it away.

"...And that makes even *less* sense," he finally said as his uncle's blurring legs carried him across the lake's surface.

"Hush," scolded Eira.

Uncle Shameless kept looking over his shoulder to see the Swamp Troll approaching. He made it to the shore but fell into the shallows and thrashed around until Zeroth and Steve came to help him up.

"What's wrong?" asked Steve.

Uncle Shameless pointed to the gruesome creature heading towards the shore, "S-S-Swamp Troll!"

Zeroth and Steve turned to look at the Swamp Troll. Instead they saw an old man riding with a passenger on a small boat carved out of a green tree trunk. Zeroth shook his head at Uncle Shameless and dragged him to the boat as Steve followed.

"It's just a man with a boat," said Zeroth.

"But he's got a Swamp Troll with him!" yelled Uncle Shameless as he pointed to the horrific passenger.

The old man steering the boat turned and looked at the passenger, and then turned to look at Uncle Shameless in disgust,

"That's not a troll, that's my wife!"

After many apologies were made, the old man agreed to transport the party to the island on his boat for no charge. This caused a huge uproar among the three bridge men, Enry, Yerlist, and Lime.

They began throwing rocks and insults at the party as they passed by the bridges in the boat with the old man and his wife.

"You're bad for business!" yelled Enry

"Why ride in a cramped boat with others when you can walk by yourself over my luxury, roomy bridge!" added Yerlist.

"*That's* his wife?" asked Lime with a nervous shudder.

The party ignored the three men with the three bridges and enjoyed the free ride. Uncle Shameless kept to the back of the boat, hiding behind Steve, away from the old man's wife. After the companions landed on the island, they thanked the old man for transporting them across.

The island was covered in a thin mist; the air was damp and humid. Steve felt sweaty and sticky under his chain mail. He once again thought of himself wearing it on the frozen lake. His daydream was interrupted by a peculiar tickling sensation around his chest.

It stopped as quickly as it had started; he looked around thinking perhaps something had been crawling on him. He did not see anything and forgot about the odd feeling, not realizing that once again his armor had shrunk.

11

Steve and the others came to the front of the village where a single guard sat half-asleep on a stool. A crudely put together wall of lumber and sticks surrounded the village. The wall did not look strong enough to stop the wind, let alone invaders.

Even the guard was not that menacing. He leaned his head against the shaft of his pitchfork as he snored softly. He was a young and scrawny looking human, a far cry from the fearsome looking bird-men guards of Da'Rahga.

Eira approached the sleeping guard and tapped him on the shoulder.

"Wha-What?" he said. After focusing on Eira and the others his snapped to attention "What's yer bidness in Uth, pelican?"

"I am a healer, and I am here to offer my services," she motioned to Steve, Uncle Shameless and Zeroth "These are my bodyguards."

The guard looked the group over. "We don't need no healers. The swamp provides us with all the healin' we need."

"Such as?" asked Eira calmly.

"Leeches," answered the guard without hesitation.

"Gros-mmphampf!" yelled Steve as Zeroth threw a clawed hand over his mouth.

"And what else?" asked Eira again.

"Bigger leeches," answered the guard. "We don't need yer kind 'round here pelican, or yer scruffy lookin' body guards."

Uncle Shameless took exception to this. He had talked his way past the guards of Da'Rahga and he wasn't going to let a smart-mouthed kid with a pitchfork stand in his way. He quietly took a drink from his wineskin and walked from behind Zeroth.

"No!" whispered Zeroth in vain. Uncle Shameless quietly asked Eira to move aside, hiked up his pants (which as always, fell right back down) and got face to face with the guard.

"Listen here..." he read the guard's poorly made nametag and poked the man hard in the chest. "Mr. Dengles, let us in."

The skinny guard gave Uncle Shameless a confused look, "Why?" he asked.

Uncle Shameless made a louder than necessary sigh, "Don't you know who I am?!" he bellowed to the guard.

The young guard looked Uncle Shameless over.

"Well, yer in ratty clothin', yer hair is a mess, and you reek of wine," The guard thought for a moment and suddenly his face expressed a sense of revelation.

"Oh, you *must* be a friend of the Alderman!" The guard hit himself on the head for being so foolish, "I am so sorry!"

The Alderman was the highest ranking member of Uth, the Last Human Village's government left after a nasty accident at the most recent 'Lookin' Good, Uth!' Charity Chili Cook-Off.

The villagers kept meaning to have special elections to refill all of the more important open positions, including the top post of village Chieftain, but no one really felt like filling out all of the paper work.

As it turned out, the Alderman was also prone to wearing ratty clothing (he preferred the term 'relaxed'), having unruly hair ("My barber's sick!") and stumbling around the village reeking of wine.

Ironically, those had been the only requirements for the job.

The guard apologized as he stood aside to let the group pass through "Please, go right in! You could have just told me who you were."

Uncle Shameless shook his head, "It was a test," he said as he put his hand on the young guard's shoulder, "And sonny – you *passed!*" Uncle Shameless punched the guard playfully in the arm. But due to his Eldercherry wine induced strength he knocked the guard easily to the ground and into a large mud puddle.

"Th-thank you sir," replied the guard as he wiped the mud away from his eyes.

Zeroth walked up to Uncle Shameless and whispered "Good work."

"No problem. Now, let's find that fortune teller!"

"Oracle," corrected Zeroth.

"Fine, Fine. Say, is that a pub?"

Back in Arx Vena'Tor, Fiach-Ra sat perched on his throne deep in the shadows. The burning flames from his eyes cast a crimson halo around his face as he did his least favorite thing of all. He waited. He had expected to hear from the raven twins by now, but no news had reached him yet.

He normally did not like sending lackeys in his place, but because of what The Boy was prophesized to do Fiach-Ra had decided to play it safe.

For now.

U'nala sat at nearby table and was going through the latest batch of Purchase Orders from Kingdom Consignment with extreme prejudice.

"New brooms for the cleaning staff?! U'nala does not think so! No, he does not!" As his old hands reached for another Purchase Order, U'nala made a mental note to find out who had ordered the brooms and to force them to lick the floors clean. This was yet another one of his many administration jobs that he abhorred - going through piles of Purchase Orders to find out what the employees of the Kingdom had been spending government funds on. He would then punish those that he felt *misused* the Kingdom's treasure, which was just about everyone.

U'nala was well aware that it would make more sense to have everyone get approval *before* buying anything, but that was not as much fun. He took great joy in personally taking away items and supplies from the Kingdom's employees after they had already been purchased and used.

Just yesterday he had taken away a brand new abacus from one of the money counters in Kingdom Finance, much to his own amusement.

U'nala scanned the next Purchase Order and wondered why this employee needed so many pieces of metal and other building supplies. He was about to order a pair of guards to fetch the employee in question when he realized it was his own Purchase Order. U'nala quietly stamped it with his 'Eprooved' stamp.

He knew that the stamp was misspelled but he did not see the point in wasting funds on a correct one. After all, *he* knew what it meant and that was all that mattered. He placed his Purchase Order in the nearly empty 'Eprooved' pile before reaching for the next sheet.

"Who is this..." U'nala squinted at the hasty writing "This, *Crammit* person? And why does he need so many yards of black cloth and," he studied the Purchase Order again "And thread?"

U'nala shook his head and was about to reach for his 'Thiseprooved' stamp when his pile of parchment was blown over by a ghostly wind blowing through the rotunda.

An eerie cloud of mist flew down from the hole in the throne room's rotunda and hovered for a moment. U'nala sighed loudly as he chased after his runaway Purchase Orders.

The mist disappeared and Delu fell hard to the floor, groaning in pain. Fiach-Ra sat up in his throne and stared down at the lone raven spy and had a feeling that he was going to be getting very angry after Delu finished speaking.

A pair of guards walked over to Delu and held him up by the steps leading to Fiach-Ra's throne.

"Speak," commanded the Hawk-King, his impatience reaching its limit.

The bruised and battered raven spy did his best to talk,

"We were…" he started, forgetting again that his brother was not around to finish his thoughts. After several moments of silence, U'nala spoke up.

"What? You were what?" asked the Wing-Master.

"We were…" started Delu once more.

"Lost?"

Delu shook his head weakly.

"Sick?"

Again, Delu shook his head.

"Tricked? Followed? Eating?"

Delu flailed his sickly head back and forth.

"Will you just say it already! U'nala commands you!" bellowed the irritable Wing-Master. From his dark throne, Fiach-Ra cleared his throat loudly "Uh…as does your King," added U'nala quickly.

"…Betrayed," Delu finally wheezed, the word oozing slowly from his beak.

"Thank you!" exclaimed U'nala "Now was that *so* hard?"

"Where is The Boy?" asked Fiach-Ra, his voice booming and heavy.

"The Boy is…" started Delu.

"Captured?" asked U'nala hopefully. A shake of Delu's head signaled otherwise.

"The Boy is…" started the raven "G..g…"

"Yes, yes," coached U'nala as he quickly grew tired of this game "That's it."

"G..g-go…go."

"The Boy is a go-go?" asked Fiach-Ra's second in command "U'nala does not understand!"

"The Boy is go...gon...nnn-nn," stuttered Delu.

His breaking point finally reached, U'nala stomped across the floor (in the old days, he would have flown) and slapped Delu across the face with all his strength.

"Get on with it!" bellowed U'nala.

"Gone. The Boy is gone," answered Delu smoothly.

"Good!" said U'nala with a smile. Seconds later the meaning of Delu's words hit him. U'nala grabbed the weak raven and shook him fiercely.

"What do you mean he's gone?!"

Delu, temporarily cured of his speech impediment, quickly informed U'nala and Fiach-Ra of the events in the Forbidden Forest.

Fiach-Ra's instincts had proven correct, he was very upset after Delu finished speaking. His clawed hands dug into the armrests of his shadowy throne. Loud cracking and scratching sounds filled the spacious rotunda.

The guards removed Delu from the throne room so that his wounds could be treated.

"Such treachery from those Hunters! U'nala is greatly shocked! Yes, he most certainly is!" barked the Wing-Master as he headed back to the desk near the base of Fiach-Ra's throne.

"U'nala is going to file a *Formal Hunter Compliant!*" bellowed the boisterous administrator.

The servants in the throne room gasped in unison. The silent Royal Guard gasped in unison as well, but silently. U'nala searched through his desk for a Formal Hunter Compliant Form – TB (Treachery, Betrayal) and promptly filled it out.

"Those Hunters will rue the day they broke their contract, they will rue it indeed! U'nala shall see to *that!*"

As U'nala rained terror upon the piece of parchment with violently dotted i's and angrily crossed t's, Fiach-Ra flew down to the throne room floor and began pacing impatiently.

"Now that they've escaped, where would they go?" the Hawk-King asked his second in command.

"U'nala does not know. U'nala is not a hu-man and does not know the type of things hu-mans like to do. U'nala hears that the south is lovely this time of the season, perhaps-"

Fiach-Ra held up a hand, U'nala stopped talking at once.

"Send in a Mystic," he commanded.

Without hesitation, two Royal Guards left to fetch a Mystic of Zuu. They returned shortly with the vulture that had visited U'nala earlier. The short and squatty Mystic entered the throne room and bowed respectfully in front of the Hawk-King. Fiach-Ra towered over the kneeling vulture, covering the Mystic with the shadows cast by the massive wings on his back.

"The Boy was here and escaped Arx Vena'Tor," spoke Fiach-Ra as he clenched his spear tightly. "Where would he have gone?"

The Mystic stood up, removed a small book from the folds of his robes and began flipping through the pages rapidly,

"Well, if he followed the same basic pattern of all heroes, and up to this point he has – coming to a strange land, getting captured, escaping…" the vulture said while skimming pages, "His next move would be to seek guidance of a super natural nature."

The pudgy vulture looked up from the book "I tell you Highness, none of these hero types can do anything on their own. They *always* need their hands held and *have* to be told what to do," he said sharply, forgetting that Fiach-Ra himself had only came to power thanks to super natural guidance.

Fiach-Ra tapped the butt of the Spear of Zuu against the floor as he thought, trying to ignore the irony of the Mystic's statement. He knew there were few places a human could seek 'super natural guidance.'

His armies had destroyed all of the major temples of Zaa, and the Mystics of Zaa, the blue herons, had been missing for hundreds of years. The Hawk-King turned to face the vulture again, his feathers flowing as he moved,

"Tell me Mystic, where would a *hu-man* seek such guidance?"

The Mystic thumbed through his book again,

"Hmmm, it is usually some eccentric old hermit, a fallen from grace holy person, or an oracle with a bizarre personally trait."

Suddenly both Fiach-Ra and U'nala looked at each other.

"Uth," they said in unison. Almost. U'nala let Fiach-Ra speak first so he'd know what to say in order to sound like he knew what the Hawk-King was thinking.

"U'nala shall muster the troops honorable Hawk-King. U'nala shall go to Uth and smite these upstarts," said the Wing-Master hopefully.

Fiach-Ra shook his head, "No, I do not want a repeat of what happened in the Forbidden Forest. I will take an attack party to Uth, the Last Human Village and I will face The Boy."

"But Lord, what of this The Prophecy?" asked U'nala, still hoping he could find a way to go into battle.

"Let me worry about that," said Fiach-Ra slyly as thunder cracked overhead.

The Hawk-King held up the Spear of Zuu and let loose a mighty cry. The spear's head burst into brilliant flame as fiery light filled the rotunda. Fiach-Ra spread his large wings, as did several members of the Royal Guard.

With another mighty cry, Fiach-Ra took flight and flew through the opening in the rotunda and his Royal Guard followed obediently. The Hawk-King flew up to towards the wicked mouth on the giant statue of Zuu atop Arx Vena'Tor. The statue stood with its giant stone wings spread in a frightful manner as its fiery mane burned in the air at the top of its head and down its back.

Fiach-Ra hovered in the air once he reached the mouth. The statue's jagged beak was agape with a dark hole at the back of its throat. Fiach-Ra pointed the Spear of Zuu towards The Mouth of Zuu and chanted a series of ancient, powerful words.

At the back of the statue's throat, faint fiery lights began to glow and come closer and closer to the hole. Terrible screeching sounds grew louder and louder, filling the sky with their horrible notes, sounding like a thousand birds screaming in anger all at once.

Fiach-Ra watched and waited as a sinister smile crossed his face.

12

Steve had been right about the Oracle.

They had walked through the mud filled streets of Uth, the Last Human Village to find the Oracle. The thin mist hung in the air like an old, ratty drape, and the ground squashed beneath their steps with loud GURGLES.

Steve kept telling himself he had been right while he listened to the Oracle ramble on, but at least they had finally found him. Steve and the others had made the mistake of just looking for a sign that said 'The Oracle' and ended up at a blacksmith's shop owned by a man named Theo Racle due to a sign maker's poor design.

Against their better judgment, they went into one village's pubs with Uncle Shameless leading the way. Halfway through a story about a talking lunch box that granted wishes, Uncle Shameless was reminded by Steve who they were looking for.

"We are lookin' for the Oracle," he slurred.

"The blacksmith? He's down by the stables," answered a man who was balding but trying to hid it with a big, silly hat.

"Nah! We've seen 'im!" answered Uncle Shameless loudly.

Uncle Shameless leaned over and put an arm around the man with the big, silly hat and moved close to him so that he could whisper in the man's ear. Unfortunately, Uncle Shameless' whispering was more like a yell.

"We're lookin' for da guy that tells the FUTURE!" he bellowed into the man's ear.

The man tried to pull away to stop having his ear shouted into, but Uncle Shameless' extra-ordinary strength kept him in place.

"Bahh!" groaned the man in pain. "You mean the weather teller?"

"No!" shouted Uncle Shameless. He then paused "Wait," he looked at Zeroth for an indication if that was correct or not. Zeroth quickly shook his head.

"No!" bellowed Uncle Shameless as he pounded a fist into the bar, causing tiny cracks to form.

"Y'know, the guy who reads your hands. Has the crystal ball?" explained Uncle Shameless.

The man with big, silly hat thought for a moment as he reached under his hat to scratch his balding head.

Steve pulled Uncle Shameless towards him and whispered in his ear, his uncle nodded.

"And has a bizarre personality trait?" added Uncle Shameless.

Clarity washed over the man with the silly hat's face, "Oh, you mean Geo!"

After learning the Oracle's name and place of residence, they began their walk to find him. Geo lived outside of the village, a distance that felt to Steve like a hundred miles. Actually it was only around two yards away from the nearest village shack but to Steve it could have just been on the other side of Eyri. He was getting tired of wearing his chain mail and walking in the mud.

They came to Geo's shack and he let them in. He had the group sit around a very small table in a very small room. Steve hated every second of it.

However, he hated this Oracle, Geo, much more.

Geo was a tall, husky human with a small round face. His hair was cropped short, yet he had a wild unmanageable beard that spread out in all directions.

"You are The Boy?" asked Geo.

"I have a name."

"That is the blue heron amulet?" Geo asked.

Steve nodded regretfully, remembering how much trouble this piece of jewelry had gotten him into earlier.

"If you were chosen to wear the amulet, then you are The Boy?"

"Isn't it your job to tell me that?" asked Steve in an agitated tone.

"You were chosen, therefore you are The Boy?" asked Geo in his light, monotone voice.

Steve groaned, "Why are you asking *me* questions? You're the Oracle, give me the answers or whatever it is you do. And I have a name y'know – stop it with all this 'The Boy' stuff."

Geo continued, "You are the one who wears the amulet?"

Steve looked around, dumbstruck and annoyed.

"Haven't you been listening to me for the past twenty minutes? We've been over that a dozen times!" yelled Steve.

Eira tried to calm Steve down, "Relax, he is an Oracle you know. They aren't always that clear."

"Well, he's not a very good one if he can't remember who I am from one minute to the next. All he does is keep asking me questions..." Steve's words trailed off as he finally realized what was going on.

Steve closed his eyes and tried to choke back his frustration, "Let me guess...everything you say sounds like a question? Is that it?"

Geo smiled and nodded, "Yes?"

Steve let out a loud groan. *This whole place is one bad joke*, he thought to himself.

"Your next step is to go to the port town of Tal?" explained Geo.

"Tal?" said Zeroth "The duck town?"

Uncle Shameless shuddered. "Not more ducks," he whispered.

"What's wrong with ducks?" asked Eira.

Steve shook his head, "It's a long story."

Geo continued, "There you must find a way to get to Dragons Well?"

"A duck town? Dragons Well?" sighed Steve as he leaned back in his chair.

"You must find the Sword of Zaa?" added Geo "Only with the Sword of Zaa can you defeat Fiach-Ra?"

Steve was about to ask what a Dragons Well was when he heard the thunder of flapping wings and hundreds of humans screaming.

Fiach-Ra normally left Uth, the Last Human Village alone since the humans there posed little threat, outside of bridge related scams. While their numbers were fewer, there were other human settlements scattered across the rest of Eyri, which made Uth, The Last Human Village somewhat of a misnomer.

The 'Last Human Village' part of Uth's name had actually been added by the Uth Chamber of Commerce Tourism Division as a marketing ploy to bring in more tourists. Being located in the middle of a swamp, deep within the Forbidden Forest had been very bad for the Uth tourism industry.

Then the three bridges scam was thought up as a way to get even more money from tourists and travelers. The marketing idea worked, and their tourism industry went up from nothing to nothing and a half.

Needless to say, neither the Uth Chamber of Commerce nor the Alderman were too happy when Fiach-Ra showed up with a small army of Hawken and Swantan troops.

"This isn't going to be good for business," lamented the Alderman, a portly bearded man, as he watched war parties of flying Hawken troops circle overhead. This was the exact reason he had only run for Alderman, all of this invasion and disaster business was left to the Chieftain, thus leaving the Alderman free to drink and stink.

However, since he was now the village leader by default, the responsibility of disaster control fell into his rather incapable hands.

But a quick-thinking, opportunistic member of the Uth Chamber of Commerce, who had been out drinking with the Alderman, disagreed with the Alderman's statement.

"Don't you see?" she said, pointing to the Hawk-King in the sky above them. "We can say we were personally visited by the Hawk-King. It'll be great for tourism!"

"I don't want to have to redo all of the village signs, we just finished having them all repainted," sighed the Alderman.

Another member of the Uth Chamber of Commerce, a small weasely looking man, jumped into the conversation, "We could just add a foot note to the signs, y'know with the little numbers?"

The Alderman nodded, his ratty hair flopping to and fro, "I like where this is going!"

The man continued, "We put a little '1' after 'Uth, Last Human Village' on the old signs and under it we put a smaller sign that says '1: Personally attacked by the Hawk-King, Fiach-Ra the Wicked and several dozen warriors.'"

The Alderman clapped the man on the shoulder, "By Donal's Beard, *that's* an idea!" he exclaimed. The Alderman turned to the other member of the Uth Chamber of Commerce, "Rally up the rest of the Chamber, we'll have a meeting later tonight at Narb's Pub to go over this footnote business."

"Uh, I think several Hawken just burned down Narb's," replied the lady as she pointed to a large pile of smoldering timbers that used to be the Alderman's favorite pub.

"Dear me, that is a shame," said the Alderman as he looked around for a building that wasn't on fire. "I guess we'll have to slum it up a bit and go to Sheao's," sighed the Alderman.

A villager ran up to the Alderman, "Sir! It's horrible!"

The Alderman nodded, "Yes I know. We have to go to Sheao's for our meeting. It is a shame about Narb's, they had these really great spicy potatoes."

The villager was dumbstruck, "Sir?!" the villager gasped, as she pointed to the attacking Hawken "Isn't there something you can do?"

The Alderman thought for several moments as flaming arrows whizzed past his head and villagers screamed all around him.

"Yes, I s'pose there is," he finally answered as he waddled over to a crowd of villagers lugging buckets of water towards an Uth library.

"Stop!" commanded the Alderman, holding his mug of wine high in the air. The would-be firefighters stopped and stared at their grubby leader.

He pointed to a nearby pub, which was also set on fire, "Save Presto's!" he commanded, earning many confused looks from the crowd. He kept pointing to the burning pub and totally ignored the flame-engulfed schoolhouse.

"It'll be a quiet night in Da'Rahga before I go to Sheao's," mumbled the Alderman as the crowd reluctantly went to save Presto's Pub.

Steve and his friends exited Geo's ramshackle house and discreetly made their way to the middle of the village. Hawken troops swarmed the skies, commanded by an angered Fiach-Ra. Hawken warriors were shooting flaming arrows into random buildings, while Swantan troops were on the ground rounding up villagers.

Steve got his first glance at the Hawk-King. He was even more terrifying in person than in Istrio's magic orb. Fiach-Ra hovered in the air above the village, flapping the huge feathered wings on his back.

Zeroth snuck up to Steve, "We have a problem," he whispered "They have taken control of the three bridges. We're stuck."

Eira moved up alongside the pair, "Could we swim to the shore?"

Zeroth shook his head, "We'd be spotted from the air."

"Not to mention the Swamp Trolls!" added Uncle Shameless.

Zeroth sighed mockingly, "Yes...the Swamp Trolls."

Fiach-Ra watched his troops from the air as they raided the village and searched every shack and shanty for The Boy. A Hawken officer flew up to the Hawk-King,

"No sign of them yet, Highness."

"Keep searching Wing-Commander, it is a small island," answered Fiach-Ra without looking at him. "But perhaps you could use some assistance."

Fiach-Ra pointed the Spear of Zuu straight up and repeated the wicked words he had spoken at the Mouth of Zuu.

Seconds later, screaming sounds were heard, coming from high above the village in a cluster of dark clouds. Suddenly, two fiery shapes burst out of the clouds in an explosion of flame and smoke. The screaming became louder and louder as the two burning shapes cut through the air at high speed and headed towards the Hawk-King.

Steve and the others looked up and watched as the twin fiery shapes flew at blazing speeds to the Hawk-King, only to stop in mid air near him. They looked like birds but, unlike the bird-people of Eyri, the two creatures looked like normal winged birds that Steve was accustomed to seeing back in Michigan.

But then they were not like regular birds either – they were gigantic bird *skeletons*. Brightly burning flames danced around their bodies. Their charred black bones stuck out against the bright red-orange flames surrounding them. Flames dressed their massive featherless wings.

Instead of eyes, crimson flames spewed out of empty sockets carved out of their coal black skulls. Their feet were armed with vicious, curved talons. Their screams pierced the air and sent chills down Steve's spine.

"We're in trouble," said Zeroth coldly as he looked up at the burning creatures "*Big* trouble."

"Oh no," gasped Eira.

"What *are* those?" asked the boy.

"They ain't pigeons," added Uncle Shameless.

Zeroth did not answer, he kept looking at Fiach-Ra as he ordered the creatures to search for Steve.

Steve shook the Hunter, "Zeroth! What are those?"

Zeroth shook his head to clear his thoughts. "Those are Pyrix, also known as Children of Zuu, or Minions of Qu-"

"Let's keep this to a one name maximum please," interrupted Steve, wondering if everything around here had to have at least three names.

"They dwell inside the statue of Zuu on top of Arx Vena'Tor," continued Zeroth.

"Oh yah, that big bird statue. Man was it ugly. An' I don't mean art museum ugly, I mean *ugly-ugly*," added Uncle Shameless.

Zeroth went on, "Fiach-Ra controls them with the Spear of Zuu, and they exit the statue from the Mouth of Zuu-"

"Zuu certainly likes to hear his name a lot," joked Steve.

Eira shushed Steve and Zeroth continued "If the Hawk-King brought them here, then you must be more important than I thought. He using them to search for us, whatever they see – he sees as well. We have to hide."

Steve did not understand how a pair of giant bird skeletons could find them any more quickly than several dozen sharp-sighted hawk warriors, "How can they even see? They don't even have eyes!" protested Steve.

But it was too late. as Steve had finished his observation about the Pyrix one spotted them from high above and started screeching. Fiach-Ra, seeing what the Pyrix saw, ordered troops over to Steve and his friends' hiding place without hesitation.

The giant flaming Pyrix swooped down and buzzed over the group. The heat from its body washed over them and set several tree branches on fire.

"Run!" Zeroth ordered as he took out his swordfish and gave it a squeeze, resulting in a loud BLEAH! Steve reluctantly did the same as he helped Eira up. Uncle Shameless took several long swigs from his bottomless wineskin and brought up the rear.

Suddenly Hawken began dropping out of the sky around the companions, and several Swantan warriors ran from the surrounding trees. The Hawken hovered in the air, jabbing at Zeroth with spears, which he expertly deflected with the use of his swordfish.

A large Swantan ran at Eira, only to be blindsided by a fast punch from Uncle Shameless. Steve looked up at hovering Hawken warrior and then looked down at his swordfish.

"Forget this!" yelled the boy as he broke into a run and looked for a hiding spot. The Hawken warrior buzzed overhead and prepared to hurl his nasty looking spear at Steve. Seeing this, Uncle Shameless darted through the melee towards his nephew. Aided by the magical effects of the Eldercherry wine, Uncle Shameless jumped high into the air and grabbed the Hawken by the legs. Surprised by the extra weight, the bird-man fell to the ground.

"Keep yer dirty claws offa my nephew!" hollered Uncle Shameless as he swung the warrior around by its legs several times, letting go at the right time to send the Hawken crashing into a pack of approaching Swantan warriors.

In the sky above them, Fiach-Ra grew tired of waiting and signaled for the Pyrix to intervene. The two Pyrix swooped down, one landed in front of the group and the other behind it. Steve once again felt the heat pouring off their bodies as the beasts landed with a ground-shaking THUD.

One Pyrix screeched its ugly cry and shot a stream of fire from its mouth at Zeroth, knocking the swordfish from his hand. Zeroth hunched over in pain and signaled Steve to throw down his swordfish, not wanting the boy to be attacked as well.

The second Pyrix approached Steve and studied him with its hollow eye sockets. Steve stared at the dancing flames in the cavernous blackened skull. The Pyrix hissed at Steve and started driving him towards the rest of the group.

Every step the Pyrix took on its burning talons left large, smoking scorch marks on the ground. Uncle Shameless charged at one of the Pyrix, refusing to hand over Steve without a fight. The beast swatted at him with its white-hot talons, knocking him to the ground and leaving deep burning scratches in his breastplate.

The group found themselves in the center of the village surrounded on all sides by Fiach-Ra's warriors and the two Pyrix. Steve and his companions stood back to back, forming a circle. A loud cry sounded as Fiach-Ra descended to the ground with such force that the ground shook even harder than when the Pyrix had landed.

Fiach-Ra towered over all his warriors and even dwarfed the tall Swantan foot soldiers. With each step he took towards the group, the ground quaked and shook. His massive wingspan of brown and black feathers cast an unnatural shadow over the group, blanketing them in darkness.

Unlike his other warriors, Fiach-Ra wore no armor. He was bare chested, clothed only in a loin cloth decorated with the symbol of Zuu that reached down to his ankles. His body was rippled with muscle that made even the strongest envious. Finally, Steve looked into the Hawk-King's fire filled eyes.

The burning hawk eyes stared intently at the young boy and at his blue heron amulet. Through the Hawk-King's left eye ran his scar. Steve remembered the scar from his dreams, the scar given to Fiach-Ra by Donal with the mythical Sword of Zaa.

The Hawk-King held the blazing Spear of Zuu valiantly above him and spoke, "So, at last we have found...*The Boy*."

"Why does everyone have to call me that?" complained Steve, growing very tired of his unwanted title.

Fiach-Ra smiled a wicked smile, "I see you are brave enough to speak to your destroyer in such a tone. Amusing. Now who do you have with you? The treacherous Hunter I assume."

Zeroth froze, finally realizing at that moment that he had broken his contract with the Hawk-King by aiding Steve. He cursed under his breath. He knew that if the Kingdom filed a Formal Hunter Compliant Form – TB (Treachery, Betrayal) against him, he would have bigger problems than the Hawk-King.

"Cam, you'd better be right about this boy…" Zeroth whispered to himself as he wondered if he had made the right choice.

"Silence!" ordered Fiach-Ra as he slammed the butt of the Spear into the ground for added impact "Now, turn and face your King."

Zeroth turned toward the Hawk-King, secretly wondering if he could talk Fiach-Ra out of filing a Formal Complaint against him.

Fiach-Ra's fire-filled eyes widened and he broke into a deep, throaty laugh. *"Zeroth?"* laughed the Hawk-King as he studied the Hunter "I have wondered over the years what came of you. I would never have expected to find you with these rabble, considering you came from such *higher* stock."

Confusion gripped Zeroth. He had never met the Hawk-King until this moment, he was certain of it.

"Does he ever shut up? Why does everyone around here have to be so melodramatic and wordy?" interrupted Steve.

"Eager to die are you?" replied Fiach-Ra, turning his attention away from the confused Zeroth "Very well. Allow me to grant your request."

Fiach-Ra waved a hand to the hovering Hawken warriors. They pulled back on their curved bows, aiming for Steve and the rest of the group.

Fiach-Ra waved again, and a cloud of arrows blocked out the sky.

13

A rrows flew at the four heroes from all directions. For a single heartbeat, the sound of flying arrows filled their ears. Steve had his eyes closed and hoped for the arrows to miss. He felt several arrows fly past him, and even felt the feathers from an arrow's shaft brush his arm. Then he felt nothing at all.

The sounds of the village filled their ears again as Steve felt himself start to breathe once more. He slowly opened his eyes, expecting to see arrows sticking into him and everyone else. Instead all of the arrows were sticking into the ground near their feet.

Not a single arrow out of the several dozen fired had struck them.

Muttering broke out within the hovering ranks of Hawken, as they tried to figure out how all of them had missed. Several warriors looked over their bows only to find them in perfect working order.

"I never knew the after-life would be so muddy," cried Uncle Shameless from his prone position in a mud puddle on the ground. He had dropped there, hoping to dodge the barrage of deadly arrows. Steve poked him in the ribs with a foot, "Get up! You're not dead!" he yelled.

Uncle Shameless slowly stood up; as he did he noticed that the arrows that had struck the ground formed a perfect outline around him.

"Is my head really that big?" he asked.

Zeroth quieted him. "What happened? There is no way they could have all missed. Hawken are expert archers.

"Unless..." Zeroth pointed to Steve's blue heron amulet, which was glowing with a faint blue light.

Fiach-Ra roared with rage and ordered one of his Hawken officers to fire a shot directly at Steve. Without hesitation and with expert skill, the Hawken aimed at Steve with his curved bow and let the shot fly. The heinous arrow flew fast and true, but the amulet's blue light shined again. The arrow altered its course and struck into the ground, harming no one.

"It's your doohickey!" bellowed Uncle Shameless.

"Excuse me?"

"I think he means your amulet," Eira said to Steve "At least I hope so."

"It must be protecting us," suggested Zeroth.

"How can a piece of ugly costume jewelry do that?" asked Steve.

Zeroth opened his beak to answer and Steve held up a hand to silence him, "Let me guess," sighed Steve, "More magic?"

"Probably."

"Magic or not, I'm just glad I don't have any extra holes in my body," remarked Uncle Shameless as he gladly found his wineskin undamaged.

Fiach-Ra watched the blue light fade from the blue heron amulet, and his rage increased. He signaled to the two Pyrix,

"Let us fight magic with magic," roared the infuriated Hawk-King.

"Oh no," gasped Eira as she watched the two Pyrix line up on either side of Fiach-Ra.

Even though Steve thought magic was silly, he secretly hoped the amulet would at least stop a few burns as the Pyrix opened their blackened beaks and shot twin streams of fire. The Pyrix fire breath cut through the air like flaming lances and headed straight towards the group.

A large blue sphere appeared around Steve and the others and the fire streams crashed into it without harm. The fire split around the party as the sphere protected them from the deadly attack. They could still feel the heat, and Steve felt sweat rolling down him.

Seeing their breath had no effect, the Pyrix stopped their assault. The semi-transparent blue sphere protecting the heroes gradually faded away. Even more muttering broke out among Fiach-Ra's troops, as they had never seen anyone withstand Pyrix breath before.

Fiach-Ra clutched the Spear of Zuu, reached back with his throwing arm, and hurled the Spear of Zuu at the group. Its flaming tip left a trail of flame as it flew towards its target.

Steve saw the spear coming towards him and thought about how badly he wanted to get away, he did not want to wait and see what else Fiach-Ra would try to throw at him.

The Hawken and Swantan troops watched in amazement as the group vanished in a flash of blue light just when the Spear of Zuu was only inches away from its target. The mighty spear struck the ground, imbedding itself deep into the cold, dark mud.

Fiach-Ra's eyes burned fiercely, yet he did not yell in fury. He stayed calm, but it was an eerie calm. He thought of what he would personally do to The Boy once he was captured. No one made him look like a fool in front of his troops and lived.

Calmly he held up his arm and unclenched a fist in the direction of the Spear of Zuu. The Spear turned into a ball of fire and flew back to Fiach-Ra. After splashing into his hand, the fireball reformed into the Spear of Zuu.

With his mighty weapon in hand, the Hawk-King looked at the idle Pyrix, "Destroy the village."

Fiach-Ra flapped his large wings and sped back to Arx Vena'Tor along with his Royal Guard. His two Pyrix took to the sky and began raining destruction down on the unlucky inhabitants of Uth, the Last Human Village.

Everyone was screaming when the blue light finally disappeared. Steve was covering his face with his arms, waiting to be struck by Fiach-Ra's spear. Like the arrows, the spear never came. Steve uncovered his face slowly and realized they were not in the village any more.

"Where are we?" he asked.

Zeroth threw back his hood and looked around, "I think we're on the road to Tal," he finally said.

"Amazing!" blurted Uncle Shameless as he slowly stood up and dusted himself off "How'd you figure that out? Some sort of tracking secret?"

"There's a sign over that says 'Tal' with an arrow pointing that way," explained Zeroth slowly, nodding towards a tall signpost along the road.

"Oh," said Uncle Shameless.

Eira noticed Zeroth's burned hand. "Let me look at that," she said as she gently inspected the injury.

She reached into her pack and pulled out the same bottle of healing potion she had used on Uncle Shameless. She poured some of the silvery liquid onto the burn wound, and it began to heal instantly. She returned the now empty bottle to her pack.

"Thank you," gasped Zeroth as he rubbed his healed hand "But you did not have to use the last of your potion on me, you should have saved it."

Eira shook her head, "No no, I have plenty more. Think nothing of it," she said with a nervous smile.

"What's it made of?" asked Steve.

"Oh, nothing special. Just-"

"Crackers!" yelled Uncle Shameless as he pointed to the eastern sky. Far in the distance, everyone saw a lofty column of dark smoke snaking skyward.

"Is that...?" began Steve.

"It *was* Uth," said a familiar voice from behind the boy.

They all turned to see Istrio sitting on a rock; his Mystic's robes blowing in the light breeze.

"Or rather, The Village Formally Known as Uth, The Last Human Village. I think that is what they are going to call it now. I overheard the Alderman discussing it with a member of the Uth Chamber of Commerce as they were trying to outrun one of the Pyrix," explained the blue heron in an obviously irritated tone.

"What do you mean 'was'?" asked Steve.

"What do you think I mean?" answered the blue heron as he approached Steve. "It has been destroyed. Wiped off the face of Eyri. Struck down by the hand of Fiach-Ra. Take your pick."

The blue heron walked up to Steve and looked down at him with his large white eyes, "And it's all *your* fault."

"No it isn't!" argued Eira.

Istrio ignored the pelican's protest, "Yes it is. I told you to go straight to Uth, and did you? No. You went to Da'Rahga, after I specifically told you not to."

Steve felt very ill and looked down at the ground, ashamed. He did not think that he would be the cause of Uth's destruction when he decided not to go there. His head shot up after he had a revelation, "That was *you* in the cell with us!"

The blue heron nodded, "Yes it was me. And you are lucky it was, otherwise...well I'd rather not think about it."

Steve nodded, remembering the villainous Hawken that had tried to trick him into going to see the Hawk-King. But the boy did think about that if he *had* gone with the Hawken, Uth would not have been destroyed.

Other scenarios began to fill Steve's mind as well. If he had gone straight to Uth, the ravens and the Hunters would have never come after him. That meant that Cam would still be alive too. All of this was very hard for the young boy to take, and his stomach felt like it was twisting into complex knots.

Istrio continued his passive-aggressive scolding, "Now Fiach-Ra knows you are here and what you look like. You could have slipped by unknown to him and made your quest a lot easier."

Steve bit his lip in thought, "C'mon I didn't think you were serious about all of that."

"Is a village burned to the ground serious enough for you?" countered Istrio.

Steve was silent and looked at the ground again. The Mystic kneeled down in front of Steve and put both hands on the boy's shoulders,

"Young Harrier, you are on a quest whether you like it or not. The sooner you accept your destiny, the easier your quest will be."

Istrio gave Steve's shoulders a friendly squeeze and stood up slowly, "You have a great power dwelling inside you, young Harrier, and once you unlock it you shall be unstoppable. Or at least *more* annoying to the Hawk-King."

"I don't think that's possible," joked Uncle Shameless.

The elderly blue heron dusted off his hands, and in a completely different tone of voice began talking to the rest of the group, "Now that all of that nasty business is out of the way, how's everyone else doing?"

The rest of the party groaned collectively, rubbing their various wounds and sore spots. "Oh *please*. You *young people*," scolded Istrio as he shook his wrinkled blue head.

"When *I* was a youngster, some 500 odd years ago, I'd pick fights with solicitors in the morning, treasure hunt in the afternoon and save beautiful bird-maidens in the evening!" he said as he shook his bony fists in the air with a strong sense of nostalgia, "And that was just a boring Relmorsday!"

"I wasn't aware that Mystics of Zaa went treasure hunting and rescued maidens," questioned Zeroth.

"...Relmorsday?" Steve said quietly to himself.

"Bah, we're not *born* pious junior," replied the wrinkled blue heron with a sly smile "All of that Mystic business comes much later. Believe me, *I* could tell you some stories! Like this one time I was..." he looked at Steve, "Uhh... never mind I'll tell that one later."

After everyone else's bumps and bruises were tended to, Istrio wished the party good luck on the next leg of their quest, which of course meant more walking.

"I'm sick of walking, that's all I've done since I came to this crazy place," whined Steve "Is that part of The Prophecy? Making us walk everywhere?"

The blue heron shook his head as thunder boomed overhead, "You'd better get used to it kid, you have a quite a few miles to go."

"Why didn't the amulet just transport us right to Tal?" asked Steve.

"Because long, boring walks through nature are a big part of quests like this. Also, it builds character," answered Istrio.

Steve groaned and started moving to catch up with the rest of the party. Istrio turned to leave as well but quickly stopped.

"Oh, I almost forgot – hang on a moment Zeroth!" cried the blue heron.

The black-feathered Hunter turned to face the Mystic of Zaa.

"I saw you've lost your swordfish, here have another," said Istrio as he tossed a new swordfish to Zeroth.

Zeroth caught the creature with ease and studied the new swordfish after forcing out its deadly tongue. Unlike his first swordfish, this one was a bright silver color and larger.

"What the-" he stuttered, surprised by the appearance of this new creature. Something about it seemed familiar to him, but he couldn't remember why. It might have been out of a story Cam had told him years ago. Then it came to him.

"This is-"

"Yes, yes. A silver swordfish, very rare, I know. Enjoy!" replied Istrio with an odd smile "Now scamper, scamper!" laughed the blue heron as he shooed the party away with his hands before disappearing in a flash of blue light.

The companions continued walking on the road to Tal, the duck port town on the coast of the Ralk Sea.

"What's so special about that swordfish?" asked Steve.

"I don't know exactly, but I think I remember Cam saying their blades were sharper and stronger," explained Zeroth. He knew that if Cam was there with him, he'd get the whole legend behind the mythical swordfish if he wanted to hear it or not. A memory flashed in Zeroth's mind.

"Now I remember," he said with a snap of his clawed fingers. "Cam told me about a legend where that human king, Donal, used one of these before he had the Sword of Zaa."

"Mhats mot ma megend, mit's mrue," said a surly voice. Everyone looked around, looking for the speaker but they could not find anyone.

"Mown Mere!" said the voice again.

Steve looked down, half expecting to see something like a short-tempered chipmunk in a funny shirt. That would have at least made a little bit of sense to the boy, instead of the true origin of the voice. Steve pointed a shaky finger at the silver swordfish in Zeroth's clawed hand.

"...I think *it* said that."

Zeroth held up his new living weapon and gave it a hefty squeeze. Its brilliant and deadly tongue shot back into its mouth.

"'Bout time, I was wonderin' how long it was gonna take you to figure that out," snapped the swordfish. Only its lips moved when it spoke, and they moved very little regardless of what the creature said, reminding Steve of a bad cartoon or a poorly dubbed movie.

"As I was sayin', that wasn't a legend. It was true, Donal did use a silver swordfish."

"How do *you* know?" asked Steve. The swordfish narrowed a large eye at Steve, "Yer a quick one, ain'tcha? How do you think? It was *me*, you ninny!"

Steve could not believe that a talking fish had just called him a ninny.

"You?" asked Eira.

"No, it was *another* talking silver swordfish. What, were your parents related or somethin'? 'Course it was me!"

"Whoa, easy there," said Uncle Shameless calmly "What's yer name?"

"Gladius," replied the silver swordfish bitterly.

"What a grouch," Steve whispered to Eira.

"I heard that!" snapped Gladius.

The party continued on to Tal as Zeroth stuck Gladius into his belt. The swordfish had calmed down a little and was talking to Steve.

"So, yer The Boy then?" asked Gladius.

"Yes," sighed the reluctant young adventurer. "My name is Steve."

"*Steve?* What kind of sissy name is that?"

"That's what I told his dad," interrupted Uncle Shameless, "I told him he needed to give the boy a really butch name, like Theodore or Gordon. 'Course if his mother woulda had her way, he woulda been named Françoise."

"You don't even have a title!" barked Gladius, ignoring Uncle Shameless. "A hero's got ta have a title, 'specially one that has such a sissy name."

Steve opened his mouth to argue but he really didn't feel like getting into a shouting match with a talking fish.

"Take Donal fer example," started Gladius "Donal the Mighty. You can't loose with that, now *there* was a good title. Much better than the one he had as a youngster."

"Which was?" asked Zeroth, looking down at the chatty creature tucked into his belt.

"Donal the Wet. He had a bit of a... *personal* problem if you get me. But he grew outta that by the time he was a teenager."

"I don't want a title," said Steve. "Besides, I can't even think of one."

"Zaa's Beak!" cursed Gladius loudly, "Ya don't give *yerself* a title kid! Ya earn it!"

"Okay, okay," replied Steve, wishing the silver swordfish would clam up. "Fine, I don't want to *earn* a title."

"You don't have any say in the matter," explained Gladius. "It just happens. Trust me." Steve knew better than to trust an irritable talking fish, but nodded anyway.

"Gladius," asked Eira politely "You were with Donal as a child?"

"Yap, sure was," answered Gladius proudly. "We had many adventures over the years...until I was *replaced* by the Sword of Zaa."

Everyone went silent, finally realizing the source of the talking weapon's hostility. "Now, I'm not bitter. No sir," lied Gladius. "I didn't mind bein' forgot about for years and years. No, of course not!"

Gladius paused for a moment; luring everyone into thinking it was finally done with its venom-drenched rant,

"I hate that home-wrecking magic sword!" yelled Gladius seconds later, startling the party. "I was a million times better than that pi-mmphpt!" Gladius' words were garbled as Zeroth stuck it into a pocket inside his cloak.

"Now I think I know *why* Gladius was replaced," said Zeroth with an annoyed sigh.

They walked for hours; so long that Eyri's two moons begin to rise in the sky.

"Are we there yet?" whined Steve. His feet ached, and he was all sweaty under his chain mail. He thought of himself walking through a cold, snowy field with his chain mail fitting him perfectly.

Steve felt the odd feeling he had felt before, a strange tickling sensation covered his chest and back. He stopped in his tracks and looked down. His chain mail was now sung against his body; it no longer hung down past his knees.

"AAAHHHH!" screamed the boy. He screamed so loud that Uncle Shameless spit out the wine he was drinking.

"Wha's wrong?!" asked Uncle Shameless, running to his nephew's side.

"Th-th-the cha-cha -" stuttered Steve.

"The Cha-Cha? This is no time for dancin' boy!" replied Uncle Shameless, very confused.

"My chain mail!" Steve yelled clearly "Look!"

Uncle Shameless stared at the armor. "Yes, it's lovely, but what's the matter?"

"It fits!"

"Well…that's great Steve-o, I'm really happy for you, but I don't see why you have to go yellin' 'bout it," Uncle Shameless turned towards Eira and signaled to her that he thought Steve was going crazy, not realizing that gesture had a completely different meaning in Eyri.

The pelican gasped loudly and covered her face with her hands.

Confused, Uncle Shameless turned back towards his nephew.

Zeroth walked up next to Steve and looked at the boy's chain mail. "Oh, it fits you."

"Thank you!" yelled Steve.

"It's about time too," said Zeroth. "I thought you'd never figure it out."

A thought exploded in Uncle Shameless' mind, "I get it," he said as he swayed and forth "You figured out how to get the armor to fitcha, just like me!"

There was suddenly a loud THUNK as Uncle Shameless' breastplate instantly increased to the size of a small car (or in Zeroth and Eira's case, a large plow).

"Ugh…" groaned Uncle Shameless as he was pulled to the ground "A little help?" Steve and Zeroth shared a gaze and shook their heads at Uncle Shameless.

14

Tal was a sailing and shipping city located in a large bay of the Ralk Sea on the west coast of Eyri. Duck-people owned and ran most of Tal and its ships. The moonlight illuminated the bay as the party entered the city and the sight was breathtaking to the newcomers. The twin moons of Eyri, one round and the other square, reflected brilliantly in the clear bay water.

The buildings were old, but sturdy looking. Most were made out of red-orange bricks, the rest hard dark colored wood. Shops, restaurants and other places of business populated the city's center. Even though it was getting later in the evening, business was still going strong.

"What are we going to do here exactly?" asked Steve. He was ready to collapse after walking the many miles to Tal after narrowly escaping Fiach-Ra and his warriors in the The Village Formally Known as Uth, The Last Human Village.

"We need to find a ship to take us to that Dragons Well, whatever it is," reminded Zeroth as they walked the duck filled streets of Tal. Hundreds of short duck-people waddled past them. Most of the ducks were barely up to Steve or Eira's waist. Zeroth and Uncle Shameless easily towered over the little citizens.

While the ducks could talk just like Eira and Zeroth, some would make quacking sounds while talking, even using it to replace words as Steve witnessed while passing a pair of duck merchants.

"Riec, you old quack! How the quack are you?" said the first.

"Eh, you know how it is Doluc. Same quack, different quack," replied the second "I just got this new quack of an assistant."

"Oh, he's that quack?" asked the first duck merchant.

"Zaa's Beak yes. That quack wouldn't quack his quack from a quack."

"That's a quack. How's your quack?"

"Dujy? Oh, she migrated to her mother's."

Steve covered his ears and started mumbling to himself "Getmeouttahere, getmeouttahere…"

Uncle Shameless found it difficult to maneuver through the sea of little duck people, and as he stopped to take drink of wine, a mother duck and several ducklings walked under him through his legs.

Uncle Shameless looked down at the tiny progression underneath him and then looked at his wineskin. He quickly tucked the wineskin away.

"And just *where* are we going to find a someone to take us to Dragons Well?" asked Steve, secretly wondering what would happen if he threw a slice of bread in the middle of the duck crowd.

"I might be able to help you with that," said a familiar voice.

The group turned around, "Mudd!" cried Steve as he recognized the duck that had helped him and Uncle Shameless escape the dungeon in Arx Vena'Tor. Mudd the duck waddled up to Steve and shook his hand. He was still wearing his stained bartender's apron.

Mudd bowed to Eira and Zeroth but gave a nervous wave to Uncle Shameless. "I have a cousin who has a ship, and he might be able to help you, but first you should all get some rest."

Mudd led the tired party to the Light House Inn, the oldest and tallest building in Tal. It sat right in the middle of the bay, close to the water's edge. As its name suggested, it was an inn but it was also the only lighthouse in Tal.

The bay was large enough to confuse sailors on unclear nights and there were many rocky spots that needed to be avoided. The Light House Inn was Tal's most famous landmark and it was renowned by many.

It was so popular, that it was a standard fixture in most sea-shanties including the very popular "The Light That Never Goes Out" and the not quite as popular "Show Me the Way."

The Inn part of the Lighthouse was made of orange bricks, like most buildings in Tal, and had many curved windows. Spires adorned the tops of the roof and windows. The lighthouse itself was taller than the Inn section, and was higher than any other building in Tal. The lighthouse was made of smooth stone and had a large reflecting crystal at the top.

A large fire pit sat underneath the crystal, the source of the light. The crystal had been created by one of the first settlers of Tal; it was the result of a failed attempt to make a new type of artificial sweetener.

Thankfully for the party – and especially Zeroth and Uncle Shameless, it was one of the few inns that had other species in mind when it was built, so not everything was duck-sized. Mudd pushed open the large double front doors and led the group into the warm Inn.

"Who have you brought me now, Mr. Mudd?" asked a calm female voice.

"Ah, greetings again Tuuga!" said Mudd to the tiny turtle Innkeeper. She was about the same height as Mudd and was smoking a corncob pipe. She wore a yellow ribbon tied into a bow at the back of her neck.

Mudd motioned for everyone to come over to meet Tuuga.

"This is Tuuga, she runs this place and the lighthouse," explained duck-man.

Tuuga nodded her wrinkled turtle head, "Yes, it's been in the family for years. Many a generation of my family have helped guide sailors from the waters of Ralk using our lighthouse."

Mudd nodded, "Tuuga would you kindly take care of those poor folks for the evening, I will return in the morrow to fetch them. They've had a long walk this day."

"It would be my pleasure Mr. Mudd. This way please," directed Tuuga with her short turtle arms. She showed the party to a large room with several beds, "Lay down and get some rest, and make sure to get up early for breakfast tomorrow!" said Tuuga as she slammed the door behind herself.

Everyone found a bed and fell asleep instantly. Steve slept soundly and dreamed of talking dragons.

Fiach-Ra lurked in the shadows of his domed throne room. He drummed his clawed fingers impatiently on the armrest of his royal seat. He had summoned another Mystic to his presence, but not just any Mystic; this was the Elder Mystic of Zuu.

He was second only to Fiach-Ra in the eyes of the followers of Zuu. The Elder Mystic was an old, powerful wizard – more powerful then he let the Hawk-King know.

The throne room doors opened and in walked the Elder Mystic. He was a bulky, fat vulture with a bald head and beady eyes. He was escorted by two Royal Guards and was led right to stairs of Fiach-Ra's throne. The oversized vulture kneeled in front of his king until Fiach-Ra told him to rise.

"You were told about what happened in Uth, correct?" asked Fiach-Ra.

The Elder Mystic nodded, "You mean of course, The Village Formally Known as Uth, The Last Human Village?" he replied with a sinister grin that ran along his aged, crooked beak.

"I'll have you know," continued the Elder Mystic "That the scribes in the library are not too happy about that. They have been working nonstop to update all the maps in Arx Vena'Tor. Not to mention the trouble of having to make such a long name fit, 'The Village Formally Known as Uth, The Last Human Village'? I'll never understand humans."

"That aside," replied Fiach-Ra "What are we to do about The Boy since he is protected by that wretched blue heron amulet?"

"Ah, very simple my lord," answered the Elder Mystic. He snapped his gnarled antiquated fingers. Two much smaller vultures waddled into the throne room carrying a hefty book. The Elder Mystic pointed to the ground in front of him with a swift jab of a clawed finger.

The two smaller vultures kneeled in front of the Elder Mystic with the large book on their backs. The Elder Mystic opened the book and gently flipped through the thin yellow pages.

"According to this, the amulet will always protect him from harm," said the vulture Mystic.

Irritated, Fiach-Ra slammed the butt of his spear into the ground.

"Patience, O favorite of Zuu," said the Elder Mystic in a slightly cynical tone. He pointed to another passage, "However there is a way."

"Go on," said Fiach-Ra, watching the Mystic's every move with his flaming eyes.

"The blue heron amulet, while filled with the magic of the eagle goddess Zaa, will not work on ground held by Zuu.

"How is that possible?" asked the Hawk-King, thankful for finally hearing some good news.

"I do not know why, I imagine it something to do with one's power canceling the other's out. Just how the Sword of Zaa is-pardon me-was the only weapon that could defeat you, Highness, and vice versa."

Fiach-Ra began to smile within the shadows as the Elder Mystic continued, "So, all you have to do is to bring The Boy back to Arx Vena'Tor...and then you can destroy him."

The Elder Mystic slammed the book shut. The force of the book closing caused one of the vultures to fall flat on the ground, with the book landing on top of his head.

"Excellent work, Rarlup," said Fiach-Ra.

Rarlup the Elder Mystic bowed and exited the throne room along with his two smaller vulture aides. As he walked down the Hall of Accomplishments outside the throne room, Rarlup thought about sacrificing The Boy to Zuu himself.

Perhaps then he would be powerful enough to topple Fiach-Ra and claim the Spear of Zuu as his own.

"*U'nala!*" bellowed Fiach-Ra from his throne. His one-winged second in command fell into the room from one of the side doors. He had been eavesdropping on to Fiach-Ra and Rarlup's conversation by the doorway.

"You called for U'nala, Mighty One?"

Fiach-Ra spread his massive hawk wings and swooped down from his throne. He landed near U'nala, causing the floor to shake.

"Old friend," spoke Fiach-Ra gently, "Spread word that The Boy is to be brought back to Arx Vena'Tor – alive. Offer a reward. A large one."

U'nala thought for a moment, trying to do some math in his head. "U'nala will have to check with Kingdom Finance, he is not sure how much we could offer."

Fiach-Ra glared at U'nala.

"But U'nala is sure they can move some numbers around to make it fit into the budget," finished the Wing-Master, nervously.

"Good. Now, prepare search parties to go out after The Boy," explained the Hawk-King as he began his impatient pacing once more "Send one in each direction, and make it known that *anyone* can claim the reward."

U'nala bowed his head in agreement.

"I will lead the search party for the West," decreed the Hawk-King "I *will* find The Boy, no matter where I have to search!" Fiach-Ra's rage added strength to his words, causing them to boom and echo in the large throne room.

Fiach-Ra continued his restless pacing, as his rant about finding Steve grew more feverish.

However, U'nala was not listening. An idea sparked in the Wing-Master's head. "Highness," began U'nala carefully "Perhaps you *shouldn't* go searching for this The Boy person."

Fiach-Ra spun on his taloned heels, insulted. "What?!"

U'nala gulped loudly and held up his hands, he knew that the Hawk-King was not very fond of being accused of weakness.

"What U'nala means to say is, perhaps it might be too dangerous for your Highness."

Fiach-Ra narrowed his flaming eyes at his old comrade, creating an unnatural tension in the room.

"Are you implying that *I* cannot handle a *child*?" asked the Hawk-King bitterly.

"Of course not, Favorite of Zuu," said U'nala, hoping to quell his king's rage by calling him by a few of his titles "It is not the child that concerns U'nala, it is the *magic* protecting him."

The Hawk-King took a deep breath and let out a loud huff, suggesting that Fiach-Ra realized he had a point.

"The...*incident* at The Village Formally Known as Uth, The Last Human Village is but one example of the power protecting him," continued U'nala, knowing he was treading on thin ice by referencing the Hawk-King's failure to capture The Boy.

"The last thing U'nala wants is to see his Highness put in danger."

The Hawk-King paced back and forth even more impatiently, thinking over U'nala's words. He came to a stop next to the one-winged warrior and let out a loud, irritated, sigh.

"Perhaps...you are right, old friend."

"You humble U'nala with your kind words, Highness," replied U'nala, who was filled with tremendous glee, which he did his best to hide. Unfortunately his best was not very good at all, and U'nala stood there giggling uncontrollably.

"I shall arrange transport for you," said Fiach-Ra, entering the pool of light pouring in from the hole in the rotunda's roof.

U'nala did not want transport arranged for him. He had been waiting to unveil his own invention and this was the prime opportunity.

"That will not be necessary Highness, U'nala has his own-"

Fiach-Ra shook his head as he interrupted his second in command, "No. You will take the transport I'll arrange for you, it will also aid in your search,"

U'nala bowed respectfully, but cursed to himself quietly.

"What was that?" asked Fiach-Ra.

"Er, um. Nothing my Lord, will that be all?"

"No. I want you to take those two *idiots* from the front gate with you. They talked to The Boy and have seen him, they may be of use to you."

U'nala nodded and exited the throne room, leaving the Hawk-King standing alone in the pool of moonlight. Fiach-Ra looked up through the rotunda's large hole at the two moons of Eyri.

"You haven't won yet…" Fiach-Ra said to the moons hatefully. He reached up with a clawed hand and pretended to crush the glowing moons.

"Okay, you were right," Kaz confessed to his partner outside the front gate of Da'Rahga.

"About what?" asked Remmit as he leaned against his spear.

Kaz held up the blindfold Remmit had lent him the night before "It worked, you were right," said Kaz sheepishly.

"I told you!" exclaimed Remmit "That blindfold works wonders, it blocks out the annoying light from the Wall of Fire. What about the earplugs?"

Kaz blinked several times, "Those were earplugs?"

"Yes," answered Remmit slowly, afraid of where the next part of the conversation was going to lead.

"Oh…well I thought I was suppose to eat them."

Remmit rolled his large hawk eyes, "No, you put those in your ears…that's kind of why they are called 'earplugs.'"

"Well," replied Kaz "They certainly plugged something up."

A look of disgust came over Remmit's face "I don't even wanna know. But this is great, now that you know they work, we can start working together."

"Yes, I would like to uh…ingest your company," said the large, slow thinking Swantan guard.

"In-*vest*," corrected Remmit "Excellent, after our shift we can go down to Wheezy's House of Pies and work out the details, I hope that –"

A pair of horrible screeches cutting through the night air interrupted Remmit.

"Look!" yelled Kaz "Pyrix!"

Above the Wall of Fire, two Pyrix flew out into the night sky. They circled around and headed towards the ground near the gate.

"It looks like they are dragging something behind them," said Remmit. He could barely make out a great chariot being pulled by the two large Pyrix. Several chains ran from collars around the necks of the fiery beasts, connecting them to the chariot.

"Whoever is driving that chariot is having a hard time keeping it level," explained Remmit as the chariot swung madly through the air.

Eventually the Pyrix landed and walked towards the two guards, dragging the chariot with them. Their burning bodies lit up the area around them. The chariot stopped in front of Remmit and Kaz. U'nala turned to face the pair, towering above them from within the chariot.

"Come with U'nala, gate guards Crammit –"

"Remmit," interrupted the Hawken guard.

U'nala narrowed his eyes as he glared at Remmit.

Kaz leaned over to his partner, "...Does this mean we're not going to Wheezy's House of Pies?"

Steve woke up the next morning with the sun shining brightly into the room.

"Ugh, what a horrible dream," he said while sitting up in bed. He was thankful all of that talking bird nonsense was only a dream and now everything was back to normal.

"Bad dream eh? What was it about?" asked a calm female voice.

"It was about this crazy..." Steve turned towards the voice to find Tuuga looking at him as she made up the other beds. The boy quickly realized he was still in Eyri and it had not been a dream, much to this his disappointment.

"...Never mind," he sighed.

"You had a bad dream about the Nevermine? I'm not surprised, tis a wicked place."

"No I...wait, what?"

"You said you have a bad dream about Nevermine," answered Tuuga softly as she tucked in a bed sheet corner "And I said-"

"I know what you said," interrupted Steve "I said 'never *mind*. Not Nevermine, what's the Never-"

"Don't interrupt adults," scolded the turtle innkeeper. Steve apologized and Tuuga continued, "Tis a wicked place, the Nevermine. You would not want to go there, trust me."

"Yes, but what *is* it?" asked the boy impatiently.

Tuuga dropped the pillow she was fluffing and looked around to see if anyone else was listening. She tiptoed close to Steve and leaned next to him, so that her wrinkled turtle face was only a few inches away from his.

"They say-"

"*They?* They who?" asked Steve. Tuuga slapped him on the hand lightly with her little turtle claw, and scolded Steve once more for interrupting.

"They say," continued Tuuga, "That it leads to a lost underground kingdom, a kingdom that was one of the first in Eyri's history."

"So...why doesn't someone just go down there and find out?" asked Steve practically.

Tuuga shook her head, "No one really knows where to find it."

"Yet everyone seems to know about it?"

"Oh yes, it is a very popular legend."

Steve shook his head. He jumped out of his bed and went to dining room of the Lighthouse Inn. He looked around for Uncle Shameless, Zeroth and Eira. He found them already sitting at a table, chatting.

"I don't know how he knew my name," Zeroth confessed over the clamor of the other patrons, "I've never met him before yesterday."

"Are you sure?" asked Eira.

"I'm fairly certain I'd remember meeting someone with flames pouring out of his eyes."

Steve walked up the table unannounced and pulled out a seat for himself, "What're you talking about?" he asked.

"Nothing," Zeroth answered coldly.

"Well g'mornin' sleepy bones!" crooned Uncle Shameless as he reached over and ruffled Steve's hair. Steve had joined the others just in time for breakfast, which consisted of a lavish spread of fruit, fish and fresh bread.

Uncle Shameless nearly caused a riot when he mistakenly asked for eggs over easy.

After breakfast, Zeroth took Gladius out to see if the silver swordfish was in a better mood. It seemed to be, for the moment at least, and treated the party to tales of high adventure from his days with the last human king, Donal the Mighty.

"So we're out in the woods, yeah? Lookin' for the proper flower arrangement to go with dinner an' Donal wanted these horrid blue flowers an' I said to him 'No! Those will clash with her dress!'...Or were they orange...Hmm, I can't remember exactly, but trust me, they were *ghastly*."

"For a talking weapon that's been around for a few hundred years, you have some really boring stories," said Uncle Shameless.

"Well *excuse* me! Maybe if I hadn't been *forsaken* for the last few centuries I would have something a little better! You g'head and spend the next hundred years or so locked in a chest and see how many adventures *you* have, drunkie!"

The other patrons of the Inn began turning their attention to the yelling silver swordfish and all other conversations stopped. Steve felt chills of embarrassment beginning to creep up his spine.

"It's all because of that lousy Sword of Zaa! I could have been the one that scarred Fiach-Ra, but *nooooo*-pmphtm!" mumbled the swordfish as Zeroth picked it up and stuffed it back inside his cloak while trying to avoid the piercing eyes of the other customers.

"Of all the magical talking swords out there, I get the only one that is emotionally unstable," sighed Zeroth.

Mudd the duck eventually showed up to collect the party. He climbed onto a high stool next to their table.

"Well my friends, I have good news and bad news."

Without waiting for anyone to say which they wanted first, Mudd started with the good news "I was able to find my cousin, he is docked in town at the moment."

"Will he help us?" asked Eira.

"Only," began Mudd as he helped himself to some unfinished food "If you ask him."

"What's the bad news?" asked Zeroth.

"It seems that your chum the Hawk-King has put out a hefty reward for young Steve's *live* capture. They want him brought back to Arx Vena'Tor kicking and screaming," explained Mudd in between bites of bread.

"So what? They want me alive, no big deal," sighed Steve.

Mudd shook his small duck head, "You do not understand. The Hawk-King rarely offers rewards, except when hiring Hunters," Mudd nodded to Zeroth before continuing "And even when he does it is only to his own warriors. But this time he has opened it up to *anyone*."

"Oh my," gasped Eira.

Zeroth nodded in agreement, "This is bad. There are enough shady characters in Eyri to make our quest a lot more interesting."

The bird-man leaned in close to Mudd and whispered, "Have you heard if the Hawk-King filed a Formal Compliant against me?"

"Yes," whispered Mudd, "I heard that someone at Arx Vena'Tor filled out a Formal Hunter Compliant Form yesterday."

Zeroth buried his face in his hands, suddenly feeling very ill, "What *type* of Form?"

Mudd leaned back on his stool, "I heard it was a...dash TB," he said mysteriously as if speaking about something blasphemous. Behind the duck, someone gasped and dropped a plate.

"Shhh!" hushed Zeroth as a concerned and hardened look crossed over his face.

"There, there," said Mudd as he patted Zeroth's muscular arm with his small hand. Everyone was worried for one reason or another, except Uncle Shameless who had fallen asleep in his chair and was snoring loudly.

"Not to mention there are not too many humans around Tal. Especially after the incident in The Village Formally Known as Uth, The Last Human Village," added Mudd "Speaking of, you might want to watch for survivors out for revenge."

Uncle Shameless fell down into his plate of fish with a loud series of snores and an even louder CRASH.

"Gwah," he said as he picked bits of fish off his face "What'd I miss?"

"We just found out that the Hawk-King put a price on our heads so large that pretty much everyone in Eyri will be looking for us. So y'know, nothing *too* new for us," Steve explained mockingly.

15

Mudd looked around the Lighthouse Inn cautiously and leaned in closer to everyone, "So where is it you have to go?"

"Some place called Dragons Well," explained Zeroth, his voice hollow and distant.

"Hmm, I do not know where that is, but my cousin might. If it is somewhere in the Ralk Sea, I'm sure it will be a dangerous quest."

"I've had enough danger already, thank you very much," whined Steve as he played with his leftover food.

"Oh, don't be such a chicken!" bellowed Uncle Shameless deafeningly.

The entire dining room of the Lighthouse Inn went silent; the only sound was someone behind Mudd dropping another plate.

Uncle Shameless looked around the silent room, "What?"

"What did you say?!" yelled an angry, husky voice from a dark corner of the dining room.

"Now what?" said Steve with a groan. He watched other patrons move out of the way as a fast moving creature headed towards Uncle Shameless. Chairs were knocked over, as were other patrons, as a shadowy figure approached their table quickly.

Uncle Shameless still had no idea what was going on.

"What?" he said to Mudd who had a look of terror on his green-feathered face.

Slowly Uncle Shameless turned to see what Mudd was looking at: a five foot tall stocky chicken. Steve could tell he was a rooster by the large crest on his head. He wore random pieces of armor, and had spurs attacked to his scaly bare feet.

On his back was a large axe covered with dark stains and scratches. Steve could tell this rooster had seen a few fights because of all the scars covering his face and the exposed parts of his feathery body.

"*What* did you say?" demanded the chicken as it stared down at Uncle Shameless in his seat.

Before Uncle Shameless could answer, the rooster continued "I do not know where you humans got the idea that we chickens are cowardly, do you want me to *prove* it to you that we are not?!"

The rooster made a fist and waved it in a threatening manner in front of Uncle Shameless' face.

Tuuga ran up as fast as her little turtle legs would let her and stood between Uncle Shameless and the angry rooster.

"Now c'mon, Jer, he didn't mean anything by that. He's from out of town," she explained, but still the rooster seemed ready to cut Uncle Shameless in two with his large axe.

Uncle Shameless leaned towards Zeroth, "I take it you guys don't use the word 'chicken' the same way we do back home huh?"

Zeroth shook his head, "How'd you guess?" he quipped as he started to stealthily reach inside his cloak for Gladius.

"I'm talking to you human!" continued Jer the rooster.

"Don't worry, I'll handle this," Uncle Shameless whispered to Zeroth, putting his hand on Zeroth's arm before the Hunter took out his weapon. Uncle Shameless leaned back towards the rooster.

"Friend, I apologize. I misspoke."

"You certainly did!"

"What I meant to say was, 'O be such a chicken!' I was trying to inspire the boy you see, to be as brave and fierce as you clearly are," explained Uncle Shameless as bits of his breakfast fell off of his face.

Jer looked confused "That does not sound grammatically correct."

"Yes, well it's an old proverb back home and they don't always translate too well into modern speech," lied Uncle Shameless.

"'O be such a chicken' is a human proverb?" asked the fowl warrior.

"You better believe it! In fact, it's practically a regular greeting back home. You'll walk down the street and people will shout 'O be such a chicken!' right boy?" Uncle Shameless said to Steve. He kicked Steve gently under the table to get the boy's attention.

"Yes, yes it is," replied Steve slowly and cynically. "In fact, it's our state motto," he added with a smile. Uncle Shameless glared at Steve quickly and then looked back at Jer,

"Y'see? A simple slip of the tongue on my part, I apologize," said Uncle Shameless with a charismatic smile.

Jer looked at Uncle Shameless for several moments and then at turned his gaze to Steve.

"You should heed his advice young one. Apology accepted friend."

Jer turned and walked back to his table slowly. Tuuga breathed a sigh of relief and proceeded to set up the chairs that the angry rooster had knocked over.

"Continue being the great big chicken you are, good sir!" Uncle Shameless yelled after Jer, before he glared at his nephew.

"State motto?" he shook his head disapprovingly at the boy's ad lib "Now *that's* just silly."

The group said their good-byes and thank-yous to Tuuga and followed Mudd to the famous docks of Tal. To hide themselves, Mudd had given everyone a long dark cloak to wear, except for Zeroth who already had one.

Unfortunately because everyone in the group was taller than most of the population of the duck town, the tall cloaked figures stood out in the crowd rather easily and the fact that it was a bright sunny day did not help either.

"I think we're getting more looks now than before," Steve noted observantly, noticing the many pairs of eyes following them.

"Nonsense," replied Mudd "You blend, don't worry."

"Too bad we don't have those ravens' mist cloaks," added Steve "Those would come in handy."

"No they wouldn't," countered Uncle Shameless "I never want to turn to mist again." He shuddered, thinking about his fight with the raven twins and turning to mist along with Delu.

"Let's keep quiet about all of that, okay?" suggested Zeroth from the back of the group. He tried not to think about his old mentor, Cam.

Eventually the group reached the Main Docks of Tal, which were a series of long wooden docks that reached far out into the bay from every direction. Boats and ships of all sizes sat tied to the docks and rocked gently in the water.

Steve had never seen so many ships and boats before. Some were very large, others were much smaller. Crews ran up and down the docks to their respective ships carrying supplies or just trying to make it to their vessel before it left without them.

The planks of the dock creaked and groaned under Steve's feet, and he felt some of them give a little under his steps.

"What's that smell?" asked Steve as a familiar odor attacked his nostrils.

"Oh, that's just the sea," answered Mudd.

Steve was fairly certain he didn't just smell the sea, but he could not be certain. He absent mindedly looked around, his head hidden under his dark cloak. He thought he caught a pair of eyes watching him from behind a pile of crates.

Steve drew his cloak tighter and walked closer to Uncle Shameless. He glanced back at the eyes again, but they were gone.

The group traveled for a while down the nearly endless alleys of docks and ships until Mudd came to a stop.

"Here is my cousin's ship," he said proudly as he gestured to next dock "But I have to warn you," Mudd whispered "He is a little...*odd.*"

Steve rolled his eyes, "I would expect nothing less."

"Wait!" yelled Uncle Shameless. He started smiling broadly and looked at Mudd.

"You say your cousin is a little odd, right?"

"Yes."

"So, would you say that he is so odd that he is," Uncle Shameless paused for effect, "'Quackers'?!" Uncle Shameless stumbled around while laughing at his bad joke.

He kept laughing until he realized everyone had left him standing by himself. Uncle Shameless took a drink from his wineskin, "Sheesh, tough crowd."

The companions walked down the rickety wooden dock and came to a stop at the last vessel. It was about medium size; not nearly as large as the massive cargo ships they had passed but bigger than most of them.

Steve noticed that at the front of the ship was a large figurehead in the shape of an eagle's face and beak. It was so large that it took up most of the bow of the ship. As the morning light gleamed off the eagle's beak, Steve realized that it was made of some kind of metal and not wood. He wondered why a ship would need a metal figurehead.

"*That's* your cousin's boat?" asked Steve skeptically.

"*Ship,*" corrected a high pitched voice with authority.

Mudd turned around, "Ah there he is! Allow me to introduce my cousin and captain of this boa-*ship*, Alexander The Small!" Mudd made a grand gesture to the green feathered duck standing on the deck of the ship.

Alexander the Small *was* in fact very small, even for a duck. He was barely three feet high and had difficulty seeing everyone over the edge of the ship. He wore a pair of ratty shorts held up by miss-matched suspenders that crossed the front of his chest forming a giant 'X.'

Alexander's eyes were wild and his feathers disheveled, suggesting he'd been out to sea far too long. On his head he wore a dented saucepan, with the long handle sticking out behind him, a string of beads tied to a feather hung from the tip of the handle.

Steve studied the little duck, paying particular attention to his dented sauce pan hat "Oh, this is just *swell*," he said sarcastically.

Alexander jumped from the deck of the ship and landed on the dock next to Mudd. They hugged briefly, and Mudd turned to leave "You are in good hands friends," he walked to Steve, "And good luck to you young sir," he said with a little bow.

Alexander the Small took careful steps around Steve and the rest of the group, looking them over.

"So, Muddy tells me you need to go somewhere," he said, looking up at Zeroth with suspiciously, "And that you need to hide from ol' Fire Eyes."

"Yes we do," answered Zeroth coldly, detecting Alexander's critical gaze.

"You certainly have an interesting name," said Eira cheerfully.

Alexander put his hands on his little duck hips and smiled widely, "Thank you, it was my mother's."

Alexander led the group onto his ship, *The Griffin*. It was then that everyone noticed the lack of sails. In the middle of the ship where the main sails should have been, was a giant tree covered with bright green leaves.

Two large paddle-wheels half sticking out of the water jutted out from both sides of the ship. It reminded Steve of the old ferry boat that River City had resting in dry dock near the Grand River, *The Ypsilanti Queen*.

Before anyone could ask where the sails were, Uncle Shameless spoke up, "So Al, what's with your metal hat there?"

Alexander turned to face the much taller human, "Oh it is very important, all of my crew wears iron pots and pans on their heads," explained Alexander, "And so will all of you when we depart."

"Why?" questioned Steve, even though he was afraid of what the answer would be.

Alexander moved in closer to the group, as if he was about to share an important secret. *"Pixie People,"* he whispered slowly and seriously.

"Excuse me?" asked Steve, almost yelling in disbelief.

"Pixie People," said Alexander again. "They don't like iron. Keeps 'em away y'know."

"O-kaaaay..." replied Steve as he looked at the others; gladly noticing that they were wearing confused looks as well.

"And why do the...*Pixie People*...bother you?" asked Steve as he looked for the nearest exit off the ship.

"Oh, they don't mean any harm," explained Alexander.

"No, of course not," answered Steve in an unconvinced tone.

"But they are a bit annoying, and it's best to just keep them away," said Alexander as he tapped on his saucepan.

"And just where do the Pixie People come from?" asked the boy, who was considering jumping off the ship as soon as possible.

"Why, the Pixie Tree of course," answered Alexander as he pointed to the large tree in the middle of the ship.

Steve nodded nervously, "Of course," he said with a fake tone of understanding. *We have to get away from this crazy duck ASAP*, Steve thought to himself.

Alexander the Small looked over the group and noticed their uneasiness. He adjusted his saucepan-hat and spoke calmly, "You don't believe me. You think I'm crazy."

"What? No, no," lied the group in unison – except for Uncle Shameless.

"Well I can't speak for everyone," grinned Uncle Shameless as he swayed to and fro on the deck, "But I think you're a little *quacker-*"

"Please. Don't," interrupted Steve.

Alexander shook his head, "I guess I'll have to show you what I mean, and then you'll tell me where you need to go."

Steve was about to tell the little duck captain that he did not have to take them anywhere when Alexander turned around and started yelling towards the cabin at the back of *The Griffin*.

"Julius! Hector! Get on deck, and bring extra head-gear!"

Alexander's two-man crew burst out of the cabin in a blur of feathers and iron. The pair made their way to Alexander and came to a quick halt, carrying iron pots and pans for Steve and the others to wear on their heads.

As his crew handed out the iron head-gear to the others, Alexander made the introductions. Hector was a small, pudgy penguin with long fin-like arms and fingers. Even though he was small, he was still taller than Alexander. He wore an iron colander on his head that covered up both his eyes, wore torn shorts not unlike Alexander's and was fist-mate of *The Griffin*.

Next was Julius, the navigator. He was the tallest of the trio at just under six feet. He was a strong looking albatross who, like most of the bird-people of Eyri, had arms but no wings.

Julius wore a flat iron frying pan tied on his head with several holes cut in it to allow feathers to stick out. Strings of beads hung from the tip of the pan's handle.

Steve and the others put the various iron cookware on their heads and followed Alexander the Small as he led them to the large tree in the center of the ship.

"It all started many years ago – the sea was angry that day my friends!" Alexander began dramatically. "We were sailing towards the North when we saw a huge cloud of smoke. Julius noticed it was coming from a secluded lagoon that was reachable from the coast.

"We entered the lagoon, and in it was a small forest filled with trees like this one," Alexander gestured to the large tree behind him "And they were all on fire. Then we saw hundreds of Pixie People flying around and around and around and around –"

Hector slapped Alexander upside the back of his head,

"...Sorry," apologized Alexander before continuing. "Anyway, it turns out the Hawk-King had decided to torch the forest, because all of those trees were their homes."

Hector and Julius nodded in unison.

"Why?" asked Eira.

"Because it was *there*," explained Alexander with a hint of a sniffle.

"That's reason enough for him," said Zeroth knowingly.

"So, we took one of the skiffs to the shore and a bunch of Pixie People flew over to us and asked us to save them. So we dug up the only tree that wasn't burning, along with some dirt and they've been with us ever since."

Hector and Julius nodded again and walked away to go get the ship ready for departure. Hector climbed a rope ladder up to the look-out post – which was nothing more than a barrel attached to a pole sticking out of the top of the Pixie Tree.

Eira smiled, "Well that certainly was an honorable thing to do, but now tell us – why doesn't your ship have any sails?"

Alexander held up his hands, "Not just yet. First, tell me where it is you want to go?"

"Dra-"

"But before that, tell me why you have a Hunter with you," demanded Alexander. Zeroth snapped to attention, caught off guard by the little duck's question.

"I spotted your pendent," explained Alexander, pointing to Zeroth's black three-ringed Hunter's pendent. The tall bird-man cursed at himself for not hiding it earlier.

"It's okay," answered Steve calmly, "He's helping us."

"I bet," snapped Alexander "For how much?"

"Nothing," replied Zeroth firmly.

"Oh, *really?*" said Alexander as he narrowed his eyes at Zeroth "And why is that?"

"It was a friend's dying wish," answered Zeroth as he tightened his yellow scarf.

Alexander the Small narrowed his eyes even more at Zeroth, so much that they were barely open. There was an eerie, awkward silence for several moments.

"Okay then, fine by me!" bellowed Alexander happily, his eyes opening to their fullest "Now, where is it you want to go?"

Zeroth leaned in, "Some place called-"

"Captain!" yelled Hector from the look-out barrel on top of the Pixie Tree.

Alexander looked up at his penguin first-mate.

"What is it?" yelled the little duck in his high pitched voice.

"Pyrix!"

U'nala held on tightly to the chains controlling the fiery Pyrix as they pulled the chariot through the air. Not that it mattered, the giant flaming skeletal birds flew wherever they wanted, making the ride in the chariot rather bumpy.

U'nala never understood how Fiach-Ra could get the beasts to fly straight when he rode his chariot. U'nala was not having any luck keeping the Pyrix under control. They had a habit of doing random high climbs into the air, only to swoop down in spiral patterns. Still, U'nala thought to himself, it was nice to be in the sky again.

Kaz the Swantan hung tightly to the edge of the chariot with his large clawed hands. Since his ancestors had bred out wings many generations ago, he was not used to flying like his Hawken companions were.

"Now I know why we decided to get rid of our wings," whined Kaz as he held his stomach.

Remmit, the Hawken warrior, was actually enjoying the wild ride through the air.

"Don't be such a hatchling," scolded Remmit. "I'll admit these Pyrix aren't the best at pulling this chariot, but it's nice to relax and let them do the work."

"Ugh, can we turn back? I think I lost my stomach on that last dive," complained Kaz.

U'nala turned to face the bickering warriors,

"U'nala would appreciate it if you would stop your complaining and start looking for this The Boy person," he said as Tal appeared underneath them.

"Okay, okay," said Kaz as he looked over the edge of the chariot and down at the crowded streets below. He scanned the screaming crowds on the ground, "There he is!"

U'nala pulled the chains of the Pyrix quickly, causing them to bank sharply in the air. As the chariot turned, the back end crashed into the top of a building, sending rubble flying to the streets.

"Where is he?! U'nala does not see him!" bellowed the Wing-Master.

"Over there!" Kaz yelled again.

U'nala turned the chariot again, and one of the Pyrix flew through a roof, setting it on fire, and emerged unharmed on the other side.

"Where?! U'nala still does not see him!" barked the angered Hawken.

"Isn't that him?" asked Kaz, pointing towards a crowd.

Both U'nala and Remmit looked, "That's not him!" yelled Remmit, "It doesn't even look like him!"

"What's he look like again?" asked Kaz as he took great pains to try and remember Steve.

"A small hu-man!"

"Yeah, that's not him. That's a duck," confessed the slow thinking swan-warrior.

The crowd below watched in horror as the flying chariot made a crash landing after Remmit lunged for Kaz's neck, causing the chariot to flip over in mid-air.

"I don't think they know you are here," said Hector as he descended the rope ladder expertly. "It looked like they were just scoutin' around. But you can bet that everyone in town will know who they are lookin' for now that they've landed."

"They landed?" asked Alexander the Small.

"*Crashed* is more like it. I don't know who was steerin' that chariot the Pyrix were pullin', but that thing was swayin' around like a ship in a storm."

Alexander turned to look at Steve and the rest of the group, "Grab a hold of somethin'! We're takin' off!"

Alexander ran as fast as his little duck legs would let him up to helm of *The Griffin*. Julius the albatross joined him and grabbed a hold of the steering wheel. Hector the penguin stood next to a panel full of levers, switches, and bells.

"Hoist anchor!" ordered Alexander from behind his crew. He made his way up a raised section of the helm's deck, which looked like a short set of stairs that went nowhere, until he was eye level with his tall navigator.

"Untie the boat!" bellowed Uncle Shameless drunkenly.

Hector pulled a lever. Gears started churning towards the bow of the ship. A heavy chain began winding up and making loud CLUNK-CLUNK sounds as it pulled up the ship's anchor.

However, once the anchor broke the surface of the water, Steve realized it was not a regular anchor. It was a large boxy, metal stove.

"Why is the anchor a *stove*?" he asked Alexander.

"Long story."

Alexander turned to Hector, "Sound the bell!" he commanded.

Hector the penguin reached up and rang a large bell several times. The loud CLANGS rang over and over. Then there was silence as the ship rocked gently in the water.

"...Should something be happening?" Steve asked as he still thought about jumping off the ship.

"Quiet you!" answered Alexander "Look!" he pointed to the Pixie Tree.

Steve looked at the Pixie Tree, the green leaves swayed gently in the sea breeze.

"Yes, it's very lovely," said Steve sarcastically.

Alexander shook his head and pointed again. Suddenly, hundreds of pin-head sized lights started glowing in the tree, and a moment later they flew out of the tree in giant swarms.

Hector rang the bell again and the giant swarm of Pixie People broke up into two smaller groups. Each flew down one of the two hatches on either side of the deck next to the paddle wheels.

"Full speed ahead!" yelled Alexander the Small.

Hector pulled two levers, one labeled for each paddle wheel to notch that said 'Full Speed Ahead.' Instantly, the two paddle wheels started turning in the water, and the ship started to move.

Gradually the wheels built up more and more speed until the ship was cutting through the water effortlessly, leaving the docks of Tal in the distance.

Zeroth's jaw dropped, amazed by the ship's mode of transportation.

"But how?" he asked Alexander.

The duck smiled and looked up at his navigator, "Take us a safe distance out Mr. Julius, I'm going to take them below," Alexander ordered.

The albatross nodded underneath his iron frying pan hat and continued steering *The Griffin* out into the open Ralk Sea.

Alexander the Small led the group down a creaky ladder into the hull of the ship. They came to a wooden door, behind which they could hear the rowdy churning of the paddle wheels.

"Just make sure to keep your hats on," reminded Alexander as he opened the door.

He opened the door and everyone was blinded for a moment by two bright swirls of light. They walked in, shielding their eyes with their hands. Alexander pointed to one of the bright swirls. It reminded Steve of spinning fireworks display.

"You see, I have the Pixie People fly down here and they turn these cranks," he pointed to the large cranks on either side of the ship that the Pixie People were turning with blazing speed, "and the cranks turn the paddle wheels." The cranks were attached to a series of gears that were connected to the axles of the paddle wheels.

"Don't they get tired?" asked Eira, amazed by the limitless energy of the Pixie People.

"No, not really but they take shifts, that's all I know and there's enough of them that each pixie only has do it once a day. They don't mind either, it's their way of saying thanks."

"Well that's somethin'," said Uncle Shameless as he walked around looking at the spinning cranks, gears and pixies.

Alexander continued describing his propulsion system, "And they can go much faster too! They aren't even workin' up a sweat right now."

"This reminds me of the time," started Uncle Shameless as he turned quickly "When I was at a speed boat race, and – Ouch!" he yelped as he banged his head against a low hanging beam.

The force of the hit knocked the iron pot off his head. It landed on the wooden floor with a loud CLUNK.

"Oh no!" gasped Alexander "Put that back on, quick!"

"Huh?" asked Uncle Shameless as he rubbed his head and tried to make the room stop spinning.

Without warning, the ship lurched sharply to the right as all of the pixies from the right side crank flew over to Uncle Shameless. Everyone was knocked to the floor by the force of the quick turn. The pixies on the left crank kept working, unaware of what was going on.

Uncle Shameless was soon surrounded by Pixie People. The pinhead size balls of light floated around him.

"Hi!" said one in an eager, squeaky voice.

"Uh, hello," answered Uncle Shameless, still dizzy from the knock to his head.

"Hi! Hi!" said another.

"Hello," said Uncle Shameless again.

"HiHiHiHiHi!" said a third Pixie rapidly.

Just then, Julius' voice came crawling through a talk tube.

"What's going on down there?! We'd be going in circles if I didn't have Hector helping me keep this wheel straight!"

Alexander ran to the talk tube and yelled into it, *"All stop! We lost a helmet!"*

Julius cursed loudly on the other end of the talk tube as Alexander went looking for Uncle Shameless' iron headgear.

Uncle Shameless was now totally surrounded by the floating Pixie People, who kept saying 'Hi!' to him over and over again. He was doing his best to return each of the 'Hi!'s but was quickly running out of breath.

On the bridge, Hector and Julius let go of *The Griffin*'s steering wheel. The ship starting going in a circle, as Hector ran over to ring the bell to disengage the paddle wheels.

In the belly of *The Griffin*, the paddle wheel gears came to a dead stop at the sound of the bell. However, now that they were free of their duties, the Pixie People from the other paddle wheel started to join their friends.

Uncle Shameless was about to black out from having to say so many 'hellos' when Alexander jumped towards him with his missing iron headgear. The little green duck slammed the cooking pot onto Uncle Shameless' head with expert aim.

"Ow!" winced Uncle Shameless.

Instantly, the Pixie People began to recoil away from the man and his iron hat. The brilliant swarm split in half and each section retreated through the hatches in the roof of the crank room and headed for the safety of the Pixie Tree.

"That," panted Alexander heavily "Was a close one."

Alexander escorted everyone to the ship's mess hall and advised them to stay there until they were further out in the Ralk Sea and safely away from Tal and the Pyrix.

Hector's ringing of the bells once more was shortly followed by the sound of churning water as the Pixie People got back to work propelling the ship. Uncle Shameless lay collapsed in a makeshift hammock, made from a now useless section of sail, still recovering from his experience with the Pixie People.

He would drift off to sleep, only to wake up occasionally to yell, "Hello!"

Steve, Zeroth and Eira all found seats for themselves made out of recycled boat parts, and enjoyed the surprisingly smooth ride.

After dark, Steve heard the paddle wheels come to a stop. Alexander and his crew joined their guests in the mess hall, finally taking the time to relax.

"Now, where is it you want to go?" asked Alexander the Small from his seat, an overstuffed chair covered in an ugly mix of yellow, brown, and green beads.

"Dragons Well," said Zeroth.

"Whatever that is," added Steve.

"You are in luck," answered Alexander proudly "I know *exactly* where that is."

"It's to the North isn't it?" asked Julius, who was leaning back in a rickety chair made of old oars.

"No, that's Dragon's *Grotto*," replied Alexander knowingly.

"Wait, is that the place with the shrieking wind?" asked Hector from a lumpy beanbag cushion, also covered in a appalling arrangement of colored beads.

"I think that's Dragon's *Mine*," suggested Julius the albatross.

"Are you sure?"

"Pretty sure," continued Julius.

"I *know* where Dragons Well is, it's to the North," interrupted Alexander, his high-pitched voice rising with frustration.

Julius scratched under the dented frying pan on his head, "I though that was Dragon's *Cove*."

"Cove? Don't you mean Cave?" asked Hector, confused.

"No, 'cove'. Y'know like a lagoon? It has this really nice bea-"

"Quiet!" yelled Alexander as he banged his little fist on the table, startling Uncle Shameless awake, causing him to yell 'hello!' once more.

"What's with all these Dragon names? Are there really dragons at all these places?" asked Steve, who's head was beginning to hurt from the absurdity of the conversation.

"They're just names. Like Forbidden Forest," explained the albatross navigator.

"Yes, nothing at all to worry about," added Hector.

16

Dawn broke the next morning with the sun igniting the sky and making it a dull red. Uncle Shameless was talking to Julius as the albatross steered *The Griffin* towards Dragons Well.

"And then the captain says 'bring me my brown pants!' Ha!" laughed Uncle Shameless as he slapped Julius hard on the back, nearly knocking the navigator over the steering wheel.

"That's a good one, eh?" Uncle Shameless asked the breathless albatross. Julius shook his head weakly, still recovering from the hard slap.

Steve exited the sleeping quarters given to him and his friends with a loud yawn and walked across the deck to the bow. He stood on top of the huge metal eagle's head that covered the bow of the ship, and looked out over the open sea.

Steve was getting tired of being on the water. After the ill-fated canoe trip that brought him and Uncle Shameless to Eyri, he was not eager to go on any more boats for a long time.

Uncle Shameless walked up beside Steve and put an arm around his nephew.

"How ya doin' kiddo?" he asked, watching the sunrise.

"How am I doing? I haven't showered in days, I have walked an insane amount of miles, and I'd give anything for a toothbrush – or even just some toothpaste!"

"Ah, just think of this like a camping trip," suggested Uncle Shameless happily.

"Camping trip? At least on a camping trip I wouldn't be the part of some crazy prophecy, or referred to only as *The Boy* by a bunch of talking animals."

Noticing Steve's bitter tone, Uncle Shameless decided to change the subject, "Y'see this red dawn out here?"

Steve sighed, "Yeah, so? It's an atmospheric thing. Big deal. *I'm* more worried about the two moons. Especially that square-shaped one."

Uncle Shameless shook his head, "There's this old sayin,' 'Red sky at night, sailor's delight. Red sky at morning,' sailor take warnin.'"

Steve looked at him, unimpressed "So? What could happen?"

Uncle Shameless shrugged, "Who knows, it's just an old sailor superstition. But stay on your toes."

Steve turned and left his uncle on the eagle's head. As the boy neared the Pixie Tree, he stared up at the two moons of Eyri, which were beginning to disappear in the early morning sky.

"The Eyes of Zaa," said Eira warmly.

Steve spun around to find the pelican behind him. "Excuse me?"

Eira pointed at what was still visible of the moons with her walking stick. "The Eyes of Zaa, that is the proper name of the Two Moons."

"Why are they called that? The sun doesn't have a fancy name."

Eira cocked her head and smiled. "Let me guess," sighed Steve, "It *does*." The pelican healer nodded slowly, "The Eye of Zuu."

Steve sighed again and leaned against the ship's rail. "Okay, I'll bite. Why?"

"The legend goes that after Eyri was created, and before Zaa and Zuu had their...disagreement."

"That whole, day of the week thing?" interjected Steve.

"Yes, before that each of them wished to keep watch over their new world. Zuu, Bringer of Fire, spared one of his burning eyes and thus created the Day."

Steve scoffed at this idea, knowing very well that a sun was nothing but a giant star.

Eira continued, "But Zaa, Bringer of Water, cared more for the protection of her creation and kept watch with both of her eyes during the Night when there was no light."

"So the two moons are Zaa watching over everyone?" asked Steve.

"Yes, like a mother watching over her sleeping child."

Steve went up to the helm to watch Julius pilot *The Griffin*. He waved to Zeroth who was up in the lookout barrel, keeping his hawk-eyes peeled for trouble.

"Where is Alexander?" asked Steve, not having seen the small duck captain that morning.

"He's got a bout o'the sea-sickness. He'll be out on deck in a bit," answered Julius, in a manner that suggested this was nothing out of the ordinary.

"Wait, he gets sea-sick?"

"Yap. All the time," answered the albatross helmsman.

Steve stared at Julius, confused "But...he's a duck."

"Mainland ducks ain't sea birds," explained Julius with a wink.

"But ducks are at least used to being on water," said Steve.

"Ah, but swimmin' and bein' on a ship are two diff'rent things, now ain't they?" replied Julius with a chuckle as he spun the steering wheel gently.

"That," said Steve with much cynicism, "Is just *ridiculous*."

"What's ridiculous?" asked Alexander as he approached the helm, wiping his mouth with a small towel. His dented iron saucepan helmet bounced up and down with each step.

"Nothing," sighed Steve. *A sea captain that gets seasick, what's next?* he thought to himself.

The Griffin paddled along at a medium pace through the clear waters of the Ralk Sea as it made its way towards the mysterious Dragons Well. Steve watched the mainland of Eyri disappear from the horizon at the back of the ship while Uncle Shameless stumbled around the deck singing 'What Do You Do With a Drunken Sailor?'

Steve watched one spot of the land in particular. It was nothing more than a blotch in the distance, but it seemed to actually be *growing* instead of shrinking. He thought nothing of it and turned back to face forward.

Hector the penguin came on deck and began handing out breakfast to everyone.

"Here you go lad, eat up," said Hector from underneath his colander head-covering. He handed Steve a plate of cooked fish and some fruit.

"What's this morning's grub?" asked Alexander as he rubbed his belly expectantly.

Hector shook his head, "No grubs today, we ran out. Fish is all we have," the penguin waved a steaming hunk of fish in front of Alexander's bill. The duck quickly covered his mouth and ran to the side of the ship. A long series of retching sounds followed for several minutes. Hector the penguin waddled over to tend to his ailing captain.

Steve looked at the seasick duck, his penguin first mate, and his uncle stumbling around singing and shook his head.

"Why *me*?" he asked aloud.

"Incoming ship!" screamed Zeroth from the lookout barrel on top of the Pixie Tree. Alexander and Hector ran to the back of the ship. Alexander held out a small hand in front of Hector.

His first mate grabbed a long looking glass and placed it in the captain's hand. Alexander held the looking glass up to his eye, and Hector extended it far for him, holding up the end of the ridiculously long spyglass.

A wily mist made it difficult for the little duck to see anything that would identify the ship. He turned towards the Pixie Tree and at Zeroth. "Can you see anything with those hawk-eyes of yours?"

Zeroth looked again carefully at the incoming ship and used his gift of hawk-sight. "I see a bunch of bird-men with white feathers and wings!"

"*Gulls!*" cursed Alexander "Anything else?"

Zeroth looked again, "One of them has a silly hat!"

"*Vanderawlt!*" Alexander cursed even louder, making his little hands into little angry fists.

The silly hat wearing Gull, Vanderawlt, was the most hated pirate in all of the Ralk Sea. He would plunder helpless ships and then sell their cargo off cheaply at the nearest town to steal business from local merchants.

His wickedness did not stop there either; Vanderawlt was also prone to taking hostages, bounty hunting, or stealing cookies from charity bake sales (and selling them elsewhere cheaper, with the money going to *his* favorite charity - himself).

The Gull pirate also was notorious for watering down his ship's gruel and only allowing one bathroom break a day.

"He probably heard about the bounty on your heads," said Alexander, his wild little eyes filling with rage.

"Can't we just out run them?" asked Steve as he watched the big, boxy ship close in on them.

"Oh sure, but where is the fun in that?" Alexander said with a smile before a dark look washed over his green face. "Besides, me an' him have unfinished business."

"What happened?" asked Eira the pelican as she and Uncle Shameless joined the tiny captain.

Alexander turned, and with his hands on his hips, told his tale of woe. "It happened many a year ago. The sea was angry that day, my friends!" he bellowed dramatically.

"…Does he always start stories like this?" Steve asked Julius. The albatross nodded slowly with a look that suggested he had heard this story ten times too many.

Alexander continued his emoting. "My poor mother, Alexandria the Not-So-Small-After-Having-Hatchlings, owned a small shop on the coast of Tal. Business was great, an' everyone was happy…until one day-*Vanderawlt!*"

Steve half expected to see a flash of lighting after Alexander's last dramatic delivery.

Hector sighed quietly to himself, "Here we go again."

Alexander went on, "He showed up with his ship full of stolen goods and sold 'em cheap! He took away all of her loyal customers! She couldn't compete with his prices and drove her out of business he did! She lost her shop because of *Vanderawlt!*"

Alexander's story hit a crescendo that almost brought Steve to tears. *Almost.* "What did your mother sell?" the boy asked.

"Beads!" exclaimed Alexander, flicking the string of beads hanging from his saucepan's handle.

"Well *that* explains a few things," said Steve, thinking of the night he spent sleeping on a beaded bed spread in the ship's belly as well as all of the beaded curtains that hung in the doorways throughout the ship.

"The same thing happened to me!" sobbed Uncle Shameless. He ran towards the little duck sniveling, picked Alexander up in his arms and hugged the little duck's head. Alexander mumbled loudly while pressed hard against Uncle Shameless' chest, his little feathered arms flailed about wildly. Eventually Uncle Shameless loosened his vice-like grip on the little duck's head.

Alexander the Small looked up at Uncle Shameless, his own wild eyes filled with tears, "So you understand! Let us join together and give Vanderawlt one for!"

"This is gonna be trouble," sighed Steve.

From the lookout barrel, Zeroth yelled again "Another ship!"

"What's it look like?" yelled Alexander as he wiped away his tears.

Zeroth looked at the patchwork ship full of angry humans heading for them. He could just barely make out writing on their flag.

"It's the Uth Chamber of Commerce!"

Julius looked at Uncle Shameless, "Would you like some brown pants?"

Vanderawlt's ship, *The Frugal Gullman*, cut through the glass-like water of the Ralk Sea towards *The Griffin*. Vanderawlt pushed up his ridiculously large brimmed hat (topped with an equally ridiculously large feather) to scan the horizon.

Vanderawlt didn't know who this The Boy was, but he didn't care. He didn't stick around to hear the rest of the one-winged Hawken's speech back in Tal. All he needed to hear was size of the bounty on The Boy's head. He would have to punish he crew for not finding out which direction The Boy had escaped Tal from sooner.

He considered watering down the ship's gruel some more, but he had a feeling if he watered it down any more, he'd be better off saying that he was grueling up the ship's water.

The Gull pirate pushed the thought of punishment aside for the moment and smiled as *The Frugal Gullman* closed in on the strange-looking ship with no sails and barked at his crew to prepare for battle.

The Alderman of The Village Formally Known as Uth, The Last Human Village nursed a severe burn on his arm, and also nursed a bottle of wine, as he watched *The Griffin* come closer into view. He stood proudly on the deck of *The Uth Chamber of Commerce All Purpose Utility Ship and Choir Annex*, and thought that he was finally get used to this whole 'being in charge' thing.

Ironically, all of the village's government positions under him (Ditch Digger, Mud Inspector, and Budget Manager respectively) had not survived the attack on The Village Formally Known as Uth, The Last Human Village, so now the Alderman was the lone authority figure. After the destruction of the village, those who survived were desperate for someone to look up to, and the Alderman recognized that *he* alone had been chosen by destiny to lead his people and to rebuild Uth.

His first decree after the destruction of *his* village had been to chase down those responsible and give them a stern talking to. He knew all about this The Boy person, thanks to a well-written letter sent to him by the Hawk-King.

The letter explained that The Boy was very dangerous and that the Hawk-King *had* to destroy Uth in order to try and save the rest of Eyri from this mentally unstable stranger from another world.

The Alderman couldn't argue with that logic. Or *any* logic for that matter.

"Turn us around!" Alexander barked at Julius.

"Why not just out run them?" Steve pleaded once more.

Alexander shook his head, "No, we must face them. We'll lure them in and strike!"

Julius nodded as Hector pulled a lever that reversed the direction of the giant paddle wheels, causing the ship to turn around to face their pursuers.

"Sir, they turned to face us head on!" cried the lookout on *The Frugal Gullman*.

"Ho ho!" laughed Vanderawlt in his irritatingly nasally voice, "If it's a fight they want, then it will be a fight they get!"

"Sir, the Look-Out Committee wishes to make a motion to inform you the ship we are following has turned around!" cried a human crewmember of the *Uth Chamber of Commerce All Purpose Utility Ship and Choir Annex*.

The Alderman looked around, "Does anyone second?"

Even though he was the only figure of government left, he *was* on the Chamber of Commerce's ship and unfortunately he had to play by their rules.

No one said anything or made any movement.

"Hmm, well if no one will second the motion, then I can't allow us to be informed about that ship turning around," he yelled back to the crewmember "I want you to forget that they have turned around!"

"But sir!"

"Tut-tut, do as I say!" commanded the Alderman. He was finally getting the hang of ordering people around, and he was enjoying it quite a bit.

"We're closing in on Vanderawlt's ship," yelled Zeroth.

"Let's surprise 'em!" suggested Uncle Shameless between sips of Eldercherry wine.

"How?" asked Alexander.

Steve's jaw dropped "You're not going to listen to him are you?!"

"Why not?" asked the duck captain.

"He can barely stand up!" yelled Steve as he pointed to his uncle, who was stumbling around the deck singing to himself.

Alexander watched Uncle Shameless and shrugged, "He just hasn't gotten his sea legs yet." The duck captain turned towards

Uncle Shameless, who was in between verses of 'What Do You Do With a Drunken Sailor?' and asked him what his plan was.

Vanderawlt's Gull-man crew readied their weapons and started flapping the wings on their backs, preparing to fly towards the ship. This was part of Vanderawlt's typical attack strategy.

His Gulls would fly to the approaching ship and board it. While the fight ensued he would move up behind and start attacking the ship itself while the defending crew was kept busy fighting the Gulls.

On the Uth Chamber of Commerce ship, the Alderman fell asleep during presentations by different Chamber of Commerce members on what their battle cry should be when attacking *The Griffin*.

"You can't be serious," protested Steve as he watched Uncle Shameless, Zeroth, and Alexander prepare themselves.

"Seriousness has nothing to do with this!" explained Alexander as he tightened his crisscrossed suspenders. Zeroth removed Gladius from the interior of his cloak.

"What's all this then?" spoke the sword with its usual venom filled tone of voice, "OH, it's sunlight! Gee I haven't seen that for awhil-pmpbpht!" Zeroth groaned as he tucked the sword back into his cloak.

Alexander turned to face Hector, "You are in command, and stick to the plan, got it?" His penguin first-mate nodded.

Uncle Shameless took a long swig of Eldercherry wine as he walked towards the rear of the ship. Zeroth followed. Uncle Shameless felt the extra-ordinary strength granted by the wine fill his muscles and bellowed a thunderous "Bru-ha!"

Zeroth jumped on Uncle Shameless' back, and the man began running towards the bow of the ship. Granted blinding speed by the Eldercherry wine, Uncle Shameless reached out and grabbed Alexander in his arms.

He zoomed by Steve in a blur of flannel, armor, and feathers as he made his way to the large metal eagle's head protruding from the bow of the ship.

Just as Uncle Shameless reached the tip of the eagle's beak, he jumped with all his might, launching himself high into the air.

When they reached the zenith of the jump, Zeroth released his wings out from under his cloak. They glided effortlessly through the air and down towards *The Frugal Gullman*.

Vanderawlt did not notice the three invaders descending onto *The Frugal Gullman* until the look out was knocked from his spot thanks to a well-placed kick from Uncle Shameless. The entire crew looked up and readied their weapons.

"Let go of me, and take Alexander," commanded Uncle Shameless "We'll split up!"

"So…you want me to *drop* you?" asked Zeroth "You do realize that ship is made of wood right?"

"I'll be fine!" yelled Uncle Shameless.

Zeroth grabbed a hold of Alexander and let go of Uncle Shameless. The bird-man tucked in his wings slightly to give him a fast, but manageable decent.

Meanwhile, Uncle Shameless dropped like a rock towards the ship's deck.

As Zeroth landed, he threw Alexander at a Gull headfirst. Alexander hit the pirate in the face with his iron-covered head, knocking the Gull to the ground.

Uncle Shameless crashed through *The Frugal Gullman*'s deck and into the belly of the ship, creating a cloud of dust and debris. As Zeroth landed, he let loose a loud hawk cry, startling some of Vanderawlt's crew. Thinking a Hawken warrior was attacking them, several Gulls flew off the ship.

"You cowards!" screamed Vanderawlt from under his silly hat. He grabbed a nearby crewman by his wings. "Form two groups! One flies to their ship, and one stays here to fight - or no bathroom breaks for a *week*!" he snapped at the crewman.

"And try to capture the black one alive! There's a big price on his head too!" added Vanderawlt.

Zeroth hid his wings away once more and took out Gladius. "What is it now hm?" said the swordfish mockingly "Need a loaf of bread sliced?"

Without saying anything, Zeroth held up Gladius so it could see the approaching Gulls with swords at the ready as he removed his shield from his magical pack.

"*Yes!*" cheered Gladius "Now that's a bit more like it! Come on then!" it taunted at the nearest pirate, a lanky Gull with a fishhook stuck in his beak.

With a sly smile, Zeroth quietly squeezed the hilt-shaped fish.

Back on the Uth Chamber of Commerce ship, the Battle Cry Committee was voting on what their battle cry was to be. The committee clerk, a kindly middle-aged woman with square shaped glasses was calling for votes, "On the matter of crying 'For Uth!' in battle, please say 'aye' or 'nay.' Mr. Alderman?"

The Alderman was still sleeping soundly in his seat until he was poked in the ribs with an oar.

"Ale!" he yelled sleepily.

"Mr. Ralson?"

"Sure."

"Mrs. Bloom?"

"Boo!"

"Ms. Gently?"

"Pass."

"Mr. Waterton?"

"Umm…well…umm. No?"

"Ms. Apeltenn?

"Maybe."

The committee clerk sighed loudly and tallied the votes. She then prepared for the vote of the next battle cry,

"On the matter of crying 'For the Alderman!' in battle, please say 'aye' or 'nay…'"

Zeroth battled the swarms of Gulls that slashed at him with their long curved swords. They were no match for Gladius. The silver swordfish's blade-tongue knocked their swords aside with ease or in most cases cut their cheaply made swords in two. Gladius mumbled a series of cheers, thankful to be in battle once more.

Alexander the Small had no problems dodging the blows of the much larger Gulls and easily passed through the legs of the tall bird-men. He wielded a heavy mallet that he used to smash their feet or knees. In no time, most of his attackers were either hopping on one foot in pain or trying in vain to move with smashed knees.

Uncle Shameless lay in the pile of rubble created by his crashing through the deck of *The Frugal Gullman*. He mumbled to himself, trying to get enough of his motor skills under control to stand up. Unfortunately between the fall and the Eldercherry wine, he could barely move. Alexander ran to the large hole left by Uncle Shameless' crash landing and looked down at him.

"Oi!" yelled the small duck.

"Whazdat?" mumbled Uncle Shameless as he slowly rolled over to look up at Alexander standing on the edge of the hole.

"Get up here! We need you!"

"I can't go Mom, they stole-ed my shoeses!" bellowed Uncle Shameless incoherently.

Alexander had been prepared for such a situation. He reached into a pocket inside his shorts and pulled out a piece of paper. Just before they had jumped off *The Griffin*, Steve gave Alexander a list of things to say if Uncle Shameless needed a little extra motivation.

The little duck unfolded the piece of paper and began to read aloud.

"Ahem, 'you know that cowboy movie star you are so fond of?'" said Alexander, even though he had no idea what a cowboy or a movie star were.

Images of a gritty, statuesque cowboy hero on a movie screen filled Uncle Shameless' mind as he smiled and nodded.

"Well," continued Alexander, "'These Gull guys just said he likes to wear dresses...'" Alexander turned the paper around as he studied the confusing words, "'and that he was a lousy actor!'"

Before Alexander even had time to wonder what a lousy actor was, Uncle Shameless jumped up through the hole in a screaming fit of rage. He landed on the deck with such force that the deck shook and knocked several Gulls over.

Uncle Shameless ran towards the nearest group of Gulls and began throwing super-human punches. Winged pirates were knocked back across the deck with each punch, while others were knocked off the ship altogether.

Alexander smiled, folded up the piece of paper, put it back in his pocket, and dusted off his hands, "Marvelous!" he exclaimed before heading towards Vanderawlt.

On *The Griffin*, Steve grew nervous as a group of Gulls flew towards the ship.

"We're gonna have company!" he yelled as he unenthusiastically reached for his swordfish.

"We'll be alright just as long as your uncle remembers the plan!" Julius howled from the steering wheel. He tied a rope around the device to keep ship heading straight.

"That's what I'm afraid of," whispered Steve.

A half dozen Gulls swooped down onto the ship. They ranged in sizes and smells, but they all wore the purple vests that were standard among Vanderawlt's crew. The small claws on their feet dug into the deck as they walked towards Steve and the others with swords drawn.

Alexander fought his way to the bridge of *The Frugal Gullman*. He swung his heavy mallet at approaching foes, knocking them out of his way with grace and practiced accuracy. The vile Gull captain stood perched on the bridge, barking orders to his remaining crew while trying to keep his ship moving towards *The Griffin*.

Alexander crouched down behind a barrel and waited for the best moment to charge at his infamous foe. He waited until Vanderawlt's face was hidden by his sizeable silly hat and charged valiantly.

Vanderawlt looked up to see the small green blur charging at him. Without hesitation, Vanderawlt lifted up a small, handheld crossbow from behind the ship's steering wheel and fired. The crossbow bolt struck Alexander the Small, causing the tiny duck to collapse lifelessly to *The Frugal Gullman*'s deck.

Vanderawlt chuckled his nasally laugh as he tossed aside the spent crossbow and kept steering.

17

Steve grudgingly squeezed his swordfish, forcing its blade-tongue out with a loud BLEAH! as he timidly prepared to fight the approaching Gulls. The attack party made their way towards Steve. Eira moved in front of Steve and held her walking stick in a threatening manner.

"You'll have to go through *me* first!" she yelled.

A Gull with an eye patch shook his white-feathered head, "We ain't inner'ested in you pelican. Just give us The Boy."

"I don't think so," Eira taunted as she started spinning her walking stick around, attempting to keep the attackers at bay.

The Gull with the eye patch smirked and lowered his sword, "A'ight then. Mooch? Take care of 'em," he ordered.

A large Gull with hulking muscles walked from the rear of the group. His barrel chest barely fit in his purple vest, and his short pants strained under the pressure of his muscle packed legs. He reminded Steve of one of the large Swantan guards he had seen in Da'Rahga.

"Mooch, smash!" bellowed the large Gull as he lumbered towards Steve. Each step he took rattled the deck and made it difficult for Steve to stand straight as Mooch's large shadow fell over him and Eira.

The boy and the pelican looked at each other worriedly, trying to hide their fear.

Everyone on the *Uth Chamber Commerce All Purpose Utility Ship and Choir Annex* enjoyed a ten minute recess before the Committee of Which Direction to Attack From was supposed to begin hearing testimony.

Gladius flashed in the morning sun as it cut down Gull after Gull. After a few more moments Zeroth would run of out of Gulls to fight. The power of Gladius amazed even Zeroth, who had used a fair amount of weapons in his career as a Hunter.

Zeroth began to lose himself in the fighting, his attacks becoming more fluid and dance like than just mere slaying. As his bloodlust grew, so did his strength and agility.

A Gull swatted at Zeroth with a top-heavy club, Zeroth leaned so far that he almost bent over backwards, letting the club sail harmlessly over him. Zeroth returned the attack with a spin of his body and flipped over another Gull, stabbed Gladius into the deck of the ship and used the leverage to hit a third Gull with a high-powered kick to the beak.

The last Gull dug into Zeroth's shield with his axe, but turned and ran away after catching a glimpse of Zeroth's red tinted eyes. Before the pirate could get away, Zeroth spun fluidly and ran Gladius through the escaping Gull's back.

The Hunter slowly withdrew Gladius, and started breathing heavily as he looked over all of his defeated foes. Zeroth took several more deep breaths and tried to quell his raging bloodlust. The red faded from his eyes as he gave Gladius a squeeze.

"Is stabbing escaping opponents in the back typical of Hunters?" snapped Gladius sourly.

Zeroth ignored the barbed words of his weapon as he glanced over at Uncle Shameless and suddenly remembered their plan.

A piercing headache brought Alexander the Small back to his senses. "Glargh…" babbled the duck as he tried to remember the last few moments.

He slowly sat up, wincing in pain as he did so. He removed his iron saucepan helmet and inspected it. Embedded in the front of the pan itself, was Vanderawlt's crossbow bolt.

Luckily, the bolt had not penetrated the iron, but the impact had left Alexander with a large bump on his head. He tried to pull the bolt free, but could not. With a shrug, he put his makeshift helmet back on.

Vanderawlt had his back to Alexander. The little duck found his large mallet and dashed at the Gull, tackling him to the ship's deck.

Alexander stood on Vanderawlt's chest with his mallet raised, ready to deliver a mighty blow.

"*This is for my mother!*" cried Alexander the Small.

"I never touched your mother!" pleaded Vanderawlt, who was considerably less menacing now that the tables were turned.

"Of course you never touched her, you just ran her out of business!" explained Alexander.

"Who?" asked the Gull in the silly hat.

"Alexandria the Not-So-Small-After-Having-Hatchlings! Don't you remember?" asked the irritated duck.

Vanderawlt thought for a moment, "Nope, doesn't ring a bell. Where and when was this?"

"Several years ago, near the coast of Tal," answered Alexander, confused. He began to lower the mallet.

"Ah, that explains it," said Vanderawlt "I've only just transferred to this district recently, it was probably one of the last guys."

"Excuse me?" replied Alexander, now *very* confused.

"I'm not the only Vanderawlt. I'm just part of the Vanderawlt Franchise," explained the pirate. "There are *dozens* of us all over Eyri."

Alexander dropped his mallet in shock. He had spent years planning for revenge against Vanderawlt, and now to find out there were more than one of him was somewhat of a surprise.

"In the old days, Vanderawlt was just a plain old pirate who fought with other pirates in the Ralk over treasure and such. But after attending a motivational seminar, he came up with the idea to incorporate all of the other pirates into one big group," clarified the would-be Vanderawlt.

"So he got them all to sail around with identical ships and identically dressed crews. He even gave each of 'em a stupid hat like this so everyone else would think all of these other ships was the same pirate," explained the Gull.

"Why?" asked Alexander.

"Because he figured it was more profitable – and safer – to have others do all of the actual piratin' for him, he gets the loot and then he pays all of us a percentage."

"Why would any pirate agree to give up their independence to work for Vanderawlt?"

"The franchise name. It's all in the name and the reputation. Every sailor knows Vanderawlt, most surrender their cargo or treasure just after seeing our purple vests. That's why I joined, I wasn't making too much as a Gull pirate named Softie Tenderhuggles."

"No, I s'pose not," agreed Alexander. "So *that's* why you joined?"

"Yap, the pay's pretty good an' there's profit sharing," answered the pirate formally known as Tenderhuggles. "Although...the health care *could* be better."

Alexander's hopes of vengeance were crushed; he had been waiting for this moment for years. Now it looked as if he would never find the *specific* Gull responsible for running his mother out of business.

But for good measure he picked up his mallet and gave the imitation Vanderawlt a hard WHACK on the head.

Steve's swordfish rattled in his hands with each of Mooch's heavy steps. Now only a few steps away, the mammoth Gull's dark shadow totally blanketed Steve and Eira.

The frightened boy raised up his weapon, but even though he now knew his blue heron amulet would protect him, he was too scared to fight. Steve tried to remember the last few sword fighting lessons Zeroth had given him, when something else distracted him.

"What's that *smell*?" choked Steve as his nostrils began to burn after being filled with a foul, yet oddly familiar, odor.

Eira hacked and wheezed next to him, "I do not know…but it is *vile*."

The Gulls began choking on the pungent stench as well; a few were blinded by tears. Even the brutish Mooch began to reel about from the foulness of the odor.

Steve covered his face as the wind suddenly picked up. He glanced passed Mooch to see a ghostly cloud of mist flying above the Pixie Tree's lookout barrel.

"Oh no!" cried Steve as he saw a pair of eyes flash within the cloud. The mist ripped away as the Hunter Arbal dropped into the empty lookout barrel.

Steve tried to run for cover, not only from Arbal, but also from the smell which had grown considerably worse after the mourning dove Hunter solidified.

Arbal stared down at Steve with his cold, black-marble eyes as he pulled his massive crossbow off his back and aimed for the boy, all in one quick motion.

A sailor tried to inform the Alderman and the Uth Chamber of Commerce that the sea battle was already well underway, and that if they didn't hurry there wouldn't be anyone *to* fight.

However, because the sailor had not filled out a testimony card prior to the current committee meeting (To Fight Dirty or Not), he was not allowed to speak.

Just as Arbal's clawed finger reached for the trigger of his crossbow, Hector rang several bells from the bridge of *The Griffin*. In an instant, hundreds of Pixie People flew out of the Pixie Tree and swarmed around Arbal, Mooch and the other Gulls.

"What dat?" asked Mooch slowly.

No one had time to answer as the Gulls and Arbal were engulfed in a huge cloud of blinding light. The Gulls tried to run away but could not escape the dense swarm of floating lights. Several even tried flying away, but met with similar bad luck. Arbal swatted at the buzzing lights with his crossbow as he tried to concentrate on his shot.

Steve lowered his swordfish and watched the odd scene. The Pixie People were not attacking the Gulls or Arbal; it looked and sounded like they were trying to make small talk with the intruders.

Unfortunately, the Pixie People were talking so fast and all at once that it was impossible to make any words out of the stew of vocabulary they were pouring on the intruders.

Aggravated, Arbal fired his shot at Steve. The lethal crossbow bolt punched through the bubble of Pixie People surrounding the Hunter, but missed Steve by only a few inches. The boy breathed a sigh of relief as the bolt buried itself harmlessly into the body of the ship.

Steve wasn't certain if Arbal had missed him because of the Pixie People or because of his blue heron amulet, but he wasn't going to stand around and give the Hunter a second chance.

Arbal continued swinging his large crossbow at the cloud of Pixie People around him, trying in vain to disperse them. His anger, stoked by the chatty Pixie People and his failed shot, caused Arbal to hack and wheeze for several moments before turning back into mist once more and flying away.

After Steve and Eira found cover on the bridge, Hector rang the bell again, causing the swarms of Pixie People to begin flying circles around the remaining Gulls. Within seconds the Gulls were encased in a swirling ball of light.

Gradually the ball of light floated into the air and hovered for a moment. Then in a blink of an eye, the giant ball of light shot towards *The Frugal Gullman*, only to stop abruptly and hover above the ship. The Pixie People slowed their flying, and the group of Gulls crashed to the deck in a pile of white feathers and ugly purple vests.

In a streaking blur of light, the Pixie People returned to *The Griffin*. Hector rang a different bell and several dozen Pixies flew down to the cranks that powered the ship.

"Hang on!" cried Julius.

Alexander joined Zeroth and Uncle Shameless in the middle of the deck as they fought several groups of irritated Gulls, including a few that had just crashed into the deck only moments before.

The small duck looked up at the much larger Zeroth, "It's time!" he yelled as he pointed to Uncle Shameless.

Zeroth dodge several burly Gulls and made his way over to Uncle Shameless, "Shameless, it's time!"

Uncle Shameless turned towards the bird-man after banging two Gulls' heads together, resulting in a loud THUNK.

"Time fer what?"

"The plan," answered Zeroth.

"What plan?" asked Uncle Shameless.

"The plan you came up with!"

Uncle Shameless thought very hard for a few moments "Okay, but where are we going to get find a giant banana costume 'round here?"

"What? No!" yelled Zeroth "The plan about *this* ship!"

"Ooooh, *right*," said Uncle Shameless "Now, what exactly was that again?"

Julius steered *The Griffin* so that it was aiming straight at *The Frugal Gullman*. By looking at Vanderawlt's ship, he could tell that Uncle Shameless had not carried out his part of the plan yet.

"What is going on over there?" the albatross wondered aloud.

"What do you mean you don't remember? It was *your* plan!" argued Zeroth, as he fought Gulls back-to-back with Uncle Shameless.

Uncle Shameless rolled a large barrel like a bowling ball at a group of Gulls, knocking them down.

"I don't 'member comin' up with any plan," confessed Uncle Shameless as he took a sip of Eldercherry wine.

Back on *The Griffin*, Julius was ready to carry out his part of the plan. The lanky navigator put a pair of goggles on over his eyes as Hector did the same. Julius nodded to Hector, and the penguin gradually began increasing the speed of the ship. Steve watched as the paddle wheels began spinning faster and faster.

The Griffin began cutting through the water smoothly as it picked up more speed. The wind blowing in Steve's face made it difficult for him to keep his eyes open. Wind screamed past his ears, drowning out all other sound, but he could just barely make out Hector yelling for Eira and him to take cover.

Eira motioned for Steve to follow her inside the cabin. Once inside, the wind howled past the wooden exterior of the cabin.

Julius glanced at Hector and yelled, "Rammin' speed!"

The penguin slammed the lever into the proper position. Julius thought to himself that Uncle Shameless had better do his part of the plan soon, otherwise this attack was not going to work.

A sickly looking Arbal materialized in the air over *The Frugal Gullman* and pulled out his small repeating crossbow. Zeroth raised his shield and blocked the volley of small arrows hungry for his flesh. After his first volley of arrows, Arbal's eyes flashed as he turned into mist once more before flying down to the deck.

"*Arbal*," growled Zeroth as his former partner threw open his stolen Caper Cape.

"Friend of yours?" asked Alexander as he struck a nearby Gull in the knee with a hard WHACK of his mallet.

"Hardly," hissed Zeroth.

The remaining Gulls cleared the space between Zeroth and Arbal, mainly to get away from the horrible smell that Arbal was giving off. The mourning dove-man pulled his large crossbow from his back and started to reload it.

Zeroth knew he'd be in trouble once Arbal got his crossbow ready, but just then he noticed *The Griffin* speeding towards *The Frugal Gullman*, and realized there was no time to waste. He grabbed Uncle Shameless, "Do it now!" he begged. Uncle Shameless swayed around in his grasp and his lazy eye swirled in his head with a mind of its own.

"I'll handle this!" cried Alexander as he grabbed Uncle Shameless. Alexander took out the sheet of insults Steve had given him once again. "Ahem, 'you know that musical group you really like?'" read the small duck.

Uncle Shameless nodded sloppily as notes from his favorite songs filled his head.

"Well, that guy over there said they are *really* overrated!" yelled Alexander as he pointed to Arbal, who was struggling with reloading his heavy crossbow.

Uncle Shameless snapped to attention, "What?!"

"Yeah, that's right," continued Alexander in a nasty tone of voice "An' he said that they are..." he struggled with the next phrase, having never heard it before, "Mainstream...sell-outs?"

Uncle Shameless roared and dashed towards Arbal. The dove-man was too busy trying to crank back the strong spring of his crossbow to notice. Seconds before Uncle Shameless was about to plow into Arbal, the Hunter glanced up to see the man charging for him.

Arbal quickly pulled his Caper Cape around him and turned into a noxious smelling cloud of mist, allowing Uncle Shameless to pass harmlessly through him.

However, Uncle Shameless did not pass harmlessly through the mast of *The Frugal Gullman*.

The top half of the mast lurched to and fro until it began toppling over, bringing *The Frugal Gullman*'s sails with it. Uncle Shameless stumbled around, taking his iron-pot helmet off for a moment to rub his sore head.

"Ugh...What happened?" he said before he looked up to see the mast crashing towards the deck. He suddenly remembered his plan, slammed the pot back onto his head and ran towards Zeroth, grabbing Alexander along the way.

Horrified Gulls ran around the deck as all the sails and riggings began snapping and dropping around them. Zeroth quickly jumped on Uncle Shameless' back before he ran towards the bow. Like before, Uncle Shameless jumped high into the air after reaching the bow of the crippled ship.

Julius steered *The Griffin* as best he could as it rocketed across the water towards *The Frugal Gullman*. Eventually he breathed a sigh of relief as he saw the main mast of Vanderawlt's ship topple over. The Gull ship was now dead in the water, and making it a very easy target.

The Griffin was going so fast that the bow was barely touching the surface of the Ralk Sea. Huge streams of water were thrown into the air by the whirling paddle wheels. From inside the cabin with Eira, Steve could see bright lights shining through the cracks in the floor boards, hinting at the blazing speed the Pixie People were spinning the paddle wheel cranks.

Julius lined up *The Griffin* with the mid-section of Vanderawlt's ship, like two lines forming a T and rammed through the side of the Gull ship. The speed of *The Griffin* shattered Vanderawlt's ship into two large pieces.

Thankfully, Uncle Shameless had jumped off the ship just before contact, allowing Zeroth to glide away from harm.

"Woooo!" cried Julius after bursting through the other side of *The Frugal Gullman*, cleaving it in half. Hector gradually began slowing the ship down as Julius turned around so Zeroth could land on the deck.

"Excellent work!" congratulated Alexander the Small as Uncle Shameless let go of him.

Steve and Eira exited the cabin. Steve pointed to the crossbow bolt lodged into Alexander's saucepan helmet, "What's with-"

"Never you mind," interrupted Alexander as he walked towards the giant metal eagle's head on the bow of the ship. He stood triumphantly as he watched the imitation Vanderawlt's ship sink into the Ralk Sea.

Alexander dusted his hands off as he slowly turned around to face Steve and the others, "I love it when a..." started Alexander, until the words left him after seeing the sky behind *The Griffin*.

"What's wrong?" asked Steve as a look of terror crawled over Alexander's face. The little duck-man pointed to the distant horizon and began stuttering "P-pp-p-p-."

"What?" asked Steve again. Alexander continued pointing to the sky, but no one turned to look. "What is it?" asked Steve once more.

"Ubb-buh-da-p-p-," stuttered Alexander as he pointed to a fiery object in the distance.

"Spit it out!" yelled Steve, not noticing that everyone else had turned around and was silent.

"*Pyrix!*" cried everyone except Steve in unison. The boy slowly turned to look. Sure enough the two gigantic, fiery skeletal birds were soaring towards *The Griffin*.

Uncle Shameless looked over at Julius; "I'll take those brown pants now."

Meanwhile, everyone on the *Uth Chamber of Commerce All Purpose Utility Ship and Choir Annex* took yet another recess as they were forced to sit through a less than rousing off-key recital by the tone-deaf Uth Chamber of Commerce Choir.

18

U'nala steered the ravenous Pyrix towards *The Griffin* while he cracked a long whip across their boney backs. Everyone had survived the crash in Tal with only minor injuries, however the same could not be said for Fiach-Ra's chariot. The custom made, elaborately decorated vehicle had been crushed by the impact, forcing U'nala come up with a quick replacement.

By the command of U'nala, Kaz searched Tal for a suitable substitute, only to return with an old fertilizer cart with misshapen wheels. Under much protest, Remmit and Kaz cleaned the cart and chained the Pyrix to it.

"It sure was easy getting those ducks to tell us where these guys went," said Kaz as he looked down at the Ralk Sea over the side of the odd smelling cart.

"Well of course it was easy, they are only about a third of your size," replied Remmit. "You could have just stepped on them if you wanted to."

Kaz nodded, "Yes I guess you are right. But it would have been fun to rough a few of 'em up."

Remmit shook his head. "Don't worry. The Hawk-King will see to that."

"What are we gonna do?" demanded. Steve "We're like sitting ducks!"

Alexander gave Steve a confused look. "Uh, figure of speech, sorry," apologized the boy.

"No, you are right!" exclaimed Alexander triumphantly. "We must even the odds!"

Julius the albatross looked at his captain with concerned eyes, "You don't mean-"

"*Yes!* All stop!" commanded the little duck with giant sized gusto. Hector pulled a lever; the giant paddle wheels on the side of the ship came to a gradual halt.

Steve looked at the idle paddle wheels and then to the now rapidly approaching Pyrix.

"Why are we stopping?!" yelled the boy. Alexander held up a hand, indicating he wished the boy to be silent.

The small green-feathered duck looked to Hector the penguin, "Now!" he ordered. Hector grasped a large lever with two hands, pressed the safety catch and pulled the heavy lever down.

Creaks and moans sounded throughout the ship and two large wooden trap doors sprang open on the deck. One was near to the eagle head at the bow, while the other was closer to the main cabin and the bridge. Steve looked over at the trap doors, seeing only what looked like piles of cloth.

"You're going to throw laundry at them?" asked Steve.

"Hush!" yelled Alexander as he nodded towards Hector.

His first-mate pulled two cables, and through the trap doors Steve heard a loud FWOOSH! It reminded him of the fire Uncle Shameless had tried to make the night before their canoe trip.

To his surprise, the cloth piles quickly began inflating and rising out of the trap doors. Steve quickly realized what they were, a pair of large patch work hot-air balloons! The balloons continued rising out of the trap doors, dragging thick ropes with them until they were floating high above the ship. Steve felt an odd sensation and looked over the edge of the ship, noticing that the whole thing was quickly rising into the air.

Before he could ask any questions, Alexander gave another command. "Ready paddle wheels!"

Hector walked to a huge crank and began turning it with all his might. Steve heard loud groans and creaks coming from throughout the ship, which was now completely out of the water and gradually rose higher and higher.

"Look!" cried Eira, pointing to the paddle wheels. Steve turned his gaze toward them. As Hector turned the crank, wooden beams connecting the wheels to the sides of *The Griffin* grew longer and longer, moving the wheels further from the ship. Hector continued cranking until there was a loud CLUNK sound. The penguin reached up, flipped a switch next to the crank, and began cranking again.

The beams swung backwards until they were parallel with the ship, transforming the paddle wheels into propellers.

"Paddle wheels ready!" yelled Hector.

"Full speed ahead!" screamed Alexander the Small.

A sailor on the *Uth Chamber of Commerce All Purpose Utility Ship and Choir Annex* tried to inform everyone that their foes had just floated into the sky and were now *flying* away. Unfortunately, everyone else was too busy suffering through the choir's horrifying rendition of 'You Break It, You Buy It' to hear him.

"U'nala is confused. Did that ship just take to the sky?" asked the one-winged Hawken officer. Remmit was equally dumbstruck "It did! Amazing!"

"Yes, U'nala agrees. Too bad we must shoot them down," U'nala said as he handed Remmit a Hawken bow and a quiver full of nasty looking arrows.

"Bring us around, Mr. Julius!" yelled Alexander.

"You're going to *attack* them?!" yelled Steve.

Alexander nodded proudly "Of course. This ship may be fast in the water but we'll never out run a pair of Pyrix in the sky."

The pair of Pyrix screamed in glee as *The Griffin* turned in the sky to face them.

"They are either really brave, or really stupid," commented Remmit as he raised his curved bow and fired a shot.

"Arrows!" yelled Zeroth just before Remmit's first shot struck the handle of Alexander's helmet, causing the saucepan to spin around on the little duck's head.

"Good eye!" congratulated Alexander as he adjusted his headgear and walked to one of the talk tubes that ran down to the crank room where the Pixie People were hard at work.

"Pixies, we have a pair of Pyrix attacking us and we need volunteers for-"

Before Alexander had even finished, several dozen pinhead sized balls of light flew from the interior of the ship and formed a circular barrier around *The Griffin*.

"Ha!" exclaimed Alexander "I knew that would get them to help!"

Remmit fired several more arrows, only to have them knocked away by pixies before they could pierce the hot air balloons.

"Enough of this," barked U'nala. He cracked his whip at the backs of the Pyrix. "Attack! This U'nala commands!" cried the Wing-Master madly. The Pyrix dropped open their blackened beaks and inhaled sharply before each fired a large fireball towards *The Griffin*.

"Incoming!" yelled Zeroth as he watched the two fireballs head towards the ship.

"Can the pixies stop those fireballs?" asked Steve nervously.

"I don't know. But I don't want to wait and see," answered Alexander the Small. He looked over at Julius. "Hard to Port!" ordered the duck captain, as he pointed to the right.

Steve did not know too much about sailing, but he did know that Port refereed to the left of the ship. Turning Port would put *The Griffin* directly in the path of the fireballs.

What confused Steve even further was that Alexander had actually pointed to the Starboard side when he ordered the turn to Port.

"Are you crazy? That will put us *more* in danger!" Steve yelled at Alexander.

A handful of seconds before the fireballs were about to hit the ship, Julius quickly spun the wheel causing *The Griffin* to turn sharply Starboard. The deadly fireballs passed harmlessly by the ship and crashed into the water below.

"Why did you turn Starboard after he told you to turn Port?" Steve asked Julius.

"Because he *pointed* Starboard," answered Julius honestly. Steve's forehead crinkled in confusion, "But...he said Port."

Hector waved Steve over with a fin-like hand "The captain always forgets the names, so he always just says 'Port' and points to the direction he wants Julius to turn," the penguin whispered to the boy.

Steve dropped his head into his hands and groaned "So you're telling me that the captain of this ship not only gets seasick, but also cannot remember Port and Starboard-"

Steve's laundry list of complaints was interrupted by Alexander rushing past him to the side of the ship, followed by a chorus of retching sounds.

"...And apparently also gets *air-sick*," finished Steve with a loud sigh.

"That reminds me of this colorblind art teacher I had in high school who tried to teach us color theory," started Uncle Shameless until he was cut off by Zeroth yelling 'incoming!' once again.

Two more fireballs screamed towards the ship. Hector pulled on a pair of cables, causing the fires under the hot air balloons to burn stronger. The ship rose abruptly out of the path of the deadly fireballs.

More retching sounds came from Alexander as he hung his head over the side of the ship.

U'nala howled with rage as he watched *The Griffin* dodge yet another attack.

"They *cannot* do that! Rising up like that, just who do they think they are? That ship does not even have wings! The *nerve!*"

Remmit continued firing arrows randomly, only to have them knocked away by the Pixie People surrounding *The Griffin*. U'nala turned around and looked at Kaz, "You there!" he yelled to the nauseous warrior, "Prepare yourself to be dropped onto that ship!"

Kaz looked around and then pointed at himself with a clawed finger, "Me?" he asked nervously.

"Yes, *you!*" barked U'nala as he pulled on the reigns controlling the Pyrix and commanded the beasts to fly above *The Griffin*.

"I don't think that's a good idea," said Kaz.

"And why not?" asked U'nala, his voice filled with anger.

"Uh," thought Kaz, thinking hard of an excuse to get out of the likely suicide mission, "I'm allergic to falling?"

"Looks like they are going fly above us!" Zeroth yelled as he watched the flying fertilizer chart wobble upward.

"Ready the cannon!" ordered Alexander.

Hector waddled toward a small cannon perched on the edge of the bridge. He wiped the thick layer of dust off the fuse and started to load it with a single fist sized cannon ball.

"What good is that going to do?" asked Steve, questioning the size of the little cannon ball.

"Not to worry," assured Alexander, "It may be old, but it's a trusty weapon."

Hector lit the fuse of the cannon, swiveled it around and aimed up at the Pyrix. The fuse burned quickly, making a loud sizzling sound before the cannon went off with a BOOM!

The cannon ball blasted up towards the Pyrix – but only for a few feet before it quickly came crashing down into the deck of *The Griffin*, creating a small fire.

"ZAA'S TALONS!" Alexander cursed loudly as he ran towards the tiny inferno. Hector ran into the cabin under the bridge to fetch a container of water and followed Alexander.

The duck captain turned to face Steve as he ran, "You stay there and help Julius!"

U'nala maneuvered the flying fertilizer cart above *The Griffin* with several tugs of the reigns. Without any warning, U'nala turned around and pushed Kaz over the edge with a hefty muscular hand. The large Swantan warrior fell from the cart, screaming as he rapidly approached the flying ship underneath him.

Right before Kaz should have hit one of the huge hot air balloons, he stopped in mid-air and hovered there for several moments.

Kaz slowly removed his hands from over his eyes.

"Am I flying?" he wondered aloud. He knew deep down that was not possible, as he did not have any wings. As he wiped tears from his eyes, he noticed several dozen tiny balls of light flying around him.

Kaz then realized *he* was flying around, not the balls of light. They were spinning him around and around, increasing the speed drastically.

From below, Steve watched as the spinning Swantan was hurled back at the flying fertilizer cart by the Pixie People, screaming loudly as he soared. He crashed into the other passengers, knocking down the driver.

As Alexander was putting out the fire on the deck of *The Griffin*, he saw the chance for an attack and yelled back to Steve, "Fire the *other* cannon!"

Steve ran to panel that contained all of the switches, levers, cables and buttons Hector had been using. He saw several switches labeled as cannons, making Steve wonder why they had used the old one on the bridge in the first place. But then he realized that very little of his voyage on *The Griffin* had made any sense at all.

"Which one?" cried Steve.

"*The Big One!*" screamed Alexander, smoke causing him to choke.

At least Alexander thought it was the smoke making him choke, though he was surprised as to just how *bad* the smoke smelled. He was even more surprised when a cloud of what he thought was smoke flew around him and headed straight for Zeroth.

"Arbal!" Zeroth yelled venomously as the mourning dove mercenary solidified near him, along with the pungent Signal Stone odor.

"Ick," choked Uncle Shameless as he recoiled from the foul odor. Zeroth's rage blocked out all of his other senses as he gave Gladius a quick squeeze and readied his shield.

Uncle Shameless cracked his knuckles and moved towards Zeroth. "No," snapped Zeroth coarsely, "He's *mine.*"

Uncle Shameless, although disappointed, understood and left Zeroth to handle Arbal alone. The black-feathered bird-man jumped at his former partner before Arbal had a chance to aim his large crossbow.

Zeroth swung Gladius downward at Arbal. The traitor managed to block the blow with the stock of his crossbow, but only barely as Gladius nearly cleaved it in two. Arbal strained against Zeroth's strength as he tried to twist Gladius to one side.

Zeroth noticed Arbal's fading strength as well as his overall sickly appearance. He was no longer the strapping and sturdy Hunter that Zeroth had come to know during their days as members of The Five.

Arbal's black marble eyes were sunken and his body appeared to be wasting away. Patches of feathers were missing and more were falling out as they struggled, revealing loose hanging flesh that looked as if it were draped over his skeleton.

"What's wrong Arbal? Is all of that turning into mist not agreeing with you?"

Without so much as a blink of his cold black eyes, Arbal managed a quick kick to one of Zeroth's knees.

As Steve watched Arbal run towards the bow of the ship and away from the momentarily disabled Zeroth, he reviewed the panel of levers and switches once more, and he noticed a lever labeled as The Big One.

Steve shrugged, released the safety catch and pulled down on the lever. Once more, the sound of large metal gears churning filled the ship and Steve felt the wooden boards beneath him rumble.

Zeroth cursed at himself for letting his guard down while taunting Arbal. He dashed down the deck of the ship towards the dove, passing by the occupied Alexander and Hector. The ship seemed to come to life under his feet as he scurried across its wooden deck.

In front of him, Arbal ducked behind the Pixie Tree and pulled out his small repeating crossbow. Ignoring the pain in his knee, Zeroth tucked and rolled to avoid the first barrage of dart-like arrows.

Zeroth let the second volley of arrows strike his shield before finding cover behind one of the large trap doors that had covered the balloon closest to the bridge.

Meanwhile, between the eyes of the giant eagle's head at the bow of the ship, a set of metal doors began to slide apart. A loud CLUNK sounded after they were completely open, and another set of gears began turning, forcing the barrel of a very large cannon to extend several yards out from the eagle's forehead.

"Now *that's* a cannon," Uncle Shameless exclaimed with a low whistle.

Zeroth spied from behind his cover to see Arbal busy loading another box of small arrows into his repeating crossbow, and decided to risk an attack. He dashed from behind the wooden trap door and headed for the other side of the Pixie Tree.

Julius suddenly spun the steering wheel to bring *The Griffin* into a better firing position. U'nala had dropped the reigns after Kaz had been thrown into him by the Pixie People, causing the Pyrix to wander aimlessly through the sky.

Julius instructed Steve from the helm to pull the cables that would raise the ship higher to get a better shot. The sudden change in altitude caused Alexander to drop his bucket of water and run once again for the side of the ship.

The unexpected lurch of the ship also caused Zeroth to loose his footing, causing him to crash into the ship's rail and nearly fell overboard.

"Zeroth!" Eira cried in shock.

Her words caught Arbal's attention. The dove dropped his small crossbow, pulled the mammoth sized crossbow from his back, aimed at Zeroth and fired all a manner of seconds. Zeroth could not dodge the heavy crossbow bolt heading for him; all he had time to do was raise his shield.

Zeroth howled as the thick bolt pierced his shield and his arm, pinning the heavy shield to him. Arbal pulled out another stake-like crossbow bolt and prepared to reload the giant weapon and finish his of former partner.

Zeroth's ear's pounded as pain coursed through his body, making him barely able to stand or hear Gladius' muffled words. The bird-man gave the swordfish a quick squeeze and held it up to his face.

"C'mon *Hunter*," jabbed Gladius, "Ya ain't gonna let a little poke like that stop ya, now are ya?"

Blinded by pain and rage, Zeroth let loose a piercing hawk cry as he charged towards Arbal, giving Gladius a hearty squeeze along the way. The cry, and Zeroth's newfound liveliness caught Arbal off guard. He quickly let go of his large crossbow and reached inside his Caper Cape for his second repeating crossbow.

Arbal's hand was a blur on the firing lever of his crossbow as he fired several shots at the charging Hunter. Undeterred, Zeroth screamed through the pain as he raised his shield arm to once again fend off most of the arrows, letting a few nick his body. Zeroth jumped at Arbal and slashed with his swordfish, cleanly slicing the dove's smaller crossbow in half.

Arbal panicked, quickly turning into mist and wafting around Zeroth, much to his annoyance. The only thing bothering Zeroth more than the indescribable pain in his arm was the indescribable smell that Arbal was giving off. He realized now the blessing and the curse of hitting Arbal with the sack of Signal Stones.

Arbal solidified behind Zeroth long enough to grab his colossal crossbow once more before retreating into his gaseous state.

Zeroth slashed angrily at the cloud of noxious mist, following it to the eagle's head on the bow of *The Griffin*.

"Arbal!' cursed Zeroth, hungry for revenge and a fight "Face me, you coward!"

As if on cue, Arbal solidified behind Zeroth and whacked him across the back with the giant crossbow, nearly knocking him overboard.

Nauseous, yet determined to win the day, Alexander the Small looked up and saw that The Big One was in the proper position to fire a deadly blast. Alexander wiped his mouth with a feathered arm and looked back towards Steve and Julius.

"Ready!" called Alexander.

"Grab a'hold of somethin'!" Julius yelled to everyone within earshot.

Weaponless, aside from his spent crossbow, Arbal lunged at Zeroth atop the metal eagle's head. The heavy crossbow met Zeroth's shield and pounded repeatedly on the bolt sticking through the shield and into Zeroth's arm, driving it like a nail.

Arbal pushed Zeroth further down the bow, until he was right on the tip of the cannon. The blows made Zeroth's legs turn to jelly, causing him to collapse as Arbal rained more blows down upon him.

The pounding in Zeroth's head quickly drowned out the CLANG CLANG of the crossbow against his shield. Time seemed to slow down to a crawl and Zeroth's vision blurred. His thoughts drifted to memories of himself and Cam, his old mentor. Zeroth's battered body went limp atop the smooth, curved surface of the large cannon.

An ancient memory clawed its way to the foreground of his thoughts. A memory of fire and pain. Zeroth let the memory take him over; his shield arm fell to his side exposing his unprotected body and face.

Realizing the moment had come to finish off his foe, Arbal towered over Zeroth's limp body, raised his massive crossbow high and prepared to deliver a lethal blow to Zeroth's head.

Suddenly Zeroth delivered a fast, well-placed kick to where most males of any species really don't like to receive fast, well-placed kicks.

Arbal collapsed on top of Zeroth, letting his colossal crossbow fall into the sea below. Zeroth narrowed his now red-tinted eyes at the traitorous mourning dove and whispered bitterly,

"This is for Cam."

In an improbable blur of motion, Zeroth swung his shield arm onto the dove's back, stabbing Arbal with the protruding crossbow bolt. The perpetually silent Arbal screamed.

Zeroth roared and used his rage-induced strength to pull his arm free, leaving the bolt embedded in Arbal's back, then flipped the mourning dove over the front of the cannon.

As Zeroth crawled back to the deck of *The Griffin*, Arbal clung to the mouth of The Big One, too weak to turn into mist and fly away.

"Fire!" cried Alexander, throwing a fist into the air to add dramatic flair. Steve gripped the firing mechanism and pulled the rusty lever down with gusto.

The barrel of the large cannon belched fire and black smoke into the sky, filling everyone's ears with a thunderous BOOM! A cannon ball the size of a boulder screamed towards the idle Pyrix and their passengers.

The recoil from the blast sent *The Griffin* spinning, though Julius did his best to keep the flying ship stable among the clouds. Steve watched as the enormous cannon ball sailed through the air on a direct path to the Pyrix.

Meanwhile in the flying old fertilizer cart, U'nala and the others wrestled around, fighting to stand up.

"Get off of U'nala!" cried the large one-winged Hawken.

"The lights! The lights!" screamed a frightened Kaz, who was still recovering from his failed attack on *The Griffin*. The large Swantan warrior flailed about on top of U'nala and Remmit.

"Uuf! Get off of us you wingless buffoon!" screamed Remmit. U'nala, who was lying on top of the prone Remmit, gave him a nasty look.

"Yipe! Not you sir!" corrected Remmit "I meant *him!*" he explained, pointing a shaking clawed finger at Kaz's white feather-covered body.

Remmit cocked his head, "What is that sound?"

"U'nala does not know, go and look," commanded the large Hawken as he pushed the still frightened Kaz off of them. Remmit dusted himself off and slowly peered over the edge of the cart.

He saw the Pyrix flapping their flaming wings, waiting for directions from the reigns of U'nala, but nothing else. Remmit turned his head in the direction of the sound he had heard, but all he saw was a large bank of white clouds.

Remmit looked over at U'nala, "Nothing unusual, but I keep hearing that strange sound," explained the younger Hawken. He looked around once more, "I still do not see anyth-BY THE EYE OF ZUU!" screamed Remmit as the giant metal cannonball burst from the clouds in front of them and went screaming towards the unaware Pyrix.

"What is going on?" asked U'nala as he pulled himself to an upright position. With horror filled eyes, he watched the mammoth cannonball crash into the Pyrix, ripping them out of their chains and collars.

The Pyrix and the cannonball plummeted into the water with an enormous splash, the screams of the fiery birds hung in the air for several moments until they finally ceased, leaving behind an eerie silence.

The old fertilizer cart hovered in the air for a few seconds, which seemed like an eternity to its passengers. The cart suddenly began falling towards the choppy Ralk Sea below them; all three passengers began screaming.

Eventually, a thought came to Remmit.

"Wait, I can fly!" he said aloud as he began flapping his wings. However, U'nala and Kaz could not fly, and grabbed onto the much smaller Hawken as he attempted to gain some lift.

"What are you doing?!" screamed the small warrior as he franticly flapped his wings.

"U'nala commands you to fly us to safety!" ordered the Wing-Master as he grabbed a hold of one of Remmit's legs.

"Yeah, what he said!" added Kaz as he grabbed Remmit's other leg.

There was no way Remmit could support both their weight for long, especially not long enough to fly all the way back to Tal. The small Hawken flapped his wings the best he could, but the trio began quickly descending toward the sea. The fertilizer cart fell out from under them, crashing into the blue waters below. Remmit strained against the massive weight of his bigger companions.

"Fly higher! U'nala commands you!" ordered the Wing-Master.

"Yeah, what he said!" added Kaz between nervous glances down at the Ralk Sea below them.

Steve and the others watched from the deck of *The Griffin* as the large cannonball knocked the Pyrix into the water, doing away with the nightmarish creatures. The water steamed for several minutes where they had splashed into the sea.

"Ew," commented Uncle Shameless as he took a swig of Eldercherry wine.

With the deck fire now extinguished, Hector returned to his post and pointed to Remmit trying to fly away with U'nala and Kaz clutching his legs. The Hawken warrior flapped and flapped his wings, but they had little effect. The strain became too great and everyone watched as Remmit could no longer move his wings. Steve's would-be captors soon went crashing into the sea, screaming all the way.

"Ouch," said Steve, knowing from experience what it was like to drop from a great height into an unforgiving body of water. A bright light caught the corner of his eye and he turned around.

Several dozen Pixie People flew toward the bridge, floating someone along with them.

"Zeroth!" cried everyone in unison as the Pixies lowered the severely wounded Hunter to the deck. Eira began treating his wounds right away, hoping she was not too late. Steve joined her at Zeroth's side as the bird-man opened his eyes slowly.

"Did I get him?" asked Zeroth.

Guessing that he was referring to Arbal, Steve told the Hunter what he wanted to hear, "Yes, you got him."

"'Bout time," wheezed Zeroth jokingly as he proceeded to pass out, too exhausted to notice a faint odor riding on the wind.

Alexander walked proudly to the helm of his ship, strutting as best he could. Uncle Shameless carried Zeroth inside the cabin so Eira could continue treating his plethora of wounds.

"Excellent, excellent," Alexander exclaimed in a congratulatory voice as Steve retracted The Big One into its hiding place with the flick of a switch.

"Good work m'boy," said Alexander the Small with a smile, "We'll make a hero out of you yet."

Steve shook his head, "No thanks," he answered. "I just didn't feel like getting burned alive by a giant chicken skeleton."

"I don't think they are chickens," answered Alexander, referring to the Pyrix and not getting Steve's joke

"I'll tell you what they are – UGLY," added Steve.

"Don't you mean, *'were'*?" joked Alexander.

"Well, at least there aren't any more of them," replied Steve with a sigh of relief.

Miles away back in Tal, the citizens of the duck-city could not share the same relief as Steve.

Ducks and other citizens fled their now blazing city, dodging streams of fire and destructive fireballs sent forth by the flight of Pyrix laying waste to Tal. Dozens of the fiery beasts clouded the sky, making the air itself look ignited.

Buildings were toppled and ships sunk by their ruthless attacks, burning away any evidence of the majestic city which had stood there only moments before.

Above the burning city of Tal, Fiach-Ra twitched for a moment as his mental link with the Pyrix following Steve was severed. His ability to see what the Pyrix see had led him to Tal. He had decided to smite the city for aiding The Boy in his escape out onto the Ralk Sea where Fiach-Ra himself could not follow.

As the Hawk-King over saw the widespread destruction, he waited for U'nala to return with Steve, secretly hoping that Zeroth would be with him as well.

The loss of his magical link with his burning minions told him something had gone wrong, causing the Hawk-King to bellow in rage. To help relieve his fuming anger, he swooped down to attack a defenseless old lighthouse.

Hours later, the Uth Chamber of Commerce and the Alderman were ready to finally launch their attack against Steve for destroying their village and forcing them to repaint all their signs with Uth's new (and much longer) name.

Battle cries of "I will be fed!" which had won the vote, roared from their mouths. The phrase actually came from a mistranslation of an old human word, but the Committee didn't feel like correcting it.

Unfortunately, no one, save the few crewmembers who had made repeated attempts to inform everyone, had realized Steve and *The Griffin* were long gone.

"Well doesn't that just take the biscuit," lamented the Alderman, who was dressed up with no place to go in his battle gear (which was nothing different then his normal clothing, with the addition of a ghastly fur coat).

The Alderman turned to his public relations advisor, a younger woman who was dressed better than the rest of the group put together.

"Loran, is there anyway this *cannot* look bad?" asked the Alderman. Loran thought for a moment, putting her weeks of public relations know-how to the test. "We could say you *scared* them away!" she exclaimed eventually.

"Donal's Beard, now that's the ticket!" gushed the Alderman, as he made his way to a comfortable chair and an equally comfortable bottle of wine.

19

With their enemies behind them, the group of adventurers relaxed and enjoyed the view of the nearly endless sea under them as *The Griffin* casually flew through the sky. Uncle Shameless unsuccessfully tried leading everyone in singing a round of 'The Deacon Went Down.'

He was unsuccessful because instead of addressing Eira, Steve, Zeroth and Alexander as he thought, he was in fact talking to a pile of old barrels and buckets.

"C'mon then, sing loud an' proud! It ain't diff-a-cult!" coached Uncle Shameless to his wooden choir. He swayed back and forth as he began singing again, "Just follow m'lead – *Well the deacon went down!*" he bellowed. He waited for the barrels and buckets to repeat the chorus and was again disappointed.

"That was terrible!" Uncle Shameless criticized between sips of Eldercherry wine. "Now let's try that again, Steve-o I'm lookin' at you!" yelled Uncle Shameless as he jabbed a finger at a rotted out barrel.

From the bridge of the ship, the real Steve watched his uncle and shook his head. He turned to face the pint-size captain of the flying ship.

"Are you sure you know where we are going?" the boy asked.

Alexander the Small looked up from a tattered map that looked as if it had been drawn with a broken crayon during an earthquake, "Oh of course!" he said with much enthusiasm, "Dragon's Cove, right?"

"No!" yelled Steve "Dragons *Well!*"

"Ha-*ha*," laughed Alexander "I know. I was only jokin', why don't you go an' check on Zeroth, hmm?" replied the duck with a broad smile. Steve sighed and went to the main cabin of the ship to visit the injured Hunter.

When Steve was out of earshot, Alexander leaned over to Julius and whispered, "Change of plan. Head North."

"*Ha!* I was right!" said Julius in a bitter tone.

"Quiet, you!" yelled Alexander as he waved a tiny fist.

Steve knocked on the door of Zeroth's cabin. "Come in," replied Eira the pelican.

The boy pushed open the sturdy wooden door and was surprised to see Zeroth up and walking around the room, which was sparse save for a simple cot and many, many boxes of beads.

"That was fast," gasped Steve, remembering the near-death state the bird-man had been in only hours ago.

"Thank her," said Zeroth with a nod to Eira, "Once again, her healing potions fixed me right up." Zeroth held up what had been his severely wounded shield arm and pulled down the sleeve of his cloak.

The gaping crossbow bolt wound was completely healed, if not for the large tear in Zeroth's cloak it would have been impossible to tell he had even been hurt.

"It was nothing at all. But I used up most of my supply, I'll have to go make some more," replied Eira modestly as she packed her things into her backpack and she let herself out of the room.

"Are we almost to Dragons Well?" asked Zeroth.

"I think so," answered Steve indifferently.

"Are you ready for this? We don't know what to expect there."

Steve shrugged as he absent-mindedly rummaged through a box of brightly colored beads. "I don't think it really matters does it? Every time I think I can get away from here, I keep getting pulled back in even deeper."

Zeroth sat down on his cot and leaned against the wall, "Is that so bad? Does it bother you that everything here is not governed by this 'science' of yours?"

Steve shrugged a second time, "Good, bad, it doesn't matter. I just want to go home, all of this stuff is just...*weird*." Steve stopped playing with the box of beads and left the room.

"Cam, you better be right about this kid," sighed Zeroth as he stared up at the ceiling of the room, thinking that his problems were probably only just beginning.

From within his cloak, Gladius started talking. Zeroth reached in and pulled out the talking silver swordfish.

"What'd you say?" asked Zeroth.

"I said, get your lousy cloak cleaned!" yelled the bitter weapon. Zeroth rolled his eyes and began to stuff Gladius back inside his cloak. "Wait!" pleaded Gladius, "I was only foolin'!"

Zeroth held up the creature and looked into its large circular eyes.

"What is it then?"

"He'll come around, they all do. Heroes, that is," explained Gladius. "But I'm more worried about you."

Zeroth's eyes flashed red for a second before he quickly stuffed Gladius away once more, leaving himself to thoughts of Cam, Arbal, and Formal Hunter Compliant Forms.

Around midday, Hector called everyone to the helm. "Land ho-ooooooo!" bellowed the penguin from underneath his colander helmet. Everyone peered over the edge of the ship, and sure enough saw a small island nearby.

Hector reached for another set of cables that would help lower the ship, but Alexander stopped him.

"Look!" said the captain, pointing to the water.

As *The Griffin* came closer to the island, they noticed it was surrounded by an impassable ring of coral reef and rocks cutting off the island from the rest of the sea.

There was wreckage from nearly a dozen ships of all shapes and sizes littering the natural barricade. Steve stepped back, surveying the ship graveyard in all of its superior glory.

"No wonder no one's ever seen this place!" mused Alexander as he glanced around at all the destroyed ships.

Steve shot the duck a confused look, "Wait, if no one's ever seen this place how come you said you've heard of it?"

"I said I heard of it, I said nothin' 'bout seenin' it," answered Alexander.

"But..." started Steve. He saw the serious look on Alexander's face and decided to forget the whole thing.

With his ridiculously long spyglass, Alexander spotted where they could land in clear water inside the foreboding ring of coral and rocks. Hector pulled on the proper cables and *The Griffin* began to descend to the strange island known as Dragons Well.

After an uneventful landing, aside from Alexander getting air-sick from the rapid decent and then sea-sick after they splashed down into the water, the team made their way to the shore. Julius stayed behind to guard *The Griffin*.

Their small landing craft ran aground on the rocky shore of the island's beach. Everyone exited and made the difficult trek over the rock filled beach.

"Ugh!" complained Steve as he tried to keep his footing on the slippery smooth rocks. "I thought beaches were s'pose to be sandy, this is nuts!"

Alexander looked at the boy "No, this is rocks," he said, picking up fist sized rock and throwing it aside.

Steve's face crinkled in confusion "What?"

"You said 'this is nuts', you are wrong. This is rocks, not nuts."

Steve shook his head, "No, that's a saying back home. When you say something is 'nuts', it means it is crazy."

"Oh, I see," nodded Alexander "So does that mean the squirrels there eat crazy?"

Steve stopped in mid-step, "What?"

"You said 'nuts' is another way of saying 'crazy', so does that mean you use 'crazy' as another way of saying 'nuts'?" asked Alexander.

Now Steve was getting very confused, "No, it doesn't work like that. We don't say someone is eating 'crazy' when they are eating nuts."

Uncle Shameless scratched his head "I dunno, I've seen people eat crazy before. There was this one time I was at this bar, and they had this hot dog eating contest. But these were not your average dogs, no sir. They were two feet long an' –"

"You're *not* helping," interrupted Steve.

Alexander's jaw dropped, "You eat dogs?! And you have contests to see who can eat the most?!"

Steve groaned, *this is going to take awhile*, he thought to himself.

After a lengthy conversation about some of the different meanings of words and phrases within Steve's own world and Eyri, the group continued their trek. Eira was having difficulty with the rocks, so Uncle Shameless decided to carry her on his back. After he nearly tripped several times in the first few steps, Eira decided to take her chances by herself.

"Where are we even going?" Steve wondered aloud. "How do we know this island isn't full mean, nasty things just waiting to jump out at us?"

Everyone ignored Steve as they finally made it off of the rocky beach of the island and onto the sandy, dirt ground that covered the interior of the island. Even though no one had been paying attention, Steve continued his verbal editorial.

"What are we s'pose to even find here? All I've seen is rocks, trees and more rocks. Geo did not exactly tell us what to look for."

"I have a feeling we'll know it when we see it," explained Zeroth calmly.

"Oh I can only imagine," added Steve sarcastically "I wonder what it'll be this time, perhaps some giant talking tree? Or wait I know, how about a piece of helpful fungus? Or perhaps even a singing plant? I can't wait to find out."

"I imagine," started Zeroth as he looked around the sandy clearing they had just entered, "It will be something like *that*," he finished as he pointed.

Steve turned to look in the direction the Hunter was pointing and skidded to a stop.

Within the sandy clearing was a ten-foot tall well, built from misshapen rocks and stones. The clearing was covered in fine white sand, and a small pond of clear water rested not far from the enormous well.

Next to the well was a small gong hanging from a wooden frame. A mallet was resting along side the frame.

"Oh, *of course*," exhaled Steve in a spiteful tone. "Well, now what?"

Everyone starred at him, their looks suggesting what to do "Oh no," started Steve as he glanced at the small gong. "I'm not ringing that thing, forget it."

"Ah c'mon it won't hurt," said Alexander as he got behind Steve and pushed the boy forward.

Steve stumbled a bit in the sand and with a loud sigh made his way to the small gong. The clearing was silent, save his sandy footsteps.

As the boy approached the well, he heard a faint groaning sound, much like that of someone blowing over a glass bottle. The well was very tall, but also very wide, nearly as wide as a house.

Reluctantly, Steve reached down and picked up the small mallet to strike the gong. Several small dents littered the face of the gong, which Steve guessed were caused by the mallet in his hand. He swung back his arm and aimed for the center of the gong.

Steve hardly touched the surface of the gong, creating a flat THUD sound. He dropped the mallet to the ground,

"Oh darn, nothing happened," gasped Steve in an urgent tone, "I s'pose we'll have to leave. What a shame."

"You barely touched it!" scolded Zeroth.

"Swing with your hips!" suggested Eira.

"You can do better than that!" Alexander the Small coached. Hector nodded in agreement next to his captain.

"Yeah, hit it with your purse Shirley!" Uncle Shameless bellowed insultingly.

Steve picked up the mallet again and scowled at his companions as he wound up his arm to give the gong a mighty blow. He swung at the gong and it sounded loudly, its unique music echoed around him for a few moments.

Uncle Shameless clapped in appreciation of Steve's little recital, but stopped after a series of nasty looks from the boy.

Steve shrugged, "Is this part of The Prophecy?" asked Steve as thunder roared in the distance. "I'm s'pose to come to this little flyspeck of an island and play a stupid gong? What do we do now, take this gong and keep banging it in front of the Hawk-King?" Steve said in a poisonous tone.

"Maybe if we're lucky, Fiach-Ra is violently allergic to gongs," joked Steve as he heard thunder roaring again, only closer. After a few moments he realized it was not thunder this time, it sounded more like the ground under him was rumbling.

The boy turned to face the well, and saw that the stones forming it were shaking. "What's going on?!" Steve yelled over the loud rumbling. He pointed to the large well "Why is that sound is coming from that thing?!"

Zeroth ran over to the well, "I'll take a look. Shameless, give me a hand."

Uncle Shameless began clapping. He eventually stopped when he noticed the nasty look Zeroth was giving him. "What? You can't take a joke?" asked Uncle Shameless as he walked over and formed a step for Zeroth with his hands and helped lift the bird-man up. Zeroth found some handholds between the rocks forming the well's walls and began to climb up.

"I'm sure it's no big deal," began Zeroth as he reached the top "Probably just some kind of..." his words trailed off as he peered into the blackness of the well. The bird-man immediately jerked his head back up and spun around.

"Run!" Zeroth bellowed as he unfurled his small wings from under his cloak and glided off the top of the well.

"What?" asked Steve confused.

Alexander ran up and grabbed the boy's hand and pulled with all his ducky strength (which wasn't that much, but it was a nice gesture), "He said run, kid!"

The companions ran to the cover of the trees and shrubs just past the edge of the sandy clearing. They turned in time to watch an enormous geyser of water explode from the mouth of the well, shooting several stories into the air. The water splashed back down to the ground in heavy sheets, soaking the surrounding area and the companions.

Everybody sputtered water from their mouths, making 'bleah' sounds and wiping the water out of their eyes before they noticed that water wasn't the only thing that came out of the well.

Sticking out of the mouth of the well and measuring a few stories high, was the upper half of a dragon.

20

"Look at the size of it!" Uncle Shameless whispered loudly as he snuck a peek at the dragon. Everyone shushed him in unison before they peered through the leaves of their hiding place.

The dragon's long body was thin and serpentine. It rested its elbows on the top of the well and looked around the clearing like a hermit crab spying from its shell. It was covered in shiny bright blue and dull purple scales.

It had a long face and big, friendly eyes. At the end of its snout were long dark blue whiskers, looking much like those of a catfish. The dragon shook its upper body as it tried to dry itself, which sent more water flying to the ground.

Steve turned and grabbed Alexander by his crisscrossed suspenders and pulled the duck over to him, "I thought you told me there weren't any dragons here!"

Alexander stared back at the boy, "When did I say that?"

"You said Dragons Well was just a name!"

Alexander shook his head, his iron-pot helmet rattled as he did so, "No, no, we meant Dragon's Mine, Dragon's Grotto, Dragon's Cove and Dragon's Cave were just names," Alexander looked to his penguin first-mate, "Right, Hector?"

Hector the penguin nodded briskly, "Oh yes, they were named after an explorer named Dragon."

"...So Dragon was his last name?" asked Steve in an irritated tone.

"An' his first name," added Hector.

Steve blinked in disbelief "...Oh you have got to be kidding-"

"An' he was a doctor too," continued Alexander.

"You mean to tell me," Steve said slowly as he tried to keep his temper, "That Dragon's Cave and Dragon's Cove are named after-"

"Yes. Dr. Dragon Dragon Agon. Agon was his mother's name," finished Hector.

"What?!" yelled Steve, finally giving into his frustration and shaking Alexander by his suspenders, "Dr. Agon?! That's the stupidest name I've ever heard!"

Uncle Shameless, never one to pass up a chance for a quick joke, joined the conversation.

"Yeah, and this Dr. Dragon Dragon Agon guy, he was known for being really long winded!"

No one responded, so Uncle Shameless tired again.

"I heard he'd talk for a long time, y'know he'd just *drag-on*! Ha!"

Steve let go of Alexander so he could scream into his hands. Everyone else rolled their eyes at Uncle Shameless' bad joke.

Hector continued his geography lesson while behind him Uncle Shameless tried to explain why his joke was funny.

"Everyone knows Dragons Well has dragons," explained Hector "It is called *Dragons* Well after all."

"Oh yes, it's common knowledge. They wouldn't have named it Dragons Well if there weren't any dragons. That'd just be silly," added Alexander.

"But how do they expect anyone to know the difference between Dragons Well and Dragon's Grotto and the rest?" asked Steve, who on the verge of a breakdown.

"Because Dragon's Grotto and the rest are *possessive*," explained Hector "Dragons Well is *plural*, meaning basically here be drag-"

Steve screamed into his hands again, his frustration knowing no limits. Uncle Shameless elbowed his nephew lightly in the ribs, "Get it? *Drag-on*? Ha!"

"Now what?" asked Zeroth as he studied the beast "It looks like it's just waiting for us."

"Don't you have anything in that pack of yours that'll kill dragons?" Steve asked Zeroth.

"Kill a dragon? Are you *serious*?" asked Alexander, revolted by the idea.

Steve couldn't believe that a duck that got seasick was asking him if he was being serious, but the boy nodded, "Isn't that a standard quest thing? Killing the dragon?"

Alexander, Eira, Hector and Zeroth all gave the boy looks of total disgust.

"Ugh!" gasped Eira, sickened by the idea.

"That's horrible!" huffed Hector, mortified.

Zeroth shook his head, "I'll never understand humans."

Alexander waddled up to Steve, "Look, I don't know how you do things back in your world," he stated as he poked the boy in the chest "But here we don't go 'round killin' dragons."

"Why?"

"W-wh-why?!" exclaimed Alexander the Small. He reached up, grabbed Steve's shirt, pulled the boy down to his eye level, and pointed at the dragon.

"Jus' look at it! How could you kill such a beautiful creature?"

"Well-" started Steve.

"Besides," added Alexander, "They are Children of Zaa, an' you don't go 'round killing a goddess' favorite things."

"No-no," said Hector with a nod "Very bad."

"But we killed them Pyrix," interrupted Uncle Shameless, coming to his nephew's defense, "Ain't they kids of Zuu or somethin'?"

"True," countered Alexander, "An' I'm sure Old Burny is mighty cheesed off 'bout that, but dragons are peaceful, helpful creatures – not winged bringers of fiery destruction. See the difference?"

Eventually, it was decided that perhaps they should attempt to talk to the dragon, since it *did* appear to be waiting for them. Alexander decided that because Steve was the one with "dragon issues," he'd better be the first one to talk to it.

"Can't we vote on this?" pleaded Steve.

"Very well," said Alexander the Small, "Who thinks Steve should go out there first?"

Everyone except Steve raised a hand.

"And who thinks he should not?"

Steve slowly raised his hand.

"There you have it, 5 to 1. Don't you just love democracy? Off you go!" sang Alexander as he pushed Steve out into the clearing.

The damp sand crunched under Steve's steps as he made his way to the well. The dragon was busy scratching itself and did not notice Steve right away.

The reluctant hero cleared his throat, but the dragon was busy scratching behind an ear with one of its arms, much like a dog would.

"Hello?" said Steve loudly, finally catching the dragon's attention.

The giant creature turned its head and looked down at the boy. Its massive head cast an ominous shadow over him. The dragon cocked its head and studied the boy with its large eyes. Eventually a long toothy grin crept across the creature's face.

"Hello there," said the dragon in a booming, refined masculine voice, "You rang?"

Steve realized the dragon was referring to the little gong he had hit with the mallet. "Y-yes," stuttered Steve as he looked in the eyes of the massive creature.

"Ah, well allow me to introduce myself. My name is Five-Toes," said the dragon. He held up one of his tree trunk sized limbs, and sure enough there were five clawed toes.

"H-hi," whimpered Steve.

Five-Toes glanced towards the trees where Uncle Shameless, Alexander, Zeroth, Hector and Eira were hiding.

"Why don't you ask your friends to join you?" asked Five-Toes warmly.

Surprised by the dragon's observation, Steve obediently motioned for everyone to join him. Slowly the others left their damp hiding places among the trees and joined Steve in front of the well.

"You certainly are a soggy lot, my apologies," Five-Toes spoke calmly. "Here, let me help."

Five-Toes opened his large mouth and began sucking in air.

"He's gonna breathe fire on us!" screamed Uncle Shameless as he ducked behind the considerably smaller Alexander and covered his head.

Five-Toes laughed a deep roaring laughter and shook his head. He then blew a mighty gust of warm breath over the group. Alexander would have been blown away, had it not been for Hector grabbing him by his suspenders. When Five-Toes stopped, everyone was surprised to find themselves completely dry.

"Thanks!" called Alexander the Small, glad to be dry once again.

"That's much better," added Eira as she smoothed out her poncho.

Steve pulled a shirt-sleeve to his nose and smelled, he moved his head away quickly, "Except we all smell like fish now, ick."

Five-Toes laughed again; his deep voice shook the ground. "Again, I am sorry little friends," said the dragon. He turned his large scaly head to look at Uncle Shameless "And for the record, I do not breathe fire," said Five-Toes with a hint of resentment.

"I thought dragons breathed fire," confessed Uncle Shameless.

Five-Toes shook its head, "Dragons breathing fire? Certainly not. You're thinking of those flaming brutes, the Pyrix."

"But back home they do," replied Uncle Shameless.

"You have dragons back home, too?" asked Five-Toes, somewhat skeptically.

"Well…in storybooks."

Five-Toes gave a knowing nod, "There you have it, only in a storybook would a dragon breath fire." The large beast scoffed loudly, "Breathing fire? Tsk, what gibberish."

Steve tried to wrap his mind about the debate on dragons Uncle Shameless was having with Five-Toes, but he quickly stopped when his brain started to hurt.

"Shall we go?" asked Five-Toes with a mighty yawn.

The party looked at each other, and then looked back at the dragon.

"Go?" they all asked in unison.

Five-Toes nodded his head and smiled another big, toothy grin.

"That is why you summoned me is it not?" answered Five-Toes with a nod towards the gong.

"Uh, well," hesitated Steve until he realized he did not have a follow-up statement. He looked at his companions, they all shrugged.

"We're here because this crazy oracle – who kept talking in questions – told us to-"

"Oh, how is Geo?" asked Five-Toes happily.

Steve stopped in mid-thought, "You know that weirdo?" he asked, "He is fine I guess."

"He was before we left The Village Formally Known as Uth, The Last Human Village anyway," added Zeroth.

"Yeah, and it was kind of burned down after that," finished Uncle Shameless.

A concerned look covered Five-Toes' face, "I had heard rumors of Uth, but had hoped for them to just be that."

Steve decided to change the subject, "When you said 'go', where exactly were you talking about?" asked the boy as the dragon lazily splashed in the water of the enormous well.

The dragon's eyes lit up "To Mininat, of course."

"Of course," said Steve sarcastically, "And what is that exactly?"

"The City Beneath the Sea," answered Five-Toes with a smile. Suddenly a thought occurred to Five-Toes. His serpentine neck swung down so that his long snout was only a few inches from Steve's face.

"Are you, The Boy?" asked the friendly dragon.

"I have a name," answered Steve regretfully.

"He is, *The Boy*," interjected Eira.

"*I have a name*," Steve said again, slightly irritated.

"Fantastical!" exclaimed Five-Toes

"...Is that even a word?" Steve asked aloud.

"At last, The Boy!" cheered Five-Toes, clapping together his massive hands.

Steve pointed to himself, "Name. I have a name, it's Steve," the boy said once more, even more irritated.

Five-Toes smiled, "We must go at once. The Queen is waiting for you."

"Excuse me? The Queen of what?" asked Steve.

"Why the Queen of Mininat of course," answered Five-Toes

"Oh, of course," said Steve, unimpressed and wondering what manner of person or creature he would be forced to meet this time.

"You sure you won't come with us?" Steve asked Alexander the Small and his penguin first-mate, Hector.

The duck captain shook his head, "My place is above the sea, not under it," he said proudly, as he shook Steve's much larger hand. "Don't worry, I'm sure we'll see each other again."

The duck and the penguin said their good-byes to the rest of the group and made their way slowly out of the sandy clearing.

"But where will you go?" Steve asked, realizing he was actually going to miss the odd little duck.

Alexander shrugged, "Nowheres special, it's up to a higher power than I."

Steve blinked at the profound statement from the little duck, "You mean fate?"

"No," answered Alexander, "Julius. He is the navigator after all, and a darn good one!" Steve rolled his eyes as he waved good-bye to the duck captain.

Five-Toes looked over the ragged group with narrowed eyes and cocked his head in confusion, "Why are you all wearing pots on your heads?"

After doing away with their pots and pans headgear, Eira, Uncle Shameless, Zeroth and Steve looked up at the large serpent-like dragon.

"Please don't tell me we have to go through more water," whined Steve as he looked at the well.

Five-Toes laughed his deep laugh, "Well Mininat is not called The City Beneath the Sea because it's above ground, young hero!"

"What is with this place and water anyway? I've nearly drowned more times in the past few..." Steve thought, and realized he did not even know how long he and Uncle Shameless had been in Eyri "How long have we been here?" he asked Uncle Shameless, who merely shrugged.

"I don't even know how long I've been here! This place is driving me crazy!" Steve yelled as he stomped around the sandy clearing.

Five-Toes reached down with a colossal clawed hand, gently grabbed the boy by the back of his chain mail and lifted him several feet off the ground.

"You must learn to relax young one and to lighten your spirits," advised the blue-scaled dragon.

Five-Toes looked at everyone else, "But there will be time for that later, for now you must prepare to travel with me under the Ralk Sea."

"Do we have to swim?" Eira asked with a hint of anticipation.

Five-Toes laughed, "No lady pelican, you will all ride on me. I shall get you to Her Majesty in no time at all."

"Good 'cause I ain't much of a swimmer," said Uncle Shameless.

"However, you cannot go as you are. You will need to be able to breathe underwater."

"Oh yeah, I forgot about that," said Uncle Shameless.

"And how," star Steve, still dangling in the dragon's grasp, "Will we do that? We don't have any underwater breathing equipment."

Five-Toes gave Steve a confused look, "I know not of this 'ee-kwip-ment' you speak of, is it magic?"

"Hardly," answered Steve. "It is science."

"Sigh-ants…hmm. You humans have strange words, you will have to teach me more some time," said Five-Toes "But it will not be these ee-kwip-ments or sigh-antses, you will be using *lungfish*," explained the dragon.

Now it was Steve's turn to give a confused look, "Excuse me?"

"Lungfish?" Zeroth asked in disbelief, "I thought those were just a legend."

"Far from it. In fact they are cousins of that chattering swordfish hidden away in your cloak," laughed Five-Toes with a knowing wink.

A loud mumble was heard from under Zeroth's cloak, and he regretfully took out Gladius. Right away the fish shaped like a sword hilt began yelling.

"How dare you!" Gladius screamed towards Five-Toes, "I am a not cousin with any lowly *lungfish!* How'd you like if I went around saying your uncle was a snake?!"

Five-Toes looked down at Gladius, "My uncle *was* a snake," he said calmly.

"Uh, yes, uh well," stumbled Gladius, "Never mind!" screamed the swordfish one last time before Zeroth put it away again.

Steve cleared his throat, hoping to get Five-Toes' attention. He was getting sore from hanging by the back of his chain mail shirt. The dragon smiled and put the boy down near a small pool filled with clear water.

"Reach in and grab a lungfish," Five-Toes instructed, motioning for everyone else to do the same.

Steve reluctantly reached into the water and was surprised that he was able to easily grab one of the large fish. Unlike the speedy swordfish, these lungfish were rather sluggish. However, when he pulled the fish out of the pool, Steve was quickly disgusted.

The fish was a dull green color, and instead of a normal scaly body like other fish had, its skin was squishy and smooth. It reminded Steve of trying to squeeze an almost empty water balloon. It had two tiny, black, beady eyes on the top of its head, and its jaw was U-shaped. Various odors and noises emitted from the fish as it lazily flopped around in Steve's grasp.

Everyone else grabbed a fish with ease, except Uncle Shameless who fell into the pool several times until he finally managed to grab one of the slow moving fish.

"Yuck!" protested Steve, holding the stinking fish as far away as he could, which did not really help.

"Excellent," said Five-Toes "Now, put them over your noses."

Everyone stared at Five-Toes in silence. "Excuse me?" asked Steve.

"Excuse you for what?" asked the large dragon.

"No," Steve said while shaking his head, "I meant, what did you say?"

"Put it over your nose," Five-Toes instructed once more.

"Yeah, that's part I don't really understand," said Steve "Or don't want to understand, honestly."

"Have you smelled these things lately?" added Uncle Shameless.

"If you want to breathe underwater, you must put them over you nose," explained Five-Toes.

"So you're saying," Steve said slowly "If I put *this*" he pointed to the slimly, smelly, squishy creature in his hand "Over my face, I can breathe underwater?"

"No, no, don't be silly," answered Five-Toes, "Just over your nose. Not your whole face."

Steve looked down at the ugly creature in his hands, "You have to be joking."

Five-Toes shook his scaly head, "If you wear these creatures over your nose, they give you the air you need underwater."

Steve looked up at Five-Toes, "Where is yours?"

"Mine?" scoffed Five-Toes "Do not jest; I have no need for one."

"Why?"

"Because I am a dragon."

"Well, I certainly can't argue with that logic," Steve answered cynically.

"Certainly not," replied Five-Toes.

With much hesitation, Steve lifted the oozing fish towards his face. It winked at him with its beady black eye. Steve shuddered in disgust.

"That's it, now pull down its jaw. Don't worry you won't hurt it," Five-Toes coached everyone.

"Gross!" cried Steve.

"Hush," scolded Five-Toes "Now simply put its mouth over your nose. That's it."

"Some of us don't exactly have noses," said Zeroth as he pointed to his beak. Eira nodded in agreement with the Hunter. Five-Toes gave them an understanding look,

"Yes I know, but just put them over your nostrils and you will be just fine," he explained as he pointed to the pair of small nostrils at the base of Zeroth's hooked beak.

Steve moved the fish's open mouth over his nose as he was told.

"Now, you might feel something a little bit…weird," warned Five-Toes.

"Huh?" was all Steve had time to say before his nose was sucked into the fish's open mouth with a loud slurp. The fish quickly secured itself tightly around Steve's nose. He felt a blast of air as the fish's mouth inflated slightly. The rest of the fish's body went limp, and merely dangled from Steve's nose, making him look like some kind of elephant boy.

Steve looked at the others, and saw that everyone had their lungfish on as well. Zeroth and Eira looked even funnier than he did since the fish only covered a part of their beaks. But then Steve realized that he probably didn't look any more normal to them.

"This doesn't make *any* kind of sense," criticized Steve as he looked down at his lungfish.

"And a talking dragon telling us to wear fish on our faces does?" said Uncle Shameless.

Steve thought about the whole concept of wearing fish that would give them air underwater, and he realized that did not make any sense either. He looked up at Five-Toes,

"How do these things even work? Is it something to do with their gills and exhaling oxygen?"

The dragon shrugged, "Mag-"

Steve cut him off "Don't say that word! Please!" he begged, as Steve was sick of 'magic' being the excuse for everything in Eyri. Steve shook his head at the whole affair, and thought about being home in good old boring Beacon Pines.

"Are we all set then?" asked Five-Toes.

Zeroth tightened his yellow scarf and nodded. Everyone waited as Five-Toes grabbed them one by one and placed them on his scale covered back.

"Grab a hold of my mane, and hang on tight!" directed the scaly dragon, referring to what looked like purple fur running the length of his spine.

"Here we go! Remember to relax and to keep breathing!" instructed the dragon as he let go of the sides of the large stone well.

Steve took one last glance at the sky before Five-Toes dunked himself under the water in the blink of an eye. The serpentine dragon snaked around the well until he was heading downward and began swimming. The sides of the well followed them for several minutes.

Warm water washed over Steve as they sank deeper and deeper into the Ralk Sea. Five-Toes swam with ease, and his pace never slowed. Eventually the sides of the well melted away as they exited into a large underwater cave.

The walls and ceilings of the cave were covered in spiky rocks, which Five-Toes had no problem swimming over and through, reminding Steve of riding a twisting roller coaster.

Five-Toes came to the mouth of the cave and burst through it out into the open seawater. The crystal clear water gave Steve an excellent view of this underwater realm. Underwater grasses and plants littered the seascape, as did more rocks and other fish. Five-Toes playfully swam through a school of multicolored fish and then through a dense jungle of sea plants.

Steve was so amazed by all of this that he had forgotten that he was breathing air through a squishy, ugly fish attached to his nose.

For about six seconds.

21

After swimming over a graveyard of sunken ships, Five-Toes came to a large canyon and dove down into it with blazing speed.

"Woo-hoo!" screamed Uncle Shameless as he held on tightly to Five-Toes' mane.

"Wait," said Steve "How were you just able to yell?"

A thought suddenly occurred to the boy after asking his question, "And how was I able to ask that?"

Five-Toes laughed deeply, "The lungfish also prevent water from entering your mouth!"

Steve sighed, "Let me guess – more magic?"

The dragon only laughed as he snaked his way along the canyon walls, dodging large rocks and sea creatures of all kinds, including striped bass the size of city buses.

As the canyon walls began to widen gradually, Steve noticed statues carved into them, as well as carvings showing scenes of underwater life. The figures in the carvings were worn down and very old, making their features hard to make out. One wall carving caught Steve's eye as they quickly traveled past it. "Was that someone *sweeping?*"

In the distance they saw that the canyon emptied into a large hole. Five-Toes' burst through it and swam over the top of the hole. He spun over, causing everyone to scream, and swam upside down.

"Behold!" he cried "Mininat!" As they rode through the water upside down, everyone looked over the grand, City Beneath the Sea.

Unfortunately, it was not nearly as grand as they had hoped. The buildings, if one could call them that, were barely anything more then misshapen piles of sand and rocks.

"Ick," Steve said loudly, before being elbowed by Eira.

"Yes," sighed Five-Toes "Sadly, Mininat is not known for its grand buildings. At least not anymore. Years ago, *many* years ago, the old city was very grand indeed," he pointed to crumbling ruins of stone buildings in the city's center, far away from the shoddy sand houses beneath them.

"But as the years went on, more and more citizens moved away from the center of the city into the cheaply built homes you see below you," said Five-Toes as he pointed to a shabby pile of sand that was supposed to be a house. "Furthermore, stores and merchants moved out of the city's Grand Market and are now scattered everywhere."

"That's a shame," said Eira.

"I'll say!" Five-Toes exclaimed. "Do you have any idea how long it takes to run errands when you have to keep traveling to different parts of the city all day? Argh, it is dreadful!"

"Aren't there shops in the center of the city anymore?" asked Eira as Steve wondered what kind of errands a dragon would have to run.

Five-Toes sighed, "Some, but they are owned by the same person and they all sell the same things. Very little variety."

"Why did everyone move away from the city in the first place?" asked Steve as he spied the majestic, yet dilapidated buildings in the distance.

"To have more property. The old city is rather cramped," explained Five-Toes as he spun right side up and passed by a swarm of brightly colored fish, "And better schools."

Five-Toes swam to what he had called the old city and sure enough it was filled with dark, empty buildings. The tightly packed buildings were all shaped like pyramids and were made from dark marble.

Time had worn away most of the buildings, sides of pyramids were missing here and there while others had lost their pointed tops. Crumbling statues littered the narrow passageways between the homes and larger buildings.

Seaweed and other plant life inched its way up and around the triangular buildings, creating green web like patterns. Tiny schools of fish swam through giant cracks in the buildings, the only sign of life Steve had seen in the city's downtown.

Eventually Five-Toes reached a dilapidated castle in the exact center of the city's layout. Steve now saw that the remainder of the buildings were all confined to three triangle sections in three different directions. Each of the giant triangles faced the castle.

The castle itself consisted of a single three sided tower made of smooth rock, and stood slanted on the seabed. The surrounding buildings and fortifications were all in various states of disrepair. Five-Toes swam down toward the entrance of the castle and slid onto the soft, sandy ground.

Everyone climbed off the back of the dragon and walked towards the entrance.

"Wait!" called Five-Toes, "I must go in and announce you to the Queen first."

Everyone moved aside as the dragon swam past them, "Come into the entryway, I shall bring the Her Majesty out to meet you," explained Five-Toes.

The group waited patiently in the small waiting area. Like the exterior of the castle, it too was in shambles and had a triangle motif.

Steve found it somewhat difficult to walk through the water, however Uncle Shameless was not having any problems thanks to the Eldercherry wine, which he was able to drink under the sea thanks to the lungfish.

"This is exciting, getting to meet the Queen," Eira eagerly as she floated around the room.

Steve shrugged, uninterested.

"Aren't you excited about meeting the Queen?" asked the pelican healer. Steve shrugged again.

"Well I think this is huge honor," replied Eira "You do realize that this is the only realm free from Fiach-Ra's yo-"

"Yoke of tyranny? Yeah yeah. I heard it the first time from the blue heron," Steve finished in an uncaring tone as he slowly floated around the waiting room's sandy floor. The room was tilted, causing large piles of sand to form on one side of the room.

Eventually Five-Toes returned, "I shall be bringing out the Queen to meet you momentarily, please bow."

"A Queen?!" Uncle Shameless exclaimed from out of nowhere. He looked himself over in a cracked, dirty mirror on the wall and pulled up his pants and did his best to brush back his hair, forgetting that he was underwater.

"I bet she's *bee-yu-ti-full!*" Uncle Shameless bellowed excitedly.

Eira and Zeroth looked at each other, "Have you even *seen* any citizens of The City Beneath the Sea before?" Zeroth asked.

Uncle Shameless shook his head causing the tail of his lungfish to flop around wildly. "But I'm sure she's a classy lady," said Uncle Shameless as he bowed to the ground in front of the large triangle that formed the door to the throne room.

"Oh, you *won't* be disappointed," Zeroth chuckled as everyone else bowed behind Uncle Shameless. Five-Toes peeked his head out to make sure everyone was bowing and swam out into the waiting area with the Queen beside him.

"I present to you, Her Royal Majesty - the Queen."

Before anyone said anything or had a chance to move, Uncle Shameless spoke up with out looking at the Queen.

"Milady, thank you for this honor to be in your magnificent presence," he said in a charming tone "We have traveled far, but to gaze upon your beauty is a reward beyond comparison."

Without looking up, Zeroth turned his head behind him to cast a quick look at Steve that suggested that he thought Uncle Shameless had lost his mind. After glancing up at the Queen, Steve agreed.

"Oh my, how charming you are," the Queen spoke in a soft, golden voice "You certainly are most welcome in my city."

With his head bowed and his eyes closed, Uncle Shameless extended a hand towards the Queen.

"My lady, might ask thee but a small favor?"

The Queen giggled happily "You might."

"May I kiss thy regal hand?" asked Uncle shameless, using words that his nephew thought he did not even know.

The Queen giggled again, "Oh my, Five-Toes you did not tell me there was such a charmer in your party." The dragon covered his long face with one of his scaly hands and shook his head.

Calmly and gracefully, the Queen slid her hand into Uncle Shameless' grasp. With his eyes still closed he leaned down and kissed her hand.

"Bleagh!" yelled Uncle Shameless after his lips touched her hand, "What was that, an old boot?!"

Uncle Shameless opened his eyes and looked down to see the Queen's leathery, scaly three-clawed hand in his. He quickly glanced up at the Queen.

"Yipe!" he shouted in fear as he jumped into arms of Zeroth, who was now standing up behind him.

Steve hid his face in his hands, "This can't be good," he said to himself.

"What is that?!" hollered Uncle Shameless as he pointed to the creature in front of him. It floated above the sea-floor in the water, propelled by waving its finned snake-like lower-half. Its upper torso was covered in several small, form fitting plates - reminding Steve of a turtle's underbelly.

It had a head similar to Five-Toes, including the whisker-like tendrils near the snout, but was a green brown color instead of Five-Toes' bright blue.

While it had no legs, it did have two long lanky arms that ended with clawed hands of two fingers and a thumb that were webbed. Two horns jutted out from its temples like a pair of sevens and two long curved teeth on either side of its top jaw escaped its leathery lips.

"*That*," Five-Toes said in a slow pace that did more than hint at his embarrassment "Is the *Queen*."

"This *really* can't be good," gasped Steve.

Several bulky guards of similar appearance to the Queen appeared from nowhere and began swimming towards Uncle Shameless with sharp spears. Silver helmets covered their heads and simple plate armor covered their chests.

Panic grabbed a hold of the companions as the guards approached with their weapons readied. Steve feared the worst, when all of a sudden the agonizing silence was broken. More of the Queen's giggling filled the room. She swam up to Uncle Shameless and patted him on the head with one of her clawed hands.

"And funny too!" she squealed. "Please," she said with a polite bow of her own "Would all of you join me in my throne room?" she turned and swam through the triangular doorway behind her. The guards lowered their spears and swam away to their hiding places.

The companions looked at one another, and Zeroth let go of Uncle Shameless. They walked past Five-Toes, who was still in shock. As Uncle Shameless walked haphazardly past him, the dragon reached down and lightly flicked the back of Uncle Shameless' head with a clawed finger as a punishment for insulting the Queen.

"Ow!" was all Uncle Shameless had time to say before Five-Toes pushed him into the throne room and pulled the door shut behind him with his whip-like tail.

The Queen was waiting for the companions and was sitting on her throne. She watched each of them enter, this time walking instead of swimming. To everyone's surprise she immediately sat up and started yelling.

"What are you doing?!"

Everyone looked at her, confused.

"Get off the floor! I just had it swept!" the Queen screamed as she quickly swam over to Steve and lifted him up off the stone floor with ease, forcing him to float. She looked down and gasped at the sand that had been tracked in by everyone.

Steve found himself confused that the Queen so easily shrugged off the insults by Uncle Shameless, yet was quick to anger over something as trivial as tracking sand onto the floor – which was underwater anyway.

Five-Toes asked everyone to swim in place as to keep off the Royal Floor while the Queen directed servants in their sweeping. This was harder than normal given the fact they were many feet underwater and the sand would only float up momentarily just to land back on the floor again.

Steve pulled on one of Five-Toes' hands. The dragon leaned down to the boy, and Steve whispered into the dragon's pointed ear, "What's her problem? We're underwater, doesn't everything just sort of wash away?"

The dragon answered the boy in a quiet whisper, "The Queen takes cleanliness *very* seriously. Especially when it comes to sand. It reminds her of the citizens who have moved out of the old city and into those poorly built sand houses I showed you."

The dragon made a quick glance around the throne room to make sure no one was watching and whispered again, "Plus, the cleanliness thing sort of runs in the family."

Sure enough, the Queen *was* taking the entire sweeping of the floor business very seriously. Her calm, smooth voice from before had been replaced by one that was loud, gruff and perhaps best suited for someone who worked at a truck stop diner.

"No! *Not like that!*" she yelled in a deep commanding voice as she swam over to a servant and showed him how to sweep properly.

Suddenly, Steve remembered the wall carving he had seen of someone sleeping a floor and realized now how much sense it made.

Finally, the Queen was satisfied, but only after she had taken a broom from a servant and swept the floor herself. She swam over to the storage closet and placed the broom back in its proper place, made sure that the closet was locked (twice) and swam back to her throne.

The Queen's throne was made of an aged metal, with a high back topped by a large triangle with the point near the Queen's head. Steve figured that the triangle was the symbol of the royal family and that was the reason everything in the city was shaped like one. The Queen got comfortable in her throne and proceeded to introduce herself.

She bowed her horned head slightly and spoke eloquently to the group, "Welcome to my city, I am Queen Lana the IV, Ruler of the Wurms, Daughter of –"

"Look, I'm never gonna remember any of that," interrupted Uncle Shameless "Can I just call you Stumpy?" he said, referring to her lack of legs.

Everyone's' jaws dropped in shock as Uncle Shameless had once again insulted the Queen. He noticed the silence, "No? Okay, how 'bout Wurmie?" He looked around for approval; he looked up and saw Five-Toes staring at him, mouth agape and shaking his head.

"What?" asked Uncle Shameless "*What?*"

The silence was quickly broken by the Queen's giggling. "You truly are a treat!" she exclaimed in-between giggles.

"Oh no, she's gonna eat me!" cried Uncle Shameless as he looked for an exit.

Queen Lana the IV laughed again, "Please, come sit by me, funny one."

"No, I'm comfortable floating here, thank you."

"Oh, please. I insist," demanded Queen Lana the IV.

"So do I," begged Uncle Shameless but he was pushed over to the throne by a swift shove from Five-Toes. He sank down to one of the small steps leading up the throne and sat nervously, still thinking the Queen wanted to eat him as a treat.

"Who else is with you?" she asked Five-Toes. The dragon motioned for everyone to step forward and show themselves to the Queen. Eira was first and she bowed respectfully.

The Queen smiled "Ah, a pelican–"

"Strange bird the pelican!" yelled Uncle Shameless as if on cue.

Queen Lana the IV looked at Uncle Shameless, confused.

"I do not understand," confessed the Queen and before Uncle Shameless could explain his joke, Zeroth stepped forward. The Queen's eyes widened at the sight of the unusual looking bird-man.

"You certainly are an interesting creature," said the Queen as she studied Zeroth's mixture of bird features.

Zeroth did not know what to say, and simply bowed his head and stepped aside allowing Steve to move forward. Steve walked to the Queen, which took some extra effort since he still was no accustomed to walking underwater.

The Queen's eyes widened even more as she looked the boy over. "Is that you, Steve, Destroyer of Cities?"

Steve was not familiar with this new title of his and he did not like the sound of it.

"What are you talking about?"

Five-Toes turned to face the Queen, "Yes Majesty, what do you mean by calling him 'Steve, Destroyer of Cities'? This is *The Boy*-"

"Just Steve is fine," interrupted Steve.

"This is Just Steve," continued Five-Toes with a nod. Steve shook his head at the dragon's misunderstanding of what he had said, "He is the one spoken of in The Prophecy."

Even though they were far beneath the waves of the Ralk Sea, Steve shook his head as he heard the familiar thunder rumble once more.

"Where did you get that title?" asked Eira.

"I don't know, I never destroyed any cities," answered Steve.

"No, I mean your title of 'Just', you didn't mention it before," she smiled at the boy "You must have done something very valiant," said the pelican.

Steve shook his head as fast as he could while underwater, "No, I didn't-"

"Silence please, Just Steve Destroyer of Cities," commanded Queen Lana.

"Great," Steve said to himself, "Now I'm one of those weirdoes with too many names." The boy was certain he heard Gladius chuckle under Zeroth's cloak.

"You have not heard then?" The Queen asked Steve. The boy shook his head.

Queen Lana the IV waved a clawed hand; three bubbles appeared and began spinning in her hand. They crashed together in a burst of white light and formed a large glowing bubble that cast the throne room in a pale white light.

"Fiach-Ra, the Hawk-King, has blamed you for the destruction of The Village Formally Known as Uth, The Last Human Village," explained the Queen as a ghostly image of the destroyed village appeared in the shining bubble, giving everyone a view of the wanton destruction caused by the Hawk-King's forces.

"In addition to putting a lofty price on your head," she said as the bubble now showed a poorly drawn wanted poster of him with equally poorly drawn letters,

"His minions have been traveling the land spreading tales of the destruction you cause and how dangerous you and your friends are."

The bubble showed even more poorly drawn wanted posters of Eira, Zeroth and Uncle Shameless, who took exception to the unnecessary detail paid to his lazy eye.

"Oh c'mon! It isn't *that* bad!" he bellowed as he looked at the poor drawing of him with one large, lopsided eye. Zeroth noticed that his poster made reference to the Formal Compliant filed against him. He clenched his beak as he tried to keep his anger in check.

Queen Lana continued, "He has also blamed you for the destruction of Tal."

"What?!" everyone cried in unison – except Uncle Shameless, who was still pretty upset about the wanted poster.

"Tis true," said the Queen regretfully, realizing they were unaware of the attack on the duck city. "Look," the bubble showed the still burning buildings of the port city. Flights of Pyrix choked the sky or sat perched on the charred remains of buildings.

A flying figure hovered above a shattered light house. It held a flaming spear and was directing Pyrix and Hawken with it. The vision moved in closer, and Steve once again looked upon Fiach-Ra. The bubble changed and showed the side of Fiach-Ra's head, Steve stared at the image without blinking.

Suddenly, Fiach-Ra turned his head and looked in Steve's direction, a loud hawk cry filled Steve's head and the bubble burst, ending the vision.

"Tal has been demolished and its citizens enslaved," sighed Queen Lana. Steve suddenly felt very bad and thought back to when Istrio had yelled at him for not going directly to Uth.

"The Hawk-King's minions continue to spread their lies that you are responsible," explained Queen Lana with a concerned look toward the boy.

Steve's eyes lit up, "Then you know I didn't destroy those cities?"

"Just because I live in a crumbling castle under the sea does not mean I don't keep up on current events," she replied. "But while you did not *directly* cause their destruction, your choice to go to Da'Rahga instead of Uth-"

"Wow, word gets around doesn't it?" interrupted Steve.

Queen Lana smiled a jagged toothy smile, "It does Just Steve, Destroyer of Cities. But what is done is done. You cannot change the past, but you can shape the future with what you choose to do next."

22

"The what?" asked Steve.

"The Temple of Arcana," Queen Lana the IV said again.

"There you will meet The Three Sisters, and they will help you on the next part of your quest."

"Woo-hoo! Three sisters!" exclaimed Uncle Shameless from his spot on the floor next to the Queen.

"Why do I have to keep going to all these different places and meeting all these different people? This is like a scavenger hunt! Why can't I just go to one place and take care of everything at once?" whined Steve.

"Convenience and simplicity do not a hero make," sang Five-Toes the dragon.

"Uh, okay," answered Steve, not completely understanding Five-Toe's meaning. "Where is this temple?" asked Steve reluctantly.

"Do not worry, Five-Toes will transport you there," explained the Queen. The great dragon nodded and smiled a toothy grin.

"But it is your choice. If you decide that you wish to go no further, Five-Toes will transport you to the surface."

"Really?" asked the boy, considering the idea.

"Yes," nodded the Queen sternly, "But if you chose not to go to the temple, who knows what will happen to the enslaved citizens of Tal, or the rest of Eyri. Or you can continue your quest and become the hero you were prophesized to be. The choice is yours."

Steve weighed the options in his head. He was not against giving up if it meant he could go home. But the Queen did not really say anything about going home, just that he'd be taken to the surface, and he could only guess what would happen then. And on the other hand, deep down he felt he owed something to Mudd, Tuuga and the others who had helped him so far.

The boy sighed and thought that the sooner he went to this temple and did whatever he had to do, the sooner he could get back on land and get rid of his lungfish. He was getting tired of breathing the breath of a squishy, ugly fish.

"Okay, let's go," he said finally, causing the Queen to break into a wide smile. Steve figured staying underwater a little while longer wouldn't be too bad, since there weren't any Pyrix or any other crazed giant monsters after him down there.

The companions turned to leave after bowing once more to Queen Lana the IV.

"Get lost!" Queen Lana the IV cried after them. The companions stopped in mid-swim and turned to face the Queen, confused by her remark.

"What'd you say?" asked Uncle Shameless.

"Get lost!" the Queen exclaimed with a wave and a smile.

"What's the big idea?!" yelled Uncle Shameless.

What Uncle Shameless did not realize was that telling someone to 'get lost' was the politest and friendliest good-bye in Wurm society. It dated back hundreds of years to when the founder of the kingdom, Derf, got lost one day and found the canyon valley that Mininat was later to be built in.

Telling someone to 'get lost' was shorthand for wishing someone luck on a journey and to benefit from something unexpected.

It would have shocked many a Wurm to find out the saying did not hold the same status among humans back in Michigan.

"Please," the Queen said proudly, "Get lost."

"Well, same to you lady!" bellowed Uncle Shameless in an angry tone.

"Why, thank you!" beamed Queen Lana as she smiled at the unsuspecting Uncle Shameless, whose anger she mistook for serious compassion.

Uncle Shameless glanced around at the rest of the Wurms in the room. "In fact, *all* of you can get lost!" he bellowed, still not realizing he was giving everyone a very high compliment. The Queen's servants and guards bowed their heads respectfully to Uncle Shameless and began applauding him as he exited.

"Go on, get lost!" cried a guard.

"Yes, get lost!" yelled several servants.

Still believing the Wurms were insulting him, Uncle Shameless continued returning the volleys one by one by pointing to individual Wurms as he swam by, saying "Get lost!" to each one.

As they exited the throne room, Queen Lana along with her servants and guards all yelled 'Get lost!' loudly in unison.

"What a bunch of jerks," snapped Uncle Shameless as the triangular doors shut behind him.

Five-Toes glanced down at Uncle Shameless in surprise, "I had no idea you were so versed in Wurm culture."

"What do you mean?"

"The Jerks were a saintly tribe of Wurms, who went around doing good deeds-"

The rest of the explanation was cut of by Steve screaming loudly in frustration.

"...And so the one cannibal says to the other, 'That was no lady, that was my lunch!'" laughed Uncle Shameless as he told jokes to pass the time while traveling to the Temple of Arcana on the back of Five-Toes. As always, he was the only who laughed.

"Here we are," Five-Toes said eventually. In the distance Steve saw a crumbling temple that looked similar to the buildings in Mininat. Unlike the castle, however, it was not leaning to one side. Five-Toes swam to a sandy outcropping and lowered himself to the ground.

"Why are you stopping here?" asked Steve "The temple is still a ways to go."

Five-Toes smiled his friendly smile, "This is as far as I go young one, from here on the journey is up to you."

"You're leaving?" asked Steve, feeling like he might miss the dragon.

Five-Toes nodded as everyone, except Steve, dismounted the dragon and swam to the sandy seabed. Five-Toes turned his blue scaly head to face the young boy,

"Fear not young hero, I have faith in you. I'm positive you will fulfill The Prophecy."

Steve ignored the distant rumble of thunder and reached out to pat Five-Toes on his snout. A rare smile crept across the boy's face as he left the safety of the dragon's back and joined his companions on the seabed.

Everyone waved to Five-Toes as he swam away and out of sight. Once he was gone, Zeroth turned to the group, "Shall we?" he said gesturing to the path ahead of them.

The path to the Temple of Arcana was surrounded on each side by tall rocks, forming a natural fence. After a few minutes of swimming, the path opened into a large open space like an empty field, surrounded on every side by the same tall rocks. Across the field, was the temple.

"It is very still and quiet here," Eira noted after not seeing any signs of underwater life for several minutes.

Zeroth nodded, as he too had noticed the lack of sea-life in the underwater field they were swimming across. The rocks surrounding the edges of the field climbed many feet up and curled inward so that it resembled a mouthful of nasty looking teeth.

Steve tried to guess how far the pointy rocks went up, but he could only guess that it would take them a long time to try and swim over the rocky fence.

Zeroth stopped in mid-stroke suddenly, "What is it?" asked Eira.

"Better not be more of those Wurm jerks, because –"

"Quiet!" Zeroth snapped at Uncle Shameless as he scanned the dark, sandy horizon. "I thought I saw some movement in the water."

"It's nothing," said Steve, although he was wondering why it had suddenly gotten darker where they were swimming. He looked at the temple ahead of them, "C'mon let's get this over with, I want to get this smelly lungfish off my nose."

Steve began swimming past Zeroth.

"Wait! Don't!" yelled the Hunter.

"Huh?" was all Steve had time to say before a giant object slammed into the ground just inches in front of him. The force of the impact threw Steve backwards into Zeroth. Huge amounts of sand were kicked up as well, clouding their vision.

"What was –"Steve asked before Zeroth quickly covered his mouth.

As the sand cleared, they saw what had almost crushed Steve. It was a massive, red lobster claw, with pointy bumps covering its surface in random places. To Steve it looked more like a huge red tree since the claw, even with part of the pinchers buried in the sand, was well over ten feet tall.

Slowly the claw moved upward as its owner began drawing it out of the ground. As the companions watched, it seemed as if the pinchers were never ending.

Finally, the pincers were free of their sandy prison and everyone saw the tips of the jagged, red pinchers.

"Crackers!" cried Uncle Shameless at the sight of the enormous claw.

Everyone was afraid to find out what the giant arm was attached to and started swimming faster, but could not out run the huge shadow looming over them like a dark storm cloud.

Steve looked up to see the attacker, but all he could see was a vague silhouette. They were trapped in the sandy field by the rocky boarder and their only hope was to head for the Temple of Arcana.

They all swam to one side, only to be stopped by another claw slamming into the sand to block their way. Any time they made a turn towards the temple they were stopped by one of the claws nearly crushing them, forcing them to turn back.

"What is attacking us?" Eira asked as she glanced upward, only to have the same result as Steve.

"I don't know," answered Zeroth "But it's clear it does not want us going to the temple."

"Then let's forget about the lousy temple!" cried Steve "I'll take the hint, let's just get out of here!"

Zeroth turned to face the boy, his eyes narrowed in anger. He reached over and grabbed the boy by his chain mail and shook him, letting his anger momentarily get the best of him "We can't do that! *You have no idea the trouble I am in for helping you!* We *will* reach that temple!"

"Oh, nuts to the temple!" yelled Steve as his sense of self-preservation kicked in after being shaken by the angered bird-man. The boy turned away from Zeroth and began swimming up, hoping to make it to the surface. Zeroth immediately regretted yelling at Steve and swam after him.

Steve and Zeroth were only able to swim a few feet upward when a powerful current from above, pushed them back down to the sand with a low THUD.

"What hit me?" asked Steve.

"Whatever that thing is, it swam right above you. It's very fast," answered Eira as she helped the boy get upright.

"It's coming..." whispered Zeroth as he righted himself.

Sure enough, the large shadow finally swam away from them, only to turn downward and begin swimming right for the group.

Its shape and features were still hidden by the shadows from the rocky wall but whatever it was, Zeroth could tell it was enormous.

"Get ready!" called Zeroth.

"For what?" asked Steve.

"Anything!"

"Brilliant strategy, General," Steve said sarcastically. Deep down, he tired to hide his own fear of the large shape cutting through the water towards them.

The creature broke from the shadows cast by the rocks and Steve did not know whether to be terrified, amazed or disgusted.

The creature was the size of a school bus, but not just any school bus. One of those super-fancy models that is extra large with a bathroom and a movie screen. It had two large, long lobster's arms; complete with the deadly crushing claws the companions had already seen.

The bright orange-red pinchers and arms were connected to the main body, which was covered in light brown feathers until the mid-section. At the halfway point of the creature, the feathers stopped and were replaced by the plated sectional body of a lobster, complete with the spindly legs underneath and a fan like tail at the rear.

From the feathered upper back sprung two giant feathery wings, which made the creature look even larger.

Adding to the creature's odd collage of body parts was its head. An eagle's head, complete with a terrifying beak, sprang from its feather-covered upper torso. On either side of the beak were two orange red, long whip-like tendrils. Lastly, its angular eyes were pupilless and glowed a dull yellow, reminding Steve of a Jack-O-Lantern.

Steve threw up his arms in protest, "Okay, that's it. I give up," he said in a cynical tone "I've had my fill of crazy, and that just put me over the limit."

Zeroth gasped, "A Roc Lobster!"

"Correction, *that* did," Steve said as he looked at Zeroth. "What did you say that thing is?"

"A Roc Lobster!" answered Zeroth "Cam told me a legend about it once."

"Drat," cursed Steve "I was hoping you were kidding."

"It's a Child of Zaa," Zeroth said "Its part Roc –

"Looks part bird to me," interrupted Uncle Shameless.

"A Roc *is* a bird!" argued Zeroth.

Uncle Shameless thought hard for a moment and glanced at the rock wall around them, then back at the oncoming Roc Lobster.

"I've never seen rocks fly before, but I have seen them roll...although there was this one time when I was playing in the back-yard and-"

"Not rock, *Roc!*" corrected Zeroth.

Uncle Shameless stared at Zeroth, "Yer talkin' crazy."

"R-o-c, not r-o-c-*k!*" yelled Zeroth.

Again, Uncle Shameless stared at the frustrated Zeroth and shook his head, "Look, I didn't spend two years in the first grade for nothin', I'm pretty sure I know how to spell-"

"I really hate to interrupt this witty banter, but we still have a very angry thing –" Steve began.

"Roc Lobster," added Zeroth "Also known as-"

"One name only please," interrupted Steve "As I as saying, it's still heading right for us."

Sure enough the Roc Lobster was still heading towards them. It swooped down to the sandy seabed and landed on its ten spindly, spider-like legs. Its landing and scuttling kicked up large amounts of sand, make it difficult for the companions to see.

"We need a plan," said Zeroth.

"Wow, you think so?" snapped Steve, still angry with Zeroth for yelling at him.

"Swim away?" asked Uncle Shameless.

"I second that," added Steve.

Zeroth swam over to Uncle Shameless, "Shameless, I have a plan and I know it's asking a lot but…I need you to drink more of your wine."

Uncle Shameless' face lit up, "I like this plan already!"

"Good, and after that all you need to do is fight the Roc Lobster while we dash for the temple," added Zeroth quickly. Uncle Shameless thought for a moment, looked down at his wine skin, then looked over at the large monster rapidly scuttling through the clouds of sand, and then looked at his wine skin one more time.

"Well, it ain't a perfect plan, but it'll do," Uncle Shameless answered.

Zeroth swam over to Steve and Eira to prepare them for their part of the plan.

"We will have to fight the creature-"

"*Roc Lobster,*" Steve interjected mockingly.

"Yes yes," replied Zeroth, "We will have to fight the Roc Lobster until Shameless can properly distract it."

Steve looked at the Roc Lobster as it scuttled nearer and nearer, "Fight *that?*"

"Yes!" commanded Zeroth, as he reached inside his cloak for his swordfish Gladius.

Steve followed Zeroth's example and reached in a pocket for his own swordfish. However, the boy had forgotten that once a swordfish is back in water, it wakes up from its state of hibernation.

"Ugh!" cried Steve as the swordfish quickly swam out of the boy's grasp.

"What's wrong?" asked Zeroth.

Steve pointed to his swordfish as it quickly swam away. The small fish darted through the water and headed for the rocky boarder of the underwater field.

However, it was not fast enough to escape the reach of one of the whip-like tendrils on either side of the Roc Lobster's face. The tendril shot out in a flash and grabbed a hold of the fish, only to whip it back to the creature's waiting mouth.

All of this happened in a matter of seconds, causing Steve to seriously rethink his idea of swimming away. The boy noticed Gladius was still in Zeroth's hand and had not swum away as well.

"How come Gladius didn't swim away?" he asked.

"Psh," hissed Gladius "He wishes I would swim away. Tough luck, freak show! Ya ain't gettin' rid of me that easily."

Zeroth shook his head and readied Gladius; the swordfish's large eyes watched the huge creature lumber towards them.

"Forget it! I'm *not* fighting that thing!" yelled the talking swordfish as it refused to extend its sword-like tongue.

"You don't have a choice," Zeroth said as he tightly squeezed Gladius' small body, causing to fish to 'Bleah!' loudly as its sharp tongue shot out. Steve and Eira hid behind Zeroth as the Roc Lobster closed in.

Meanwhile, Uncle Shameless floated around drunkenly, trying to remember what it was Zeroth had asked him to do.

The speed of the Roc Lobster's approach caused a powerful current to wash over the companions. They tightly hung on to each other, except Uncle Shameless.

Zeroth praised Uncle Shameless' strategic thinking, although he failed to realize that Uncle Shameless was too busy singing to himself and was not paying any attention to the events going on.

When the Roc Lobster was within a few feet of Zeroth and the others, it reared up onto some of its rear legs. It gave a mighty bellow, and its two front legs began stabbing downwards at the group, like large orange-red spears.

Each blow struck the ground, and only the ground thanks to some quick swimming by the web-footed Eira and Zeroth.

Zeroth swung Gladius at the legs but they were too quick to strike. The bird-man dodged out of the way of a large claw as it swung at him before swimming over to Eira, who was hanging on to Steve.

"You keep hanging on to him. When Shameless distracts the beast, swim towards the temple as fast as you can," Zeroth ordered as he kept his eyes on the scuttling Roc Lobster. Eira nodded and tightened her grasp on Steve.

The group did their best to dodge blows from the Roc Lobster and patiently waited for the unseen Uncle Shameless to strike.

Sadly, Uncle Shameless had dozed off and was floating through the water sound asleep.

The Roc Lobster attacked again with its giant claws, each time coming within mere inches of crushing Steve and the others. They continued to swim out of the way of the creature's dangerous, but slow moving, claws. Zeroth batted at the hard claws with his swordfish, but it had no effect.

Meanwhile, Uncle Shameless continued his nap.

No matter where the companions swam to, the Roc Lobster scuttled around to cut them off from their destination. Zeroth had enough, and pushed off from the sandy ground, launching upwards in the water until he was eye-to-eye with the attacking Roc Lobster.

The creature opened its mighty beak and roared as one of the two tendrils near its beak lashed out at Zeroth. The bird-man dodged the giant fleshy whip and swung at it with his swordfish, cleaving off several feet from the tip.

As Uncle Shameless dreamt during his nap, he heard within his dream a loud roar as if something had been hurt. Then he heard more yelling and someone kept calling his name. He did not like this dream, as it was noisy and it smelled bad too, like a fish market on a hot day.

He was jarred from his slumber when something hit him.

"What's the big idea?!" Uncle Shameless called out and felt around to see what had hit him. He grabbed a large squishy object in his hand and opened his eyes.

"What the-" he started as he looked down at the cleaved section of the Roc Lobster's tendril that had floated into him while he was sleeping.

"Sea-Snake!" Uncle Shameless cried in fear as he fought the lifeless tendril. The tendril had managed to wrap itself around part of his body, and after a few minutes Uncle Shameless was free. He was annoyed at being woken up, but since he had been dreaming a rather boring dream he did not mind too much.

Then Uncle Shameless heard the screams and roars from his dream and looked over to see Zeroth and the others fighting the Roc Lobster.

"What the heck is *that* thing?" he asked aloud, completely forgetting his conversation with Zeroth from only a few minutes before.

Whatever it was the man thought, it was harassing his nephew and friends. Uncle Shameless decided quickly to put a stop to that.

"I think you made it mad," Steve said to Zeroth after the Hunter cut off part of one of the Roc Lobster's tendrils. The beast roared again and again as it continued trying to impale the trio with its, spidery legs.

Gladius began mumbling, all of which was impossible to understand with its tongue extended. Zeroth gave the silver swordfish a squeeze, retracting its tongue.

"Way to go genius! What are you going to do next, insult its mother? If you ask me I-"

"I still want to know why you didn't swim away," Steve asked "All you've done is complain since Istrio gave you to Zeroth. I figured this would be your big chance to get away."

"I ain't goin' nowhere, he's stuck with me!" gloated the talking swordfish. "Besides," continued Gladius "Common swordfish like yours are cowards anyway, they don't have the steel courage that I – LOOK OUT!" screamed Gladius as a large lobster claw swung into Zeroth, knocking him back through the water and forcing Gladius out of his clawed hand.

"Help!" Gladius pleaded from the seafloor.

"What do you mean, 'help'?" Steve asked "You're a fish."

"I can't swim!" confessed Gladius.

Steve rolled his eyes. *A fish that can't swim, what's next?* he thought to himself.

As Eira kicked her way through the water to help Zeroth up, Steve swam down and picked up Gladius.

"Steve!" cried Eira.

The boy quickly turned to see the Roc Lobster only a few feet away. Steve squeezed Gladius to extend its blade with a loud 'bleah!' and held the sword in a threatening manner. Of course, had Steve been holding Gladius correctly, instead of upside down, it would have been threatening. Instead, it was just plain silly.

The Roc Lobster reared up on its back legs and roared a battle cry that sounded like an irritable whale that had been smoking for years. Its intact mouth tendril shot out at Steve like a huge bullwhip and pushed Steve down to the ground so that he was lying flat.

The boy fought against the leathery tendril but it held him fast to the seafloor. The mythic beast leaned close to Steve so that its huge beak was only inches away. It tilted its head and studied Steve with one of its glowing yellow eyes.

The Roc Lobster brought its head back as it roared again and sent a crushing lobster claw down at the helpless Steve.

As Steve watched the enormous jagged claw fall down, he was glad he was underwater, because he was certain he had just wet himself.

23

The next second or so for Steve felt more like ten or perhaps even fifteen. The Roc Lobster's claw hurled down toward him, intent on putting an end to his quest. He thought of home, his parents, and even Uncle Shameless.

"If they had just sent me to computer camp, none of this would have happened," Steve thought aloud, remembering the argument he'd had with his parents about spending the summer in River City with Uncle Shameless.

The frightened thirteen year old glanced up at the Roc Lobster's claw in time to see a plaid-colored torpedo dash its way through the water over him and stop the claw only a few feet above his body.

"Pick on someone yer own size!" cried a voice that put the emphasis on all the wrong syllables, as if it were hiccupping.

Steve looked up to see Uncle Shameless above him, holding apart the giant lobster pinchers so that they formed a U.

The Roc Lobster roared at this intrusion, to which Uncle Shameless replied by pushing up on the creature's arm with all his Eldercherry wine induced strength. The force of this caused the Roc Lobster to lose its footing in the sand and sent it floating back several yards.

"Okay," answered Uncle Shameless, "Hows 'bout just me then?" he said as he cracked his knuckles and pushed off from the seabed towards the Roc Lobster.

Uncle Shameless crashed into the Roc Lobster with such force that it was knocked onto its back. He then proceeded to wrestle the creature.

"I'll handle this guy!" called Uncle Shameless as he rained thundering blows down upon the Roc Lobster, "Get lost!"

"Hurry!" Zeroth ordered, after Eira helped him up so he could swim. She swam quickly to Steve, grabbed him and they both began swimming for the now unprotected Temple of Arcana.

"I'll take that," Zeroth said, reaching for Gladius. He gave the silver swordfish a squeeze, causing the hilt shaped creature to draw its deadly tongue back in with a loud slurp.

"Thank you!" said Gladius, grateful to be away from Steve, "I couldn't stand another minute with him. He was holdin' me back'ards for Zaa's sake!"

Zeroth ignored his annoying weapon and tucked it away inside his cloak. The two bird-people and the boy swam towards the Temple of Arcana as the sounds of Uncle Shameless' clash with the Roc Lobster echoed around them.

Uncle Shameless was thankful for the extra-ordinary strength he had in Eyri. Otherwise he knew that the Roc Lobster would have made short work of him quickly. Uncle Shameless worked his way onto the creature's back by grabbing handfuls of feathers. This only irritated the creature more, as it did not like having its feathers harshly pulled on or yanked out.

Uncle Shameless tried to get his hands around the creature's neck, but was unsuccessful because its neck was the size of a tree trunk. The Roc Lobster rolled around in the water, trying in vain to shake Uncle Shameless loose.

"Ha!" bellowed Uncle Shameless "You'll have to do better than that!"

As if answering the challenge, the Roc Lobster spun upside down and dragged its back along the sandy seabed. "Pbbt!" sputtered Uncle Shameless with a mouthful of sand.

"That's dirty pool!" he yelled at the back of the Roc Lobster's head as it continued swimming upside down across the sand.

Uncle Shameless started crawling from the upside down creature's neck, until he was standing on its chest. Since the Roc Lobster was so large, it could not look down to see Uncle Shameless, and was caught off guard when the man dove at its large beak.

With all his might, Uncle Shameless shot himself at the large beak and tackled it. The Roc Lobster's head was driven into the sandy sea floor until it was almost completely submerged in sand.

The Roc Lobster's body flailed about as it fought to get free, but it could not get any leverage due to being upside down.

"That's right!" Uncle Shameless taunted in a bragging manner as he continued to hold the creature's head against the sandy seafloor.

Uncle Shameless gathered all his might and lifted the creature's head out of the sand and he bellowed, "Had enough?"

The Roc Lobster only roared and continued flailing around.

"Guess not!" yelled Uncle Shameless as he pushed the creature's head back into the sand. A few moments later Uncle Shameless once again freed the feathery head from its sandy prison.

"How 'bout now?" asked Uncle Shameless.

Again, the Roc Lobster answered with a loud roar. Uncle Shameless shook his head and pushed the creature's head into the sand once more. "Talk about stubborn," he said.

"*What* is he doing to that thing?" Steve asked as he glanced back at Uncle Shameless while frantically swimming towards the Temple of Arcana.

"I'd rather not think about it," answered Zeroth.

Steve agreed and continued swimming along side Eira, who was easily the best swimmer in the group. Even as she hung onto Steve with one hand, she cut through the water with stunning expertise. It reminded Steve of the day she saved Uncle Shameless and himself from drowning.

With the Roc Lobster detained by Uncle Shameless, the three adventurers had no problems crossing the barren sandy field that was between them and the Temple of Arcana.

The temple looked ancient, even older than the stone buildings in Mininat. The building was egg shaped, with a high domed roof. A covered entryway extended out from the front of the temple, supported by chipped and worn stone columns. In the center of each of the columns was a figure carved out of the rock with its hands above its head, supporting the weight of the rest of the column. Seven columns filled each row, and followed the same pattern of figures. First two Wurms, then two humans, followed by two blue herons, and lastly a single owl-person on each side, right by the large stone door.

The last figures intrigued Steve, as he had yet to see any owl people while in Eyri.

The trio floated under the entryway and stopped in front of the main door. It was easily twenty feet high and made of very thick rock. "Well, now what?" asked Steve.

Zeroth shrugged, as did Eira. Steve swam over to the large stone door and knocked against the hard surface.

"Hello?" he called. Nothing happened.

Discouraged, Steve turned to the others, "Well that's just dandy. We go through all the hassle to get here and we can't even get in!"

"I'm sure there is a way," Eira said calmly.

"Yes, we were sent here for a reason," agreed Zeroth "Let's look around."

Steve sighed and rolled his eyes as he looked around the entryway for some hint of a way into the mysterious temple.

Zeroth began inspecting the various statues in the columns and Eira went to study the door. Steve floated around, dispirited. His eyes fell to a stone sandbox in the center of the roofed entryway to the temple. He swam over to the unnatural looking sandbox to examine it in more detail.

The sand in the sandbox was not like the sand on the sea floor. It was pure white, almost snow-like in color. Steve noticed that any lines or shapes he made in the sand stayed in place even though the sand was underwater.

"Weird," whispered Steve as he looked around the edge of the sandbox.

As he floated over the edge, he saw an oddly shaped stone sticking out a few inches above the rest. He swam down to it and inspected it with more care.

There was a hole cut into the center of the rock and it was filled with sand from the seafloor. Steve reached down and brushed out the hole, reveling its true shape.

"What is this?" he said aloud as he looked at the odd shape. It was indented, as if something were to be put into it. Steve turned his head and looked at the shape upside down. His eyes widened.

He had seen this shape before.

The boy looked around for Zeroth and Eira, "Uh, I think I may of have found something."

Zeroth and Eira joined the confused teenager by the stone sandbox. Steve pointed to his discovery.

Zeroth cocked his head and peered down, "Looks like a hole."

Steve nodded sarcastically, "Very good."

"What is it for?" asked Eira.

"Dunno," confessed Steve, "But what I do know is that *this*," he pulled out his blue heron amulet and held it up, "Fits into *that*," he pointed to the jagged hole that was a perfect outline of the amulet.

Steve took off the amulet and kneeled down next to the hole. He gently placed the amulet into the hole – it fit snugly.

"So, now what do we do?" asked Steve. Both Eira and Zeroth shrugged, neither having the slightest idea.

Suddenly, the amulet began glowing a bright blue light and before the trio could react they were completely bathed in the peculiar azure glow.

"Bah!" Steve cried in alarm, not knowing what to expect.

In the distance a series of rumbles sounded and began moving towards the temple.

"Ah, crumbs!" Steve cursed, "It better not be that Roc Lobster after us!"

In a flash the temple and the companions were hit by a powerful underwater current. Zeroth, Eira and Steve were knocked back through the water and saved themselves by grabbing onto whatever they could find.

Steve looked in the direction of the rumbling and saw three bright blue blurs traveling through the water towards him and his friends.

"Now what?!" Steve yelled.

The powerful currents continued as the three blurs grew closer and closer. Steve felt as if he was going to be dragged off by the current and tightened his grip on a nearby statue. Sand began blowing into his face, making it hard to see.

For the first time he was thankful for the lungfish on his nose which let him breathe without inhaling sand.

"Look!" yelled Zeroth, pointing to the area just in front of the temple's entryway. Steve squinted his eyes in the swirling sandstorm and saw three small cyclones.

"Oh, marvelous," Steve said cynically.

The three cyclones grew larger and larger until they were around eight feet tall. They came to a stop just before the covered entryway of the Temple of Arcana and spun in place.

"I don't like this," Steve said loudly as the cyclones began spinning faster and faster until they were nothing more than blurs of sand and blue light.

As they cyclones spun, an odd sound filled the companions ears. It sounded like low chanting and a choir going 'Ahhhh' in unison. The cyclones began glowing blue, Steve's eyes widened.

When the three cyclones suddenly exploded into huge flashes of blue light, blinding Steve and the others with their brightness.

Steve kept blinking until his vision returned, even though he hated opening his eyes underwater. He glanced over at Eira and Zeroth, to see that they were also okay.

Steve noticed the whole area was blanketed in a shimmering blue light. He slowly turned his head towards where the three cyclones had been. His jaw dropped.

Hovering in the water were three very tall ghostly visages of blue herons, dressed in the same kind of robes as Istrio's. But these three looked different from Istrio, they looked like they were female.

Their arms were crossed over their chests and they were looking at Steve with blank glowing eyes.

Steve remembered this time *not* to throw any rocks.

"Uh, hello?" Steve finally said to the three Mystics of Zaa.

"You-" said the first in a delicate feminine voice.

"Are-" continued the second in a similar tone.

"The Boy?" finished the third, in a voice just like the others

"Yes," Steve sighed reluctantly. He still hated being called 'The Boy'.

"So, it was-" started one blue heron-lady.

"Foreseen by us-," continued another in an supernatural tone

"That The-" started the last blue heron, before being cut off by Steve.

"Okay look. I hate to be a killjoy, but I really can't handle the three of you talking like that," he said, irritated. *Geo had been bad enough with his questions*, thought Steve, there was no way he was going to put up with another long winded story split up between three talkers.

"Seriously, can we just skip all of the over the top dramatics and just get down to the point?" asked the boy.

The three blue heron Mystics looked at each other and then looked back at Steve.

"Fine by me," said the first in a more casual tone.

"Ditto," said the second.

"Yes, that'll work," finished the third.

Steve smiled, "Good, I'm sure you're all very busy-"

"Well, not really," started one of the ghostly blue herons, "We've actually been asleep for-" she started before Steve cut her off.

"-And I'd like to get things moving along, because I really want to get this lungfish off my nose."

One of the blue herons smiled, "Very well, let's get right to it then."

24

Steve, Eira and Zeroth swam over to the tall shimmering visages of the blue heron Mystics. Zeroth tried to apologize to Steve for yelling at him earlier, but the boy ignored him.

"What are your names?" Steve asked as he looked up at the semi-transparent giant images.

"We are The Three Sisters," answered the first. "I am Reshyl, Daughter of-"

"Let's keep this to a one name maximum," said Steve.

Reshyl blinked and stared at Steve, "You're one to talk, Just Steve Destroyer of Cities," she countered with a hint of venom.

Steve rolled his eyes, "Please don't call me that. Besides, how did you even about that?"

Reshyl smiled, "Five-Toes told us. What he hears, we know," she answered.

"Wait a second," started Steve "If you 'know' what he hears, then why did we have to come all the way to this old temple? Why didn't you just come to Queen Lana's castle and save us the hassle?"

Reshyl looked at Steve calmly, "That just isn't how these things are done."

"What kind of answer is that?"

"Listen here little mister, there are certain rules and ways of acting when it comes to quests such as yours," began Reshyl.

"-You're not going to start talking about that stupid Prophecy again are you?" Steve asked over the rumble of distant thunder.

The other two blue herons cleared their throats at the same time, attempting to derail the growing argument.

The ghostly image of Reshyl rubbed her eyes, "Ahem, yes anyway..." she pointed the sister on her left "This is Alura," Alura bowed her head slightly. Reshyl then pointed to the sister on her right "And finally this is Akyrn, and we are The Three Sisters."

"You already said that part," added Steve

"Oh, yes. Sorry," confessed Reshyl. "We are Mystics of Zaa, and guardians of the Temple of Arcana."

Reshyl waved a hand and a globe of light appeared in her palm. It flashed and began showing moving pictures, just like Istrio and Queen Lana had done.

"Long ago before The Fall, the skies were ruled by –"

"Sorry, but can we skip all that too?" asked Steve. "I'm not in the mood for a boring, long-winded back-story."

Reshyl narrowed her blank eyes and crushed the glowing globe in her hand, shattering it like an old Christmas ornament.

"*Fine*," hissed Reshyl, "Because its not like I've only been waiting, oh three hundred some odd years for this moment. But fine! I'll skip the 'boring back-story'."

"Good, I'm glad you understand," answered Steve, choosing to ignore her sarcasm.

Akyrn pointed to the temple's door, "You see that door over there?"

"Yes," answered Steve.

"You must open it."

"…You don't say," sighed Steve.

"I do say," continued Akyrn. "And you must open it to enter."

Reshyl's semi-transparent image floated over to Akyrn's, "What are you doing? It's *my* job to instruct him, not yours!" Reshyl yelled at her sister "It's bad enough he wants to skip the one thing I've been waiting centuries to tell. I don't need you stepping on my toes!"

"But why do you get to do both?" asked Akyrn nastily, "That isn't really fair."

"Because I'm the *oldest!*"

Alura covered her face in embarrassment as she watched her sisters argue.

Zeroth swam towards the arguing Reshyl and Akyrn, "Ladies please," Zeroth spoke in a rare gentlemanly tone, "Let's try and stay focused."

"Argh!" yelled Reshyl as she hovered away from her sister "Very well," she calmed down slightly and continued, "As my sister was saying, you need to open the door to the temple."

"Yes, yes. I got that part," said Steve "But how?"

"That is your challenge," began Reshyl "It is the –

"CHALLENGE OF ARCANA!" all three sisters cried in unison as they threw up their hands and flashes of light exploded around them.

Steve stared at the three semi-transparent sisters, unfazed by the over the top theatrics. "I thought we agreed to leave out all of the crazy talking stuff."

"Sorry, we couldn't help it," confessed Alura.

The Three Sisters hovered over to the stone sandbox that Steve had found earlier, and they beckoned the companions over. Akyrn waved a glowing hand to the sandbox, "Behold, The Box of Arcana, and in it The-"

"Sand of Arcana?" Steve finished flatly.

"Why, yes," said Akyrn, surprised, "How did you know?"

"Lucky guess."

Akyrn continued, "You will open the door to the temple using this sand."

Steve looked down at the sand and then over to the door. "Uh, and how do I do that?"

Alura waved a clawed hand over the blue heron amulet that was still stuck into stone at the base of The Box of Arcana. The amulet reacted and began flashing.

"Very pretty, but-" Steve started until the Three Sisters shushed him. A beam of light shot up from the jeweled eye of the amulet. The beam then quickly began turning solid.

"Impossible..." whispered Steve.

"Oh, my..." gasped Eira.

"What the..." added Zeroth.

Alura reached down and grabbed the object; it was only a few inches long and resembled a pencil. She held it out to Steve.

"Use this," she explained, "In The Sand of Arcana." Alura motioned to the sand with a nod.

"...And do what exactly?" Steve asked as he held the pencil made of solid light.

Akyrn spoke, "Whatever you create in the Sand of Arcana using that," she pointed to the object Steve held, "Will alter the door and allow you inside. That is The Challenge of Arcana."

"So, The Challenge of Arcana is for me to draw in the sand with a stick?" asked Steve in a suspicious tone.

All of the Three Sisters nodded in unison.

"Oh you have got to be kidding."

"What do you mean you don't know how to draw?" Eira asked Steve a few minutes later.

"I've never done it before, we weren't taught how to draw in school," explained Steve "The closest thing to drawing we ever did was when we made bar graphs to show the rise in unemployment."

"Oh," replied Eira and Zeroth, not understanding most of what Steve had just said.

"Just give it a shot, what do you have to loose?" coached Zeroth.

"Yes, just try," Eira added supportively.

Steve shrugged and swam down to the pure white sand and stared at it. He had never drawn anything. His school had done away with the art program in favor of Double Nuclear Chemistry. He began to dip the make-shift pencil into the sand but hesitated.

He did not know what to do, or even how to begin.

Steve thought for a moment and jabbed the pencil into the sand. He moved his hand around quickly, forming the shapes he wanted. When he was finished, he looked at it and smiled.

He had written 'Open' in the sand. He looked up, expecting to see the large stone door swung open to allow him in. Instead, all he saw was the word 'Open' carved into the old rock.

"Oh, c'mon," whined Steve.

"Try again," directed Alura.

Discouraged, Steve brushed away the words with a free hand. The carved word disappeared from the stone door.

His lack of art experience certainly was making the Challenge very much a *challenge*. He tried to think of what to draw. He thought of what an open door looked like in his mind.

Steve closed his eyes and thought hard. The clouds of reason began to part within his mind's eye and he imagined a picture of an open door. He thought hard to keep the image in mind as he opened his eyes and set to work to draw a copy of this open door in the sand.

He slowly jabbed the make-shift pencil into the sand and moved it away from him, and drew the left side of a doorframe. He stopped and moved the pencil to the right, creating a backwards seven until he reached a certain point.

Then he moved the pencil back towards himself, forming a lowercase n shape. His lines were uneven and shaky, but he tried not to focus on his lack of talent, and was only concerned with finishing.

Steve then drew the bottom of the door frame, completing an uneven, lopsided rectangle. He glanced up at the actual temple door and did not notice any changes, but he was not discouraged since he was not yet finished. He thought hard again to bring the image of a door back into his mind, and immediately knew what he had to add.

On the right side towards the middle, he drew a simple door knob. Instantly, there was a loud cracking sound and Steve looked up from his sand drawing to the temple door.

A door knob, identical to the one in his drawing, had appeared. Steve looked up at the Three Sisters for a sign of approval, but the eerie blue herons just stared back at him, unmoving.

Eira spoke up, "Why not go try it?" pointing to the door knob he had created. Steve shrugged and swam over to the temple door and grabbed a hold of the simple knob and twisted it. To his surprise, the knob turned.

"This isn't possible…" he whispered to himself as he pulled on the knob.

The door did not move.

"It didn't work!" he yelled, annoyed.

"Are you sure you don't have to push it in first and then turn?" called Zeroth as he floated over the Box of Arcana.

"Did you turn it the correct way?" asked Eira, "Because sometimes that can –"

"I don't think it matters!" Steve yelled back, trying unsuccessfully to hide his annoyance with the situation. Zeroth studied the door with his sharp eyes and thought that maybe something was missing.

"Maybe you forgot something?"

Steve tried to ignore Zeroth as he swam back to the sandbox. He stared hard at the door and tried to think of what he needed to add. *The door has a knob, what else could it need?* he thought to himself.

Steve thought hard again to bring the image of a real door back into his mind. He studied the image with his budding imagination and thought of all of the parts of the door. Eventually inspiration struck and he got to work fast.

On the left side of his door drawn in the sand, he added hinges at the top, the bottom and in the middle. Just like before with the doorknob, the hinges instantly appeared on the temple door. Steve smiled, satisfied and swam over to the temple door.

He grasped the door knob once again, turned it and pulled. To his amazement and surprise, the door swung open easily as its new hinges groaned loudly.

"Well done," praised Reshyl as her sisters joined her in clapping, although their ghostly hands did not make any sound.

Steve looked down at his poorly drawn door with its equally poorly drawn knob and hinges, and smiled. He had enjoyed his first experience with drawing.

"Shall we go inside?" asked Alura as she and her sisters floated through the water towards the now open temple door.

Zeroth, Eira and Steve followed the giant shimmering images of the Three Sisters into the waiting temple.

The glow of the Three Sister's iridescent bodies lit up the interior of the ancient Temple of Arcana. It was more like a cave than a temple, with jagged rocky walls and floors. Steve swam carefully to avoid hitting any of the larger, sharper rocks and tried to stay within the eerie glowing light given off by the blue heron Mystics.

The Three Sisters came to a stop near a large stone box that sat in the center of the room atop a tall column. The base of the column was carved into a large eagle with its wings spread.

Akyrn pointed to the box, "Go there and open the box. The tool you need to defeat the Hawk-King will be inside."

Finally, Steve thought to himself, even though he did not want to fight the Hawk-King or even see him again. He swam to the stone box that sat proudly on top of its stone column.

Steve pushed the lid off of the box with all his might, causing it to fall off and sink to the floor of the temple. Dust and sand spilled out of the box, and instead of waiting for it to clear Steve reached blindly inside for the fabled Sword of Zaa.

However, what he pulled out of the box was not the Sword of Zaa. In fact, it was not even a sword.

25

"A *stick*?!" Steve yelled loudly as he swam back down to the Three Sisters. He waved his find in front of them. It was a simple wooden sick, several inches long and the thickness of a broom handle. It had a pair of twigs sticking out from the sides; one even had a tiny green leaf.

"Is this some kind of joke?" asked Steve bitterly.

"No," answered Reshyl plainly.

"You mean to tell me I fought Gulls, rode a crazy flying boat, put a smelly fish over my nose and almost got crushed by a bird-lobster, just to get a beat-up old stick?"

The Three Sisters were silent for a moment, then answered, "Yes," in unison.

"What am I going to do to the Hawk-King with this thing?" asked Steve in a very angry tone *"Give him splinters?!"*

"Perhaps," answered Reshyl.

"What do you mean *'perhaps'*?!" Steve screamed.

Reshyl floated over to Steve, "This is not just an ordinary stick, it is a weapon that is only limited by your imagination."

"Huh?" replied Steve as he looked at the stick in his hand.

Akyrn floated down next to her sister, "This stick is The Staff of Arcana, it will help you on your quest."

"I thought my quest was to get this thing."

"Dear me, no," replied Alura, with a chuckle "Who told you that?"

"Your brother," snapped Steve.

"Brother?" asked Akyrn.

"Yeah, Istrio."

The Three Sisters laughed in unison, "Istrio is not our brother," explained Alura "But it is not unlike him to be a little misleading in these matters. That is his way."

"What, do you think all of us blue herons are related just because we look similar?" demanded Akyrn.

"Uh, well…uh…no," stumbled Steve, embarrassed at his mistake. He had a sinking feeling he was going to have to go to yet another strange, far away place.

Reshyl placed a glowing ghostly hand on Steve's shoulder, "Young Harrier, you must go to Arx A'Quila."

"Ah *c'mon!*" protested Steve. "How many more stupid places do I have to go before I'm done with all this crazy stuff!" He swam away from the Three Sisters and headed towards Eira and Zeroth.

"It never ends!" he yelled to the blue heron sisters. "I'll tell you one thing, I'm not walking anymore. I've had my fill of walking, that's all I seem to do around here is walk *everywhere.*"

"Fear not Just Steve, Destroyer of Cities," replied Reshyl calmly. "Upon exiting this temple you shall find the transportation you desire." Before Steve could ask what she meant, Reshyl and her sisters disappeared in a flash of vaporous blue light.

After exiting the temple, Steve swam over to the Box of Arcana and grabbed his mysterious blue heron amulet. He thought about how he was collecting an odd assortment of talismans and relics while in Eyri, and wondered if he could take them back to Michigan with him when he left.

Steve rolled his eyes at the thought, since he wondered *if* he'd even get home. It seemed to him that every time he got close to finally leaving Eyri, he had yet another task given to him. Being in Eyri for him was almost as bad as doing weekend chores with his dad back home in Beacon Pines.

As the trio swam away from the Temple of Arcana, they heard an odd chorus of yells and roars. They hurried to where they had last seen Uncle Shameless, only to find him trying to teach the Roc Lobster how to sing 'What Do You Do With a Drunken Sailor.'

"No, no, no, not like *that!* Listen to me dang-nab-it," scolded Uncle Shameless as he sat on one of the Roc Lobster's claws. Uncle Shameless cleared his throat and began singing again, "What do ya do with a drunken sailor-" he pointed to the Roc Lobster, and the creature opened its beak to sing,

"Arrr, oor oarr awwwk!" the Roc Lobster roared deafeningly.

"No! No! NO!" coached Uncle Shameless, making the creature try again.

"Arr, woo woa aww ark!"

"*Better!*" smiled Uncle Shameless, who did not notice that Steve had swam up behind him with a very disapproving look on his face.

"What," Steve spoke slowly, "Are you doing?"

"Steve m'boy! Glad you could stop by!"

Steve rolled his eyes and gestured to the Roc Lobster.

"Oh," continued Uncle Shameless "I'm just teaching Rosco how to sing –"

Steve covered his face with a hand, "...Rosco?" asked Steve even though he did not want to know the answer.

"Yeah Rosco," Uncle Shameless pointed to the Roc Lobster. "I gave him a new name, he seems to like it. Don'tcha Rosco?"

Rosco the Roc Lobster roared a cheerful cry and flapped his wings.

"And *why* are you teaching him to sing?" asked Steve.

"Well I sure couldn't teach him to dance, look at how many legs he has!"

Steve groaned loudly and thought about getting back to the surface as soon as possible.

"But we saw you fighting when we left," said Zeroth as the studied the enormous creature.

"Oh, that. Heck, weren't nuttin, just had to take a little of the fight out of ol' Rosco here. We tumbled a bit, but when I held him down and told him why we were here he stopped fighting."

"He stopped fighting after you said why we were here?" asked Eira.

"Yep, ain't that something?"

"Oh, it's *something* alright," Steve replied sarcastically.

As Eira and Zeroth looked over the now tame Roc Lobster, Steve searched around for the transportation the Three Sisters had so cryptically told him about. Discouraged, he swam back to the group to find them listening to Uncle Shameless tell a story about the time he tried unsuccessfully to kayak across Lake Superior.

After the part about him getting picked up by shipping vessel and being forced to dance for the crew (which he proudly demonstrated), everyone broke out in laughter.

Rosco flapped his large wings as a sign of approval. Steve stared at the wings on the back of the odd creature and a feeling of knowing and dread washed over him.

"Oh they have got to be kidding," he said to himself as he finally realized what the Three Sisters had been referring to. Steve swam over to Uncle Shameless and interrupted his story, much to everyone's displeasure.

"What is it boy? Can't it wait until I'm done? I'm almost to the part were I had to fight off a swarm of lampreys."

"Do you think the Roc Lobster–" started Steve.

"Rosco," Uncle Shameless interrupted.

Steve rolled his eyes and continued "Do you think *Rosco*, could fly us out of here?"

"I dunno, why don't you ask him?" Uncle Shameless said as he nodded towards the large creature behind him.

Steve sighed and could not believe what he was about to do. He looked up at Rosco and stared into his large glowing eyes, "Rosco," Steve said very formally and without any emotion, "Could you fly us to Arx A'Quila?"

Rosco reared up on his legs and roared,"Arrrrooooooo!"

Uncle Shameless looked back at Steve and smiled, "That's a yes."

"Swim faster, U'nala commands you!" U'nala ordered from the back of the hastily repaired old fertilizer cart. The lackluster craft was being pulled through the water by a very tired Remmit and Kaz both swimming to the best of their ability. Kaz, with his webbed swan feet, was having a much easier time than Remmit.

This difference in swimming ability led Remmit to under steer while Kaz over steered, which resulted in the cart going in a circle most of the time until U'nala yelled at them to straighten their course, which happened about every five minutes or so.

"Are we any closer to shore yet?" Remmit asked as he reluctantly kicked with his taloned feet.

"You asked U'nala that only moments ago and the answer is still the same!" hollered the bitter Wing-Master. "No!"

"I don't mind," said Kaz with a wide smile across his orange bill "I like swimmin'!"

Remmit narrowed his eyes at the large Swantan warrior, "You *would*."

Kaz returned the nasty gaze to the smaller Hawken, "What's *that* s'pose to mean?"

"Oh nothing," Remmit started in a calm tone, "Only that you're too *stupid* to know any better. This isn't fun, this is *work*!"

"Oh yeah?" countered Kaz, "Well at least I *can* swim!"

"Big deal, I'll take flying over swimming any day," Remmit said proudly.

"Yeah, well I'd take having a fancy lunch with your mother over flying *any day*!" yelled Kaz.

Remmit's eyes filled with rage, "You take that back!"

"Never!"

The small Hawken dove at the Swantan and they began wrestling in the water while exchanging insults. From the back of the old fertilizer cart, U'nala rolled his eyes as he stood up.

"Stop that at once! U'nala commands you!" he cried, but the two warriors ignored their superior officer and continued fighting. U'nala growled as he leaned over the front of the cart to grab the two fighting bird-men. However this was harder then he had imagined and he nearly fell in the water several times.

All the while, the dimwitted trio failed to notice an ever-growing rumbling sound underneath the sea. U'nala reached out and finally grabbed the shoulders of each of his warriors and banged their heads together.

"Ow!" cried Remmit.

"That wasn't nice!" Kaz yelled as he winced.

"It wasn't s'pose to be nice!" U'nala bellowed as he banged their heads together again, creating a loud knocking sound.

"Ow!" Remmit cried again.

"That still wasn't nice!" yelled Kaz

"Silence!" bellowed the angered Wing-Master, "U'nala grows tired of your fighting, you two must work together if we are ever to…" he paused for a moment and cocked his head to one side "Do you two hear that?"

"All *I* hear is a bunch of hot air," Remmit joked.

"No, it is most definitely not hot air," replied U'nala, not understanding Remmit's remark "It is something underneath us…something in the water."

Remmit and Kaz waded in the water, silent.

"I don't hear anything," said Kaz.

U'nala listened again, "No, U'nala does not hear anything either, perhaps it was nothing…now where was U'nala?"

"*Working together,*" sighed Remmit.

"Yes, that's right…as U'nala was saying, it is important for-"

Right before U'nala got to the point of his speech, the Roc Lobster blasted into the sky from the water underneath the shabby cart. The force of the creature's giant head and beak shattered the cart and sent its former passengers flying in all directions.

U'nala, Remmit and Kaz landed safely in the water with several large splashes, and surfaced in enough time to see the Roc Lobster – with several passengers on its back – fly off into the horizon.

The three minions of Fiach-Ra stared at the magnificent beast as it soared through the sky, and U'nala did not know what the creature was, but he had a feeling the Hawk-King was not going to like hearing about it.

26

"...And so the second man says, 'Well then how does he smell?' and the first man answers 'terrible!'" Uncle Shameless joked as Rosco the Roc Lobster soared through the crimson sky.

Everyone except Steve laughed. The boy was too busy getting his lungfish off his face. After some struggling, he was about to give up.

"What's the deal with this thing?"

"Having problems?" asked Eira. Steve nodded. She gripped the lungfish with her slender hands and pulled with all her might.

"Stop! Stop!" screeched Steve, as it felt like his nose was about to be ripped off his face. Eira let go and apologized.

"Great, I'll be stuck with this thing forever. I'll spend the rest of my life looking like a weird elephant boy."

Steve heard muffled laughter come from inside Zeroth's cloak as Gladius laughed at the conversation. Zeroth reached into his cloak and pulled out his irritable talking weapon.

"I'm glad you find this amusing," snapped Steve.

"After spending a few hundred years locked away, I needed a good laugh," chuckled Gladius.

"What did you do over all of those years?" asked Zeroth.

"Thought about things. Mostly about Donal and the good ol' days."

"That sounds very...boring," confessed Steve as he tried once again to remove his lungfish while hanging onto Rosco's back.

"Well, I also worked on rhymes," said Gladius with a hint of excitement. "Would you like to hear one?"

"No, not rea-" started Steve before Gladius went ahead anyway.

> *"Darkness is my darkly home,*
> *Blackness is my blackened cage,*
> *Even though it has no bones,*
> *A fearsome beast, is my rage,"*

"Wow," gasped Steve, doing his best to pretend to be impressed by the senseless drivel he had just heard "How long did you spend on that?"

Gladius thought for a moment. "I don't know, maybe thirteen years."

"I think you shoulda spent *fourteen*," joked Steve.

"Let's see you find inspiration while locked away in a box for a few hundred years! I was going to tell you how to get them lungfish off ya, but fergitit!" snapped Gladius. Steve quit tugging on his lungfish and crawled over to Gladius, "Oh c'mon! Please!"

"Alright. But on one condition."

"Anything!" begged Steve.

"You have to listen to my free verse poem, *What I Did In The Dark*."

After a lengthy dose of *vers libre* torture, Steve was happy to learn that all it took to remove a lungfish was a quick tickle to its side. The odd-looking fish let out a raspy laugh and let go of the boy's nose, causing him to rejoice as he breathed in fresh air once more.

Everyone else followed Steve's example and removed their lungfish in the same manner. Uncle Shameless asked Rosco to stop at Dragons Well so they could return the helpful fish to their small pond.

Zeroth and Steve jumped down from the massive creature's back and walked to lungfishes' home. After dropping the squishy fish into the water, Zeroth took Steve aside before they made their way back to Rosco and the others.

"Look, I'm sorry I yelled at you earlier," the Hunter apologized in an awkward tone that suggested it wasn't something he did too often. Steve looked up at Zeroth and could tell the bird-man truly meant what he said. His sharp hawk's eyes were filled with regret, and his expression did not have his usual hardened edge.

"It's okay," Steve replied calmly, "But what did you mean when you said I had no idea the kind of trouble you were in?"

"I'm in big trouble kid, *big* trouble."

"Because the Hawk-King is after us?"

Zeroth shook his head. "Because he knows you for some reason?" the boy asked.

"No, and I don't even know what all of that is about."

"Then what's the problem?" asked Steve as they passed the giant stone well in the center of the island.

"The Kingdom filed a Formal Hunter Compliant Form dash TB against me," explained Zeroth. Steve gave him a very confused look. "That's bad. Very bad," replied Zeroth.

"Why?"

"Because, it means that the Hunter's headquarters, known as The Lodge, will be very upset with me."

"I still don't understand," confessed the boy as he kicked at a rock.

"The Lodge has zero tolerance for Hunters who breach their contracts and commit treachery or betrayal – which I did by helping you."

"So?"

"*So,*" began Zeroth uneasily as he struggled to find the words, "It means that the Lodge will-"

"Hey!" bellowed Uncle Shameless from his spot on Rosco's back "Put a wiggle on it you two! We ain't got all day!"

After they had climbed back onto Rosco, the mighty beast roared and took flight once again. The Roc Lobster's speed and strength still surprised Steve. He held tightly onto his glasses so that they would not fly from his face during the trip. He looked out toward the distant horizon and wondered what his next destination was going to be like.

"What is this place we're going to?" asked Steve.

"Arx A'Quila," answered Zeroth "It was the seat of the old owl kingdom. It's a palace, not too different from Fiach-Ra's Arx Vena'Tor."

"Yes," added Eira, "But no one has set foot in it for hundreds of years."

"That's right, not since Fiach-Ra usurped Fel-Ra's throne," finished Zeroth.

Steve looked over at Uncle Shameless, who was sharing yet another story with Rosco, "Did Rosco say how long this trip would take?" asked Steve as the wind blew through his hair.

"He said it shouldn't take too long. With wings as big as his I imagine we'd get there in no time."

Eira gasped suddenly. Everyone turned to face her (except Rosco, as he was too busy flying). The pelican pointed down to the ground below.

Smoke and burning buildings littered the scenery they flew over. The coastline and the docks showed that it could only be one place, "*Tal,*" whispered Zeroth, "What is left of it anyway."

Rosco's body cast a large shadow over the skeletons of the burned out buildings of the once proud duck city.

"Looks like a few fires are still burning," Steve said as he watched flames jump a few buildings.

"Where?" asked Zeroth as he looked to spot Steve pointed. As the bird-man scanned the buildings with his hawk-eyes, what he saw sent a chill over him, "*Pyrix*," he spat.

Horrible shrieks clouded the air as a flight of Pyrix took to the sky after the Roc Lobster.

"I thought we finished them off!" yelled Steve.

"Looks like the Hawk-King had a few more than we thought," said Zeroth as he thought up a plan.

"Don't worry, ol' Rosco here will take care of them, won't you Rosco?" added Uncle Shameless as he patted the Roc Lobster's feathery head. Rosco roared and turned his huge body around so that he was flying toward the approaching Pyrix.

"I don't think this is a good ide-aaaaaah!" Steve screamed as Rosco dove towards a Pyrix.

"Hang on everyone!" advised Uncle Shameless, a moment too late.

"Let us know a little sooner please," begged Steve.

The lead Pyrix broke off from the rest of the flight and headed towards Rosco. Its black bones and ever burning flames blended in with the crimson sunset. The Pyrix opened its jagged beak and shot a giant fireball towards its target. Rosco roared and spun to avoid the fiery missile, Steve felt the heat as it blazed past them.

Annoyed, the attacking Pyrix flapped its flaming wings and streaked towards Rosco. The smaller creature had a slight speed advantage over the large and bulky Roc Lobster, not to mention the four passengers he was carrying. The Pyrix dove underneath its prey and pulled up quickly so that it flew right in front of the Roc Lobster.

"What are we gonna do?!" cried Steve as he watched the flame-covered beast open its beak to use its breath weapon. Before Steve could blink, a powerful stream of fire shoot out of the Pyrix's mouth, and was aimed right for Rosco's face.

Without hesitation, Rosco held up one of his lobster-like claws to use as a shield. The stream of fire bounced harmlessly off the tough exoskeleton, and before the Pyrix had time to more or react, Rosco swung at it with his other enormous pincher, grabbing the villainous creature effortlessly. Rosco roared loudly as he crushed monstrous bird with a simple squeeze of his giant claw.

Back at Arx Vena'Tor, the Hawk-King blinked as his magical link with the Pyrix was severed, but not before he had a good look at the Roc Lobster and its passengers. Fiach-Ra slammed the bottom the Spear of Zuu against the floor in his throne room out of frustration, as he had not expected Steve to have the aid of such a powerful creature.

The Hawk-King relaxed and opened his mind to the surviving Pyrix in hopes of learning as much as he could about what The Boy was planning next.

"I think I'm gonna be sick," said Steve as he looked over the edge of Rosco. Seeing the Roc Lobster crush the Pyrix in his huge pincher had been somewhat unsettling.

Uncle Shameless reached over and slapped Steve on the back, "Buck up boy, an' hang on tight!" he yelled before adding a heart-felt "Woooooo!" as Rosco dove towards the three remaining Pyrix.

The three fiery birds shot up at the Roc Lobster, screaming their horrible screams.

"Enough foolin' around there Rosco," commanded Uncle Shameless as he peered over the Roc Lobster's forehead "Let's get a move on to that Archa...Ackuh...Archie..."

"Arx A'Quila," corrected Eira.

"What she said," smiled Uncle Shameless.

Rosco roared again and did a sharp turn away from the trailing Pyrix, flapping his mighty wings to gain speed. The three remaining Pyrix continued their pursuit, screeching all the way.

One shot a stream of fire at Rosco, but he dodged it – much to the discomfort of Steve and his uneasy stomach.

"We can't have them attacking us from behind," said Zeroth as he began to stand up.

"What are you doing?!" exclaimed Steve.

"You and Eira, hold onto my legs, I'll try and scare them off from our tail," ordered Zeroth.

"And just how are you going to do that? Yell at them?" Steve asked in disbelief.

Zeroth ignored the boy and pulled out Gladius, "'Bout time!" yelled the swordfish as it scanned the sky with its large eyes and spied the three angry Pyrix.

"*Wings On A Swantan!*" exclaimed the swordfish. "A fine mess you've gotten us into! Why, if ol' Donal were here he'd-*BLEAH!*" was all Gladius had to time to say before Zeroth gave him a hefty squeeze and pulled his shield out of his magical pack.

The boy watched as Zeroth tried in vain to scare the Pyrix off by waving his swordfish around, Gladius' sharp blade clashed with the Pyrixs' flaming talons, showering Rosco's back with sparks. Zeroth's battle scared shield was able to withstand some of the flames the Pyrix shot at him, but Steve could see that his shield would not hold out much longer and had caught fire.

Steve wished that he could help, even though he did not like the idea of standing up while they were flying, since Rosco did not exactly have seat belts. Since Steve had lost his own swordfish when it swam away, now all he had was an old stick that was supposed to be some sort of magical weapon.

He thought the whole idea of a stick being a magical weapon was ridiculous. He held the Staff of Arcana in his hand, and wondered what kind of magic it could *possibly* possess that made it so special.

A red-orange glow caught his attention, and he saw one of the Pyrix had broken off from the others and flown along the side of Rosco, unknown to Zeroth, as he was busy with the other two. It glanced at Steve as flames poured out of the empty eye-sockets of its blackened skull.

The Pyrix dropped open its pointy beak, ready to shoot a fiery blast at the unsuspecting Zeroth. The air hissed as the stream of fire shot towards the Hunter.

"No!" Steve yelled, and without thinking jumped in front of the flames to protect Zeroth. He closed his eyes and thought of something, anything that could shelter them from the wicked flames.

Abruptly, Steve felt something heavy in his hand that felt like cold metal. He felt the force of the Pyrix's breath weapon, but not the heat. He opened his eyes.

In the hand where he had been holding the Staff of Arcana, was now something else. Steve blinked, not understanding, but realized quickly that it was protecting him and Zeroth from the Pyrix's flames.

"What the…" he started to say as he looked over the new item.

Zeroth pushed Steve aside and swung his swordfish in the direction of the attacking Pyrix. It had the effect he'd hoped for; the Pyrix flew around the front of Rosco.

The Roc Lobster made short work of the would-be attacker with a swing of mighty pincher. The Pyrix exploded after being struck by the giant claw, spraying fire and bone all over Rosco and his passengers.

"Well that's a new one," said Uncle Shameless as he beat out the tiny flames around him and tossed shards of bone over the side "I didn't know they could 'splode like that."

"Yes, we'll have to be careful about that next time," noted Zeroth.

"Um, hello?" Steve said to get everyone's attention "Can someone tell me why am I holding a beat up trash can lid?"

27

Zeroth inspected the trash can lid; it was dented and dull silver in color. "This…*trash can*… you didn't have it with you?"

Steve gave Zeroth a look that said 'what do you think?'

"No, I s'pose not," whispered Zeroth as he inspected the large metal object once again.

"Here, let me take a closer look," he held out a clawed hand Steve handed the trash can lid to him. Instantly there was a flash and the lid disappeared. All that remained in Zeroth's hand was the Staff of Arcana.

"Ah-ha!" Eira cried out from behind Steve.

"What do you mean 'ah-ha'?" asked Steve as he turned to face the pelican.

"Isn't it obvious?" she asked.

"*Enlighten me,*" said Steve curtly.

"The Staff of Arcana can turn into different objects."

"How? It's just a stick," replied Steve.

"Mag-" started Eira happily.

"*Yes, yes.* Magic," Steve sighed as Zeroth handed the Staff back to him.

"I hate to interrupt, but we still have two visitors behind us," called Uncle Shameless. Rosco emitted a low mumble – which was still very loud given the creature's enormous size. Uncle Shameless nodded, "Hold on to your potatoes!" he yelled back to the rest of the group.

Everyone grabbed onto Rosco's body as the Roc Lobster did a quick roll in mid-air in order to face one of the Pyrix. The fiery attacker screeched and dove at Rosco, but the Roc Lobster struck first. One of Rosco's mouth tendrils – the one that Zeroth had not cut– whipped out at the Pyrix and coiled around it like an angry snake.

With a quick snap, the tendril whipped the Pyrix back towards Rosco, and into his waiting, massive beak, which crushed the Pyrix with a mighty bite. Rosco roared with delight.

"I've heard of spicy food, but that's just ridiculous," joked Uncle Shameless.

"This whole *place* is ridiculous if you haven't noticed," replied his nephew.

"Oh, I have," answered Uncle Shameless, "But I decided just to sit back and enjoy the ride."

Steve crossed his arms and glared at his uncle, "And just what do you mean by that?"

"Lighten up," answered Uncle Shameless with a wink. "You might just have some fun by accident."

A volley of fireballs whizzed over their heads as the last Pyrix chased after them. It was keeping its distance, having learned from watching the destruction of its companions.

"Let's just continue on," ordered Zeroth.

"Good idea," said Uncle Shameless as he ducked to avoid a fireball. He crawled to the top of Rosco's head, "Fly us as fast as you can buddy! Let's dust that sucker!"

Rosco chirped a pleasant response and sped up the beating of his forceful wings. As the wind roared around them, Steve had a hard time keeping his eyes open even though he was wearing glasses, and Zeroth's yellow scarf flapped violently behind him.

The ground far below them was rapidly turning from forested to bleak and barren. "Where are we going?" asked Steve as gazed down at the changing landscape.

"The Smoldering Wastes," explained Zeroth with a hint of concern "It is the desert that surrounds Arx A'Quila."

"Why would anyone want to take over a kingdom in the middle of a desert?" asked Steve.

"It wasn't always a desert," Eira said in a sad tone as she gripped tightly onto Rosco's back. "Fiach-Ra used his dark magic to put a blight on the land around the castle to keep everyone away."

"Oh yes, that old trick," said Steve sarcastically.

The plants and trees abruptly disappeared and an endless sea of sand stretched far into the horizon.

"Look!" cried Eira as she pointed behind them. The last of the Pyrix had stopped at the edge of the desert and was flying in place.

"Why won't it follow us over the desert?" asked Steve even though he did not really mind, since he was tired of dodging fireballs.

"Dunno," said Uncle Shameless "Musta forgot its sun block! Ha!" he slapped Steve on the back as he laughed at his own joke.

From the edge of the desert, the Pyrix screeched loudly, turned and flew away leaving a trail of flame in the sky.

The sun was setting but it was still light enough to clearly glimpse the sea of sand beneath them. While Steve surveyed the surroundings, Zeroth put Gladius and his shield away.

The bird-man looked at Steve's new magical item and a thought struck him, "We're not being attacked for the moment, why don't you try using the Staff again?"

"Fine," sighed Steve as he took out the simple wooden stick that had only moments ago turned into a trash can lid. Steve held it and waved it around. Nothing happened.

"Why isn't it working?"

"Maybe you have to think of something," suggested Eira.

"Yes, think of a weapon," said Zeroth "Think of something really nasty looking."

Steve tried as hard as he could to think of a weapon, but was not really sure what to think about. He looked away and a quick image popped into his head. There was a flash, and the staff was replaced by the thought of weapon.

Zeroth stared at Steve's conjured weapon with great interest, "*Okay*," he said, choosing his words carefully, "I think you're going to need some practice with this."

Steve blinked and looked over to see an old, rusty rake in his hand. Its handle was a boring orange color, long and full of deep scratches. The blue metal rake part at the end was virtually covered in rust. Several of the spokes were missing and more than a few were bent backwards, making it absolutely useless in the task of raking up leaves.

However, the most bizarre part was that it was the same exact rake Steve used back home in Beacon Pines.

"This...this is the rake I use back home when my dad makes me rake up the leaves," explained Steve.

"Hmm, it does not look like it would be well suited for that task," Zeroth noted as he studied the worn out tool.

"You got that right," agreed Steve. "But my dad refuses to buy a new one because it was a wedding present. The rotten thing is older than I am."

"That sounds like your dad all right," added Uncle Shameless with a knowing nod.

"But, why did you think of that?" asked Eira, "Why not something else?"

Steve shrugged, "It's the first thing I thought of. I have to clean up the yard a lot back home. Dad is kinda nuts about his yard."

Zeroth smiled as he tried to hide his amusement, "Don't worry, it'll be fine for now." Zeroth looked around and took notice of the wind, as it had picked up considerably the last few minutes.

"Is it getting windier?" he asked.

"I think so," said Eira.

"Lots of sand blowin' around too," added Uncle Shameless.

Everyone looked around them and realized that a sandstorm was forming about the Roc Lobster. The wind began howling like a deranged wolf as sharp grains of sand began to cut into everyone. Rosco was having problems seeing and was practically flying with his eyes closed.

"Pa-tooie!" spit Uncle Shameless, trying to get the sand out of his mouth, "What's goin' on?"

"Sandstorm must have kicked up," Zeroth said, spitting sand out of his beak.

"This isn't a regular sandstorm," Eira realized "The whole sky is blocked out!"

Everyone looked above and around them, only seeing sand and more sand. Sure enough they were caught in a violent sandstorm. Rosco began swaying back and forth as he fought to stay level in the air.

"Y.u..re t.esp..sin.!" bellowed a booming woman's voice, but no one could understand a single word over the howling wind.

"What was that?" Steve asked as he looked around. The voice seemed to come from all directions.

"I ...aid..u..re...re..ssing!" yelled the voice again over the loud wind.

"Did you say 'ressing?'" called Uncle Shameless, "I don't know what you mean!"

"No!" yelled the deep voice again. "I sa.. .o. a.. .re…ssing!"

"*The wind's too loud!*" answered Uncle Shameless as he put his hands over his ears and shook his head to illustrate the point.

"Oh for the love of…" muttered the woman's voice. Instantly the wind stopped and all the sand blowing around in the air froze in place.

A cloud of sand appeared in front of Rosco as he hovered in mid-air and solidified into the body of an old, craggy faced woman with bad posture. Her skin and body were made entirely out of sand.

"Ewwww," winced Steve, looking her over, "I hope she at least has a good personality."

The woman pointed a long, skinny finger with an equally long and skinny nail at the group.

"I said, all of you are trespassing!" she bellowed in a deep gravely voice.

"Oh!" exclaimed Uncle Shameless, finally understanding what the woman had been saying "*Trespassin'*. Yeah that makes sense," then he thought about the statement as he sipped his Eldercherry wine "Wait, no it doesn't. Trespassin' where?"

"On my desert!" yelled the woman made of sand.

"Look here lady," Uncle Shameless replied smoothly. "I don't know nuthin' 'bout this so-called dessert of yours. I know better than to take food from a lady, especially one with such...interesting features as yours."

Steve pulled on his uncle's sleeve to get his attention, so he could point out his mistake.

"Not now boy, grownups are talking," answered Uncle Shameless. "An' further more, how dare you accuse us of somethin' we didn't even do. What's your problem lady?"

The woman made of sand merely floated in mid-air, confused. She finally spoke, "What do you mean *didn't do*? Look where you are! You're *in* it!" she said, referring to the desert.

Uncle Shameless looked around, thinking perhaps he stepped on her dessert, but could not see any signs of a dessert anywhere. He reached into his pocket and pulled out a tattered dollar bill. "Look lady, here's a dollar. You can just scoot yourself down to the Bridge Candy an' Cone and get yourself an ice cream on me," he said thinking of his favorite frozen treat stand back in River City.

"Uncle-" started Steve.

"Hush boy," said Uncle Shameless as he continued to wave the dollar around and smiled broadly.

The woman made of sand narrowed her sandy eyes and her mouth melted into a nasty sneer. She pointed a long, sandy finger at the dollar bill. A blast of sharp, rocky sand shot at the dollar, ripping it to shreds.

"Hey!" cried Uncle Shameless, "What'd you do that for?!"

"She said *desert* not *dessert*," Steve explained finally.

Uncle Shameless thought for a moment as he took another sip of Eldercherry wine. He then looked at the woman and to the still stationary wall of sand around them.

"*Oh,*" he said. "Yeah, I guess we are kinda trespassin'.'"

The woman made of sand bellowed an evil laugh and snapped her fingers. The wind and the sand began blowing around the Roc Lobster again. Steve watched as the woman drew back her arms as if she was preparing to push something.

"Have a nice trip!" she cackled.

"Why, thank you!" answered Uncle Shameless, not realizing what was about to happen.

The woman made of sand shot her arms forward in a pushing motion. A huge gust of wind and sand flew at Rosco, throwing him and his passengers backwards through the air. All the while, they heard the woman's deep gravely laugh.

They were knocked clear out of the Smoldering Wastes by the mighty wind, and Rosco could not control his flying. Everyone held tightly onto his back and screamed. Except Uncle Shameless, who was actually enjoying the ride.

The mighty wind sent Rosco flying into a forest on the outskirts of the Smoldering Wastes, and the large creature was able to control his crash landing just enough so that he did not land on his back. He skidded into the forest floor, knocking over several trees with his bulky body.

Uncle Shameless, somewhat numb to pain due to his level of intoxication, dusted himself off and stood up on Rosco's back. "A'ight then, who ain't dead?" Thankfully, he was answered with three groans and a low growl.

Steve rolled over and coughed sand out of his mouth, "Yeah, she definitely does *not* have a good personality."

"Well that could have went better," groaned Zeroth as he lowered himself from Rosco's back and dusted himself off.

"Aw, I thought it went swell," Steve said sarcastically.

Steve helped Eira climb down to the forest floor; the pelican woman coughed up sand and wiped her eyes. "Ick," she coughed "What I wouldn't give to be underwater again."

Steve shook his head, "No thank you, I've had my fill of underwater adventures."

Uncle Shameless joined everyone on the forest floor, he inhaled deeply only to cough violently for a few moments as he too coughed up sand and dirt from his lungs.

"Oh man, this reminds me of the time I worked at a gravel pit. Now *that* was some dirty work, let me tell you. Y'see, I was in charge of filling these sand bags and one day this giant of a man, by the name of Hondo-"

"Can we save that for later, please?" begged Steve.

Uncle Shameless shrugged and helped himself to more Eldercherry wine as he walked over to check on Rosco. Steve looked up at Zeroth and Eira, "I guess that sand-lady is not going to just let us fly over the Smoldering Wastes, huh?"

Zeroth shook his head, "Not likely."

Eira agreed, "There must be another way around."

Zeroth shook his head, "I doubt it. Arx A'Quila is in the *center* of the Smoldering Wastes, atop Tyton Mountain, said to be-"

Steve interrupted Zeroth, because the last thing he wanted to hear about at that moment was some kind of magic mountain in the middle of a cursed desert.

"Uh, anyway who was that lady?"

"The Sand Witch."

"The *Sand Witch*?" Steve asked, looking at Zeroth, "You're kidding right?"

The bird-man gave Steve a puzzled look, "I didn't say anything."

Steve looked at Eira; she shook her head as well.

"Well if you didn't," Steve pointed to Zeroth "and if *you* didn't," he pointed to Eira, he glanced behind him back at Uncle Shameless to see him stumbling around Rosco, "And he didn't... then who...?"

"Over here!" called the mysterious voice.

Steve looked in the direction of the voice only to find a tree, "Oh no, not a talking tree. That's all I need," he sighed.

"I am not a tree. A tree is not nearly as amazing as I am," boasted the voice.

"Great. So it's a shrub with an ego problem," mumbled Steve as he walked toward his illusive advisor.

Steve reached where the voice had come from and looked around, but he did not see anyone or anything. His head was starting to hurt as he was getting tired of all the crazy things that had happened so far. It was bad enough have just gone through a crash landing atop a giant bird-lobster; he was not in mood for playing blind man's bluff with a mysterious creature. Also, with the sun almost set, a spooky blanket of darkness was starting to drape itself over the forest.

"Over here," the voice called again.

Steve turned and looked in the direction of the voice, it was coming from straight in front of him yet he could not see anything.

"Okay," Steve sighed, "I give up, where are you?"

"Right here in front of you," answered the voice with an authoritative tone.

Steve was beginning to get irritated, "Look, I don't have time for this," said the boy. "It's getting dark out and we still have to figure out how to get past that crazy sand lady-"

"Sand *Witch*," corrected the voice.

"Whatever. Regardless I'm not in the mood," snapped Steve as he turned to leave.

"Silly me!" called the voice. "I know what the problem is, you can't see me!"

Steve stopped in mid-step, "Were you even listening to me?" said the boy, who couldn't believe he was arguing with a mysterious voice. But then he thought to himself that it was perhaps the least crazy thing he had done all day.

"I'll fix everything, just stay there," explained the voice "I just need to turn a bit."

"What are you talkin…" was all that escaped Steve's mouth before his jaw dropped in amazement.

28

In front of Steve stood a great orange tiger, complete with black and white stripes. But this was no ordinary looking tiger. It was completely flat, yet stood upright. Its body was constructed of floating squares and rectangles.

One large rectangle formed the body of the irregular tiger, while columns of smaller squares formed the limbs and tail. A medium sized square formed the head and was topped by two smaller squares for a set of boxy ears.

Steve thought to himself that it looked like a tiger that had been rolled flat by a giant rolling pin. Now he knew why he had not seen the tiger when it claimed to be standing in front of him. Because it was flat and turned edgewise, he could not see the tiger at all. Once it moved so that Steve was looking at its front side, the tiger stood out plainly.

Zeroth, carrying a hastily made torch, along with Eira joined Steve next to the Paper Tiger. Zeroth studied the odd creature in the flickering torchlight and Eira's large beak dropped in wonder.

Steve looked the tiger over and over before finally asking, "…And what are you exactly?"

"Why I'm a Paper Tiger of course."

Steve rolled his eyes and nodded slowly. "Yes. Of *course*."

"Surely you've heard of me?" asked the Paper Tiger in a proud tone.

Steve, Zeroth and Eira all shook their heads in unison. The Paper Tiger blinked his square eyes in disbelief, "But I am the most ferocious of felines,"

Steve and his two companions shook their heads once more.

"I am most canny of cats!"

Steve merely shrugged.

"The most terrifying of tigers!" yelled the Paper Tiger, baring his flat paper teeth.

Steve and the others once again shook their heads collectively, having never heard of the two-dimensional feline.

"But-but," muttered the Paper Tiger, unable to grasp the situation of these strangers not knowing who he was.

Just then, Uncle Shameless stumbled over, "What's with all the yelling over here?" he said as he joined Steve, Eira and Zeroth. He turned his head to see the new and odd creature before him.

"Oh, hi there Mr. Paper Tiger," Uncle Shameless sang with a polite wave.

Everyone turned in surprise towards Uncle Shameless, except the Paper Tiger who's flat face broke into a large smile, "See! I told you I was well known!" The Paper Tiger bowed politely, causing part of his body to curl back and forth.

Steve leaned in close to his uncle, "How did you know who he was?"

Uncle Shameless stared at Steve and blinked slowly before saying, "He's a tiger made of paper. What else was I going to call him? Susan?"

The Paper Tiger followed the others back toward Rosco, who was laying low on the ground and making odd chirping sounds.

"We got a little problem kids," began Uncle Shameless, "Poor ol' Rosco busted up one of his wings in our little landing," he pointed to the Roc Lobster's right wing which was hanging limply.

"Where is this Rosco character?" asked the Paper Tiger, "Perhaps I can help the little fellow out, I am after all the most canny of-"

"Cats. Yes, we know," Steve said with a groan. He pointed to the Roc Lobster "There he is."

The Paper Tiger turned his body in the direction of Steve's pointing and immediately jumped back. "What is that thing?!" he yelled, looking nervously at Rosco's scissor-like claws.

"That's Rosco," Uncle Shameless explained proudly. "He's a Roc Lobster."

"A *Rock* Lobster you say?" said the Paper Tiger with a broad, flat smile, "Well I have nothing to fear from him then!" boasted the tiger as he hopped over towards the wounded Rosco. "Fear me, O beast! *For I am mighty!*" the Paper Tiger yelled loudly as he lashed out at the helpless Roc Lobster with a paper claw.

His claw struck Rosco's body and had no effect. In fact, his paw was bent backwards from the force of the blow. The Paper Tiger kept swatting at Rosco but because he was made of flat paper, only ended up fanning Rosco with each strike.

Steve gave Zeroth a confused look as the Paper Tiger continued his two-dimensional assault, "Who *is* this fruitcake?" Steve asked Zeroth.

Rosco paid no attention to the odd creature, although he did enjoy the cool air that the funny creature was fanning towards him. The Paper Tiger eventually stopped after Rosco fell asleep, "And let *that* be a lesson to you!" boasted the flat feline.

"...This guy is all talk," commented Steve. "He couldn't hurt a house of cards." Zeroth nodded, agreeing with Steve's opinion of the Paper Tiger's uselessness. The two-dimensional beast trotted over to Steve, "Now, where were we?"

Steve stared at the tiger, "I don't think we were anywhere actually."

"Oh I remember!" shouted the flat creature, "The Sand Witch!"

Steve sighed, "Yes, *that*."

"Can you...help us?" Zeroth asked somewhat reluctantly.

"Oh I certainly can!" answered the tiger smugly.

Steve pulled Zeroth aside, "What's he gonna do? Fan her to death?"

"What do we have to loose? He obviously knows something we don't," whispered Zeroth.

"Fine, you can help us," sighed Steve.

"We still have one problem," added Zeroth "Rosco is hurt and we need him to fly us to Arx A'Quila."

"I can help with that," stated Eira as she hobbled over to the wounded creature and climbed on top of Rosco with help from Zeroth. Steve and the Paper Tiger ambled over to watch. Steve wondered what Eira was going to do to heal Rosco, he was certain he had heard Eira say she was out of her healing potion back on *The Griffin*.

Eira lifted up her cane and grabbed a hold of one of the sides of the T shaped handle. She pulled on it quickly, and part of the handle came off in her hand. To Steve's surprise, the handle was actually a hidden knife. It was not a fancy knife, or very big, but it certainly looked sharp to Steve, and he wondered what she was going to do with it.

The lady pelican pulled up part of her poncho and revealed a bare, feathered arm. Steve gasped as he saw it was covered with many scars and a couple of bandages. He gasped even louder when he saw Eira make a quick slash against her arm.

"What is she doing?!" cried Steve, confused.

A thick liquid began to flow out of the cut. Steve looked at the liquid and realized that it was Eira's blood. Her blood was not red like his or Zeroth's; it was silver - the same color as her healing potions.

Eira dripped her silvery blood over Rosco's broken wing. Steve stared at Eira, "What-" Zeroth shushed Steve as he watched Eira.

After a few moments she dug a bandage out of a pocket in her bulky backpack and wrapped the cut on her arm.

"Gross!" cried Steve, "What good did that do?"

Zeroth pointed to Rosco's wound, "Look."

Steve studied the wing, but all he saw was Eira's blood covering it, "Big deal, its not doing anything except looking gross."

"Just wait."

Steve sighed and looked again. To his amazement, the wound began absorbing the blood and, even more to his amazement, it began healing instantly.

"How…?" gasped Steve, refusing to believe his eyes.

"Whoa!" bellowed Uncle Shameless.

"I say!" shouted the Paper Tiger, who was equally impressed "You are a very peculiar pelican!"

Eira smiled weakly and nodded a thanks to the Paper Tiger.

"That's incredible," gasped Steve, his eyes wide with disbelief.

"Yes, it is handy," Eira said as Zeroth helped her down from Rosco's back. "But is also a curse."

"Huh?" asked Steve.

"The Hawk-King made it *seem* like a curse," Eira explained nervously as if she just recalled a bad memory. "All female pelicans have this ability, and many years ago the Hawk-King sent his minions all over Eyri searching for every pelican they could find."

Steve shuddered, knowing first-hand what it felt like to be chased after by swarms of Fiach-Ra's cronies.

"That is why there are not that many pelicans around these parts anymore," Eira continued. "Those who could escape his forces went into hiding. He eventually stopped rounding up every pelican he could find, but the damage had already been done."

"But why did he want all these pelicans? I thought he was immortal," asked Steve. "He certainly wouldn't need the healing powers."

Eira sniffed loudly "I don't know, but there were tales that he needed our blood for some sort of spell or experiment."

"What kinda experiment?" asked Uncle Shameless.

Eira shook her head, "I do not know."

The pelican put her secret knife away before turning towards Steve, "Now do you see why you must fulfill The Prophecy?" she asked over the distant rumbles of thunder. "Fiach-Ra is mad with power and who knows what unspeakable evil he will commit next."

Steve gave a weak nod. He looked down at the Staff of Arcana, "But how am I going to fight unspeakable evil with an old rusty rake?"

"Don't' worry, we'll work on that," smirked Zeroth.

Rosco roared softly and flapped his mended wing as he woke from his nap near the campfire.

"Amazing," gasped Steve as he studied the beast's completely healed wing.

"I agree," said the Paper Tiger, "But not nearly as amazing as me!" he jumped up on his flat rear legs and gave a flat sounding roar. One of his paper back legs bent in sharply due to a gust of wind, causing the tiger to fall to the ground flat on his face.

"I can honestly say, no one is as *amazing* as you," teased Steve.

"So, are we going back to the desert now?" asked Uncle Shameless as he patted the side of Rosco's head.

"I think it'd be best to let Rosco get some rest," suggested Eira "Who knows what the Sand Witch will do the next time we face her."

Zeroth nodded "I agree. We should all get some rest."

"I like the sound of that plan," yawned Steve. Zeroth dropped a clawed hand to the boy's shoulder "Not yet, you need to practice with the Staff."

"You want me to practice the ancient art of rake fighting?" joked Steve.

"Some other time," replied Zeroth, not getting Steve's joke. "You need to try thinking of other weapons. *Real* weapons."

Steve held the rusty rake in his hand, "Okay…so what should I do?"

"Just imagine something, like you did before, but try to think of a weapon this time," suggested Zeroth.

Steve held the battered rake in front of him and kick started his imagination, but nothing happened.

"*Concentrate,*" coached Zeroth.

Steve closed his eyes and thought hard until he felt the rake in his hand jiggle. He opened his eyes to find that the rake had turned into something else.

"Excellent!" applauded Zeroth as he studied the object in Steve's grasp. "But...what *is* it?"

Steve sighed, unhappy with his result "It's called an edger. You use it to trim grass along the sidewalk." Like the rake, it looked exactly like the old edger his dad made him use back home while doing weekend chores.

It was about the length of the rake, and the handle was covered with a chipped green paint. Crowning the top of the edger was a heavy metal wheel covered with small, rusty, dull blades. Steve tried to demonstrate the tool's use on the ground, but the wheel would not turn because as it was as rusty as the rake.

"Hmm," thought Zeroth as he studied the ineffective garden tool "You might have been better off with the rake."

As Steve tried harder to think of weapons or at least something more useful than rusty garden tools, Uncle Shameless stumbled over. "Rosco says he'll be rested enough to fly in the morn..." he began to say as he watched Steve swing around an old shovel with a large hole in the center of the blade.

"Boy, what are you doin'?" asked Uncle Shameless.

"Trying to get this stupid Staff of Arcana to turn into something useful," explained a frustrated Steve.

"Fine, fine," said Uncle Shameless as he pretended to understand even though he did not.

Steve closed his eyes again and thought hard, only to end up with the old rusty rake once more.

"I give up," whined Steve as he balanced the rusty old rake over his shoulder.

"Fine, fine," sang Uncle Shameless in a cheerful tone, unaware he was repeating himself "So...where are we going tomorrow?"

"To fight the Sand Witch again," explained Zeroth as he searched his magical pack for cooking supplies.

"Fight the sandwich?" asked Uncle Shameless as visions of a mammoth club sandwich with a bad attitude filled his mind.

"Yes, and I am going to help!" boasted the Paper Tiger.

"I don't think I'll need your help for that," scoffed Uncle Shameless, unaware that everyone was referring to the woman in the desert that they had already encountered.

"No?" asked the Paper Tiger, surprised.

"I should hope not. I manage to eat them by myself all the time."

Both Zeroth and the Paper Tiger gasped, "You *eat* Sand Witches?"

"Well yes, don't you guys eat 'em 'round here?"

"Certainly not!" exclaimed the Paper Tiger.

"Well, ya should, they are *mighty* tasty!"

"How can you eat a Sand Witch?" asked a mortified Zeroth.

"Easy!" cheered Uncle Shameless, "All you do is grab it with both hands, pull it towards ya and take a big ol' bite out of it!" explained Uncle Shameless as he acted out the scene.

"Ugh!" groaned Zeroth in disgust.

"Ghastly!" cried the Paper Tiger.

The Paper Tiger leaned over to Steve and whispered, "I say, is there anything *wrong* with him?"

Steve looked over his shoulder at the flat creature and smiled. "Do you want a list?"

After Zeroth cooked a satisfying and filling dinner, everyone made camp for the night and tried to get some rest near the slow burning fire. Rosco's deep breathing filled the camp and rustled the nearby trees and bushes.

Zeroth leaned against Rosco's side, his hand resting on Gladius inside his cloak out of habit, ready to draw his weapon at a moment's notice. His hood was pulled up over his head, covering his face with blackness and making it impossible for anyone to see if his eyes were open or not.

Rosco's gentle inhaling and exhaling soothingly rocked Zeroth to sleep. Just before he gave into sleep's siren song, he felt the wind pick up around the camp.

Zeroth rarely dreamed but tonight, visions fought on the battlefield of his mind. None of the visions were clear, but they seemed familiar and unfamiliar at the same time. Dark red flames framed the images as they marched past him like an army.

His body began to shake as he tried to fight the dreams, his unconscious mind trying to force him awake. Then came a ghostly, chilly voice, "*Zeroth...*"

The bird-man's eyes shot open as he jumped into a standing position, his body shaking. Nothing. He saw and heard nothing. But just as he began to sit down, "*Zeroth...*" gasped the voice once more.

"*Over...here,*" chanted the voice.

Against his better judgment, Zeroth snuck his way through the camp, careful not to wake any of his companions. He followed the voice to a dark, gloomy clearing several yards away from his camp and the safety of the fire. Skeletal black trees surrounded the clearing, adding to the spookiness of the situation.

"...*Zeroth*..." echoed the voice once more.

The bird-man searched the clearing as best he could in the darkness, "What do you want?" he called out, on the verge of screaming.

"*I bring you, an offer,*" gasped the phantom speaker, the words drawn out and uneven in volume.

"An offer?" scoffed Zeroth "You woke me up, and dragged me away to ask me about a job?"

"*No,*" corrected the voice, "*An offer for a deal.*"

"A deal?" Zeroth called out as he spun around the clearing, chasing the voice that seemed to surround him. "I don't make deals with someone I can't see.'

Responding to the taunt, a ghostly cloud flew by Zeroth and hovered in front of him. Zeroth's eyes widened and he reached instinctually for Gladius as a pair of white eyes flashed from within the cloud of mist.

"I thought you were dead," Zeroth said with a crooked smile as Delu finished solidifying in front of him. The raven's body and clothing still carried the scars from their previous meeting, and the spy did not look fully recovered. Zeroth pulled out Gladius and gave the swordfish a quick squeeze, shaking the creature from its sleep.

"Far...from it," hacked Delu, still getting accustomed to talking by himself "I am not...here to attack...you." The raven held up his empty hands to show he was weaponless.

"Then why *are* you here?" snapped Zeroth as he pointed the tip of Gladius' deadly tongue at Delu's chest. "The last time I checked, you and I weren't exactly friends."

"As I...said," stumbled Delu, coughing madly between the words, "I am here...to...offer you...a deal."

Zeroth narrowed his eyes deep in the depths of his hood, "What makes you think I'd make a deal with you?"

"Because," coughed Delu, forcing him to drop his arms and grab his chest, "It concerns you...and the Formal...Hunter Compliant...Form dash TB."

The Hunter instantly lowered his weapon and took a step closer, "I'm listening."

29

"And...that...is the...deal the Hawk-King asked me...to give you," Delu wheezed in-between sickly, wet coughs.

"So I hand over The Boy, and the Hawk-King will cancel the TB compliant?" recited Zeroth.

"Corr...ect."

Zeroth rested Gladius on one of his shoulders as he stared at the ailing spy in front of him. "How did you even find us?"

"I am...a...spy y'know, that is...my job," replied Delu. "Plus you aren't...exactly keeping...a...low profile with...that...*beast.*"

"True, Shameless can be rather loud-"

"No!" snapped Delu. "The Roc Lob...ster."

Zeroth reluctantly nodded in agreement. "The Hawk-King...had his own...methods as...well," added Delu.

"*The Pyrix,*" cursed Zeroth, earning a nod from the raven spy. "Why not just take The Boy now?" Zeroth said teasingly.

Delu shook his head weakly. "I am not strong enough to...transport...him with...me. The Hawk...King also...feared his...blue...heron amulet might...prevent such a...thing. The Boy must...come to Arx...Vena'Tor. See that...he...gets there and we...have a -"

"Alright, alright. I get the idea," interrupted Zeroth, finally having his fill of Delu's chilly, drawn out speaking. Without hesitating, Delu turned back into mist and sickly wheezed one last message to Zeroth, "*Bring...him to...Arx Vena'Tor...no...Boy...no deal...*"

The unnatural cloud rocketed away through the night sky as Zeroth slowly made his way back to the camp. He gave Gladius a squeeze, retracting its tongue with a loud slurp.

"Well you certainly are a piece of work," snapped Gladius "I knew you Hunters were a crafty lot, but I would have never thought-"

"Say one word about this to anyone and I'll bury you in the Smoldering Wastes," snapped Zeroth. Terrified and surprised by the threat, Gladius became silent as Zeroth tucked him away into his black cloak.

The next morning after a quick breakfast, prepared expertly by Zeroth, everyone climbed onto the back of Rosco and readied themselves for another encounter with the Sand Witch - except for Uncle Shameless who still thought they were going to eat a giant sandwich. Zeroth and Steve held on tightly to the Paper Tiger so he would not be carried away by the wind as Rosco roared and flapped his newly healed wings.

They flew over the Smoldering Wastes for no more than a few minutes before the terrible wind that had preceded the Sand Witch's earlier arrival started up once again.

"Don't let go!" begged the Paper Tiger as the wind roared fiercely all around Rosco. Steve still did not see how the nearly useless creature was going to help them defeat the powerful sand-wielding witch. As before, the Sand Witch appeared before them and her powerful gusts of wind kept Rosco flying in place, no matter how hard he flapped his wings.

A massive cloud of sand flew in front of Rosco and formed into a giant version of the Sand Witch's face. Uncle Shameless studied the giant craggy, grit-covered visage before turning away in disgust, "Lady I got one word for you," Uncle Shameless yelled from his perch on top of Rosco's head. "Moisturizers!"

The Sand Witch's eyes narrowed, but Uncle Shameless continued his taunting, "Seriously, your face is grittier than a bad detective novel!"

"Silence!" bellowed the enormous face, spewing sand and dirt all over Rosco and his passengers.

"Ugh! Gross!" yelled Steve as he wiped the debris off himself.

"You are trespassing!" bellowed the Sand Witch as loose sand ran off the edges of the giant floating head.

"Yeah, we know!" answered Uncle Shameless. "You told us already!"

The giant face paused and blinked for a moment as if she was trying to remember the previous encounter. "I did?" the giant face finally asked.

"Yes," all of Rosco's passengers said in unison, sounding like a group of students being asked if they finished last night's homework.

"Are you sure?" asked the Sand Witch.

"Oh c'mon lady, there aren't that many deserts around here!" yelled Uncle Shameless "Where else could we have been?"

"Tsk, just a minute," snapped the Sand Witch bitterly. Steve and the others watched as a giant pair of glasses constructed themselves out of the sand on the witch's face, complete with glass.

The giant eyes behind the glasses scanned over the group for several minutes.

"Oh that's right!" exclaimed the Sand Witch in a pleased tone as the recent memories came back to her. "I remember now, the ugly kid with the weird crab-bird," bellowed the Sand Witch in a gravely, booming voice.

"Hey!" Steve yelled in protest as he eventually realized that 'ugly kid' referred to him.

"Didn't you get the message last time?" asked the giant bespectacled face of the Sand Witch. She did not wait for anyone to answer before she continued, "No matter! If I must cast you down once again – So be it!"

The Sand Witch began laughing her evil laugh as she surveyed the group once more and decided how to dispose of them. But when her eyes landed on the Paper Tiger, her laughter stopped abruptly.

"*Zuu's Talons!*" she cursed, "*Is that a Paper Tiger?!*"

The Paper Tiger gave a loud, but flat sounding roar.

Confused, Steve looked at the Paper Tiger then back at the Sand Witch as her previous expression of powerful supremacy quickly changed to one of absolute terror.

In a flash, the giant head of the Sand Witch changed into an equally giant hand made of sand. It flew towards Rosco and grabbed a hold of him. The giant hand then hurled itself, and Rosco, to the floor of the barren desert. Rosco crash landed in a giant cloud of sand.

Everyone jumped off Rosco's back, who was thankfully unhurt this time. Steve started brushing himself off and tried to get sand out of his mouth, "Pbbt! I'm sick of all this sand!" he yelled, frustrated.

"Watch your mouth!" hollered the familiar gravely voice of the Sand Witch "Some of that sand you are spitting out was part of me!"

"…I think I'm gonna be sick," Steve replied in a disgusted tone.

"Not in my desert ya ain't!" bellowed the voice of the Sand Witch from all directions.

Not too far away, a mound of sand began to grow larger and larger, finally taking the form of the Sand Witch's body, complete with bad posture.

"You may think you are clever for bringing a Paper Tiger, but it won't help!" she screamed.

"That's what I tried to tell everyone," said Steve as he reached under his chain mail and t-shirt to get rid of more sand.

"I am all powerful!" shrieked the Sand Witch with a slight hint of fear. She held out a hand, and a ball made of sand formed instantly. She then threw the ball towards the companions, striking Uncle Shameless in the chest and knocking him down.

"What's the big idea?!" the man yelled back as he tried to stand up. Uncle Shameless quickly realized that for some reason, he was having more trouble than usual standing up. "Help me boy!" he cried to Steve.

"Oh for cryin'…" answered Steve as he began to walk over to his uncle. However, Steve soon found out that he could not move either.

"What gives?" he said as he looked down at his feet and saw that he was *very* slowly sinking into the sand.

The Sand Witch began laughing her evil laugh once more. "Fools!" she bellowed, causing sand to tumble off her face, "You are caught in…*Slowsand!*"

Steve looked down at the sand at his feet and then looked up at the Sand Witch, "Don't you mean, Quicksand?"

"Psh, not on my salary! Slowsand is all you get!" countered the Sand Witch.

Steve didn't even want to waste the time thinking about who actually employed the Sand Witch, let alone how much she made. He was more concerned with getting out of the Slowsand. Luckily for him however, the name was correct.

The sand was pulling him down so slowly that it was barely past his toes. Still, the sand did hold him firmly in place. He glanced around to see Eira, Zeroth and Rosco in the same situation. Zeroth tried in vain to flap his weak wings, hoping he could gain some kind of lift.

The only one who was not stuck, ironically, was the Paper Tiger. He sat down on his haunches and began grooming himself.

"Nuts to this," spat Steve, fed up with being stuck in the sand. He took out the Staff of Arcana and though of his old rake once again. He blinked and like before, the Staff was replaced by the old rusty rake.

Steve jabbed the rake into the ground nearby and used the leverage to free himself from the Slowsand and jumped onto a regular patch of sand.

"Hey!" protested the Sand Witch "You can't do that!"

"Too bad, I just did," countered Steve.

"Why you little...I'll get you!" growled the Sand Witch as she began forming large balls of sand in mid air.

"What's stopping you?" Steve taunted with angry eyes.

"Argh!" yelled the Sand Witch as she hurled balls of sand towards Steve. He dodged one and then a second before swinging at the third with the rake. As he swung the rake, he had a brief flashback to a summer's afternoon when his father had attempted to teach him baseball.

To Steve's amazement, the rake instantly turned into an old wooden baseball bat, and as he hit the ball of sand it went sailing back towards the Sand Witch. The sandy missile struck the Sand Witch harmlessly in the face. The pseudo-baseball was quickly absorbed into her sandy body, causing Steve to grimace in disgust.

"It's so great to see a kid usin' a wooden bat," sniffed Uncle Shameless with a nostalgic tear in his eye.

The Sand Witch continued her volleys of sand and dirt spheroids, only to have them knocked aside by Steve's magically summoned bat, which only further annoyed the Sand Witch.

"Enough!" cried the Sand Witch.

"You're givin' up?" asked Steve in a mocking manner. "'Bout time."

"Silence!" bellowed the Sand Witch.

"You certainly are a woman of few words," added Steve as he readied his bat for another swing.

"Quiet!" responded the Sand Witch.

"Like I said..."

The Sand Witch let out a loud snarl of frustration and waved a gritty hand. The ground under Steve turned into a gigantic sandy hand and grabbed the boy tightly in its sandy grasp.

"No fair!" Steve yelled from his fingery prison.

"Fear not young one!" shouted the Paper Tiger.

"Oh, are you still here?" asked Steve, having forgotten about his flat companion.

"Very much so!" roared the Paper Tiger as it leapt over the pools of Slowsand towards the Sand Witch.

"No, that's okay, you don't have to...help," replied Steve, who was still convinced there was nothing the paper creature could do, other than take up space.

The Sand Witch sent balls of sand flying at the Paper Tiger, which he dodged easily by curling his flat body this way and that. When he was within a few yards of the Sand Witch, he gave a mighty growl and pounced upon her.

To Steve – and everyone's – amazement, the Paper Tiger toppled the witch over and stood on top of her, growling. The Sand Witch twitched and turned, trying to free herself but the Paper Tiger held her tightly to the ground.

The hand holding Steve crumbled and sent the boy tumbling to the ground. He got up, dusted himself off before pulling his companions out of the glue-like hold of the Slowsand.

Steve studied the odd scene of the Paper Tiger towering over the prone Sand Witch, "Okay, so how did that happen?"

Zeroth shrugged, and began to answer but Steve interrupted him quickly, "...and if any of you say 'magic', so help me I'm going to give you a one way ticket to Sluggerville," finished Steve as he repeatedly hit his bat against the palm of his open hand.

Zeroth noticed the name on the side of Steve's bat and, realizing what the boy meant, decided to remain silent.

"I know how," said Uncle Shameless knowingly "It's easy."

"Oh, please...*enlighten* us," Steve said sarcastically.

"It all comes down to one of those ancient rules of life," began Uncle Shameless.

"Silence is golden?" asked Steve.

"No," answered Uncle Shameless.

"Glory is fleeting?" asked Eira.

"No."

"Always look out for number one?" tried Zeroth.

"*No!*" yelled Uncle Shameless.

"A bird in the hand is worth two in the bush?" asked Steve.

Eira and Zeroth both stared at Steve in silence with confused expressions on their faces.

"Uh...never mind," replied Steve as he pretended to look at something else.

"No!" yelled Uncle Shameless again. He pointed at the Paper Tiger and yelled "Paper beats rock!"

Silence again crept over the group, and if there had been any crickets in the Smoldering Wastes, they would have been deafening.

"C'mon people!" screamed Uncle Shameless, "Do I have to draw ya a picture?"

"That wouldn't help," joked Steve, "Unless the reason involves stick figures."

"Paper!" yelled Uncle Shameless as he pointed to the Paper Tiger once more "Rock!" he yelled as he pointed to the now helpless Sand Witch. *"Paper beats rock!"* Uncle Shameless explained once more.

"But...she's made of sand..." said Steve, confused.

"Sand is just little rocks!" explained Uncle Shameless loudly as he wiggled his fingers in the air.

"What I want to know," asked the Paper Tiger from afar, "Is why could I not hurt your big bird friend over there?" he said as he nodded towards Rosco.

"Because he's a Roc, not a rock," explained Steve.

The Paper Tiger stared at Steve and blinked, lost in deep thought.

"You are talking in circles young one, I-"

"Never-*mind!*" Steve groaned loudly.

The Sand Witch cleared her throat loudly, sounding like a large rock breaking into tiny pieces, as she tried to get the group's attention. Everyone looked down to face her, as she was still held firmly in place by the Paper Tiger's two-dimensional paws.

"You may have stopped me, but you'll never stop – *The Kractus!*" she screamed, spewing grit and gravel as she pounded on the desert floor with a steady beat while chanting a few wicked words.

Eira gasped in terror and Zeroth cursed under his breath, Steve however was not scared. Although this only because he had no idea to what the Sand Witch was referring to.

"Lady, if you think pounding on the ground is going to scare me, then you must have more than one screw loose," Steve said eventually.

"It's got a nice beat tho!" blurted Uncle Shameless as he started to do a poorly improvised dance. Steve covered his eyes, *"Please* stop," he asked his dancing uncle.

Suddenly a distant rumbling filled everyone's ears and the ground beneath them began to quake violently. Steve turned to Zeroth and Eira, "You guys weren't talking about that prophecy just now were you?"

The two bird-people shook their heads, "Then what-" started Steve.

"The Kractus!" screamed the Sand Witch in glee, "Approacheth!"

The ground shook more and more, making it hard to stand up straight. Uncle Shameless kept falling over, but continued his poorly choreographed dance.

"What is she talking about?" Steve asked as he continued to ignore his uncle's dancing.

"*The Kractus!*" exclaimed Zeroth as he looked around expectantly.

"And that is...?" asked Steve in a disinterested tone.

Zeroth did not have time to answer before the ground erupted several dozen yards beyond them. Sand and dirt exploded into the air as the ground quaked relentlessly. Everyone who was standing was sent falling to the ground as a cloud of sand descended upon them like a dirty blanket.

A deafening, garbled screeching sound cut through the air, only to be followed by the Sand Witch's gritty laughter. "Behold!" she bellowed in-between wicked laughter, "The Kractus!"

Steve looked up from his place on the ground and all he could see was a large, drab green colored object that looked like a gargantuan cactus that had been knocked over, complete with sharp pointed thorns the size of spears.

To Steve's amazement, the object began to move slowly through the sand as if it were swimming. Then, with another eruption of sand and piercing screams, the object shot up in the air casting a long shadow over them.

Steve could see now that it was some manner of beast and that what he had seen swimming through the sand was only the top of the creature's head. The green, thorn covered beast now towered above them, its long limbless body coiled like an attacking snake.

"What," said Steve slowly as he took in the sight before him "Is *that?*"

"A Kractus," answered Zeroth in a knowing tone, "Cam told me about it once, and they can be really nasty."

Steve looked up at the shrieking creature as it poised to attack. Its head looked like a cross between that of a squid and an overgrown cactus. At the front of the long head was a vile mouth covered in a web of thick, thorny green tentacles.

Under the tentacles, Steve could see a rather nasty looking sharp beak. Unlike a squid however, it had a long snake-like body extending from the base of its skull, which seemed to coil endlessly underneath it. Thorns and spines covered the rest of the Kractus' body, making it look very frightening.

"Okay...but what is it?"

"It's part kraken, part cactus!" exclaimed Zeroth as he dug out Gladius.

"It's a sea-sand monster!" Eira added as she covered her head to block out the Kractus' shrieking.

"…A sea-sand monster?" asked Steve. "Wouldn't it just be a *sand* monster?"

"Oh that's just silly," said Eira.

"Yes, there's no such thing as a *sand* monster," added Zeroth "Everyone knows that."

Steve pointed at the still captive Sand Witch, "What about her?"

"I *heard* that!" bellowed the Sand Witch in an annoyed voice.

"She's not a monster," answered Zeroth.

Eira nodded, "That's right, she's a *witch*."

Steve covered his face with his hands and groaned loudly.

30

A tree-sized thorny tentacle slammed into the desert ground near Steve and his companions, causing them to almost lose their footing. "What is it doing?" asked Steve as he watched the tentacle move around and burrow into the sand.

The ground rumbled as the tentacle dug its way through the sand, only to emerge next to the Sand Witch. The tentacle burst through the surface of the desert and curled around to grab the Sand Witch, freeing her from the Paper Tiger's grasp.

The Sand Witch laughed her wicked laugh as the Kractus' tentacle carried her high into the air and away from her captors.

"Fools!" she bellowed from her safe place in the air.

"Does she only know five different words?" joked Steve, poking fun at the Sand Witch's lack of a thrilling vocabulary.

"This isn't good," observed Zeroth as he looked up at the large creature that towered above them.

"Nothin' gits by you," quipped Gladius from his place in Zeroth's hand.

"Help me up, boy!" pleaded Uncle Shameless, who had fallen down again. The boy ran over and helped his uncle, hoping that his uncle's extraordinary strength might come in handy again.

"Ah good work," praised Uncle Shameless as he stood up and dusted himself off.

"Now, what's all the ruckus about?" he said as he looked up at the Kractus. The creature snarled and shrieked loudly as the tentacles surrounding its deadly mouth whipped wildly to and fro.

"Talk about falling out of the ugly tree, ick," said Uncle Shameless in a show of disgust.

"Yeah it is a scary looking beast," added Steve.

"Hm? Oh, I was talking about that dried up sand lady up there," explained Uncle Shameless. In the distance, Steve could swear he heard the Sand Witch yell 'I *heard* that!'

Uncle Shameless looked over the Kractus a second time. "Yeah, I guess that's *kinda* ugly too. But did you see that lady's face? It looked like bowl of oatmeal with a nose."

Steve rolled his eyes "Moving on," the boy began as he pointed to the Kractus, "What are we gonna do about *that*?"

"Hey, I told her to get some moisturizers-"

"Not the lady, the Kractus!" yelled Steve.

"Kractus? What's a Kractus?" asked Uncle Shameless.

"That!" yelled Steve as he jabbed his finger upward.

"...I thought she was a witch."

"Not her!" Steve yelled again, frustrated "The creature holding her!"

Uncle Shameless looked again as he took a quick sip of Eldercherry wine, "Oh. Yeah, I could see how that would be a problem."

Rosco warbled loudly nearby and Uncle Shameless moved towards the Roc Lobster, being careful to avoid the Slowsand.

"Rosco says that if we can get him loose, he'll fight that giant critter," explained Uncle Shameless as he helped himself to another swig of wine.

"He's too big. I can't just pull him loose like I did with everyone else," said Steve. Zeroth, Eira and the Paper Tiger joined Steve along side Rosco.

"We have to think of something," stated Zeroth as the Kractus hissed loudly behind them.

Zeroth studied Rosco and thought for a moment, "Well maybe we can – " he never got to finish his thought, because the Kractus slithered close to them quickly and sent a swarm of thorny tentacles hurling towards the ground like a rain of green lances.

The tentacles crashed into the ground like jackhammers and sent the companions running for cover.

"Look out!" cried Zeroth as he rolled to avoid being smashed by a thorn covered tentacle. He looked at the tentacle stuck in the ground and inspiration struck him.

"Steve, Shameless, Eira – do your best to free Rosco," ordered Zeroth as he looked up at the looming Kractus "I'll handle Ugly until then."

Zeroth tightened his yellow scarf and dashed towards the Kractus, giving Gladius a quick squeeze along the way.

"What are you-" began Steve, but quickly became silent as he watched Zeroth put his plan into action. The Kractus shrieked its garbled cry and dove its head down at Zeroth. It snapped its massive crushing beak at the bird-man, but Zeroth rolled out of the way in time.

The beak clapped shut loudly behind him, catching a fragment of his cloak and sounding like cracking thunder. The snarling Kractus followed Zeroth's movement with its large, angry eyes and prepared another deadly attack.

As Zeroth ran as fast as he could through the loose sand, he stealthily reached into his magical pack. He felt the Kractus' wind-like breath on his back; he turned around and threw the object at one of the Kractus' expansive eyes.

The bulging sack burst against the creature's spiny face right under its eye, exploding in a cloud of extra strong cooking spices and fiery pepper.

The Kractus' wailed as it was momentarily and painfully blinded by the bird-man's surprise attack. Above the Kractus' head, still clutched safely in the creature's grasp, the Sand Witch bellowed "What a dirty trick!"

"I guess I won't be making my thirteen alarm chili again anytime soon," Zeroth thought aloud as he lamented over his lost pack of fancy spices and peppers.

The Kractus flailed its deadly tentacles around blindly as it blinked to clear its eye of the heinous cooking ingredients. One of its tentacles smashed into the sand near Zeroth and, seeing an opportunity, the Hunter ran for it. He slashed at a tentacle that swung towards him and ducked another.

Just before reaching the idle tentacle in front of him, Zeroth squeezed Gladius and put the swordfish away. He then reached into his magical pack once more and pulled out a pair of objects. After retrieving what he needed, Zeroth jumped through the air towards the tentacle.

As the Hunter landed carefully in a gap between several spear-like thorns, he dug the climbing hooks he had removed from his pack into the Kractus' tough flesh.

The Kractus wailed again as Zeroth began to climb up its tentacle with the aid of the long, curved hooks in his hands. Each was secured to his wrists by a simple loop of rope. This allowed him to drop the hooks from one or both of his hands to fight, without fear of losing the useful tools.

No matter how fast the tentacle flew through the air, the hooks kept Zeroth securely attached.

"He's crazy," gasped Steve as he watched Zeroth dig his climbing hooks into the thrashing tentacle and scale it, heading for the Kractus' head.

"No," countered Eira, "He's *brave*."

Uncle Shameless stood on the edge of the Slowsand, coaxing Rosco to move a large claw towards him. "That a'boy, c'mon you can do it," sang Uncle Shameless.

Rosco stretched his body and was finally able to extend a tip of a large lobster claw far enough for Uncle Shameless to grab it.

"Are you sure this is going to work?" Steve asked skeptically.

"Nope," answered Uncle Shameless honestly, "But we don't' have much of a choice." Uncle Shameless grunted and groaned as he tried to lift Rosco out of the sand without much luck.

"You don't have enough leverage," explained Steve.

"Walking in sand don't make it any easier neither," added Uncle Shameless "What we need is a sand buggy!"

"A what?" asked Steve.

"A sand buggy, it's a car that has special tires, that helps you get more grip in the sand. Did I ever tell you about the time at Sleeping Bear Dunes when-"

"Not now please," Steve begged as he glanced over at Zeroth and the Kractus.

"There I was!" continued Uncle Shameless "In a to-the-death race with the leader of the most vile, heinous sand buggy gang in all of northern Michigan, The Sand Angles!"

"I don't think this is the time for stories," pleaded Steve. "Wait...The Sand *Angles*?"

"Well y'see it was s'pose to be the Sand Angels, but the place they got their jackets from spelled it wrong and their leader was kind of a cheap skate. He decided just to stick with it instead of buying all new jackets," explained Uncle Shameless.

"That's the stupidest thin-"

"Hey, Steve-o," prodded Uncle Shameless.

Steve sighed, "What?"

"Are you hot?" laughed Uncle Shameless loudly, slapping his nephew on the back.

"I hate to interrupt," Eira said patiently, "But you might want to move out of the way," she pointed to an incoming spiny tentacle. The tentacle swung madly over the companions, barely missing them.

After the attack Uncle Shameless helped Steve and Eira up.

"Well enough screwin' around boys and..." he glanced at Eira, "Uh, pelicans. Let's see about helpin' ol' Rosco here."

Uncle Shameless looked over the nearly helpless creature and thought hard for a moment. "Maybe if we built some sort of rudimentary pulley system we can lift him out," he mused.

"And just *how* are we going to do that?" asked Steve; surprised his uncle even knew what the word rudimentary meant.

"Easy! We'll find some coconut trees an' some bamboo, Eira you start making some rope..."

"There aren't any coconut trees or bamboo around here!" yelled Steve, "Besides, that would take hours!"

Uncle Shameless scratched his head, "Hmm, that's funny it only takes about five minutes on TV."

"This isn't TV, this is..." Steve was about to say *real life*, but changed his mind as he looked over the giant bird-lobster stuck in Slowsand and then over at the giant cactus-squid attacking them, "Never mind."

Inspiration struck Uncle Shameless a few moments later as he glanced up at Rosco's wings.

"Fly!" commanded Uncle Shameless as he flapped his arms in front of Rosco.

"...Are you trying to fly?" asked Steve, "I hate to break it to you, but you are kind of ill equipped."

"Yes, you do not even have any feathers," added the Paper Tiger.

"No!" yelled Uncle Shameless as he jabbed a finger towards Rosco "I'm tellin' *him* to fly!"

Rosco chirped loudly and began flapping his massive wings.

"There ya go!" coached Uncle Shameless as the Roc Lobster began ascending. However the victory was short lived as everyone quickly realized that even though Rosco was gaining altitude, he could not break free of the Slowsand's glue-like hold.

"Well this is a fine how-ya-do," lamented Uncle Shameless as he watched Rosco struggle.

Zeroth climbed the thorn covered tentacle, hoping to reach the head of the Kractus without much of a fight. But luck was not on his side. The Kractus whipped the tentacle Zeroth was climbing in all directions trying to knock him off.

Had it not been for his climbing hooks, he would have been thrown to the ground easily.

"Now I'm glad I did that Hunt in the mountains," Zeroth confessed aloud. The climbing hooks, had been part of his payment.

Determined to get rid of its unwanted guest, the Kractus swung a thick tentacle at Zeroth.

"Oh, *great*," gasped Zeroth as he let go of one of his climbing hooks and pulled out Gladius.

"Where are we?!" yelled the swordfish before Zeroth gave him a hard squeeze and slashed at the incoming tentacle, nearly slicing it in two.

The Kractus howled in pain as the tip of its severed tentacle hung limply in the air. Zeroth smirked as he placed Gladius in his beak, and continued his dangerous climb with both of his hands.

The Kractus lifted the tentacle Zeroth was climbing to its beak, snapping at the Hunter. Just before the sharp beak closed on the tentacle, Zeroth pulled his climbing hooks free from the tough green flesh and jumped.

As the Kractus painfully bit one of its own tentacles in half, Zeroth pierced the side of a different tentacle and pulled himself up. While the Sand Witch berated the Kractus for its foolishness, Zeroth continued his climb towards the monster's head.

"I know!" Uncle Shameless exclaimed after several minutes of Eldercherry wine fueled brain storming. "We'll make a rudimentary pulley system. All we need is a coconut tree an' some bamboo-"

"You said that already," groaned Steve.

"I did?"

Eira, The Paper Tiger and Steve nodded.

"Really?" asked Uncle Shameless, looking at the Paper Tiger for confirmation. The creature curled its flat paper head in a nod.

Uncle Shameless thought again for a few moments, taking a few sips of wine. Eventually he turned and faced the group, "I have it, all we need is a – DUCK!" screamed Uncle Shameless.

"I don't see how that will help," Steve said before Eira quickly pulled him to the ground. One of the Kractus' tentacles whipped uncontrollably over their heads and smacked Rosco in the side.

Steve looked up to see Zeroth hanging from the bottom of the tentacle as it whipped through the air. A roar sounded behind them, but it was not from the Kractus. Steve looked up to see Rosco, freed from the glue-like grip of the Slowsand, taking to the sky above them.

The Roc Lobster roared again and flew straight at the Kractus, head butting it in its fleshy underbelly. Zeroth used this distraction to continue his climb to the villainous creature's head.

Another tentacle whipped at the bird-man and buzzed over his head. He swiftly pulled his swordfish from his beak and in one fluid motion slashed at the attacking tentacle.

The sliced limb fell many stories until it crashed onto the desert floor. Zeroth jumped to another nearby tentacle and continued his ascent to the creature's snapping jaws.

Even though the pain of another lost tentacle angered the Kractus, it was focused on fighting the Roc Lobster. The giant creature lowered the Sand Witch to the ground so that it could fight and not worry about hurting its gritty mistress.

Rosco took the to air with blinding speed and spun so that he could launch another attack against the Kractus. In anticipation of the attack, the Kractus reared up and hissed loudly.

Rosco dive bombed his thorn-covered foe, his stony lobster claws at the ready. Zeroth sensed an opportunity, formed a strategy and waited for the right moment. As Zeroth had expected, the Kractus lifted up all of its mouth tentacles to expose its sharp, nasty beak. This brought Zeroth closer to the creature's large head, where he waited to carry out his plan.

Moments before the Kractus was about to lunge at Rosco with its deadly beak, Zeroth pulled his climbing hooks free and jumped from the uplifted tentacle. He aimed his free-fall towards the creature's head and at the right moment, released his wings to control his dive.

With expert timing and aim, Zeroth zipped past the Kractus' face, plunging his climbing hooks into the centers of the large disk-shaped eyes.

The Kractus shrieked in pain and thrashed as it tried in vain to see through its now useless eyes. This gave Rosco the chance he needed, and the giant Roc Lobster flew right into the blinded creature's chest, causing it to topple over.

The Sand Witch tried to move out of the way, but due to the Kractus' giant size and being weak from magically summoning her spiny pet, this was rather difficult.

Zeroth glided safely out of the way as Rosco grabbed the Kractus' neck between his mighty claws and crushed it. The Kractus fell to the desert floor, lifeless.

As the giant green body of the Kractus landed on top of her, the Sand Witch mumbled to herself, "I knew I should have taken that Vanderawlt job."

The Roc Lobster stood perched upon the body of the defeated Kractus and let loose a mighty, ground shaking roar.

"Well I'm glad that's over with," Uncle Shameless said as he dusted his hands off and looked over the massive carcass of the Kractus.

"Its not like you did anything to help," snapped Steve.

"Didn't I?" replied Uncle Shameless with an exaggerated wink.

"No," answered Steve strictly, "You didn't."

"...Yeah, I guess you're right," Uncle Shameless finished with a shrug. Zeroth approached his companions, winded. Steve ran up to him, "That was amazing!" exclaimed the boy in a rare show of excitement.

"Eh, I've fought worse," sighed Zeroth, casting an exhausted glance at the Kractus' crumbled body. "But now I'm short one pack of spices." Zeroth kicked a rock bitterly, emphasizing his annoyance.

"I just hope we can avoid any more bothersome distractions," Steve wished aloud as everyone climbed onto Rosco and prepared for the flight to the mysterious castle, Arx A'Quila.

Fiach-Ra sat in the dark, spacious shrine of Zuu and mixed together a foul-smelling compound. The only light in the shrine came from a single fire pit built in the center of the room.

The dancing fire cast eerie shadows on the shrine's walls and ceiling. After his compound was finished, Fiach-Ra reached into the red stone mixing bowl and grabbed the squishy, pungent substance with a clawed hand. Without hesitating, he quickly swallowed it in one gulp.

The Hawk-King turned around to face the lonely fire in the center of the room and stared at the flames with unblinking eyes. He began chanting the dark words of Zuu and maintained his focus on the dancing flames.

When his chanting hit its crescendo, the shrine flashed with a brilliant white light. The flames of the fire erupted upward in a tall column of white flames. Fiach-Ra's own fire-filled eyes burned with white flames as well.

"Mighty Zuu, Bringer of Fire, hear me," Fiach-Ra spoke slowly. "Your Favorite requests your aid."

The fire crackled loudly, almost shaking the shrine.

"My spy tells me The Boy has crossed the Smoldering Wastes," Fiach-Ra explained to the fire, which only crackled a response.

"No, Mighty Zuu. He has defeated the Sand Witch *and* the Kractus. He is on his way to Arx A'Quila. I have made an offer to that treacherous Hunter with him, hoping that he will turn The Boy over to me," Fiach-Ra paused for a moment before continuing, "The Hunter is Zeroth, Mighty Zuu."

The fire snapped madly for several seconds, "Yes, I know," replied Fiach-Ra, "But still, I do not entirely trust him to deliver The Boy to me. I seek guidance, I wish to dispose of The Boy, but I fear the strength of his protective amulet."

The Hawk-King sat in silence for several moments as the white flames danced in front of him. Fiach-Ra nodded, as if understanding each snap and pop.

"Ah, I understand Mighty Zuu. Because your dark magic cursed Arx A'Quila, The Boy's blue heron amulet will not protect him there," the Hawk-King smiled at this pleasant turn of events. "But should I fly to the castle and eliminate The Boy myself?"

The fire snapped loudly several times.

"Yes Mighty Zuu, yes," Fiach-Ra smiled wickedly "*They,* are still there." Fiach-Ra nodded rapidly as the flames danced higher and higher, "Yes, I agree Mighty Zuu. I shall let *them* destroy The Boy."

The Hawk-King chanted a thanks to the eagle god and finally blinked his eyes, turning the fire in them back to normal. Fiach-Ra picked up the Spear of Zuu, which had been lying on the floor next to him, and stood up. The winged tyrant laughed madly as he left the ominous shrine, leaving a normal looking fire burning away in its center.

31

Steve yawned and looked out over the horizon. Through the hazy desert sky, he saw a steep mountain not too far ahead. The mountain's peak extended high over the clouds, obscured from view.

"That's it," said Zeroth.

"What a beat up castle, it looks like an old mountain," slurred Uncle Shameless.

"The castle is on *top* of the mountain," explained Zeroth.

"Wow, I'd hate to be their paperboy," Uncle Shameless joked as he sipped from his wineskin.

While the mountain grew larger as they neared it, everyone was surprised that Rosco began heading toward the ground instead of the mountaintop.

"Why is he landing here?" Steve asked Uncle Shameless.

The boy's uncle climbed to the top of the Roc Lobster's head and listened to the creature's chirps and growls. "He says it's too dangerous for him to fly up that far," Uncle Shameless yelled back to the waiting group.

"Aw, c'mon…" hissed Steve.

"Oh, an' somethin' about the castle being haunted," Uncle Shameless added a few seconds later.

Everyone reluctantly climbed off their feathery transport after reaching the sandy desert floor once again. The Roc Lobster let loose a long screech and flapped his wings.

"Rosco said he'll stick around and wait for us," translated Uncle Shameless.

"Well, now what?" Steve asked to no one in particular.

"You *walk*," commanded a familiar voice that came from every direction. There was a flash of blue light and Istrio the blue heron appeared.

"Oh, *you* again?" whined Steve.

"Nice to see you too," countered the Elder Mystic of Zaa. Istrio walked around the group, studying everyone with his pale, empty eyes. "Everyone seems to be doing well.." Istrio stopped when he came to the Paper Tiger. "Hello, and who might you be?"

"I'm the Paper Tiger," answered the flat cat proudly.

"Yes, of course you are," replied Istrio as he continued looking everyone over "Shamus, how's the wine treating you?"

"Oh just fine! It's a fine wine!" bellowed Uncle Shameless. "Hey, I rhymed!"

"Fine, fine," replied Istrio as he waved a hand, trying to ignore Uncle Shameless' rhyming. He reached Steve and slapped the boy hard on the back, "How ya doin' kid? You all seem to be keeping it together. That was some nice work with the Sand Witch."

"Easy for you to say," winced Steve as he reached under his chain mail to rub his back.

Istrio pointed off into the distance. "Well kids, I hope you are ready for a hike because you certainly have one in front of you," everyone looked to where the blue heron was pointing.

The lanky bird-man pointed to the tallest mountain Steve had ever seen, although being from the suburbs that wasn't really saying much. Still, it was a very tall piece of rock. Everyone strained their necks to look up as high as they could, but none of them could see the top, not even Zeroth with his hawk-sight.

"We have to *climb* that?!" yelled Steve.

"Of course not. Don't be silly," answered Istrio as Steve breathed a sigh of relief. "There are stairs," explained the blue heron, adjusting his pointing to guide their eyes to a staircase cut into the rock.

"Oh, *c'mon!*" whined Steve as he saw the staircase climb the mountain side up into infinity. The steps were jagged, narrow and rather steep. Steve's legs began to ache just looking at them. A concerned look crossed Istrio's wrinkled face as he studied the staircase as well, "Hmm. You all might want to do a bit of stretching first."

As Steve climbed the narrow steps carved into the mountain several minutes later, Istrio final words still rang in his ears.

"You must climb the Steps of J'La to the top of Tyton Mountain, there you will-"

"Excuse me, the Steps of *what?*" Steve had asked.

"The Steps of J'La. Now pay attention."

"Why do these steps even have a name? Why can't they just be called 'steps'? Now *there's* an idea," snapped Steve. "Seriously, why does *everything* around here have to named after someone or something?"

"*Just climb the bloody steps!*" Istrio hollered before disappearing in a flash of light and disgust. Steve was certain he heard the Mystic of Zaa mumble "Kids today..." as he vanished.

Now, as Steve climbed the steep steps further and further up the mountain, he thought about who this J'La person might be, and how bad they were at making steps.

Steve's legs burned and ached. With each step he took, he felt his leg muscles cramp up and tighten like a vise. He looked behind him to see how everyone else was doing. Eira was having some difficulty, but was aided by her cane and Uncle Shameless was lost in a wine-induced stupor.

After almost getting blown away by a strong mountain wind, the Paper Tiger had been tied to Zeroth's back. The bird-man did not mind, since the flat feline weighed almost nothing.

"This is cruel and unusual punishment," Steve complained, as he took a short break to massage his sore legs.

"But think of all the money we're savin'!" exclaimed Uncle Shameless, his voiced booming around the steep mountain walls.

Steve turned slowly to face his staggering uncle, "*What* are you talking about?" asked the boy, even though he was afraid of the answer. Uncle Shameless causally jumped up a pair of steps and stood beside Steve.

"Fat people spend hundreds of hundreds of dollars-"

"They call those 'thousands,'" corrected Steve.

"Don't interrupt me, boy...Where was I?" asked Uncle Shameless.

"Fat people..." sighed Steve as he started to rub his temples.

"Ah, yes!" exclaimed Uncle Shameless, "*Fat people!* They spend stacks of money on machines that simulate walkin' up and down stairs, and we're gettin' it for free!"

Uncle Shameless spun around and started whistling off-key as he continued ascending the staircase. Steve turned to see everyone else staring at him, as if looking for some kind of explanation for his uncle's reasoning.

"I *have* to be adopted," sighed Steve.

The staircase circled the perimeter of Tyton Mountain, slowly climbing upward in a gradual spiral. Steve fought to ignore the sharp pain in his legs. He peeked over the edge of the staircase to the distant ground below.

Steve could see the giant Roc Lobster, Rosco, below searching for food. From far up the great beast looked like a child's toy. Uncle Shameless hopped down a few steps with a look of delight on his face.

"We're near the top, just a little bit more to go!" his words echoing loudly. Steve hopped off the last step onto a smooth landing cut into the mountain, and began to cheer.

However, as he looked to the other side of the landing his cheers quickly turned into a swarm of curses.

Across the smooth stone landing, stood a well worn wooden sign. In elaborately painted, flowing letters, the sign read 'The Steps of J'La' followed by an arrow pointing to a nearby set of ascending stairs, even steeper and in worse condition than those he had just climbed.

Zeroth (still carrying the Paper Tiger) and Eira ran to join the angered boy, wondering what the problem was. Steve could only manage an angry pointing gesture in the direction of the new set of stairs, causing his friends' spirits to fall as well.

Uncle Shameless meanwhile amused himself by bellowing and listening to his echo.

Steve looked at the sign, and then remembered what Istrio had said. "Wait, if *those* are the Steps of J'La, then what did we just climb?"

Uncle Shameless scratched his head of shaggy hair and thought aloud, "Maybe…" he started "Maybe…those were just the steps to *get* to the steps."

Steve narrowed his eyes and stared at his uncle, "Steps to get to the steps? That has to be the most absurd…" he thought for a moment before finishing his sentence.

"Oh forget it," sighed Steve as he threw up his hands. "Let's get this over with."

The weary group made their way up the *real* Steps of J'La, trying not to think about the sharp pains in their legs.

Due to his over-indulgence of the Eldercherry wine, Uncle Shameless was immune to the effects of all of the stair climbing. This only added to Steve's annoyance with the whole ordeal.

"Why are these steps so tall anyway?" Steve complained aloud.

"Not everything was built with humans in mind," explained Eira.

Without looking behind him, Steve asked, "What do you mean?"

"Arx A'Quila *was* the castle of the owls, the previous rulers of the animal kingdom."

"So?" asked Steve, gritting his teeth while climbing more and more steps.

"Well, the owls were tall and had very strong legs. Steps like these would not have bothered them."

Steve thought for a moment of the statues of the owls he had seen at the Temple of Arcana "But didn't they have wings? Why not just fly up?"

"They ruled *all* of the animals, not just the birds. Those who could not fly would have to come to the castle like we are," explained Eira.

Steve turned his head towards Eira. "What happened to the owls anyway?"

Before Eira could answer, Steve walked right into Uncle Shameless' back, knocking his glasses loose.

Uncle Shameless turned his head slowly and in a very sober tone said, "I think I know," as he pointed a shaky finger to the top of the staircase.

Steve fixed his glasses and looked to where his uncle pointed.

At the top of the staircase, hunched over against the mountain side sat two large bird-people skeletons, dressed in rust covered armor.

Steve slowly made his way past Uncle Shameless and reached the top of the stairs. Old, cruel looking arrows jutted out from the chest armor of one of the skeleton warriors, reminding Steve of his close call with the Hawken archers in Uth.

The warriors were large, much bigger than the Hawken, but not nearly as bulky as the Swantan. Steve noticed the skeletal remains of wings sticking through large openings on the back of the armor they wore.

"*Owl warriors*," said Zeroth as he examined the remains. "Probably left here after Fiach-Ra's assault on Arx A'Quila long ago."

Uncle Shameless walked over to the second fallen owl warrior, who was filled with arrows like its counterpart. "Was this littler one a squire?" he asked, due to the warrior's smaller stature and lighter armor.

"No," answered Zeroth truthfully, "Just a male."

"Oh," whistled Uncle Shameless. "Wait...then that big fella by you...*ain't* a fella?"

"Yes, this one," said Zeroth as he pointed to the larger warrior next to him dressed in heavier armor, "Was a female. Owl females were bigger, stronger and better warriors than the males."

Steve's jaw dropped, "You're joking right?"

Both Zeroth and Eira looked at Steve with puzzled expressions. "Of course not," answered Zeroth seriously, sounding insulted. "That is the way it has always been. Owl leaders have always been warrior-queens."

"Yes, in fact it was Fel-Ra herself who united all of the animals into one kingdom after the War of Fire," added Eira. "Just as Donal did with all of the human tribes."

"That's right," continued Zeroth. "And it was not until Fiach-Ra overthrew Fel-Ra that there was a male ruler of the birds."

"Well, there was that short-lived takeover by the Badger-King about 400 years ago," said Eira.

"I forgot about that little guy," laughed Zeroth.

"The...*Badger*-King?" asked Steve.

Zeroth nodded, "Yeah, he was probably Alexander's size, maybe smaller. The legend goes that he showed up on the front steps of Arx A'Quila, armed with the Trowel of Zuu and took over the castle."

"The *Trowel* of Zuu? You can't be serious," Steve questioned skeptically.

"Oh yes," answered Eira, "But it wasn't as strong as the *Spear* of Zuu. It was only slightly more dangerous than a normal trowel."

A vision of a tiny, cantankerous badger with fiery eyes wielding a flaming garden trowel filled Steve's mind. He couldn't help but smile. "Wait, how did he take over the castle?" asked Steve.

Zeroth shook his head and tried to fight back a chuckle, "He was so small, that no one noticed that he had in."

Eira nodded and continued, "And Fel-Ra was out on royal business, so the throne room was empty."

"Right," laughed Zeroth "So this pint-sized revolutionary scurried his way to the throne room unnoticed, climbed up on the throne, and declared himself Badger-King of Eyri."

"You're joking. *Please* tell me you're joking," said Steve.

"Hardly," continued Eira "But his reign didn't last long. Fel-Ra came back about three minutes later and promptly threw him from the highest tower."

Uncle Shameless ran ahead to see what was around the bend in the path. Eira helped untie the Paper Tiger, who was all too happy to be walking around again, from Zeroth's back.

"Dear me, I'm all wrinkled and creased!" complained the Paper Tiger as he studied his crumpled mid-section.

Steve studied the remains of the owl warriors, wondering if there were more lying around the mountain. The idea scared him a little, as the dirty white bones and empty eyes of those in front of him reminded him of Fiach-Ra's fiery Pyrix monsters.

As Steve walked away from the remains and closer to the path Uncle Shameless had taken, he noticed a thick fog growing in the air. It started just near his feet and extended high into the sky, cloaking the top of the mountain.

Steve remembered that Rosco had mentioned that the mountain top and the owl castle, Arx A'Quila, were haunted. After staring into the spooky, swirling fog for a few moments, Steve ran to join his companions.

"Any sign of your uncle?" asked Eira as Steve ran up to her.

"Hm? Oh, no."

"I hope he's okay."

"I'm sure he's fine," replied Steve confidently "After all, he's the one with super strength."

Uncle Shameless stumbled blindly through the thick fog. "Where'd all this come from?" he said aloud.

Uncle Shameless felt his way through the fog with his hands, following the curve of the rocky mountainside along the path. "This is exhausting!" he bellowed, again only to himself. He leaned against the mountain wall and took out his wineskin. The crimson liquid fought his strong thirst as he glanced around at his surroundings, trying to peer through the fog.

A breeze kicked up and the wind howled around Uncle Shameless, sending chills down his spine. From within the fog he heard a loud SNAP! Uncle Shameless jerked his head in the direction of the sound.

"...Hello?" Uncle Shameless called out as he blindly felt his way through the fog once more.

The wind began to howl near Steve as well, creating a chorus of odd sounds around him. Steve noticed the fog thickening to the point where he was having a difficult time seeing everyone, even though they were close by.

Steve blindly bumped into Zeroth, "Sorry," the boy apologized.

"No worries," replied Zeroth "But I think we should look for your uncle. The fog could make walking around the top of this mountain very dangerous."

Steve nodded and turned to go look for Uncle Shameless. After he stumbled around for a several minutes, Steve bumped into Zeroth once more.

"Sorry," the boy apologized again "Did you see my uncle at all?"

Zeroth did not answer. The young hero tried again, "Look, I said I was sorry."

Steve could just barely see the outline of Zeroth's body turn to face him. It moved very slowly, and with odd jerky motions.

"Are you okay?" asked Steve, growing concerned.

A faint, red-orange glow began emitting from Zeroth's eyes. The glow began flickering, like a fire.

"C'mon, I said I was sorry for bumping into you. You don't have to take it so hard," Steve said with a nervous smile.

The bird-man's head swung down to Steve's eye-level, moaning a low, eerie cry as flames poured out from its eyes, illuminating the face like a beacon.

"Ahhhh!" screamed Steve as he came face to face with one of the owl skeletons. The creature lashed out at Steve with a boney hand, grabbing a hold of a shirt sleeve. Steve screamed again and ran, ripping the sleeve.

Deep within the sea of fog, Steve saw another pair of eyes ignite, followed by another, and another. Fire began pouring out of so many skull eyes, that Steve could not keep count.

As Steve ran blindly through the fog, he bumped into one of the warriors. It quickly tried to grab him. Steve readied the Staff of Arcana and again imagined it was a baseball bat. He swung at his attacker's knees.

"OW!" yelped a familiar voice.

"Zeroth?"

"Of course!" yelled the bird-man "Why'd you hit me?"

"We have a *problem!*" Steve yelled as he turned to point to a quintet of skeletal shapes in the fog. Zeroth's eyes widened with fear and he hands began to shake, "No…it can't be, not yet."

Steve looked up at the bird-man, very confused.

"They couldn't have found me yet..." the Hunter gasped nervously.

"*What* are you talking about?" snapped Steve.

Several words built up in Zeroth's beak but he could not bring himself to speak them. He was about to stutter the first word when he noticed the fire in the eyes of the skeletons in the fog.

"...it isn't them..." Zeroth whispered with a sigh of relief as he stopped shaking and regained control of his senses.

"What do you mean, 'it isn't them'?" demanded Steve.

"Zaa's Talons!" cursed Zeroth as he again noticed the countless fiery eyes marching through the fog erratically and realized now whom they belonged to. He looked down at Steve, "What did you do?"

"Me? I didn't *do* anything!"

Zeroth grabbed the boy's arm and broke into a run, pulling Steve with him. The undead warriors quickly followed, moaning and groaning all the way.

Steve panted heavily as he ran behind Zeroth. "What are those things?" asked the boy, "And what were you yelling about?"

"More than just skeletons, that is certain," answered Zeroth, ignoring the boy's second question.

The pair met up with Eira and the Paper Tiger, who were quickly ordered by Zeroth to get up and start running. "What's going on?" asked Eira. Zeroth pointed to the sea of fire filled eyes pursuing them in the dense fog.

"*Oh*," replied the pelican-lady. She looked down at Steve "What did you do?"

"Why is everyone blaming me?!" screamed the boy.

The cohorts ran toward the path Uncle Shameless had taken earlier, hanging on to each other so that they would not lose one another in the swirling fog. An owl screeched loudly, jumped into the air and flapped its tattered wings. It landed near the group and swung a rust covered sword at Zeroth, who dodged the attack easily.

Another skeletal warrior dropped down from above and took a swing at Steve with a broken sword. In a flash, his baseball bat once again turned into a trash can lid to deflect the blow. With a quick thought, the trash can lid switched back to a baseball bat, and Steve swung it hard towards the crouched owl's head.

The bat connected to the creature's skull with a loud CRACK! and the skull was sent flying through the air, flames trailing behind it as it soared deep into the fog. The now headless owl warrior stumbled around aimlessly, feeling the ground for its missing head.

"Good job!" complimented Zeroth as he took out Gladius.

"*Now* what?" scoffed the swordfish curtly, looking up at the attacking skeleton. The creature let loose a chilling growl as it prepared to attack Zeroth.

"Yikes, it's almost as ugly as you!" joked Gladius.

"*Quiet,*" snapped Zeroth as he prepared to release the swordfish's deadly tongue.

"I see how it is," whined Gladius "You only take me out of your cloak when you *need* something."

Zeroth held up his moody weapon and stared into its large eyes. "You *can't* be serious..." said the Hunter.

"Oh, I am. You never take me out to just chat it up, no no. Only when you need something."

"We don't have time for this-"

"Well, when will we?!" screamed the swordfish, its emotions boiling. Zeroth groaned and gave Gladius a hard squeeze. Gladius mumbled its disapproval loudly but more moaning from approaching owl skeletons quickly drowned it out.

Zeroth plunged his swordfish into an attacking owl's boney rib cage, sliding harmlessly between the bare ribs, only to poke out its back. Zeroth shook his head as his attack did nothing to harm the undead owl.

Steve watched as more and more pairs of fiery eyes lurched toward him and his friends through the fog. Eira was fending off attackers with her walking stick, smacking the owls in their heads as hard as she could.

The Paper Tiger growled at the skeletal attackers and swiped at them with his flat paws. Much to the flat feline's surprise, his parchment claws did nothing to hinder their advance.

"They must be protected by *powerful* magic!" exclaimed the clueless cat.

Zeroth grabbed Gladius in his clawed hands and pulled on the stuck swordfish. This only brought the undead owl closer as he repeatedly tried to pull Gladius free. Zeroth ducked swing after swing from the attacking skeleton.

The frustrated bird-man tried to ignore his talking weapon's muffled laughter and threw a punch at the owl's hard skull, which had no effect other than hurting his own hand.

"Ow!" yelped Zeroth as he rubbed his hand and ignored more of Gladius' laughter.

With an agitated grunt, Zeroth squeezed Gladius tightly, causing its tongue to recoil sharply.

"Now why didn't ya think of that b'fore?" criticized the talking weapon. Zeroth squeezed Gladius again, causing the swordfish to let loose a loud BLEAH!

The bird-man struck the attacking skeleton's skull with the flat side of his blade. The force of the blow caused the skull to spin around like a top on the creature's neck, eventually coming to a stop facing backwards. The confused skeleton stumbled around, not able to see where it was going.

Steve had turned the Staff of Arcana into an old rake once again and was using it to trip approaching skeletons. He swung the long handle of the rusty rake under the legs of a tall owl and knocked the legs out from under it. Several of the creature's bones became loose and fell off as it tried to right itself.

"Eww..." winced Steve, disgusted by the sight.

A clawed hand gripped Steve's shoulder and his instinctively swung the rake hard at the creature's legs.

"OW!" yelped Zeroth.

"Sorry!" apologized Steve, realizing his mistake. "We need a plan," The boy said to the bird-man

"Don't worry I have one," answered Zeroth as he rubbed his sore leg.

"What is it?"

"A cunning piece of strategy, relying on ancient tried and true tactics."

32

As the group ran away as fast as they could, Steve glanced over at Zeroth, "Run away? *That* was your plan?"

"It's working ain't it?" Zeroth countered defensively.

As Steve ran, he thought he heard footsteps coming from in front of him. However, before he had time to think about it, he ran right into Uncle Shameless. The pair fell to the ground, and as uncle and nephew saw each other they both yelled 'Am I glad to see you!' in unison.

Uncle Shameless narrowed his eyes in thought for a moment and then looked down at Steve. "What'd you do?"

Steve threw up his arms, "Ugh! I didn't do anything! It's not my fault we're being chased by skeletons!"

"You're bein' chased by skeletons too?"

"Yes, and we've only just now got away from…*wait*…what do you mean 'too'?" Steve asked bitterly.

"Uh, well…"

The boy leaned past his uncle and looked into the fog. Dozens of fire-filled eyes stomped through the cloudy murkiness towards them. Steve buried his face into his hands. "What did *you* do?" asked Steve through his hands.

"Look, it ain't my fault these things can't take a joke, all I was doin' was-"

"I don't want to know," interrupted Steve.

"I think you do, it's a pretty funny story."

"Perhaps we should discuss this some other time?" suggested the Paper Tiger, "We are about to be surrounded."

Uncle Shameless ran off in a different direction, everyone else followed and tried not to lose one another in the thick fog. "Where are you leading us?" asked Steve.

"You're following me?" asked Uncle Shameless.

"Of course!"

"Oh, I thought we were gonna split up."

Steve groaned loudly.

Zeroth looked behind them, "They are closing in." The Hunter reached into his magical pack and pulled out a large package of what looked like marbles and dumped the contents on the ground behind him. As the owl skeletons tried to shamble over the tiny orbs, they easily tripped and crashed into one another, creating a large pile up of bone and armor.

"That'll buy us a few minutes," said Zeroth as more skeletons collided into each other in the distance.

"What were those?" asked Eira.

"They're hard candy," explained Zeroth. "I got them as part of a payment for a job."

"Are you ever paid with anything other than food stuffs and random objects?" asked Steve.

"Over there!" interrupted Uncle Shameless, pointing to a new rocky path ahead of them. The group rounded the corner and stopped dead in their tracks.

In front of them rested a stone castle, crumbling in its isolation atop Tyton Mountain. The main building was a pyramid, joined by two smaller pyramids on the side.

The castle looked very old and was falling apart before their eyes. Steve saw several pieces crumble and fall off thanks to a heavy gust of wind. The pieces crashed to the ground many miles below.

Crowning the castle was an enormous eagle statue, made of bluish silver. Its wings were spread in a majestic span like some sort of avian airplane. Its body was expertly crafted and all of the edges were rounded and smooth. The giant eagle clutched the top of the pyramid in its mighty talons, perching for all of Eyri to see. It reminded Steve of the statue on top of Arx Vena'Tor, only this was not a menacing, snarling effigy.

This statue gave off an impression of peace and protection as its head looked down at them with a powerful, vigilant gaze.

"Arx A'Quila!" gasped Eira as she kneeled respectfully.

Uncle Shameless scratched his head and smiled a crooked grin as he patted Steve's head. "Now that wasn't so hard, was it?"

The companions' enjoyment was short lived as a chorus of low moans and groans echoed behind them.

"Crumbs!" cursed Steve, "How'd they find us?"

"Well we did just stay on the main path," Uncle Shameless pointed out "It ain't like we made it too hard for 'em."

"Let's just get inside and away from those things," said Steve as he pointed to the main pyramid.

As Steve and his friends headed for the front door, the small army of undead owls shuffled and moaned along the path after them. The path to the main pyramid was formed by a series of stone staircases criss-crossing among the cliffs and peaks leading up to the main peak of the mountain.

Like Arx A'Quila itself, the stairs were crumbling in front of the group's eyes.

"I should report this to the landlord!" complained Uncle Shameless as a step broke underneath him.

Steve ignored his uncle and continued climbing the crumbling steps. He could feel some of the steps beginning to give way under his feet. Steve turned around to see a score of fire-filled eyes heading up the path. His foot slipped and the boy found himself falling off the stairs into the endless fog.

Visions of being splattered among the sharp rocks below ran through Steve's mind. Even though he was growing tired of this quest, he did not want it to end like this.

A hand shot out and grabbed him, "Easy there!" yelled Uncle Shameless as he effortlessly lifted the boy back up. Steve had only fallen for a few seconds, but it had felt like an eternity.

Steve tried to ignore the panic inside him as they continued up the steps. The moans of the owls grew louder and louder. Steve could hear their bone feet going clickity-clack against the stone steps.

All of sudden, Uncle Shameless stopped in his tracks.

"Why are you stopping?!" yelled Steve.

"I had a thought."

"Now?!"

"How can those things move if they are just bone? They ain't got no muscle," Uncle Shameless pondered aloud. "I seem to remember from school that bones needed muscle to move."

"We really don't have time for this," snapped Steve.

"Hush, we have plenty of time for science," smiled Uncle Shameless. "I would think *you* of all people would appreciate that."

"Science has *nothing* to do with walking, undead skeletons!" yelled Steve, "It's magic!" the boy's voice rang with frustration over using his least favorite word.

Uncle Shameless looked down at the boy and then back over at the army of the undead and scratched his head. "*Yeah,* I s'pose you got a point there."

"*Shall we?*" Steve said curtly, motioning to the path ahead in a sarcastic tone.

The group continued their flight up the stairs with the owls still in hot pursuit. A pair of owls took to the air and flew down in front of the companions, swinging their rusty swords wildly. Uncle Shameless pushed one of the boney attackers over the stairs easily with a hard shoulder tackle, crushing the creature's brittle bone wings in the process.

"That's another thing," Uncle Shameless pondered as Steve blocked a sword attack by the second owl, "How can they fly without feathers?"

"How can *anything* around here do *anything?*" answered Steve knowingly as he swatted at the second owl with a quickly summoned baseball bat.

"True, true," replied Uncle Shameless as he grabbed the owl's arm as it reached back to swing at Steve again. With a quick jerk, Uncle Shameless pulled the skeletal arm out of its socket and whacked its owner upside the head with it, knocking the owl over the edge of the staircase.

"I see the top of the stairs!" cried Zeroth.

"Finally!" cheered Steve as he cast a quick glance at the countless owls closing in on them.

The group cleared the top of the stairs. Followed by the stream of undead warriors seconds later. Eira felt a boney hand grab at her poncho, ripping it.

"Head for the front door!" commanded Zeroth, pointing to the large elaborately decorated front entrance of the main pyramid. The moans of the owls turned into piercing shrieks as the group came up to the door.

"Shameless, hold them off while we open the door!" yelled Zeroth.

"Right!" Uncle Shameless bellowed as he hiked up his pants, which quickly settled back down again. The man took a quick swig of wine and prepared to fight the horde of undead warriors.

"Alright! Who wants some of this?!"

A burly owl took a swipe at Uncle Shameless, striking him in the side of the head with its large fist.

"Ow!" cried Uncle Shameless as the blow knocked him over. Before he could get up, many of the owls were either punching him or trying to pull him in different directions.

"Lemme go!" Uncle Shameless cried as two owls pulled his legs this way and that.

By the door, Steve shook his head. "Well at least he's keeping them distracted."

"Help me with the door," asked Zeroth as he grabbed a hold of one of the large wing-shaped handles.

The pair grunted loudly as they pulled with all their might, yet the door did not budge. Eira joined in and still nothing happened. The Paper Tiger grabbed the back of Steve's chain mail in his jaws and pulled as well, but the door would not move an inch.

"There must be some secret way to open it!" said Steve in a burst of inspiration.

"Possibly," said Zeroth "But how?"

Steve thought for a moment, "Maybe Gladius knows."

Zeroth nodded and took the temperamental talking weapon out of his cloak.

"What now?" asked Gladius in very annoyed tone.

"Can you hurry up!" cried Uncle Shameless in between punches and kicks from the owls, "Please!…Hey! *No biting!*"

Zeroth held Gladius up to the front door of Arx A'Quila, "Have you ever been here before?"

The swordfish scanned the large door with its eyes, "Oh yeah, this is Fel-Ra's castle. Donal an' me came here a few times back in the ol' days."

"Good, now do you know-"

"'Course, that was until he got that no-good Sword of Zaa. After that, he never took me anywh-"

"We really do not have time for this," Steve begged as he pointed to Uncle Shameless being beaten silly by the owl warriors.

Gladius sighed, "Fine. What is it then?"

"We can't get this door open!" yelled Zeroth.

"Well 'course you can't."

"What do you mean?" asked Steve, trying to ignore the sound of his uncle being pummeled.

"It's just fer decoration. This door don't open," explained Gladius.

Steve looked over the large door with its hand-carved details and shook his head, "Typical."

"So, how *do* we get in?" asked Zeroth.

"The side entrance, 'course," answered Gladius.

"Of *course*," added Steve sarcastically.

"Ooof!" puffed Uncle Shameless as he used his extra-ordinary strength to push the pile of owls off himself. "I've had just about enough of this!" He made his way back up the stairs to join the group. Along the way, an owl jumped and tackled Uncle Shameless.

Steve watched as his uncle pried the skeleton's fingers off his neck and picked the owl up. Uncle Shameless spun the owl around and around before sending the creature sailing into the crowd of other skeletons marching up the stairs, knocking them all down like a set of decayed bowling pins.

"Let's go now!" yelled Steve, realizing they had only moments to spare before their pursuers regrouped. A small, wooden bridge led them around the outer edge of the pyramid toward the side entrance.

"I'm shocked. Fel-Ra's really let this place go ta pieces," lamented Gladius.

"Fel-Ra is dead," said Zeroth as he ran down the rickety walkway.

"Dead?!" the talking swordfish exclaimed in surprise. "I didn't even know she was sick!"

The group eventually reached the side entrance. While the front door had been a grand piece of exquisite architecture, this side entrance – as Uncle Shameless crassly put it – was a grand piece of something else.

Set into the crumbling stone side of the pyramid was an average size wooden door. It had been shoddily made of uneven warped planks of wood. The hinges were not evenly spaced, and the doorknob was crooked.

"Ew," Steve criticized while looking over the shoddy excuse for a door. The bottom of the door dug into the ground and the top had an uneven angle that would dig into the door jam above it when opened or closed.

"Here we are then," said Gladius. "The Queen's Entrance."

"You can't be serious, this is called The Queen's Entrance?" asked Steve as he made a face of disgust.

"It's an owl thing," explained Gladius. "It is suppose ta show how humble the Queen is – er...*was*."

"Who cares, let's just get in-saaahh!" screamed Uncle Shameless as an undead owl jumped onto his back and tried biting his shoulder.

Steve turned to see other owls close behind them on the wobbly walkway.

"Open the door!" the boy called to Zeroth as he went to help his uncle.

"Get offa me!" cried Uncle Shameless as he thrashed around with the owl on his back. "No, not in the face!" he yelled as his unwanted passenger punched his face with a hard, boney hand.

Steve felt the heat from the owl's fire-filled eyes as he approached his uncle. The owl saw Steve and lashed out at him with a free hand. Steve closed his eyes as he swung the Staff of Arcana and thought of a weapon.

The owl moaned loudly as an axe blade cut through its fleshless arm. Steve opened his eyes to see himself holding an axe. It resembled the axe he had used to cut wood back on Uncle Shameless' farm, but this one was different. The blade was made of brilliant silver and the handle was made of finely crafted wood.

"'Bout time!" cheered Zeroth as he and Eira pulled on the door. It creaked loudly and scratched against the top of the door jam. "Ooooh, Fel-Ra's not gonna like *that*," said Gladius as he watched the top of the door leave a long scrape mark on the stone above it.

The arm Steve had cut off started moving around, using the fingers of the hand like little spindly legs. "Gross!" yelled Steve as he swung his axe wildly at the scuttling hand.

The low bottom of the door skipped along the floor, causing it to jerk sharply. Zeroth and Eira pulled hard, but the door had become stuck after only opening a few inches.

The Paper Tiger watched more and more owls funnel down the rickety bridge towards them. "We'd better hurry!"

"OW!" screamed Uncle Shameless. "Hey! Not the hair!" he screamed again as the owl on his back began pulling his scraggily hair.

Steve kept trying to hit the hand chasing him, and he was growing frustrated as the fast moving hand easily dodged the axe blade. Steve roared and swung again, imagining something else. The clawed owl hand was crushed by the large head of a sledgehammer. Steve lifted the hammer up to inspect it. The hammer was similar in design to the axe he had used moments before.

The owl's hand was nothing more than dust and the stone floor by the Queen's Entrance now had a sizeable crack in it.

"Thata boy!" called Uncle Shameless as he repeatedly threw himself backwards into the side of the pyramid, trying to knock the hand's owner off.

Steve looked back at Zeroth and the others at the door. "Is it open yet?"

"It's stuck!" cried Eira.

Steve looked back at Uncle Shameless and then at the other owls only seconds away. "Hurry up!" the boy yelled back as he went to help Uncle Shameless.

The teenage adventurer ran up alongside Uncle Shameless. The owl was having a hard time hanging onto Uncle Shameless and attacking with only one arm.

Steve readied the hammer, "Hey!" he yelled to Uncle Shameless, who stopped and looked at Steve.

Without hesitating, Steve swung the large hammer at the owl on his uncle's back, striking the creature in the rib cage. The impact knocked the owl loose and broke the fiend in two.

"Let's go!" yelled Uncle Shameless as he grabbed Steve's hand and ran towards the door. Zeroth pulled on the door again and again but it would not budge.

"Is dat the best ya can do?" chided Gladius, who was still in Zeroth's free hand. Inspired by frustration, with a quick flash Zeroth squeezed Gladius, releasing his tongue and rammed the blade between the door and the wall.

"Push with me!" Zeroth commanded Eira and the Paper Tiger, using the swordfish as a wedge. To their amazement, the door began to creak and flex.

A pair of owls closed in on Uncle Shameless and Steve. The boy prepared to take a swing at them but Uncle Shameless stopped him. "Just keep movin'!"

"Push!" yelled Zeroth again as the trio tried to force the old door open on its rusted hinges. It jerked sharply, and was open another inch "Good! Keep going!"

Only a few feet from the door, Uncle Shameless tripped on the crack Steve had created and went crashing into Zeroth, Eira and the Paper Tiger. This caused the door to swing open sharply and Steve jumped aside so that the freed door hit the two owls right in the face, knocking them down.

Zeroth stood up quickly, "Inside, now!"

Everyone dove through the dark doorway and into the black void that waited beyond the Queen's Entrance. Zeroth slammed the door shut and relaxed for a moment. The room was dark and smelled very old.

"Is everyone okay?" the bird-man asked, panting heavily. His companions answered him with a chorus of sore grunts and painful murmurs.

33

Uncle Shameless leaned against the shoddy wooden door while Zeroth searched for a torch or some other light source. Steve walked around the dark chamber, his footsteps echoing loudly. "Are we in the main part of the castle?"

"I'm not sure," answered Eira. "It's hard to tell, this place is enormous."

Thin shafts of light came down from several broken skylights near the top of the pyramid, creating random pools of light in the blackness of the room.

Steve walked up to an old tapestry on a cracked wall that was partially illuminated by a shaft of light. What remained of the weaving showed a flight of owls ascending from Arx A'Quila. At least it looked like the castle.

The pyramid in the weaving was missing the giant eagle that Steve had seen perched on top. Steve studied the rest of the weaving and noticed a section of the tapestry had been torn. All Steve could see was one large bluish silver wing.

"Hurry up will y-ahhh!" cried Uncle Shameless as he felt a pounding from the other side of the Queen's Entrance. A series of moans and cries came from outside as the owls began pounding on the door. Uncle Shameless braced the door with his back, trying to keep it shut.

"What are you doing?!" yelled Steve.

"I'm keeping the door shut!"

"That door opens outward!"

"So?"

"So," explained Steve "You're pushing on it with your back!"

A look of total cluelessness washed over Uncle Shameless' face. "And...?" asked Uncle Shameless as he unsuccessfully tried to figure out the problem.

"*And* you're pushing the door open!"

Uncle Shameless' eyes widened as he turned his head slightly. Sure enough, the door had opened several inches. A decayed skeleton hand rammed through the opening and grabbed at him.

"Aieeeee!" yelped Uncle Shameless as he repeatedly slapped the hand away. In the commotion, Uncle Shameless lost his balance and fell backwards into the door, knocking it open even more.

"*Oh*, for the love of..." started Steve as he shook his head, dismayed (but not surprised) with the whole scene.

An owl stuck its head through the opening and moaned loudly, the fire from its eyes lit up the room. Zeroth and Steve ran over to the door and grabbed on to the handle. Steve kicked Uncle Shameless to get him to stand up and help.

All three pulled on the handle quickly, trapping the owl's skull in the doorway, causing the undead creature to thrash around. Its dry and brittle beak snapped at Steve from above, nearly taking a bite out of his head.

"*Pull!*" yelled Zeroth as they pulled hard on the handle once more. There was a loud scraping sound followed by an even louder POP!

Steve looked down at the floor. The owl's skull had been pulled loose from the rest of its undead body on the other side of the door. The still moving skull snapped its beak at Steve's feet.

"Ugh, gross!" cried Steve as he kicked the skull away.

"Wait!" yelled Zeroth as he walked over the skull. "I have an idea."

"That," Steve said slowly, "Is *disgusting*."

"Do you have a better idea?" asked Zeroth. Steve rolled his eyes and shook his head.

Zeroth held up his makeshift torch proudly. He had tied the owl's skull to a piece of wood and was using the fire pouring from the creature's empty eye sockets to light their way. However, the skull was still alive (or undead), so he had tied the sharp beak shut with the extra rope.

Zeroth held the flaming skull in front of him as he led the group through the castle. The skull tried to wiggle free, but could not break its tight bonds.

Using the light, they had found a locking mechanism for the Queen's Entrance, although Zeroth did not think it would last too long against the angry mob outside. He hoped it would at least buy them a little more time to look for the long lost Sword of Zaa.

The immeasurable castle was silent except for their footsteps and the crackling of fire coming from Zeroth's undead torch. Steve's face contorted as he breathed in the musty, old air inside the castle.

"Do you even know *where* you are going?" Steve asked Zeroth.

"Of course," explained Zeroth. "To the end of this hallway."

Steve rolled his eyes. "Where are we s'pose to find this sword anyway?" asked Steve.

"I'm sure it'll be pretty obvious," slurred Uncle Shameless as he stumble down the hallway.

"How do you know?"

"It always is in the story books!" bellowed Uncle Shameless. "Like stuck in a stone, or hidden in some huge treasure room or guarded by some nasty, ugly creature!"

The narrow stone hallway opened up into a large circular rotunda in the middle of the castle. Steve looked up as far as he could, but could not see all the way to the top. The flames from the owl skull cast spooky shadows around the circular room as Zeroth waved his improvised torch around.

Broken carvings and statues lined the walls of the rotunda, giving Steve the feeling that he was being watched from all sides. More tattered tapestries were hung in the room as well, but centuries of neglect had turned them into illegible smears or smudges.

Zeroth swung his undead torch downward to get a look at the rotunda's expansive floor.

"Aggh!" screamed Steve after getting a peek of what they were standing on. The floor was made of what looked like solid, but flowing, dark water.

"Th-that's water," gasped Steve, lifting up his foot to see tiny waves and ripples dancing underneath him "But it isn't ice…so how are we standing on it?"

"Hm, maybe there's glass?" suggested Uncle Shameless.

Steve kneeled down to knock on the water, expecting to hear the telltale sound of glass. Instead, his fist dunked into the cold darkness under him. He lifted his fist up again, it was soaking wet.

"Okay," gasped Steve slowly as he shook his hand dry. "This is *really* starting to freak me out."

Zeroth walked next to the boy "If that freaks you out, look at *this,*" Zeroth lowered the torch and pointed to a dark shape moving slowly through the water they were standing on.

Without looking away from the water, Steve reached over and quickly pushed the torch upwards, obscuring the thing in the water once more. "Correction, *that* really freaked me out," Steve replied through his clenched teeth.

On the other side of the circular room was a large set of double doors. Like everything else in Arx A'Quila, with the exception of the Queen's Entrance, it was elaborately decorated and beautifully made.

"Y'see?" said Uncle Shameless as he pointed to the doors, "That sword *has* to be in there!"

"Just because it's a room with really big doors? Oh, *please* that is the worst logic I have ever heard," said Steve.

"Ah, I see you've found the sword room," spoke a familiar, ghostly voice.

"Oh no," whined Steve as he realized who the voice belonged to.

"Oh *yes*," replied the voice as a blast of blue light went off in the middle of the rotunda. Steve sighed as Istrio, the blue heron, appeared before them as the blue light faded away.

"And how is everyone doing?" asked the ancient Elder Mystic of Zaa, bowing respectfully to the group.

"You didn't say anything about running into an army of zombie owls," snapped Steve resentfully.

"Well of course I didn't say anything about zombie owls young Harrier."

"Why not!"

"Because those were *skeleton* owls," answered Istrio. "Trust me, you don't want to mess with zombies."

"What's the difference?!"

The blue heron snorted, "If you have ever had to deal with zombies, you'd *know* the difference. They are some nasty business."

Zeroth looked over at Istrio, "Is the Sword of Zaa in that room?" he asked, jerking a clawed thumb towards the large doors.

"Almost positive."

Steve's jaw dropped, "What do you mean *almost positive*?!"

The blue heron looked at Steve with his blank eyes and shook his head, "You really need to learn how to relax kid." Istrio ambled over to the double doors, his robes hiding his feet so it looked as if he was floating.

"I haven't been here in a few hundred years, anything could have happened."

"That reminds me of the time I went looking for a pair of pants after I got home from vacation, and they weren't where I left 'em," explained Uncle Shameless.

"What does *that* have to do with anything?" asked Steve.

"You see?" added Istrio, "Things happen over time."

"I'll say," said Uncle Shameless as he swayed around the rotunda. "I really needed those pants!"

"Why?" asked Eira.

"Because I lost the pair I wore on vacation."

"*Anyway*," continued Istrio, "I'm here to get you back on schedule."

"What do you mean back on schedule?" asked Steve.

"I told you when I first met you that we were on a timetable."

"You weren't really specific!" argued Steve.

"I wasn't?"

"No!"

"Oh," the blue heron shrugged, "You have to confront Fiach-Ra before dawn."

"I don't even know what time it is!" Steve yelled truthfully.

"The sun is setting soon, Fiach-Ra is vulnerable during the night to the power of Zaa."

"Since when?" asked Steve bitterly.

"...I didn't mention this before?" asked Istrio. "No!" everyone yelled in unison.

"Oh, so sorry. I thought I had."

"You said no such thing," grumbled Steve.

"Well, I'm telling you now. So you had better get on with it," the Mystic made a shooing motion with his hands. "C'mon then, quick quick. We haven't got all night!"

"But why tonight?" asked Steve as he looked up at Istrio's wrinkled face.

"Oh, just some nonsense with the alignment of the moons and such. You know, more of the *magic* business you just can't stand, so I won't bore you with the details," explained Istrio as he crossed his long arms and returned the boy's grumpy stare.

Steve sighed and headed for the doors to the room that may or may not contain the Sword of Zaa. As he passed by the blue heron, the ancient bird-Mystic spoke one last time.

"Oh, one last thing - if you don't defeat him by sunrise, we'll have to suffer his rule for another 313 years. Have fun!" smiled Istrio, waving a hand and disappearing in a flash of blue light.

"He's so *strange*," mumbled Steve as he avoided looking down at the watery floor beneath him.

"Well, this sword ain't gonna find itself," sighed Steve as he tucked the Staff of Arcana into his belt and headed for the impressive doors. Once at the door, Zeroth joined him with his makeshift torch, which illuminated a big sign on the wall.

Steve brushed the dust and grime off of the letters with the palm of his hand. It read "Sword Room."

"Oh you *have* to be kidding," Steve said with a sigh.

Uncle Shameless stumbled over next to Steve and read the sign. "See! I told you!"

The boy shook his head and pushed on one of the doors with Zeroth. The rusty hinges creaked and moaned but finally gave way and the door slowly opened.

Uncle Shameless grabbed the owl-skull torch from Zeroth and walked into the room. "This'll be simple, we'll be outta here in five min…"

"What is it?" asked Steve as he walked in after his Uncle. His eyes widened at the sight before him. "I give up," sighed the boy.

The room, around the size of a large school gym, was filled with piles upon piles of swords of different shapes and sizes.

Eira and the Paper Tiger joined the others inside the aptly named Sword Room.

"Well, at least the sign wasn't lying," said the pelican optimistically as she patted Steve on the shoulder trying to comfort him.

Steve glanced up at the slanted ceiling of the room to a large skylight. He could see that the sun was starting to set. He then looked down at the roomful of swords and shook his head.

"What are we going to do? I don't even know what it looks like!" Steve kicked at a nearby pile of swords, stubbing his toes on the ebony blade of a rune-covered longsword.

"I know someone who might," said Zeroth as he took out Gladius.

"Wings On A Swantan!" exclaimed the swordfish. "The Sword Room!"

"Your observation skills never fail to amaze me," quipped Steve as he rubbed his sore foot.

Zeroth held Gladius up to his eye level, "You have seen the Sword of Zaa before right?"

"Sadly, yes…on the day it was given to Donal."

"Well?" asked Zeroth intently.

"Well *what?*"

"What does it look like?" demanded Zeroth.

"It looks like a sword," answered Gladius cynically.

Steve narrowed his eyes at the irritable silver swordfish, "Could you be a *tad* more specific?" the boy said bitterly.

"Not really, remember after Donal was given that sword I didn't get out much."

"Don't you remember anything at all about it?" pleaded Zeroth.

Gladius was silent for several moments and blinked its large eyes while he thought. "I seem to recall," Gladius coughed and cleared its throat "That its hilt and handle were shaped like...hmm...like a..."

"A dragon?" suggested Zeroth.

"An owl?" tried Eira.

"A tiger?" added the Paper Tiger proudly.

"A badger?" asked Uncle Shameless. Everyone looked at him and shook their heads.

"No, no," said Gladius "Not any of those."

Steve thought of the giant statue at the top of the castle, "An eagle?" he said.

"Yes!" exclaimed Gladius, "That's the one! An' its blade looks like a feather."

"Okay," began Zeroth "Let's split up and everyone look for a sword in the shape of an eagle."

Zeroth took the owl-skull torch from Uncle Shameless and placed it in the center of the room to illuminate as much of it as possible.

Looking through a pile of swords was harder than Steve had thought it would be. At one point, when he pulled a sword free the rest of the pile crashed down to the floor with a ground-shattering racket. A free-falling short sword with a cat eye-like jewel in its hilt nearly cut off his toes.

Steve's fingers were suffering as well; some of the swords were surprisingly sharp even after all the years they had been sitting in the dark room. He would hear random cries from the rest of the group, signally that he was not the only one suffering.

The lone companion who wasn't getting hurt was the Paper Tiger, who refused to touch any of the swords.

After an hour or so, Steve called everyone to the center of the room by the still moving owl skull to share what they had found.

"I couldn't find it, did you?" Steve asked Eira.

The pelican-lady shook her head, as did Zeroth. Uncle Shameless had not joined the group and was passed out next to his pile of unexamined swords. Steve walked over and nudged him with his foot.

"It wasn't me!" yelled his uncle, half asleep.

"Wake up!" yelled Steve.

"Mergh?" mumbled Uncle Shameless as he slowly stood up. "What's goin' on?"

"Did you find the sword?" asked Steve.

"No."

"Did you even look?"

Uncle Shameless scratched his head and thought hard for several moments. A few times he began to answer but then stopped. Finally he answered, "No."

"Well that's just great!" yelled Steve, his loud voice echoing madly around the gym-sized room.

"We're trying to find this stupid sword so we can get outta here!" yelled Steve again "And here you are, passed out on the floor!"

"Uh..." started Uncle Shameless, with a very distant look on his face.

"Look at this!" yelled Steve as he held up his nicked hands, "We're all cut up, and you're over here sleeping!"

"Uh..." said Uncle Shameless, who was not paying any attention to Steve or his loud rant.

Steve was about to ask what Uncle Shameless' problem was, when all of a sudden the room was plunged into darkness. Steve stumbled around in the inky blackness, trying not to fall into a pile of swords.

"What's going on?" asked Eira, a nervous tone in her voice.

"The owl's eyes went out," said Zeroth "That's all."

"Uh-uh..." negated Uncle Shameless, who was pointing but no one could tell because of the darkness.

"What *is* your problem?" Steve asked finally and just as he did, the owl's eyes lit up again.

Only this time, the light was coming from the *other* side of the Sword Room. The light was higher up, about seven feet, and was moving quickly towards the adventurers.

"I was trying to tell you," began Uncle Shameless in a panic, "We ain't alone!"

34

Heavy footsteps thundered around the Sword Room as they headed toward Steve and his friends. The light was moving behind tall piles of swords, and Steve could barely see the top of the flames over the piled up weapons. In-between the heavy footsteps, the boy heard the crackling of fire as well. A long and low eerie moan flooded the room.

"What is that?" asked Steve, before being quickly shushed by everyone else. Steve did not have to wait long to find out. The creature rounded a sword pile and looked right at the group.

It was another owl skeleton, but much larger than the others, and wearing very heavy armor. Fire spilled out of the skull's empty eye sockets and climbed upward towards the ceiling. After seeing the group, it let out a high pitched screech.

"Not another one!" cried Steve as everyone began heading for the large double doors that led back out to the rotunda. As they reached the doors Steve stopped and turned around even though the owl was very close. "Wait, we don't have the sword!" he yelled to the others.

"We don't have a choice," bellowed Zeroth. "That thing is after us!" He grabbed on to the boy and dragged him into the hall. Zeroth and Uncle Shameless pulled the heavy door closed.

Just before it shut, a large skeleton hand slid through the opening and grabbed the edge of the door.

"Get back!" yelled Zeroth.

The hand easily flung the door open and it crashed into the wall, cracking it. The spacious rotunda amplified the loud BOOM, making it sound like a cannon had just been fired.

"Move!" yelled Steve as he helped Uncle Shameless run.

The owl hissed madly, flapped open its skeletal wings and jumped into the center of the rotunda, causing the water-floor to ripple under its weight.

Steve thought of heading back to the Queen's Entrance but the large owl was blocking the way. The creature produced a lethal looking blazing sword, and began moving towards Steve and the others.

"Run!" commanded Zeroth.

"But where?" asked Eira looking down three other possible hallways.

Steve looked at each hallway, and something inside him made him think they should head down the left hallway. "This way!" he yelled as ran, everyone quickly followed.

"Why this way?" asked Zeroth.

"Just a gut feeling!" answered Steve.

The large owl paused for a moment and let loose a loud series of eerie WHOOTs that lasted several seconds.

"What is it doing?" asked Steve, stopping to watch. In the distance behind the colossal owl, they heard a loud sound like wood being split.

"The door!" cried Zeroth.

"You mean..." started Steve.

"Look! It's calling the other owls!" yelled Eira.

In different parts of the hallway and back in the rotunda everyone watched as pair after pair of fire-filled eyes lit up and started moving with the larger owl. A trio of owls jumped out of the mysterious water in the rotunda's floor, and landed near their much larger cohort.

"Zaa's Talons!" cursed Zeroth, "This place is *filled* with skeletons!"

"Let's get outta here!" Uncle Shameless suggested loudly.

They all started running again as the legion of undead owls followed closely behind. Zeroth pulled out his battered shield from his magical pack. He then took out Gladius and squeezed the living weapon hard before it had a chance to make any nasty comments. Steve followed Zeroth's example and readied the Staff of Arcana.

Everyone continued running down the long hallway, not knowing where it would lead. The owls kept up their pursuit, with the large owl from the Sword Room leading the charge and inspiring its counterparts to move faster.

The dark hallway was now lit brightly from the many pairs of fiery eyes, which made running away a little easier for the companions.

"At least we can see where we are," Eira noted optimistically.

"Yeah, *in trouble,*" added Steve.

From a hidden burrow an owl skeleton jumped out at Steve and grabbed him by his arms. The ghastly creature's sharp claws dug into the boy painfully.

"Ahhh!" screamed Steve as the owl-person lifted him up with its strong hands.

Zeroth ran the skeleton through with his sword, forgetting what had happened the last time. After seeing the skeleton was unaffected, he remembered his previous blunder, "Oh yeah…that doesn't work."

"Well *duh!*" yelled Steve as he tried to wiggle himself free from his boney bonds.

"I'm comin' boy!" bellowed Uncle Shameless loudly as he lumbered toward the skeleton. Uncle Shameless failed to see a loose stone sticking up out of the floor and tripped over it. He went flying through the air, and crashed into the owl. The three of them fell to the ground.

The impact knocked the arms holding Steve loose and the boy was able to get away, although one of the hands was stilling hanging onto him.

"Ouch!" yelled Steve as he painfully peeled the dirty-white claw off his arm. Uncle Shameless got up slowly and dusted himself off, "I meant to do that."

A piercing screech from behind reminded everyone that they were still being followed.

"Shameless, you bring up the rear and I'll take the lead!" ordered Zeroth "Steve, you stay in the middle and help Eira."

The boy nodded and assisted Eira in moving faster. The pelican gasped as she noticed the wounds on Steve's arms from where the owl skeleton had grabbed him, "You're hurt!" She stopped and quickly reached into an inside pocket of her poncho, pulling out a few bandages.

"I thought I *couldn't* get hurt," said Steve as Eira dressed his wounds as quickly as possible. He looked down at his blue heron amulet. "This thing is s'pose to protect me, that's what Istrio said."

"Just be careful from now on," suggested Eira as she put her leftover bandages back into her pocket "It's never a good idea to rely on magic to the point where you get careless."

"What shall I do?" asked the Paper Tiger proudly as Eira and Steve started moving again.

"Oh, are you still here?" said Zeroth, having forgotten about the nearly useless creature.

"What do you mean by that?" asked the Paper Tiger, hurt by Zeroth's words.

"I'm sorry, what I meant was 'Oh, you are still here!' I'm glad nothing happened to you," Zeroth lied confidently.

"Oh, how very nice of you!" exclaimed the Paper Tiger with a flat smile, not realizing the bird-man was lying to him.

"Anyway, you can…umm…" Zeroth tried to think of something for the parchment cat to do. "You can…just be *you*."

"Well, I am very excellent at that. After all I am the most courageous of c-"

"*OWLS!*" Steve screamed to get everyone to continue their run down the hall. The heavy footsteps of the colossal owl from the Sword Room echoed off the old stone walls and kept the party moving out of fear of its blazing sword and sharp claws.

As they ran, Steve felt as if they were climbing upward gradually. He wondered how that was possible, but he was beginning to accept the fact that things were not always what they seemed in Eyri.

"Door!" cried Zeroth as he pointed. Several feet ahead was a simple wooden door with a large eagle carved into it.

"Shameless, keep them busy while we open the door!" ordered Zeroth.

"Aw c'mon, not again," whimpered the man, remembering what had happened last time. Reluctantly, Uncle Shameless took a long drink of Eldercherry wine and prepared to hold off the owls, or at least slow them down.

He grabbed a loose stone from the wall and threw it like a fast ball at the incoming horde of undead warriors. The stone smacked an owl right in the skull, causing it to collapse.

"*Batter up!*" bellowed Uncle Shameless as he picked up another stone and struck a sloppy pitcher's pose.

Steve, Eira and the Paper Tiger joined Zeroth at the door, "Where do you think it leads?" asked the boy.

"Dunno, but any place is better than this hallway," answered Zeroth as he slung his shield on to his back and reached for the rusty handle. He gave the handle a hard pull, and there was a loud SNAP! it handle broke off in his clawed hand.

"It *never* ends," griped Steve loudly as he kicked at the now inoperable door.

Uncle Shameless was running out of loose stones to throw at the owls, and he didn't think he would have time to try and pry any more loose. He skillfully threw the last one at the owl from the Sword Room, but the creature dodged the stone with ease, letting the masonry projectile hit a minion behind it.

Uncle Shameless made a quick glance over his shoulder to see if the door was open yet. All he could see was Zeroth and Steve arguing. He suddenly felt very hot and saw a bright flash in the corner of his eye. Uncle Shameless glanced back to the owls and realized the large one was only a few feet away and was swinging its blazing sword at him.

"Gahh!" exclaimed Uncle Shameless as he dodged to one side. The vile sword skimmed the top of his shaggy hair, burning the tips of the wild strands.

"Woo woo woo woo!" yelled Uncle Shameless as he patted the flames on his head out in time to dodge another sword attack from the huge owl warrior. He jumped back in time so that the swipe from the sword just barely scratched his heavy breast plate, leaving a long burn mark across it.

"Hurry, *please!*" Uncle Shameless shouted.

Steve inspected the broken handle on the door. It looked like there was a lock of some sort and that the handle was needed to unlock the door, the handle which had just broken off in Zeroth's hand.

"Now what?" asked Zeroth as he studied the door.

"We're in trouble," answered Steve.

Down the hall, they heard Uncle Shameless bellow "Hurry, *please!*" and Steve saw the owl with the blazing sword attack him.

"Correction – we're in *big* trouble."

Steve gasped as he saw the huge owl swing its deadly sword at Uncle Shameless again and again. The boy could not stand it any longer, he grabbed the Staff of Arcana and thought of the axe he had summoned earlier.

The simple piece of wood flashed and turned into the majestic axe once more. "What are you doing?" asked Eira as the boy held the axe high.

"Nahhaahhaa!" yelped Uncle Shameless as he dodged another sword attack. Behind the large owl, its undead cohorts watched the fight with empty eyes.

Uncle Shameless was waiting for the owl to get tired from swinging the large sword over and over again, but then he had a thought: undead skeletons probably do not get tired.

The man dodged another sword swing; the blade crashed into the stone wall, sending a shower of sparks and rocks everywhere. Sparks got into Uncle Shameless' eyes and he lost his footing and fell to the ground. His undead attacker shrieked, grasped its blazing sword with both hands, and prepared to deliver a fatal blow.

Steve swung his axe. It cut through several of the wooden planks of the door with ease. Bright light poured through the hole and filled the hallway. Steve kept swinging, destroying the rest of the door and allowing more and more light through.

The mysterious light hit the large owl in the face, causing the creature to wince and howl in pain. Uncle Shameless used this distraction to kick the attacking owl's legs out from under it. The tall creature crashed to the ground, giving Uncle Shameless enough time to get up and join the others by the door.

With the door destroyed, everyone ran up the stairs that had previously been hidden behind it. The hallway and stairs were all made of see-through bricks, which had allowed the stairwell to be filled with ghostly moonlight.

The large owl finally righted itself and ran after them, with several of its minions close behind. The stairs began spiraling upward and grew more and more cramped. Steve glanced behind and saw light from his pursuers' eyes growing brighter and brighter as they closed in.

Steve was breathing heavy, and so was everyone else as the steps became steeper and steeper. A loud, piercing shriek from behind kept their legs moving and made them ignore the burning in their lungs.

Uncle Shameless saw several loose bricks and using his super-strength pulled them loose, "Keep going!" he yelled to everyone else.

"But-" started Steve, remembering how his uncle had only just barley escaped harm a few moments ago. "Don't mind me boy, I'll be fine!" Uncle Shameless said with a sloppy smile.

Eira grabbed a hold of Steve, "We must keep going, your uncle will be fine." The boy nodded reluctantly and continued his climb.

Uncle Shameless waited until he saw the fire from the owls' eyes grow the brightest and lobbed brick after brick down the stairs. The spiral of the stair case caused the attack to take the skeletons by surprise. The sound of dry bones falling against the hard stone steps let Uncle Shameless know his plan had worked.

Eventually Steve, Zeroth, Eira and the Paper Tiger reached the top of the spiral staircase.

"Not another door!" yelled Steve as a new door blocked their escape, "This place has doors like they're going outta style!"

Zeroth inspected the door, "There's no handle or knob."

"Well that's just *great!*" yelled Steve.

Uncle Shameless joined his nephew a few moments later, out of breath "Whew!" he panted, "How's...that...open?" he said in-between heavy breaths.

"No idea!" Steve yelled again as he threw up his hands in frustration.

Uncle Shameless nodded back to the staircase, "Well...you...better...get...one...fast," he said as he tried to catch his breath. A faint shriek told everyone he was not kidding.

Steve walked over to the door and inspected it in the eerie moonlight. It was not made of wood, he was certain of that. He knocked on the door, and it sounded like metal. He used a hand to brush away several centuries worth of the dust and grime, the surface underneath shined brightly. It was made of silver.

"A silver door?" he mumbled to himself. He looked over the rest of the door. There was no knob or handle just like Zeroth had said.

However, he noticed something just off center of the middle of the door. It was covered with dirt and cobwebs. He brushed it all away to reveal a small, circular hole.

"What the...?" the boy thought aloud.

"Did you find something?" asked Zeroth as a louder shriek echoed from the spiral staircase.

"I hope so," said Steve as he pointed to the hole.

"Looks like a keyhole," said Zeroth as he kneeled down to get a closer look at Steve's discovery.

"That'd have to be a pretty big key," replied Steve, "Heck, it's almost the size of the Staff of..."

"*Arcana,*" Zeroth and Steve said in unison. "Try it!" suggested the Hunter, standing up to get out of Steve's way.

Steve reverted the Staff back to its original shape with a quick thought. Without hesitation, he carefully placed it in the key hole as far as he could.

Please open, Steve thought to himself as he turned the Staff clockwise slowly.

Suddenly, the keyhole began glowing. There was a dazzling flash as the glowing light spread its way through the rest of the door. Everyone shielded their eyes from the brightness and tried to ignore the tell-tale moans of the owls in the stair case.

When everyone's sight returned, the door was open.

35

Steve ran first into the room beyond the silver door. It was circular in shape and had a large hole in the ceiling, through which the night sky was visible. This new room was built with regular bricks instead of the bizarre see-through bricks that the spiral staircase had been made of.

Descending from the hole in the ceiling was a simple ladder; it glittered like a diamond in the moonlight pouring through the open ceiling.

"Where does that thing go?" asked Steve, pointing to the ladder.

"Who cares?" said Uncle Shameless. "*Climb!*"

Steve shrugged and began climbing the ladder as fast as he could. He soon found himself outside, on a flat platform at the top of the pyramid right under the giant eagle statue.

The chilly night air made Steve shiver, but the idea of being so far up made him shake even more. He tried not to look down and kept his gaze locked on the twin moons that hung in the sky above.

Steve wondered what time it was and long he had until dawn.

"What's up there?" called Zeroth who was halfway up the ladder.

"Nothing, just the eagle statue!"

"Are you sure that's all?" yelled Zeroth.

"What else could...*wait*," said Steve. He *did* see something. "...It looks like we can go *inside* the statue!" he yelled back down.

"Do it!" commanded Zeroth as he began climbing. "Shameless, help Eira!"

"Will do!" hollered Uncle Shameless with a quick salute. He helped Eira onto the ladder and started climbing behind her. Uncle Shameless glanced behind him and saw the Paper Tiger just standing below the ladder.

"C'mon! Let's get goin' there, Stripes!" Uncle Shameless bellowed to the Paper Tiger.

"No-no, I can't," whimpered the flat paper feline.

"What's going on down there?" called Zeroth, keeping an eye on Eira's slow ascent.

"Stripes won't climb!" Uncle Shameless shouted up.

"I can't!" whined the Paper Tiger, "The wind! I'll be blown away!"

"You'll be okay!" Uncle Shameless coached. "I'll hang onto ya! But hurry!"

The Paper Tiger hesitated for a moment and then stood on his hind legs and wrapped his flimsy limbs around the bottom rung.

Steve kept climbing up towards the blue-silver eagle statue, resting briefly when he reached the talons that rested on top of Arx A'Quila's main pyramid. Again the boy noticed that unlike the eagle that had been on top of Fiach-Ra's castle, which was standing upright, this eagle rested horizontally on its perch.

As Steve started climbing again, he wondered why that was, but he quickly found out. The boy glanced down at Zeroth and yelled over the wind, "There's a door on the back of this thing!"

"Go inside then!" yelled Zeroth from further down the ladder.

Steve kept climbing the ladder and eventually reached a flat area of the eagle's back just past where its expansive wings met the body. While the rest of the eagle statue was round and smooth, this section of the colossal bird was flat with a guard rail surrounding its edge. The sight reminded Steve of the main deck onboard *The Griffin*.

After pulling himself onto the blue-silver deck, Steve ran to the door that was led to the inside of the eagle. The heavy looking door had a circular keyhole just like the last door, so Steve used the Staff of Arcana once more. The door effortlessly slid into the body of the eagle, granting the boy entrance.

Steve gasped loudly as the interior of the eagle was revealed.

"You're doin' fine!" called Uncle Shameless as the Paper Tiger slowly pulled itself up the first rung of the ladder.

"Just take your time, you got nothi-" Uncle Shameless was interrupted by a wicked sounding, piercing shriek. The Paper Tiger's eyes widened.

"Forget what I said, move it!" yelled Uncle Shameless, waving the Paper Tiger towards him.

Steve entered the back of the eagle and was astounded. The interior was enormous, elaborately decorated and nicely furnished. He passed various storage compartments filled with weapons, armor and other supplies. Another area was covered with maps and there was even a small library.

On a wall he saw what looked like a blueprint of the entire statue. It included a cross section, which showed additional areas underneath where Steve was standing and what was in the head of the eagle.

Steve gasped again, even louder.

"What is it?" asked Zeroth as he ran into the eagle after finishing his climb up the ladder. The boy turned toward the bird-man slowly and swallowed hard before answering, "It can *fly*."

"C'mon you can do it!" Uncle Shameless yelled down at the Paper Tiger.

"How's he doing?" Eira asked.

"Not too good and he has to hurry, those things will be here any second!" A chill went down Uncle Shameless' spine as he saw fiery light growing near the doorway.

"What do you mean it can fly?" asked Zeroth. Cam had told the bird-man many legends and myths about the old kingdoms, but his mentor had never mentioned an eagle airship.

"Look!" Steve pointed to the blueprint of the eagle, "These things here are gears and such, and this," he pointed to a series of drawings near the wings, "Shows how the wings move!" Steve pointed to an engraved silver plate under the blueprints and drawings "This thing even has a name, *The Defender!*"

"But..." started Zeroth.

"Follow me!" yelled Steve as he ran towards the head of the eagle. Zeroth followed close behind. As they neared the head, a series of seats were lined up on either side, much like on an airplane.

They reached what looked like the section just before the head, but another door greeted them. This door slid open automatically, much to their surprise. Both Steve and Zeroth gasped as they walked into the eagle's head.

A single seat rested in the middle of the spacious head. In front of it was a panoramic view of the world outside through a long and tall window that followed the shape of the eagle's face. A metal and wood control panel filled with knobs, levers and other devices sat in front of the seat.

"I think," gasped Zeroth, "I believe you."

"But how does it work?" Steve wondered aloud as he walked towards the pilot's seat. The control panel was filled with plenty of knobs and buttons but he did not see anything that looked like it would be used to steer.

Steve studied the control panel again. He noticed a circular groove towards the center of the panel. He sat down in the pilot's seat and looked at it again. It was a jagged shape that looked like a broken clockwork gear with three protruding triangles in the center.

Inspiration struck Steve and he took off his blue heron amulet.

"What are you doing?" asked Zeroth.

"Testing a hunch."

"Are you sure that's a good idea?" Zeroth asked cautiously.

Steve ignored the bird-man and gently placed the blue heron amulet in the strange looking groove, lining up the three protruding triangles with the three triangular holes in the blue heron amulet.

It fit perfectly.

36

Streams of light, like tiny rivers, poured from the blue heron amulet after Steve placed it into the control panel. As the light flowed over the control panel, the panel began to make noises and loud clicking sounds. The circular groove began turning underneath the amulet, sounding like someone spinning a very old combination lock.

Steve watched in amazement as a series of tiny silver pins began to rise out the spinning groove. Two separate rings of the silver pins, one on the inside of the amulet and the other on the outside, began moving in opposite directions. The inner ring came to a stop with a loud SNAP! and Steve noticed that the tiny pins from the groove filled in all of the gaps of the amulet's inner ring.

Shortly after that there was another loud SNAP! as the pins moving around the amulet's outer ring found their desired position. Suddenly *The Defender* lurched, causing Steve and Zeroth to lose their footing. The pair slowly looked at each other.

"What was that?" asked Zeroth.

"I think I just turned it on," Steve replied excitedly.

Loud clicks and whirls began going off everywhere inside the airship, and not just by the pilot's seat in the head. It sounded like a train trying to start up after not being used for many years.

There was a loud CLUNK, followed by a series of ratcheting sounds.

"What is it doing?" wondered Steve.

"I'll check it out," offered Zeroth as he headed towards the entrance at the back of the eagle. Steve let out an exhausted sigh and sat in the pilot's seat. He stared out at the night sky.

The view was breathtaking; he had never seen so many stars. As he looked at the stars, he wondered why they were moving. They were not moving fast, just creeping upward very slowly.

An unpleasant thought struck Steve and he jumped up from the pilot's seat and pressed his face against the large continuous window that made up the eagle's eyes. He yelped loudly after he realized his fear was correct; the stars had not been moving, the eagle was.

The Defender was slowly tipping downward and in a few moments, it would fall headfirst off its perch atop Arx A'Quila into the jagged mountain canyons below.

Zeroth reached the entrance at the back of the eagle and saw to his amazement that the ladder they had climbed was pulling itself up. He exited the eagle and stood in the indented entry way and saw that the ladder was in fact *part* of the airship, and that it was being drawn up into a hidden compartment much like an anchor on a ship.

"Whoa!" said Uncle Shameless as the ladder lurched to life and began lifting him upward. He glanced up at Eira, "Any idea what's happenin'?"

The Pelican lady shouted the same question up to Zeroth, who was keeping an eye on them from the deck. She relayed the information to Uncle Shameless after Zeroth explained the situation.

"Well that makes things a little easier," said Uncle Shameless as he stopped climbing and decided to enjoy the free ride. Eira asked him how the Paper Tiger was doing and Uncle Shameless glanced down to share the information with his flat feline friend.

"Just hang on there, this ladder will take us all the way up!" explained Uncle Shameless with a smile. The Paper Tiger did his best to wrap his parchment paws tightly around the rungs of the moving ladder.

Uncle Shameless looked down at the tiger, "I told you it'd be okay!"

But the man's smile quickly turned to a face of alarm as he watched a clawed skeleton hand grab the Paper Tiger by the neck. The large owl from the Sword Room tore the Paper Tiger from the ladder with ease.

The owl shrieked loudly as it crumpled up the Paper Tiger and tossed it heartlessly to the cold, stone floor.

"Stripes, *no-oooo!*" yelled Uncle Shameless, fighting back tears. The beastly owl began climbing with one hand, the other still wielded its lethal blazing sword.

"What happened?" asked Eira as she glanced down.

"*Climb!*" bellowed Uncle Shameless, trying to increase the distance between him and the relentless owl warrior.

Eira gasped as she saw the colossal skeleton scaling the ladder and swinging its sword upward at Uncle Shameless. She had not seen what the owl had done to the Paper Tiger, but she feared the worst.

The courageous pelican pushed aside her feelings and focused on climbing.

Zeroth had seen the whole scene with the owl and the Paper Tiger, thanks to his powerful hawk-sight. He ran into the cockpit, only now noticing that the airship was angled downward more than he remembered.

"We have a problem!" Zeroth yelled to Steve.

"What kind of problem?" asked the boy.

"An *owl* kind of problem!"

Steve whirled to face Zeroth, "Not the big one from the Sword Room-"

"The same," confirmed Zeroth.

"Crumbs!" cursed Steve, banging a fist on the control panel.

"But tell me," Zeroth tried to ask coolly, "Why are we tipping over?"

Uncle Shameless felt the heat from the owl's blazing sword as it swung near him, nearly hitting his ankles.

"Enough of this," Uncle Shameless said aloud as he wasted precious seconds to take a drink of Eldercherry wine. He stopped climbing and waited for the owl to move in closer, but still kept his eyes on the sword (which had already done permanent damage to his hairdo).

Uncle Shameless shot a quick glance up to Eira, "Start moving fast – now!"

Eira heard the man and did the best she could to ascend even faster. Uncle Shameless turned around so his back was against the rungs of the ladder and waited. The owl hissed and shrieked, fire bursting from its empty eyes, showcasing its fury.

Uncle Shameless swung back his leg and with expert timing and super-human strength, landed a powerful kick right into the owl's skull. He felt the fire from the owl's eyes burn his shoe and tried to ignore the pain as the kick sent the owl falling down towards the floor.

Not waiting to see the outcome of his attack, Uncle Shameless quickly scaled the ladder and caught up with Eira before she reached the airship's deck. With the power still granted by the wine, Uncle Shameless picked up Eira with one hand and continued climbing with the other. He gently placed Eira onto the flat deck and then lifted himself up.

Zeroth and Steve joined the others near the entrance of *The Defender*. Steve noticed the absence of the Paper Tiger and began to ask where he was. Zeroth stopped him and explained what had happened. Steve stared off into the night sky, sad for the first time in a long while. Losing a friend was a new experience for him, since back home he did not have any friends *to* lose.

"What in the name of…what *is* this thing?" bellowed Uncle Shameless as he peered past Steve to see the inside of *The Defender*.

"It's some kind of airship," explained Steve.

"Bully!" beamed Uncle Shameless, ready to go on yet another adventure. "How does it work?"

"No idea. It has started to work itself free from whatever was holding it in place all these years," added Steve.

"Uh…" slurred Uncle Shameless.

"That's *bad*," said Steve. He demonstrated what was going to happen by having one hand crash into the other.

"Oh, that is definitely *un*-bully," whimpered Uncle Shameless.

The airship suddenly tilted sharply downward, causing Uncle Shameless to fall down. "Whoa Nelly!" he bellowed.

The ratcheting sound of the retracting ladder began to slow down.

"I think once that thing is completely up, we might be in trouble," suggested Steve, referring to the impending tipping over of the eagle.

Everyone stared at the ladder as it clicked-clicked upward and into a hidden compartment inside the airship. Steve watched the silver ladder slowly creep upward, and as it did he could swear he saw a light growing brighter and brighter just beyond the edge of the eagle's rear deck.

To everyone's horror, a large skeletal hand swung up onto *The Defender*'s deck. It dug its cruel claws into the metal body of the eagle.

"*No!*" screamed Steve as he watched the hulking owl from the Sword Room pull itself up onto the back of *The Defender*. It had lost its blazing sword, but was not any less vicious. It jumped into a menacing stance and shrieked loudly, hurting everyone's ears.

Eira moved to run away, but the airship shook again, causing her to lose her footing. The owl lashed out with a wicked, boney hand and tore open her pack at the bottom. Many things fell from her pack and littered the rear deck of the airship.

The undead owl then picked up Eira and prepared to toss her over the side. Uncle Shameless got up to help, but due to his intoxicated state, he tripped on some of the spilled items from Eira's pack and painfully landed flat on his face.

Zeroth readied Gladius and charged the owl. Even while holding Eira and without a weapon, the skeletal behemoth was able to dodge Zeroth's blows and to land several punches onto the bird-man.

Steve did not know what to do. His friends were in trouble, and this creature would surely come after him next. Then there was the problem of the airship, which was rocking more and more.

Before he had time to make up his mind, the airship dropped several feet abruptly. A large bottle from Eira's pack rolled down the deck right to Steve, he picked it up and quickly formed an idea. He called to Zeroth to get his attention and signaled what he wanted to do.

With a nod, Zeroth dodged a blow from the owl and sliced off the hand the held Eira captive. The airship rocked again as the owl howled and wailed. Steve thought of all the summer afternoons his dad had spent trying to teach him the proper way to throw a fastball – or as his dad liked to call it, a Harrier Heater.

Steve closed his eyes and thought of what to do and hurled the bottle at the owl's face.

The glass bottle crashed into the creature's skull, covering it with the silver liquid that had been stored inside. The force of the hit caused the owl to stumble backwards and as the airship lurched once more, the owl fell over the deck's guard rail and down to its doom.

But now the ship was free from its holdings and was free falling.

"Get inside!" Steve yelled.

The boy helped his uncle up and pushed the him into the cabin of the airship. Zeroth helped Eira gather most of her possessions while she took a few seconds to peel the lifeless owl hand off of her and toss it overboard.

The airship picked up more speed as it fell from the top of Arx A'Quila, making it difficult for everyone to get safely inside. Steve, aided by gravity, made it to the pilot's seat quickly. The boy looked over the controls frantically, Zeroth quickly joined him.

A loud CA-CHUNK filled the airship as the eagle's legs tucked themselves under its body, adding to its airplane-like appearance.

"I don't know what to do!" screamed Steve as he randomly pushed buttons and pulled levers. He tried not to look at the rapidly approaching mountain side through the main window of the cockpit.

The teenage pilot was not having any luck; the buttons he was pushing and the levers he was pulling all seemed to do random things. A green switch caused a few extra seats to raise out of the floor behind the pilot's chair. A tan colored lever activated a sort of large, ancient windshield wiper system and a red, shiny button started up a hot drink machine near the entrance to the cockpit. Steve was certain he smelled coffee brewing.

"Try that one!" suggested Zeroth, pointing to the lever that had activated the windshield wiper-like device.

"I already did!" yelled Steve.

"What about that-"

"That one too!" Steve screamed, pointing to the tray of mints that had slid out of the control panel after pushing the button. "I've tried everything except-" the boy's jaw dropped as he finally noticed a familiar looking hole just below where he had placed the blue heron amulet.

Without hesitating, Steve slammed the Staff of Arcana into the hole. Nothing happened.

"Crumbs!" yelled Steve.

"Try it again!" bellowed Zeroth.

Steve took the Staff of Arcana out and tried again. Once more, nothing happened.

"Argh!" yelled Steve as he prepared to try the Staff for what would most likely be the last time before smashing into the side of the mountain.

"C'mon! All I need is something to steer with!" Steve yelled, thinking of a control stick that could be used for flying as he tried a third time.

The Staff of Arcana flashed and turned into what looked like a metal joystick adorned with an eagle's head. There was a loud CLICK followed by an even louder whirling sound. Part of the control panel that the joystick was attached to slid out from the rest of the panel so that it rested just above Steve's lap.

It reminded Steve of a fighter jet he had seen at an air show once. Other components rose from the floor around him and surrounded him on almost all sides.

Zeroth stared in amazement. A huge smile crept across Steve's face as he pulled back on the stick, causing the airship to pull up from its deadly free-fall.

"*Woooooo!*" yelled Steve as he skimmed the top of a mountain by only a few yards.

Steve couldn't believe it; he was flying. More than that, he was flying a giant airship that was *his* to control and command. He tested the controls, attempting several types of loops and rolls.

A very befuddled Uncle Shameless stumbled into the cockpit, "What in Sam Hill are you – holy cats! *We're flyin'!*"

Uncle Shameless glanced at the hot drink machine Steve had accidentally turned on and sniffed the air, "…Is that coffee?"

Steve took the airship above the clouds and gasped at the lovely view of the night sky. He wondered how much time was left until dawn. "Hey look!" bellowed Uncle Shameless as he pointed out the main window of the cockpit, "Rosco!"

Everyone glanced over to see the Roc Lobster joining them in the sky. Rosco roared and playfully flew around the airship, which was even bigger than he was.

Uncle Shameless looked over at Steve and watched him effortlessly work the controls.

"How do ya know how to fly this thing anyway?" he asked his nephew.

Steve merely shrugged, "It just came naturally to me I guess. I can't explain it. Heck, I don't even know what makes this thing fly, let alone why I can fly it."

"I know the answer to that question, but I'm sure you won't like it," said a familiar ominous voice.

Steve's face scrunched up in annoyance and he sighed, "Not *you* again."

"Oh hush," snapped Istrio as he appeared as a ghostly visage in front of the main window.

"Let me guess," said Steve with a sigh, "Magic makes it fly?"

"Among other things, but yes that's the long and short of it," explained the floating see-through visage of the blue heron Mystic "You are flying *The Defender* –"

"I know, I read the nameplate," interrupted Steve.

"-The airship used by Donal and Fel-Ra during the War of Fire," continued Istrio as he ignored Steve's rudeness "After that, it was used by the owls to help keep peace throughout the kingdoms and...*say*, is that a fresh pot?" asked Istrio as he spied the hot drink machine percolating in the corner.

Before Steve or anyone else could answer, the ghost-like image of Istrio floated over to the machine. He reached for a tall, blue-silver mug in a latched cabinet and filled it with coffee from the eagle head shaped pot.

Everyone gasped as Istrio took a sip, expecting the hot liquid to pass through his ghostly body and spill on the floor. To their collective amazement, it did not.

"Mmm-*mmm*, now *that's* a cup of coffee," praised the Elder Mystic of Zaa. Steve cleared his throat to get the blue heron's attention once more.

"Yes?" asked Istrio between sips.

"You were talking about the airship?"

"Ah yes," continued Istrio as he leaned on the top of the hot drink machine, looking like an office employee who was about to ask a co-worker if they had watched the big game last night. "*The Defender* can only be flown by those who are pure of mind...*and* so on and so forth."

"What does that mean?" asked Steve.

"It flies because you believe it can," answered Istrio with a wink "How 'bout that?"

"So you showed up just to tell me to make sure that I believe this thing will fly?"

"And to check up on you...wait a moment...aren't we missing someone?" asked the blue heron. Almost on cue, Eira joined the others in the cockpit.

"Ah good, that's everyone," said Istrio with a vacant smile as he refilled his tall mug.

"We're still missing someone," explained Eira.

"No, it's quite alright. I talked with Rosco outside," started Istrio as he took a long drink of coffee.

"Someone else," said Zeroth as he shook his head.

"Not that little duck fellow? I thought he left you all a long time ago."

"No, not him," said Steve.

"Well, who then?" asked the blue heron, giving up.

"The Paper Tiger," answered Eira.

"Excuse me, the Paper what?"

"Tiger."

"Huh," Istrio thought for several moments as he refilled his mug a third time. "Was he the one that lived in the well?"

"That was Five-Toes the Dragon!" yelled Steve.

"Well *excuse* me. I can't help it I can't keep track off all of your traveling companions, it seems like you get a new one or two every time I see you," retorted the blue heron. "So, where is he?"

A blubbering Uncle Shameless retold the story of the Sword Room, the large owl with the blazing sword, how the Paper Tiger had been left behind and the demise of the large owl.

"Dear me, that is unfortunate," replied the Mystic in a somewhat lackluster tone. "Well," he produced a see-through hour-glass, "I s'pose I should get moving along then."

Istrio put away his tall mug and started to fade away. "Keep up the good work kids! I'll see you soon!" And with that, the blue heron blinked into nothingness.

A thought instantly struck Steve after Istrio had vanished, "Crumbs!" he yelled, "I forgot to say we weren't able to find the Sword of Zaa!"

"So?" asked Uncle Shameless as he wiped his eyes dry on a sleeve of his flannel shirt.

"…That was the reason we went to Arx A'Quila in the first place," explained Steve as he shook his head at his forgetful uncle. "I was s'pose to get that sword and then go fight the Hawk-King." Steve shuddered at the idea of facing Fiach-Ra again. "I guess I should just fly somewhere else-"

"No!" Zeroth interrupted loudly.

Steve turned his head slowly to face the Hunter. "Huh?" asked Steve "Are you okay?"

Zeroth kneeled down next to the boy, "I'm fine. But I think we should go straight to Da'Rahga, we'll think of something once we get there."

"But I don't have the Sword of Zaa and Istrio said it was the only-"

"Don't worry about it," replied Zeroth coldly as he stood up.

"But-" started Steve again.

"Don't you remember what happened to every other place you've visited?" explained Zeroth, "Uth? Tal? The Hawk-King has already destroyed two cities in his search for you-"

"Well, I think Uth was technically only a village," interrupted Uncle Shameless "So I don't think-"

"*Regardless*," hissed Zeroth through a tightly clenched beak, "You don't want another place to feel the Hawk-King's wrath because you didn't do what Istrio said again, do you?"

A feeling of extreme guilt crept over Steve and his head dropped, heavy with grief "No," he answered weakly.

"It's settled then," replied Zeroth as he placed a reassuring hand on Steve's shoulder. "We'll head to Da'Rahga."

Steve agreed reluctantly and turned his head back around to face the main window of the cockpit. It was at this time at the he realized that he had not kept *The Defender* level and that the airship was heading straight for the ground.

"This is demeaning," bellowed U'nala as he marched down an endless dirt road with Remmit and Kaz.

"Y'know sir, I could just fly to the castle and get us-" started Remmit. "No!" yelled the Wing-Master "U'nala asks for help from no one!"

"But you'll hitchhike down the road asking for rides from total strangers?"

"That's different!" bellowed U'nala.

"Yeah, that's different," added Kaz.

"Do either of you even know where we are?" said Remmit with a sneer.

Kaz stopped and looked around for several moments, as if searching for a familiar landmark. He was fairly certain the tree they had just passed looked familiar, but then all trees looked familiar to the muscle-headed swan-man.

"Uh…" he stuttered since Swantans were not exactly known for their sharp memories.

"We are in Fiach-Ra's Kingdom, that is all we ever need to know," answered U'nala proudly.

"Oh, *nice* answer," said Remmit sarcastically. The Hawken warrior kicked at some rocks along the road, lost in thought. "Well at least this has given me a new business idea."

"Giving up on the blindfold project?" asked Kaz.

"No no, but I have another idea that might work just as well."

Kaz sighed, "What is it this time?"

"Some sort of public transportation system," explained Remmit.

"A what?"

"Public transportation," Remmit said again. "Y'see, all I would have to do is set up these carts that would pick customers up at specified locations on a continuous loop, a route of sorts."

"How would that make any money?"

"Someone would go to the location and pay to get on, easy."

Kaz laughed a deep laugh, "Why would anyone pay to sit on a cramped cart with strangers when they could just buy their own cart and travel alone?"

"But it'd be cheaper than owning your own cart and creatures to pull it, plus it would cut down on congestion on the roads," explained Remmit.

"It sounds silly," answered Kaz in a critical tone.

"*No* it doesn't!" countered Remmit.

"*Yes* it does!"

"You take that back!"

"Silly! Silly! Silly! IT SOUNDS SILLY!" Kaz screamed loudly.

"*That's it!*" yelled Remmit as he jumped to tackle the larger Swantan warrior. At the last second before contact, Remmit was pulled backwards by the strong hands of U'nala.

"U'nala has had enough of this ridiculous fighting!"

Remmit fought uselessly against the iron grip of U'nala, even swinging his fists around. "Lemme at him! C'mon!" Remmit yelled as he flapped his wings robustly.

"C'mon little Hawken!" taunted Kaz with his fists raised, "Let's go!"

U'nala roared in frustration and once again slammed both of his subordinates' heads against each other. The arguing warriors yelped in pain and became silent as they fell to the ground.

U'nala bent down and stared at both of the warriors, "There will be no more of this useless fighting among yourselves!" U'nala paced back and forth, giving the pair a mean stare down.

"You are comrades in arms, you should save your anger for the enemy!"

Both Remmit and Kaz's eyes widened. U'nala took this as his speech having a big impact on them.

"That's right, the *enemy!*" articulated U'nala as he placed his hands behind his back and struck an authoritative, iconic pose. "The Boy is the enemy! Not each other!"

Kaz opened his beak to say something. The Wing-Master held up his hand to silence the swan-man, "No, no. Don't say anything, U'nala knows what you are thinking."

"Sir-" started Remmit until U'nala reached over and clamped his beak shut tightly with a clawed hand.

"Years from now, when all of this Prophecy nonsense is over with," U'nala continued over the thunder in the sky, "You'll be sitting at home with a little grand-hatchling on your knee, and he's going to ask 'What did you do-"

"But sir!" interrupted Kaz, looking up at the sky above them.

"Silence!" bellowed U'nala as he lashed out with his other hand and clamped Kaz's beak shut as well.

"As U'nala was saying, he's going to ask 'What did you do in the War Against The Boy'..." U'nala trailed off and looked around, confusion creeping over his aged and graying face.

"What is that sound?" he said, practically yelling over the ever growing roaring sound coming from above. Remmit and Kaz pointed in unison to the sky.

"Hurm?" uttered U'nala, wondering what they were pointing at. He slowly turned his head in the direction of their pointing in time to see a large metal eagle about to crash into them.

"Pull up! Pull up!" yelled Uncle Shameless as Steve grabbed the controls of *The Defender*.

The boy pulled back hard on the control stick and held his breath as he watched the tip of the eagle's beak start rising. However, it was not rising fast enough to avoid a total disaster.

Steve looked over the knobs and levers and pulled back on a heavy lever, he then banked the airship hard to one side, slicing the tops off several trees with the wings.

U'nala slowly rolled over. He had been blown several yards away from where he had been standing due to the force of the airship buzzing over him. Kaz had been knocked back several yards as well, and Remmit was hanging in a nearby tree.

U'nala rolled over again so that he could see the Hawken warrior in the tree, "Mr. Crammit-"

"Remmit, sir."

"Mr. *Remmit*, would you please fly to the castle and get some help. U'nala has had enough."

The Hawken groaned loudly and dropped from the tree. He prepared to fly off, but U'nala asked him to wait a moment.

"When they ask what happened, say we were ambushed by this The Boy person...but make it sound heroic," ordered the Wing-Master. Remmit gave a less than perfect salute and took flight.

U'nala painfully dropped his head back down onto the dirt of the road, "U'nala is getting too old for this," he lamented, thinking that being stuck behind a desk filling out forms was not as bad as he had originally thought it was.

37

"An' so then he stops in the middle of his speech, walks over to me, smacks the flask outta my hand and yells, 'There will be no more of that!'" Uncle Shameless shared as he sipped from his wineskin.

"Then what happened?" asked Eira as she listened intently.

"You *don't* want to know, trust me," suggested Steve as he focused on flying the airship. After their near disaster, Steve had become lost and it had taken him some time to figure out how to fly to Fiach-Ra's castle in the city of Da'Rahga.

"Oh hush," scolded Eira, "I do want to know."

"Well," started Uncle Shameless as he stumbled around the cockpit, "Y'see, the problem was I didn't know he was a priest. So I-"

"What's that?" interrupted Steve, staring out into the distance through the main window of *The Defender*. On the horizon he saw an orange glow.

"Oh no!" yelled Steve, "The sun is rising!" A deep feeling of guilt filled Steve as he realized he had missed his chance to defeat Fiach-Ra. Furthermore he was worried that now he would not be able to return to Michigan.

Zeroth entered the cabin from the airship's kitchen, wearing a food-splattered chef's apron and holding an impressive looking ladle. He saw Steve was upset. "What's wrong?"

"The sun is rising!" Steve pointed to the orange glow on the horizon.

Zeroth blinked and looked out to the horizon, "That isn't the sun."

"What?" asked Steve in disbelief.

"That's no sun, just wait."

Steve frowned but kept flying toward the orange glow. A few minutes later he realized that Zeroth was right, it was not the sun at all.

"Crackers!" yelled Uncle Shameless "It's-"

"Da'Rahga!" finished Steve.

"It is called the City of Flame for a reason y'know," explained Zeroth. "That was the Wall of Fire you were seeing."

Steve wished he could get a closer look at the City of Flame as he squinted at the blazing Wall of Fire. He then noticed a lever he had not seen before on the armrest of his pilot's chair. It had a picture of an open eye next to it and without thinking he pulled the lever.

Gears above the boy started coming to life and before he had time to ask what the sound was, an odd object had lowered itself down in front of his face.

The object looked like the device his eye doctor used to check his eyes; it was squatty and diamond shaped. It had two large holes for eyes to look through and two handles on the side to move it around. Above one of the handles was a dial.

"What is that?" asked Zeroth, lightly poking the object with his ladle.

"One way to find out," said Steve as he moved his face closer and looked through the lenses.

He was instantly treated to a much closer view of Da'Rahga; he could see the top of the Wall of Fire and watch the flames jump around. He felt for the dial on the side and turned it.

With each click forward, the image zoomed in, and every click backward zoomed the image out. "It's some kind of telescope!" exclaimed Steve as he moved the viewer around to inspect other parts of the city.

"Good," said Zeroth slyly, "We can use it to plan our attack on the city. Do you see a way in?"

"Not really," answered Steve, "And I don't know how fireproof this airship is."

While Zeroth and Steve discussed strategy, Uncle Shameless heard Rosco roaring from the outside. He walked over to the main window in the cockpit and pressed his face against the glass to look at the giant bird-lobster.

"I think Rosco is trying to tell us somethin'," said Uncle Shameless.

"That's nice," replied Steve as he ignored his uncle and kept looking at the castle through the telescopic viewer.

"Uh, I think-" Uncle Shameless started again.

"Not now," pleaded Steve as Zeroth reassured the boy that he did not have to worry about not having the Sword of Zaa.

"But-"

Steve shushed his Uncle as Zeroth started talking about a possible attack plan from the rear of the city. Uncle Shameless watched as

Rosco began flying erratically and making obvious attempts to get their attention.

After a few moments, Rosco decided to get a little more drastic. He flew under one *The Defender*'s wings and gently bumped it with his head.

Everyone in the cockpit, except Steve who was strapped into his pilot's seat, was knocked around.

"What's the big idea?!" yelled Steve.

"I think he wants you to see something," advised Uncle Shameless.

"Fine!" snapped Steve as he rapidly clicked backwards on the viewer's dial, getting a wider and wider view of what was up ahead, "I don't see what there could possibly be that would..." Steve's words trailed off as he stared out through the viewer, seeing a flight of Pyrix heading right for *The Defender*.

"We're in trouble," said Steve coldly as he pushed the button to raise the viewer. The device climbed back up into the roof the cockpit and hid itself in its compartment.

"What is it?" asked Zeroth.

"Pyrix. Heading right for us," Steve answered painfully.

Even from within the confines of the airship's cockpit, everyone could hear the unmistakable piercing shrieks of the flaming Pyrix.

"We can't let them stop us," Zeroth stated authoritatively. "We *must* get to Da'Rahga."

Steve sighed and a feeling of dread washed over him. He wanted to go home, even if deep down this place was growing on him. He considered just turning the airship around and heading somewhere far away with it, regardless of Zeroth's determination to fight their way into the city.

The boy then thought of all the tasks he'd done since arriving and all the friends he had made. He thought of the amazing statues he had seen at the temple of Arcana of what the owls had looked like before they had been cursed.

Lastly, he thought of all the destruction that he had been blamed for. His eyes narrowed in determination. *Enough was enough*, Steve thought to himself.

"Get back in the cabin and strap yourselves in," he said to Zeroth and Eira. He turned to Uncle Shameless "Figure out a way to signal to Rosco to help us fight those things," he pushed up his glasses with steady finger as a very serious look crossed his face.

As Steve reached for the throttle and shifted to full speed, he tried to think of a heroic metaphorical, inspirational cliché to use at that moment but unfortunately all he could come up with was:

"*Time to mow the lawn.*"

"What was that?" asked Zeroth as he was leaving the cockpit.

"…Nothing," Steve replied sheepishly.

"Its looking like this is the final show down, the big dance, the uh…last…*thing*," Uncle Shameless exclaimed heroically.

Steve rolled his eyes, "So?"

"*So*, I have to change."

Steve turned his head slowly towards Uncle Shameless, "No."

"Yes, I hafta."

"Please, no," Steve begged, knowing what his uncle had in mind.

"I'll be right back," Uncle Shameless said proudly. He exited the cockpit like a knight preparing for battle. Steve banged his head against the control panel in frustration.

Uncle Shameless found a private room and emerged moments later. He gallantly strutted down the aisle of the airship past Zeroth and Eira. He looked the same as far as they could tell. Until they glanced down.

"Why is he wearing fur leggings…*Oh my*," Eira exclaimed in a shocked tone.

Instead of the pants he had been wearing for the entire adventure, Uncle Shameless was now wearing a ratty pair of beat up, khaki short-shorts. Even though he had done away with his tattered jeans, he still wore his leg armor over his now bare and very hairy legs.

Zeroth gave Uncle Shameless a confused look, "Where did you get those?"

"I had 'em with me the whole time," explained Uncle Shameless "Y'see, these are my lucky shorts."

Steve groaned loudly from the cockpit, showing his contempt for yet another of his uncle's odd quirks. Uncle Shameless shrugged and marched proudly towards the entrance to the rear deck of *The Defender*. Eira leaned over to whisper to Zeroth, "Humans are so…*odd*."

Uncle Shameless worked his way to the back of the airship. The door leading the back deck of *The Defender*, which was just past its wings, had a large circular lock. He grabbed the lock with both hands and turned it like a steering wheel until there were several loud clicks. The door became unlocked and was ready to be opened.

Not wanting to be blown away by the strong air currents, Uncle Shameless searched for a rope to tie himself to the airship. He found a smelly old rope in a storage locker and proceeded to tie one end around his waist. The other end he tied to the circular handle on the back of the door.

Uncle Shameless slowly turned the handle and pushed. The howling air started to snake through the open door. The air current made it difficult to merely throw the door open, but due to his Eldercherry wine-enhanced state, Uncle Shameless did not have too many problems.

The wind caught the door as it was halfway open and pushed it the rest of the way. Air whipped around Uncle Shameless' face as he walked onto the back deck.

"This is gonna do a number on my hair!" the man said to himself as he felt his ratty hair whipping around madly. Uncle Shameless worked his way to the edge of the deck and started waving at the Roc Lobster and began bellowing "*Rosco-oooooo!*"

Back in the cockpit, Steve watched as Rosco left his place near the front of the airship. Steve did not need any help to see the Pyrix now; they were closing in – and *fast*. The burning bird creatures stuck out brightly against the night sky, making them easy to see.

"You got all that?" Uncle Shameless yelled to Rosco over the roaring air. The Roc Lobster chirped a loud yes.

"That a boy!" bellowed Uncle Shameless as he gave Rosco an enthusiastic thumbs up "...I'm glad someone does," he mumbled to himself as he fished out his wineskin. A loud shriek sounded nearby, causing Uncle Shameless to spit out some of his wine, most of which landed on the front of his battered armor.

Uncle Shameless glanced behind him and decided quickly to run back into *The Defender*, but a well-placed fireball slammed into the door first, forcing it closed.

"What is he doing back there?" asked Steve, wondering why Uncle Shameless hadn't come back yet. Everyone heard the door slam shut loudly, but saw no sign of Uncle Shameless stumbling down the aisle in his ugly khaki shorts.

There was however, a great amount of loud pounding on the door.

Steve sighed as he realized what the problem was, "He locked himself out, will someone go let him in?" Zeroth got up, took off his chef's apron and ran down the aisle to the backdoor.

But he did not stay there long.

"We have a problem," Zeroth explained as he made his way into the cockpit.

"What's wrong?" asked Eira.

"The backdoor is melted shut."

A Pyrix landed its fiery body on the back deck of the airship, which creaked and moaned under the weight of the creature. Uncle Shameless was still trapped outside with the blazing beast.

"Well this is a fine how to do," Uncle Shameless said aloud. The Pyrix snapped its blackened beak at Uncle Shameless, but he rolled out of the way.

"This is bad," Uncle Shameless noted as the creature stared him down with its burning eyes.

As Uncle Shameless tried to come up with a way of fighting the creature barehanded, he watched as two Hawken warriors dropped out of the clouds above the ship and flew down to the deck.

"This is *really* bad," sighed Uncle Shameless as he reached for his wineskin.

"We have to do something," Eira said from her seat just beyond the cockpit.

"I just wish we could see what was going on back there," replied Steve from his pilot's seat.

"Look over the controls, maybe there is something," suggested Eira as Zeroth looked over a diagram of the airship attached to the wall near the airship's midsection, trying to find another way out.

Steve quickly scanned the control panel and did not see anything that looked like it would help. He looked at the armrest of his pilot's seat once more. Next to the control for the telescope viewer he had used earlier, Steve saw another button. It had a drawing of a person's face, but with a second set of eyes in the back.

Steve shrugged and pushed the button.

The Pyrix by itself had been bad enough, but now Uncle Shameless had two Hawken warriors added to the mix. One of the Hawken stepped forward, his deadly talons digging into the deck.

"Surrender hu-man!" the Hawken shouted as he leveled his spear at his flannel wearing target.

Uncle Shameless made a quick glance backward at the door. He gave his rope a quick tug to find out that it was still tied, even with the door closed over it. He took a quick swig from his wineskin and cracked his knuckles,

"Not t'day, shorty."

Several clicks and whirls went off over Steve's head after he pushed the new button. Another viewer, not unlike the telescope viewer he had used earlier, lowered from the cockpit's ceiling.

"What the...another one?" Steve pondered aloud as he looked into the new device. He found himself looking at the back deck, and saw Uncle Shameless talking to someone. He tilted the viewer up to see more of the deck.

"Crumbs!" Steve yelled as he saw the Pyrix and the two Hawken warriors attacking his uncle.

Uncle Shameless dodged a spear thrust from one of the Hawken.

"Shorty?!" yelled the insulted warrior.

"Would you prefer stubby?" Uncle Shameless cracked as he jumped out of the way of another spear.

The Hawken warrior screamed and his comrade joined in on the fight, wielding a sword.

"What's yer pal's name? Shrimp basket?"

Both warriors stopped in mid-attack, "What's a shrimp basket?" asked one of the Hawken. Not knowing the answer, other warrior shrugged.

"Shuddup, short-stack!" taunted Uncle Shameless, re-igniting their rage.

Steve watched the battle through the rear viewer as Zeroth ran into the cockpit, "I think I found a way to get outside...what are you doing?" he asked, seeing the new viewer Steve was using.

"We have trouble on the back deck," Steve explained as he watched Uncle Shameless grab one of the Hawken's spears.

"Look out!" yelled Zeroth.

Steve leaned his head away from the rear viewer in time to see a volley of fireballs heading right for *The Defender*. He quickly pushed the button to raise the viewer and grabbed the control stick.

"Hang on!" Steve yelled as he pulled hard on the control stick.

Outside on the rear deck, Uncle Shameless swung his stolen spear as he tried to trip the Hawken warriors. Behind the two bird-men, the Pyrix opened its beak and began inhaling loudly.

"Uh-oh," whimpered Uncle Shameless, not looking forward to getting a face full of fire. Suddenly the deck spun underneath him.

"Whoa!" yelled Uncle Shameless as the airship abruptly banked hard to one side. The move had caught Uncle Shameless' attackers off guard, causing them to fall of the deck.

Uncle Shameless was saved by his rope. As he watched several fireballs sail overhead, he breathed a sigh of relief.

That was until he remembered that all three of his attackers could fly.

"That was close!" yelled Zeroth.

"I'm *aware!*" answered Steve as he watched the Pyrix close in on him. He saw Rosco engage a pair of the fiery bird skeletons and lead them away from *The Defender* as Steve leveled the airship again.

"Aw, crackers!" Uncle Shameless cursed as the airship righted itself, causing him to crash down to the hard floor of the deck. His attackers landed on the deck shortly after, undeterred.

"Surrender hu-man!" yelled one of the warriors as the Pyrix readied its breath weapon once more.

"You guys need a better writer," joked Uncle Shameless, who was getting tired of being told to surrender and being called 'hu-man.' "Come an' get me, stubby!" he hollered at the short Hawken troops.

The Hawken with the sword roared and charged. Uncle Shameless lightly thrust his spear into the chest of the furious warrior, barely penetrating the hawk-man's chest armor. The warrior readied his sword to make a swing at Uncle Shameless' head, but at the last second, Uncle Shameless swung the spear towards the Pyrix as it shot a stream of fire at Uncle Shameless.

The fire struck the Hawken in the back, protecting Uncle Shameless from the lethal flames. The warrior screamed as fire covered his feathery body. Uncle Shameless used his extra-ordinary strength to spin the burning Hawken around and around.

He built up enough speed and let go of the spear, sending the warrior into his unarmed comrade. Both of the Hawken fell over the edge of the deck, falling many feet to the ground below.

Uncle Shameless breathed heavily as he looked up at the flaming Pyrix and dusted off his hands, "Guess it's just you an' me now Tiny."

"Incoming!" Eira hollered from her seat.

Steve looked off to one side to see several more fireballs heading for the ship. The fiery projectiles whined louder and louder as they approached.

Steve pushed the control stick to one side, making the airship bank sharply. A pair of fireballs passed harmlessly over *The Defender*, but another struck near the head of the eagle.

Part of the large window that acted as a windshield for the cockpit, shattered, filling the cockpit with broken glass. Steve, Zeroth and Eira did their best to shield themselves from the flying shards. Steve righted the airship once more, having been knocked around after that last volley.

"How's Shameless doing?" Zeroth yelled over the loud wind as he looked at the now broken main window. Steve lowered the rear viewer and inspected his uncle's status. "He's fighting a Pyrix."

"Zaa's Beak!" exclaimed Zeroth.

"Barehanded."

"No!...Really?"

"See for yourself," Steve turned the viewer toward Zeroth; the bird-man looked through it and sure enough saw Uncle Shameless throwing punches at the fire covered bird.

"Your uncle certainly is amazing," Zeroth said as he took his eyes away from the viewer.

"Oh, he's certainly *something* alright," Steve answered sarcastically.

Zeroth headed towards the broken window and yelled over the wind, "See if this thing has any weapons, we must make it to Da'Rahga. I'm going to help Shameless!"

Steve diverted his gaze from the night sky over to Zeroth, "What? Are you crazy?" he yelled as Zeroth climbed out the window and on to the top of the eagle's head.

"...He *is* crazy," whispered Steve.

"C'mon big boy!" Uncle Shameless yelled as he landed another punch on the Pyrix's fire covered beak. Uncle Shameless had guessed correctly that if he got close enough, the Pyrix could not successfully hit him with its breath weapon.

Uncle Shameless had taken one of his armored elbow guards off and was using it to protect his fist against the Pyrix's fire covered skeleton as he punched it. Even with the metal guard covering his hand, he could feel the burning heat from the beast's body, but Uncle Shameless did his best to ignore the pain and kept punching.

The Pyrix jumped into the air and swatted at Uncle Shameless with a fiery talon, raking him across the back. The burning hot claws cut into his armor like a knife through butter.

"So that's how it is, huh?" Uncle Shameless growled at the hovering creature. He took a deep breath, squatted slightly and made a jumping upper-cut, "Wor-ba!" he yelled.

The blow caught the creature on the bottom of its beak and knocked it back down to the deck. The creature slowly got up, shaking its head to regain its senses.

"That's what happens when you mess with someone from Michigan!"

Zeroth made his way to the topmost part of the eagle's head. He dug his claws into the body of the airship as much as he could to keep from falling off. The bird-man kneeled so he faced forward, looking out at the Wall of Fire. He exhaled quickly as he took out Gladius.

"I see we're at Da'Rahga, so are you gonna turn in Steve now?" asked the prickly swordfish.

Zeroth gave his weapon a cold, dark stare, "That is my business, and if you say anything I'll drop you off this airship right here and now." The Hunter reached over the side of *The Defender* and dangled Gladius from his hand.

"I'll be good!" Gladius whimpered weakly. "So what are we doin' then?"

"We're going to help Shameless. He's fighting a Pyrix."

"Hermf," scoffed the silver swordfish. "Very honorable for a likely traitor...wait, is he really?"

"Barehanded," added Zeroth.

"This I *hafta* see," Gladius said right before Zeroth gave him an enthusiastic squeeze.

Steve poured over the control panel of the airship, looking for something that might be a weapon. He looked at the pilot's seat armrests again, but he still could not find anything. The boy sighed loudly, frustrated. He mindlessly ran his hands over the control stick. Steve stopped when he came to something that felt like a button. He looked down and realized that one of the eyes of the eagle's head that adorned the control stick *was* a button.

Without hesitation, the intrepid teenager pushed it.

Zeroth lifted his wings out from under his cloak and opened them up to the wind. He held onto Gladius tightly and let go of the airship. The Hunter floated backwards through the air, looking down as he did. The airship quickly passed underneath him and he soon saw the back deck below.

Zeroth saw the Pyrix attacking Uncle Shameless and immediately tucked in his wings and pointed his sword downward.

"Whatsamatter there Tiny?" taunted Uncle Shameless. The fiery minion of evil looked exhausted after a series of powerful blows from the man in the ugly khaki shorts.

The creature flapped its wings and prepared to escape, but just as it spread its wings to take flight, Zeroth dropped from above and sliced one of its boney wings off.

Zeroth ran over to Uncle Shameless, "Are you okay?"

"'Course I'm okay."

Zeroth looked over Uncle Shameless, who aside from some deep cuts in his armor and a few burns, did not look too bad at all.

"Really?"

"Uh, *Yeah*," countered Uncle Shameless, his hands on his hips.

"Amazing," whistled Zeroth.

There was a loud clickity click sound coming from the floor by the middle of what was left of the main window. Steve tried to see what was happening but he could not see from his seat. His curiosity was soon satisfied.

A targeting cross hair rose from the floor and stopped so that it was positioned in the middle of the front view. Before Steve could even think about what that was all about, he felt the eagle's head on the control stick move. He looked down and saw that the eagle's mouth was now open enough for him to fit his index finger in, like a trigger on a gun.

Steve decided to give this new find a try. He called to Eira to join him in the cockpit so she could act as a spotter. "How am I going to do that?" she asked.

"Watch," Steve pushed a button on the control panel in front of him. A ladder dropped down from above as a section of the ceiling slid back to reveal a small observation dome at the top of the cockpit.

Eira scaled the ladder as fast as she could and strapped herself into the seat, which was able to spin in a circle, making it easier for her to see everything.

"Why didn't you use this earlier?" she asked from her lookout seat.

"I only just found it a few minutes ago, I'm still figuring this whole thing out. But find me some Pyrix," ordered the boy.

"Over to the left!" called the pelican.

"I see it!" yelled Steve as he banked the airship in the direction of his target.

"So what do you want to do about *that* thing?" Zeroth asked Uncle Shameless as he pointed a clawed finger at the wounded Pyrix thrashing around on *The Defender*'s deck.

"Well, I reckon-" Uncle Shameless started before he was cut off as the airship banked sharply to one side. Uncle Shameless and Zeroth lost their footing as *The Defender* flew in its tilted state through the night sky. Uncle Shameless, still tied to the airship door, jumped and grabbed Zeroth, swinging through the air on his improvised life-line.

The now single winged Pyrix began to slide off the deck, towards the dark ground below. It screeched as it clawed at the deck with its single wing and foot talons, trying in vain to stay on board.

Uncle Shameless and Zeroth watched while they swung back and forth as the fiery creature toppled over the deck's guard rail, lighting the night sky as it fell like a lost comet.

"Glad that's over with," Uncle Shameless said as he watched the creature's light fade away in the distance. Zeroth nodded in agreement as he clutched both of Uncle Shameless' hands tightly.

The Pyrix let loose one last mighty shriek and Uncle Shameless glanced up in time to see a fireball crash into the door, setting the rope holding him and Zeroth to the ship aflame.

38

Steve lined up the Pyrix in the crosshairs in front of him. At least, he tried to. The creature was very wily and quick moving. Every time he would get it centered, the creature darted this way or that.

"C'mon!" the boy yelled in frustration, as he grew tired of chasing the creature through the night sky, almost running into Rosco in the process. The Roc Lobster was busy chasing down some of the other attacking Pyrix.

"To the *right!*" yelled Eira, "It's moving to the right!" Steve directed the craft accordingly, cutting through a bank of clouds.

"Why are you going into the clouds?" asked Eira.

"We'll surprise it. Keep your eyes open," Steve ordered as he eased back on the airship's throttle, slowing it down. He piloted the craft through the thick clouds, looking for a tell-tale hint of orange and yellow. Eira spun her lookout's seat around, looking for the fire-covered creature against the dark night sky as well.

"There!" the pelican yelled, pointing.

"...Y'know, I can't see where you are pointing," explained Steve, trying to remain calm.

"Oh, sorry. Back and to the left!"

Steve punched the throttle forward, increasing his speed as he skimmed through the clouds. Just beyond the edge of the dark fluffy forms, he saw the tips of fire-covered wings.

"We're in trouble," Uncle Shameless explained as he nodded up at the burning rope.

"What else is new?" Zeroth joked as he leaned his head back and looked up. He saw the fire eating away at the old, smelly rope. He looked around, trying to figure out an escape plan.

"If the boy weren't flying all crazy like, we'd be okay," Uncle Shameless replied, commenting on the airship's current sideways state.

"I'm *sure* he has a reason," answered Zeroth as he fought the strain growing in his arms.

"Wait. You have wings, can't ya just fly us outta here?" asked Uncle Shameless as he watched the rope begin to give way.

"I can only glide."

"Fine, can you *glide* us out of here?"

"I don't even know where or how high up we are. We could easily get lost," explained Zeroth. "But I'm thinking of something."

Uncle Shameless and Zeroth fell sharply as part of the rope weakened.

"Think. *Faster*," Uncle Shameless said nervously through clenched teeth.

The front of *The Defender* breached the boarder of the cloud bank and Steve instantly saw the Pyrix. He lined up the creature in the crosshairs and pulled the trigger on the control stick.

"*Whoa!*" Steve exclaimed, as he watched a blast of glowing blue liquid rocket from the eagle's beak. The blast struck the Pyrix in the back. Steve's jaw dropped as he watched the fiery beast disappear in front of him.

"Well that was *something*," Steve said, wondering what it was he had shot the vile creature with.

"Good shot!" Eira cried from her lookout dome just before another fireball flew overhead, nearly striking the pelican in her seat. She spun around, "Another, right behind us!"

"Did you see that?" asked Zeroth, after seeing the glowing blast fire from *The Defender*'s beak. "See what?" asked Uncle shameless, trying to ignore the pain in his arms.

"I think Steve found a weapon," replied Zeroth.

"Bully!" bellowed Uncle Shameless happily. "Now, if he'd only level this thing out so we wouldn't fall thousands of feet after that rope gives out."

The airship rolled sharply and leveled out quickly, as if answering Uncle Shameless' wish. The duo crash landed on the deck.

"Ugh," winced a sore Uncle Shameless, turning to see how much longer the rope would have held out. It was down to only a handful of strands. "Good timin', we were about to-"

The airship rolled sharply again, sending the pair tumbling. Zeroth banged his head against the rail lining the edge of the deck, and was knocked out cold. Uncle Shameless managed to grab the unconscious Zeroth by a leg and hoped that the rope would hold. It did.

For about three seconds.

The last thing Uncle Shameless heard was a loud SNAP! as the rope finally broke. He suddenly felt the odd sensation that comes with falling, as if his stomach was trying to escape his body through his throat. The wind ripping around Uncle Shameless as he fell forced his eyes closed.

Tears streaked the man's face as he tried not to think about what was going to happen to him and Zeroth after the hard ground caught up with them.

Uncle Shameless willed his eyes open and watched as the ground moved closer and closer, like a camera zooming in on a subject. Uncle Shameless closed his eyes and maintained his tight grip on Zeroth's leg.

Uncle Shameless felt an odd feeling around his stomach. He felt like his entire midsection was contracting and loosening over and over. He then felt an even stranger sensation.

He felt like he was falling *up*.

Uncle Shameless forced open his eyes once again and saw the he was in fact whipping through the air on a wide arc.

"What the-" he started. He looked at his stomach and saw a thick snake-like thing wrapped around his midsection. Uncle Shameless looked at it again and realized whatever it was, it was alive.

"Bah!" Uncle Shameless yelled as he beat at the thing with his free hand. The creature let go of him, and he started falling toward the ground again.

"There, that's *better*," the man said, proud of himself. He quickly realized that he was falling to his doom once more.

"Oh yeah…" Uncle Shameless sighed, his error occurring to him. The snake-like thing whipped through the air at him again, pulling him up through the air.

"*Waaaaa!*" Uncle Shameless yelled during his odd trip, finally stopping when he landed hard onto the feathered back of Rosco.

Steve squeezed the trigger again and like before, a glowing blast thundered out of the eagle's beak and shot a Pyrix out of the air.

"Look!" Eira cried.

"…*Where?*" Steve sighed.

"Sorry. To your right," Eira replied.

The boy glanced over and saw Rosco cutting through the air with Uncle Shameless and Zeroth on his back. His Uncle waved with both hands, forgetting he needed at least one to hang onto the Roc Lobster's feathered back. Steve shook his head as he watched his uncle almost fall off before quickly grabbing onto Rosco's back once more.

Rosco tucked his wings in and dove at a rogue Pyrix, swatting at it with an enormous lobster claw. The black-boned skeleton exploded in a burst of flames as the heavy claw crushed its body. Rosco let out a roar of accomplishment; Uncle Shameless patted the creature on the head.

The sound of the exploding Pyrix woke Zeroth from his altered state "Ahh!" he cried, not remembering anything that had happened in the past few minutes.

"Easy there!" Uncle Shameless said as he grabbed the startled bird-man.

"We're okay. Rosco saved us."

Zeroth let out a loud sigh of relief. He had Uncle Shameless ask Rosco to return him to the airship. The Roc Lobster reached back and wrapped a thick tentacle around Zeroth. He expertly flew close to *The Defender* and held Zeroth near the hole in the cockpit's shattered windshield.

Zeroth climbed through the hole and waved a thanks to the Roc Lobster. The colossal creature chirped loudly and climbed into the air with Uncle Shameless still on his back.

"Where's Eira?" Zeroth asked as he dusted broken glass off his cloak.

"Up here!" cheered the pelican-lady from the spinning chair in the observation dome. Zeroth glanced up at the cheery Eira. He then glanced over at the crosshairs sticking in front of the main window.

"You've been busy," Zeroth said to Steve with a sly smirk. "Now what?" asked Zeroth as he strapped himself tightly into what looked like a co-pilot's seat near Steve.

"I've been thinking," Steve began as he looked over the night sky outside the airship.

"You do that a lot," joked Zeroth.

Steve rolled his eyes at the bird-man, "*Anyway*, this weapon is able to destroy the Pyrix."

"Really?" Zeroth asked intently.

"Yes," continued Steve, "And I have a hypothesis."

"On no," Zeroth replied in a concerned tone. "I hope it's not contagious."

"What?" answered Steve, forgetting that the bird-man did not know too much in the ways of science. "No, a hypothesis is an idea or theory."

"Then why not just say 'idea' or 'theory'?" asked Zeroth.

"Because..." Steve thought for a moment, "Well, just because. It has to do with science."

"Ah, more of this 'science' you are so fond of," Zeroth added cynically. "So tell me, is part of science coming up with bigger words to explain simple things just so you'll sound smarter?"

"Okay *fine*. I have this *idea* I came up with," Steve countered in a grumpy tone.

"Which is?" Zeroth asked with a smirk.

Steve paused for dramatic effect, "I think I can use this to bring down the Wall of Fire."

The Defender rocketed through the dark night sky towards the glowing Wall of Fire that protected Fiach-Ra's city, Da'Rahga. Rosco, along with Uncle Shameless, flew in front of the colossal airship. Steve and the Roc Lobster had chased down the last of the Pyrix, and now had clear flying towards the menacing City of Flame.

Steve did not know if the Pyrix that had attacked had been sent out after him and his friends or had only been standing guard. Since the battles had taken place far away from the city, Steve decided to assume no one in Da'Rahga knew they were approaching.

In his dark throne room, Fiach-Ra sat and thought. Steve had forgotten that what the Pyrix saw, Fiach-Ra also saw. The Hawk-King had been witness to every single battle that took place in the shadowy skies near his burning city.

"*The Defender*..." the Hawk-King whispered to himself as the Spear of Zuu rattled in his clenched hand, the words painfully snaking their way out of his vile beak.

U'nala, now safely back in Da'Rahga, entered the throne room. The Hawk-King looked up, surprised to see the one-winged commander of his armies. "And just *where* have you been?"

"A better question, O Favorite of Zuu, would be where U'nala has *not* been," the jaded second in command replied.

Fiach-Ra flew down at U'nala, his eyes full of fire and anger.

"Do *not* take that tone with me," barked the irritated Hawk-King in a subdued yet terrifying voice.

U'nala quickly dropped to one knee, "Apologies my Lord. U'nala has had a long and difficult journey," the Wing-Master said as he summarized his many misadventures with Remmit and Kaz while pursuing The Boy. "...And then there was this huge eagle...*thing*. U'nala does not know how to describe it."

The Hawk-King flapped his wings and walked away from his old friend. "I have seen it," Fiach-Ra replied resentfully. "It is at this moment heading right for my city."

U'nala stood up quickly, "Are we to go into battle?" U'nala asked in a very excited tone. He thought of the special project he had been working on in his quarters and figured now would be the time to unveil it.

"We are not going to do anything," explained Fiach-Ra.

"But-" U'nala started, disappointment creeping into his voice.

"No, we are not going to do anything – *yet*," the Hawk-King started with a wicked smirk. He began walking back to his throne as U'nala made for the exit.

"By the way," Fiach-Ra added with his back to U'nala, "Where is my chariot?"

U'nala pretended not to hear the question and quickly ran out of the room.

As Steve flew *The Defender* closer to the Wall of Fire, the light from it grew more and more intense. The boy squinted, trying to see through the brilliant light.

"Well," Steve sighed, "Here goes nothing."

He moved the airship so that it was flying alongside the Wall of Fire and pulled the trigger on the control stick. A glowing blue light exploded outward in a mighty blast. The blast struck the top of the Wall of Fire and Steve held his breath.

Nothing happened.

Steve tried again and again, but only met with the same results. He pounded on the control panel angrily, drawing Zeroth's attention. "What's wrong?"

"It didn't work!"

Zeroth watched as Steve tried again with no luck, "Of course it didn't work."

Steve spun in his pilot's seat, "What do you mean?"

"Haven't you ever put out a fire before?" asked Zeroth.

"Uh...well," Steve started, realizing that he had not, except for that fire caused by a mishap with his home chemistry set when he was much younger.

He had resorted to making multiple trips with cereal bowls filled with water to extinguish the flames, but his mother ended up making short work of the inferno with the garden hose.

"You never aim for the *top* of the fire," explained Zeroth "You have to put it out at the base of the flames, where the embers are."

Steve didn't think that really mattered considering it was a *magical* fire, but he kept his mouth shut and decided to try it anyway. He turned the airship around so he could start his attack again and this time aimed for the bottom of the Wall of Fire. He squeezed the trigger and held it, causing the blast to keep firing, like a hose watering a lawn.

The glowing blue blast struck the base of the flames and there was a dazzling flash. Smoke began billowing into the air wherever the blast hit the flames, and as the smoke cleared Steve could see that the Wall of Fire was becoming extinguished.

With one section of the Wall of Fire down, Steve banked *The Defender*, aimed for another section and easily extinguished the magical flames.

In Da'Rahga, Remmit and Kaz exited one of the many adobe buildings that littered the city with their arms full of boxes.

"You're never going to regret this," Remmit said convincingly, as he carried boxes piled up higher than his head.

"I gave you all of my savings for this blindfold plan of yours, it better work," Kaz responded from behind his own stack of boxes.

"Trust me, this is the best investment you'll ever make. I even used some of the money to get us a booth in the downtown bazaar. After a few months of selling this stuff, we'll be rolling in money," Remmit explained cheerfully.

Kaz nodded behind his load of boxes, "I can't believe I'm saying this, but it's nice to be back in Da'Rahga..." his words trailed off as he looked around the city square.

"Is it just me, or is it darker than usual?"

Remmit looked around as well, "Y'know, I think you might be..." his beak dropped open as he saw that half of the Wall of Fire was extinguished. His eyes noticed the giant blue-silver eagle circling the city, which with one final swoop, put out the rest of the Wall of Fire.

The boxes of blindfolds cascaded from Remmit's hands and he fell to his knees as Kaz did the same. A box broke open, and several dozen blindfolds spilled out onto the stonework of the city square.

Remmit buried his face into his clawed hands and sobbed loudly, "It isn't fair!"

Kaz visualized piles of money disappearing in his mind as he realized he had wasted all his savings on the now useless blindfolds.

Remmit's sobbing quickly changed to gagging as Kaz wrapped his muscular hands around his feathery neck and squeezed. Remmit skillfully kicked Kaz in the shin, causing the large Swantan to loosen his grip long enough for Remmit to run away.

Kaz chased after the enterprising bird-man, wielding a sword and yelling laments about his lost fortune as well as unsavory remarks about Remmit's ancestry.

Everyone in the cockpit cheered loudly as the Wall of Fire at last became totally extinguished. Da'Rahga, City of Flame, now sat in darkness and was defenseless. Steve felt very proud of himself and thought that finally things were going his way for a change.

That was until he turned *The Defender* around and found himself staring at a massive armada of Pyrix and Hawken warriors, led by none other than the Hawk-King himself.

39

"Bring down the airship!" Fiach-Ra commanded as he flapped his mighty wings and pointed to *The Defender* with the flaming Spear of Zuu.

Steve stared at the enormous force heading towards him, thinking that all of the Pyrix in the sky looked like a constellation of fiery stars.

A volley of fireballs headed for the airship and Steve tried to dodge most of them, but several struck the craft, knocking it around in the air. Steve fired at Pyrix after Pyrix, but their numbers seemed endless.

"Enough of this!" yelled Steve as he banked the airship sharply and turned to fly away.

"What are you doing?!" exclaimed Zeroth as Steve started to fly away from Da'Rahga.

"A strategic withdrawal."

"What?"

"Flying away."

"You can't do that!" Zeroth yelled, anger rising in his voice.

"Watch me," countered Steve. However, after he turned *The Defender* around, he found himself facing more Pyrix and Hawken warriors.

"Well that's just great," Steve sighed as disappointment filled him.

"You can't give up," Eira called down from the lookout dome.

"Yes, we've come this far," Zeroth added, trying to control his temper.

"But we're outnumbered! And I'm not even going to bother counting by how much!" Steve yelled.

"That didn't stop Rooster McGrew in the Battle of Ib'okk," said Zeroth.

"Rooster McGrew? I don't even know *who* that is," responded a very confused Steve. "What happened to him?"

"…He died," Zeroth confessed.

"Yes, he was greatly outnumbered," Eira added from above.

Steve rolled his eyes "And this is s'pose to encourage me, *how?"*

"He didn't give up!" Zeroth explained emotionally.

"Look!" yelled Eira.

"*Where?*" Steve and Zeroth asked in unison.

"Oh, sorry. Back and to the left," Eira said, correcting herself.

Steve and Zeroth looked out to see Rosco and Uncle Shameless fighting the numerous Pyrix and Hawken warriors. One of the Hawken landed on Rosco's back and slashed at Uncle Shameless with a spear.

Uncle Shameless caught the spear and knocked the bird-man off. As Rosco swatted at attacking Pyrix with his might claws, Uncle Shameless thrust the spear at Hawken warriors like a knight of old on horseback.

"You see?" Zeroth said, "Rosco and your uncle aren't giving up."

"Well, for the record, my uncle is probably too drunk to count past five at the moment," Steve joked sarcastically.

Zeroth gave Steve an intense stare and pointed a clawed finger back at Da'Rahga. The boy sighed, "*Fine*, here we go," he said as he increased the ship's speed and dove into a flight of Pyrix.

Fire lit up the night sky as Pyrix swarmed around *The Defender*. Hawken warriors tried in vain to shoot the airship with their arrows and spears. Several fireballs had struck the ship, leaving craters and burn marks in *The Defender*'s smooth body.

Flying above his city, Fiach-Ra watched as Pyrix fell victim to Rosco's claws and Steve's shooting. Even though the boy and his friends were still outnumbered, the Hawk-King decided to keep it that way.

Fiach-Ra flapped his wings and flew closer to the Statue of Zuu that sat atop Arx Vena'Tor. He was followed by several members of his Royal Guard, who flew in a tight V formation behind him. The Hawk-King flew towards the Mouth of Zuu, the open beak of the statue, and chanted several wicked words as he held up his magic spear.

A heinous chorus of shrieks and screams sounded from within the darkness of the Mouth. Soon the darkness was replaced by fire as dozens of new Pyrix shoot out from the Mouth and took to the sky, chasing after The Boy and the Roc Lobster.

Steve saw all of this from the airship thanks to the telescopic viewer he had discovered earlier.

"Aw, *c'mon!*" he whined, "Talk about overkill!"

Steve swallowed his anger and went into a fast dive to try and loose a group of new Pyrix that was chasing him. The boy banked the airship here and there, cutting over trees and skimming hills and mountains.

"At least we can out fly these things," whispered Steve.

As if hearing Steve's inner thoughts, Fiach-Ra decided to gain even more of an advantage. He pulled back a mighty arm and with expert skill hurled the Spear of Zuu towards *The Defender*.

The Spear of Zuu was nothing more than a fiery blur as it cut through the night sky like a comet. Fiach-Ra had timed his shot just right, and the heinous spear struck one of the airship's wings as Steve turned the large aircraft.

The spear blasted clear through the wing, bursting out through the other side. The impact knocked the airship into a spin and Steve fought hard to correct it while having a damaged wing.

The Hawk-King held up an open palm. There was a flash of fire and the Spear returned to his grasp. Fiach-Ra's eyes burned as he watched the airship correct itself even as smoke poured out of the hole in the broken wing. His plan had succeeded however – the ship's speed was halved.

"Not good! Not good!" Steve hollered as he felt the airship's speed dropping, causing the Pyrix behind him to gain on him instantly. He could hear the many piercing shrieks behind him.

"We have trouble ahead!" Eira called out.

"Now what?" Steve and Zeroth cried in unison.

The pelican lady explained that she saw a trio of Pyrix heading for them, and that they were carrying burly Swantan warriors equipped with special carrying harnesses.

"I don't get it," confessed Steve.

"The Pyrix are going to drop them on the ship!" Zeroth realized as he undid his straps so he could get on top of the ship.

"Eira! Get down here!" Zeroth called up.

Eira spun her seat around so she could reach the ladder to descend. As she did, one of the Pyrix shot a fireball close to her lookout dome. The missile crashed into the metal body of the airship. Shards of heavy metal smashed through the glass surrounding the pelican. A large hunk of metal hit Eira the head, knocking her senseless.

"No!" Steve cried as he watched his friend helplessly hunch over in her seat. He soon heard three heavy thumps on the ceiling of the airship – the Swantan warriors had landed on top of *The Defender*.

"I'll stop them. Keep flying and shooting down those Pyrix carrying warriors," Zeroth ordered. "We *must* reach the city."

The Hunter was about to climb out through the shattered main window but decided against it since the vile swan-men on top would easily spot him. Instead, he headed towards a hatch he had found earlier by studying the blueprint of the airship.

Zeroth made his way to the midsection of the massive airship. There were two hatches on either side of the ship, which Zeroth had learned led out onto the wings. He went to the hatch that led out onto the damaged wing, hoping that the smoke pouring out of it would conceal him.

Zeroth groaned as he turned the handle of the hatch and flung it open. The night sky whipped past him as he looked outside. He tightened his yellow scarf and stealthily wormed his way out of the hatch, finding a series of indented handholds in the bluish-silver body of *The Defender*.

The bird-man crawled onto the eagle's back, and moved towards the trio of Swantan warriors that were heading for Eira.

The three Swantan warriors slowly made their way over the top of the airship. The leader of the trio, an older squatty Swantan with an array of white and gray feathers, was the first to find the unconscious Eira.

"W'at do we 'ave 'ere?" said the warrior, his words oozing through his cracked beak. The Swantan lifted up his heinous looking spear with a crooked, rusty blade. He spun it around in one hand and prepared to throw it at the helpless pelican trapped in the shattered observation dome.

Just before letting his weapon fly, the Swantan felt a tap on his shoulder. He turned and saw no one. While his head was turned, Zeroth grabbed the thick spear out of the muscle headed warrior's upturned claw. In a blur of robes and wood, Zeroth spun the spear around and whacked the giant swan across the face.

The warrior fell down onto the airship, disoriented. His companions quickly reacted, drawing swords and swinging them at Zeroth, who spun the spear and let both sword blades dig into thick wood. Zeroth gathered power in his muscular legs and quickly pushed back on the spear, twisting the warriors' hands so they were forced to let go of their weapons.

This maneuver also caused the two warriors to lose their footing. One fell down onto his back and screamed as he slid off the back of *The Defender*. The second slipped and fell, knocking his head against the hard body of the airship before falling over the edge.

Zeroth tossed the spear over the side of the airship and dropped down to a crawl. As he moved towards Eira, the ship banked to one side to avoid a volley of fireballs. Zeroth felt their heat as they passed over his body as he continued crawling.

A few feet behind Zeroth, the Swantan with the cracked beak finally righted himself and moved stealthily towards Zeroth, pausing only to draw a long, rusty knife.

Fiach-Ra watched over the chaos in the night air that he conducted like a symphony. With a wave of his spear, he directed troops and Pyrix to do his bidding. The Hawk-King knew he had to lure The Boy into Da'Rahga in order to destroy him and was waiting for the airship to fly directly over the city so he could strike it again with the Spear of Zuu. He watched as flights of Pyrix led The Boy closer to the city and closer to his doom.

In *The Defender*, Steve franticly bobbed and weaved the large aircraft through the sky, trying to avoid the Pyrix behind him and trying to shoot down those in front.

"This is crazy! How did I ever get mixed up in this?" the boy said to no one. He blinked repeatedly, "And who am I even talking to?"

Steve bellowed loudly as he shot down another Pyrix with the airship's mighty cannon. He was trying not to think of the wing that had been severely damaged, not to mention the rest of the damage the ship had already taken. It was no where near the perfect condition he had found it in originally.

The boy heard a loud CLUNK! and the ship dropped several feet instantly, knocking Steve around in his pilot's seat.

"Great, now what?!" he yelled as the airship began to make a loud CHUGGA-CHUGGA sound as if it were straining to stay in the air. Steve realized he wouldn't even know what was wrong anyway – he didn't even know how the airship was powered or how it stayed in the air, other than the magic nonsense Istrio had told him about.

Steve decided he was happier *not* knowing. He figured that it would be just his luck that *The Defender* was run on something really crazy, like ill-tempered wolverines on a tread mill or worse yet – annoying, chatty Pixie People.

Zeroth lost his grip for a second as *The Defender* suddenly lurched, only to right itself moments later. The bird-man's claws and talons dug into the airship as he regained his grip and slowly maneuvered towards Eira. He reached the shattered observation dome and started calling Eira's name and gently tapping her on the shoulder.

The Swantan with the cracked beak crawled low against the body of the airship. His rusty knife was clamped tightly in his orange beak as he used both of his muscular hands to maneuver forward unnoticed.

"Mergh..?" Eira whimpered as she slowly came around.

"Easy there," Zeroth said. "You got a nasty bump on the head." He leaned over the lip of the observation dome and looked down at Steve, "She'll be okay," he looked back at Eira. "Can you climb down okay?"

Eira groaned a weak yes and started to climb down from the demolished observation dome.

The flight of Pyrix Steve was chasing turned sharply towards Da'Rahga. Thinking nothing of it, the boy followed them.

Not too far away, Fiach-Ra's eyes narrowed as he prepared to fire a deadly blast from the Spear of Zuu at the unsuspecting airship as it headed towards the city. He pointed the spear at *The Defender* and its obelisk shaped blade became engulfed in flame. The light pouring off the spear grew brighter and brighter as the Hawk-King prepared to fire a shot at the already crippled airship.

Eira took the rungs of the ladder slowly, her head still ached but she was determined to get down safely.

"That's it, take your time," Zeroth coached as he cracked a smile, noticing Steve was heading for Da'Rahga once again. The pelican-lady glanced upwards towards Zeroth and her beak dropped open as she saw a rusty knife blade flash in the night sky, heading right for Zeroth's back.

The Hawk-King flapped his wings and glided to a better firing position as he watched *The Defender* soar over the dark city of Da'Rahga. A piercing burning beam cut through the night sky as it left the tip of the Spear of Zuu and rocketed relentlessly towards the unsuspecting airship.

"Look out!" Eira cried as she saw the hungry knife blade plunge towards Zeroth's unprotected back. Zeroth spun quickly and reached for Gladius.

A swift sword strike knocked the knife loose from the attacking Swantan's hand, sending it flying overboard. But the strike had not come from Zeroth.

In the cockpit, Steve heard a voice yell "Pull up!" He did as quickly as he could, figuring it was Eira and that she saw something he did not. As he did, he wondered if the knock to the head had done something to the pelican's voice.

Zeroth grabbed on to the edge of the observation dome as the airship pulled up abruptly, his other hand still clutching Gladius – but its bladetongue had not yet been released.

The bird-man watched as a tall, shadowy shape pulled up the Swantan with the cracked beak and threw him overboard.

"Who…?" Zeroth gasped.

The backstabbing Swantan fell from *The Defender* and right into the path of Fiach-Ra's beam of fire, which had been meant for the airship.

As the night sky lit up with a small explosion, Zeroth shielded his eyes from the bright light. He looked at up as his anonymous savior flew away on a large set of wings, now illuminated by the flash of light coming from Fiach-Ra's failed attack.

"It can't be…" Zeroth whispered.

Gladius looked up at the figure with its big eyes and laughed, "Ha! I *knew* she wasn't dead!"

40

Fiach-Ra bellowed with rage as his attack missed. His eyes burned as he watched the airship fly away from Da'Rahga.

An eerie cry pierced the night air and a chill washed over Fiach-Ra as it was repeated by more and more unseen criers. The Hawk-King did not have to see the criers to know whom they belonged to; he knew the battle cry well. But it was a battle cry he had not heard it in over 300 years.

"*Impossible!*" The Hawk-King roared angrily.

Back on *The Defender*, Zeroth and Eira joined Steve in the cockpit.

"Thanks for the tip," Steve said to Eira.

"What are you talking about?"

"You told me to pull up, good thing too or else it would have been us who exploded."

"…That wasn't me," Eira explained.

"But if it wasn't you…" Steve started before his words trailed off. He was positive he had heard a female voice.

Zeroth moved over to Steve, still in awe from his encounter on top of the airship. "It was-"

"Look!" Eira yelled, pointing straight ahead.

Zeroth and Steve slowly turned in the direction of the pelican's point. What he saw almost made Steve let go of the airship's control stick.

The boy watched as a flight of owl warriors descended from the clouds to engage a squad of Hawken warriors in the night sky. But these were not the undead skeletal monsters he had fought at Arx A'Quila. These were living breathing bird people, covered with flesh, muscle and flowing feathers.

Steve watched as a flight of owl warriors, led by a much larger owl covered in elaborate armor, sliced through several Pyrix in mid-air. Their battle cries drowned out the vile shrieking of the Pyrix.

The large owl yelled orders and commands to different owls of all sizes in-between swift attacks with its blue-bladed longsword.

The boy quickly turned to Zeroth, "Is that-"

"The Owl-Queen herself, Fel-Ra," Gladius blurted out, answering for Zeroth.

Steve watched as the winged warrior queen expertly fought off foe after foe with a series of quick dives and climbs in the sky, powered by strong flaps of the massive wings on her back. She looked just like the statues of the owl-people Steve had seen at the Temple of Arcana.

She had a strong, muscular body covered in a dazzling pattern of white, black and brown feathers. Fel-Ra's arms and legs ended with clawed hands and powerful taloned feet. Her orange, circular eyes stood out against the black night sky, as did the two horn-like tuffs of feathers that crowned her head.

"Wow, she looks *mad*," Steve noted, commenting on Fel-Ra's relentless fighting.

"You would be too if you had been dead for over 300 years," Eira said.

"This certainly helps us out," Zeroth added as he scanned the battle in the air – hawk and owl clashed against one another, neither side holding back.

"Look!" Eira yelled, "On the ground!" the pelican added before Steve had a chance to ask where.

Steve banked the craft slightly so he could get a better view of the ground. He watched as the city gates opened and hundreds of Swantan warriors poured out to meet another group of white feathered bird-people in battle.

Steve blinked, "Are those..?"

"Chickens!" finished Eira. "Roosters, to be specific."

"...Seriously?" Steve asked in disbelief.

"Why not?" Zeroth said. "Don't you remember that chicken you met in Tal?"

Steve thought back to Jer, the scar covered rooster warrior that Uncle Shameless had insulted back at the Lighthouse Inn. Steve remembered that had it not been for some smooth talking and quick thinking by Uncle Shameless, he probably wouldn't have an uncle right now.

The boy watched a tide of furious rooster warriors plow into the advancing Swantan horde, creating a thunderous symphony of steel against steel.

A fireball skimmed across *The Defender*'s beak, reminding Steve that he was still in the middle of a massive air battle. He spun the craft around quickly and shot at a group of Pyrix. He was aided by a pair of owls that swooped down and took out a Pyrix each as he blasted the last with the airship's beak cannon.

Steve spun the airship around to shoot down another fiery Pyrix that was chasing after a flight of owls. A bright blue shot knocked down yet another Pyrix. But the shot had not come from the airship.

Steve turned his head quickly, "Five-Toes!" he exclaimed as he saw the blue dragon snaking his way through the sky. On his back rode Queen Lana the IV. She waved a glowing hand and fired another magical blue blast at a nearby Hawken, striking it in the face.

Beyond the Queen, Steve saw a small army of Wurm troops riding flying beasts that seemed to be part bird and part fish, and perhaps even related to Rosco. A portion of her army joined the chickens on the ground, fighting alongside them.

The Wurms wielded swords with blades that looked to made of bubbling water, but had no problem cutting through Swantan and Hawken armor. It reminded Steve of the solid water floor in Arx A'Quila.

The airship rocked again, and began making more peculiar sounds. Steve quickly regained control and shook his head "Why did everyone take so long to get here? This ship might still be in one piece if they had shown up sooner."

"All that matters is that they are here now," Eira said optimistically.

Steve agreed, enjoying that *The Defender* was no longer the lone target for Pyrix fireballs. "Yeah yeah, I know. Don't look a gift horse in the mouth."

Eira and Zeroth both stared at the boy, very confused. Steve rolled his eyes, forgetting there are not any horses in Eyri. "Uh, I mean – beggars can't be choosers," he corrected.

"Ah, yes. That makes sense," Zeroth replied as he and Eira nodded.

Steve wiped imaginary sweat off his brow and aimed for another Pyrix.

Fiach-Ra swatted at an attacking owl with his flaming spear, slicing one of its wings off with ease. His Royal Guard formed a perimeter around him and fought off any more owls foolish enough to attack.

"This cannot be!" the Hawk-King screamed in disbelief as he randomly fired blasts of fire at the army of chickens fighting his brawny swan troops on the ground. Pillars of smoke and fire cut through the chicken ranks. Those who survived continued their unyielding battle against the larger Swantans.

A blast of blue grazed over Fiach-Ra's head. He spun in mid-air and saw Five-Toes and Queen Lana heading for him. With a wave of his spear, a flight of Pyrix closed in upon the Wurm Queen and her dragon, but they were easily dispatched by her magic and Five-Toe's many sharp claws.

The Hawk-King looked over the scores of battles around him and decided to swing the odds back in his favor once more. He flapped his massive wings and sped off. His Royal Guard trailed after him, a few pausing to rain arrows down on the chicken warriors below.

As Fiach-Ra dashed through the night air, a pair of owls dropped down in front of him with swords swinging. Even with his much larger size, the Hawk-King was able to dodge around them while his Royal Guard took out the attackers with a hail of arrows.

The Hawk-King reached the snarling Mouth of Zuu and held his spear with both hands as he began chanting more evil words. There was a thunderous clash behind him, but he did not bother to turn and see who was fighting his Royal Guard. The Hawk-King closed his burning eyes in deep thought as he continued his chant.

"Fiach!" a powerful voice yelled behind him.

The Hawk-King's eyes shot open, remembering the authoritative voice.

"I do not know how your curse was broken, but it does not matter. You are too late *Fel*," Fiach-Ra spat, addressing the former Owl-Queen. Fel-Ra hovered in mid-air, flapping her massive wings. She wore heavy armor and wielded a longsword, her orange owl eyes narrowed in rage as she looked upon her usurper.

Fel-Ra dove at Fiach-Ra, her sword splitting the air. He easily blocked the attack and spun the Spear of Zuu, knocking Fel-Ra in the ribs with the flat end. Fel-Ra shook off the blow and raised her sword high. As she did, a column of flame erupted out of the Mouth of Zuu. *"Behold!"* the Hawk-King yelled at his old foe, pointing with the Spear of Zuu.

The blast of fire from the Mouth shot out into the night air. Suddenly, all of the Pyrix that were fighting turned and flew towards the ominous column of flame.

"What are they doing?" Steve asked as he watched all of the Pyrix crash into each other with blazing speed, creating a great ball of fire and smoke in the dark sky over Da'Rahga.

"I don't..." Zeroth began as he watched the ball of fire grow and grow. His eyes widened as the flames began to form into an eerily familiar shape, "Oh no!" he yelled.

The fighting stopped on both sides as foes and allies watched the transformation that looked like the creation of a small sun.

Shapes quickly formed inside the flames, the shapes of blackened bones, monstrous talons and massive wings. Steve cried out as he watched a gargantuan Pyrix come to life right in front of his eyes.

The colossal creature dwarfed even *The Defender* and nearly filled the night sky. The fiery behemoth's beak was sharp, jagged and looked like it could easily swallow up the airship in one bite. Unlike the Pyrix, this beast had arms with vicious three-clawed hands.

Hot, molten lava dripped from the creature's angry jaws, falling to the ground below and melting all in its path. The burning eye sockets resembled a pair of twin suns and its blazing, skeletal wingspan blocked out scores of stars from view.

The fiery fiend's mighty beak flung open and it let out a shriek that chilled Steve to the bone, sounding as if hundreds of Pyrix were screaming at once.

Fiach-Ra flapped his wings and sped off towards his newly summoned minion.

"Hail Quorix, Pyrix Overlord!" the Hawk-King bellowed as he approached the mountain sized Pyrix.

Fel-Ra, brought back to her senses by Quorix's piercing shriek, raised her blue-bladed sword and chased after her Hawken foe. Fiach-Ra laughed and waved the Spear of Zuu. An enormous skeletal arm swatted at the Owl-Queen, knocking her out of the air easily.

The Hawken tyrant laughed as he reached Quorix's fire covered skull and stood upon it. Fiach-Ra raised a clawed hand and reigns of fire shot out, wrapping themselves around Quorix's vast beak. He then pointed the Spear of Zuu down at the army of chickens and gave the reigns a hard pull.

Quorix howled madly and flung his head around towards the fowl warriors below. Quorix's mighty jaw opened and after a quick inhale, let loose a forceful blast of scorching lava at the chickens, instantly incinerating those caught in its path.

Rosco and Uncle Shameless circled in the air near Quorix and Uncle Shameless recoiled in horror as he watched sight below him and decided that he would never eat barbequed chicken again.

"What is *that* thing?!" Steve exclaimed loudly as he whirled *The Defender* around quickly to avoid running into the giant creature.

"I don't know," Zeroth said "But we have to do something –fast."

Steve looked over the mammoth creature with its massive bone jaws that dripped smoldering hot lava. "Like *what*?" asked Steve sarcastically "Call it names?"

The Hawk-King pulled on the reigns controlling Quorix and the fiery creature swatted at *The Defender* with one of its large clawed hands.

"Bahhh!" Steve screamed as he saw the enormous claw heading towards him. Without any other option, Steve pushed the throttle to maximum speed and flew the airship between the gaps of two boney fingers.

Quorix roared in rage and spattered out a shower of molten lava at the airship. The lava rained down on *The Defender* like large burning rain drops.

"Gross!" Steve yelled as he banked the airship and tried to get behind the monster. Fiach-Ra directed Quorix as it began firing blasts of powerful fire from its mouth at owls and Wurms scattered across the sky and ground.

"Our help is disappearing rather quickly," Zeroth noted as he watched Quorix effortlessly incinerate a group of owl warriors.

The colossal Pyrix then turned its aim once again to the airship as Fiach-Ra spun the large creature around with a hard pull on the fiery reigns. Wherever Fiach-Ra looked, Quorix looked while the Hawk-King pushed his powers to the limit to keep control of the beast.

Quorix inhaled deeply, with a noise like a violent windstorm. After a long inhale, the beast became silent. The silence lasted for a single heartbeat before the sky thundered as a stream of fire blasted towards Steve and his friends.

The boy pulled hard on the control stick to move out of the way, but the blast of fire was too fast for the damaged aircraft. The night sky grew brighter and brighter as the fire grew closer to striking the airship.

Steve knew he could not outrun the fire chasing him, so he decided to try one last desperation move. He quickly spun the craft around to face the blast, and as Zeroth began to ask what he was doing, the boy pulled the trigger for *The Defender*'s beak cannon.

A bright blue blast shot out of the eagle's beak and rocketed through the sky to meet Quorix's fire breath. The two energies collided and a brilliant flash lit up the dark sky. *The Defender*'s blast held off the burning fire and started pushing it backwards.

The airborne stalemate ended as Quorix snapped its beak shut and let loose a loud piercing shriek. Steve let go of the airship's trigger and banked the craft quickly to one side as not to be in the line of fire anymore.

As the aircraft darted past Quorix, Steve decided to fire a short blast from the beak cannon at the beast itself. Steve did not have a hard time aiming his shot since the creature was so large in size; it was literally like trying to hit the broad side of a barn. *The Defender*'s blast caught the minion of evil in its rib cage.

Quorix roared and shrieked as it bucked around in pain, almost knocking Fiach-Ra off its head.

"He sure didn't like that," noted Steve, glad that his improvised plans had worked. However, his victory was short lived, as Quorix quickly recovered and started flying towards *The Defender*. Steve flew the airship behind Quorix and prepared to fire another blast.

"What is that?" Zeroth asked while pointing out the window.

"You're picking up Eira's bad habit," Steve said "What are you pointing at?"

Zeroth told Steve where to look, the boy engaged his telescopic viewer to get a better view since he was not gifted with hawk-sight like Zeroth.

"What the..." Steve mumbled, thinking aloud. He saw what Zeroth had spotted – a thick strand of fire sticking out of Quorix's back like a tail. In fact, that is what Steve thought it was at first. As he moved the viewer around, he saw that the strand ran from the small of Quorix's back all the way to the Mouth of Zuu, like a electrical cord plugged into a wall outlet.

"He's attached to that ugly statue," Steve noted as he focused his telescopic viewer "But why?"

"Maybe it has something to do with all that fire that shot out of the statue," Eira suggested.

"That's it!" Steve said, snapping his fingers for emphasis before he quickly formed a plan.

"Look out!" yelled Eira.

Steve pushed the button to send the telescopic viewer back up into the ceiling. As the device rose, Steve saw himself staring at the Quorix's building-sized boney face.

"Neheheh!" Steve screamed as he quickly pulled up to escape the massive snapping beak of the creature. Steve rolled the airship here and there, dodging the repeated attempts by Quorix to make a meal out *The Defender*. As he flew the airship out of harm's way, Steve kept heading for the snarling statue of the eagle god Zuu.

"*Watch it!*" Zeroth yelled as Quorix closed in again.

"Do you wanna fly this thing?" snapped Steve, "Be my guest."

"Sorry, sorry," Zeroth pleaded as he clung tightly to his seat.

The colossal beast of fire and bone maneuvered more quickly than Steve had expected, and was moments away from chomping the airship in two.

A spear cut through the air, hitting Fiach-Ra in the back of the head. The metal tip bent as it struck the Hawk-King's magically protected body. The Hawk-King was so focused on directing Quorix that he had let his guard down. The attack did not harm Fiach-Ra, but it did anger him greatly.

Fiach-Ra pulled sharply on Quorix's reigns and turned the creature to see who had attacked him. Steve and his friends breathed a heavy sigh of relief as the massive black beak turned away.

"Leave my nephew alone!" Uncle Shameless yelled as Rosco flapped his large wings, flying away from the infuriated Hawk-King and his fiery mount. Uncle Shameless' plan worked - Quorix left *The Defender* alone for the moment.

"Thata boy Rosco, make 'em chase ya!" Uncle Shameless shouted as he patted the Roc Lobster's large head. His attitude quickly changed when he looked behind him and saw a mountainous bird skeleton covered in flames only a few yards away.

Uncle Shameless leaned in close to Rosco's head, "Faster! Faster!" he screamed as he heard Quorix starting to inhale a deep breath before spewing fire from its wicked beak.

With Quorix distracted, Steve headed right for the Statue of Zuu that sat on top of Arx Vena'Tor. The lack of Pyrix in the sky made the trip considerably easier, as the remaining Hawken were occupied fighting chickens, owls and Wurms.

Steve centered the Mouth of Zuu in his firing crosshairs. The strand of fire that connected the Mouth and Quorix hung in the air like a blazing power cord. Steve took a deep breath and pulled the firing trigger.

"Faster! *Faster!*" Uncle Shameless screamed again and again as he heard Quorix preparing to toast him and Rosco in mid-air. The Roc Lobster flapped its massive wings, but could not out fly the colossal Quorix. Uncle Shameless felt the intense heat pouring off of the beast's body behind him.

Quorix stopped inhaling and there was a second long pause before a torrent of fire shot from its mouth at Uncle Shameless and Rosco.

A blast of magical blue light exploded in the sky just behind Rosco, blocking the flames like a shield. Uncle Shameless looked over and saw Queen Lana the IV casting a spell from the back of Five-Toes.

Uncle Shameless waved a thank you to the Wurm Queen. She responded by blowing Uncle Shameless a kiss.

"*Ehgggh,*" Uncle Shameless cringed as he tried not to think of what a real kiss from the scaly lady would be like.

Quorix and Fiach-Ra roared angrily at the new attackers. Five-Toes buzzed past Quorix's face, baiting it to follow. Quorix and Fiach-Ra quickly gave chase, forgetting about Steve and the airship once again.

The radiant blast of blue liquid erupted from *The Defender*'s beak and rocketed across the night sky towards the unprotected Mouth of Zuu. Quorix and the Hawk-King were too busy chasing Five-Toes and the Roc Lobster to notice.

But they did notice when Steve's shot hit its target.

The blast struck the Mouth of Zuu and there was an enormous flash, followed by Quorix shrieking madly, clearly in pain.

"It worked!" yelled Steve.

The boy looked at the strand connecting the Mouth to Quorix – it was not as thick or as bright as before, and looked weakened. Steve circled around the statue of Zuu and quickly fired once more.

Steve witnessed the same result as before, Quorix roared in pain and appeared to be weakened. He noticed this time that the fire burning in the Mouth of Zuu was growing dimmer as well. The boy banked the aircraft, headed straight for the Mouth of Zuu and fired repeatedly.

Finally Quorix came to its senses and headed for Steve, roaring all the way. Steve could hear the beast behind him and figured this might be his last chance for attack and came up with another plan.

"What?" Zeroth asked, surprised by the boy's inventiveness.

"We have to destroy that statue," explained Steve, almost shouting over Quorix's shrieking behind the airship.

"But...how?" asked Zeroth.

"I'll think of something," Steve explained, "Just hold on." Eira and Zeroth tightened their seat straps, neither of them knowing what Steve was going to do next.

The boy kept firing at the Mouth of Zuu and the strand of fire that was coming out of it. As he got closer, the boy pulled a lever he had found a few moments ago. Next to it was a picture of eagle talons, and he had a pretty good idea what the lever would do.

A loud clanking sound echoed in the cabin as the two giant legs of the eagle airship lowered from their tucked in position under the body. As they lowered, the taloned metal feet fanned outward like hands getting ready to grab something.

The sky around the airship almost looked like day as Quorix closed in, but this did not hinder Steve one bit. He stayed focused as he approached the vile statue of the eagle god, Zuu.

Steve increased *The Defender*'s speed in an attempt to put a little more distance between him and his fiery pursuer. Not wanting to be outdone, Fiach-Ra ordered Quorix to shoot his flame breath at the aircraft.

As Quorix began his tell-tale inhale, Steve lowered the ships legs into the position he wanted and held his breath. *"Whoa!"* Zeroth shouted, figuring out what Steve was planning. Steve ignored the bird-man and stayed focused on his approach. He eased back on the throttle, hoping he could finish his plan before Quorix roasted them alive inside the airship.

The Defender slowed down greatly and there was a loud CLUNK! as the taloned feet of the airship latched onto the towering statue of Zuu. Fiach-Ra's fire-filled eyes opened to their widest as he realized what The Boy was trying to do – to topple over the statue, the source of Quorix's power.

After Steve was sure the talons were dug into the stonework of the statue, he pushed the throttle to maximum speed. The ship whined and strained against the load as it tried to pull the statue over.

"C'mon!" Steve yelled, trying not to think about being on the business end of Quorix's breath attack.

A thunderous CRACK filled the night sky as the statue began breaking at the base. It was not falling over fast enough, as Quorix was seconds away from burning *The Defender* to ashes with its villainous breath.

The airship lurched sharply as more of the statue gave way, but it still would not totally topple over. The airship began groaning around Steve and his friends. There were several loud pops and crashes inside as the airship's mechanical parts began to give way under the stress. An overhead panel in the rear hallway burst open, filling the hall with steam and bits of metal.

"C'mon!" Steve yelled again. The little sky he could see through the shattered main window grew incredibly bright as Quorix flew up right behind the airship, making a deafening inhaling sound before pausing to let loose a deadly blast of fire.

Tears welled up in Steve's eyes. He had failed.

41

Steve felt the temperature in the cockpit raise quickly, the result of Quorix painting the airship with red-hot flames. But the boy continued to lean on the control stick, hoping that maybe the statue would topple.

Over the crackling of flames, Steve heard a whistle in the air. He ignored it at first but it grew louder and louder. He wondered what it was, it sounded like something traveling through the air very fast. Steve looked out the main window of the cockpit and down at the snarling face of the statue of Zuu.

Just as he did – BOOM! the face of the statue shattered into a million pieces as a large cannon ball smashed into it.

Instantly the strand of fire connecting the Mouth of Zuu to Quorix disappeared. The massive beast let out a roar of extreme pain, which was second only to Fiach-Ra's hollow bellowing. Steve watched as the strand, like a fuse on a bomb, began disappearing until it reached Quorix's back.

And like a bomb, when there was no more strand, – Quorix exploded.

A volcano exploding would have been quieter and perhaps even less fiery. The mountain sized Pyrix combusted, lighting up the night sky to the brightness of a summer afternoon. Steve and the others shielded their eyes, but even with their eyes closed they felt as if they were staring into the sun.

Fire and lava rained down on everything, causing wanton destruction in Da'Rahga and the immediate surrounding area. Then a new sensation came over Steve.

The Defender was falling.

Steve grabbed the controls and tried to get *The Defender* airborne again, but he could not. The airship was too heavily damaged after the last attack from Quorix and from the beast exploding.

"Hang on!" Steve yelled as the airship tumbled towards the stone courtyard outside of Arx Vena'Tor. He knew the aircraft could not fly anymore, but he tried to steer it as it fell. He managed to stabilize *The*

Defender enough that it would not land upside down, and Steve closed his eyes as the ground began coming in closer and closer.

There was a loud crash and the sound of something breaking as *The Defender* landed hard on the ground. Steve felt himself being tossed around and was thankful for the straps that kept him locked into his pilot's seat.

Then everything went quiet.

Steve slowly opened one eye. Everything was blurry. He opened up his other eye and everything near him was still blurry. His hands shot to his face as a sense of dread filled him. He felt for his glasses – they were gone.

"Ah, crumbs!" he cursed loudly as he undid the straps of his pilot seat and jumped onto the floor of the cockpit. As he did, the cockpit tilted suddenly.

Steve looked around as best he could without his glasses. The airship tilted again.

"Uh-oh," The boy said quietly. He crawled around looking for his glasses; he heard Eira and Zeroth undoing their seat straps as their senses returned to them. The airship groaned loudly as Eira and Zeroth began moving. Steve turned around and faced the two blurry shapes.

"I think we should get out of this thing – *fast*," the boy suggested.

Eira and Zeroth began moving towards the shattered 'eyes' of the eagle airship, causing *The Defender* to rock back and forth as it groaned loudly.

"Careful!" Steve yelled as quietly as possible.

"Sorry," Zeroth apologized as he looked out of the main window and saw why the airship was tilting to and fro. The eagle feet and legs had broken part of the fall, but one had snapped off in the crash. The side that had lost a leg was lying on top of a large statue of Fiach-Ra that was ready to give out at any second.

Zeroth urged Steve to hurry up as the boy continued looking for his lost glasses. Steve ignored Zeroth while he and Eira climbed out of the cockpit. Zeroth's wings flapped out from under his cloak and he held Eira so they could glide to the ground safely.

After landing in the stone square, Zeroth noticed that Steve was still in the cockpit.

"Hurry up!" he yelled, "That thing is going to fall over!"

"Do you want me to be blind?" Steve yelled. He could still see without his glasses, but not well.

"I'd rather you be blind than crushed!" Eira hollered in an uncharacteristic scolding tone.

With that, Steve gave up and was about to leave the cockpit. He got to the window and looked down at Zeroth. The bird-man held out his arms, expecting Steve to jump down so he could catch him.

"…You have to be kidding," Steve said.

"I'll catch you," assured Zeroth.

"Uh, *yeah*," replied Steve. "I don't think so. I'll climb down."

"There's no time!" Eira said, pointing to the crumbling statue.

"*Fine*," sighed Steve as he lifted one leg up. Just before he jumped, a thought came to him. "Wait just a second!" he yelled down to Zeroth and Eira as he climbed back through the shattered window of the cockpit. Both Eira and Zeroth sighed as they watched the boy disappear into the damaged airship.

Steve walked lightly across the floor, but as fast he could. He scolded himself; he had almost left the airship without the Staff of Arcana and his blue heron amulet. He was almost to the control panel when he heard a loud CRACK and the airship began to tip over to one side.

"Get out of there!" Zeroth bellowed from the outside.

Steve lunged for the Staff of Arcana, which reverted to its normal shape as he pulled it out of the control panel. He made it to the shattered window and quickly jumped out just before the airship crashed to the ground. Zeroth caught the boy as promised with his outstretched arms.

"Ooof," Zeroth grunted as he let Steve down. "You're heavier than you look."

"Nice to see you too," Steve replied sarcastically as he squinted at his feathered friend.

Steve turned and surveyed the damage done to *The Defender*. The once majestic airship now laid sprawled out on the stone court yard, resembling a bluish-silver scrap pile.

"Eeeugh," winced Steve as he looked at the tattered airship. "I hope whoever owned that has insurance and a decent deductible."

"Speaking of ducks," started Zeroth.

"No, not a duck. A deduc…wait what do you mean?"

Zeroth pointed up to the night sky. Steve crossed his arms and cleared his throat loudly. After Zeroth looked back at him confused, Steve pointed out his lack of glasses.

"Oh right," apologized Zeroth. "Alexander," he said pointing to *The Griffin* floating in the air over the city.

"Ah-ha, so it was his cannon ball that destroyed the statue," Steve said, thankful that another friend had shown up to help. Steve glanced around the wicked city of Da'Rahga. Most of the buildings were destroyed or heavily damaged as a result of Quorix exploding and *The Defender*'s crash landing.

"I really hope I don't get blamed for this," said Steve, who had already earned the title Destroyer of Cities thanks to the Hawk-King.

Steve looked up and saw that the only building not damaged from Quorix's fire and lava was Fiach-Ra's castle, Arx Vena'Tor. The statue of Zuu that had sat on top of the castle's egg shaped rotunda had been destroyed, but other than that, the castle looked unscathed.

"I found your glasses!" called Eira.

Steve turned quickly and ran to join the pelican-lady. "Where are they?" asked Steve.

"Down there," she said, pointing to section of the airship on the ground. Steve looked down. He saw one black plastic arm of his glasses sticking out from under the wreckage.

"Uh," started Steve "Forget it."

"Well, at least you know where they are," Eira added with a smile.

"…*Yeah*."

A massive BOOM shook the air and everyone looked in the direction of the sound. A giant ball of flame exploded from under a distant pile of rubble and shot up into the air. As the ball of fire climbed higher, a set of large feathery wings sprang from it. After the wings flapped, a loud angry bellow echoed across the night sky.

It was the Hawk-King, and as he darted through the sky, the flames covering him disappeared, revealing his unharmed body. High above Da'Rahga, he looked down at the destruction done to his city, causing him to bellow angrily once more.

With a thunderous flap of his wings Fiach-Ra took off for his castle, diving down through the open roof of his throne room.

Steve held up the Staff of Arcana and adjusted his chain mail vest. He glanced up at the ominous castle and then back at his two friends, "Well, I guess this is it," he said, referring to his impending showdown with the Hawk-King.

Eira joined the boy and they began walking towards the castle. He noticed Zeroth was still next to the airship, "Are you coming?" asked the boy. Zeroth nodded slowly but avoided Steve's gaze, "I need something from my pack. I'll catch up, don't worry."

Steve nodded and grasped the Staff of Arcana tightly, wondering how he was going to battle the Hawk-King without the Sword of Zaa. He was so preoccupied about not having the mythical sword that he completely forgot that his protective blue heron amulet was left behind in the wreckage of *The Defender*.

42

"**W**ait for me!" Uncle Shameless bellowed from above. Rosco chirped loudly as he glided down to the stone courtyard near Steve and Eira, while Zeroth remained near the wreckage of *The Defender*, rummaging through his magical pack.

"'Bout time you showed up," Steve said. Uncle Shameless tried to carefully climb down from Rosco's back, but slipped and landed hard on the stone ground. "Ow!" he yelled loudly, his voice bouncing around the stone courtyard.

"Keep it down, will ya?" snapped Steve, "We're kinda trying to sneak in."

Uncle Shameless rubbed his sore back as he slowly stood up. He looked up at Arx Vena'Tor and shuddered, remembering his last visit. "Why do you wanna go in there again?"

"I have to go inside there and stick it to the Hawk-King...Y'know, the *whole* reason we've been on this quest from the beginning."

Uncle Shameless took several sips of wine while he thought about what Steve had just explained, "Oooh *yeah*," Uncle Shameless answered eventually.

"Good, now as I was saying – we're trying to sneak in so try and keep it dow-"

"*HEY!*" screamed Uncle Shameless, his voice echoing wildly off the remains of the city. "You lost your glasses!"

Steve held back the urge to yell at his uncle, "Yes, I know. Now, please – *be quiet*."

Uncle Shameless stumbled over to Steve and wrapped a noodle like arm around his nephew.

"Don't worry boy, you can count on yer ol' uncle," he whispered.

Steve nodded, "Good, I'm glad-"

"*RIGHT ROSCO?!*" Uncle Shameless hollered at the top of his lungs. Rosco let loose a thunderous roar, which rattled the courtyard.

Steve threw up his arms, "Why don't you just yell 'Hey, Hawk-King, we're here'? Y'know, and make it even easier for him?" the boy snapped in a nasty tone. "And another thing-" started Steve.

"Uh..." Uncle Shameless rambled, lifting up an arm to point.

"Let me finish-"

"Uh…" Uncle Shameless rambled again.

"Will you stop interrupting me?" yelled Steve, slapping his uncle's arm down.

"Uh…" began Uncle Shameless, lifting his arm and pointing again.

"What?" asked Steve, following his uncle's point to a sizable group of Hawken and Swantan warriors that had formed around Steve, Eira, Uncle Shameless and Rosco.

"Oh, *crumbs*," sighed Steve.

"Silence hu-man!" yelled a burly Hawken warrior as he jabbed a spear at Steve.

The boy held up his hands, "Okay okay, take it easy."

The Hawken blinked several times, confused. "Take *what* easy?"

"It's just a saying," answered Steve.

"It doesn't make much sense," said the burly Hawken. Several of his comrades nodded in agreement.

"Yes, well I didn't make it up-"

"Silence!" the burly warrior yelled again as he gently prodded Steve's chain mail with the tip of his spear.

"You guys really need to get a thesaurus," Steve, who was growing tired of hearing one word sentences, joked.

The Hawken warrior lowered his spear and thought for a moment. "A what?"

"A *thesaurus*."

"Ain't they dead?" asked a hefty Swantan warrior with an eye patch.

"No-" started Steve, shaking his head.

"I think you mean *extinct*," added a lanky Hawken with a fancy belt "They are all *extinct*."

"*No-ooo!*" yelled Steve, "They aren't extinct!"

"Wait, so they ain't dead…but they smells bad?" asked a pudgy Swantan who was scratching his back with a spiked club.

"No-" Steve tried again.

"Extinct means something is gone forever, not that they smell," explained the lanky Hawken.

"I dunno," said the pudgy Swantan, "I heard them thesauruses could smell pretty bad."

"I'm confused," confessed the burly Hawken with the spear.

"Yeah, me too," added the Swantan with the eye-patch.

"IT'S A BOOK!" Steve screamed.

"Oh that's *right*," agreed the burly Hawken. "You were thinking of those really old creatures," he said to the Swantan with the eye-patch, "*They* are the things that are extra stinky-"

"Extinct," corrected the lanky Hawken.

"Right, right," replied the burly Hawken as he turned to face Steve "So, you mean we need to – *HEY!*" he yelled at Steve and the others who had been silently sneaking away (which was impressive considering that Rosco was the size of a bus), "Stop right there!"

The companions all looked at the menagerie of warriors behind them before simultaneously breaking into a run and heading for the front entrance of Arx Vena'Tor.

"Halt!" bellowed a mighty voice from above. Steve sighed as he skidded to a stop, "Now *what*?"

"You shall not enter! U'nala forbids it!" bellowed the aged Wing-Master. He was standing on a balcony several stories above Steve.

"Oh yeah? And what are *you* gonna do about it?" Steve taunted.

"Wh-wha-who..." U'nala stuttered, caught off guard by Steve's taunting. "Why, you little...U'nala shall show you a new meaning of pain! Prepare to be conquered!" U'nala proudly stepped from the shadows of the balcony and stood up on the stone railing.

"Oh...*my*," Eira gasped as she looked up at U'nala.

The Wing-Master had strapped to his body a harness made of thick metal. On the back of the harness a series of cables and pulleys ran to his remaining wing and to an oddly shaped, poorly built fake metal wing on the other side of U'nala's back.

"Behold!" U'nala yelled into the night sky, "As U'nala flies again!"

U'nala began flapping both of his wings and then jumped into the sky, ready to take flight thanks to his homemade wing.

Sadly, he fell like a rock.

"Ouch!" cried Steve, as U'nala painfully crashed into the ground with a sound like a suit of armor falling down several flights of stair, leaving an U'nala-shaped crater in the courtyard.

"Ow!" added Uncle Shameless, as he cringed thinking about how much that must have hurt.

"That couldn't have felt good," said Eira.

U'nala very slowly and very painfully lifted his head up from the stone floor of the courtyard. "G...gu...guards...," he whimpered before collapsing again.

The Hawken and Swantan guards that Steve and his companions had been running away from gave chase once more.

"Gahh!" yelled Steve as he turned to flee from a hissing swan-man wielding a filthy looking net.

"Uggh," whimpered the fallen Wing-Master. "U'nala landed on his keys."

Steve, Uncle Shameless, and Eira were just about scurry onto Rosco when there was a loud CRACK as something struck the ground in front of them. They all coughed and choked as they were enveloped in a thick, white gaseous cloud.

"What…" was all Steve had time to gasp before he collapsed to the stone courtyard, fast asleep. Uncle Shameless and Eira fell down next to him, also fast asleep, as did Rosco. The Hawken and Swantan warriors stopped short of their targets, keeping away from the swirling cloud of sleeping gas.

As the wind blew away the villainous cloud, the Hawk-King's warriors spied a cloaked shape approaching, with a yellow scarf flapping around his neck. The warriors snarled at the approaching stranger and readied their weapons. There was a flash of silver as the cloaked stranger readied his swordfish and jumped at the warriors, disabling all of their weapons with as series of blurry slashes.

"Delu," Zeroth commanded distantly as the warriors looked over their now useless weapons. "I want to see *Delu*."

43

The Hawk-King's loyal spy solidified in front of Zeroth moments later, hacking and wheezing sickly the whole time. After throwing open his Caper Cape, the wraith-like raven clutched his chest and wheezed loudly for several moments before settling down.

"You're sounding better," Zeroth joked as Delu shambled over to him. The raven spy ignored the Hunter's taunt and looked over at the rest of the companions sleeping soundly on the stone courtyard.

"Impres...sive," wheezed Delu. "I did...not...th...ink...you would actually do...it."

"You have to look out for number one," Zeroth recited without emotion "I'm sure you would have done the same if you were me."

"True...tr...ue," agreed Delu, the words oozing slowly out of his beak. "A For...mal Hun..ter Complaint dash TB is...a hard...thing to live...with."

The raven laughed hollowly as he snapped his brittle, stick-like fingers and motioned for a pair of Swantan warriors to grab Steve.

"Hold it," snapped Zeroth as he pointed the tip of Gladius' bladetongue at Delu's neck. "Aren't you forgetting something?"

Delu coughed wetly as he reached into a pocket and pulled out a sealed parchment envelope "Sil...ly me," he wheezed as he held it out for Zeroth. "A deal...is...a de...al."

Zeroth smirked slyly as he snatched the envelope out of the raven's boney hand. He lowered Gladius away from Delu's neck and began to open the envelope.

"You won't mind if I make sure you're holding up you're end of the deal?" asked Zeroth as he broke the seal on the envelope, "Nothing personal."

Delu shook his head weakly, "Of course...not," his eerie saucer-like eyes stayed focused on the Hunter as he took a letter out of the envelope.

"Good, I'm glad you-"

Zeroth hacked loudly as a small cloud of glittery dust exploded in his face after he unfolded the letter. His eyes instantly grew heavy and his limbs started to go weak as he breathed in the mysterious dust, forcing him to drop the blank letter from his clawed hand.

Zeroth tried to swing Gladius at the cackling Delu but the swordfish fell from his hand and clanged loudly on the ground.

"*Delu!*" Zeroth cursed as he was gripped by a vengeful, unnatural sleep. The raven spy gave the sleeping Zeroth a swift quick to the midsection as he lay passed out on the ground, "Nev...er trust...a spy," cackled Delu as he ordered the Hawken and Swantan guards around him to collect their new prisoners.

High above the courtyard aboard *The Griffin*, Alexander the Small lowered his spyglass as a fierce look of anger washed over his face.

44

Zeroth awoke later to someone poking him with a stick. "Wha's dat?" asked a voice over him.

"Dunno, but he shar is oogly," answered another voice as Zeroth was prodded with the stick again. Zeroth's eyes snapped open; he grabbed the stick from its owner and quickly sat up.

"Eeek! It *lives!*" screamed one of the voices as Zeroth growled loudly and swung the stick madly.

As the bird-man's eyes adjusted to the darkness around him, he saw two little ducks scurry away to the other side of what looked like a dungeon cell. Zeroth held his pounding head as he stood up and studied his new surroundings.

"*Great,*" Zeroth sighed as he realized he was in the dungeon of Arx Vena'Tor. A series of loud, shocked gasps told him that he was not alone in his cell.

The Hunter spun around to see at least twenty duck-people of various sizes, ages and genders in the cell with him. For the moment they were all huddled together and collectively wearing terrified looks as Zeroth approached them.

"Easy there," Zeroth spoke calmly as he dropped the stick. "I'm not your enemy."

"Den who is ya?" asked a crotchety sounding older duck with faded brown feathers, pointing at Zeroth with his corncob pipe.

"I'm a..." Zeroth almost said Hunter but decided against it, not wanting to cause anymore problems. "I'm a prisoner, just like all of you." The huddling ducks all breathed a sigh of relief in unison and went back to idly walking around the cell or sitting on the damp floor.

Zeroth walked over to the bars of the cell and inspected the lock. It was old, rusty and complicated looking. But, Zeroth figured he might be able to pick it as he instinctively reached for his magical pack.

"Argh!" he yelled as he realized his pack had been taken away. The Hunter gently banged his head against the bars of the cell in frustration.

"This wasn't s'pose to happen," he sighed, cursing his own carelessness for trusting Delu. His lamenting came to a stop when he heard a crowd of ducks in a nearby cell erupt into a roar of quack-like laughter.

Zeroth glanced down the hallway of the dungeon and peered into the cell diagonally across from him. Moments later, he heard a familiar voice tell a familiarly bad joke.

"And so then the first guy says, 'rectum? I darn near killed 'em!'"

The crowd of ducks erupted once more into thunderous roar of quacking laughter.

"Shameless?" called Zeroth.

"Zeroth!" answered Uncle Shameless from the cell on the other side of the dungeon. He ran to the bars, towering over his small ducky audience. "They got you too, eh?"

"Ye-yes," Zeroth stuttered as he lied to Uncle Shameless, "Yes they did. I tried to help all of you, but I was ambushed. What are you doing?"

"Just tellin' some jokes to these duckies to pass the time, they can't get enough of 'em!" Uncle Shameless beamed, happy to finally have found an appreciative audience.

"I see," replied Zeroth. "Where is everyone else?"

"I'm here too!" Eira called from the cell next to Uncle Shameless', which was also packed full of duck-people.

"Why are all of these ducks down here?" asked Zeroth, spying several more cells packed full of the tiny bird-people.

"They are from Tal," explained a familiar voice at the back of Zeroth's cell. The bird-man spun around to see the duck Mudd as he emerged from the shadows with Tuuga, the owner of the Lighthouse Inn, next to him.

"Mudd!" Zeroth exclaimed as he knelt down next to the duck and the turtle innkeeper. "So it was true that the survivors from Tal were brought back to Arx Vena'Tor?"

Mudd held out his arms, "Well this ain't a family reunion," joked the webbed-footed barkeep.

"I don't know what the Hawk-King plans to do with us, and honestly I don't want to," added Tuuga.

"Don't worry, I'll think of something," assured Zeroth as he walked back to the front of the cell. He tried to get Uncle Shameless' attention, but the man was too busy leading his cell-mates in a loud chorus of 'What Do You Do With a Drunken Sailor?'

"*Shameless!*" Zeroth yelled forcefully.

"-*Early in the mornin'!*" Uncle Shameless sang before noticing Zeroth's shouting. "Oh, sorry. Yes?"

"What about Steve and Rosco?" Zeroth asked, with a hint of fear in his voice.

"I dunno, when I woke up I was in 'ere," explained Uncle Shameless.

"Me too," Eira added from the neighboring cell.

Mudd walked up to Zeroth and pulled on the sleeve of his black cloak, "I saw them carry The Boy off down the hall, through that door," the duck pointed to a creepy looking door at the other end of the hallway.

A thought occurred to Zeroth, "How long have we been here?" he asked.

Mudd shrugged, "Not too long, less than a hour I think."

Zeroth thought for a moment. He knew enough about the Hawk-King to know if Fiach-Ra had done something to Steve already, he would have come down here to gloat about it in front of them. Or he would have dragged them out of the dungeon to witness whatever he had in store for Steve firsthand.

Zeroth smirked as he realized that there was an advantage to being the prisoner of a megalomaniac: he was very predictable.

"Shameless, can you bend those bars?" Zeroth asked.

"*Stick 'em in a long boat 'til he's sober! Stick 'em in a long boat 'til he's sober!*" Uncle Shameless sang along with a score of feathered back-up singers.

"*SHAMELESS!*" Zeroth screamed loudly.

"Oops, sorry. Whatcha need?"

Zeroth rolled his eyes, beginning to understand why Steve did it so often, and repeated himself "Can you bend those bars?"

"Nuthin' doin'" answered Uncle Shameless. "They wised up and took my wine away."

Zeroth eyes widened, "Wait, so you've been telling jokes and singing while sober?"

"'Course."

"Why?"

"'Cause it's fun!" Uncle Shameless answered truthfully. "Right everyone?!" he asked his cellmates as they all jumped back into their song, much to Zeroth's annoyance. The loud singing was quickly interrupted by a pair of hefty Swantan guards running down the hall towards Uncle Shameless' cell.

"For the last time, *no singing!*" yelled a guard with breath that smelled like a dirty mop bucket. As the guard had his back to Zeroth, the Hunter noticed Uncle Shameless' wine skin and Gladius tucked into the guard's belt.

"Hmm," thought Zeroth, trying to think of a plan.

After the guards clanged their heavy swords against the bars of the cell, Uncle Shameless and the ducks finally stopped their dungeon cell concert. "Sheesh, everyone's a critic," mumbled Uncle Shameless.

"Where is The Boy?" Zeroth demanded as the guards passed by his cell.

"Don't worry," one of the guards laughed wickedly "You'll see him soon – when he's sacrificed to Zuu at dawn."

"No!" Eira and Uncle Shameless yelled from their cells. Zeroth let out a sigh of relief after learning they had until dawn to save Steve from wherever he was being kept.

Steve groggily opened his eyes and groaned. He slowly sat up on the cold stone floor, wondering where he was.

"Ugh," moaned the boy as he lifted his arms to rub his sore head. As he did, there was a rattle of chains. He looked down to see that his arms were chained to the wall by a set of long, rusty chains. Steve looked for the Staff of Arcana and was glad to see it was still in his pocket. He decided to keep it there for now.

He looked around and guessed that he was in some sort of cell as he noticed the lone stone window in the wall. It had thick bars criss-crossing through it.

"*Swell,*" Steve said sarcastically after figuring out he was in yet another of Arx Vena'Tor's cells. He slowly stood up and looked out the window. He looked out over a courtyard that was lit by dozens of torches.

By the torchlight Steve noticed that the courtyard was made of a circular pattern of colored bricks. The outermost ring was a deep, fire-red, the next orange and the last a brilliant yellow.

On the edge of the courtyard was a tall section of wall with a large circle cut into it and Steve wondered what it was for. A deep moan from the side of the courtyard caught the boy's attention and he looked as best he could without his glasses. Even without his necessary spectacles, he had no problem making out the bulky shape of the Roc Lobster chained to the floor of the courtyard.

"Rosco!" the boy exclaimed, hoping that somehow the creature might be able to hear him. Rosco looked like he was asleep in addition to being chained down. Steve could just barely make out what look liked primitive rubber bands wrapped around the beast's massive pincher claws, rendering them useless.

From his lookout, Steve could see that even Rosco's whip-like tendrils had been tied down, and heavy chains were wrapped around his crushing beak.

Steve saw Hawken scurrying around the courtyard and looking like they were getting ready for something. He was so busy watching the warriors work that he did not notice the door open behind him.

"What are they doing?" Steve said aloud, still thinking he was alone.

"Preparing," replied a gruff voice behind him.

"Ahhh!" Steve screamed as he spun around to see a short, squatty vulture in red robes. "Who're you?!"

"A Mystic of Zuu," answered the vulture in fire-red robes. "I am to be your...*attendant*."

Steve did not understand what the Mystic meant by that, but he had a feeling it was not anything good. The boy pointed a thumb towards the courtyard beyond his window, "What is that?"

"The Altar of Zuu," answered the Mystic as he set down a dirty cup of water and a plate of fuzzy bread. He joined Steve by the window and pointed a clawed finger at the wall with the circular hole. "When the Eye of Zuu rises at dawn, its light shines through that hole and illuminates the center of the circular Altar."

Steve shuddered involuntarily and decided he had been happier not knowing what had been lying outside his window. The Mystic turned to leave, but Steve had one more question,

"You said the warriors outside were preparing, what for?"

The Mystic stopped and slowly turned to face Steve in a very eerie manner, "What for? Why, a sacrifice of course."

"What kind of sacrifice?"

"*Yours*."

A few moments later, after the guards had returned to their post Uncle Shameless thought he saw something dash by his cell. He rubbed his eyes and looked again, only seeing the endless shadows of the hallway. The man shrugged and sat on a moldy cot.

Uncle Shameless started to doze off until he heard what sounded like someone trying to get his attention. He sat up and peered into the hallway again. "Hello?" he said.

"*Shameless,*" a high pitched voice faintly responded from the shadows. Uncle Shameless gulped loudly; afraid of whom the voice belonged to "Y-y-yes?"

"*We're here to help,*" the faint voice explained replied, sounding as if it was moving closer to the cell, which did nothing to ease Uncle Shameless' fears.

"G-gg-ga-ga-gg-!" Uncle Shameless stuttered, pointing to the shadows just outside his cell.

"*Shhh!*" shushed the voice as it approached the cell again. "*Keep it down!*"

Eira looked over at Uncle Shameless from her cell, "Are you okay over there?"

"GHOSTS!" Uncle Shameless answered, biting his nails out of terror.

"Oh forget it," snapped the mystery voice "C'mon," the voice continued as two short shapes clad in what looked like black pajamas, stepped into the circle of torch light next to Uncle Shameless' cell.

But all the man could see were eyes through a slit in the black masks and cooking implements resting on top of their heads.

Even though the head accessories seemed somewhat familiar to Uncle Shameless, he still felt the need to let out a loud, frightened shriek.

"Keep it down!" commanded one of the black-clad strangers. "We're trying to rescue you!"

"Who're you?!" Uncle Shameless asked as he peered at the pair through the hand covering his eyes.

"It's *me,*" started the very short stranger as he pulled the bottom of his black mask to reveal a familiar duck face. "Alexander the Small!" the pint-sized duck captain finished dramatically.

"Oh, hello," replied Uncle Shameless, finally recognizing his former traveling companion. Next to Alexander, Hector pulled down his black mask as well.

"I'm so glad to see you!" Eira called from the neighboring cell. Alexander walked over and bowed respectfully. "And I you, lady pelican."

Zeroth snapped to attention and ran to the bars, "Alexander I need you to-"

The short duck spun around and gave Zeroth a defiant look, "I'm not helping you do anything, *traitor*."

A chill shot down Zeroth's spine as Alexander waddled closer to his cell, "You can *rot* in here for all I care," the duck captain cursed. Next to him Hector nodded in agreement.

"What do you mean?" Eira asked as she leaned as far out of the bars as she could.

"Oh, you don't know?" Alexander replied cynically. "He's the reason you all got captured, he betrayed you and turned you in."

Zeroth said nothing as he lowered his head and stared at the floor of his cell.

"No," Eira gasped.

"Whatcha talkin' 'bout?!" Uncle Shameless demanded.

"It's true, I saw it all through my spyglass on *The Griffin*. He knocked all of you out with some kinda sleeping gas and turned you over to the Hawk-King's spy. They had some sort of deal it seemed," explained Alexander as he trotted confidently back and forth in front of Zeroth's cell. Inside the cell, all of the ducks around Zeroth quickly moved away, shaking their heads in disapproval.

"But things didn't go as planned did they?" Alexander snapped, straining his neck as he looked up at the considerably taller Zeroth, "'cause that spy double-crossed him."

In the other cells, Uncle Shameless' jaw had dropped and Eira gasped speechlessly.

"The only thing I don't know is *why*," Alexander continued. "After all you've been through with The Boy, why would you do that?"

Zeroth sighed loudly as he looked down at Alexander. "Because, the Kingdom filed a Formal Hunter Compliant Form against me."

Alexander shook his head, "So?"

"A Form dash TB," Zeroth finished. Alexander and Hectors' eyes widened with shock. "And Delu said if I brought Steve to Arx Vena'Tor, he would give me the Form before it was sent out."

"*Oooh*," Alexander and Hector said in unison, understanding instantly. Uncle Shameless rested his head against the bars of his cell, "What's so bad about a piece of paper that you'd hand over my nephew?!" he spat angrily.

"It isn't the Form itself," explained Zeroth. "It is what happens after the Form is received by the Lodge is what I am worried about," he sighed loudly "And just so we're clear, my plan was after I got the Form from Delu, I was going to rescue all of you."

"That's a pretty reckless plan," snapped Eira. "Why didn't you tell any of us?"

"It couldn't look like you were in on it, I'm sorry," apologized Zeroth. "I should have known Delu would double-cross me, I was careless."

Uncle Shameless cleared his throat loudly, "I'm a little out of the loop here, but what happens after this Lodge gets that Form?" he asked, making Zeroth, Alexander and Hector noticeably shudder in unison.

"Listen," began Zeroth as he hesitated to say what he was about to say. "And listen *well*."

45

"Long ago," Zeroth began eerily, "Hunters were undisciplined and wild. Some would change sides in battles just because the opposing side offered them more money, or they wouldn't capture their targets because of bribery."

Alexander and Hector nodded in agreement as Zeroth continued, "After the bloody Hunter Wars, the few remaining Hunters decided changes had to be made. Thus the Lodge was formed and would act as a governing body for all Hunters, and all jobs would require contracts."

"Okay," yawned Uncle Shameless, "But I don't see why you got so worked up."

"I'm getting to that," explained Zeroth. "In order to thwart Hunters from breaking their signed contracts with clients, it was decided by the Lodge that there needed to be someone to enforce the Hunter's Code, someone to scare the ranks of Hunters into behaving."

Uncle Shameless sat down again but kept listening to Zeroth's history of the Hunters.

"Five Hunters, from five of the best bands of Hunters, were chosen to form a *super* band."

"So?" asked Uncle Shameless.

"*So* pay attention, this part is important," answered Zeroth. "These five then had a magic spell put upon them to increase their abilities-"

"Big deal," interrupted Uncle Shameless.

"*And* this spell also made them nigh-immortal, so that no other Hunter could stop them."

"Oh," answered Uncle Shameless, starting to figure out why Zeroth had been so worried.

"Yes," replied Zeroth, noticing the understanding look on Uncle Shameless' face. "The only side effect was that the spell turned them into living skeletons, but very different and far more dangerous from those we fought at Arx A'Quila."

It was Uncle Shameless' turn to shudder as he recalled his many fights with the relentless owl skeletons at Fel-Ra's castle atop Tyton Mountain.

"And it was from this side effect that the band got their infamous name," Zeroth hesitated, afraid to utter the cursed words, *The Roving Bones.*" All of the ducks nearby gasped in unison at the mention of the notorious band of Hunters.

Zeroth let out a worried sigh. "Any Hunter that has a Formal Hunter Complaint Form dash TB filed against them faces the wrath of The Roving Bones," Zeroth gripped the bars of his cell uneasily "They hunt you down, no matter where you are, no matter who you are, they will find you. They cannot be stopped."

"Then what?" asked Uncle Shameless "They kill ya?"

Zeroth shook his head as he continued his gloomy story. "No, you aren't that lucky."

Uncle Shameless' teeth started chattering nervously, "Well, what happens?"

Zeroth shuddered "No one really knows for sure, but I've heard stories. *Terrifying* stories."

"Like what?"

Zeroth answered in a distant somber tone, nearly choking on the words. He shared stories of the fates of those caught by the infamous band of Hunters. Everyone in the dungeon screamed in unison, terrified beyond belief. Alexander jumped into Hector's arms, mortified. His penguin first-mate patted him reassuringly on the back.

"Th-that's *horrid!*" yelled Uncle Shameless, suddenly feeling very ill.

"Yes," Zeroth nodded weakly. "So now you know why I had to try and stop Fiach-Ra from sending away that Form."

Uncle Shameless stood up and leaned against the bars of his cell, "No one should have to suffer through somethin' like that," replied Uncle Shameless as he shook his head and looked Zeroth in the eyes. "I forgive ya."

"As do I," added Alexander the Small, climbing down from Hector's arms.

"You should have just told us," Eira scolded, "But I forgive you too."

"Thank you everyone," Zeroth answered with an appreciative smile. "Now, let's get outta here."

"What do you mean, 'yours'?" Steve asked the vulture Mystic of Zuu, as he tried to remain calm.

The squatty Mystic shook his featherless head. "What do you think I mean? You are going to be sacrificed by the Hawk-King at dawn."

"Bu-but *why?*"

"Sacrificing you to Zuu will stop the Prophecy," explained the Mystic as thunder cracked in the distance, "And allow the Hawk-King to continue his glorious reign."

"*Oh,*" answered Steve as the Mystic chuckled coldly and left the cell, slamming the door behind him. Steve immediately took the Staff of Arcana out of his pocket and thought of a sharp axe. With all his remaining strength, Steve swung the conjured axe at one of the brackets holding his chains to the wall. There was a flash of red light as the axe bounced off the metal bracket, leaving it unharmed.

Steve blinked his eyes in silence several times and grabbed a hold of the cell's bars. He stared out into the night sky. "Just keep cool, everything will be fine," he assured himself. "They'll rescue me before…before I'm sacrificed at dawn to an eagle made of fire."

One of Steve's eyes twitched wildly several times before he finally lost control, "*GET ME OUTTA HERE!*" he screamed loudly.

"Don't worry," Alexander the Small assured proudly, "I have a plan. Hector, the bomb please."

"Bomb?" asked Zeroth, "You can't be serious!"

"I'm always serious when it comes to explosives," replied Alexander as he held out a hand, waiting for the bomb.

"You'll hurt someone, not to mention you'll let everyone in the castle know we've escaped!" yelled Zeroth.

"Never you mind," countered Alexander as he turned to face his taller first-mate "Hector, *the bomb!*"

Hector the penguin looked at his captain and shrugged.

"What?! Don't tell me you forgot it!" yelled Alexander. Hector shrugged again.

"Keep it down," shushed Zeroth, "You'll alert the guards."

"Sorry, sorry," Alexander replied quietly, but still visibly irritated "Well, that was my only plan."

"Don't worry," Zeroth said. "I'll think of something, but I just wish I had my magical pack."

"What, this old thing?" asked Alexander as he held up Zeroth's small pack.

"Yes!" Zeroth exclaimed quietly, "But how'd you get it?"

Alexander passed the small pack through the bars of the cell to Zeroth "When those guards came to yell at Shameless for singing, they left it on their table. I was going to keep it, y'know out of spite."

"I'm glad you changed your mind," said Zeroth, relieved to have his pack returned. The Hunter looked at his many cell mates, and then at the other citizens from Tal imprisoned in the rest of the dungeon. Zeroth decided that he needed to help them escape as well.

But he did not know if he'd have time to pick all of the locks of each of the cells (assuming he could even pick his own cell's lock), or if he wanted to risk attacking the guards to get the keys.

As the Hunter looked down at his magical pack again, inspiration quickly struck him.

"I will say this tops the list of zaniest plans that I have ever been a part of," Alexander the Small exclaimed as duck after duck disappeared into Zeroth's magical pack.

"Just keep quiet and we'll all be out of here in no time," ordered Zeroth as he lowered the last of his cellmates into the magic pack. The Hunter then set the pack on the ground close to the bars and climbed into the science defying pack himself, pulling the lid shut as his arm disappeared into the bread loaf sized pack.

"Well, here goes," Alexander said as he reached through the bars, grabbed the pack, and pulled it out of the cell. The small duck captain spun around in the hallway and set the pack on the ground as Zeroth had instructed, opened the lid, reached inside and pulled Zeroth out by the top his head.

Once Zeroth was out of the pack past his beak, the Hunter lifted out his arms and pulled himself up out of the pack.

"Zaa's Beak, that is *peculiar*," Alexander added as Zeroth began pulling his webbed footed cell mates out of the pack one by one.

"Just try hidin' in that thing for a spell," Uncle Shameless called from his cell, "Now that's *really* weird."

"Shhh," shushed Zeroth as he continued pulling ducks out of his pack and setting them down. Pretty soon the hallway was littered with little duck prisoners.

"So, yer gonna do that to *every* cell?" Uncle Shameless asked as he looked up and down the hallway at the scores of ducks locked up in numerous cells.

"*Yes!*" Zeroth snapped, "*Now keep quiet!*"

Everyone froze as Zeroth's loud words echoed down the hallway. After several tense heartbeats, Zeroth decided everything was safe and continued removing ducks from his pack.

Luckily for Zeroth, the two burly Swantan guards were locked in a fierce game of 'X's an' O's.' It was fierce because both of the muscle-headed guards kept forgetting who was the X and who was the O.

After being taken out Zeroth's pack, Mudd quickly waddled over and hugged his cousin Alexander. However, as he grabbed a hold of his smaller cousin, Mudd accidentally knocked the dented cooking pot (with Vanderawlt's crossbow bolt still stuck in it) off his head. The iron pot clanged loudly on the floor of the dungeon.

"Wazzdat?" said one of the Swantan guards, standing up and drawing his sword as his partner tried to decide to draw a X or an O.

The guard ran quickly to the block of cells holding the ducks and Steve's companions. As the guard turned the corner he saw Zeroth pulling ducks out of his pack and yelled "Stop right there!"

"*Great*," Zeroth mumbled, realizing he was still weaponless as the hefty guard charged towards him. Zeroth quickly picked up his pack, turned it upside down and shook out the last of the ducks. The surprised mallards quickly waddled away to join the others. Zeroth flipped up his pack so that the opening faced the yelling guard and waited.

When the Swantan guard was only a few feet away, Zeroth jumped at the brute and pushed the pack down onto the guard's swan-like head, making it disappear. Zeroth then quickly pulled the pack down to the ground, making the rest of the guard's body enter the small pack. After reaching the guard's large, webbed feet, Zeroth flipped the pack right side up and snapped the lid closed.

The black-feathered Hunter then began swinging the pack around wildly and smacking it against the bars of the surrounding cells. In the distance Zeroth heard the guard's partner heading for him, and after hitting his pack against more bars, flipped it upside down again and opened the lid.

The bird-man shook the hefty guard out of his magical pack, leaving the Swantan, dazed from his wild ride inside Zeroth's pack, collapsed on the floor of the dungeon. Zeroth then placed a taloned, webbed foot under the Swantan's sword and kicked it up at the second guard. The heavy sword spun in the air and its large hilt smacked the charging Swantan right it the face.

The bulky guard swayed to and fro for a second before dropping to the floor like a ton of bricks. Zeroth quickly wrapped his pack around his waist and secured it as the Tal ducks broke into a thunderous applause around him. Zeroth modestly disregarded the ducks' applause as he removed Uncle Shameless' wineskin and Gladius from one of the knocked out guard's belts.

Zeroth tossed Uncle Shameless his wineskin and gave Gladius a hard squeeze. He looked over the ducks in front of him and those still waiting to be freed and then down at the door that Steve had been taken through.

In the hallway beyond the door Steve had been taken through to get to his cell, a Hawken warrior sat in an uncomfortable chair, with his taloned feet resting on the table next to him. Instead of keeping watch like he had been ordered to, he was busy reading the Late Late Edition of Da'Rahga's own newspaper, *The Da'Rahga Daily*, which was written by the Hawk-King's loyal scribes.

The big, friendly seal on the front page informed every reader that each page was approved by the Hawk-King himself, which made all of the readers feel much better, knowing that they were only getting the best news.

The Da'Rahga Daily was a fairly new idea of Fiach-Ra's, however according to the Hall of Accomplishments the Hawk-King had invented the printing press hundreds of years ago, but had only recently decided to share it with his subjects.

That explained a few things to the guard reading the newspaper, a middle-aged low-ranking Hawken by the name of Ka'nae. He had been to the Hall of Accomplishments when he was younger, and he did not remember seeing a tapestry portraying the Accomplishment of inventing the printing press back then. But he figured the Hawk-King had his reasons for waiting to share his great invention with his people. He was *King* after all.

As Ka'nae was staring down at an article detailing just how badly the Hawk-King had once again defeated the owls in battle earlier that night, Ka'nae thought he heard metal groaning in the distance, as if it were being bent. Ka'nae quickly lowered his paper and glanced around the hallway, but he did not see or hear anything.

The guard shrugged and continued reading about the earlier battle outside the castle. Ka'nae had thought the Hawk-King had cursed and banished the owls forever, but according to the article Fiach-Ra had brought the owls back just so he could defeat them once more and teach them a proper lesson all over again.

Ka'nae thought that did not make much sense, but he just shrugged and decided if it was in *The Da'Rahga Daily*, it had to be true. The sound of little webbed feet slapping against the stone floor caught Ka'nae's attention. He dropped his paper again and looked. Nothing.

Ka'nae put the paper down on the table and got up, picking up his spear in the process. The Hawken guard looked down both ends of the long, dark hallway. All he saw were torches along the walls and shadows.

Ka'nae leaned his spear against the table and took up his reading position once again and set to work on the paper's crossword puzzle. He was about to fill in the answer for a seven letter word for "Favorite of Zuu," when the sound of webbed feet scurrying across the floor in front of him was heard again.

Ka'nae angrily pulled down his newspaper and just in time to see the tail feathers of a duck waddling quickly past him. The Hawken guard clumsily jumped from his uncomfortable chair, grabbed his spear and yelled at the duck running away.

"Hey! Stop right-" Ka'nae began as he heard even more noise coming from behind him and turned around in mid-sentence "There?"

Just as the last word escaped Ka'nae's hooked beak, he was plowed into by a flood of escaping ducks, knocking him to the ground. Hundreds of little webbed feet trampled the Hawken guard as the escaping prisoners ran down the hall to freedom.

Even so, Ka'nae did his best to try and stop the escaping brown and green water fowl.

"Ha-halt!" Ka'nae tried to yell as scores of ducks walked over his face, "Oof! Ack!"

At the end of the hall the Hawken guard heard yelling.

"That's the last of 'em!" yelled a voice that sounded like it was drenched in wine.

"Right, *let's go!*" replied a sober, commanding voice.

Ka'nae was able to sit up slightly as the tide of webbed feet thinned out, but just as he did, a human in tattered shorts carrying a pelican stepped on his stomach. "Comin' through!" Uncle Shameless bellowed.

"Uggaha!" Ka'nae groaned, struggling to sit up again. No sooner had the lazy guard propped himself up, than his face was stepped on by a large webbed foot with talons, sending his head crashing into the floor.

"Make way!" Zeroth yelled as he followed the duck horde down the rest of the hall.

Ka'nae groaned loudly minutes later as he slowly crawled toward the alarm bell on the nearby wall and tried in vain to ring it before passing out.

"No, no, *no!*" scolded an excessively pudgy Mystic of Zuu at a trio of Hawken warriors trying unsuccessfully to set up a buffet table on the circular Altar of Zuu. "The desert buffet goes *there*," explained the Mystic as he waddled around with the aid of a red cane. He pointed to far side of the Altar. "The dinner buffet goes *here!*" he commanded, banging his cane against the stone courtyard for emphasis.

The three armor-clad warriors mumbled and grumbled as they swapped one bare, wooden table for its identical twin.

"Honestly, how do you expect to have a proper sacrifice without a proper buffet?" the Mystic asked rhetorically. The torches lining the courtyard flickered away in the fading night as Hawken warriors and Mystics of Zuu rushed to have the Altar of Zuu prepared before dawn.

The grossly overweight Mystic, a vulture by the name of Morlavo, waddled over to another group of Hawken warriors who were busy working at a nearby table.

"How're the flower arrangements coming, Wing-Commander?" Morlavo demanded.

A muscular Hawken officer held up a bouquet of flowers so wretched looking, that even a blind honey bee would have been appalled. "*No!*" Morlavo screamed in anger as he slapped the officer with his cane. "Do it over!" the heavyset Mystic of Zuu commanded as he waddled away.

"You there!" Morlavo barked at a pair of gangly Hawken warriors near the entrance to the courtyard, "Quit loafing and set up the sacrificial altar!" The two guards groaned disapprovingly and left their guard post by the entrance.

High above the courtyard, from the window in his cell, Steve watched the events below and wondered why a pair of Hawken warriors were setting up a comfortable looking hammock in the middle of the Altar of Zuu.

Zeroth caught up with Alexander the Small at the front of the throng of escaped ducks, "I think that door will lead us outside,"

Zeroth explained as he peeked around the corner and spotted a door guarded by a pair of Swantan guards.

"Uncanny!" exclaimed Alexander, "How can you tell?"

"The sign next to the door that says 'Exit to Courtyard,'" Zeroth replied plainly.

"...*Uncanny!*"

Zeroth rolled his eyes and held up Gladius as he prepared to take on the guards, alone.

"Wait!" Alexander yelled, grabbing a hold of Zeroth's cloak.

"What now?" asked the much bigger bird-man.

"Allow *me*," demanded the pint-sized, black pajama wearing duck. Zeroth glanced back at the pair of mean looking guards who were leaning on equally mean looking swords.

"I don't think that's a good idea," Zeroth began, but it was too late; Alexander was already heading for the mountainous guards alone. Zeroth tried to give chase, but Hector grabbed his arm and shook his head, "Let him go," replied the penguin.

Alexander strutted confidently around the corner and headed right for the guards. The hefty Swantans immediately noticed the tiny duck and began raising their immense swords.

The guards had not even raised their swords halfway when Alexander let out a deafening battle cry and sprang through the air towards one of them. The little duck spun in mid air and landed a well placed flying kick to the beak of the Swantan on the right.

Alexander spun again after knocking down the guard, stealthy removed his iron cookware helmet and promptly smashed the remaining guard on the head. Alexander did a back flip, landed on his feet and replaced his headgear as the guard collapsed like a fallen tree.

Zeroth's eyes widened to their fullest, amazed by the little duck's abilities. He joined Alexander by the door. Uncle Shameless ran up to the door as well and was followed by Eira a few moments later. Uncle Shameless reached down and picked up Alexander and gave him a sloppy hug, "Good job, li'l buddy!"

Alexander tried to give his thanks, but had a hard time doing so with his beak pressed tightly against Uncle Shameless' chest. Meanwhile, Zeroth inspected the door and was annoyed to find it locked. He searched the two incapacitated guards but could not find a key.

"Drat," Zeroth cursed as he tried the door again in vain.

"What's wrong?" asked Uncle Shameless as he released Alexander from his suffocating grasp.

"The exit's locked and neither of the guards had the key."

Uncle Shameless looked down at the two burly guards and then at the exit, "No key?" he bellowed, cracking his knuckles *"No problem!"*

Zeroth instantly realized what Uncle Shameless had in mind and threw up his arms in protest, "No Shameless, wait!"

"Who put this *here*?!" Morlavo bellowed to no one specific as he tapped a battered wooden podium with his cane. "The podium goes over *there!*" he gestured to the section of the courtyard wall with the large circular hole. The Mystic of Zuu waddled over to a dozing Hawken guard and whacked him upside the head with his cane, "WAKE UP!"

"Who, me?" the guard asked slowly.

"Yes *you!* Move that podium!"

The guard got up lazily and shambled over towards the misplaced podium. "Sorry, I'm not used to workin' nights."

"Keep this up and you won't have to worry about working days *or* nights!" Morlavo screamed as his impatience with the incompetent warriors reached his limit.

"Fools! Slackers! *Loafers!*" Morlavo screamed as he waddled around and inspected the poorly prepared Altar of Zuu. "You imbeciles wouldn't know your dessert from your dinner if it weren't for me! You should all be kissing the ground I walk on!" the Mystic of Zuu screamed, causing all of the Hawken in the courtyard to shudder in unison.

Morlavo turned to look upon the warriors in his charge, prepared to let loose another volley of insults, when suddenly the door he was standing in front of crashed down upon him.

Uncle Shameless jumped through the doorway and landed on the fallen door. He turned and looked back inside the hallway and waved to his scores of companions, "Ducks, *ho-ooooo!*"

An unrelenting stream of brown and green ducks poured out of the castle, each running across the fallen door and into the courtyard. The surprised Hawken warriors dropped their garden shears and salad tongs as they went for their weapons.

The ruckus in the courtyard got Steve's attention and he began yelling as loud as he could when he spotted Uncle Shameless and the others. He wondered where all of the ducks had come from, but decided he didn't have time to worry about that now.

Zeroth slashed at a Hawken as it prepared to fire arrows into a group of escaping ducks. Eira did the best she could with her walking stick, and Uncle Shameless kept jumping up and down on the fallen door, directing the torrent of fleeing ducks into the courtyard.

A low moan across the multicolored courtyard caught Uncle Shameless' ear, "Rosco?" he mumbled as he staggered across the Altar of Zuu.

"O-ooo! *Nice* hammock!" Uncle Shameless exclaimed.

From his lofty cell, Steve continued yelling. But now he was yelling at his uncle to get out of the hammock in the center of the Altar of Zuu.

Zeroth kicked a tall Hawken warrior in the chest and sent him crashing into the desert buffet. The force of the warrior landing on the end of the table catapulted a large bowl of fruit salad through the air. It landed upside down on the napping Uncle Shameless.

"Pbbt!" sputtered Uncle Shameless as he was rudely awoken from his nap in the comfortable hammock by a shower of diced fruit "What's the big idea?!" he bellowed, looking at a nearby Hawken warrior who was holding a ceremonial melon baller. The bird-man fled quickly as Uncle Shameless promptly gave chase.

Up in his cell Steve shook his head as he watched his uncle chase the confused Hawken around the courtyard, "Well, at least he's out of the hammock."

46

Alexander the Small ran up to Zeroth, joined by Mudd, Tugga and his first-mate Hector, "We've found a way out of the castle's grounds."

"Good," answered Zeroth as he threw a ghastly flower arrangement at a Hawken chasing a pair of ducks.

"I'll lead my fellow ducks to safety and then, I shall return!" Alexander shouted with gusto as he charged off into the distance, an endless tide of ducks following closely behind.

Steve watched the odd-battle below him intently, failing to notice the door of his cell opening behind him.

More and more of the Hawk-King's warriors began to join the battle in the courtyard, making things harder for Zeroth and the others.

"Shameless!" Zeroth barked, "Free Rosco!"

"Free Rosco?" asked Uncle Shameless as he stopped chasing the Hawken with the melon baller. He heard a familiar low moan once again and immediately snapped to attention *"Rosco!"*

Uncle Shameless ran for the colossal beast, who was still chained down on the other side of the courtyard. He dashed by menacing Hawken warriors and grabbed a hold of one of the gigantic metal stakes attached to Rosco's chains. Uncle Shameless grunted and groaned loudly as he pulled on the huge stakes, but they would not give.

Uncle Shameless quickly drank some more Eldercherry wine, hoping to increase his strength even more, but he still could not pull out the giant stake. As he hunched over next to the stake and panted heavily from exhaustion, Uncle Shameless notice that the stake was covered with a faint red light.

Zeroth, seeing that Shameless was not having any luck, made a quick dash towards the imprisoned Rosco. Dozens of Hawken warriors began surrounding the trapped Roc Lobster and prepared to move in on Uncle Shameless and Zeroth.

Behind Steve, a Mystic of Zuu snuck into his cell and drew a jagged knife from the folds of his fire-red robes.

Rosco began to wake up and tried to break his bonds but had no luck. He chirped as loudly as he could with his chained beak at Uncle Shameless. The man nodded and ran to Zeroth, taking time to clobber a few Hawken along the way. Uncle Shameless stood back to back with Zeroth as the bird-man sliced and diced with his swordfish.

"Rosco says to cut them things wrapped 'round his claws!" Uncle Shameless yelled over the fighting.

"Right!" Zeroth answered as he finished off another Hawken warrior and jumped towards one of Rosco's massive claws, slashing downward at the primitive looking rubber band with Gladius.

"They are too late," cackled Steve's vulture attendant from behind as he raised his jagged knife. The boy spun around in time to see the deadly weapon glisten in the moon light and made one last scream for help.

Gladius' sharp tongue bit into the primitive rubber band around one of Rosco's claws, instantly snapping it in two and falling off. Zeroth then leapt for the remaining claw and did the same, freeing it from its rubbery prison. The expressions on the Hawken guards faces' immediately turned from smug cockiness to one of complete terror as the Roc Lobster's colossal pincher claws were now free.

Just as Rosco's second claw was freed, Steve's scream was clearly heard in the courtyard.

"Steve?" gasped Uncle Shameless, looking up to the cell window "Rosco! Help 'im!"

Without hesitating, the gigantic beast cut the thick chains holding him to the ground with his freed claws and quickly took to the air.

"I thought I had until dawn!" Steve yelled at the attacking vulture, as he began to reach for the Staff of Arcana, which he had reverted back to its normal stick-like appearance.

"Your friends have changed all of that!" countered the Mystic of Zuu. The beady-eyed vulture lifted the knife higher and began to stab it downward at the boy. Just as he did, one of Rosco's enormous pinchers smashed through the cell wall and pinned the attacking Mystic against the far wall.

"Rosco!" Steve cheered happily as the giant creature cut the chains around his beak with his other claw and let out a thundering roar as he broke down the rest of the cell's outer wall.

The Roc Lobster grabbed Steve with one of his mouth tendrils and flew down to the courtyard. The Mystic of Zuu cursed Steve loudly and threw his knife at Rosco, but it bounced harmlessly off his hard lobster tail.

The Roc Lobster swatted at groups of Hawken warriors with his freed claws as Zeroth climbed on to his back. Steve was placed next to him by Rosco's mouth tendril as the beast scuttled over to pick up Uncle Shameless and Eira.

A Hawken warrior jumped at Eira as she climbed up Rosco's side, but Steve turned the Staff of Arcana into a long hockey stick and bonked the bird-man on the head. Eira waved a thank you to the boy as she finished climbing onto Rosco.

Uncle Shameless hugged his nephew tightly, "Am I glad to see you boy!"

"Me too, me too," Steve replied with a warm smile.

"Look out!" Eira cried as a squad of Hawken archers prepared to fire a massive volley of wicked arrows at Rosco. Right before the squad's commanding officer gave the order to fire, an axe flew through the air and struck the Hawken in the back.

Everyone turned as a chorus of rooster crows filled the courtyard.

"Chickens!" Steve said as a tide of stocky, battle-hardened rooster warriors poured into the courtyard and fought the remaining Hawken troops. "But how?" asked the boy.

"Alexander must have showed them the way," explained Eira.

Steve smiled as he was glad to hear that the little duck captain was safe after helping him destroy the Statue of Zuu. Uncle Shameless looked over at Zeroth as Hawken and chicken clashed in the background, "Now what?"

"Just get us in the air so we can come up with a plan," Zeroth instructed. Uncle Shameless passed the command on to Rosco, who let out a roar and took to the sky above Arx Vena'Tor.

As Rosco soared overhead and dodged stray Hawken arrows, Zeroth confessed his failed plan to Steve and apologized. The boy was angry at first, but after Zeroth explained why he had done it, Steve forgave the Hunter.

"Are you serious?" Steve asked, uneasy after hearing about the dreadful punishment in store for the bird-man.

Zeroth shuddered and nodded, "That's how the stories go."

"*Ick,*" Steve replied, sticking out his tongue in disgust "Heck, I'd turn *him* in to get out of that," Steve finished as he jerked a thumb towards Uncle Shameless.

Even without his glasses, Steve could see a faint crimson glow far off in the horizon. "Dawn is coming!" he yelled as he reached over and shook Uncle Shameless, who was drinking more wine, "We have to hurry!"

Uncle Shameless wiped his mouth on his arm and patted Steve on the head, "Don't worry boy, everything's gonna be just fine."

Zeroth quickly interrupted with, "Something tells me it isn't."

The bird-man pointed down at a large fireball that was heading right for them as Rosco flew over the open ceiling of the Hawk-King's throne room.

Before the Roc Lobster could dodge it, the fireball turned into a gigantic, fiery clawed hand. The blazing hand grabbed a hold of Rosco and effortlessly pulled him down towards the throne room.

Everyone screamed as they were quickly pulled down through the large hole in the throne room's ceiling. The hand of fire slammed Rosco into the floor with such force that the floor cracked, and all his passengers were tossed around the room.

Right before Steve blacked out, he saw a pair of fiery eyes moving towards him in the darkness.

A villainous laugh filled the throne room and brought Steve out of his daze. He hurt all over and had been thrown far across the stone floor by Rosco's crash landing. The mighty beast laid motionless on the floor except for staggered deep breaths. Steve saw Eira not too far from him, but could not see Zeroth or Uncle Shameless in the spacious room.

The laughter caught Steve's attention and drew his eyes towards a pair of red eyes heading toward him, brimming with fire. He tried to stand up but was too scared, all he could manage was to scoot backwards on the floor.

Steve scolded himself. He was finally meeting up with the Hawk-King but did not have the courage to face him alone. Steve stared at the fire-filled eyes and became confused. The eyes in the darkness were not that high up, perhaps only slightly taller than Steve.

The boy finally found his voice and addressed the approaching eyes in the darkness.

"I thought you were taller."

"Silence!" bellowed an unfamiliar voice.

The boy had heard the Hawk-King speak before and he was certain that it was not Fiach-Ra in front of him. The eye's owner entered a pool of light and Steve saw an ugly looking vulture dressed in red robes. This vulture was larger than Steve's attendant had been, and his robes were more elaborately decorated.

"Oh, hello," Steve replied casually, not thinking this new creature would be much of a threat, since most of Fiach-Ra's cronies ranged from bungling to inept.

"Quiet!" yelled the vulture, the jowls around his beak flapping madly.

"What's the deal? Are you guys charged by the word or something?" Steve. joked

The vulture grunted and shot a blast of fire from a clawed hand.

"Eep!" yelped Steve as he tried to move away but the fire wrapped around him like a rope. It did not burn him, or even feel all that hot, but it pulled the boy towards the vulture.

The ugly vulture reached down and picked up the boy, or at least tried to. The obese vulture grunted and groaned several times before successfully picking the teenager up.

"You are heavier than you look," grunted the vulture as he carried Steve towards the center of the throne room.

"You're one to talk, Chubby," Steve teased. "Who are you? And why are you carrying me?"

"I am Rarlup, Elder Mystic of Zuu! Second only to-"

"Okay, *okay*," sighed Steve, "Sorry I asked."

Rarlup narrowed his beady eyes at Steve, "But, moments from now *I* shall be King after I sacrifice you to Zuu!"

Steve's eyes widened, "Hey, listen Burlap, can we talk about this?"

"Rarlup!" corrected the chubby Elder Mystic.

"Right. Anyway, can we talk about this?"

"*No!*"

Steve could just barley make out groaning sounds in the distance and figured that his companions were slowly waking up. The boy thought that if he kept the portly Mystic talking, someone might wake up in time to save him.

"Wait, did you say that you are going to be King?"

"Yes!" laughed the fat vulture, "After you are sacrificed, Zuu will grant me the power to topple Fiach-Ra."

Steve heard movement in the darkness and decided to keep trying his plan. "That was some trick you did with that giant hand of fire," Steve said in a fake impressed tone.

"You liked that, huh?" boasted Rarlup as he looked over the boy with his fire-filled eyes.

Zeroth came to and quickly saw what was going on. Uncle Shameless also woke up and was about to dash towards Steve, but Zeroth held him back, waiting for just the right moment to attack the magic wielding Mystic of Zuu.

"Oh yes, it was very…uh..very," Steve tried to think of how to drag this conversation out, "Very, very, very impressive. *Very.*"

"*I agree,*" added an authoritative, booming voice from the shadows.

The flames pouring from Rarlup's eyes extinguished and returned to normal pools of white with tiny dots of black. The fat vulture turned his bald head in the direction of the unmistakable voice.

Steve swallowed hard. He had recognized the voice as well.

Fiach-Ra's eyes lit up brightly within the shadows above his throne. Steve could see the bright burning eyes in the sea of shadows as they moved towards him and the vulture Mystic.

Zeroth did his best to keep Uncle Shameless quiet as he tried to think of a way to save Steve.

"There is more to you, Elder Mystic," Fiach-Ra spoke slowly as he descended the steps that led up to his lofty throne, "Than meets the eye."

The Hawk-King entered a pool of moonlight pouring through the hole in the rotunda's ceiling. The lethal talons on his feet clicked against the stone floor as he closed in on Rarlup and Steve.

"I should have known you'd turn against me. You vultures are all the same – scavengers till the end," Fiach-Ra snapped.

"You are too late, *O Favorite of Zuu!*" Rarlup yelled condescendingly as he clutched Steve with one hand. The obese vulture reached inside his robe and pulled out a gruesome looking knife. "I will sacrifice The Boy to Zuu, and unbelievable power shall be *mine!*"

"'Unbelievable power'? Would you listen to yourself?" Steve said as he fought against the flame ropes that held him. "You sound like a-"

"*SILENCE!*" Rarlup and Fiach-Ra yelled in unison.

"Y'know what? You guys need to get a word of the day calendar," Steve sighed as he shook his head.

"Enough!" the fat vulture bellowed as he prepared to stab Steve with the knife.

"Or at least some kind of a vocabulary builder," added the boy.

Without hesitating, the Hawk-King fired a blast of flame from the Spear of Zuu, knocking the knife out of Rarlup's hand.

The Elder Mystic of Zuu howled and dropped Steve as he tended to his burnt hand. In the shadows, Zeroth whispered to Uncle Shameless to get ready as he took out Gladius.

Rarlup hissed at Fiach-Ra, conjured a fireball with a wave of a clawed hand and tossed it at his King. The giant hawk-man blocked the missile with the Spear of Zuu, sending sparks and flames showering down around him. Fiach-Ra counter-attacked by firing another blast from his spear.

As the blast of fire neared the fat vulture, the Elder Mystic waved his good hand and the fire curved around him. Rarlup waved his hand again and shot Fiach-Ra's magical fire back at him.

Just before hitting the Hawk-King, the fire once again turned into a giant burning hand. The flaming fingers held Fiach-Ra tightly in their red-orange grasp. Meanwhile Steve watched from his place on the floor, unable to sit up or to move away.

"You should not have doubted my power, *O Favorite of Zuu*," snorted Rarlup. "My magical skills have reached even your godly level."

Fiach-Ra narrowed his fire filled eyes at the gloating creature before him. "Perhaps. But you are forgetting one thing," the Hawk-King said, never flinching as the fiery fingers attempted to crush him.

"What?"

The Hawk-King did not reply, but merely leaned the Spear of Zuu so that it touched the flaming hand. There was a flash as the Spear suddenly began absorbing the flames into its sinister tip.

Rarlup's beak dropped open as the giant hand of flame was completely absorbed by the Spear of Zuu, freeing Fiach-Ra. The portly vulture tried to waddle away as the flame covered spear illuminated the dark throne room.

Rarlup managed to get to the other side of the room, near Zeroth and Uncle Shameless before Fiach-Ra hurled his fire-tipped spear at the Elder Mystic.

The Spear of Zuu hit its mark. The force flung Rarlup back through the air, his heavy body landing on top of Uncle Shameless and Zeroth. The burning spear laid embedded in the Elder Mystic's chest, setting fire to his elegant robes. Fiach-Ra waved a clawed hand and the spear disappeared in a burst of flame, only to reappear in the Hawk-King's grip a second later.

Zeroth tried to push Rarlup's heavy body off of him with no luck. Uncle Shameless had bumped his head after being knocked over and that combined with the Eldercherry wine made him very groggy and unable to move.

Zeroth fought against the excessive heaviness of the overweight Mystic as he watched the Hawk-King stomp across the floor towards the helpless Steve.

"Now," Fiach-Ra said in a deep, booming voice *"You."*

The Hawk-King waved the Spear of Zuu, conjuring a bubble of fire around himself and Steve.

"So we aren't disturbed," the villainous bird-man with flaming eyes explained. Realizing now that the element of surprise was not an option, Zeroth began yelling to bring Uncle Shameless back to his senses and perhaps even Eira or Rosco.

The idea worked, Uncle Shameless began mumbling as he regained his senses. "No Mom, I didn't put the spittoon in the dishwasher," Uncle Shameless muttered as his eyes adjusted. He saw the bubble of fire around Fiach-Ra and Steve, and tried to sit up. He was unable to with Rarlup's heavy body on top of him.

"What the...?" Uncle Shameless exclaimed. *"Who is this?"*

"Just get him off!" Zeroth ordered.

"Gladly. He stinks!"

On the other side of the room, Eira began to stir. She held a hand to her head, still dizzy from the crash landing. She gasped when she saw Steve trapped in the massive bubble of fire with Fiach-Ra.

Steve was frozen with fear as he stared up from the ground at the Hawk-King, still bound by Rarlup's magical rope. Fiach-Ra's villainous eyes stared at Steve with a piercing gaze. Fear choked the boy's voice as Fiach-Ra raised the Spear of Zuu.

Through tear filled eyes, Steve saw Uncle Shameless and Zeroth trying to break through the bubble of fire without any luck. Uncle Shameless punched the bubble until his knuckles became charred and blistered.

Seconds dragged as the next few moments seemed to flow in slow-motion. Deep inside himself, Steve accepted his fate and blinked away his tears. He decided, if this was how his quest was going to end, he wasn't going to go out crying.

Steve stared up at Fiach-Ra and called him the nastiest word he could think of.

47

"Nooo!" screamed Eira.

Zeroth grabbed on to Uncle Shameless and did what he could to keep the super-strong man from throwing himself into the bubble of fire.

Fiach-Ra grinned a wicked grin as he turned away from Steve and raised his spear. The bubble of fire burst, sending Uncle Shameless, Zeroth, and Eira flying backwards several feet. The Hawk-King flapped his wings and flew off through a large passageway behind his throne.

Everyone ran to Steve, Uncle Shameless tried to pick him up, but Eira stopped him.

"Don't move him!" she yelled, looking over the wound in the boy's chest. The Spear of Zuu had easily cut through Steve's magical chain mail vest, mortally wounding him.

Uncle Shameless looked at Eira with tear filled eyes and eventually gave in to her command. He left Steve alone as Eira ran her hands over Steve's neck, looking for a pulse.

"He's not gone yet!" she exclaimed after finding a faint heartbeat "...but he could go at any second."

"Do something!" Uncle shameless bellowed loud enough to wake up Rosco. The large beast stirred slowly and turned to see what was going on. He cooed a sad sound, as if he knew everything that had happened.

"I can't do anything with you yelling at me," Eira replied in a firm but calm voice.

"Okay, okay," Zeroth started as he tried to remain calm. "Shameless, you and I will go after the Hawk-King. Eira, you do...whatever you can for Steve. Shameless, tell Rosco to stay here and keep an eye on Eira and Steve."

Uncle Shameless ran a hand through his ratty hair and hesitated. *"Shameless!"* Zeroth yelled in a very authoritative tone. "Uh...right, sorry," whispered Uncle Shameless as he stumbled over toward Rosco.

Zeroth placed a clawed hand on Eira's shoulder, "I have faith in you," he said truthfully. He quickly stood up, took out Gladius and gave the swordfish a quick squeeze.

"Shameless!" he yelled, *"Let's go!"*

Zeroth and Uncle Shameless climbed the steps leading to the Hawk-King's throne and dashed out of the room through the hidden door Fiach-Ra had used.

Rosco cooed loudly as he slowly crawled over to Eira on his spindly lobster legs and formed a semi-circle around her with his body.

Eira wiped away a tear and slid off her back pack.

"First, I'm gonna punch him in the face. *Then* I'm gonna clip his wings. *Then* I'm gonna kick him in the-"

"Shameless, quiet!" Zeroth barked as they ran down a tall stone hallway, their footsteps echoing loudly.

"Where does this lead anyway?" asked Uncle Shameless, noticing an odd smell filling the hallway. Zeroth pretended not to hear the question, but the smell in the hallway seemed oddly familiar to him.

The pair came to a large door that was wide open. Flashes of light and smoke could be seen coming from the inside of the room as they approached.

"Prepare yourself," Zeroth suggested quietly.

"For what?" asked Uncle Shameless before taking a sip of wine.

"Anything."

Eira dumped the contents of her pack on the floor in front of her. She franticly searched through the pile of odds and ends. She groaned in frustration when she did not find what she was looking for, startling Rosco in the process.

She forced herself to calm down as she again checked Steve's pulse. She could barely feel it this time. She took a deep breath and searched the contents of her pack once more.

Uncle Shameless and Zeroth jumped through the wide doorway, ready for a fight. They saw Fiach-Ra dipping the Spear of Zuu into a cauldron covered with grotesque cravings. A pillar of foul smelling black smoke poured out of it. His back was turned to them.

"Stop!" yelled Zeroth.

The Hawk-King slowly turned to face the pair of intruders.

"What a nice surprise," Fiach-Ra said in his deep voice "My favorite failed experiment and..." he watched Uncle Shameless stumble around the cavernous room. "The town drunk."

Zeroth did not know what the Hawk-King meant by saying he was failed experiment, but at the moment he couldn't care less. The Hunter raised Gladius and prepared to attack, "You'll pay for what you did!" he yelled.

"This coming from a treacherous Hunter who even turned against his friends?" Fiach-Ra replied harshly. "Please, skip the heroic nonsense," the Hawk-King's voice boomed as he lifted the Spear of Zuu. "It is beneath you."

"No!" yelled Zeroth.

Fiach-Ra sighed, "So be it." He slyly reached over and pulled a lever, opening a large hole in the floor behind Uncle Shameless and Zeroth.

"Shameless, watch out for that hole!" yelled Zeroth.

"Whazdat?" mumbled Uncle Shameless.

"It's the Pit of Big Nasty Things!"

Uncle Shameless looked over his shoulder at the gaping hole in the floor, "How do you know that?"

Without taking his eyes off the Hawk-King, Zeroth pointed to a big, hand painted sign dangling above the expansive hole. It read 'Pit of Big Nasty Things' and in very small letters under that 'Caution.'

Uncle Shameless' lips moved slowly as he read the words to himself, "Oh," he said finally.

Eira slumped back against Rosco's feathered body, still unable to find the item she was looking for. She was positive she had a large bottle of her healing blood left at the bottom of her pack just for this type of emergency, yet she could not find it. She closed her eyes and thought for a moment.

A memory came back to her in a flash. She remembered Steve picking up a bottle that had rolled out of her pack onto the deck of *The Defender* after she had been grabbed by the owl skeleton from the Sword Room. She then remembered him throwing it at the undead creature, causing it to topple off the back of the airship and down to its doom .

She cursed loudly after realizing what had happened and tried to think about what to do. The bottle Steve had thrown would have had more than enough of her healing blood in it to save him. But the large bottle only had that much because she had slowly filled it up over a long time. She could not just simply nick herself and use a few drops like she had done with Rosco on the outskirts of the Smoldering Wastes.

A wound such as Steve's would require a great amount of her healing blood, and there was no way she could save the wounded boy. Eira sighed loudly and shook her head. There *was* a way, and as she felt Steve's pulse come to a stop, she quickly grabbed her knife and made her choice.

Zeroth and Uncle Shameless charged Fiach-Ra. The Hawk-King spun his wicked weapon and blocked Zeroth's sword strike. He pushed Zeroth away and swung his spear again so that shaft hit Uncle Shameless in the ribs.

Zeroth madly slashed at Fiach-Ra with his swordfish, but each strike was either blocked or dodged. Uncle Shameless slowly got to his feet and made a dive for Fiach-Ra. The Hawk-King flapped his large wings and flew up just as Uncle Shameless was about to tackle him.

Uncle Shameless landed near the edge of the Pit of Big Nasty Things. He slowly got up, trying not to tip over. Before he had a chance to move, Fiach-Ra flew towards Uncle Shameless and kicked him in the back, knocking the man down the hole.

"Shame-*less!*" Zeroth cried as he ran towards the hole. Fiach-Ra fired a blast from the Spear of Zuu, burning a spot in the floor just in front of Zeroth.

"I have other plans for you," the Hawk-King said as he landed near the switch that operated the cover of the Pit of Big Nasty Things. He pulled the switch again. The cranking of ancient gears and chains filled the cavernous room as the pit became covered once more.

Uncle Shameless fell for what felt like several minutes. All he could see was never ending blackness below him. Eventually, he landed in a small pool at the bottom of the Pit of Big Nasty Things. The water was ice cold and had a sobering effect on him.

Uncle Shameless crawled out of the water onto the sandy floor of the endless pit. He saw several torches lining the walls. Near the torches, he saw large arched passage ways. He didn't want to know what was beyond them.

Uncle Shameless sniffed the damp air, "Blagh, this place smells like moldy fish heads!" he exclaimed, his voice bouncing around the walls. As his echoes faded, Uncle Shameless began hearing movement in the arched passage ways surrounding him on all sides. In one he heard a low slithering sound, in another he heard heavy footsteps. He also noticed glowing eyes beginning to appear in the shadows.

"Oh boy," Uncle Shameless whispered to himself as more and more eyes lit up around him. His last drink of wine had worn off, so he decided to have a few sips to regain his super strength.

Uncle Shameless lifted up his wineskin to take a long swig, but nothing came out. He tried not to look at a large shadow moving towards him as he inspected his wineskin in the torch light.

It was empty.

"No!" he yelled as he looked over the wineskin again. He saw a large hole had been ripped in the bottom during his fall.

"You weren't a total failure," Fiach-Ra said with his spear pointed at Zeroth. "I learned so much after making you."

Zeroth ignored Fiach-Ra, trying to think of a plan.

"I'm serious," the Hawk-King said with a wicked chuckle. "One learns from their mistakes. I can honestly say you were an excellent learning experience."

Zeroth roared and swung his swordfish at the Hawk-King, which was easily dodged. Fiach-Ra spun around and struck Zeroth across the back hard with the shaft of the Spear of Zuu. Zeroth toppled over, hurt. He quickly regained his fighting stance and readied his sword.

Fiach-Ra shot a blast of flame from the Spear of Zuu, knocking Gladius from Zeroth's hand. It rattled as it hit the hard stone floor.

"I don't know what you're talking about," snapped Zeroth.

"Isn't it obvious?"

"You're my father?" replied Zeroth, guessing at his mysterious heritage. Fiach-Ra broke into a thunderous, booming laughter. *"Father? Do not make me laugh. I am no more a father to you than a farmer is to his crops."*

Zeroth narrowed his eyes at the Hawk-King, now even more confused, "But…"

Fiach-Ra sighed loudly, "I *created* you, here, in this place," the hawk-man waved the Spear of Zuu around as he gestured. "I wanted to combine the strength of the Swantan with the agility, brains and flying ability of the Hawken."

"Why?" asked Zeroth.

"Do you have any idea how difficult it is to maintain two separate armies?" asked Fiach-Ra. "To make things easier, I created you – with a little help from Zuu, his minions and several dozen pelicans, of course." The Hawk-King chuckled a low, evil laugh.

Zeroth's eyes widened as he remembered Eira's tale about the Hawk-King rounding up scores of pelicans years ago, "No..." he gasped.

"Oh yes," the Hawk-King replied "But sadly, you were not strong enough, nor could you fly with those pathetic wings of yours. So I cast a spell to cloud your memories, banished you, and started over. I would not accept anything less than perfection."

Zeroth suddenly felt very ill, but he was relieved to know that he was not descended from the Hawk-King. Being born out of a dirty cauldron was much more appealing to him than being Fiach-Ra's son.

Zeroth clenched his sore hand and glanced down at Gladius. But before he could make a move for it, Fiach-Ra fired another blast from his spear, knocking the swordfish further away.

"Now," the Hawk-King started, leaning on his spear, "It is time for you to witness what I learned from the mistakes I made with you...and the others."

Zeroth had a gut feeling he wasn't going to like whatever it was Fiach-Ra was talking about. Without a word, the Hawk-King reached over and pulled another lever.

Chains hanging from the ceiling began moving behind Zeroth. They made a loud clinking sound as they pulled something up from a chamber below the floor. A metal grate slid aside with a loud BANG! Smoke began pouring out of the hole, creeping eerily over the floor like smoky tendrils.

Zeroth turned to face the object being brought up by the chains. He could not make out any details through the thick smoke pouring out of the hole, but he could see a large shape within the cloud. The chains eventually came to a stop with a sharp jerk.

The room became silent, except for the slight jingle of the chains swaying back and forth from the ceiling. The smoke began clearing away, giving Zeroth a good view of what had been lifted up through the hole.

His beak dropped open with a loud, disgusted gasp.

48

Steve felt groggy and weird. Everything was hazy around him and the last thing he saw was his companions leaning over him and yelling about something. Their voices were muffled and he could not hear what they were saying. Steve blinked and they were gone.

Light surrounded the boy and he felt funny again. He blinked once more and suddenly he was in a garden next to an old, simple looking castle near an even older looking aqueduct.

"Where am I?" he said, his words echoed around him.

Steve walked through the garden, confused. He could have sworn he was just inside Arx Vena'Tor only moments ago. He did not know where he was, but the castle nearby did not look anything like the Hawk-King's wicked home. He looked down and saw he was on a rocky path and wondered where it led. He turned a corner under a large tree, and was surprised to find someone else in the garden.

A old man dressed in light armor with long, gray hair and poorly kept facial hair stood by himself in the garden. Steve was unsure what the man was doing, but it looked like he was trying to cut down a tree with a long stick.

Steve approached slowly, his footsteps drowned out by the sound of the man's repeated whacks against the tree. The sound echoed around them in the garden as did the man's heavy breathing.

"Uh, hello?" Steve said.

The man stopped in mid-swing and looked at Steve, "Oh, Hello there."

"What are you doing?"

The man stood his stick up vertically and leaned against it. "Trying to cut down this tree. It's harder than I thought," he explained as he scratched his scruffy, wrinkled face.

"Well, *duh*. You are using a stick," Steve said, still confused.

The man took the stick and held it in his hands. He studied it for several minutes.

"No I'm not," he finally said.

In the Pit of Big Nasty Things, Uncle Shameless started to panic. Unknown horrors surrounded him and he did not have any more strength enhancing Eldercherry wine. The creatures that inhabited the Pit began creeping into the torch light.

In one corner he saw the side of a giant hairy beast, making him think of his encounter with the solicitor back in the Forbidden Forest.

"Great that's all I need, ta get eaten by a giant shrew," Uncle Shameless said as the creature began stomping towards him with heavy footsteps.

On another side of the room Uncle Shameless saw pair of glowing, beady eyes floating in the darkness.

"Now what?!" Uncle Shameless blurted out loud, putting up his fists. The creature entered the light, and nearly caused Uncle Shameless to retch.

It looked like a big floating brain with a tiny set of jaws and eyes at the bottom. The exposed brain throbbed and oozed as it floated through the air.

It reminded Uncle Shameless of a giant blimp with a tiny cabin at the bottom. Out of the back of the brain, a long and nasty looking tendril whipped around like a tail.

"*Gross!*" Uncle Shameless yelled, taken aback by the revolting creature.

The hairy beast from before now came into the torch light, and his fears were true – it was a solicitor. The giant shrew looked at Uncle Shameless with its beady eyes. It sniffed the air with its long snout, as if trying to figure out what Uncle Shameless was.

The massive beast's jaws opened, revealing lopsided teeth the size of bananas as saliva poured out all over the floor. The tail it swung around was as thick as a tree trunk and just as hard. The furry beast hissed loudly at Uncle Shameless.

"Easy, easy," Uncle Shameless said soothingly to the tank-sized rodent. He started backing up away from the hissing solicitor, until he realized he was getting closer to the floating brain-creature.

"Eep!" Uncle Shameless exclaimed as he backed up in a different direction. He kept his eyes forward on the creatures moving towards him. The man stopped when he reached the wall of the Pit of Big Nasty Things, and pressed his back tightly against it.

At least Uncle Shameless thought it was the wall, until it started moving.

Zeroth looked upon the thing that had risen from the floor and was filled with disgust.

The creature was bound in chains that were attached to the bottom of the platform it stood on. It was bulky and very tall, even taller than the Hawk-King. Zeroth could not see all of its features, because a pair of massive black wings were wrapped around the front of the body like a feathery cocoon. The creature's head was lowered and it breathed slowly, as if it were sleeping.

Fiach-Ra knocked his spear against the hard floor loudly several times, causing the creature to stir and slowly wake. The creature's eyes shot open and its large, black wings spread out away from its body with a loud WOOSH.

Zeroth's eyes widened again after seeing the rest of the creature's body. Its appearance sickened him and he wanted to look away, but he could not.

Its head was like a hawk's, with angular piercing eyes. Fire filled them and flowed outward, just like Fiach-Ra's eyes. Its body was covered in black feathers and it had a sharp beak that looked like an odd blend of a hawk's and a swan's, just like Zeroth.

Again, like Zeroth the beak had a ring of black around it, mirroring a swan's. Its beak was hooked and wicked looking, smoke poured out of it whenever it opened even for the slightest exhale. But those were not its most shocking features.

At its shoulders shot out thick muscular arms, reminding Zeroth of the arms of a Swantan warrior. However, underneath those arms, was a second set of arms closer to the creature's midsection.

Unlike the larger arms above them, these arms were thinner and lanky, but looked muscular and agile. The creature stood on powerful looking legs that ended with large curved talons on its webbed feet.

The creature's wrists – all four of them – and his ankles were bound in heavy bracelets, through which the thick chains that kept the creature subdued were attached. The ghastly creature hissed at Zeroth, smoke shooting out of its sharp beak and fire burning in its eyes.

"What is *that*?!" Zeroth yelled, trying to look away from the abomination in front of him.

"*That*," Fiach-Ra said proudly "Is your brother."

"No," Steve replied, looking over the scurfy, elderly man in front of him "*That* is a stick."

The man dressed in armor swung the stick around, "No, it is more than just a 'stick.'"

"Okay...," Steve began, fearing he was about to be treated to some sort of long-winded speech about sticks.

"To *you*, it is just a stick because you have been taught that it is nothing but a stick," the bearded man explained.

"Well, I -" started Steve, quickly regretting talking to this man in the first place.

"But what if you were taught that it could be many things?" asked the man.

"Uh...," stumbled Steve as he tried to answer, not really sure what point the man was trying to make.

The man did not wait for Steve to answer and continued. "It can be a cane," he walked around, hunched over using the stick as a cane. "Or a pointer," he pointed to a piece of fruit hanging in a tree with the stick. "Or an artist's tool," he drew a square in the dirt with the stick.

"Or something to write with," he wrote 'square' in the dirt next to his drawing, "Or-"

"Okay, *okay*," Steve said finally "I get the point."

"Do you?" asked the man, lifting the stick up and poking Steve lightly in the chest.

Uncle Shameless lost track of all the creatures that were skulking towards him. The wall he had leaned against had turned out to be some manner of giant slug-creature with the scaly body and rattling tail of a snake.

"Egeeh!" Uncle Shameless yelped as he ran away again. He tripped over a pile of discarded bones and landed face first in a puddle. Uncle Shameless looked up and saw two solicitors moving toward him, followed by one of the floating brain creatures.

Uncle Shameless jumped up and started running again, but one of brain creatures lashed out with its odd tendril, wrapping it around the man's chest. Uncle Shameless ran in place for a few seconds before he realized what he wasn't getting anywhere. The creature lifted him up with its tendril and spun Uncle Shameless around to face him.

"Yuck!" Uncle Shameless yelled as he received a close up view of the floating brain and its snapping jaws. Uncle Shameless swung a fist at the brain, but the creature lifted him away at the last second, causing his blow to miss.

"Well, this is most un-bully," Uncle Shameless lamented. "What a way to go, eaten by flying brains and giant shrews." Uncle Shameless sighed loudly as the creatures around him licked their lips and snapped their jaws as he swung back and forth in the slimy tendril's grip.

"This is worse than the time I got kicked out of that petting zoo."

"What?!" Zeroth yelled after hearing he was somehow related to the monstrosity in front of him.

"I created him some time after you were banished, you could say he's your *little* brother," Fiach-Ra laughed.

"There's nothing *little* about him," Zeroth snapped bitterly.

The room suddenly shook as something struck the castle. Fiach-Ra's eyes narrowed as he looked off in the distance, as if sensing what was happening. There was another deafening shake as the castle was struck once more.

"I'll leave you two alone to play. It looks like I have some pests to deal with," the Hawk-King snapped. He waved the Spear of Zuu and chanted a few wicked words, the shackles holding the creature released themselves and fell to the floor.

"Secundus," the Hawk-King barked, addressing the freed creature, "*Kill.*"

Secundus, sprang forward with surprising speed. Zeroth managed to roll out of the way of the colossal bird-man's tackle, but just barely.

Behind the dueling pair, Fiach-Ra laughed and flew away through a hole in the ceiling. Zeroth, now alone with the furious creature, looked around for Gladius. Secundus ran at Zeroth again, shrieking loudly, causing smoke to pour out of his monstrous beak.

Zeroth looked over and saw a tall pole with a candle stick on top. He quickly grabbed the pole and swung it at Secundus, candle end first. The beastly creature snapped at the pole with his mighty beak, biting off the burning candle and swallowing it whole.

Zeroth pulled back the pole and inspected the bit off candle, "*Okay...*" he said, thinking carefully about his next attack. He swung the pole at Secundus' side, but the creature reached out with one of its large arms and easily grabbed it.

Secundus threw a mighty punch with his other large arm. Zeroth leaned back quickly and let go of the pole, dodging the punch. The Hunter spun around fast and kicked at Secundus' midsection. Zeroth's attack was stopped by the larger bird-man's set of smaller arms. The quicker arms grabbed onto Zeroth's leg and pulled hard, sending Zeroth crashing into a nearby table.

Zeroth got up slowly from the shattered remains of the table, his leg now very sore. "This isn't fair," Zeroth snapped, looking at Secundus' two sets of arms.

Secundus spread out his wings and all his arms and let loose a loud hawk cry, spewing smoke everywhere from his mouth. Zeroth looked around for another quick weapon. He picked up a thick leg from the table he had just crashed into. He stared down Secundus and held up the hard hunk of wood.

"*C'mon!*" Zeroth taunted.

Secundus snapped his beak several times and inhaled sharply. He then spewed a stream of fire from his mouth, hitting the table leg in Zeroth's hands and setting it on fire.

Zeroth dropped the flaming bit of wood instantly and decided he'd had enough. "Gladius! Where are you?!" Zeroth hollered, trying to hide his panic. He heard a loud sigh from across the room, "Now what?" answered the silver swordfish bitterly.

"I need you!" Zeroth bellowed. Secundus shrieked loudly. In unison, all four of his arms reached for his back and pulled out four swords from four sheaths.

" I *really* need you!" Zeroth added.

"Yeah, I get it," sighed Steve "A stick can be more than just a stick, right?"

"Not with *that* attitude," replied the old man in the garden.

Steve rolled his eyes "Look beardo, are you going somewhere with all of this? Because you are talking really weir-"

"I do not need to go anywhere," the man said in a regal tone. "It is you that has to."

Steve blinked and stared at the man "Huh?"

"I can only show you the path, you are the one that-"

"Y'see? *That* is what I was talking about," interrupted Steve "You are not making any sen– OW!" Steve yelped as the man struck him sharply on the leg with the stick. The boy hopped up and down for a few seconds in pain.

"What was that for?!" yelled Steve.

"I found another use for this so called 'stick'," explained the man in a stately voice. "An instructional tool."

Steve rolled his eyes "Oh, there's a *tool* here all righ – OUCH!"

Zeroth ran across the room to find Gladius, the swordfish told the bird-man it had slid under a table after being knocked from his grip. Zeroth reached the table, trying to avoid Secundus for at least a minute or two.

The table was tall, wide and very heavy and Zeroth did not see Gladius right away.

"Where are you?!" Zeroth yelled as he snatched random objects off the table and threw them at the approaching Secundus.

"Under here!" Gladius yelled back, irritated that it had to keep repeating itself.

Zeroth hesitated and got down on the floor and looked under the large table. He could see his living weapon, far back under the table and against the wall. Zeroth reached as far as he could with his arms, but could not reach Gladius.

"C'mon, ya pansy!" Gladius taunted.

"Can't you move yourself closer?"

"Hello-ooo! I'm a *fish!*" Gladius yelled, now irritated even more.

"Right, right," Zeroth conceded, forgetting that swordfish became paralyzed outside of water. The bird-man stuck his head under the table as far as he could and reached again, still unable to grab the creature.

"You can do better than that!" coached Gladius.

"Listen, I don't need-"

"Look out!"

Zeroth pulled his head out from under the table right before Secundus dropped from above him, swinging the ironing board shaped swords he had in his larger arms. The table shattered into a hundred pieces under the brutal attack.

Zeroth jumped up and dodged a series of quick slashes from the smaller swords in Secundus' lower set of arms. Zeroth reached blindly behind him and felt a bottle of liquid and threw it at the giant brute's face. The bottle hit Secundus' beak and shattered, distracting him long enough for Zeroth to dive into the rubble of the table and grab Gladius.

The smaller bird-man rolled out of the bits of shattered wood in time to avoid two crushing blows from Secundus' larger swords. The wide, heavy blades cut into the stone floor, sending chips of stone flying in every direction.

Zeroth gave Gladius a hard squeeze, releasing its sharp bladetongue with a loud BLEAH! He then quickly reached into his magic pack and took out his battered shield. Secundus cocked his head in confusion at the sight of Zeroth producing a shield from nowhere.

The giant, fiendish Secundus then spun his swords around in a show offish manner, shrieking loudly as flames danced in his eyes.

Zeroth narrowed his hawk eyes at his sizeable foe and prepared to strike.

Steve rubbed the many sore spots on his body as he stood in a peaceful garden in the shadow of an old castle. "Will you please stop hitting me?" Steve pleaded, giving the elderly man with the stick a nasty look. "Are you ready to pay attention?" asked the man as he leaned on the stick.

"I've *been* paying attention! I don't know – OW!" Steve yelped again, "Stop that!"

The man sighed and held up the stick. "What is this?"

"*A stick.*"

"Wrong," sighed the man.

Steve prepared himself to get hit again, but the blow never came. The man held the stick up again. "What is *this*?" he asked.

"It's a stick!" Steve yelled, frustrated, "S-T-I-C-K, stick!"

"Wrong," replied the man, this time lightly striking Steve on the leg.

"Ow!" yelled Steve, rubbing a new bruise, "What's your problem?!"

"What is *your* problem?" asked the man with a stately tone.

"I don't have a problem," Steve explained as he thought about running away from the crazy old geezer.

The man sighed again and shook his head, "With all the education you posses you cannot answer a simple question."

"There is one I *can* answer – what *your* problem is. You're crazy!"

"Does thinking differently make one crazy?" the man asked truthfully. Before Steve could answer with a loud 'yes' the man continued, "Does seeing things differently make one crazy?"

Steve opened his mouth to make a nasty comment but stopped. He thought for a moment. The man saw Steve deep in thought and held up the stick again.

"What is this?"

"Whatever you want it to be?" Steve answered carefully, wincing as he expected to be hit again.

"*Ah,*" the man said gladly, "Now you are beginning to understand."

Steve smiled and breathed a sigh of relief. "Ow!" yelled Steve as the man hit him on the head with a quick strike. "Now what?!"

"Sorry," the old man confessed, "Force of habit."

Zeroth blocked one of Secundus' swinging swords with a quick parry. Unfortunately, that left him open to three additional sword strikes. Zeroth let two of the other sword attacks bounce off his shield, but one of the smaller swords in Secundus' lower set of hands slashed at Zeroth's arm, cutting him.

Zeroth winced and stepped to one side to avoid a second barrage of sword strikes. Zeroth's heart was pumping so fast that he felt like it would burst through his chest at any moment.

Secundus attacked with his lower set of swords and sheathed his two larger swords, leaving his upper mighty arms available for hand to hand attacks. Even with half as many weapons, Secundus was still difficult for Zeroth to hold off.

Zeroth was having to dodge multiple sword attacks as well as ferocious punches. The Hunter got backed up against a wall, and he ducked under a mighty punch, causing Secundus' meaty fist to crash into the stone, cracking it.

Secundus quickly sheathed his lower set of swords with a quick spin of his wrists and grabbed Zeroth with his lower arms, trapping him. Zeroth was not only caught in the creature's iron-grip, but was also backed up against the wall. Secundus began landing a barrage of body blows on Zeroth with his stronger upper arms. Zeroth felt the air being knocked out his lungs and thought he was going to faint from the copious clobbering.

The colossal mutant bird-man landed a fierce punch to Zeroth's face, causing him to falter back and forth unsteadily. Before Zeroth could recover, Secundus wrapped his lower arms around Zeroth's waist in a vise-like bear hug and lifted him up.

Zeroth tried to wiggle out of the grip but could not. Smoke pouring from Secundus' beak choked the smaller bird-man's lungs and watered his eyes. Trapped in the creature's strong hold, Zeroth was subjected to a series of severe strikes to the body and head.

The Hunter could not take much more of this and decided he had to do something. Zeroth felt rage growing inside him as Secundus rained blows upon him, a rage he always fought to control.

A lucky break came to the battered bird-man as Secundus lifted Zeroth up and hurled him across the room into a set of tables and chairs. Secundus flapped his wings and flung out all four of his arms as he shrieked loudly in a boasting manner. His celebrating stopped as it was drowned out by a loud, piercing battle cry.

Zeroth jumped from the rubble, bloodied and bruised. His normally calm eyes were now a sea of crackling fire and rage. The flames poured out of his eyes into the air around his head, burning brightly just like Secundus' and Fiach-Ra's. Zeroth put away his shield so he had use of both of his arms. He let loose another rage filled battle cry as he raised Gladius and charged the surprised Secundus.

The old man clad in armor lifted up his stick and walked back over to the tree he had been trying to cut down when Steve had appeared in the garden.

"What are you doing?" asked Steve.

"Trying again," the man answered.

"Why? It won't work."

The man shook his head, "And why is that?"

"It isn't scientifically possible!"

"Not everything is," explained the old man. "There are things *beyond* science and logic, I thought you had come to accept that over the course of your quest."

Steve shrugged, wondering how the old man knew about his quest. "Well...I guess, but-"

The man turned to face Steve, "You have a power that you have not yet realized," he lifted up the stick and pointed to Steve's head, "In here."

"You're talking all crazy again-"

The bearded man spun around and ran at the tree with speed that did not suggest his age. He swung his stick upwards, cleaving a tree branch in half effortlessly.

Steve stumbled backwards, his mouth agape in disbelief. He looked down at the severed branch, very confused, "But...how?"

"Because I believed I could. In here," he pointed to his own head with the stick, but he swung the stick too hard and gave himself a nasty whack in the temple.

"Ow!" the man yelped, rubbing his sore temple. "That *does* hurt."

"I told you!"

49

Secundus unsheathed all four of his swords in time to block a speedy sword strike from Zeroth. Secundus' swords rattled loudly as Gladius bit into the blades. Zeroth attacked again, and again, driving Secundus backwards.

Untamable rage burned inside Zeroth like the fire now filling his eyes. He rained this rage down upon Secundus, swiftly striking with Gladius. Zeroth's attacks were nothing but a blur of silver and a crash of steel. His speed aided him against the much larger bird-man, allowing him to attack quickly from different angles.

Secundus lashed out with one of his larger swords. Zeroth side-stepped and avoided the strike, swatting at the arm with his swordfish, knocking the sword out of the mutant's hand. The heavy weapon fell to the floor with a loud CLANG.

Zeroth kicked the sword away as Secundus responded by shooting a blast of fire from his mouth at his foe. Zeroth ducked under the blast and sprang at Secundus, his shoulder catching the giant creature under the creature's smoke spewing beak.

Reeling from the blow, Secundus jumped at a thick stone column in the middle of the room. His talons and many claws dug into the rock as he scaled up the column. Zeroth began throwing random objects from around the room, causing Secundus to counter attack with a volley of small fireballs.

With a quick swing of his silvery swordfish, Zeroth sent one of the fireballs sailing back at Secundus. The four-armed beast shrieked as the fireball struck a part of the column above him. Secundus flapped his expansive black wings and took flight in the high ceilinged cavernous room.

Not being able to do more than glide, Zeroth found himself in trouble once more as Secundus continued launching fireballs from his malicious beak from the safety of the ceiling. Zeroth quickly grew tired of dodging the fiery missiles and jumped for cover in a pile of rubble.

Zeroth found another bottle of unknown liquid. He waited for Secundus to fly above him and hurled the bottle at his flying attacker.

Like before, the bottle struck the beast near his face, granting Zeroth the several seconds he needed.

As Secundus flew around aimlessly in pain, Zeroth jumped at another column and quickly scaled it with his own claws and talons. Summoning all his strength, The Hunter leapt at the temporarily hindered Secundus. Zeroth landed on the monstrosity's back and struck him on the head with Gladius' hard hilt-like body.

Secundus crashed to the unforgiving floor along with his unwanted passenger. The pair got up quickly, but not unharmed. Secundus screamed with pain as he tried to move a wing that been broken by the fall.

Zeroth granted no quarter to his foe and immediately attacked with his swordfish, slashing open a nasty wound on one of the creature's large arms. Zeroth summoned all of his burning rage and bombarded the four-armed creature with a flurry of slashes.

Countless attacks came in-between the blinks of Zeroth's fire-filled eyes, and the attacks never slowed. Secundus began breathing heavily, spewing smoke everywhere with each deep breath. The beastly bird-man was weakening and Zeroth could sense it.

Secundus swiped at Zeroth with his remaining large sword but Zeroth leaned backwards at the last second to allow the blade to pass harmlessly over his chest. Zeroth took a chance and stabbed the arm with his sword, disabling it.

Both of Secundus' muscular upper arms were now wounded and practically useless. However, this still left his lower set of agile arms with their own set of deadly swords. Zeroth battled with these weapons in a blur of metal and rage. Even though the agile arms were lower on Secundus' body, because the beast was so tall they were about even height with Zeroth's own arms.

The black feathered Hunter bobbed and weaved to avoid the attacks or used his own weapon to parry the blows. Zeroth swung at Secundus, only to have his blade stuck in-between Secundus' swords, thanks to a quick move by the snarling creature. Zeroth was about to pull the weapon free but Secundus used what strength he had left to wrench the swordfish out of Zeroth's hands and sent it flying.

Gladius flew through the air until it hit the side of one of the stone columns supporting the ceiling of the room. The knock caused Gladius to retract its deadly tongue with a loud slurp.

Zeroth narrowed his burning eyes at Secundus as he dodged a pair of sword strikes. Zeroth spun quickly and grabbed one of Secundus' hands with one of his own. Zeroth used his other hand to land a solid punch to his foe's face.

Zeroth then twisted Secundus' wrist and pried the sword he held free. After stealing the weapon, Zeroth gave the large creature a hard kick to his broken wing.

Secundus stumbled backwards in great pain, shrieking and spewing smoke everywhere. He gave a loud battle cry as he charged at Zeroth once more. The smaller bird-man blocked this sword attack with his stolen weapon. The block knocked Secundus' weapon away momentarily, allowing Zeroth to land several nasty cuts on Secundus' already tattered body.

The creature howled in pain and swung his sword with all the strength he had left. Zeroth swung his weapon as well. The two swords connected, but Zeroth's cut Secundus' blade in two.

Zeroth kicked the weaponless Secundus in the chest with a mighty taloned foot. The creature fell to the ground with a loud thud, beaten. However, Zeroth was not finished with his foe. He lifted up his sword and ran towards the fallen beast.

Zeroth spun his sword around as fire leapt from his eyes and prepared to plunge the hungry blade into Secundus' heart.

"Stop!" a voice cried just seconds before Zeroth ended his foe.

Zeroth snarled and ignored the voice and raised his sword again.

"Zeroth, stop!" Gladius yelled again, "This isn't the way!"

Zeroth shook his head as if trying to regain his senses. The fire in his eyes burned lower as he relaxed slightly. He looked at the weapon in his hands and then down at his defeated foe.

"What am I doing?" he said in a shaky voice before his rage took over again. His eyes filled with flame and he raised the sword once more.

"Mercy!" Gladius called from across the room. "Your foe is beaten, leave him be!"

The conflicted bird-man could not decide what to do.

"Anyone can take a life," Gladius explained in a uncharacteristically gentle tone, "But only a true hero can grant it."

Zeroth's hands relaxed and the sword fell freely down to the floor, crashing loudly against the hard stone. The flames in Zeroth's eyes died away as Zeroth fell to his knees, exhausted and ashamed that he had given in to his rage.

Zeroth double checked the chains and ropes from his magical pack that he had used to tie up Secundus. The creature sat tied to one of the immense stone columns in the room, groggy and weak. After he was confident the chains and ropes would hold, Zeroth bandaged up his own wounds as best he could by ripping strips of cloth from his cloak. His left arm was severely hurt, requiring him to make a make-shift sling out of his long yellow scarf.

With the adrenaline from the battle gone, Zeroth suddenly felt very sore and weak.

"Thank you," Zeroth said to Gladius.

"That was a close one," replied Gladius. Zeroth nodded as he turned to go pick up the talking swordfish. "What was all that about anyway?"

"What do you mean?"

"The anger, the fire in your eyes, all of that business," explained the chatty weapon.

Zeroth sighed as he picked up Gladius, "It runs in the family," he answered with a glance back at Secundus.

Zeroth's words sparked a memory, "Shameless!" he exclaimed as he ran over to the covered hole that led down to the Pit of Big Nasty Things. He ran over to where the lever the Hawk-King had used to open and close the cover of the pit was and pulled it.

As the cover of the Pit of Big Nasty Things opened up next to him, Zeroth stuck Gladius back inside his cloak and searched his pack for more rope. He cursed loudly as he realized that he had used all of the available rope to tie up Secundus.

The injured bird-man paced back and forth, trying to think about what to do. He cursed loudly again and made up his mind. He lifted his small wings out from under his cloak and flapped them open. As he prepared to glide down to the bottom of the Pit of Big Nasty Things, he heard a mumbling from inside his cloak. Zeroth took out his talking weapon.

"What now?" Zeroth asked.

"*What* do you think you are doing?" Gladius answered in a bitter tone.

"I'm going to glide down to the bottom to save Shameless."

"Glide down? To the bottom of the Pit of Big Nasty Things?"

"Yes-"

"Then what?"

"Well-"

"I'll tell you what – You'll be attacked and or eaten by any number of different horrors."

"I s'pose but-"

"But nuttin'," Gladius snapped "What if Shameless has already been eaten?"

"Well-"

"*Well*, then you will have gone down there for no reason. No sir, this is a bad idea in my hon-"

"Shhh!" Zeroth interrupted as he leaned his head closer to the Pit.

"I will do no such thing, you adventurers today never think things out bef-mmmfffm!" Gladius yelled as Zeroth stuck the swordfish back in his cloak.

Zeroth listened carefully, he thought he heard something clawing at the sides of the Pit of Big Nasty Things. Against his better judgment, Zeroth leaned over the edge of the Pit and looked down.

To his shock and amazement, he saw a solicitor clawing its way up the side of the Pit of Big Nasty Things. Zeroth's blood ran cold as the massive, hairy beast slowly made it's way up towards him.

The Hunter knew he was in no condition to take on a solicitor by himself, and tried to think of an escape plan. Zeroth pulled out Gladius quickly.

"Changed your mind?" Gladius started.

"I didn't have to, look," Zeroth held the swordfish over the edge so it could see the approaching solicitor.

"Well that certainly is convenient," Gladius noted "Now you don't have ta go all the way to the bottom ta get eaten."

"Thank you for the observation," Zeroth snapped sarcastically as he gave the swordfish a quick squeeze to extend its bladetongue. Zeroth backed up and raised his weapon. Before he had time to think up any kind of strategy, the giant killer shrew hopped out of the Pit of Big Nasty Things. Zeroth readied his weapon, trying to ignore all of the pain he was in.

The giant solicitor moved closer to Zeroth, hissed loudly and reared up on its strong back legs like a bear. Saliva poured from its angry mouth as it prepared to attack.

Zeroth took a step back and swung Gladius.

"Whoa, easy there!" yelled a voice as the solicitor dodged the attack. Zeroth stopped and lowered Gladius "...Shameless?" he said, looking up at the solicitor. Zeroth heard a series of grunts and groans until he saw Uncle Shameless climb on top of the giant shrew's head.

"Hiya!" Uncle Shameless said with a smile.

"You're alive?!"

"Last time I checked."

"But...how?"

Uncle Shameless told Zeroth everything that had happened, including losing the Eldercherry wine. Zeroth looked at the frightening creature that had carried the now sober Uncle Shameless out of the Pit of Big Nasty Things.

"But...what about that?" Zeroth asked, still expecting the giant beast to attack him.

"Oh, well it was the darndest thing. I just started talkin' to them and they just kept listenin'!"

Zeroth all but dropped Gladius, "...You're joking."

"Oh no, all of them critters couldn't get enough of my stories. Ain't that right?" Uncle Shameless asked as he scratched the solicitor behind its large ears. The giant shrew wore an expression of contentment and even looked like it was smiling.

"They just loved my stories. Even the stories that Steve is sick of..." Uncle Shameless' words trailed off as he remembered what had happened to his young nephew. Uncle Shameless wiped a tear from his lazy eye and looked at Zeroth, "What's the plan?"

Zeroth looked up at the hole in the ceiling that Fiach-Ra had flown away through, "We go *up*."

Zeroth held on tightly to Uncle Shameless with his good arm as the solicitor scaled the walls and eventually climbed up the hole in the ceiling.

"Any idea where this goes?" Uncle Shameless asked.

"Your guess is as good as mine," confessed the bird-man.

As the hairy solicitor continued his vertical climb, Zeroth glanced upward and made out a few random stars at the top of the hole, guessing they would end up on the roof of the castle. He leaned close to Uncle Shameless, "So...this solicitor really likes you?"

"You bet. Their nice critters...except..."

"Except what?"

"They smell like gym class."

"Jim...Class? Who is Jim Class?" Zeroth asked, confused.

Uncle Shameless shook his head, "Naw, not Jim Class. *Gym class.*"

Zeroth thought hard for a moment, "I don't understand...Is this someone you know?"

Uncle Shameless was about to explain when they heard a deafening explosion above them, followed by a loud smashing sound.

"Let's put a wiggle on it!" Uncle Shameless yelled to the solicitor. The giant shrew squeaked a loud reply.

"I don't care 'bout that, just get us up there – *now!*" countered Uncle Shameless.

"What did he say?" Zeroth asked, amazed that Uncle Shameless could understand the odd creature.

"Nothing major," Uncle Shameless explained calmly, "Just that someone is firing cannonballs at the castle."

"What!"

"Relax, we'll be okay!" Uncle Shameless said, turning around to pat Zeroth reassuringly on his feathered head, but his voice was drowned out by another loud cannon blast.

Zeroth held onto Uncle Shameless even tighter as the odd party exited the mouth of the hole and they found themselves on a flat section of Arx Vena'Tor's roof. A cannonball whizzed through the air in front of them and crashed into the roof only a few yards away.

"Let me down!" Zeroth pleaded, having had his fill of riding the colossal rodent. But the solicitor scurried across the roof towards what looked like a battle as Zeroth and Uncle Shameless saw Hawken and owls fighting each other once more. In the distance, Zeroth saw *The Griffin* and knew at once who had been firing at the castle.

"This isn't good," Zeroth said as he scanned the sky.

"What's not good about it?" Uncle Shameless asked, "Besides the obvious."

"Dawn is approaching and remember the blue heron told us we only had until dawn to defeat the Hawk-King," Zeroth explained.

"Oooh yeah," said Uncle Shameless, "I forgot about that part. You kind of lose track of time at the bottom of a giant pit."

"Look out!" Zeroth cried as a trio of Hawken warriors landed on the roof in front of them. The solicitor reared up on its mighty legs and swatted at the warriors, striking one down easily. It bit into a second with its razor sharp teeth and knocked down the third with a swing from its heavy tail.

"Good work, Mr. Nibbles!" Uncle Shameless said encouragingly.

Zeroth leaned in closer to Uncle Shameless, "...Mr. Nibbles?"

"Aw, well I used to have a pet mouse called that, so I –"

"So you decided to name a giant, rabid killing machine after your childhood pet?"

"It seemed like a good idea at the time," Uncle Shameless replied with a shrug. Zeroth smiled and shook his head.

Mr. Nibbles eventually came to the place where the main battle was being fought. Hawken and owls were locked in fierce combat, their clashing weapons creating an odd symphony as some fought on the rooftop, some in the air.

The battle was broken up occasionally as cannonballs from *The Griffin* would crash into the roof but for the most part everyone was busy fighting one another. Zeroth wished to join in but was too weak from his fight with Secundus.

Zeroth soon realized he was not needed, as Mr. Nibbles crashed through a crowd of Hawken and easily took them out of the fight as well as a few random Swantan that had somehow made it to the roof. Mr. Nibbles jumped over the large cannonball craters that littered the rooftop as he headed toward the Hawk-King.

Fiach-Ra was once again locked in battle with Fel-Ra, who had organized the survivors of the earlier battle.

"C'mon Mr. Nibbles, let's give her a hand!" Uncle Shameless bellowed.

Fiach-Ra blocked a sword attack from Fel-Ra with his spear. He used all his might and lifted up her sword, leaving her momentarily vulnerable. He used this opening and quickly thrust his spear into her shoulder.

Fel-Ra ignored the pain and pulled away from the Hawk-King. She promptly moved her blue bladed longsword to her good arm and continued her assault. Fel-Ra ducked a second spear thrust and slashed at the Hawk-King's leg. She opened up a long wound on his leg as she landed her first hit on the tyrant.

Fiach-Ra did not even flinch after the attack and to Fel-Ra's shock the wound ignited in flame and was burned away without a trace. The Hawk-King laughed wickedly and struck Fel-Ra across the face with the bottom of his spear while she was distracted. "You cannot defeat me Fel," the Hawk-King snapped.

The Owl-Queen stumbled a bit after the blow to her face but quickly regained her composure. After seeing Fiach-Ra heal himself, she was beginning to believe Fiach-Ra's taunt that she could not stop him. But Fel-Ra persisted, taking to the sky with a quick flap of her expansive wings. The Hawk-King quickly gave chase, flying after his old foe.

The winged pair clashed in mid-air as Fel-Ra brought her long sword down upon the Spear of Zuu, but failed to best Fiach-Ra.

Unable to use both hands with her long sword, Fel-Ra did the best she could with only one usable arm and led Fiach-Ra high into the clouds above Arx Vena'Tor. The vengeful Hawk-King followed her into a bank of thick, rolling dark clouds, his fire-filled eyes casting a hazy halo around his face.

Fel-Ra glided patiently through the clouds and darted silently above the unsuspecting Hawk-King. When Fiach-Ra's head was turned, the warrior queen tucked in her wings and dove at the bird-man as he began shooting fireballs from the Spear of Zuu in random directions within the opaque clouds.

Fel-Ra's sneak attack allowed her to slice through one of Fiach-Ra's large wings, cleaving most of the feathers off. To the Owl-Queen's horror, the wing instantly healed itself in the same fiery manner that Fiach-Ra's leg had before.

Once more, the Hawk-King did not so much as flinch during the attack. He spun to shoot a stream of fire across Fel-Ra's stomach, which sent her crashing into the roof of Arx Vena'Tor.

Not one to give up not matter how bad things were, Fel-Ra, using her sword for leverage, righted herself on the roof. She narrowed her circular orange eyes at the Hawk-King as she prepared to continue her fight with him until one of them was no more.

Impressed by the former Queen's persistence, Fiach-Ra dropped to the roof and prepared to finish off his old foe once and for all. Just as Fiach-Ra began to rush towards Fel-Ra, a roar cut through the air behind the Hawk-King as Mr. Nibbles jumped at his former master.

"What?!" the Hawk-King bellowed as the colossal beast headed for him.

"Miss us?" Uncle Shameless taunted.

Without hesitation, Fiach-Ra fired a blast from his spear into the belly of Mr. Nibbles. The giant shrew collapsed to the roof, severely hurt. Uncle Shameless and Zeroth were thrown onto the roof as the large creature bucked.

Uncle Shameless ran over to his wounded friend, "Don't worry Mr. Nibbles! We'll take care of you," Uncle Shameless promised as the huge creature whimpered and whined in pain.

"You should be more concerned with yourself," retorted the Hawk-King "I don't know how you got out of the Pit-" Fiach-Ra stopped when he noticed Zeroth.

"Impossible!" the Hawk-King snapped loudly, his eyes ablaze with anger after seeing that Zeroth had somehow defeated Secundus.

Zeroth took out Gladius and tried not to look as injured as he was.

"*Enough!*" bellowed the Hawk-King, fire pouring out of his eyes. He raised the Spear of Zuu and stabbed it at Zeroth, who was too weak to dodge the attack. Fel-Ra flew over in front of Zeroth, letting the spear pierce one of her wings.

The wounded Fel-Ra slumped down in front of Zeroth and Uncle Shameless, burdened by her injuries. The proud warrior queen fought back all of her pain and forced herself to stand up between Fiach-Ra and Zeroth.

Despite her unrelenting persistence, the Owl-Queen's strength was quickly leaving her, causing her majestic long sword to dangle loosely in her grip. The Owl-Queen's spirit remained strong, even if her body could not. But she knew that was not enough to topple the powerful Fiach-Ra. Zeroth was too weak to battle as well and Uncle Shameless was all but useless against the likes of the Hawk-King without his Eldercherry wine.

They were beaten.

Fiach-Ra laughed maniacally as he raised the Spear of Zuu and prepared to mercilessly finish off the intrepid trio.

Steve held the stick in his hands and looked at the tree.

"You can do it. All you have to do is believe you can," the old man coached.

Steve exhaled sharply and readied the stick. He looked at the tree and swung hard. His body shook as the stick struck the thick tree, hurting his hands. The boy shook his head, discouraged by his failure.

"Try again," the bearded man said calmly, "Remember – it is more than a stick. It is *whatever* you want it to be."

Steve took a deep breath and closed his eyes, realizing that the old man's instructions reminded him of the Staff of Arcana. He did not think of the stick as a stick. He thought of it as just something that *could* slice through the tree's trunk.

With his eyes closed, Steve swung. He felt no contact and assumed he had missed. He opened his eyes and sure enough the tree still stood.

Steve spun the stick upside down and leaned on it, dejected but prepared to try again. The man watched silently. Just before Steve was ready to swing once more, a slight wind blew through the garden and shook the branches of the tree.

The old tree began making a low creaking sound which grew louder and louder. Steve jumped back as the thick tree fell over and crashed onto the ground. All that remained was part of the trunk with a clean diagonal cut through it.

The old man smiled, but Steve did not see it. The boy suddenly felt very odd and the garden began disappearing around him. Everything went black and he felt cold. Then, just as quickly he felt warm again and felt himself blinking.

Steve groggily woke up and saw that he was staring up at the red tinted early morning sky through the throne room's open roof.

"Ugh, I need to stop landing on my head," Steve said while thinking about the odd dream he had just had. At least he thought it was a dream. A creepy chill went through his spine as he looked down to find the Staff of Arcana in his right hand, giving off a soft blue glow.

Steve began looking around the throne room from his spot on the floor. He thought he was alone until he heard a low chirp behind him and he quickly turned to find Rosco behind him.

A thought quickly struck the boy. He had seen the sky clearly as he had just seen Rosco and the rest of the throne room. For some reason, his vision was better, even without his glasses.

Steve groaned sorely as he turned to his other side, and his eyes widened as he saw Eira.

She was laying on the floor next to him, dead.

50

A flight of owl warriors landed around the Hawk-King as he prepared to finish off Fel-Ra, Uncle Shameless and Zeroth. "Stop!" yelled one of the larger female warriors.

Fiach-Ra bellowed loudly as he charged the would-be rescuers. He cut through two owls effortlessly with the tip of his spear and smashed another in the head with the butt end all in a series of frenzied swings.

A cannonball crashed into the roof nearby, giving the last few owls a chance to escape. Without moving from his spot, the Hawk-King fired a volley of fireballs at *The Griffin*, hitting the front main cannon and disabling it. He then shot at the escaping owls, hitting all of them in the back.

"This ends *now*," Fiach-Ra snarled as he turned around and hovered the wicked Spear of Zuu above the helpless Zeroth, Fel-Ra and Uncle Shameless.

The Hawk-King thrust his spear at Zeroth, but stopped short when a loud roar echoed across the pre-dawn sky.

Everyone turned and saw the Roc Lobster burst from the open ceiling of the throne room with Steve riding bravely on the creature's back, carrying the Staff of Arcana.

Blind with rage, Fiach-Ra threw his spear at Rosco. The vile weapon grazed the side of the giant creature, forcing Rosco to make a hasty landing on the roof. The spear returned to the Hawk-King's hand magically and he prepared to threw it again, this time at the young hero.

"Steve!" Zeroth and Uncle Shameless yelled in unison.

The Hawk-King roared as Steve jumped down from Rosco and headed towards him. Fel-Ra looked over at Zeroth, "Is that The Boy?"

"You bet it is," Zeroth replied with a sly smile.

The Spear of Zuu rattled in the Fiach-Ra's grasp as Steve bounded across the roof. "Impossible!" the Hawk-King yelled.

"You still haven't picked up that vocabulary builder, huh?" Steve joked.

Fiach-Ra narrowed his burning eyes at the young boy and hurled the Spear of Zuu. Instantaneously, Steve turned the Staff of Arcana into a sizeable diamond shaped shield, elaborately decorated with scenes of everyday life in Beacon Pines.

The Spear bounced harmlessly off the conjured shield, much to Fiach-Ra's annoyance "What?!" the Hawk-King bellowed in disbelief as the spear returned to his hand.

Steve ran at his foe and turned the shield into a long, wooden hockey stick with a quick picture in his head. Fiach-Ra stabbed his evil weapon at the boy, only the have it knocked aside by Steve.

"Go get 'em boy!" Uncle Shameless cheered.

"Don't give up!" Zeroth added as he helped the wounded Fel-Ra to her feet. The bird-man glanced to the horizon and saw the tell-tale signs of dawn's rapid approach "Hurry!" he yelled to Steve, "Dawn is coming!"

The Hawk-King crashed the Spear down on Steve, but the boy turned it back to the diamond shaped shield once more to block the hit. As Fiach-Ra became more angered, his attacks became more and more careless. Steve kept switching back and forth between the shield and the long, wooden hockey stick as he fought back.

"What's wrong?" Steve taunted as he noticed Fiach-Ra's lack of banter, "Did you already use up all four of the words you know?"

"Blarrgh!" Fiach-Ra growled venomously.

"I don't think that's a word, but nice try," Steve joked as he slapped the Hawk-King across the face with the blade of the hockey stick. This attack angered the Hawk-King and fire jumped from Fiach-Ra's burning eyes as he made a sloppy thrust with the Spear of Zuu.

Steve easily dodged the sloppy thrust and slashed at the Spear of Zuu as he thought of a different weapon.

There was a brilliant flash that filled the sky, making everything go silent. The Spear of Zuu fell to the roof, its obelisk shaped blade cut in two. Fiach-Ra fell to his knees, defeated. In Steve's hands rested a glowing mighty silver sword with an eagle shaped hilt and a feather shaped blade– the Sword of Zaa.

The owls and Hawken stopped their fighting as they all landed on the roof and stared in awe. There stood Steve with the mythical Sword of Zaa and in front of him, Fiach-Ra the Hawk-King on his knees in defeat. Whispers ran through the crowd of Hawken and owls, neither side knowing what to do next.

"So, now what'll we do?" a scar covered Hawken asked his comrade. "Bein' a goon is all I know. I've been gooin' since I was a hatchlin'!"

His comrade shrugged, "I've always liked basket weaving."

The scar covered Hawken gave his comrade a concerned look before slowly sneaking away into the crowd.

"That a boy, Steve!" Uncle Shameless cheered.

With the Spear of Zuu destroyed, Fiach-Ra's powers quickly faded. The fire began fading away in his eyes, but did not disappear completely.

"Impossible...," the defeated tyrant whispered, sounding like a balloon deflating.

Steve pointed the Sword of Zaa at the defeated tyrant. More allies began landing on the roof, including Five-Toes and Queen Lana the IV.

Everyone waited to see what Steve would do next. The boy felt the dozens of eyes on him and quickly made his choice.

"Leave," Steve said, pointing to the horizon with his sword.

"What?" the Hawk-King replied weakly.

"Okay, first get a thesaurus. *Then* leave."

Steve turned his back on the once powerful Hawk-King and walked over to Uncle Shameless.

"Why are you letting him go?" his uncle asked.

"Too many have died already," Steve replied in a hollow voice, thinking of Eira and her sacrifice, "Besides, forcing him to live a normal life after hundreds of years as an immortal tyrant is a worse punishment than anything I could ever do to him."

"That is very wise of you," Fel-Ra said as she willed herself to stand on her own.

"Yeah, well-"

"Look out!" Zeroth cried, pointing behind Steve.

The boy turned quickly enough to see Fiach-Ra trying to stab him in the back with the broken tip of the Spear of Zuu. Steve defensively slashed upward with his blade. The Sword of Zaa cut across Fiach-Ra's eyes, blinding him and finishing the job Donal had started over three hundred years ago.

Fiach-Ra dropped the spear head, fell to the roof and clawed at his useless eyes. He howled in pain as his once loyal Hawken troops began muttering among themselves.

"Zuu's Beak, he blinded him!" a lanky Hawken warrior cried from behind Five-Toes.

"Maybe basket weaving *isn't* such a bad idea," the scar-covered Hawken warrior thought aloud as he and his comrades began flying away, refusing to serve the blinded Fiach-Ra.

"Come back!" Fiach-Ra barked as he heard his warriors leaving him alone on the roof, helpless. Fiach-Ra roared angrily, started flapping his wings and took off into the sky, taking the tip of the Spear of Zuu with him.

The lower half of the obelisk-like blade and the shaft of the infamous spear remained on the roof near Steve's feet.

A pair of owls flapped their wings open to pursue the defeated Hawk-King, "Leave him be," ordered Fel-Ra as she managed to walk over to Steve despite her numerous injuries. She placed a clawed hand on the boy's shoulder and gave it a strong squeeze. The Owl-Queen smiled as she reached down and grabbed the boy's sword hand by the wrist and lifted it upward.

"Hail Steve! Hero of Eyri!" Fel-Ra bellowed in a royal tone. Everyone formed a circle around the boy and joined in on the chant, creating a deafening roar.

Queen Lana the IV snaked her way over to the broken remains of the Spear of Zuu. She waved her scaly hands and chanted until the Spear became incased in a solid cylinder of flowing water.

"Why'd you do that?" Uncle Shameless asked.

"To keep the Spear from being used," answered the Wurm Queen.

"But Steve destroyed the Spear," Zeroth added. Queen Lana shook her head, "Magic weapons are not so easily destroyed."

As the cheering raged on around Steve, Fel-Ra leaned in close to the boy, "By the way – where is my airship?"

Steve pretended that he could not hear the Owl-Queen, no matter how many times she asked.

After dropping off all of his friends and family safely back in Tal, Alexander the Small returned to the ruins of Arx Vena'Tor to gather Steve and his companions.

"But where are we going?" Steve asked, watching Five-Toes and a bandaged Rosco fly behind *The Griffin*. "Back to Arx A'Quila," Fel-Ra explained calmly as a pair of owl warriors tended to her wounds.

"Why? It's a dump," Steve replied frankly, his hand resting on the Sword of Zaa, which was tucked into his belt. The regal warrior queen narrowed her orange eyes at the boy in confusion, "Are you insulting my home?"

"Oop!" gasped Steve "No, I mean, what's left to go home to? All that's left is the Smoldering Wastes and a run down castle."

Fel-Ra smiled warmly and nodded to the horizon. "See for yourself."

Steve wandered over to the rail on the deck of *The Griffin* and peered overboard. What he saw almost made him fall over.

Where the Smoldering Wastes had once laid was now a lush never ending forest of trees covered in shimmering blue-green leaves. A healthy, sky blue river cut its way through where there had only been nothing but sand.

"But-but," Steve stuttered as Fel-Ra joined him by the rail. The Owl-Queen smiled again as she pointed to her castle while *The Griffin* raised up through a bank of puffy white clouds.

Arx A'Quila shined majestically in the early morning sun, looking as if the past thirty decades had never passed. Lush foliage and gardens circled the pyramid shaped castle, and best of all, there were no skeletons to be found anywhere.

A large celebration was held at Arx A'Quila shortly after everyone arrived. Wounds were bandaged (even Mr. Nibbles'), bones mended and a time for rebuilding was at hand. Steve and Fel-Ra stood on a balcony as the celebrating went on both inside and outside the majestic castle.

"So I have to know," Steve said.

"What's the deal with the Queen's Entrance?"

"No," answered Steve, even though he thought about it for a moment. "Where did you and your owls come from?"

"Our mothers," the Owl-Queen replied truthfully, with a hint of sarcasm.

Steve rolled his eyes, "No, I mean you guys were all turned into those skeleton things..." his words trailed off as he remembered the many battles with the undead owls.

"Ah, *that*," the warrior queen answered with a smile. "Do you remember that owl you threw the bottle at on the deck of *The Defender*?"

Yes," answered Steve "...That was you?!" he exclaimed, finally putting it all together.

Fel-Ra nodded reluctantly. "Sadly yes, I was cursed – as were my warriors. Doomed to guard Arx A'Quila as the undead minions of the Hawk-King."

"But, you tried to kill us!"

Fel-Ra nodded again, "True. But you must remember my people and I were under a spell. We could only do one thing – attack those who dared to enter Arx A'Quila."

Steve gave an understanding nod, even though the whole idea gave him a creepy feeling. Suddenly Steve remembered the fate of the Paper Tiger, "But what about –"

"Me?" asked a voice from behind. Steve turned and saw the flat feline alive and well.

"But I thought-"

"No real harm done," the Paper Tiger explained. "Once Fel-Ra was revived, she had her people flatten me out and I was good as new!"

Steve turned back to face Fel-Ra, "Revived?"

"Of course. Did you not realize what you hit me with?"

Steve thought for a moment, he remembered that the bottle had fallen out of Eira's pack. His eye's widened, "You mean-"

"Yes," Fel-Ra answered, predicting the boy's response. "It was a large bottle of her healing blood. Enough to break Fiach-Ra's curse."

Steve thought about the warrior queen's explanation, "But what about the rest of the owls? How did they change back? And what happened to the Smoldering Wastes and your castle?"

"You broke the curse on the land when you destroyed the Spear of Zuu," Fel-Ra explained, "But it was your reviving me that turned all of us owls back to normal. That is the problem with curses, they are taken *very* literally."

"I don't understand."

Fel-Ra looked out over the celebration and festivities, "I don't recall all of the exact wording, but it basically went that we were to remain skeletons until 'the undead became living.' Fiach-Ra thought he was being smart by using those words, he did not think there was a way to revive the *undead*, even with pelican blood."

"I wasn't aware Eira's blood could do that either," confessed Steve.

"A pelican's blood is a tricky thing. Some pelicans are stronger healers than others," the owl finished as a sad expression fell over her face, "But, do not worry. Because Eira sacrificed herself to save you," Fel-Ra placed a comforting arm around Steve, "She will honored by all of us, and never forgotten."

Steve looked out into the horizon with tear filled eyes. In the distance, he thought he saw a pelican shaped cloud.

After a lavish meal, Fel-Ra spoke to those gathered in Arx A'Quila's cavernous dining hall. She told of the trials ahead. They were now free from Fiach-Ra but there was much work to be done. Cities and towns needed to be rebuilt and peace and order had to be maintained.

Later on, Steve walked around the castle inspecting the magically restored tapestries, the Sword of Zaa still tucked into his belt.

"Well, you did it," said a familiar ghostly voice.

Steve sighed, recognizing the voice as one that had caused him much annoyance. He turned and saw the Istrio appear in flash of blue light.

"Good work kid. You pulled it off," the blue heron said, giving the boy a thumb's up.

Steve took out the Sword of Zaa and held it up, "You knew the whole time didn't you?" he said, shaking the sword at the Elder Mystic of Zaa.

"Knew what?"

"That the Staff of Arcana was actually the Sword of Zaa!"

"Eh...*maybe*," Istrio answered with a wink.

"Why didn't you say so!" Steve yelled.

"Well, where's the fun in that?" the blue heron countered. "It would have made for a very boring quest."

Steve sighed and shook his head. Uncle Shameless, Zeroth and Fel-Ra caught up with the boy and joined him.

"Well, at least I beat him before sunrise," Steve added, thankful that his laborious quest was finally over.

"Oh yeah, *that*," snickered Istrio.

"Now what?"

"I was just pulling your leg on that one. It didn't matter when you defeated him," the lanky bird-man explained.

"What?!" Steve yelled. "Why did you lie to me?"

"To give you a little extra motivation. Plus it made things more exciting, didn't it?"

"More *exciting?!*" Steve screamed.

"Take it easy boy," Uncle Shameless said as he patted Steve on the back. Steve took a few deep breaths and tried to calm down. He remembered what the Three Sisters had told him about Istrio having a habit of being misleading.

"So now what?" Steve asked eventually. "Are you going to make me a king or something?"

Fel-Ra and Istrio both laughed loudly. "*You?* A king?" chuckled the blue heron "Yeah, we're going to make some thirteen year-old, who has only been here for a few days, King of All the Land," Istrio said sarcastically. "What do you think we are, stupid or something?"

"Well, I," Steve started before he was interrupted by the blue feathered Mystic.

"You still have to be told to clean up after yourself, what would you know about running an entire kingdom?" Istrio added in between laughs. Steve narrowed his eyes at the ancient looking bird-man, not amused by his joking.

"Trust me, other places have tried that and it *never* works," Istrio added as he wiped away tears of laughter.

The Elder Mystic of Zaa turned and started walking away, "I must get going everyone. Fel, always a pleasure, Zeroth keep your head on straight, Shamus keep telling those stories, and young Harrier...we'll be in touch," Istrio finished with a wink of an all white eye.

Before Steve could ask what Istrio meant by that, the blue heron quickly turned a corner and was out of sight.

As Istrio trotted down the hall, a ghostly visage of a bearded old man in armor appeared along side him.

"I knew he could do it," the old man said.

"Yes. He certainly came through," answered Istrio.

"Now, you know what that means – you owe me dinner."

"Dinner? But you're dead!" the bird-man countered.

"So? A bet is a bet," replied the ghost.

"What are you going to do? *Look at it?*" Istrio replied. "Last time I checked, ghosts couldn't exactly *eat.*"

"Look, you said 'I'll bet you a fancy dinner that he –"

"I know what I said," Istrio sighed reluctantly. "But I was only joking."

The bearded ghost gave Istrio a nasty stare. Eventually the Elder Mystic of Zaa shook his head and sighed, "Fine, fine. A dinner it is," the blue heron said as he shook his head again. "I swear Donal, you were always such a stickler."

"I have one more question," Steve said to Fel-Ra as they walked over the solid, flowing water floor in the castle's main rotunda. The water was a crystal clear blue, instead of the murky black it had been the last time Steve had walked on it.

"How come there weren't any humans with you at Arx Vena'Tor?"

Fel-Ra shrugged her bandaged, muscular shoulders. "I sent a messenger to The Village Formally Known as Uth, The Last Human Village just like I did to my other allies before we attacked the wicked castle. But I never received a response..."

Miles away, in The Village Formally Known as Uth, The Last Human Village, a male owl warrior stood next to the Alderman in a hastily repaired Presto's Pub, still trying to convince the portly man to help.

"Sir, *please*. Will you help us?" the owl asked again.

The Alderman quickly emptied his mug of wine and spun in his seat to get up and to face the lean-looking bird-man. However, this caused the Alderman to fall out of his seat and to crash onto the floor of Presto's.

"Ugh, I tried to get up but my legs didn't work," the wine soaked elected official wheezed as the owl warrior closed his orange eyes in embarrassment. A pair of sycophantic members of the Uth Chamber of Commerce ran over and helped the rotund man to his feet, eventually.

"You must forgive the Alderman," Loran, the Alderman's well-dressed public relations advisor, quietly whispered. "He's been in the bubbly."

The owl warrior gave the well-dressed young woman a nasty look "He's *'been in the bubbly'* ever since I got here!" the owl yelled, his voice almost shrieking. "Now, please! Will you join our cause?"

"Hmm, I dunno," the Alderman mused as he thought over the owl-man's request for the umpteenth time. "What's in it for us?"

"Wh-what's in it for you?" asked the owl warrior, mortified by the Alderman's response. "We're finally going to topple the Hawk-King, and free all of Eyri from the yoke of tyranny!"

"Yoke of tyranny?" the Alderman pondered as he reached over the counter and helped himself a bottle of wine decorated with a blue ribbon. "What do eggs have to do with this?" the Alderman asked as he pulled the cork out of the bottle with his teeth.

The owl-warrior groaned loudly, "I mean we finally won't have the Hawk-King ruling over us!"

"Oh, I don't like that sound of that," added the weasely looking member of the Uth Chamber of Commerce from his usual spot next to the Alderman.

"How can you say that?!" bellowed the owl, banging his clawed fist on the rickety bar.

"'Cause, we'd have to get rid all our footnote signs," replied the weasely looking man as he did his best to keep the Alderman from swaying back and forth.

"DONAL'S BEARD!" the Alderman bellowed thunderously. "Yer right! An' we just had those made!"

Fel-Ra's messenger gave the Alderman a blank, confused look. "Fergitit," the Alderman slurred. "You need ta recognize that we want none 'o that. You best be on yer way." The Alderman accented his profound statement by promptly falling over once again.

Steve eventually confessed the fate of *The Defender* to Fel-Ra, and after a long string of curses and yelling, the Owl-Queen, Steve and his friends returned to Arx Vena'Tor aboard Alexander the Small's flying ship.

As they floated over the dark castle aboard *The Griffin*, Steve noticed that the once impenetrable stronghold looked as if it was decaying in front of their eyes. After landing, Steve was surprised to see that a pair of familiar looking warriors had set up a business in front of the now crumbling ruins of Arx Vena'Tor.

"Hey kid, wanna buy a piece of the Hawk-King's wicked castle?" Remmit called out from behind a shoddy looking small booth as Steve and Uncle Shameless walked by. "C'mon they are cheap!" the Hawken barked as he held up different handfuls of rubble "Hey c'mon, get back here and take advantage of 2 for 1 deal, today only!"

Remmit slammed the hunks of rock down on the booth's make-shift countertop. Kaz walked up next to Remmit and dropped a large basket of rubble next to him in the booth.

"This isn't working as well as I'd hoped," Remmit confessed.

"Maybe we need a better location?" suggested the large Swantan warrior.

Remmit snapped his clawed fingers, *"That's it!* We'll take it on the road!"

"Huh?"

"We'll travel the land and sell pieces of that stinking old castle to customers who have never even seen it! *Genius!*" Remmit exclaimed as he began packing.

Steve and Zeroth walked through the charred ruins of Da'Rahga. Zeroth's signature yellow scarf was still tied up in a make-shift sling. "So what are you going to do now?" asked Steve.

Zeroth sighed, "I can't stay here. That Formal Hunter Compliant Form dash TB will reach the Lodge soon, if it hasn't already, and then…" The Hunter shuddered as he thought of the Roving Bones coming after him.

"Is there anything you can do?" the boy asked in a concerned tone.

"Don't worry," interrupted Gladius from Zeroth's hand, "I'll keep an eye on 'im, Donal an' me got outta some tough spots back in the ol' days. It'll take more than a few piles of bones to shut me up."

"I doubt there's *anything* that could ever shut you up," Steve joked. "But the Hawk-King is gone, wouldn't that void his compliant?"

"No," Zeroth began as he stepped over a the wreckage of a destroyed house "The Lodge can show no quarter when it comes to these matters, otherwise the whole system fails. I must be made an example of…because honorable or not, I *did* go against my contract," Zeroth stared off into the distance, trying not to think of the trials ahead. "Besides, the Hawk-King is not *gone*. He is wounded, and powerless, but not gone."

A wall crumbled near them, causing Zeroth to instinctively ready Gladius. After seeing there was no danger, he continued. "And, Fiach-Ra is not alone either."

Steve did not understand what Zeroth meant until the bird-man told him of the Hawk-King's mutant warrior, Secundus.

"I went back to where I'd tied him up, and he was gone. I'd bet Secundus is out there somewhere, probably with Fiach-Ra plotting revenge."

"But how, I thought all of his troops abandoned him," added Steve.

"He still has followers I'm sure, and perhaps even a few who are no fans of yours," explained Zeroth.

The pair reached the outskirts of Da'Rahga and Zeroth turned to leave.

"Where will you go? I thought those Bones guys could find you no matter where you are?" asked Steve, trying not to act as upset as he was feeling. Zeroth shrugged as he tightened his sling, "I'll travel far away and hope I get lucky."

Steve looked down at the ground, sad to see his friend leave.

"Just remember everything I taught you," Zeroth said with a smile. "And remember to believe in yourself. Your power lies in here," Zeroth pointed to Steve's head, "And *here*," he pointed to Steve's chest.

"In my lungs?" asked the boy.

"Sorry, I meant *here*."

"...My kidney?"

"No, your heart," Zeroth said.

"You didn't point to my heart."

"Sorry, I'm no expert on human anatomy."

After a strong hug, Steve watched the half-hawk half-swan wander off into the horizon as Gladius subjected him to an endless supply of bad rhymes and even worse free verse poetry.

Once *The Defender* was repaired, thanks to a little bit of magic and a lot of hard work, Fel-Ra told Steve that Queen Lana the IV (with some help from the Three Sisters) had discovered a way to send him back home to Michigan.

The Defender flew over the Ralk Sea until it came to a giant swirling whirlpool. Fel-Ra and Uncle Shameless walked with Steve to the back deck of the airship. Uncle Shameless had decided to stay and pass on his knowledge of modern farming to the peoples of Eyri.

"There's nothing back home for me Steve-o," Uncle Shameless said tearfully "At least here, I can do what I love, an' help others too."

"I'm going to miss you," Steve said to his uncle, sad that their adventure together had finally come to an end.

"Aw shucks, me too boy. Me *too*." They shared a long hug before Steve walked over the Fel-Ra, finally ready to leave.

"Oh, and Steve?" Uncle Shameless called.

"Yeah?"

"When they ask what happened to me, come up with a good story! Make me proud!" The boy smiled sadly as he promised to fulfill his uncle's request.

Steve looked up at Fel-Ra the Owl-Queen, "So let me guess, there is some kind of magic you have to do for this to work?"

Fel-Ra shook her head, the horn-like tuffs of feathers flapped in the blowing wind, "No. Not really."

A confused look crossed Steve's face, "Well, then wha-"

Without hesitation, Fel-Ra quickly grabbed Steve by the shirt, lifted him up effortlessly with a powerful arm and tossed the boy over the side of *The Defender* into the giant whirlpool many feet below.

A very groggy (and soggy) Steve woke up on a sandy bank along the Grand River. He slowly stood and squinted to see where he was. He then realized that not only had he lost his chain mail vest but that he needed glasses to see again. He grumbled a bit as he walked up the river bank.

Steve's parents were rather shocked when the boy called them from a pay phone outside a convenience store near the bank of the Grand River that used to be an old speak easy. His parents even more shocked when the boy explained that Uncle Shameless had disappeared after saving him from a pack of delusional, bloodthirsty wolverines.

Weeks passed and one day Steve walked to an all but forgotten park in Beacon Pines and found a comfortable spot under a tall, gnarled oak tree and started doodling in a little sketch book. As he finished adding a long scarf to an elaborate drawing of a bird-man, a group of children his own age approached him.

One of the group, a boy with a dinosaur t-shirt, walked up to him, "Hey wanna play with us?"

"What are you playing?" Steve asked as he put the little sketch book in a pocket.

"We can't decide, either ninjas or pirates."

Steve thought for a moment about the conundrum, "Well how about we mix 'em together and play Ninja-Pirates?" he suggested. All of the children instantly loved the idea.

Steve played with the other children for the rest of the warm summer day, only stopping when the street lights came on.

The End (for now).

About the author –

Daniel J. Hogan is a life-long Michigan resident. He was born in Detroit but later grew up in the nearby suburb of Harper Woods. He currently lives and works in the greater Lansing area. His other interests include animation, filmmaking, photography, drawing and the Detroit Red Wings. *The Magic of Eyri* is his first novel and he is anxious to continue the adventures of Steve and his friends.

To learn more about the author or to send him an email, please visit **www.danieljhogan.com**.

About the artists –

Michael Church (front cover art), a Michigan resident as well, studied painting and illustration at Grand Valley State University. While in college, he met Daniel J. Hogan while living in the same dorm building.

To see more samples of his work, please visit **www.drakered.com**.

Romel Clawson (back cover background art) studied film and animation along with Daniel J. Hogan at Grand Valley State University. He grew up in Hopkins, Michigan.

To learn more about Romel, visit **www.danieljhogan.com/romel**

Kevin Knipstein (title logo and caricature of the author on the back cover) is one of Daniel J. Hogan's oldest friends and grew up around the block from him in Harper Woods. He also attended Grand Valley State University where he studied illustration. Kevin currently lives in Chicago.

You can see more of his work at **www.prettyokayproductions.com**